BOOKS 1 – 3

THE
JADE HARRINGTON
SERIES

J. L. BROWN

Printed in Seattle, Washington, United States of America.

For information address JAB Press, P.O. Box 9462, Seattle, WA 98109.

Cover Design by Damonza

First Omnibus Edition, 2019
Library of Congress Control Number: 2019913302
ISBN 978-0-9969772-8-9 (paperback)
ISBN 978-0-9969772-9-6 (Kindle)
ISBN 978-1-7354750-0-4 (EPUB)

Don't Speak © 2016 by Julie L. Brown
Library of Congress Control Number: 2015918331
ISBN 978-0-9969772-1-0 (paperback)
ISBN 978-0-9969772-0-3 (Kindle)
ISBN 978-0-9969772-2-7 (EPUB)
ISBN 979-8-9917654-0-4 (audiobook)

Rule of Law © 2017 by Julie L. Brown
Library of Congress Control Number: 2017901223
ISBN 978-0-9969772-3-4 (paperback)
ISBN 978-0-9969772-4-1 (Kindle)
ISBN 978-1-7354750-2-8 (EPUB)

The Divide © 2019 by Julie L. Brown
Library of Congress Control Number: 2018915314
ISBN 978-0-9969772-6-5 (paperback)
ISBN 978-0-9969772-7-2 (Kindle)
ISBN 978-1-7354750-1-1 (EPUB)

Few Are Chosen © 2017 by Julie L. Brown
ISBN 978-0-9969772-5-8 (Kindle)
ISBN 978-1-7354750-9-7 (EPUB)

First Edition: October 2019

THE
JADE HARRINGTON
NOVELS

DON'T SPEAK   *   RULE OF LAW   *   THE DIVIDE

J. L. BROWN

DON'T SPEAK

A JADE HARRINGTON NOVEL

To Audi, for everything

*If we don't believe in freedom of expression for people we despise,
we don't believe in it at all.*

- Noam Chomsky

PART I

CHAPTER ONE

Present Day, Arlington, Virginia

JADE HARRINGTON STARED down at her opponent. He was four inches shorter than she but built like a linebacker. For this Tae Kwon Do testing, she had already defeated six opponents—all men—and at one point, took down two fighters simultaneously. At the beginning of this final match of the day, a few onlookers stood outside the ring. As the match progressed, however, more spectators from around the arena gravitated from other contests to observe this fight between two highly ranked competitors.

Jade pushed up the front of her protective headgear, which had inched down again. Sweat streamed into her eyes, and her bulky sparring gloves could not wipe it away. The pungent mixture of sweat and the scent of Tiger Balm tingled her senses.

Five judges sat with stoic expressions at a table on the dais to her right. The senior judge, in a quiet voice, said, "*Sijak,*" Korean for "start," to begin the fifth round.

Jade's opponent launched a rear round kick. She expected the move. He had been using the same technique for most of the match, and had landed a few blows with it. At first. But now she was on to him. She blocked his shin with her left forearm while jabbing a front kick to his stomach. It connected. He expelled a short breath, surprised, and hunched back to his sparring position.

They circled, breathing hard, eyes locked.

Jade had been training for this moment for three years, but after six matches and five rounds in this one, she was exhausted. She had to end this. Now.

He began to raise his back leg for another round kick. *Doesn't he know any other kicks?* Jade didn't wait. She jumped up, her lithe body coiling as she turned clockwise. At the apex of her twenty-inch vertical jump, her right leg straightened and whipped across her opponent's head, connecting at his temple. As he fell, Jade completed the 360-degree spinning hook kick, landing softly on the mat in her original stance, her gloves near her head in a protective position.

She held her stance, then relaxed. He was not getting up.

Jade removed her headgear and released her ponytail. Her light brown hair, wet and clumpy, fell to her shoulders. *Lovely*, she thought, sarcastically. The spectators had been holding a collective breath, but they began buzzing when they realized she was a woman. The *dobok* (uniform) was not the most flattering attire for the female anatomy. As a biracial woman—thanks to a Japanese mother and a black father—her looks often drew the appreciative stares of strangers. Or, maybe this crowd just appreciated a good kick.

She crouched over her fallen competitor, concerned that she had hurt him. She offered her hand to help him up.

"Are you all right?"

He nodded, not meeting her eyes. He waved away her hand and struggled to his feet. Jade knew he was disappointed. This was his third time testing for this rank. *Whatever.* She had tried to be nice.

They both stood at attention, feet together, hands at their sides, facing the panel of judges.

"Mr. Randall," said the senior instructor, Master Won Ho. "I'm sorry. You didn't pass. Not because you lost, but because you forgot our core tenet of courtesy. I would like to have a word with you after this testing."

He turned to Jade.

"Ms. Harrington, by the power vested in me by the Tae Kwon Do Association, I now bestow upon you the rank of fourth-degree black belt. Congratulations."

Jade's chest swelled, but she didn't smile. The skin around Master Won Ho's eyes crinkled, and he nodded at her. She nodded in return, the beginning of a smile creeping onto her face.

The spectators clapped. Jade surveyed the crowd, not recognizing anyone except for a few classmates. But she didn't know them well enough to share in the glow of this accomplishment. Her past made it hard for her to make friends. Ever since she was a kid, after what happened, she found it hard to trust anyone. Still.

As she packed her gear, spectators came up to congratulate her and relive her spinning hook kick.

She thanked them and left the arena.

Alone.

CHAPTER TWO

Pittsburgh, Pennsylvania

I SAT IN a rental car across the street, watching.

They had already consumed several rounds of drinks at an Italian restaurant on the bottom floor of a downtown skyscraper that housed radio station KABC up on the top floor. The dinner rush was gone, except for seven station employees still going strong at a table near the front.

Most of the conversation was directed at a tall, broad-shouldered man. Whenever he spoke, his companions laughed as if he were a comedian. This funny man was named Randy Sells.

Sells stood and drained the rest of his beer before stumbling toward the back of the restaurant, bumping into chairs along the way. The restaurant didn't have its own restrooms, so patrons had to use the ones in the office building. I had scouted that out earlier.

I got out of my car, and sprinted across the street and through the lobby. I had to beat him to the restroom. I turned right and then left down a long hallway. I won. I heard his footsteps echoing behind me.

He stopped. I stopped, too. He may have heard me, but he could not see me.

Sells started walking again. His footsteps rounded the corner, toward me. I slipped out the back door next to the bathroom and into the alley behind the building. I left the outside door ajar.

The stench of rotten food and urine hit me. Nauseated me. I kept my composure and remained silent. And I waited.

Sells entered the restroom.

A few minutes later he came out, shaking his hands dry.

I eased the door open, took two quick steps, and put my arm around his neck. And squeezed.

He brought his arms up to free his throat and began to writhe away from me. He was bigger than I thought.

"What the hell do you—"

I re-established my grip, took the stun gun out of my pocket, placed it under his rib cage, and fired.

I held him tight and close as the electrical current pulsed through his body. After a time, he stopped struggling.

I whispered in his ear, as if to a lover, "There are consequences to what you say."

He sagged into me, and I dragged him outside and laid him on the pavement. I stared at the handsome face and reached for my trusted bat, where I'd hidden it earlier. Time for batting practice.

My swing was getting better.

CHAPTER THREE

Washington, DC

WHITNEY FAIRCHILD, JUNIOR Democratic senator from Missouri, strode down the steps of the Capitol. Landon Phillips, her legislative director, struggled to keep up despite his long legs.

Landon briefed her on her remaining schedule for the day, reading from his electronic tablet as they crossed Constitution Avenue toward the Russell Senate Office Building.

"You shouldn't read that while crossing the street," Whitney said.

"You're right, Senator. Bad habit." He stopped reading and carried the tablet like a book. "At three o'clock, you're scheduled for a photo op with kids from the elementary school with the highest points under the new Missouri scoring system. This will give you a chance to say a few words about education reform."

"Such as my plan to eliminate scoring systems?"

Landon ran his fingers through his long hair. "Uh . . . , that might not be appropriate for the occasion."

"How about my plan to let teachers teach children how to learn rather than how to take a test?"

"Not enough time."

"How about firing nonperforming teachers?"

"Ditto."

"You're no fun."

"You're having lunch today with Senator Sampson at the Four Seasons," Landon continued, "ostensibly to discuss Agricultural Committee work, but really his goal is to convince you not to separate farm subsidies from your welfare reform bill."

"He wants to break bread now after everything he's been saying about me?" Whitney said. Sampson was Whitney's rival for the Democratic nomination in the upcoming presidential primaries. Turning serious, she said, "Email his LD and work on a separate bill capping subsidies. The subsidies should be directed toward small- and mid-sized farmers only."

"Will do."

"Wait until after lunch."

A trim, fit man with black hair, a dark business suit and red tie, caught up to them.

"Senator Fairchild, may I speak with you?"

"Of course, Senator Hampton." To Landon: "Give us a moment."

Landon walked a few paces away, finding something, as always, to read on his electronic tablet.

She smiled at Hampton, his professorial glasses augmenting his self-proclaimed intellectual persona. "What can I do for you, Senator?"

"I can deliver the votes on welfare reform, if you back off supporting the anti-personhood legislation."

"You know I can't do that."

The Virginia Republican smiled as if it pained him. "But this is a state issue."

"No, this is a civil-rights issue."

"What about backing off the ERA? The deadline expired in 1982. It's dead already, for God's sake."

Whitney was shaking her head before he had finished speaking. "That's because most people think equal rights is already the law. Eric, you're wasting your breath. Give me something we can work together on. What about education? Immigration? The deficit?"

His lips parted to say something else, but he closed them.

"Maybe. I'll see what I can do. I'll be in touch. Good day, Senator."

He walked away. Landon rejoined her.

"What did he want?"

She filled him in.

"That's not going to happen."

"Not in my lifetime."

CHAPTER FOUR

Washington, DC

THE BIGGEST STUDIO at the Patriot News Network was painted orange and yellow. Loud colors for a loud man. Cole Brennan sat behind the microphone during his fourth commercial break of the hour, watching CNN, ABC, FOX, CBS, and NBC on the TV monitors on the wall opposite him. There was no breaking news.

Cole surveyed the guest list, waiting for his music intro to fade out. He put on his headphones. His producer said, "Our next caller is Frank from New York City."

"Frank from New York City. What's on your mind?" Cole asked.

"With all due respect, Cole, I disagree with what you just said. Income inequality isn't a recent phenomenon. The difference in wealth between the haves and have-nots widened over the last forty years. The rich continue to migrate to gated communities, cutting them off from the rest of us. If something isn't done, the divide will be permanent. The resentment between the rich and everyone else will only get worse. I believe . . ."

Cole, the number one-rated radio talk-show host in the United States, sipped his ice-cold sweet tea while Frank jabbered on. He believed that when someone began a sentence with "With all due respect," he wasn't being respected at all.

"Well, Frank," he interrupted, "what you neglected to say is the so-called rich create the jobs and pay the most taxes in this country."

"But that's not true—"

He hung up on Frank and spoke into the microphone.

"He also neglected to say education makes a difference. Not for those people who graduate from college with philosophy or African-American studies degrees and wonder why they can't get a job, default on their student loans, and stick us with the bill. I paid off my student loans, and so did you. Our kids can do the same."

The next caller asked about welfare reform.

"Good question," Cole said. "I believe it's far more compassionate to help people become self-reliant rather than dependent on the government. Don't you agree? The Commiecrats' grand scheme is to expand the number of folks on welfare and working in Big Government, ensuring them two voting blocs for life."

His producer signaled him: five seconds left.

"Well, everyone, we've run out of time. This is Cole Brennan protecting your life, liberty, and pursuit of happiness. Join us again tomorrow for 'The Conservative Voice.'"

He stood.

"That's a wrap."

He left the studio. "Great show, Mr. Brennan," said several of his young employees. He ignored them as he sauntered down the hall to his spacious office.

Cole sunk into the leather executive chair behind his desk and spun to remove a cigarette from the humidor on the credenza behind him. He didn't light it because of the stupid regulations that governed the workplace. How could the government tell him he couldn't smoke in his own office?

He scanned the walls lined with pictures of him with former Republican presidents, the current Senate minority leader and Speaker of the House, every important new person in the conservative establishment, and celebrities like Clint Eastwood and Arnold Schwarzenegger. Most celebrities were Socialists, but some, like Clint and Arnold, weren't afraid to come out of the closet and stand up for American conservative values.

His eyes rested on the photograph of his hero, former President Ronald Reagan. Well, he was trying to "win one for the Gipper," all right. Next, he settled on a picture he had taken with singer Gloria Estefan. Unlike some conservatives who preached family values, but lived quite the opposite, Cole believed in them and had never cheated on his wife. The singer was beautiful and charming, though. He smiled at the memory of meeting her.

Cole's eyes landed on a photograph of himself with President Richard Ellison. He scowled and shook his head. Ellison needed to get with the program. He hit the speed-dial button for the White House residence.

The president came on the line. "This better be good."

"We need to meet."

"Why?"

"I want to make sure we're on the same page."

"About what?"

"The game plan."

"This isn't a damn football game." Ellison exhaled. "Never mind. When?"

"Tomorrow. I'll leave instructions with your secretary."

Cole hung up, grabbed his jacket, and put it on over his pale green polo shirt. Ellison didn't like being told what to do, but so what. Ellison owed Cole. Cole was the kingmaker. With the support of his millions of listeners, and his influence on the financiers of Republican candidates, he put Ellison in office. And he could take him out. Ellison sometimes forgot that.

He should take the stairs from the third floor, but he had never met an elevator he didn't like. Yes, he needed to lose a few pounds—okay, maybe a hundred—but he was, as they say, fat and happy. Except when he thought about Ellison.

As the elevator car descended, Cole thought about ways to eradicate income inequality from the nation's political discourse. The country had more important issues to address.

Correction: more important conservative issues.

CHAPTER FIVE

Arlington, Virginia

"WHAT'S THAT NOISE?" Jade's boss, Supervisory Special Agent Ethan Lawson, said through the cell phone. "What are you doing?"

Jade glanced down at her gray Stanford basketball shorts and her black sports bra. The sweat glistened on her triceps and flat stomach. She stopped dancing.

"Nothing," she said, muting "Holiday" by Madonna.

He hesitated. "Okay . . . I hope you've been enjoying your vacation."

She looked around the living room of her two-story Arlington townhouse. Her collection of '70s and '80s albums were spread over the hardwood floor. A stack of books she planned to read this week towered high on the coffee table. She normally didn't have time for her favorite things.

"It's a staycation, and it hasn't started yet."

"It's already over, I'm afraid."

She sat on the sofa. "What happened?"

"The Pittsburgh Police Department needs a consult on the murder of a local radio personality. You are it. I've booked you and Merritt on a flight out of Dulles. You leave in three hours." He hung up.

She moved to the kitchen where Card, her cocoa-colored cat, squatted, attacking the Purina ONE in his bowl, as if he hadn't eaten in weeks. Card was short for Cardinal, the nickname of her alma mater.

Jade wasn't close to a lot of people, but she loved this cat.

She picked him up and stared into his eyes.

"Sorry to interrupt our vacation, but I need to go. I'll call your girlfriend to look after you while I'm gone."

She gave him a squeeze and a kiss and set him down. He rushed back to his bowl to resume eating, as if he had never been interrupted. Jade tried not to take it personally.

She called as she left the kitchen.

"You rang?" said a female voice, sleepy, playful.

"I need you to check on him."

"Card?" Zoe, her best friend, asked.

"Just for a few days."

"You owe me one."

The sudden silence indicated she had hung up.

CHAPTER SIX

Andrews Air Force Base, Maryland

PRESIDENT RICHARD ELLISON settled into his driving stance. Everyone around him remained library-quiet as he twisted his hips and raised his golf club high overhead. The whacking sound as the club met its target at the wrong angle was followed by the cracking sound of the ball slicing to the right and into the trees. A high-pitched squeal emitted from behind the president. The sound seemed incongruous with the big body from which it came.

Laughing, Cole Brennan said, "You can't drive worth a shit, Richard."

The rest of the foursome, Senator Eric Hampton and Representative Howard Bell, remained stoic as Ellison walked off the tee.

Cole swaggered up, placed the ball on the tee, and swung. The sound was true, and the ball sailed straight down the fairway.

Hampton and Bell took off in one cart. The president folded his tall, lanky frame into the passenger side, next to Cole. As he drove, Cole marveled at the championship golf course of Andrews Air Force base on this lovely spring day, basking in its military presence: the servicemen in uniform, the flags, order.

The Secret Service followed them in a cart at a discreet distance.

Ellison remained silent.

The president had the lean, sinewy build and handsome, rugged, weather-lined face of a cowboy. What one would expect of a man from Wyoming. Still sporting his tan, despite his many years in Washington, Ellison's lined forehead illustrated his troubles. With the country's deficit problems and the rising tensions with China, who could blame him?

Cole regarded the president. "Richard, I'm glad you sliced the ball again, because I needed a little word with you. One on one."

Ellison continued to stare through the cart's windshield.

Cole cleared his throat. "Even though this is an election year, I feel you're straying off the reservation."

"Get to the point." Ellison's Wyoming drawl was more pronounced when he was irritated.

"Okay, then. You need to stop talking about this left-wing income-inequality bullshit. Why do we always let the other side frame the political discussion? The rich get richer, because they work harder. They deserve to keep the spoils from their efforts. I never saw my dad growing up. He worked on Wall Street. He worked all the time to provide his family a better way of life. He doesn't owe anyone anything."

"Interesting word choice, Cole. 'Spoils' means plunder, taken from an enemy in a war or from a victim in a robbery. Don't say that in public or you'll give some activists the ammunition to resurrect the 'Occupy Wall Street' movement."

"Cut the shit, Richard. You know you're not my first choice, but you were the only alternative at the time. None of the wingnuts could win the general election. But I put you in office, and I can take you out."

"Are you threatening the president of the United States?"

Cole realized he needed to tone it down. He stole a glance at the Secret Service men in their cart. One of them may have been a woman, but he wasn't sure. "I know you're tired of Washington and want to retire to your ranch, but we need you for four more years. This election is bigger than you and me. The future of our country depends on you."

"I'd stop pointing your finger at me if I were you."

Cole dropped his hand back on the steering wheel. "No more income-inequality BS. Your constituents don't care about it."

"They should."

"What're you going to do? Raise taxes on the rich? Increase the federal minimum wage? Switch parties?"

The president remained silent.

"Listen to me. I need you to be vocal in your support of pro-life issues. At least two justices will be named to the Court next term, and we'll finally be able to overturn *Roe v. Wade*. We're close on passing 'personhood amendments' in Mississippi, Louisiana, Arkansas, Montana, and Colorado. Why can't you be more like Hampton?" Cole smiled and waved at Senator Hampton standing near the green. The senator returned the wave. "Richard, if you don't get with the program, I swear I'll support someone else."

"Who? The uncontrollable billionaire businesswoman? The Libertarian wingnut? Or the governor who has destroyed his state, but has the saving grace of being a minority?" He laughed. "Although he doesn't seem to remember he's a minority."

The knuckles on Cole's hand were white against the black steering wheel. He seethed inside, afraid to release his grip. He stopped the cart at the edge of the fairway.

Ellison was staring at him. "Face it, Cole, you're stuck with me."

Cole released his tight grip, glanced at Ellison, and then into the trees where the president's ball had disappeared. "This is your stop."

The president paused before alighting from the cart, turning to face Cole. "You're right. This election is bigger than you and I. Maybe we should cease pushing the social issues and focus on important things. Like the deficit and entitlements." Ellison's jaw clenched. "By the way, I'm a pretty good hunter. Next time, why don't we go hunting? I don't miss."

Ellison stepped out of the cart to hunt for his golf ball.

"Ellison," Cole said. He waited for the president to turn around. "Don't make me run."

CHAPTER SEVEN

Miami Gardens, Florida

"I AM COMMITTED to helping the poor and the disenfranchised realize the American Dream. Yes, we will extend a hand in need, but the American ideal will not be handed to you on a silver platter. You must earn it."

Whitney scanned the huge crowd at Sun Life Stadium, home of the Miami Dolphins and the University of Miami Hurricanes football team.

"Welfare is not a permanent solution. All of us must take personal responsibility for our own lives. That's the best way to strengthen our families, our communities, and our nation. Under the Fairchild administration, workfare programs will be created to help welfare recipients receive the training they need to facilitate their return to the workforce.

"My administration will not forget that creating legislation is the fundamental job of Congress. It's appalling to me that every year this body is creating fewer and fewer laws. The role of lawmakers seems to have been forgotten among all the politics. Our major issues must be resolved, and the journey will not be easy. But as John F. Kennedy once said, 'Let us not seek the Republican answer or the Democratic answer, but the right answer. Let us not seek to fix the blame for the past. Let us accept our own responsibility for the future.'

"Ladies and gentlemen, as your president, I will accept the responsibility of restoring the United States of America to a country we can be proud of once again. A nation respected and admired by every other nation as the greatest and most powerful on earth."

The crowd stood and applauded. Whitney waved in its direction and left the podium. She shook hands with people lined up on either side of the red carpet laid down for the occasion. The hot Florida sun pressed down on her in her cream blouse and navy-blue suit. After posing for pictures, she walked into the coolness of the large, cavernous hallway of the stadium where her advance team waited. Sarah, her body woman, handed her a bottle of water.

Whitney gave her a grateful nod, took a long sip, and turned to her campaign manager, Ted Bowling.

"That seemed to go well."

Ted shook his head. "Well? Better than well . . . that was great! You were great!"

Ted had the remarkable ability to cough and talk at the same time. He lit a cigarette, and lifted his chin to exhale.

"They loved you! And your hair looked fabulous. The way the wind teased it, . . . it was majestic. Magnificent. We'll poll it, but I think you should wear your hair down from now on."

"And, perhaps, the speech resonated with them as well."

Ted missed the rebuke. He touched her elbow.

"We need to get going. Xavi is meeting us at the next stop." Xavier "Xavi" Fernandez was the Independent governor of Florida.

They walked past the player locker rooms and headed outside to a Lincoln Town Car. Ted took a final puff on his cigarette and threw the butt on the ground, and began to grind it with the ball of his shoe.

Whitney stopped. "Pick that up."

Ted paused in mid-grind and bent to retrieve it.

Whitney turned and smiled and waved to the people seeking one last glimpse of her before ducking into the car. Ted climbed in the other side. She patted her forehead with a handkerchief and smoothed her hair before leaning her head back on the headrest and closing her eyes.

Her cell phone rang. She eyed the digital display before hitting the button. "Yes?"

"Senator? Landon. Senator Sampson called. He has a proposition for you."

"Did he tell you what it is?"

"No, but he wants to meet with you first thing when you get back from your trip."

"Anything else?"

"We're getting calls."

"About my speech?"

"A lot of people aren't too happy with the workfare program idea. Some are complaining you sound like a Republican."

"Hillary Clinton once said, 'I have a conservative mind and a liberal heart. I fight for change within the system.'"

"What do you want me to tell Sampson?"

"Tell Sean to set up a meeting." Sean was Whitney's receptionist and scheduler.

"Yes, Senator."

She hung up.

"What did Mr. Perfect want?" Ted asked.

"Not now, Ted."

"As you wish. Here are the talking points for your meeting with Xavi." He started to hand her a sheet of paper.

Whitney raised her hand to ward him off. "Give me a minute."

She turned from him and gazed out the window at the bleak landscape. Florida had broken a record for its number of days without rain. The land was dry, everything brittle. Scientists attributed the lack of rain to global warming. She needed to develop a centrist global warming message for her platform.

As she continued to gaze out the window, she wondered, *What was Senator Sampson up to now?*

Pittsburgh, Pennsylvania

PITTSBURGH POLICE LIEUTENANT John Cooper held the door for Jade and fellow special agent, Christian Merritt, as they entered Angelo's. It was an Italian restaurant in the Golden Triangle, Pittsburgh's downtown center.

Cooper, in his late forties, had an almost transparent complexion and a slight paunch. He nodded at the hostess.

"We're looking around."

She smiled and they headed toward a table close to the entrance.

"The group sat at this table. Sells sat here." He put his hands on the back of a chair facing the front of the restaurant.

Jade removed a red peanut M&M from the small bag she kept in her gray slacks and slipped it into her mouth. She glanced through the window.

"The UNSUB must have been watching him through the window." She scanned the restaurant, eying the waitstaff. "Did you check out all the employees, Lieutenant?"

Cooper stared at her longer than appropriate. Jade, accustomed to stares, ignored it.

He found his voice. "Uh . . . , call me Coop. My friends do."

Was he blushing?

"Yes, we did," Cooper continued. "They were either working or had an alibi."

"Were the alibis verified?" Jade asked. "Corroborated by others?"

"Of course," Cooper said, his words clipped.

Christian, his hair cut military-short, crossed his arms in front of his muscular chest. "What was the radio show about?"

"The rich getting richer and the poor getting poorer." Cooper shrugged. "I'm not sure why that's news to anyone."

"What about the callers that night?" Christian asked. "Any that caught your attention?"

"None, yet, but we're still checking. Most of them weren't too happy with the topic of the show. Heck, Sells didn't seem to want to talk about it, either. He was a pretty big deal around here. He was singlehandedly trying to revive conservative talk radio in Pittsburgh. Could've made some enemies along the way. After dinner, he told everyone he needed to use the john and to order another round of beers. He never returned." He cocked his head. "This way." He led them toward the back. "The restaurant doesn't have its own restrooms, so customers use the ones in the building."

He held the door open to a hallway and turned right. They arrived at the bathroom at the end of a long hall. Cooper knocked on the door and peeked in.

"Anyone here?" He motioned for Jade and Christian to follow. "We know Sells used the bathroom. We found a partial print on the inside door handle and a handprint on the wall over the urinal. His co-workers said he was drunk. We figured he needed the wall for support. No prints on the faucet; it's automatic."

A man, who appeared as if he had had several drinks himself, entered the restroom. He stared at Cooper, Jade, and Christian. Then he muttered, "Sorry, dudes," and stumbled out the door. Christian laughed. Cooper blushed again. Jade rolled her eyes. They went back out into the hallway.

"We think he was incapacitated in some way here—maybe tased—and dragged outside." He pushed the release bar on the back door, which opened into an alley. The narrow alley stunk of trash and urine. Farther down, a large dumpster took up most of the narrow lane. "When he didn't return, his co-workers went looking for him. One checked the bathroom and then out here, thinking Sells may have come out to talk on his cell phone or grab a smoke. He didn't see him. It gets pretty dark out here at night. Another co-worker checked the front of the building. After a while, they all figured he went home. You can leave the bathroom and go out the front of the building without going through the restaurant." He pointed to the pavement. "The victim was killed here."

Jade bent down a few yards from the door. Flecks of blood still dotted the pavement. "Cause of death?"

"Severe blows to the head. He lost a lot of blood."

"Spatter?"

"Cast-off pattern on the wall and the ground."

"So, you're thinking he was most likely hit with a blunt instrument."

Cooper nodded.

"Did you recover the murder weapon, Lieutenant Cooper?"

"Coop. And no."

"Any defensive wounds?"

"Nope. The victim's head looked like mush. He didn't put up much of a fight."

"Is this where you found him?"

"Not exactly." Cooper started walking down the alley. Jade and Christian glanced at each other and followed.

Cooper stopped at the dark green dumpster. "We found him in here. Someone threw him away with the restaurant's nightly trash. His tongue had been cut out."

✻

"Jesus," Christian breathed.

Jade stared down at the body on the stainless steel table at the Allegheny County Medical Examiner's office. Although it had been cleaned up, the face of Randy Sells had been beaten beyond recognition. *Was that the point?* Sells would have a closed casket at his funeral.

"No question as to the manner of death," Cooper said.

Jade scanned the length of the corpse and returned to his face. Almost all the damage had been inflicted to the right side of his face. "The UNSUB is left-handed."

Christian nodded. "And has anger management issues."

Jade's eyes didn't leave the victim. "Sells was a big boy. Our suspect must be strong."

"Or had help," Christian said. He turned to Cooper. "Who found him?"

"One of Angelo's busboys. He had started to swing the trash into the container when he noticed the vic. He dropped the bag, ran back into the restaurant, and told the manager, who called 911. The kid was shaking so hard during our interview, we had difficulty getting the story out of him."

"Time of death?"

"Between nine p.m. and midnight. Sells's friends were still drinking while he lay dying in the alley."

Jade continued to stare at Sells's face.

"Anything back on the tongue?"

"Sent to the lab. Results aren't back, yet."

"Cutting out someone's tongue is extreme," Jade said. "This seems personal."

"We agree," Cooper said. "We don't think the victim was chosen at random. Nothing was stolen as far as we could tell. He still had his wallet and cell phone on him."

Christian pointed at the corpse's bare neck. "According to the autopsy report you showed us, the victim wore a necklace with a crucifix. Maybe this is connected to his religion or church. A hate crime. Did you check it out?"

Cooper's cheeks reddened, a vein throbbed on the right side of his pale forehead.

"We're in the process of checking it out now. We've just started this investigation. We haven't even completed our interviews, yet. My boss called you in. Premature, if you ask me. He's nervous because Sells was a rising celebrity in this town, and Pittsburgh is ranked as one of the safest big cities in the country every year. There's a lot of pressure for us to solve this case quickly and protect our ranking. But this isn't some damn TV show. We need more than forty-eight hours to solve the crime."

Jade touched Christian's forearm before he reacted. She smiled at Cooper in apology.

"I think we've seen enough here, . . . Coop. We need to catch a flight. Is there anything else you want to tell us?"

Cooper broke his stare with Christian and turned to Jade. "Yeah, about the tongue. When we arrived on the scene, the vic was clasping it in his own hands. Like a rosary."

CHAPTER NINE

Athens, Georgia

"YOU SOUND TIRED," said Grayson, her husband.

"Sometimes I wake up with no idea which state I'm in, much less which city." Whitney lay back on the king-size bed in her hotel suite, cell phone pressed to her ear. "People seem to be receptive to our message," she said, "though some of my base may be disappointed."

"When are you coming home?"

"I thought we could meet in Ohio in a few days for dinner. A romantic dinner."

Grayson had always understood the demands of her career and never been resentful that she had to fit him into her schedule. As the CEO of Fairchild Industries, a St. Louis-based biotechnology and agricultural conglomerate, Grayson didn't enjoy much free time either.

"Sounds good to me," he said. "I need to see you. Hold you. What's wrong?" He knew her.

Grayson was normally too busy to miss her. "I could ask the same of you."

"I just miss you. That's all." He paused. "Is it Hampton? The women's rights bill?"

"Have you spoken to the children?" Whitney asked. She didn't want to talk about work.

"I spoke with Chandler today. He decided to intern with us this summer. I'm not sure why he wants to work for the family firm all of a sudden. I rarely talked to him last semester. He only calls when he needs—"

"—money," they said at the same time and laughed.

"And Emma," Grayson continued, "is freaking out about her final exams, and they're still three months away. Again, not sure why. She inherited her mother's brains."

Whitney scoffed. "Please . . . ." She thought of her son, Chandler, a junior at the University of Missouri, his hair falling on his forehead no matter how many times he pushed it back and her daughter, Emma, a freshman at Princeton, whose nose was the same as Grayson's. "I miss my babies."

"They aren't babies, anymore."

"I know. I talk to Emma every day about nothing at all, and those calls mean everything to me." She paused, sighed. "Dear, I need to run. My audience awaits. I'll call you tomorrow about dinner. I love you."

"I love you, too. I'm so proud of you."

She held the cell phone next to her heart.

At the discreet knock on her door, she placed the phone on the nightstand. "Coming."

Whitney rose, smoothed her shirt and skirt, and put her heels back on. She went out into the living room of the hotel suite. Ted Bowling and several others on her campaign staff sat on the beige sofas and chairs with laptops and papers spread out everywhere. Easels with white boards were placed throughout the room for a strategy session.

A presidential candidate was never alone, and the lack of privacy would only become worse when she became president. Yes, she was able to grab a few minutes on occasion, such as just now with Grayson, but most of the time she was surrounded by the individuals in this room.

Whitney sat, crossed her legs, as she thought again of the unusual anxiousness in Grayson's voice. Scanning the faces of her team, she forced the thoughts of her husband from her mind. "What's the plan for tomorrow?"

CHAPTER TEN

Washington, DC

"HEY, COLE. THIS is Carl from Lubbock, Texas. Love your show. The reason for my call is I'm not too happy with Ellison. Why does he feel the need to compromise with the Socialist Democrats? Why isn't he doing more to protect and promote our conservative values?"

"Good questions, Carl. Sometimes, and I think you would agree, some of the folks in our party aren't 'right' enough for me. They don't stand up for our conservative heritage. They're either weak and willing to compromise with the Commies or they flip-flop as Romney did back in the day. Romney flipped more times than an Olympic high diver on steroids. I think President Richard Ellison sometimes forgets where he came from and who elected him to office. He may need help getting in touch with his 'inner conservative.' That's what I'm here for."

"Why don't you run, Cole? We need a man like you in the White House."

"Because my calling is to spread the word to you good folks. Thanks for the call, Carl. Next caller."

"Cole, this is Fred from Nebraska. Senator Sampson is trying to keep the farm and welfare reform bills together. Do you support this?"

"Absolutely not. The federal government pays around thirty-two billion dollars per year to farmers, whether they grow crops or not. Our US Department of Agriculture—it's not a coincidence its acronym is DOA, dead on arrival—also provides subsidized crop insurance and marketing support for the farming industry at a cost to American taxpayers of five billion dollars a year. Crop insurance guarantees eighty percent of their revenue. Most other businesses must pay these expenses out of pocket without government help and with no revenue guarantees. Why should farmers be the exception?"

"Yeah, but Cole, I'm a farmer. I need that money—"

"Listen, Ted. You farmers resisted subsidy reductions for decades. Subsidies made sense when we were a country of farmers, but now you all represent a small percentage of the population. These subsidies are costly and transfer income from general taxpayers to farmers, who then overproduce, resulting in lower prices, and more subsidies. It's a vicious circle, Ted. Worse, these handouts hinder you guys from taking the actions needed to compete in the global economy. We want a free market, where those who invest and innovate reap the rewards. Prices should be set by supply and demand, not subsidies."

"But—"

"Did you know the average farmer makes more than the average US industrial worker?"

"Uh, no, I didn't, but—"

"Did you know millions of dollars in farm subsidies and crop insurance are paid to dead farmers? I'm talking fourteen million dollars per year of our money. Our government doesn't know whether you're dead or alive. It's not capable of managing this."

"But—"

"A fraud ring in North Carolina bilked the government for over one hundred million dollars. Listen here, Ted—"

"Fred."

"Senator Sampson is pushing this bill because his family owns farming corporations. He and his cronies in Congress are all farmers or ex-farmers, and they're trying to stuff their own pockets. Farmers need to be disciplined and self-reliant like the rest of us. Sorry, Fred, the subsidies must go. This is tough love, my friend. I'm not even going to answer your question about welfare reform. You all know how I feel about it. Next caller."

"Yo, Cole, this is Adam from St. Cloud, Minnesota. What do you think of Senator Fairchild as a candidate?"

"Well, Adam, from St. Cloud, Minnesooooooooooooooota. I think she is the chick version of Mitt Romney. She was a bleeding-heart liberal when she was in the House. Now, all of a sudden, she is talking about compromise and making lazy people work? I don't buy it, and the American people won't buy it. Liberals think the public is dumb. That we don't understand what's in our best interest, so they need to make decisions for us. The Commiecrats love her, because the women's libbers have been nagging them to death to nominate a female candidate. She doesn't stand a chance.

"Before we go, remember to pre-order my book coming out this summer, *Communism in Russia is Dead, but Alive and Well in the USA*. Ain't that the truth! You can also purchase my other books, newsletters, apparel, and DVDs on my website, www.theconservativevoiceonline.com.

"This is Cole Brennan protecting your life, liberty, and pursuit of happiness. Join us again tomorrow for 'The Conservative Voice.'"

❋

The black limousine was at the curb in front of the studio, and the driver held the door open for him. Cole Brennan lifted his bulk and sat in the seat facing the front, a glass of cognac in the cup holder. On the short drive to his home in Bethesda, Maryland, he sipped the brandy as he made a quick call to his agent, who had been pestering him for the final manuscript of his new book. Cole had no problems pre-selling the book, but finding the time to write these days was proving problematic. He completed the call by assuring his agent it was almost finished—*Not!*—as the limo ascended the long driveway to his sprawling home. Before the car had stopped, five of his six children ran toward him. The oldest, Cole Jr., followed them, too cool to run.

Cole hugged each of his kids and held the hands of his youngest two as they strolled toward the front door. His wife, Ashley, still retaining the figure of the fashion model she once was, stood in the doorway, smiling, holding his second cognac of the evening.

He grinned and gave her a quick kiss, and stepped inside the massive foyer. They shuffled down the hallway and entered the large family room at the back of the house. Cole plopped on the overstuffed sofa. The kids gathered around him and all started to speak at once.

"Dad! I got an 'A' on my test."

"Dad! Don't forget my game this Saturday!"

"Dad! Boys are gross."

"Dad, watch this!" another of his sons said, and he tumbled into a forward roll.

Cole laughed. "Very good, Ronnie. One at a time. What was your test in, Madeline?"

"English."

"Who are you playing this weekend, Sport?"

"The Spartans!" Ryan, his seven-year-old, said.

Cole turned to his eight-year-old daughter. "Kaitlin, I'm a boy, and I'm not gross."

She continued to stare at him with an expression as if she'd eaten something distasteful.

"What is it, sweetheart?"

"Dad, some kids were talking about you at school today."

"Sweetheart, people are always talking about me. Go on. What did they say?"

Kaitlin hesitated, then said, "They said you only like rich people and people who look like you."

Cole was stunned. "What? That's not true. I-"

Ashley clapped her hands. "All right, kids. Dad just got home. Let him rest for a minute. Go wash your hands for dinner."

"Okay!" the four youngest said, as they raced out of the room. The two eldest children sauntered after them.

"No running!" Ashley called after them. She glanced at Cole, uncertain. She tried her best to eliminate conflict in their home, since his job was stressful enough. He smiled and moved his hand holding the drink to the side, providing room for her to climb into his lap. She gave him a kiss.

He squeezed her to him.

"Why do kids run everywhere? My last inclination is to run anywhere. Unless someone's chasing me." He laughed, but it sounded forced even to him.

Kaitlin's words didn't bother him. He had heard worse many times before. Given his profession, he had grown immune to what people said about him.

No, it wasn't what she said that hurt him. It was the expression on her face that tore at his heart. He was rich and revered in this country because millions of Americans agreed with his values and where he stood on the issues, while here in his own household, he saw doubt about his character on his daughter's face for the first time.

CHAPTER ELEVEN

Washington, DC

THE HEADQUARTERS OF the Federal Bureau of Investigation took up the entire block between Ninth and Tenth Streets on Pennsylvania Avenue in Northwest Washington, DC. The J. Edgar Hoover Building's Brutalist architectural style, popular in the mid-twentieth century, was now listed by *Washingtonian* magazine as one of the "Buildings I'd Tear Down." A travel website proclaimed it "the ugliest building in the world." Although Jade Harrington agreed with the widespread assessment, her affinity was strong for the historical building and the twelve flags in front depicting the evolution of the United States flag since before it became a republic.

The first floor, built to accommodate commercial businesses that never materialized, remained empty—and now, for security reasons, always would. Two red barricades blocked the entry into the parking garage. Yellow chains and ten-foot high barricades cordoned off the stairs. Tours of HQ, once a popular DC tourist attraction, were canceled indefinitely for renovations. Those renovations would never be completed.

The building appeared to be a fortress. And it was.

The Monday after returning from Pittsburgh, Jade dropped her briefcase beside her desk in her fourth-floor office, grabbed her favorite FBI mug, and headed for the break room for coffee. On her way back, she stopped by Christian Merritt's cubicle, or rather his pictorial shrine to his wife, four kids, and golden retriever. "Hey. How was your weekend?"

Christian shifted his solid frame in his desk chair. "Good. You?"

"Watched the Wizards."

"Why do you think they're called the Wizards? I don't understand why they don't use their magic to win a game."

"There's always next season. What are you working on today?"

"The Morales case. You?"

"Doing some research on Sells. See if I can dig up anything to help Cooper."

"Don't you mean 'Coop?'" Christian batted his eyes like a coquettish female. "Uh . . . , 'Call me Coop. My friends do.'"

"Shut up," Jade said, giving Christian a playful push. His rock-solid body did not budge.

She returned to her office and straightened the files and other items on her desk, making sure the stacks aligned with the desk's edge.

An overpowering cologne announced the arrival of Special Agent Dante Carlucci. He leaned against her door frame, watching her.

"A tidy desk makes a tidy mind?"

Jade continued to straighten the items.

"Something like that," she said, not looking up.

Dante had curly brown hair, a long nose, and one ear higher than the other. All of his features were a little off, but in combination made him handsome. And he knew it. He wasn't her type, though. He knew that, too.

Dante had been a rising star at the Bureau. That is, until Jade arrived in the division. Since then, his star had fallen, while hers continued to rise. During her first week, he had also hit on her, as he did with every woman he met under fifty. He had not taken the rejection kindly.

"How come you never ask me what I did on the weekends?" he asked.

"Why should I? You always do the same thing."

"You're jealous 'cause I'm getting some."

She booted up her computer. "So you say."

"How's Zoe? Man, she's fine. I sure wish she didn't swing on the other side of the fence."

Jade ignored him and popped a red peanut M&M into her mouth. Dante couldn't stay quiet for long.

"Why do you eat one M&M at a time? Who does that?"

"Me." Jade began perusing her emails until Dante gave up and left. She typed "Randy Sells" in the search bar. Thousands of hits came up. She clicked on one.

Randy Sells, KABC Talk-Show Host, Murdered

Popular Pittsburgh talk-radio host Randy Sells was found dead Friday night behind a downtown restaurant in what police are calling a homicide.

The body of the 28-year-old Sells, a political conservative whose talk show aired the last three years on KABC-AM, was discovered in an alley behind Angelo's Restaurant at 600 Grant Street at about 10:30 p.m. The body was beaten almost beyond recognition, according to police sources.

Jade read several more news items on the Sells murder but didn't learn anything new.

She paused for a moment and then typed "conservative talk show host" into the Google search bar. Four million hits. Jade perused the first few pages, most of the links referring to Cole Brennan. She knew of Cole—everyone did, and everyone called him by his first name—but didn't listen to his program.

Jade took a break, refreshed her coffee, and wandered over to Pat's cubicle. Patricia "Pat" Turner, fiftyish and overweight, looked like someone's grandmother. Individuals who met her were fooled by her appearance. Jade was not. Pat had been with the FBI forever. She could run the place.

"What're you up to?" Jade asked.

Pat finished typing on her computer. "Nothing now. What do you need?"

Jade leaned against a filing cabinet. "Looking into this Sells murder." She brought Pat up to speed on what she had done so far. Pat tapped the keys on her keyboard as Jade talked.

Pat added "murder" to the search request. Randy Sells's murder topped the search results.

She clicked through the next several pages and the links changed to stories about conservative talk-show hosts in general. Nothing helpful.

"What about 'killed?'" Jade asked.

Pat clicked through a few pages of search results. She clicked to the next page. Jade leaned over her shoulder, expecting another dead end.

Halfway down the page, she pointed to a link for Pat to click on.

The story was dated ten years ago.

Chattenham College Radio Personality Killed

A Chattenham College talk-radio personality was found dead earlier today next to his car in the campus radio station's Main Street parking lot in what police are calling a homicide.

Kyle Williams, 22, a Chattenham student who hosted a controversial conservative talk-radio show at campus station WCCO-AM, was found on the ground beside his car. Police say Williams suffered at least one blow to the head with a blunt instrument.

The Chattenham County Police Department requests that anyone with any information about this crime call 215-555-5555. Grief counselors will be available to talk to students and staff. A candlelight vigil will be held on the campus's Quad on Friday.

There weren't any follow-up articles on progress or suspects or arrests.

Jade looked at Pat. "Are there others?"

They spent the next two hours searching the Internet and other databases without success. By this time, Jade had pulled up a chair and her coffee sat on Pat's desk, cold and half-full. Forgotten.

Jade stood and paced the corridor between Pat's cubicle and the cubicles of other agents. *Were the two murders connected? Why ten years apart? Were there others?*

She popped her head back into Pat's cubicle. "I gotta run. I'm late. Keep working this."

❄

An hour later, Jade Harrington paced the sideline, glaring at LaKeisha, her point guard.

"LaKeisha, run the offense!"

LaKeisha smiled at her as she dribbled in place near the half-court line. She gave Jade a thumbs-up.

"You got it, Coach."

Jade tried hard to hold the glare and prevent the smile trying to form on her face. LaKeisha's smile never failed to produce one of her own.

Jade coached a girls' basketball team made up of preteens from Anacostia, a rough DC neighborhood. Some people called the players on her team "at risk" kids. Jade thought of them as kids who had gotten the short end of the stick in the universal draw of circumstances that dictated where one was born. They just needed a break.

The old high-school gym in Southeast DC sported sagging nets, crooked rims, and dead spots on the court floor, but these kids didn't care. They just wanted their own place to play.

LaKeisha passed the ball to her teammate on the wing, faked as if she were going to set a pick for the other wing, and then sprinted toward the basket for a give-and-go pass. After receiving the ball, she went up for a shot, but instead passed it behind her back with her left hand—LaKeisha was right-handed—to a forward cutting down the lane. The forward made the easy layup.

Jade shook her head and laughed. LaKeisha never did things the easy way.

For her, the more difficult the shot or the pass, the better. Sounded like someone else Jade knew. Herself.

Jade, a former All-America basketball player at Stanford University, enjoyed her time with these kids. No matter how busy she was, she tried her best not to break her commitments with them—and to be present. For the next hour, she would not think of Sells, Kyle Williams, or the work piling up on her desk. In truth, she never felt as free as when she was on a basketball court. Whether the court was in Palo Alto, Madison Square Garden, Japan, or on the playground.

It was home.

The sight of the teams running up and down the court dredged up the memory of that day after elementary school. That day was never too far from her thoughts. The day she thought of as "before."

Three girls in her eighth-grade class had followed her home and beaten her up. They called her "Bink"—and worse—although Jade was black and Japanese, not Chinese. She didn't bother to correct them. After her attackers left, she stayed on the ground for a long time, bleeding and bruised and broken. Through her tears, she recognized another girl from school whom she did not know.

The girl reached down and helped her up.

Jade realized many things that day. Her parents couldn't protect her. Her teachers couldn't protect her. With no brothers or sisters, she had to learn how to protect herself. She also learned that kindness could come from strangers. The next day—"after"—she decided: never again. She hadn't cried since.

Jade convinced her parents to enroll her in Tae Kwon Do, and she learned to defend herself. She started practicing basketball. Every day. She slimmed down and her body became stronger. She got rid of her glasses, replacing them with contact lenses. After she'd been named an All-America her junior year in high school, with scholarship offers from every major college in the country, all the kids who had teased her wanted to be her friend.

No one ever messed with her again—or became her friend.

The whistle sounded, ending the game.

Most of her players left the gym as Jade stuffed basketballs into a bag. LaKeisha dawdled nearby before coming up to her.

"You know I like messing with you, Coach."

Jade straightened, holding a ball.

"I know you do, but would it hurt you to make the easy shot for once instead of the fancy pass?"

LaKeisha was a talented player—Jade's best—with an excellent chance of going far in the sport, if she didn't get pregnant, go to jail, or end up dead—the three fates all too common for female students at this school. The girl smiled, her mini-twist hairstyle springing from her head in every direction.

"Did you always take the easy shot, Coach?"

No. "Just do it, LaKeisha. Okay?"

"I'll try, but it's not in my nature." She grew serious, a foreign emotion for her. "You know what I like best about you, Coach?"

"What's that?"

"I can work on my skills, close to home, and I feel safe. And it's not because you're an FBI agent."

Jade froze, beating back the emotions from her childhood. LaKeisha broke into a big smile, serious time over, the moment broken. She grabbed the basketball from under Jade's arm and sprinted for the door under the Exit sign. Over her shoulder, she yelled, "You need to protect the ball better, Coach!"

Jade called out after her as the door slammed shut.

"You better bring it back to the next practice!"

Jade sat on the bench and laughed, stuffing the last ball into the bag. She sobered as her thoughts returned to work. To the two murders. *Why so long between them?*

She thought about what Lakeisha said. She liked working on her skills close to home.

Jade stopped closing the bag in mid-zip.

Maybe the killer was honing his mission close to home, with the Williams murder, and then decided to branch out.

She whipped the cell phone out of her pocket and texted Pat.

Try conservative television commentator, blogger, journalist, columnist.

Got it, came the response.

❉

Jade, still in the black Adidas track suit she had worn to the game, was sprawled out on the wicker sofa in her best friend's apartment in Adams Morgan, a diverse neighborhood in Northwest DC.

Zoe, kicked back in an adjacent chair, had her feet up on the coffee table. The television was on, muted, and African music quietly played on the stereo. The apartment sported walls splashed with different hues—indigo, eggplant, and lime—and displayed art she purchased in Senegal and framed posters from various local and national political campaigns Zoe had worked on: marriage equality, the equal rights of women, Occupy DC, and the taxation without representation of DC citizens.

The bookshelves contained Nigerian statues, mementos from Zoe's time in Ghana with the Peace Corps, and Ivory Coast knickknacks, including swaths of Kente cloth, reflecting Zoe's fascination with all things African. The aroma of patchouli wafted throughout the living room.

Jade lay on her back, shooting a round pillow into the air like a basketball. "Who sings this?"

"Shantae Ndiaye. The hottest singer in Africa right now."

"Don't you own any Prince?"

"No. Unlike you, I live in the present decade. You need to expand your horizons, including your musical tastes. So, how was your vacation?"

Jade rolled her eyes. "One day a vacation does not make. I had started planning what I was going to do for the week when Ethan called and sent me to Pittsburgh for a consult." She caught Zoe staring at her. "What?"

"I wish I had your high cheekbones."

Jade eyed her former college roommate with the funky hair and the game-show-host smile, and threw the pillow at her.

"Shut up."

Zoe caught the pillow as the doorbell rang. She returned with two brown paper bags, a thin layer of grease on the bottom of each. She put the Chinese takeout on a pile of magazines on the coffee table, picked up their empty beer bottles, and went to the kitchen for replacements.

Jade grabbed the carton labeled Kung Pao Chicken and a pair of chopsticks and ate straight from the container. She chased the food with a sip of Zoe's ice-cold Tsingtao. They enjoyed the meal in comfortable silence.

"How's work?" Jade asked.

"Tough. Most of our candidates are in tight races with lots of money on the other side. We don't receive enough funds to support all of them. Of course, we're working on Senator Fairchild's presidential campaign." Zoe's nonprofit organization helped elect pro-choice, Democratic female politicians.

"She's still behind in the polls. Do you think she'll win the nomination?"

Zoe smiled. "You're such a jock. It's always about winning for you."

Jade gave a wry smile. "What else is there? Besides, you're a little competitive yourself."

"True. I wouldn't count out Senator Fairchild. She's smart, attractive, politically savvy, with a better chance against Ellison than Sampson. It's also about time the US had a woman president. We're one of the last developed countries who haven't." Zoe got up and moved toward the bathroom. "We share that dubious honor with Japan and Italy, by the way. Be right back."

Jade picked up their empties and headed to the kitchen. She must have bumped Zoe's desk as she passed it, because the sleeper screen disappeared and the laptop sprang to life. She started to pass by, but something made her stop. Jade placed the bottles on the desk and began to read.

AlextheGreat: *I've been searching for a job for two years. I have a college degree. Sent out thousands of resumes. I can't even get hired at McDonald's. I don't have enough money for food. I don't want to be on food stamps or collect unemployment. I want to work. What should I do?*

PittFan: *That sucks.*

JoanofArc: *What was your major?*

AlextheGreat: *History.*

PittFan: *Ouch.*

A chat room. Jade continued to read.

JoanofArc: *Have you tried temping? That could be a way for you to earn money and an assignment may turn into a full-time job.*

AlextheGreat: *Good idea.*

SusanB: *What about teaching?*

Oedipus: *Why would anyone enter the teaching profession today? Teachers are vilified as lazy, union employees who make the rest of us pay more in taxes. With cutbacks at the state level, it is difficult to land a teaching job much less keep one.*

PittFan: *Agreed. And teachers don't make shit. They're disrespected, glorified babysitters.*

SusanB: *I wouldn't go that far. Who taught you how to write and express yourself so eloquently?*

PittFan: *True. Hey, did you just slam me?*

Oedipus: *The fundamental issue is, because of the Great Recession, millions of our elderly are forced to work into their golden years, crowding out young workers like Alex. If things don't change, we will be the first generation worse off than the generation before us.*

SusanB: *During this downtime, Alex, why don't you become more involved* *with Senator Fairchild's campaign? Instead of sitting around feeling sorry for yourself, make yourself useful. Go out and do something.*

PittFan: *Ouch. How do you really feel, SusanB?*

Oedipus: *I think volunteering is a good idea. 'Letting the market work' is not working. The 1% keeps getting richer while the rest of us keep falling behind. People still can't find work, toil in jobs for which they are overqualified, or have given up. The key is removing Ellison from office.*

PittFan: *Right on, brother. Hey, did you all hear about the conservative talk-show host in Pittsburgh who got whacked the other day? I couldn't stand the guy, but . . . man!*

Jade froze.

SusanB: *One fewer preacher of hate.*

JoanofArc: *That's awful, SusanB.*

The chat continued, but Jade's eyes started to lose focus. The cursor on the monitor was next to SusanB, which, knowing Zoe, could only be short for Susan B. Anthony.

Who were these people? What was the point of this chat room?

Zoe came back into the living room and stood still.

Taking the offensive, Jade pointed to the screen. "What's this?"

Zoe waved her hand dismissively and sank deep into her chair. "It's a liberal chat group I belong to. Something I do for fun. Like minds and all that."

Jade's eyes scrolled down the text. "Seems pretty intense."

"It can be, yeah."

Jade grabbed the empties and headed to the kitchen. She returned, handing Zoe a fresh Tsingtao.

Jade settled on the sofa and took a long pull of her beer. "Was that the last chat conversation?"

"We were in the middle of a discussion when you got here."

"'One fewer preacher of hate?'"

Zoe gave her a small, shy smile. "Am I being interrogated for something?"

Jade carefully placed her beer on the coffee table. "I don't know. Should you be?"

"Why are you so interested in the murder of a radio talk-show host in—" Then, Zoe made the connection. "—Pittsburgh."

Jade leaned forward. "How involved are you with this chat group?" *Could Zoe be involved in this murder, even tangentially? She can't be. Right?*

"What do you mean, involved?" Zoe sat up. "I don't like where this conversation is going."

"Why aren't you answering the question?"

"Why are you snooping through my things?"

"Zoe . . . ."

Zoe stood. "I think you should leave."

Jade rose and stared at her best friend. Zoe's eyes were bright, her eyelids blinking rapidly.

"I'm just doing my job," Jade said.

"I'm not your job." Zoe pointed toward the front door. "Leave."

CHAPTER TWELVE

Columbus, Ohio

THE RESTAURANT'S OAK tables and dark decor complemented the enticing aroma of Tuscan cuisine. Whitney spotted Grayson at a table near the back of the restaurant, and her heart fluttered at the sight of him. Other patrons began the inevitable whispers and pointing as she glided toward his table. Whitney smiled and nodded at them, but did not stop. Grayson stood, smiling, as she came nearer. He gave her a quick hug, a chaste kiss, and pulled a chair out for her.

"Darling," Grayson said, grabbing her hand. "You look amazing."

She glanced down at her beige wool and cashmere coat and back at her husband. He was still handsome, with light brown hair, a slender face, and a straight-edged nose. If she didn't know how much he loved her, she would worry about him with other women.

"You're not so bad yourself, although you look tired. Are you getting enough sleep?"

He shrugged. "There's a lot going on . . . at work."

Grayson ordered wine.

"I'm so glad you could get away," Whitney said.

"Fairchild Industries can survive without its CEO for one day."

"How's business?"

"The lab developed a genetically engineered seed we think will do well in the marketplace. We think it'll be ready next quarter. Revenues for existing products are up. We froze hiring and wages so profits are up, and cash reserves are high. Business is good."

"So many companies are taking the same approach. Or they're outsourcing jobs overseas, two of the reasons why the real unemployment rate is not budging. Perhaps you can hire a lot of people once I become president. Help me drive down the unemployment rate."

The waiter offered them the bottle Grayson had selected. Grayson swirled, sniffed, and tasted the wine. "Excellent."

The waiter poured and left.

They raised their glasses. "To us!" Always the same toast.

"Darling," Grayson said, "the private sector's responsibility isn't to lower unemployment, but to provide the most value to its shareholders." He sipped his drink. "For me, that means our family."

"I know." She sighed. "Unemployment is a long-term problem with no easy answers. The infrastructure bill I co-wrote would repair decrepit roads and bridges and create thousands of jobs. It could solve so many ills. Instead, it's languishing in committee. You would think my colleagues would act after the number of collapsed bridges over the last few years."

"All I know is you're a fighter. Keep fighting." He frowned. "Are you okay?"

"I'm fine. Really." She paused. "It's Hampton. He's using the classic Overton Window, and I'm not sure how to fight him."

"What Window?"

"The Overton Window. A theory postulating a range of ideas considered viable politically and acceptable to the public. By proposing a radical idea, you either expand or move the window until it becomes acceptable public opinion."

Grayson was trying to catch up. "Okay . . . ."

"For example, a politician may try to expand the window of narrowing a woman's right to choose by banning abortions except in the cases of rape and incest. Another candidate comes along and advocates no abortions under any circumstances. This position will be dismissed as extreme under current public opinion, but makes a ban on abortions except in cases of rape and incest seem more reasonable and more acceptable. The window has been shifting and expanding for years. To change a political outcome, you must expand your constituents. That's Senator Hampton's game plan."

Grayson had caught up with her. "And, if Ellison is re-elected, he'll be able to appoint one or two justices to the Court and *Roe v. Wade* will be overturned."

"To paraphrase Bill Clinton, 'Abortions should be safe, legal, and rare.' If *Roe v. Wade* is overturned, abortion will be none of those things. The rights of women ebbed away over the last decade. But things won't change until some women are faced with hard, individual choices, and then realize they don't have a choice."

"Darling, this issue is so controversial. Do you think you should focus so much on it? You're not the only one responsible for solving it. Perhaps you're taking it too personally."

"I'm a woman. I must take it personally."

They remained quiet for a moment.

"So," Grayson said, "the primaries are down to the two of you. Senator Paul Sampson doesn't seem like the kind of guy who'll give up, though."

"And I'm not that kind of woman."

He raised his glass to her. "This I know."

"I'll need you and the children to make some appearances with me. I don't want them to miss a lot of school, but Ted says it's important that people see us as a family. See me as a mother."

"You are a mother. A good one." He touched her hand. "We'll work it out."

A woman came up to them, blushing. "I'm sorry to interrupt. We admire you so much, and my daughter, Bella, here wants to be like you someday. Wants to be president. Can I please take a picture of you with her?"

Whitney leaned toward Grayson and away from the woman. "I did not think I would live to see the day when every child in the United States, regardless of race or gender, could grow up believing she or he could become president. Isn't it wonderful?"

To the woman, she said, "It would be my pleasure."

She rose and put her arm around the young girl. Her mother snapped their picture with her smartphone camera. Other diners moved toward their table. Another woman shoved a baby into Whitney's arms. Whitney never understood why parents would hand their baby over to a stranger, even a stranger running for the Democratic nomination for president of the United States. She pasted on a smile, turned toward the woman who had whipped out her smartphone, and kissed the baby.

Whitney scanned the people now waiting in the impromptu line and exchanged a glance with her husband.

So much for a quiet, romantic dinner alone.

Washington, DC

THE NEXT MORNING, she passed Pat's cubicle on the way to her office.
"It's in your inbox," Pat called after her.
Jade hurried to her office.

Jade,

I found these two articles. There were no follow-ups on the investigation or subsequent arrests.

Pat

Jade clicked on the first link.

Popular Columnist Taylor LeBlanc Found Dead

Advocate columnist Taylor LeBlanc was found dead today in his condo in Perkins Rowe. Baton Rouge Police confirmed that the case is being investigated as a suspected homicide.

LeBlanc, 30, who interned with The Advocate while a student at Louisiana State University, worked for the newspaper his entire career.

The date line was two years ago. The next article was dated five years ago.

Pete Paxson Found Dead

Conservative blogger Pete Paxson of Houston had a date last night. He never made it. Paxson, 34, was found dead this morning in the parking garage of his apartment building. The Houston Police Department has ruled his death a homicide.

Paxson was an engineer for the Shell Oil Company by day and wrote his blog at night. Paxson, divorced, is survived by a daughter.

She looked up to find Pat standing in the doorway. Pat handed her a piece of paper. "Names and phone numbers of the lead detective for each case."

She turned and left.

Jade shook her head, smiling. Pat was a godsend.

Jade called the detectives on the list. No suspects, no arrests. It didn't appear robbery was the motive in any of the cases. In the Houston case, Paxson's Rolex watch was still on his wrist and the keys to his late-model BMW in his pocket when he was discovered.

She came across a gruesome discovery that connected all the cases.

All the victims' tongues had been cut out.

None of the police departments had disclosed this fact to the media. Criminal investigators often kept a salient detail secret to screen out anyone making a false confession or providing deliberate, misleading information. A sensational detail like a missing tongue would have lit up the police tips' hotline numbers.

Jade skipped lunch and spent the rest of the afternoon building her case. Near the end of the day, she picked up a stack of printouts and headed down the hallway to her boss's office. Ethan Lawson was talking to Dante. She knocked on his door frame.

"I need to talk to you," Jade said to Lawson.

Lawson looked at Dante. "Give us a minute."

"I'd like to finish this conversation later," Dante said.

Lawson nodded.

Dante stood as she crossed to the other guest chair. With his back to Lawson, Dante bestowed on her a bright insincere smile.

"Always the teacher's pet, I see."

Jade gave him her winning smile. "Just trying to follow in your footsteps."

He frowned and hesitated before walking out.

She admired the large FBI emblem on the wall behind Lawson depicting the scales of justice and the words Fidelity, Bravery, Integrity. On either side hung his diplomas: a bachelor's degree from the University of Florida and a Juris Doctor from George Washington University.

"J. Edgar Hoover went to GWU Law School, you know," Ethan said.

"I know. You tell me every time I come into your office." She handed him a summary she had written with a few of the articles she had printed out. "The Sells case. I think there are others."

Lawson began reading. He took his time.

Jade waited.

He finished the last page, leaned back in his chair, and considered her. He twirled the wedding ring around his finger.

"What do you need?"

"Not what," Jade said. "Who."

Lawson nodded. He knew whom she meant and picked up the phone.

He stared at Jade while he spoke. "Max, we have something. It's right up your alley." He listened. "Agent Harrington's on her way."

❁

An hour later, Jade drove past the replica of the US Marine Corps War Memorial at the entrance to the FBI training academy at Quantico, Virginia, thirty-six miles south of Washington, DC.

She entered Max Stover's small, cramped office without knocking. Max was a special agent for the Behavioral Analysis Unit 4 of the National Center for the Analysis of Violent Crime, which provided behavioral-based support to the FBI and other federal, state, local, and international agencies in the investigation of unusual or repetitive violent crimes against adults. The public would call him a profiler, although the FBI didn't list an official position by that name.

Max looked up from reading the report Lawson had emailed to him. Pale, slender, with short, fair hair balding on top, Max was newly single after his wife left him six months ago following thirty years of marriage. He had thought they had come to an agreement of civil co-existence. His job came first; she came second. He provided a good home for her with everything she needed. Except him. She decided she wanted more. He had heard that her new boyfriend wasn't making the same mistake.

Jade moved some papers and files from a chair and sat down across from him. "Thanks for seeing me right away."

"Of course," Max said.

"I discovered four cases that may be related," Jade said.

She described her trip to Pittsburgh, her conversation with Lieutenant John Cooper of the Pittsburgh PD, and the preliminary information she and

Pat had found through the Internet and the FBI databases on the murders of the other three conservative media personalities.

"The time between the murders is shortening," Max said.

"I realized that, too."

Max pushed up his glasses. "Who would have the motive to kill conservative commentators?"

"A liberal or someone who disagrees with conservative ideology?"

"Perhaps. Or another conservative who may be envious. Or for some larger agenda we may be unaware of. It's too soon to tell. We need more."

"The removal of the tongues is significant."

Max nodded, as if she were a student answering a question in class. He leaned back in his chair, thoughtful. "He silences them. Forever. Because of their profession? Did they know something the perp wanted to remain a secret? Or something else?"

Basketball players have those nights when every shot goes in. It's called being in the zone. Max, too, tended to get into a zone when he analyzed motives. Jade could have walked out the door now, and he wouldn't have realized it.

"All the tongues were left at the scene. He doesn't keep them as trophies unlike some serial killers," Max continued. "If we're dealing with a serial killer. It's possible anything associated with the victims would make him angry or uncomfortable."

"Or be a painful reminder of something," Jade said. "What about the UNSUB putting the tongue in Sells's hands like a rosary?"

"He was unconcerned the body would be found and took the time to stage the victim's presentation. The staging was important to him. He's trying to communicate a message to someone. The police? The media? The public? The victim's family? Someone else? All the above?"

"What about the removal of the crucifix?"

"A lot of religious possibilities with both the tongue and the crucifix. The tongue symbolizing a rosary is conjecture. It may mean something entirely different. The stolen crucifix may not have anything to do with the victim's or the perpetrator's religion."

"Or lack of religion," Jade pointed out.

"Was the necklace valuable?"

"A couple hundred dollars."

"Conceivably, it was a shiny object that caught his attention. Like impulse shopping. Impulse stealing. But according to your information, the

UNSUB didn't steal anything from the other victims. Why did he deviate from the pattern?"

"You're raising more questions than answers."

"That's my job." Max smiled, which always appeared more like a grimace to Jade. "The UNSUB is a planner. He studies his victims' daily patterns and knows when they'll be alone. He possesses some degree of superior intelligence." Max snapped out of it. His tone changed. "How are you, by the way?"

"I'm fine."

"As one of my best students ever at the academy, I doubt you're just fine."

"You're only saying that because I'm your goddaughter." It wasn't true. Max was harder on her because he was her godfather. And more like a father to her, since her parents had been killed by a drunk driver when she was in college.

She couldn't think about them now.

They sat in silence for a few moments.

"My gut tells me these crimes were committed by the same person," Jade said. When Max didn't respond, she continued. "And he's still out there." Jade waited. "He can't get away with this."

"I know," he said.

"I need to go after him."

"I know that, too," he said.

CHAPTER FOURTEEN

Washington, DC

SENATOR WHITNEY FAIRCHILD arrived at the door of the United States Senate chamber at the same time as Senator Eric Hampton. He paused, and with a quick hand gesture, indicated for her to proceed first.

"How are you this fine morning, Senator Fairchild?"

The man was charming.

"Never better, Senator Hampton." They walked down the aisle together. Whitney asked, "Are we in agreement?"

Hampton, his hair parted on the side and slicked into place, pushed his glasses up on his nose with his index finger. He clutched a black leather folio in his other arm. "Yes, we are."

They parted midway, and Whitney squeezed her way through to her assigned desk. She greeted the senators on either side of her as a new legislative day began. After an hour of bill introductions, joint resolutions, and committee reports, she listened as the education bill was called to the floor for consideration and to the opening statement by the chairman of the committee that introduced the bill. Another senator from the same committee offered an amendment.

Pleased that Hampton promised to deliver sufficient votes from his side on her welfare reform bill, Whitney was happy to cast her vote for education reform, which she supported. It was better for her that the bill was proposed by the Republicans; her support demonstrated to the American people her willingness to reach across the aisle. Everything was proceeding as they had agreed. As planned.

Senator Hampton rose and addressed the presiding officer, who granted him permission to speak.

"Thank you, Senator. I'm happy to support the education reform bill put forth," he paused, "and I'd also like to propose an amendment, if I may, entitled

The Protection of Rights for All Citizens. Over the last two hundred years, our nation made extraordinary strides in providing equal rights for all citizens. Now, is the time for us to extend this legacy of fairness to a group that cannot speak for itself, but who is crucial to the future of this nation. The unborn."

The lull of the proceedings had relaxed Whitney, but she jolted to full alert at Hampton's last statements. His amendment was not unusual; senators introduced nongermane amendments to bills all the time. This was not why she sat up in her seat and stared at him in shock and surprise.

He had lied to her.

He continued to address the presiding officer: "My amendment will extend equal rights to all persons at the moment of conception in every state of the land."

He went on to explain that his proposed legislation would defund Planned Parenthood and eliminate all its facilities in the United States.

When he finished, Whitney stood. She forced herself to appear calm to everyone else, but she placed her hand on the desk for support to stop it from trembling. Even though Hampton had given his word, she should not have been surprised. She should have known better.

Whitney allowed a brief thought on how the course of her own life would have been different, if she had had access to Planned Parenthood as a teen.

After the presiding officer recognized her, Whitney took a deep breath. "With all due respect to the senator from Virginia, the rights of one group are being ignored by his amendment, the group who makes up the majority in this country. I am speaking of the rights of women and their right to make decisions about what happens to their own bodies."

Whitney spoke for over an hour. She spoke of the Equal Rights Amendment, which fell three states short of ratification in 1982. She proposed repealing the deadline and attaining the ratification of the remaining three states. She spoke of pay equity; today, women were still paid, on average, seventy-seven percent of what men were paid for the same job.

As she took a sip of water, her phone vibrated on the desk. It was a text from her daughter, Emma.

Thinking of U. I luv U, Momma.

Whitney willed her eyes from tearing. Emma's words could not have come at a better time. This was why she kept fighting. For her daughter and all the daughters in this country.

Whitney remained standing and spoke in the Senate chamber for the rest of the afternoon.

CHAPTER FIFTEEN

Washington, DC

"MY LONG-TIME LISTENERS know I don't invite guests onto the show often, because you all tune in to listen to me. But today, we have a very special guest. The president of the United States of America, Richard Ellison. Mr. President, welcome." Cole Brennan glanced at Ellison sitting in the swivel chair across from him in the studio.

"Thank you, Cole. It's a pleasure to be here today."

"Now, Mr. President. You're up fifteen points on whoever the Commiecrats nominate, and one may think you can put the campaign on cruise control and win this thing. But what are you doing, sir, to ensure victory?"

"Well, Cole, I'm not taking anything for granted. In my travels all over America, I have listened to people and heard their problems. Financially, people are still hurting, and we're doing everything we can to help ease their anxieties about the economy. Our economic plan is a good one and we believe we're on the right path to restore this country to economic prosperity."

"One way I think we can help ease their anxieties, Mr. President, is to eliminate regulations on our wealth creators. Think of all the jobs that'll be created when business owners can spend more time growing their businesses and less time filling out forms."

"That's right, Cole. My administration tried to repeal Dodd-Frank, Sarbanes-Oxley, and all the financial regulations enacted during the Great Recession. We've not been successful yet, but when I'm re-elected, and our party controls Congress, we will be. We'll eliminate environmental regulations that hinder development and hamper job growth. A free-market economy produces greater economic growth in the long run, more jobs, and greater prosperity for all."

"I couldn't agree more. President Ellison, how can we assure my listeners and good conservative folk everywhere that you are the man to lead the conservative movement for the next four years?"

"Examine my record. I believe our party is best suited to reduce the budget deficit. During my first term, wasteful spending has been reduced and the government shrunk by fifteen percent. In my second term, I hope to eliminate the progressive income tax structure, which punishes the American Dream, and enact my flat-tax proposal."

"What about passing the second Defense of Marriage Act?"

The president hesitated. "That may be difficult in the current environment. As I said, my administration is focused on the economic prosperity of our citizens, and—"

"—which starts with the nuclear family," Cole said. "One man, one woman in a union recognized by God. Switching gears, Whitney Fairchild seems to be moving up in the polls and gaining with independent and women voters. She's taken a centrist approach and abandoned the Socialist policies she is known for. If she becomes the other party's nominee, what's your strategy, Mr. President, for putting this woman in her place?"

"Senator Fairchild is a well-meaning, and, I believe, good person, but she doesn't possess the experience, character, or the fortitude to be president. She has flip-flopped on many issues. I've been consistent in my views since I was the governor of Wyoming, then as a US senator, and now as president. The American people want someone who will stand by his principles. I am that man."

"A 'personhood' amendment has been proposed in the United States Senate. The federal government is finally realizing that the unborn are entitled to the same rights and freedoms we enjoy. Do you support this amendment?"

Ellison hesitated again. "I believe this issue is best decided by the states."

"But you do believe life begins at conception?"

Ellison glared at him. Cole stared back, glad this interview was being conducted on the radio rather than television. He motioned with his hand for Ellison to answer.

Ellison pursed his lips and spat out, "Yes."

"I want to thank you, Mr. President, for coming on our show today. Godspeed."

The president didn't respond.

"We're going to a commercial break and will be back in a minute. Don't go anywhere. This is 'The Conservative Voice' with Cole Brennan."

The ON AIR light went dark. They stared at each other for several moments. President Richard Ellison bowed his head, stood, and left the studio without another word.

CHAPTER SIXTEEN

Crystal City, Virginia

THE VODKA SLID through the blocks of ice as I poured the liquid into a glass and took the drink over to one of the floor-to-ceiling windows. My penthouse condo afforded a stunning, panoramic view of the Potomac River, the Kennedy Center, and the Washington Monument. On a clear day, the US Capitol was visible in the distance. Traffic, still snarled at this time of the evening, snaked up the GW Parkway. I soaked in the beauty of my city—our city—as I sipped my drink.

Cole Brennan's broadcast just ended. Why do I continue to listen to him? Why do I torture myself? Because I must. It is my duty. That is the curse of every great person throughout history, is it not? To suffer? Joan of Arc suffered. As did Martin Luther King Jr., Gandhi, and John F. Kennedy. Perhaps they were great because they suffered. Why should I be any different?

I thought back to Brennan's broadcast. President Ellison was not a bad man, but his moderate views didn't stand a chance against Brennan and people of his ilk. I didn't like how he put words into the president's mouth. I did not like it at all. I needed to do something about it.

Like Kyle. Kyle had been a good start. A success. It was good training. Then, I extended my reach. I was disappointed with the lack of media attention after LeBlanc and Paxson. The journalist and the blogger. Now Sells. Doesn't anyone care?

I shook my head, turned from the window, and wandered to the space I used as an office, next to the dining room. I sat in my gray Herman Miller Mirra chair and tapped the touchpad. The three computer monitors on my desk sprang to life.

Good. My friends were here.

Some might think you cannot call people you have never met your "friends." I could make friends in the physical world. I choose not to. I much prefer the characters I meet in books. They are more interesting and more genuine than the people I meet in real life. But I had something in common with my online friends. The issues. Only the issues. The issues that mattered.

The cursor was next to my name. I typed: *Sorry, I'm late. What are we discussing tonight?*

SusanB: *Women's rights.*

PART II

Washington, DC

ETHAN LAWSON, IN a pressed white shirt and dark gray tie, leaned back in his office chair.

Jade sat across from him.

"What's the latest?" Lawson asked.

Jade recited without notes, "I followed up again with the detectives assigned to each case. Kyle Williams, from Chattenham, Pennsylvania was killed ten years ago with a blunt instrument. Pete Paxson of Houston, Texas, was also killed with a blunt instrument five years ago. Carpet fibers were found at the scene. Taylor LeBlanc was murdered in Baton Rouge two years ago with a blunt instrument. A hair and carpet fibers were found at the scene."

Unlike hair, trace evidence such as carpet fibers might not lead them to the suspect, but would help convict a suspect once he was identified.

"Did they match the Paxson fibers?"

"No," Jade said. "Randy Sells, the latest victim, was also killed with a blunt instrument. No carpet fibers, but a hair was found in the blood at the scene. Test results aren't back yet."

"Not much to go on."

Jade leaned forward. "Ethan, all of them had their tongues cut out."

"Yes, there's that."

"And all the victims were conservative media commentators."

"Yeah, there's that, too. Okay. What do you propose we do?"

"I need a task force. We need to go after this person."

"Jade, you have a pretty full caseload as it is. At this point, these killings may be tragic coincidences."

Her back straightened and she gave Lawson a look. Her look. "You're kidding, right?"

"I know. It's not funny."

"No, it's not," Jade said. "I have a feeling about this. I'm going to investigate it with or without your support. On my own time, if I have to."

Ethan twirled his wedding ring and sighed. "I'm sure you will. Who do you need?"

"Christian, Max, Pat, and Austin."

"I see you haven't thought about this."

Ethan came from around his desk and sat in the guest chair next to her. His brown shoes glistened. Jade bet she would see her reflection in them if she bent for a closer inspection. The faint whiff of shoe polish brought back memories of her father, an Army colonel, sitting on a small, wooden stool in the kitchen of their split-level home, surrounded by rags, brushes, shoes, and tins of black and brown Kiwi polish. She loved watching the care he demonstrated with every brush.

Ethan said, "I'll authorize the task force . . ."

"Thank you." She started to get up.

". . . as long as Dante is included."

Ethan knew how she felt about Dante. "I know what you're thinking," he said, "but that's nonnegotiable. Dante possesses useful qualities you don't appreciate. You'll see."

She didn't bother to argue. She had what she wanted.

CHAPTER EIGHTEEN

Washington, DC

SENATOR WHITNEY FAIRCHILD rose from the chair in her office and walked around the large mahogany desk. She gave Senator Paul Sampson, her opponent in the Democratic primary campaign, a wide smile, took his right hand in both of hers, and squeezed. She had read once that Bill Clinton had shaken hands this way with those individuals who meant something to him. She was sure Sampson knew that as well. Although her gesture was disingenuous, she hoped he would be flattered by it.

She motioned for him to sit as she returned to the high-backed brown leather chair behind her desk.

Sampson arranged his massive frame in the guest chair. "Quite a speech the other day."

"Thank you for the filibuster threat. It shut Hampton down." *And is the reason for your visit today.* "I owe you one."

"Yes, you do." He stared at an oil painting of Susan B. Anthony high on the wall behind her.

Whitney glanced over her shoulder. "Before Susan B. Anthony retired, she said, 'Failure is impossible,' encouraging her fellow suffragettes to keep up the good fight. She believed one half of the American people should not be kept in bondage." She turned back to Sampson. "We need her now."

Sampson appraised her. "Maybe she's here."

Whitney was surprised by the compliment.

"I'll support your welfare reform bill," Sampson continued, "even with its silly little workfare program, but I need you to combine the bills. Those farm subsidies are essential to the people of the great state of Nebraska."

Whitney rose and moved to a cabinet built into the wall. She opened its doors to a stocked bar and turned to him. "The usual?"

He nodded. She picked up a bottle of whiskey she reserved for guests and filled a glass a quarter full. She poured a glass of red wine for herself. She handed him his drink. Instead of returning to her desk chair, Whitney sat next to him and crossed her legs. Sampson gave them a quick, appreciative glance as Whitney sipped her wine. "A combined bill will die in the House," Whitney said, "and you know it."

His eyes were like pinpoints over his ruddy cheeks, his love of drink an open secret on the Hill.

"The bill can pass with full Democratic support. Otherwise, farmers will suffer. What's the alternative? What are all those people going to *do*? Do we plan to retrain them? To do what? Think of the national security risk and economic threat of becoming dependent on foreign sources for our food." His voice softened. "My people need those subsidies. If you do this for me," he paused, peering into his glass, "I'll drop out of the race."

This caught Whitney off guard. She and Sampson were separated by a few points in the polls, less than the margin of error. He was handing her the nomination.

"That's a heavy price to pay."

"But I want to be considered for VP."

Of course. Sampson was a seasoned pro and would never give without taking. Whitney calculated the costs versus benefits of his proposal. His request went against the platform on which she was campaigning, and everything she believed in.

She shifted her drink to her right hand and extended her left to him. "You have a deal."

CHAPTER NINETEEN

Baton Rouge, Louisiana

A MAN WITH a complexion of dark, roasted coffee stood outside the security station, holding a sign with the word Harrington written in block letters. His eyes never strayed from hers as she walked toward him.

Jade stopped in front of him, peering down slightly. "Detective Miles Thomas?"

The man offered his hand. "That's me. Agent Harrington?" He tilted his head and glanced down and back up at her. "No heels."

"Nope."

"Huh. Welcome to Baton Rouge." He extended his arm toward the exit. "This way."

They were traveling down I-110 South in his unmarked Chevrolet Caprice within minutes. The early-model vehicle was well kept; Detective Thomas took pride in his car.

"Good flight?"

"Not too bad. As usual, I was stuck fighting for space on the armrest with the guy next to me. I'm not sure why guys think the armrest is theirs. Do you?"

Thomas kept his eyes forward, moving his muscular forearm from the armrest between them. "No idea. I know you're in a big hurry, so let's get to it. Where to?"

"I'd like to see the crime scene."

"The condo was empty for a long time, but someone lives there now. Let me make a call."

After he hung up, Thomas said, "This case received a lot of local media attention at the time. Taylor LeBlanc was *the* torchbearer for conservative politics in Baton Rouge."

"Who called it in?"

"We received an anonymous tip."

"How?"

"Text."

"Did you trace it?"

Thomas shook his head. "The texting program allows the public to send in anonymous tips."

After merging onto I-10 East toward New Orleans, he took the second exit, Bluebonnet Boulevard. They passed a six-story building on the left, and Thomas waved his hand. "LeBlanc worked there."

A mile later, he turned into Perkins Rowe, an upscale commercial and residential development. He parked in front of the Barnes & Noble. They walked through the bookstore, its back entrance opening to the rest of the shopping complex and residences.

Jade stared at the numbers above the door as the elevator ascended. "Any luck with the neighbors?"

"We interviewed all of them living on his floor. No one saw anything on the night in question. Although they live close together, these neighbors don't socialize with each other much. A few would run into LeBlanc every once in a while in the neighborhood. The consensus was he was a nice enough guy, kept to himself, but had many female visitors."

A representative of the leasing company, a skinny woman with hair over-processed and dyed blonde, waited at the end of the hall.

"Hello! Hello!"

"Hello, again." Thomas whipped the gold badge from his belt. The rep waved it off and smiled at both of them without bothering to look at it. She turned and opened the front door.

"The occupants are at work, so you shouldn't be disturbed. The place appears a lot different from the last time you were here, Detective. Thank God! Please lock up when you leave."

He nodded. "Thank you."

Jade took in the condo's lofty ceilings, hardwood floors, and open floor plan.

Thomas scanned the room.

"She's right. LeBlanc had a gigantic flat-screen television on that wall. Black furniture: leather sofa, coffee table ottoman, TV console, bookcases. Not a flower, throw pillow, or family photograph in sight. He did, however, own an extensive game collection with every iteration of Madden Football, NBA, and FIFA soccer. Oh, yeah, and lots of action movies." To her expected question,

"Never married. No girlfriend at the time, although he had an on-again, off-again relationship with a young female co-worker at the paper."

"Fingerprints?"

"About forty sets. We processed all of them through IAFIS"—the Integrated Automated Fingerprint Identification System, an FBI database containing thousands of fingerprints. "Nothing." Meaning none of the owners of the fingerprints had ever been arrested for a crime or worked for the government. "After ruling out the cleaning lady, we determined the thirty-nine remaining prints belonged to Caucasian women."

"Using the latest fingerprint technology, I see. What else?"

"No sign of forced entry. No sign of a struggle. We found the victim fully clothed, bound by rope. He was lying in front of the stereo system, arms crossed over his chest."

"In what condition was the body?"

"A complete mess. Head battered. Only the right side, though. There were blood and brains everywhere."

"Tongue?"

"I'll show you the photos when we get back to my office," Thomas said.

"Who found him?"

"A few of the neighbors called the leasing company complaining about the loud noise coming from the condo."

"What was it? Music? An argument?"

Thomas grunted. "A recording of a speech he gave. Burned to CD. It was set to replay over and over again."

Jade paused to absorb that. "Tell me about his column."

"Published weekly. Dedicated to conservative issues. Readers could write in and comment."

She nodded toward the CD player. "What was the speech about?"

"I don't recall. I'll check on that for you."

"Any of his readers ever disagree with or become angry at LeBlanc?"

"LeBlanc could be obnoxious. He'd write articles some people found politically incorrect—sexist or racist—but his friends and co-workers said he was neither of those things."

"What about the women he dated? Did any of them feel betrayed or angry?"

"As far as we can tell, not enough to kill him. His co-workers said he was okay to work with and he got along with everyone. He received the occasional hate mail. We checked out the senders, but came up with nothing. He wasn't depressed or anxious about anything. He had a core following, active in local charity work. He had everything going for him."

"Where did he hang out?"

❊

They strode toward The Wine Shoppe two blocks away.

Jade downshifted her gait to allow Thomas to keep pace. Despite the short walk, her silk shirt stuck to her back from the humidity. "What do we know about his movements that night?"

"His editor said LeBlanc left sometime after eight. We believe he parked his car in the residence lot over there"—he waved to his right—"and walked to The Wine Shoppe and had several glasses of wine and some bar food."

"Time of death?"

"The coroner estimated between midnight and three a.m."

"You told me on the phone a witness—the ex-girlfriend—saw him leave with another man. No one else saw him?"

"We couldn't find a corroborating witness. The manager said LeBlanc was a frequent customer, but the place is usually packed and he couldn't swear LeBlanc came in the night of the murder."

They entered the bar and walked around so Jade could get a sense of the place. She shielded her eyes when they came out, the sun brighter after the bar's dark interior.

Thomas gestured at the retail establishments around them. "LeBlanc's co-workers said he loved Perkins Rowe because it had everything: restaurants, a grocery store, clothing stores, a gym, and a movie theater. He used to always tell them he never had to 'stray too far from the reservation.'"

Thomas stopped and faced Jade. "Murders like this don't happen in this part of Baton Rouge. He probably felt safe here."

Jade shrugged. "He was wrong." They resumed walking toward the car. "I'm hungry," she said. "Do you mind?"

❊

Detective Miles Thomas stopped at a squat building, the paint long since peeled away, squeezed between two modern office buildings. Jade tried to hide her surprise as she emerged cautiously from the car.

Thomas shut the car door. "Don't let the decor fool you."

A small sign, the same color as the faded paint, hung on a nail at a crooked angle next to the door: Momma's. The hole-in-the-wall exterior opened up to a cozy interior of ten small wooden tables. The cheap wood-paneled walls were filled with pictures of different individuals with Momma, the thin, light-skinned woman behind the counter at the rear of the restaurant. Jade recognized some of the individuals in the photographs: Former Senator Mary Landrieu and her brother, New Orleans Mayor Mitch Landrieu, former Governor Bobby Jindal, New Orleans Saints quarterback Drew Brees, NBA greats Shaquille O'Neal and Pete Maravich, and WNBA all-star Seimone Augustus.

Thomas pointed. "Our mayor, Kip Holden, former Governor Kathleen Blanco, and, of course, you know, Lolo Jones and Glen 'Big Baby' Davis."

"Instead of who has eaten here," Jade said, "the better question is who hasn't?"

Thomas ordered a Coke. She asked for a Pepsi. Thomas shook his head, disappointed.

She eyed him and then the waitress. "What?"

Thomas tried to stifle a grin. "You're in Coke country."

The waitress nodded a slow, all-knowing confirmation.

Jade conceded. "I'll have a Coke then."

After the server brought their drinks, Thomas raised an eyebrow at Jade. She was about to take a drink. "What?"

He inclined his head at her extended pinkie as she held her soda.

She smiled. "Don't let the pinkie fool you." She sipped the drink, trying not to grimace at the sharp flavor.

He laughed.

Since this was Jade's first time in Baton Rouge, Thomas ordered a sampling of everything: gumbo for an appetizer, jambalaya, red beans and rice, and crawfish étouffée. She put her foot down when he attempted to order alligator. She developed an instant philosophy of not eating anything that could eat her.

The waitress placed their meal on the table. The aroma of the dishes made Jade's mouth moist.

Thomas glanced at her plate. "Do you always separate your food like that?"

Jade shrugged. "I don't like different foods touching each other."

Thomas shook his head, and, as if to prove a point, mixed all his food together. He popped a forkful into his mouth.

Jade shook her head. "That's disgusting."

Thomas smiled. "You look like you can still play ball." He had done his homework.

"A little."

He laughed. "Yeah, right. I'll let it go or next thing I know you'll be challenging me to a game."

Jade took a sip of her Coke. "What about your name? Miles Davis?"

"My mother, a jazz fan, wanted me to be a musician. I always wanted to be a cop. When I was growing up, playing 'cops and robbers' with toy guns was still okay. I was always on the side of the good guys." The light in his eye dimmed. "When I became a teenager, some of my friends started playing with guns for real."

"How'd you get out?"

"My mother enrolled me in a Big Brother program. Someone took an interest in me and saved me from the fate of most of my friends who are either in jail, on drugs, or dead. This city earned the distinction as one of the top US cities for murders per capita. Mostly black-on-black homicides." His shoulders inched down, as if he alone bore the burden to save his black brethren.

Thomas, though a big man, had a certain gentleness. They discussed their careers and his eyes lit up when he talked about his wife, Tracy. His wife was a lucky woman. During the conversation, he remarked she was light-skinned, which still seemed to matter in the Deep South.

Later, at the police station, Thomas signed Jade in as a guest. The atmosphere buzzed as they weaved their way between the desks of the other officers.

In his office, he pointed at the conference table in front of his desk. "I pulled the case files. Let me grab them."

She peered around him at the mess on his desk, the top covered with stacks of paper, towering in some cases a foot high. Coffee cups of various life spans acted as a buffer between the stacks. *How could anyone work like that?*

She dropped her briefcase on a chair and stretched her arms and rotated her neck. The big Creole lunch had started taking its toll. She wanted to take a nap. Thomas returned with the files and a laptop.

He sat next to her and tapped on the keyboard.

He brought up an autopsy picture of LeBlanc. "Not the easiest thing to look at after lunch."

"Occupational hazard," she said.

She examined the photograph. The right side of LeBlanc's head, matted with blood and brains, was unrecognizable but similar to the damage inflicted upon Randy Sells, the Pittsburgh victim. Thomas pulled a manila folder out of the stack, in an expert motion like the one Jade used to use in the game KerPlunk as a kid. He handed the folder to her.

"The autopsy report confirms he was killed by blunt-force trauma to the head."

Jade began clicking through the crime-scene photographs on the computer. Thomas moved to the window, and closed the blinds halfway to block out the afternoon Louisiana sun. His action also removed the glare from the screen. Thoughtful.

"What do you think about the tongue?"

Thomas sat down in a chair and parked a foot on the table, his shoes scuffed and worn. "It's significant. To silence him forever? Retribution? It was cut after he died."

"Did you find it?"

"Keep clicking."

Jade scooted back in her chair when she came to the photo. "Wow." A vinyl album sat in a new turntable record player, ready to play. In place of the tonearm rested LeBlanc's tongue. "Is he playing with us or is this a clue?" She squinted at the photograph. "What was the vinyl?"

"*Tragic Kingdom.*"

"No Doubt? Really?"

"You've heard of them?"

"Of course." She clicked to another page. "What about the arms crossed over his chest?"

Thomas dropped his foot from the table. "Prepping him for his funeral? Some religious significance? How could there be an open casket with that much damage? Who knows? I still have more questions than answers about this case."

"I know the feeling."

Jade thought of the Pittsburgh commentator holding his tongue in his hands like a rosary.

Do the victims' religious beliefs have something to do with this? Or the killer's? Or possibly his lack of religion?

She finished perusing the photos and opened the folder with the autopsy report. She started to read. "Anything come up on the rope?"

"Made out of nylon and polyester. Manufactured by Everbilt. This particular rope can be found in any Home Depot store in the country."

"That narrows it down." She continued reading. "Not much food in his stomach and his blood-alcohol content was point-one-six."

"Twice the legal limit here."

She flipped another page, and eyed him, eyebrow raised. "Rohypnol?"

He nodded.

"Could he have ingested it unintentionally?" she asked.

"According to the lab, yes. In pill form, it's tasteless and dissolves in liquid. If the liquid is clear, the drug turns bright blue. But in dark liquids, such as the red wine the victim drank, it becomes cloudy. In a dark room, like The Wine Shoppe bar, he wouldn't have noticed."

"How long would it have taken for him to feel the effects?"

"Within thirty minutes up to several hours."

"So your witness may not have seen someone helping a drunk friend home, but rather a killer who had drugged his victim."

"And before you ask, we were too late to obtain fingerprints at the restaurant. They'd sanitized the glasses before we got there the next day."

Jade examined a close-up photo of a strand of hair. Light brown, Caucasian, human.

"Where was the hair found?"

"On the victim's shirt. No match came up in CODIS." CODIS was the Combined DNA Index System database managed by the FBI.

She closed the file. "What about his finances?"

Thomas grabbed another file midway down the stack. Jade was glad she would never play him in KerPlunk.

"Nothing jumped out at me. He earned a pretty decent salary and lived within his means. Owned the condo and made his mortgage payments on time. He had one credit card he rarely used and paid off his balance every month. His credit report, unenlightening. He paid all his bills on time, but only had an average credit score. He probably didn't have *enough* credit. Only in America. He didn't owe anyone any money as far as we can tell, and he didn't gamble."

"Do you think someone killed him for his political views?"

"Possibly. During my research I also discovered"—he got up, searched through a stack, and handed her a file—"this. In 1984, members of a white nationalist group killed a Jewish, liberal radio talk-show host in Denver, Colorado. So, yes, it's possible."

Jade read the article and the police report. "Anything on LeBlanc's computer? Phone records?"

"Nothing on the hard drive. Checked out his Twitter and Facebook accounts. Some followers disagreed with his viewpoint, but most comments were benign. He didn't use his home phone much. We found the ex-girlfriend through his cell. A graduate of LSU, she'd been with the paper only a few months before she and LeBlanc started dating."

"But she was at The Wine Shoppe that night."

"Yes, but they weren't together. She saw LeBlanc talking to some guy at the bar. Didn't introduce her. She said LeBlanc and the guy were in a heated discussion."

"An argument?"

"No. More like a debate. She thought it had something to do with LeBlanc's work."

"Did she give a description?"

"She believed he had brown hair, but the bar was dark. And, oh, he was kind of cute."

Jade rolled her eyes. "Any way she could've been involved?"

"We didn't think so. We checked her out. She was pretty shaken up by his death."

"What time did LeBlanc and this guy leave the bar?"

"Eleven thirty."

"Consistent with the time of death."

"I tried everything. Even asked for the public's help through pleas on television, radio, and billboards throughout Baton Rouge and New Orleans. Nothing."

It looked to Jade like the case still ate away at him.

They spent the rest of the afternoon reviewing every file and photo in detail and brainstorming ideas. Later, he leaned back in his chair and gave her a tired smile. "I'd better be getting you to the airport. Oh, before you go, let me check on that speech for you. The one playing in his condo when we found him."

She gathered her things while he rummaged through his files.

"Here it is," he said.

She stopped and eyed him, expectant.

He returned her stare and shrugged. "Income inequality."

CHAPTER TWENTY

Bethesda, Maryland

THE DC AREA doesn't enjoy many perfect-weather days, with winter sometimes switching to summer with only a brief touch of spring. Today, however, was one of them. The sound of what seemed like hundreds of happy, laughing kids running around filled the air. A soccer ball was kicked down the field, chased by twelve kids, six from each team. The coaches on both sides yelled "Spacing!" to no avail.

Cole Brennan loved the crisp scent of recently mown grass. He stood on the sidelines with his wife, Ashley, and a few of their children watching their son, Ryan, play. Blond hair flying, Ryan sported a huge smile on his face. Cole's heart filled with love and pride as he gazed upon his son. Cole envied him. To be innocent and carefree. When the worst thing in the world that could happen to you was that no one passed you the ball or you didn't score a goal. Much preferable to having the fate of your country's future weighing on your mind. He glanced at his wife, reached for her hand, and turned back to the game.

Hannah, the best player on the team, sent a perfect pass down the left side of the field. Ryan sprinted his little heart out to arrive first, slowing as he approached the ball. He dribbled it toward the opponent's goal.

Cole dropped Ashley's hand and cupped his hands around his mouth.

"Go, Ryan! Go! Go! Go!"

Cole wanted to run down the sidelines along with his son as other fathers did.

Ryan shifted the ball to his strong foot. He was now one-on-one with the goalie. He reared back his right foot and shot the ball with all the power he had, almost falling down in the process. The ball veered to the right, missing the goal by ten yards.

Cole's heart fell as Ryan shuffled back up the field, his head down.

"That's all right, Ryan! You'll score next time! Keep your head up!"

The game ended a few minutes later. Cole was grateful these games were short. Ryan wouldn't miss another shot and Cole would be able to sit down soon. He was not accustomed to standing for long periods of time.

"Dad?"

Cole tore his gaze away from his son to find his daughter, Kaitlin, staring at him with the look she had been giving him on a regular basis as of late.

"Yes?"

"Some kids at school were talking about you again today."

"Don't they have anything better to do?"

"They said you don't have a heart."

"They're wrong, sweetheart. I do have a heart. It's just not a bleeding heart."

Cole's high-pitched giggle faded away when Kaitlin's expression didn't change. He stole a quick glance at Ashley, but before he could say anything else, Ryan ran to where they stood.

Cole mussed Ryan's hair.

"Good game, Champ."

Ryan beamed, remnants from the post-game strawberry juice box forming a red circle around his lips.

"Thanks, Dad. I almost scored!"

"Yes, you almost did, son."

Cole and Ashley sauntered toward the parking lot, Ryan between them, and the other children a few steps behind. None of the other players' parents had said "hello" when they arrived or spoke to them during the game. He had picked up on the furtive glances. Maybe even dirty looks, he couldn't be sure.

That is what I get for living in a liberal city. Now, these people are poisoning my daughter with their liberal way of thinking. We need to move.

CHAPTER TWENTY-ONE

Washington, DC

WHITNEY SPENT THE afternoon in her office reviewing briefing books and pending legislation. A little after seven p.m., Landon knocked on her open door and stood in the doorway.

She affixed her signature to the document she had just read and looked up him. "How is the reading going?"

He sighed. "Not well."

Whitney extended her arm to place the pen in its gold-plated holder in the center of her desk. "Why not?"

"Because every time I make a dent in my stack of books," he said, "you give me more work to do. It isn't fair."

She leaned back in her chair and smiled at him. "When I proposed this reading contest, I wanted it to be predicated on the number of books read." Whitney and Landon shared a love of reading, particularly books on history, politics, and current events. "You should have made it easy on yourself and read all the short books on your Kindle. But instead, you had the idea to change the contest to number of pages. Bragging rights are at stake. Are you raising the white flag?"

Landon was never one to back down from a challenge. "Do you need anything else, Senator?"

"What are you doing this evening?"

"Reading."

She rose. "Join me for dinner and then a meeting with Ted later."

"Yes, Senator," he said. "Is this invitation another ploy to prevent me from winning the contest?"

❉

Whitney and Landon sat at a table in the back of the American cuisine restaurant enjoying an after-dinner coffee. An older establishment, the restaurant had not changed with the times and, in consequence, was nearly empty. The social climbers and power players in DC did not dine here, which was okay with Whitney.

Landon took a sip from his cup. "How does it feel being the de facto nominee?"

"As if the fight has just begun."

"The campaign will start to get ugly. Their PACs are flush. Expect an avalanche of negative ads."

"Could be worse. We could still be resolving our differences by dueling."

"Can you imagine the Capitol surrounded by a mass of duelists?"

"The American people would need to elect a new Congress." She paused. "Perhaps that's not such a bad idea."

They shared a laugh. Landon's smile no doubt drove the young women crazy. He would go far in politics.

"You haven't mentioned how you feel about my compromise with Sampson," Whitney said.

"Not my place, Senator. You did what you felt like you had to do."

"I wanted to talk to you about the campaign. I need something substantial to make a move."

"I thought you were focused on women's rights."

"I am, but I need something else. Something with a broader appeal."

"Health care reform's been taken. Education reform appropriated by the other party. Campaign finance?"

"People don't care about campaign finance reform, and politicians have no incentive to change the status quo."

"The deficit? It's a financial reality. We must reduce spending, and you would be perceived as doing what is best for the country rather than for your party."

"After the election."

"Social Security?"

"Can't win."

"Income inequality."

"The country's not ready."

"Climate change?"

Whitney sighed. "I know firsthand the impact of climate change on my state. The increased ice storms, droughts, and extreme hot and cold temperatures have hurt Missouri's agricultural production. We need to reduce greenhouse-gas emissions, but the regulatory impact may hurt middle-class families."

"And ship jobs overseas."

"Climate change is important to me, but not the issue I want to bet my campaign on. The sad part is, Al Gore will end up having the last laugh, but our grandchildren won't find the joke funny."

Landon shook his head. "Combating the untruths. Used to be facts were facts. Now, facts are relative to which party you belong to. What did Senator Moynihan always say?"

"'Everyone is entitled to his own opinion, but not to his own facts.' Some politicians and organizations, like Patriot News, realized their agenda could be propagated by what Lenin once said: 'A lie told often enough becomes the truth.'" Whitney sipped her coffee. "I also believe it comes down to the 'Genius of the And.' People are oppressed by the 'Tyranny of the Or'; that you must believe in one idea or the other but not both. F. Scott Fitzgerald said, 'The test of a first-rate intelligence is the ability to hold two opposed ideas in the mind at the same time, and still retain the ability to function.'"

Landon nodded. "The conservatives have mastered the formula of a simple message repeated over and over again: pro-life, pro-family, pro-guns, pro-smaller government. If only our party would craft a consistent, coherent, and simple message that could compete. The problem is trying to distill complex issues down to simple-minded sound bites."

Whitney set her cup in the saucer. "Corralling individual Democrats to stay on message is harder than herding cats."

She glimpsed the pink wristband underneath his shirt cuff as he also replaced his cup. Someone in his immediate family was a breast-cancer survivor. Mother? Sister? She needed to be better about remembering these things.

Landon hesitated. "I've been working on something." When she remained silent, he hurried on. "A transaction tax on hedge-fund managers." He described how his proposal would work and how much tax revenue would be generated.

Whitney was skeptical, but listened in silence. When he finished, she gave him her most serious expression. Or at least, she tried. "We would never want to put forth a proposal for political reasons."

He didn't try to conceal his smile. "Of course, we wouldn't."

✻

Her driver dropped them off at her national campaign headquarters, in an office building on K Street in Northwest Washington, DC. The outer area, where the phone bank was located, had been bursting with activity an hour ago. The volunteers—calling citizens at home and interrupting their dinners, TV watching, video-game playing, or tweeting—had left. The walls displayed several oversized pictures of her. Whitney still found gigantic close-ups of her face disconcerting.

They entered the conference room. On one wall, a large sign read, Senator Whitney Fairchild for President - Our America, Our Future. Ted Bowling glanced up from his laptop, an almost imperceptible shadow darkening his face when he saw her companion.

Whitney waved her hand in front of her nose. "This room smells like an ashtray, Ted. You know you're not supposed to smoke in here."

"Sorry, Senator, stressful day."

She sat and crossed her legs, as Landon sat next to her, removing the electronic tablet from his briefcase.

Ted began speaking.

"I just emailed the numbers to you. We're down twenty points against Ellison. Your approval rating with women is trending higher—I think the ERA is helping—but the numbers are still soft in other categories: young voters, Latinos, middle-class white men. We need to do something big."

"I agree. Go on."

Ted coughed. "Income inequality. Talked about in the media for years. Over the last forty years, the top one percent of the US population is seven hundred and fifty percent better off, while the middle- and the lower-income classes' wealth—"

"I know the numbers, Ted."

"There are a lot of voters in that ninety-nine percent." He rapped the table with his knuckles on each word. "The 'wealth creators create jobs' line is a lie, which is becoming more apparent every year. The only thing wealth creators create is more wealth for themselves. We must develop a policy that won't be considered a 'wealth distribution' tactic or 'class warfare,' terms that turn off independents, moderates, blue-collar workers, and all those afraid of anything reeking of Socialism."

"Be that as it may, what do you suggest?"

"Poll after poll shows the majority of Americans are not opposed to tax increases on the rich. We've enacted increases before; we can do it again. This would result in a small increase in taxes for the rich, relative to their incomes, but billions of dollars in additional revenue."

Whitney brought her right index finger to her lips with her thumb under her chin, her thinking position. "Hmm . . . ."

Ted continued in earnest. "The strategists and I also think we should propose increasing estate taxes to pre-George W. levels."

She remained silent.

Landon cleared his throat. "May I make a suggestion?" He waited until he had their attention. "There are a lot of ways to increase revenues. One idea I had was to impose a tax on the financial markets. The original purpose of financial firms was to raise capital for the private sector. Instead, they focused on making as much money as they could trading for themselves; helping businesses find capital became an afterthought. To generate higher returns, these firms took on increased risks. Our lost decade showed the awful, sometimes irreparable consequences of speculation on our markets and our economy."

"What do you propose?" she asked, although he had told her at dinner earlier.

"Levying a transaction tax on hedge-fund managers and other large, complicated financial transactions. This would decrease speculation and create an incentive for long-term investment. In the short term, tax revenues will rise."

"Why do you think your plan will work?" Ted asked, in a tone indicating he believed quite the opposite.

"The European Union implemented a similar tax several years ago. Yes, the financial markets took a hit at first, but, as their economies recovered, investors began to consider the tax as another cost of doing business."

Whitney shifted in her chair. "Why hedge-fund managers?"

"I don't believe we should tax every transaction, which would hurt individual investors. To Ted's point, the Republicans oppose any increase in taxes or regulations on the 'wealth creators.' Most hedge-fund companies employ five employees or fewer. Sometimes, it's one person, a computer, and an algorithm that buys and sells based on discrepancies of supply and demand in the market. These firms generate billions of dollars a year. One firm during the Aughts generated a billion dollars in one day."

"The Aughts?" Ted asked.

Landon ignored the sarcasm. "The last decade."

Whitney nodded. "So you're saying these fund managers don't create jobs or *make* anything."

"Well, not exactly. But they don't create the jobs ascribed to them by the other party. And, to top it all off, they're taxed at the capital-gains rate, which is a third of the ordinary rate, or what a normal business person pays." Landon pulled an accordion folder from his briefcase and handed it to her. "I took the liberty of running some numbers under various scenarios."

Ted still did not try to hide the sarcasm in his voice. "Of course you did."

Landon ignored him. "I also propose a change in tax policy to discourage short-term investment. Capital gains on stocks sold within one year would be taxed at seventy-five percent; one to three years, fifty percent; twenty percent after five years; and zero percent beyond that. We should also eliminate capital-gains taxes for those Americans making less than, say, one hundred thousand. This will bring in new investment and allow investors' wealth to grow tax-free. It's all in my analysis."

Ted stared at Whitney, his face flushed. "We should poll this first."

"Who in the ninety-nine percent would be against this proposal?" she asked.

Ted and Landon did not answer her rhetorical question while she perused the proposal she had read in the restaurant earlier. Landon had written a one-page summary with supporting analysis, data, and charts. She closed the report cover.

"No one." She answered her own question. "I like it." Whitney gave Ted a sweet smile. "Polls be damned."

CHAPTER TWENTY-TWO

Chattenham, Pennsylvania

JADE HARRINGTON LISTENED to the computerized female voice guide her as she drove down the Delaware Expressway, thinking about the Baton Rouge, Pittsburgh, Houston, and Chattenham cases. No explicit evidence tied the cases together so far, besides all four victims' involvement in conservative media.

Oh . . . and they all had their heads bashed in and their tongues cut out.

Jade turned onto Interstate 476 and headed north. Her cell phone rang.

"Hey, you." Zoe.

"How's my kitty?" Jade asked.

"Card's fine. Lonely. Meowed he wanted to come home and live with me, but I told him you needed him."

"He'd come back once he found out you'd try to turn him into a vegan."

"He'd live longer. And I'm not a vegan."

"Thanks again for taking care of him. After what happened at your apartment . . ."

Silence, then, Zoe said, "We're best friends. It's going to take a lot more than you being a knucklehead to drive me away. Where are you?"

"On a case."

"I know, silly."

Jade did not respond for a moment. "I may need your help with something."

"Really?"

"Don't sound so happy. Talk to me about income inequality."

"What about it?"

"It was a major issue during the Occupy Movement, but you don't hear about it as much now. Why not?"

"Depends on where you live. The problem's still there. Simmering. And one day it will boil over."

"Why?"

"The issue hasn't gone away. When the poor and the middle class realize the American Dream is just that—a dream—they'll revolt."

"What's the solution?"

"How much time do you have?"

Jade glanced at the navigation system display. "Not much."

"When are you coming home? We can discuss it then."

"Not sure," Jade said, "but I'll let you know. I'm flying into Reagan."

"National."

"Sorry, I forgot." Zoe refused to call the former National airport by its proper name. Jade passed the sign indicating her exit was one mile away. "Listen, I need to go."

Driving through a quaint town of pizza joints, cafés, a Dunkin' Donuts, bars, restaurants, and a dry cleaner's—everything a college student could ever need or want—she turned right a half mile later at the small wooden sign: Chattenham College, Home of the Eagles. Founded 1863.

Jade drove down a long, paved drive with oak trees on both sides interspersed with tall, black, old-fashioned street lights. She veered right, around an administration building made of fieldstone and meandered through the heart of the campus: rolling lawns, a plethora of trees and shrubs, wooded hills, classrooms, and dormitories. Students sporting backpacks ambled along the sidewalks in ones, twos, and threes. A peaceful campus.

She located the college radio station in one of the older buildings and parked behind a campus police car. A uniformed black gentleman with short gray hair waited for her in the cramped, barren lobby, reading a copy of *Sports Illustrated*.

The officer eyed her and nodded with approval. "You must be Agent Harrington."

Jade, not sure what test she had passed, said, "Yes."

"Nice to meet you. I'm Nate." He stuck out his hand. "I'll be honest with you. I was surprised to learn of the FBI's interest in this old case. Come on. I'll take you up to the studio." Nate headed down a hallway and led her up a narrow flight of stairs.

"The campus is about four hundred acres with two thousand students," Nate said over his shoulder. "Founded in 1863 by Quakers. The station has been around since 1939, six years after the invention of FM radio. It's one of the oldest college radio stations in the country."

"Who manages it?"

"It's always been run by the students."

On the second floor, Nate opened a door to a modest room. The term "studio" was generous. The room consisted of a small area with engineering equipment and a space for the DJ. Vinyl albums and CDs packed the scuffed white shelves.

She examined a mural on the wall displaying an impressive pictorial history of the school. She peered closer. In the corner of the drawing, a woman held a basketball with laces, wearing an early twentieth-century uniform, skirt and all. Jade was thankful she never had to play ball in a skirt. Her penchant for diving after loose balls could have been problematic.

"This mural is amazing," she said. "It's a shame it's tucked away in here. It should be in a museum."

After a moment, she straightened and turned to Nate.

"What can you tell me about the victim, Kyle Williams?"

"I remember Kyle. A loner. Although the school's mission is to be fiercely independent, it's still pretty liberal. He never fit in. Kyle was the only person who ever had a conservative program at the station. He often got into heated discussions with his co-workers."

"Anyone in particular?"

"We interviewed all of them at the time. They didn't care much for his politics, but they liked him well enough. None of them seemed to have a motive for murder and their alibis checked out."

Nate started toward another staircase.

"Kyle had just completed his show and went down these stairs and out the back door. That's the last time anyone saw him." Nate paused. "Except for his killer, of course." He exited the building and Jade followed him toward the corner of the parking lot. He stopped at the farthest space under a huge American elm tree in full bloom. "His car was parked here. His body was a couple of feet from the driver's side door. His car keys were found next to him and he still had his wallet on him."

"On the phone, you said the weapon was a blunt instrument."

"According to the medical examiner and my personal observations."

"Any evidence?"

"No murder weapon. No fingerprints. No evidence. The victim was a good kid. I knew him and liked him. He didn't deserve this."

"Do you have much crime here?"

"No, except for the typical college stuff: underage drinking, public intoxication, disorderly conduct. We had a huge problem with date rape many years ago. More so than now, anyway. Around the time Kyle was killed, now that I think about it." He shook his head. "I've worked here for almost twenty years." He stared down at the asphalt. "Never saw anything like what happened here. Before or since."

Jade glanced back toward the building and scanned the grounds. Her eyes settled on Nate. "I'm going to spend some time out here, if you don't mind."

"Take all the time you want. Call me if you need anything else."

Nate ambled away, rounding the building to his car parked out front.

Jade stood for a long time on the spot where Kyle Williams had died. When working a case, she always tried to use the name of the person as much as possible rather than "the victim." Sometimes, the essence of a murdered person was lost during an investigation.

Jade never wanted to forget who she was working for.

❖

The foundation of the house was built with the same fieldstone as the buildings at the college, the siding of the house once white. Green shutters hung next to the windows, paint chipped, one crooked, as if it didn't want to be like the others. The yard boasted more brown patches than green.

Jade knocked at the wooden, weathered door. And waited. No footsteps approached, although someone was at home. She was expected. She knocked again.

The door opened with effort, partially concealing a woman who appeared close to seventy but, according to her file, was in her mid-fifties.

"Mrs. Williams?"

The woman nodded.

Jade held up her badge. "I'm Special Agent Jade Harrington. We talked on the phone." No response. "May I come in?"

The woman half nodded, stepped back, and swung the door open the rest of the way. Jade entered a darkened foyer and followed Mrs. Williams as she shuffled a few steps into the sitting room. A large bay window faced the front yard. The woman sat on a sofa with her back to the window. She clasped her hands on her lap. She didn't offer refreshments.

"Mrs. Williams, as I told you on the phone, we're investigating the death of your son."

"Why?"

Not the question Jade had expected. *Didn't she want her son's killer found?*

No matter how long it took to solve the case? "There's evidence that his death may be related to others."

She continued to gaze at Jade, but didn't ask the obvious question. After a moment, she broke eye contact with Jade and stared at her hands.

"He was such a good boy. Had such a bright future. He could've been anything he wanted to be. I died, too, the day my son was taken from me."

Jade waited a beat. "Mrs. Williams, can you tell me anything about what happened that day?"

"He still lived at home. Before school, he ate breakfast, kissed me on the cheek, and told me to have a good day. I never saw him again." She looked at Jade, her eyes pleading for forgiveness. "I should have told him I loved him."

"Did he write, make notes, keep a journal? Anything like that?"

The older woman glanced to the left before shaking her head.

She was lying.

Jade pressed. "Are you sure?"

The woman's lips formed a hard line, another quick shake of the head.

Jade let it go and asked her many questions, but didn't learn much more than what she had learned from Nate. After a half hour, Jade realized the trip to this house was a waste of time. She started to get up. "Thank you, Mrs. Williams, for your time. I won't keep you any longer. I can show myself out."

She was still examining her hands. "I didn't tell . . . He did. He did keep a journal."

Jade sat back down. "Do you still have it?"

Mrs. Williams nodded. "I found it in his room."

Jade remained cool. "May I see it?"

Kyle's room appeared unchanged since his death. A poster of Kid Rock pointing an index finger straight ahead hovered above the headboard of the neat, twin-size bed. Other than the poster and a small desk, the room was bereft of trophies or personal items. A thin book lay on the nightstand. His mother picked it up and handed it to Jade.

"I found it a few months after his death under the mattress." She shrugged her shoulders and gave Jade a weak smile. "I finally got around to washing his sheets."

"Did you read it?"

With a slight shake of her head, no, Mrs. Williams looked away.

Jade didn't think she was telling the truth again. It didn't matter. She held the journal, and then opened it, flipping through the pages until she came to the last entry, written the night before Kyle died.

I don't know for sure, but I think someone's been following me. It's creeping me out. For some reason, I think it's C. But why? I should tell someone, but who? What would I say? Everyone would think I was paranoid. That I'm the creep.

Jade sat on Kyle's bed, ignoring Mrs. Williams' quick intake of breath. She scanned several entries. More of the same. "Mrs. Williams, why didn't you take this to the police?"

The woman was back to staring at her hands again. The silence dragged on for so long, Jade thought she hadn't heard the question. Jade was about to repeat it.

"I couldn't," Mrs. Williams said, her eyes filled with anguish. "It's the only part of my son I have left."

Jade nodded and closed the journal. She moved toward the desk. Textbooks were intermingled with books on Ronald Reagan, Barry Goldwater, and other conservative thinkers. Towering above them all was a Chattenham College yearbook.

Jade's pulse quickened. She opened the yearbook to the index and scrolled down until she located the radio station. She turned to the appropriate page. In a corner, among the text and the large motto of the station, was a photograph of the radio station crew. She found Kyle Williams: short, slight build, blond hair, smiling. She read the names under the picture. The crew had a couple of "Cs."

Jade glanced up at the older woman, trying to appear nonchalant. "May I borrow these?"

Mrs. Williams shifted, uncomfortable.

"I'll bring them back." Jade stared into her eyes. "I promise."

CHAPTER TWENTY-THREE

Columbus, Ohio

WHITNEY ROLLED OVER, knowing she should be getting ready for another day of campaigning. She was exhausted, even though presidential candidates were not allowed to get tired. If that leaked out, she could imagine Ellison's camp airing an ad of her sleeping, with the sonorous voiceover: "*What will happen when Senator Whitney Fairchild receives the call at three a.m.? Will she hit the snooze button, roll over, and go back to sleep?*"

She heard an insistent knock on the door of the hotel suite. A few minutes later, Sarah, her body woman, knocked on her bedroom door. "Senator, Ted's here. He says it's urgent."

Isn't it always? "I'll be right there."

Whitney sighed and went to the bathroom to freshen up. Still in her pajamas, she threw on the cream-colored, hotel-provided robe and slippers. In the living room, Ted sat on a sofa, his suit rumpled, his tie skewed, and his hair uncombed. *Was that the same shirt he wore yesterday?*

"Good morning, Ted."

"Good morning, Senator."

She turned to Sarah. "Please order breakfast. The usual. Thank you." Sarah nodded and left. Whitney turned to Ted. "What is it?"

"You need to start going to church."

"Why?"

"Americans expect their president to go to church."

"Why does the faith of the president matter? I thought this country was founded on the principle of freedom of religion, which denotes a freedom *from* religion."

"Optics, Senator."

"Ted, did you really wake me up for this?"

"And this." He flung the *Columbus Dispatch* down on the coffee table, a large photograph of Grayson and her smiling above the newspaper's fold. The photo was taken at an event earlier this year, a rare occasion when her husband had joined her on the campaign trail. The headline screamed Personal Bailout? Below, in a smaller font, read Graysongate: Husband of Presidential Candidate Benefited from Federal Funds.

She picked up the paper. The news item explained in detail how Grayson's company avoided paying millions of dollars in taxes as a result of a bill she had sponsored as a member of the powerful Appropriations Committee. In the article, Senator Eric Hampton accused Whitney of nepotism and implored her to withdraw from the presidential campaign. The bill in question was passed years ago, which Hampton knew. The article insinuated she proposed and pushed this bill through for her husband's benefit. Of course, she knew Fairchild Industries would be a beneficiary of the bill. But that was not her intent, only a consequence. A lot of American businesses benefited. That was the point.

She dropped the paper back down on the coffee table. "Hmm . . . , I wonder why this is coming out now."

Ted eyed her. "Is that it? Will anything else come out?"

Sarah had let in the room service server who placed the breakfast items on the table and left as quietly as he had arrived.

Whitney poured herself a cup of coffee, grateful for the interruption. "No."

"Obviously, this is from Ellison's camp," Ted said. "It's already on *Drudge.*"

She reached for a croissant. "Ah . . . then it must be true."

Ted overlooked her sarcasm. "We must issue a strong denial and nip this in the bud. We can say when you introduced this bill, you were trying to help companies keep jobs in the United States. You had no way of knowing your husband's company would benefit. Yada, yada, yada. I've scheduled a press conference for you this morning."

She nodded, wondering how long she would need to ride the elliptical to work off the croissant. She had to find more time to work out. Constituents did not like overweight female politicians. "Okay. I will do one press conference on this subject. With the twenty-four-hour news cycle, this story will be forgotten with the next 'Breaking News' headline."

She finished the croissant.

"So, our president wants to play hardball," Whitney continued. She disliked negative politics. But she disliked losing more. Whitney had learned her profession in the rough-and-tough arena of Chicago politics. She didn't back down from anyone. She smiled at Ted, the smile that had helped her to become the most powerful woman in DC.

"I read somewhere that when you are a female US senator, people tend to underestimate and trivialize you." Her smile evaporated. "But I can play hardball, too. What do we have on him?"

Ted didn't hesitate. "When Ellison was in high school, he and a bunch of his popular friends got drunk and went from ranch to ranch punching and kicking pigs. I think one was set on fire. Many of the pigs died."

Whitney took a sip of her coffee. "Was he arrested?"

Ted shook his head. "The farmers were paid off by the boys' rich daddies. 'Boys will be boys' and all that. The kids left for different colleges the next year, everyone sworn to secrecy. The incident forgotten."

"What an awful story." She replaced her cup on the table. "I never liked that saying. 'Boys will be boys.' As if they possess a license to do whatever they want."

"Unfortunately, we didn't have cell phones back then to capture it on video, but the public still doesn't like cruelty inflicted on animals. This would hurt Ellison. Bad."

Whitney did not hesitate. "Use it."

CHAPTER TWENTY-FOUR

Washington, DC

IN A WINDOWLESS conference room at the Bureau, Jade popped an M&M into her mouth and scanned the faces around the table: her task force, code named CONFAB. Jade came up with the name herself: to honor the victims' profession.

CONFAB consisted of Christian Merritt, Dante Carlucci, Max Stover, Pat Turner, and a hungry, freckle-faced rookie agent named Austin Miller.

Jade brought everyone up to speed on the case. "We can presume our victims were killed because they were conservative media personalities. Who would have a reason to kill them?"

"Every liberal in this country," Pat said, typing notes into her computer as she talked.

"We may need to narrow it down," Jade deadpanned.

"Someone who was offended by something each of the victims had said?" This from Christian.

Dante, his chair leaning against the wall at a precarious forty-five-degree angle, said, "A rival who wants to be the top dog?"

Jade nodded. "Possibly." She turned to Max. "Talk to me."

"The UNSUB has complete disdain for his victims. He makes no attempt to hide the bodies and leaves them in disrespectful states. The multiple blows with a blunt instrument are overkill, demonstrating his rage. Something is causing him to accelerate the murders. The time between them is getting shorter. He will strike again."

Max had the team's full attention. Jade motioned with her hand for him to continue.

"He cuts out the victims' tongues, but doesn't keep them as trophies. Why?"

"He's in a hurry?" Christian asked.

"No room in his refrigerator?" Pat asked.

Jade frowned at Pat. "He doesn't want them."

"Perhaps," Max said.

"Why wouldn't he want them?" Austin asked.

Max shrugged. "He doesn't want anything to do with the victims after the act."

"Or maybe he doesn't like trophies," Jade said.

Christian crossed his arms in front of his chest. "Where was the tongue of the Houston victim found?"

Jade responded without glancing at her notes. "In a trash can by the elevator in the parking garage."

"Complete disdain is right." Christian eyed Max. "Best guess of what kind of person we're searching for?"

"A highly organized individual with advanced social and planning skills. I believe he possesses above-average intelligence and comes from an upper middle- to high-income family."

Dante leaned forward, allowing his chair to drop to the floor without softening the landing, startling Austin. "Is he also a loner who wet the bed and picked the wings off insects as a kid?"

"I bet the UNSUB felt unloved growing up," Max continued, ignoring Dante. "May be an only child. He suffers from depression and feelings of despair."

"I'm curious, Max," Dante said. "What do you do away from work? What're your hobbies?"

"I don't have any hobbies."

"Everyone has a hobby."

Pat said, as she continued to type, "Dressing up like the characters on *Miami Vice* on the weekend and asking out as many women as you can is not a hobby."

Dante's face reddened. He leaned his chair back.

"What's *Miami Vice*?" Austin asked.

Christian laughed.

"Let's get to work," Jade said, turning to Christian. "I want you to focus on the three latest killings: Pittsburgh, Baton Rouge, and Houston. Let's see if we can track the UNSUB by where he's been. Check out the manifests for flights, hotels, and rental-car agencies in those cities around the dates of the murders. Maybe we'll get lucky and he used the same name."

Christian nodded. "Got it."

"Pat, you research the lives of the four victims and create a dossier on each of them. Besides their occupation, were they connected in some other way? Were they ever in the same place, such as a conference? Did they belong to the same professional organizations? Where did they go to school? Where did they work before? Subpoena email, cell phone, computer records, anything you need."

Pat started typing at a different pace, already working on the assignment.

"Dante, I want you to check out the college yearbook. Interview everyone who worked at the Chattenham station at the time, all Kyle Williams's friends, and cross-reference your lists with Christian's."

Dante's eyes bored into hers. "I know how to do my job."

"Then, you also know why your job is the most important."

Austin glanced at Dante and back at Jade. "I'll bite. Why?"

Jade answered him, without breaking eye contact with Dante. "Serial killers often end up living near their first victim."

Dante looked away first.

"How do we know he was the first victim?" Christian said.

"We don't," Jade said, "but we must start somewhere. I think Chattenham may be the key."

Jade turned to Austin. "I want you to listen to every broadcast of the victims for the last few years of their lives. Did the same person call more than one of them or become mad or upset? The college station may not have kept its recordings but find out. Same with the blogs and columns for Paxson and LeBlanc. Read them and readers' comments."

Austin threw up his hands. "That'll take months!"

"Then you better get started," she said.

Dante smirked at Austin.

"Dante can help you, if you need it," Jade said.

Dante's smirk disappeared. "What are you going to do, Chiefette?"

She tensed and willed herself not to punch him in the face. Her voice softened to a low, dangerous level.

"Don't call me that, Dante. Belittling me is unacceptable. And I won't stand for it."

He mumbled a response.

"What was that?" she asked. *One word. Just say one word.*

His eyes tried to hold hers and failed. He stared at the table. She addressed the rest of the group.

"I'm going to get in touch with the MEs and ask them to review their cases again in light of the new evidence. Inform them that their cases may be connected to others."

"We need to make sure all the evidence gets entered into the database," Christian said.

"Good point," she said. "Everything should be entered into the database before you leave for the day. Any leads, evidence, suppositions, wild theories, anything, needs to be entered, even if the info doesn't seem important. Got it?"

Everyone nodded, except for Dante.

She stood and started gathering her materials. "Okay. This is our room for the duration. When in town, I want us to meet here twice a day: nine a.m. and five p.m. Be prepared to debrief me on anything since the prior meeting. If you discover anything important between meetings, don't wait. Tell me immediately. Any questions?"

"Are we keeping our base here or moving to Pittsburgh?" Christian asked.

"Here for now until we determine how big this thing is and depending on what we find. You and I may head to Pittsburgh again to lend support to the local police force." She stared briefly at each of them in turn, ending with Dante, whose gaze she held. "I shouldn't need to say this, but I will. This case is highly sensitive. Do not discuss it with anyone outside of law enforcement, especially the media."

CHAPTER TWENTY-FIVE

Washington, DC

HER DRIVER BACKED out the Lincoln Town Car in a cautious crawl. Whitney glanced over her shoulder at the reporters in front of the gate to her driveway. Most of them hesitated before moving aside grudgingly. One brave soul stood behind the car until the last second, unaware of how her driver felt about reporters.

Whitney couldn't hear what they were saying, but she could read their lips.

"Senator! Did you realize the bill would benefit your husband?"

"How much money did you and your husband personally make from the bill?"

"Are you going to drop out of the race?"

She almost laughed at the silent movie playing out around her. The intense faces, the animated mouths.

A man pounded his fist on the glass. She recoiled, despite the unlikelihood of his breaking through. Her driver put the car in drive. She caught his eye in the rearview mirror and nodded her thanks.

He gave her a reassuring nod.

Whitney disliked Washington's love for "-gate" scandals. FOX News had been covering Graysongate nonstop since the story broke. The network demanded she quit the campaign. CNN was neutral. MSNBC supported her. Most of its commentators maintained that with all the legislation she considered, she had no way of knowing which particular bill would benefit her husband. A congressional ethics investigation was underway, and she wondered how long it would be until she received a subpoena.

Any momentum she had been building in the polls had stopped.

Her cell phone rang. She checked the screen. Her son.

"Mom!"

"Chandler, this is a nice surprise."

"I'm checking to make sure you're all right."

"I am. Why?"

"Because we're getting harassed, Mom. Emma's being followed around campus. The press is following me here like I'm on *The Voice*. And I saw on the news a crowd protesting in front of Dad's company."

Whitney's heart dropped. "Is Emma okay? Are you okay?"

"She's dealing with it like the rest of us. We're tough. Like you. Why do they call it Graysongate? Can't they be more original?"

"The media are often as original as Hollywood."

"Like *Fast & Furious*? How many sequels can you make? Well, I wanted to call and tell you that I love you."

"Thanks. I appreciate that. I love you too, son."

"Mom? Guess what?"

"What?"

"You've arrived in Washington."

"How so?"

"You've got your own scandal! Maybe you need to hire Olivia Pope."

He laughed and hung up.

Whitney gazed out the window, smiling. No, she did not need a fixer like Olivia Pope, but, like Olivia, she would indulge in a generous pour of wine later at home. She replayed the conversation with Chandler in her mind and realized something. Her son had not asked whether the allegations were true.

CHAPTER TWENTY-SIX

Washington, DC

COLE BRENNAN SETTLED into his studio chair. He was in a good mood. The ratings for Cole's show were higher than ever, and Ellison's poll numbers had ticked up during Graysongate. Then, the unfortunate Piggygate surfaced. Cole shook his head with regret.

Graysongate could have been Whitney's Whitewater. What a missed opportunity. He never understood why the media made such a big deal out of boys being boys. Why did they care so much about a few pigs? People ate pigs, didn't they? The incident happened so long ago. The media wouldn't be satisfied until they turned all men into—*what do they call them?*—metrosexuals. In other words, girls.

He received the "Go" signal from his producer.

"Good evening, everyone. I'm Cole Brennan and next I want to talk to you about the good ol' Post Office.

"Liberals have said for years we must keep the United States Postal Service open. Our country was brought together by those carriers who delivered your mail and neither snow, or rain, or heat could stop them. The liberal elite's main argument is that those people living in remote areas need the post office to pay their bills, send letters, and to receive prescriptions. For some of these small towns, the liberals moan, an inverse relationship exists between the size of the post office and its importance to the community. If we eliminate their post offices, these towns will die.

"Well, here's my suggestion for people living in those remote communities. Move!"

Cole laughed.

"The Postal Service was formed to run like a business, but it's a money-losing business. Lots of money. When a company brings in less money than it spends, its management—or the bank, or its creditors—eventually shuts the operation down.

"Like everything else in Washington, the Postal Service is broken. The use of email and private carriers resulted in declining volume, which is never coming back, folks. People only go to the post office when it's absolutely necessary or during Christmastime. Furthermore, its costly, inflexible unionized workforce doesn't give a crap about the institution it represents and continues to receive lucrative compensation packages despite the service's horrific financial condition. Remember the good ol' days, when President Reagan fired the air traffic controllers? That's the kind of courage we need now.

"To top it all off, the unions and Congress joined together in their resistance to consolidating or closing facilities or decreasing delivery from six to five days a week. A lot of this resistance from Congress, the Super Committee, and the Super Super Committee comes from those weak legislators afraid of receiving a call from Ethel Humperdinck from Podunk, Oklahoma who is upset because her post office, which services five people in a hundred-mile radius, might have to cut back its services.

"The liberals are always saying we should be more like Europe. Europe is perfect and sophisticated and humane. Well, for once, they're right. Let's be more like Europe. Many countries in Europe privatized or partially privatized their mail service using good, effective management and common-sense labor practices. Privatization and competition increased productivity, decreased costs, improved on-time delivery, and provided better service to everyone.

"The Democrats want to form a committee to figure out what to do about the Postal Service. I'll save them the time and the taxpayers' their money. Privatize it! And do it now!

"I only have time for one caller today. Go!"

Cole listened to a question about Whitney's financial tax proposal.

"Well, I think the idea is idiotic. One, if you assess a tax on financial transactions in the US, global investors will invest elsewhere, so our stock market will shrink. Two, hedge-fund managers will trade less. Therefore, revenue will decrease, shrinking our overall economy at a time when we can least afford it. Hedge-fund managers create wealth for this country, which creates jobs. It's a myth they're all rich billionaires. Most of them are everyday Joes, like you and me, trying to make a living.

"This financial transactions tax is a bad idea. Next! And I don't mean next caller, I mean next election. You must help me defeat Whitney Fairchild at all costs."

CHAPTER TWENTY-SEVEN

Fairfax, Virginia

WHITNEY SURVEYED THE crowd in the massive high school gym in Fairfax County, Virginia, the first in the United States to surpass six figures in median household income. Large blue and gold banners hung from the ceiling displaying years of district, regional, and state championships in a wide variety of sports. The students were engaged this morning, although she suspected their enthusiasm was more from getting out of class rather than hearing her speak. No matter. Her audience was not only them, but their parents and the numerous cameras representing all the major cable news networks and local television stations.

She gripped the podium. "Some of you will be old enough to vote in this election, which is a good thing because this election is about you and your future. Why?" She paused. "There's a lot at stake, such as the future of our country's educational system and how we make higher education affordable. Whether you'll be able to find a decent, well-paying job when you graduate from college. Whether you will be able to afford to buy a home. You don't want to live with your parents forever, do you?"

"No!" every student yelled, as if they had rehearsed together.

Whitney staggered back as if the volume of their voices had pushed her. She waited for the laughter to die down before returning to the podium. She smiled.

"I didn't think so. Just checking to see if you were paying attention." She paused again for the appreciative laughter to subside. Her expression turned serious. "For our country, the status quo is no longer an option and no longer acceptable. We need broad, sweeping reforms in education, in how we manage the economy, in how we create a comprehensive domestic clean energy program, which will eliminate the national security risk of relying on foreign oil. We need to invest in our infrastructure, science, technology, and the middle class. We need to make sure you and your children and your grandchildren live in an environment with clean water and without pollution. At the rate we are polluting this country, it won't be long before a medical face mask will be required to venture outside. With your help and your parents' help, we can make the needed changes to prevent that from happening.

"I want all of you to do something for me now. Take out your cell phone." She paused. "I want you to post to Instagram or Snapchat your story, telling your friends to vote. If they're not registered, tell them to register. Let's see how many people we can reach!"

The students cheered.

"When you're finished," Whitney continued, "hold your phone in the air."

Whitney waited.

A few minutes later, a sea of arms was raised, cell phones held high. The sight was overwhelming. She was glad the moment was captured on camera. "Amazing. Look around you," she said. "You just made a difference in this election. Thank you."

Whitney scanned the room and leaned forward into the microphone as if she were sharing a secret with them. She softened her voice.

"My husband and I have two children. As their mother, I am concerned about their future. 'Our America, Our Future' is not merely a campaign slogan to me. It's my promise to you and to my children." She spoke louder. "America has always been the beacon of hope. The land of opportunity where everyone through hard work and education can be whatever he or she wants to be. You can be whatever you want to be. This is your future and what I promise to give you when I am elected president of the United States of America."

Throughout the auditorium, students stood and gave her a standing ovation. Most were shouting, "Whitney! Whitney! Whitney!"

She smiled and waved for a long time, before allowing Ted and her recently assigned Secret Service agents to escort her off the stage. The special agent in charge, Josh McPherson, closed in next to her. His conservative dark suit could not minimize his bulk or the gun concealed underneath his arm. Upon meeting him last month, she had developed an immediate rapport with this man and trusted his warm, confident manner.

Outside of the high school, reporters asked if she would take a few questions. She shielded her eyes from the early June afternoon sun and nodded.

"Senator Fairchild, what do you think of the rumor Ellison is considering privatizing the US Postal Service?"

She gave the reporter her characteristic wry smile. "I normally don't comment on rumors, but I find it interesting Ellison is taking policy advice from Cole Brennan."

The reporters chuckled. Behind her, some of the camera operators had followed her outside.

"The history of the United States Postal Service is inseparable from the history of our country," she continued. "I believe a role for the Postal Service in America still exists. I do not believe privatization is the answer. Small, rural towns and island communities would suffer irreparable harm. Private companies will find these areas unprofitable to do business, so they won't deliver to those locations."

"If you were president, what would you do?" shouted a reporter in the back.

"*When* I am president," she said, "I would consider partial privatization as a possibility, but only in combination with compensation reforms and a reduction in overhead costs. Consolidating post offices, reducing hours, and approving select retailers to offer mail services will save taxpayers five hundred million dollars per year. We must end prefunding requirements for retirees and allow the Postal Service to manage its own health-care costs, instead of Congress. My team is evaluating all of our options and putting together a plan to save the Postal Service while making the agency more efficient and cost-effective."

"Senator Fairchild," said an older, female reporter named Judy, "how come your family is never on the campaign trail with you?"

"Well, as you know, both of my children are away at college, receiving an education and having a great time. The last thing they want to do is hang out with Mom on the campaign trail. Campaigning may be fun for us, but not so much for them."

The reporters laughed.

Whitney smiled and continued. "As for my husband, he has a pretty important job himself and employees who depend on him. Well, thank you all, I must be—"

Judy persisted. "Senator, I have one more question."

"Okay, one more, but then I must be going."

"Senator, speaking of your husband, is there any truth to the rumor he is having an affair?"

Whitney hesitated for a moment—only a moment—and recovered. She turned to face Judy, who had been covering her campaign for the last nineteen months.

"I haven't heard that one, but no, none whatsoever. Whoever planted that lie does not know my husband. Or me. You surprise me, Judy. I would think for as long as you've been in this business, your sources would be better."

Judy stood her ground, but with compassion in her eyes. "With all due respect, Senator, why don't you ask your neighbor in Missouri about it?"

For the first time, Whitney's voice faltered. "My neighbor?"

Washington, DC

JADE EXAMINED HER own notes before glancing at her team seated around the conference-room table.

"I called all the medical examiners and didn't find out anything new," Jade reported. "Williams, Sells, LeBlanc, and Paxson were killed as a result of blows to the head by a blunt instrument. Strands of hair were found at the LeBlanc and Sells scenes. The hairs found at the LeBlanc scene were Caucasian. No results back, yet, from the Sells case. And we know all the victims' tongues had been cut out."

"Since there's been no evidence of resistance, could the killer have known all his victims?" Christian asked.

Max nodded, thoughtful. "It's possible. Or he—or she—could be one of those trustworthy or charming, Ted Bundy-looking types."

Jade turned to Christian. "What do you have?"

"So far, not much. We scoured thousands of reservations at airports, hotels, and rental car agencies in both Baton Rouge and Houston. Nothing. The perp could've used assumed names." He threw his pen on his notebook. "If only we had a photo."

"Agreed," Jade said. "Get a list of the students who attended the school at the time of the murder. Maybe a name will jump out at us or we can cross-reference it later."

She glanced at Pat.

Pat shook her head. "None of them went to the same school, lived in the same location, or worked together previously. None belonged to the same associations or attended the same conferences, as far as I can determine."

"Austin?"

"I've listened to hours of tapes and haven't found any instances where the same person called both victims, yet."

"What about the college radio station?"

"The good news is the station did keep its recordings. I talked to the current manager and he said its audience back then was limited, mostly students at Chattenham and residents who lived in the town. The audience for the Pittsburgh radio station is also local."

Christian leaned in, peering over at Austin. "Any calls stand out to you?"

"The majority of the callers agreed with the radio talk-show hosts. It's almost cult-like; it's scary. Sometimes callers disagreed with the host and were shouted down by other callers. Few disagreed. I am trying to follow up on them as best I can, but these callers only give a first name. Bottom line, nothing."

"What about the blogs and newspaper articles?" Jade asked.

Austin shook his head and sat back.

The theme song from *Miami Vice* trilled from a cell phone. Everyone glanced at each other and then at Dante, who seemed more surprised than anyone. He fished the phone out of his pocket and pressed the ignore button. He glared at Pat.

Pat was typing on her computer. "Don't look at me."

Dante glowered at Jade.

Jade cracked a smile. "Don't look at me, either."

Austin joined in the laughter, holding up his arms as if surrendering. "I don't even know what that is."

Christian stared at something interesting in the file on the table in front of him.

Dante scowled. "Very funny, Merritt."

Christian winked at Jade.

Jade never allowed herself to depend on anyone, but Christian always seemed to know the right thing to do or say at the right time. Zoe was her only friend, but at work, Christian was her rock. She turned to Dante. "Talk to me."

Dante glared at Christian one more time before flipping through the pages of his notebook. He leaned back in his chair and began to read. "As you recall, the victim—"

"Kyle Williams," Jade interjected.

Dante continued, as if he hadn't been interrupted, "—wrote in his diary he thought a 'C' was following him. I found two 'Cs' in the yearbook picture: a Carly Simms and a Christie Yardley."

Christian murmured, "I don't believe a woman is behind this."

"I don't either," Jade said.

Max took off his glasses and used a handkerchief to polish them. "It would be unlikely this is the work of a woman, but I wouldn't rule it out."

"Can I finish?" Dante asked.

Jade nodded.

"I was able to get in touch with the ten students in the photograph," Dante said, "including Carly and Christie. None of them could imagine who would do such a thing. One of the students died in a car crash three years ago, which would rule him out for the LeBlanc and the latest killing."

Pat, typing, said, "Alibis?"

"All of them had alibis, but . . ."

"What?" Jade said.

"There's a problem."

Jade tried not to roll her eyes in frustration. Working with Dante sometimes was like pulling teeth. "What is it?"

"Ten students posed for the picture. But in order to staff a twenty-four-hours-a-day radio station, the school accepts applications from any student who wants to be a DJ. Students are selected based on their competency, style of music or talk-show format, and maintaining a certain GPA."

Jade motioned her hand for him to hurry up.

"How many students were on the staff at the time of the Chattenham killing?"

Dante closed his notebook, an incongruous grin on his face. "Over one hundred."

CHAPTER TWENTY-NINE

Washington, DC

"SO, WHITNEY SAYS this election is about their future? The way things are going, these students won't have a future. Student debt, not to mention the national debt, will be a yoke around their necks for the rest of their lives. Our educational system is broken. We are in the middle of the pack among developed countries. Our students couldn't do a math or science problem if we wrote the answers on the back of their hands. Where's her plan?

"And, yes, our kids want to live with their parents forever. We allow them to stay on their parents' health insurance policies until they're twenty-six. Twenty-six! At twenty-six, you're no longer a child! You should be having children of your own. Health insurance is a privilege, not a right. The Socialists are always talking about rights. A right to health insurance, a right to marry whoever we want, a right to clean air, a right to a first-class education, while I don't have the right to smoke in my own freakin' office?

"And concerning President Richard Ellison taking his policy advice from me, well . . . it's about damn time!" Cole laughed into the microphone.

"The United States Postal Service, as we know it, is dead. We can't bring back those nostalgic times of the men and women—I know I mustn't forget about the women—mail carriers in their blue sweaters, blue shirts, blue shorts, and blue socks bringing us our mail in a blue bag rain or shine. But listen: email is not going away, folks. The volume the Postal Service enjoyed back in the day is never coming back. Never. As a country, we must accept this and move on. A piecemeal approach won't work. Partial privatization isn't the answer. We must privatize the whole thing. The Postal Service is like a cancer. You can't remove a little bit of the cancer or the disease will continue to spread. You must remove all of it.

"I need you to do something for me. Make sure you call or write President Ellison about this issue. I know for a fact he enjoys hearing from you."

CHAPTER THIRTY

Washington, DC

WHITNEY SETTLED INTO the back seat of the Lincoln Town Car. She should be making phone calls to donors, but she didn't feel like it. Instead she leaned her head back against the headrest, leaving her cell phone in her purse. Her driver had taken a circuitous route from the Capitol to avoid the press, this time because of the allegations of Grayson having had an affair. Sensing her mood, the driver remained silent for the duration of their drive home. She gazed out the window at a city even more stunning at night, thanks to The Height of Buildings Act of 1899, which allowed for the unobstructed view of the city's many historical buildings. She didn't notice them tonight.

Before she left the office, Landon told her the campaign event at Randolph High school broke the Internet, her Twitter account adding one million followers in less than three hours. The kids talked about how cool she was, although they probably used a different adjective. Overall, an overwhelming success. For once, she didn't care.

The rumors had turned out to be true.

Grayson admitted to her on the phone that he had slept with the woman next door, whose husband died young of a heart attack five years ago. She hadn't been a friend of Whitney's, but was a good neighbor who had done a lot for their family over the years. Someone she had trusted.

Her thoughts, though, were mostly of Grayson. She now wondered when he had asked her when she was coming home in that conversation long ago, whether it was eagerness or something else. Maybe, he didn't want to be surprised.

This was not the first time her faith had been shattered by someone she loved. Someone she trusted. She had been raped as a teenager by a boyfriend who was "tired of waiting." She had become pregnant. With the boyfriend long gone, Whitney wanted an abortion. Her liberal parents wouldn't give their legal consent, surprising her. Instead, they sent her to live with an aunt outside of Chicago for the nine-month duration. The aunt died a year before Whitney was elected to Congress.

She gave the baby up for adoption and returned to her life in Missouri, telling her classmates she had spent a year at boarding school. Whitney decided then to never put herself in another situation where her choices in life were not hers to make. And she became a lifelong pro-choice advocate. She never tried to find her rapist's offspring.

After high school, Whitney attended Northwestern University on an academic scholarship and during the summers interned for local Chicago politicians. There, she caught the political bug, and after graduation, enrolled in Harvard Law School. Whitney ruminated now on how many individuals ran for Congress today without a legal background and no knowledge of the Constitution. She believed this was part of the problem in Washington.

After Harvard, she returned to Chicago and volunteered for Brad Davis's mayoral campaign. She served on Davis's staff after the election, which was how she met Grayson Fairchild. Whitney walked into a meeting between the mayor and Grayson regarding tax incentives to move a large subsidiary of his father's company to the city. She gazed into Grayson's blue eyes; he stared at her, and it was all over for both of them. They had a long-distance relationship for a year before he proposed. After a beautiful wedding for a match that pleased both sets of parents, the newlyweds settled in St. Louis, the headquarters of Fairchild Industries.

Whitney had Chandler about a year after the wedding and Emma two years later. Although she enjoyed being a mother, the political bug never left her. Grayson understood when she explained she wanted to help people. Whitney entered and won her first political race for a seat on the county council. A couple of years later, she campaigned and narrowly won a state representative seat. When the US House representative for her district died in a car accident, Whitney ran in the special election to replace him. Her opponent painted her as an inexperienced legislator and a housewife, but the voters in her district responded to her honesty, her sincere willingness to help people, and her intelligence. Her attractiveness didn't hurt either. The women turned out to vote for her in droves, and so did the men. She won by a landslide.

Four terms later, she ran for the US Senate when one of the senators retired. The people of Missouri loved her. She was one of their own. She won again by a wide margin.

Whitney decided to run for president to stop the erosion of women's rights and to express her frustration with the country's direction. She believed she could bring a divided country back together. People trusted her. She did not offer pie-in-the-sky rhetoric, but practical solutions and results, as evidenced by her many accomplishments in the House and Senate.

Now, her campaign was no longer about proving a point.

It was about winning.

Their neighbor had always been there for Whitney. When Whitney was away on state business and then in DC, the woman had checked on her family, brought them warm meals, shuttled Chandler to lacrosse practice in a pinch, helped Emma get ready for a homecoming dance.

When Judy, the reporter, had first asked Whitney about the affair, she couldn't conceive that it might be true. Now, she had a decision to make. Divorcing Grayson in the middle of a presidential run was out of the question, wasn't it? She fell back on the question that guided her political life. WWHD? *What would Hillary do?* She knew exactly what HRC would do.

Landon had informed her about the chatter on Twitter and other online sites, the additional rumors spawned, the vicious talk, and the few-and-far-between calls for the couple's privacy.

The most remarkable development was that although the affair was killing her on the inside, it was helping her poll numbers. The American public loved a scorned woman.

The vehicle stopped, jolting her from her thoughts. The driver came around and opened the door, extending a hand to help her out. She took it and thanked him as she stepped by him. He hustled to the other side to retrieve her bulging briefcase and followed her into her Georgetown home. He placed the briefcase on a stand for that purpose in the elegant foyer, tipped his hat, nodded, and left without a word.

The house was quiet. Unlike most of her colleagues, she lived primarily in DC, refusing to be in perpetual campaign mode. She was sent to DC to do a job, and to do it she needed to be here. At first, living apart from Grayson was hard, but over the years she welcomed the solitude after days spent with ever-demanding constituents, colleagues, the media, and lobbyists.

Leaving the lights off, she kicked off her shoes and padded to the library off the foyer. The curtains remained open and the moonlight provided sufficient visibility to navigate the furniture. She walked around the rolling ladder for the books on the highest shelves and past the large, unlit stone fireplace. She went to her music collection in a section of one of the bookcases. Selecting a CD at random, she slipped it into the player. Skipping the bottles of wine, she selected the bottle of Yamazaki Single Malt Sherry Cask 2013 and a tulip glass and moved to the sofa. She poured several ounces into the glass, then sat back and drew her legs up under her. She swirled and sniffed the whiskey, took a sip, and cradled the glass in her hands.

She had to use two hands to keep the glass from shaking.

This was her favorite room in the house, the shelves filled with first editions whose titles she couldn't read in the dark.

Despite Chopin's "Nocturnes, Op. 9, No. 2" and the liquor, she couldn't relax.

She started to reach for the humidor on the coffee table; indulging in a Cohiba cigar seemed appropriate for the occasion.

"Hello, darling."

A lamp clicked on next to a chair, revealing her husband, Grayson, sitting there in his suit and overcoat, a bittersweet smile on his face.

✿

Whitney rose without speaking. She grasped a highball glass from the cabinet above the bar and filled it with ice cubes, pouring an even dose of gin and tonic water.

She glided to Grayson's chair and dangled the drink before his face.

"Sorry, I'm out of fresh lime. I wasn't expecting you." She resumed her position on the sofa and brought her glass to her lips. She peered at her husband over the rim and sipped while he swallowed most of his drink.

He placed the glass on the cherry end table next to his chair. His hair was uncombed, spiking on top. He had been crying.

"It wasn't an *affair*. It was just one night."

"So what would you call it?"

"A mistake."

She bent forward, placing her own glass on the coffee table in front of her. "I see," she said. "How did it happen?"

He sighed. "Do you really want to know?"

"I need to know what I'm up against. How did this *mistake* occur?"

He was silent for a long time. "With you gone, with the kids gone, she still brings dinner over." A quick, reassuring gesture with his hands. "Brought. Brought dinner over. Especially when I worked late. We'd talk. When you're the boss, you have few people you can talk to about what's going on at work. She was so far removed from what was going on there. Easy to talk to . . . One night, we had a bottle of wine, and then another . . ." He shrugged, knowing nothing more needed to be said.

Whitney took in the pain of each word and swallowed her grief. "Have you spoken to the children?"

Grayson grabbed his drink and drained it. "Chandler's angry. And Emma is not speaking to me. Always protective of her mother. The press had left them alone for the last week, but now they're back in full force."

"They've been through enough," she said, her words harsh. "They don't deserve this, Grayson. Affairs are harder on the children than the couple."

"Mistake."

"I wish they had Secret Service protection."

He stared into his empty glass. "I know. Me, too. This is my fault. What can I do to make this right?"

She said nothing.

After a while, he indicated with his chin. "What're you reading?"

Whitney glanced at the book on the coffee table, for once, not interested in books. "Another Abraham Lincoln biography. I don't know how much more can be written about the man, but writers always find something."

Lincoln was her favorite president, leading the country during its deadliest war and through its greatest moral and constitutional challenges. She loved reading biographies: Churchill, Thatcher, the Roosevelts, Gandhi, Martin Luther King Jr., Hitler, Gorbachev. She never understood those people who did not like to read; she pitied them for what they were missing. Whitney learned from the mistakes and successes of others. A lifetime wasn't long enough to make all the mistakes yourself.

Grayson placed his highball glass on the end table and stood. "I need to get to the airport. Board meeting tomorrow. But I needed to see you in person. To talk about this face to face."

Whitney didn't bother to get up. "Lock the front door on your way out."

He hesitated, continuing to search her face, and then left the room. She heard the front door close.

Whitney reached for the bottle and poured a refill.

She grabbed a cigar, cut the cap, and struck a wooden match. Opening one of the large windows facing the street, she sat on the cushioned window seat. She puffed as she stared out into the cool night thinking about how to use Grayson's "mistake" to her political advantage, ignoring the tears streaming down her face.

CHAPTER THIRTY-ONE

Crystal City, Virginia

MY PLACE WAS dark, except for the light emanating from the three computer monitors on my desk. A news report video played on the monitor to my right, reporters shouting questions as the senator left her office building.

"Senator Fairchild, why aren't you speaking out against the person or persons who leaked to the media about your husband's affair?"

"Are you getting a divorce, Senator?"

"Senator, how do you feel?"

"Senator, if you were in a room alone with the other woman, what would you say to her?"

I frowned. Reporters were not my favorite people.

Senator Whitney Fairchild, her posture perfect, stopped. She faced the reporters and the cameras.

"This is a very difficult time for my family and me. We are dealing with a personal situation and would be grateful if you would honor our privacy." She glanced down briefly, before scanning the faces of those around her. "We are all human. We all make mistakes. That's all I'm going to say about this matter."

The senator started to walk away, before turning back. "Oh, one more thing." Her voice hardened. "Leave my children alone."

She walked to the waiting black car at a brisk pace. She shook her head and waved to the press, her expression unreadable.

God, she's beautiful.

I laughed when I realized what I had just thought. How can you talk to someone in whom you do not believe?

I paused the video, her face turned toward the camera, as she was about to duck into the car. I traced my finger down her forehead, her nose, her lips, and brought it to my lips. I yanked my finger away, surprised.

Her husband was a fool.

After I wiped my finger with the handkerchief I kept on my desk, I pressed play and ignored the rest of the news program. I turned to the center monitor.

My friends had arrived. I found it curious, yes, and a little sad, that conversing with them was the best part of my home life. I felt closer to my online friends, whom I had never met, than to anyone else. But I did not have time to think about that now. I caught up on the conversation. Pittfan, of course, was leading the discussion topic about the affair.

I lurked as the chat continued, waiting a few minutes before typing.

Good evening. I waited for everyone to return the greeting and typed, Entertainment Tonight *is over. We have more important things to discuss. We need to take it up a notch.*

Washington, DC

WHITNEY BREEZED THROUGH the anteroom of her office suite in the Russell Senate Office Building. Sean, her receptionist and scheduler, stopped typing and grinned.

"Welcome back, Senator."

"Thank you, Sean." She kept walking. "Give me five minutes and then send Landon in, please. Afterward, you and I can go over my schedule."

"Yes, Senator."

She put her purse in the lower right-hand drawer and scanned the top of her desk. She never checked her email first thing. She liked to find her equilibrium before dealing with all the messages that needed an immediate reply and the overwhelming majority that did not. She eyed the briefing books stacked on the right top corner of the desk, in order of priority. Sean had printed out her messages, also in the priority of whom she needed to call back first. She nodded her approval. She had a good team.

She did not think about Grayson.

At the knock on the door, she looked up. Landon stood in the doorway, a smile on his face.

"Come in."

He sat across from her.

She stared at his hair. Someone had taken an ax to it.

He rubbed his buzzed head. "My barber got a little carried away."

She squinted. "It'll grow out. Someday." She picked up some papers and started skimming through them. "Bring me up to speed."

Whitney had been out of the office for a few days on a road show through Michigan, Indiana, and, of course, Ohio. She had told Ted before the campaign began she was not going to stop doing her job even though she was running for president of the United States. During the previous election primary, a congresswoman from the other party missed almost half of the votes that came to the floor and had a two-month stretch when she didn't vote at all. Although Whitney suffered from perpetual jet lag, she flew back to the Hill for every vote. Representing her constituents was important to her. And why she was here.

Landon finished his briefing and left. She thought about the last couple of months and how the media had jumped all over the Graysongate story, the bill that benefited Grayson's business, and the negative impact on her polling numbers. Then, the president's animal cruelty scandal broke—Piggygate—and her poll numbers started to rise again. Finally, her husband's affair had catapulted her numbers through the roof. *What a crazy profession I have chosen.*

She returned to the memorandum in front of her. Another rap on her door.

"Senator," Landon said, a strange expression on his face. "I think you'd better come see this."

She held his gaze and frowned, but followed him into the anteroom. He stopped a few feet from the television where Sean and other members of her staff stood. She refused to have a TV in her office. Sometimes she needed a break from the noise.

The Breaking News flash was crawling across the bottom of the screen. An impressive graphic with the words Talk Show Killer at the upper right hovered next to the commentator's head.

"In an exclusive breaking news story, a person claiming to be the Talk Show Killer sent an email message to this network. Our investigative reporters now believe the murders of conservative blogger Pete Paxson of Houston five years ago, conservative newspaper columnist Taylor LeBlanc of Baton Rouge two years ago, and Pittsburgh conservative radio personality Randy Sells this past January are all related.

"The killer claims to have murdered Randy Sells because conservative talk radio dominates the airwaves and the time has come for moderates and the left to be heard." The pretty anchorwoman, whose hair seemed incapable of moving, glanced down at a sheet of paper and back up to the camera. "This person goes on to state that the public is being brainwashed and likens right-wing radio programs to the Nazi propaganda machine. Until the Federal Communications Commission brings back the Fairness Doctrine or news networks take it upon themselves to present both sides of significant issues, the murders will continue, according to this self-proclaimed killer. We will be reading the full email on the air at the top of the hour. We will also post it on our website, www.msnbc.com. MSNBC will keep you updated on this important story.

"After the break, we'll talk to a panel of experts about how MSNBC is the leader in providing fair and balanced reporting."

The group stood in silence for a few moments. Landon muted the television. Whitney's employees turned to her, studying her reaction. She shook her head.

"This is terrible news." She took in each of her staff members, her eyes resting on Landon.

"My office."

"Yes, Senator."

Sean went back to his desk and resumed working. The other staffers drifted back to their offices.

Landon put the television remote down on a *Roll Call* newspaper on the coffee table and followed Whitney into her office. He closed the door behind him. She sat behind her desk. He remained standing.

She stared at him. "Find out anything you can about the killings and whether they're related."

"Yes, Senator."

"And get a copy of the email."

"Yes, Senator." He stopped at the door and turned. "Do you want this closed?"

"Yes."

She leaned back in her chair and crossed her legs. She abhorred violence. The next thought—she could not help herself; she was a politician after all—was about the impact this news would have on her campaign. Would it help or hurt?

One thing she knew for sure: her husband's affair had become yesterday's news.

CHAPTER THIRTY-THREE

Washington, DC

COLE BRENNAN ENTERED the small, quaint church near the White House. The nave was quiet and empty, except for the lone man sitting in the front row. Cole ignored the beautiful, stained-glass windows he had admired on a previous visit and sauntered down the center aisle. He sat down, a little too close to the man. The man scooted away from him.

"Funny you asked to meet me in a church," the president of the United States said. "When was the last time you were inside one without the cameras present?"

"Ha, ha. Your sense of humor has always been underrated."

"What do you want, Cole?"

"Why didn't you tell me about your animal troubles? Why did I hear about it for the first time on the news?"

President Richard Ellison examined his hands. "I barely remember the incident. It was a long time ago. I was young. Sixteen. The court records were supposed to have been sealed."

"You didn't think it was going to come out? In this day and age? Everything you did from elementary school on is fair game."

"My daddy paid off a lot of people. Most people thought it was my brother, anyway. He was the one always in trouble." Ellison sighed. "There's nothing I can do about it now. If I could go back and change it, I would. It happened. My friends and I were drunk. Out-of-our-minds drunk. I made a stupid, youthful mistake, which I now deeply regret."

Cole laughed. "Save the speech for the cameras. I'm not saying it was a mistake, only you should've told me about it." He leaned back and crossed one ankle over the other and interlocked his hands over his belly. "In high school, my buddies and I talked this crane operator into putting an old Volkswagen

Beetle on the roof of the school. The principal freaked out, not knowing how the car got there or how he was going to get it down. I was one of the ones he questioned, of course—I was always up to something—but talked my way out of trouble. I learned from that situation that I can convince anyone of anything, which is why I'm in the profession I am today."

"Fascinating," Ellison snapped. "Shit,"—the word coming out in two syllables—"Cole, I don't have time for—or care about—your glory days. Get to the point of why I'm here."

"You must get out ahead of this Postal Service issue. I set everything up for you. All you need to do is take the ball and cross the goal line."

"You're always telling me what I *must* do. Right now, I have other pressing matters."

"You always have other pressing matters."

The president's voice softened. "This time may be different."

"How so?"

"We've intercepted a threat."

"What kind of threat?"

"Terrorist."

"Where?"

Ellison shrugged, distracted. "That's all I can tell you."

"Have you seen the latest numbers? Your approval rating is down to forty-three percent. The race shouldn't be this close. She's inexperienced and a woman, for God's sake."

"I've seen the numbers. We're fine. Just a blip."

"I can't believe her husband's affair is helping her."

"Did you have something to do with that? The affair?"

Cole sat back, smug. "Like I said, everything from elementary school on is fair game. He should've known we're always watching."

Ellison shook his head in disgust.

"She's showing she's not tough enough to be president," Cole said. "'No comment. No comment.'" He mimicked Whitney. "Anyway, she'll be out of the office for a week once a month."

The president gave him a quizzical expression.

Cole shook his head, as if the president were an idiot. "Her period."

Ellison turned from Cole and said nothing.

The two men remained silent for a long time, lost in their own thoughts. The president stared up at the intricate sculpture of Jesus nailed to the cross. Cole, at the floor.

Cole lifted his head, a slow thoughtful movement. He looked into Ellison's eyes. "Maybe a terrorist attack wouldn't be such a bad thing."

"You're not joking," Ellison said.

"Presidents win elections because of wars and conflicts all the time. You can demonstrate your leadership skills in our time of need."

"Then I would rather lose this election than hope for an attack that could kill thousands of our people," Ellison said. "What do you know about this serial killer going after conservative talk-show hosts?"

"Nothing much. Why?"

"Because the right-wing extremism of you and your brethren has something to do with it. That's why. The rhetoric has gotten out of hand, and I believe it hurts the party and galvanizes their base."

"Bullshit. Without me, you wouldn't have been nominated, and you wouldn't be where you are today. And don't you forget it."

Ellison gave Cole a sideways glance. "What if there is a serial killer out there? How would your show go on without you?"

The sarcasm wasn't lost on Cole. "There's that sense of humor again."

Ellison leaned forward, about to rise. "Do you remember how we met?"

"No, I don't."

"It was at a fundraiser. You sidled up next to me at a urinal in the restroom. That's when you made your first demand." He laughed without mirth. "Thinking back on it now, what an appropriate place." The president stood. "I'm done taking orders from you, Cole. Go ahead and run."

He walked toward the empty choir chairs and the side door, where his Secret Service detail was waiting.

For once, Cole Brennan had no response.

CHAPTER THIRTY-FOUR

Washington, DC

JADE SAT AT her desk, Christian and Dante hovering behind her. After being alerted by another agent, they watched the MSNBC broadcast on the Internet. Within minutes, the president of the network, at Jade's request, had forwarded her the email in its entirety. CART—the FBI's Computer Analysis and Response Team—was tracing its origins.

The three of them read in silence.

To Whom It May Concern,

Several years ago, a movement swept across this country called "Occupy Wall Street." The people participating in these protests did so for many reasons, but the main reason was to protest the unfairness of America's wealth belonging to the top one percent of the population while the other ninety-nine percent struggled during the Great Recession. The movement was not against capitalism per se, but against a system that was rigged to favor the few. The same could be said for talk radio.

Conservative talk radio controls 76% of the market, which means a majority of US citizens are hearing one side of the argument on our myriad of complex issues. How is this different from the propaganda machine propagated by Goebbels under Hitler? Our citizens, some of them uneducated, functionally illiterate, or lazy, listen to this propaganda as if it were news. It is not.

There is a lot of big money behind conservative talk radio. The government must regain some control and make sure the media are serving the informational needs of all Americans. Our citizens deserve the right to hear both sides of an argument so they can engage in intelligent discussions and make informed decisions. Some would argue that citizens can just "Change the channel," but since a significant number of talk-radio stations are conservative, finding a liberal talk-radio station is difficult and a moderate one impossible. In addition, what if one does not want to change the channel? What if one wants to receive fair and equitable reporting like the good old days?

The party in power wants to turn back the clock. I agree. Let us do so in the following ways:

1) Restore requirements that broadcasting ownership must include local owners. Talk radio has been ambushed by large group owners holding multiple licenses in different markets. These owners are more likely to air conservative programming;

2) Provide incentives to women and minorities to own broadcasting licenses. Minorities and women are more likely to air liberal or moderate programming; and

3) Bring back the Fairness Doctrine requiring broadcasters to present both sides of controversial issues and give fair and balanced reporting.

If the above suggestions, or something similar, are not implemented immediately, then more conservative talk-show hosts are going to die. And there is nothing the FBI can do to stop me.

Sincerely,

TSK

Jade didn't take her eyes off the screen. "TSK?"

"His initials?" Christian said.

"Or a message like 'tsk, tsk,' as if he were scolding the reader," Dante said. He straightened. "All I know is this is a bunch of liberal B.S."

"What else?" she asked, ignoring Dante.

"Max said the killer has above-average intelligence. That jibes with whoever wrote this email," Christian said. "Check out the style, word choice, and sentence structure."

"I'm not sure how intelligent he is," Jade said, "if he thinks killing radio personalities is the best way to attain what he wants. I need to get this to Max."

She leaned back in her chair. "Let's look at this from a broader perspective. What is he trying to tell us?"

Dante circled around her desk and moved into her field of vision. "More people are going to die."

CHAPTER THIRTY-FIVE

Arlington, Virginia

THAT EVENING, JADE sat on the couch in her living room surrounded by files and papers, her cat, Card, on her lap.

An Earth, Wind & Fire album played on the turntable, the volume low. She paused to listen to the much-needed rain falling outside. This was her favorite room in the house, its hardwood floors in need of polish, the sparse but comfortable espresso-colored furniture, her shelves crammed with books and her precious album collection. She came out of her reverie when a key was inserted into the lock of the front door.

A moment later, Zoe poked her head around the wall that separated the foyer from the living room. "Hey, you. Hard at work, I presume?"

Jade gave her a tired smile. "Of course."

Zoe shook off her raincoat.

Jade did a double take at the clothes Zoe wore on her short, thin body. Skin-tight green leggings, a bright colorful African shirt, and some of the largest earrings Jade had ever seen. "Does that outfit even go together?"

Zoe laughed and held up a bag. "Food!"

"What is it?"

"Healthy takeout. Imagine!"

Jade pretended to whine. "Do we have to?" Zoe was always bugging Jade to improve her eating habits.

"Just because you look healthy doesn't mean you are healthy."

Zoe moved toward the kitchen at the back of the house, and Jade turned her attention back to the file she had been reading. Zoe came out with a tray holding a paper plate with two chicken wraps, a side salad, and a glass of water for Jade. Zoe left and returned with the same meal and a Hoegaarden beer for herself.

"How did you know?" Jade said, setting the file down beside her on one side and the cat on the other.

Zoe scrunched up her face and rolled her eyes. "I know how you are when you're on a case. You forget to eat, call your friends, and do all the other things us mere mortals do."

Jade stood. "Be right back."

She went to the half bathroom in the foyer, washed her hands, and double-checked that Zoe had locked the front door behind her. Jade returned, placing the tray in her lap, and took a bite of the chicken wrap. It was delicious. She realized she had forgotten to eat breakfast. And lunch.

"This is right on time. Thank you. How're things with you?"

"Fine. Busy. The possibility of being a part of helping to elect the first woman president and passage of the ERA has everyone at the office fired up and motivated."

"How's your friend?"

"She's fine. I haven't seen her much, because of work, but we're okay." Zoe paused. "I think." She laughed.

Jade had long ago stopped calling Zoe's partners "girlfriends." Her relationships didn't last long enough. Zoe went through girlfriends like Imelda Marcos went through shoes. Jade, of course, heard the rumors about Zoe and her in college, the conventional wisdom that if you were a woman basketball player, you must be gay. She didn't care about the rumors or what other people said about her. Her business was her own. Jade's only significant relationships in college had been with a basketball, her coach, and her teammates. Zoe was the one person she allowed to get close to her—sort of—and she wasn't going to change that to please others.

"What do you expect?" Zoe continued. "I grew up in a free love, peace, and happiness household with a father named Harry and a mother named Moon. Let's say I didn't have great role models for committed relationships. Anyway, enough about me. I know I can't ask what you're working on, but how's it going?"

"Actually, you may be able to help me with this case."

"Moi?"

"Yes, you. What are the chances of Congress bringing back the Fairness Doctrine?"

"Ah . . . so, that's your case." Zoe put down her wrap and thought for a moment. "Slim. Conservatives and libertarians don't want it back. They say it violates First Amendment rights and that it's an attack on conservative radio."

"Why do we label everyone?"

"Because that's what Americans do. Otherwise, we'd have to listen to each other."

"What about public opinion?"

"According to the latest polls, forty-seven percent of Americans want the Doctrine reinstated, thirty-nine percent don't. Regardless, the public doesn't care enough about the issue. The economy, immigration, health care, and national security are in the forefront of people's minds. Maybe with these killings and the issue getting more exposure, there could be some movement, but I doubt it."

"Did you read the TSK email?"

"Sure, and I can't say I disagree with any of it. You and I talked about this before. The gap between the haves and the have-nots will only get worse, and social unrest will increase as a result. I believe the Great Recession is payback for unbridled greed and capitalism."

"But how do you really feel?" Jade said. They shared a laugh at this.

Zoe finished the rest of her wrap. "You know I belong to this online chat room and we were discussing the email last night."

Jade remembered the chat room Zoe frequented and had a vague recollection of the discussion on the Pittsburgh killing right after she had started her investigation. She did remember their argument; one of the few they had had over the last decade. Jade realized Zoe was still talking.

"—can be intense, but the conversations are exhilarating. I love having discussions with like-minded, intelligent individuals."

Jade smiled at her friend. "I'm sorry. What can be intense?"

"Not what. Who. One of the chat members. Never mind, it's not important. You have more important things on your mind than my online discussions." Zoe got up with her beer and strolled over to the shelves displaying Jade's extensive album collection. "The Bee Gees, Janet Jackson, MJ, George Michael, Lionel Richie . . . I used to make fun of you for buying these old albums and now vinyls are back in. This collection is probably worth a fortune." Zoe shook her head in admiration. She turned to Jade dazzling her with a toothbrush-commercial smile and game-show host voice: "And the most amazing thing of all, they're all in alphabetical order!"

Jade laughed. She was inured to Zoe's teasing about her OCD tendencies.

Zoe reached for a brown journal. "What's this?" Her forefinger tipped the top of the book downward to a thirty-degree angle.

"Don't," Jade said. She hadn't told her best friend about her latest hobby, writing haiku poetry in this Japanese-style journal. The poetry was awful, but writing it brought her peace.

Zoe froze.

They knew each other well. By the tone of Jade's voice, Zoe knew not to disobey her. Jade knew Zoe had to exercise all of her willpower not to open it. Finally, Zoe slid the journal back in its place, turned to pick up their trays, and walked to the kitchen as if their last exchange hadn't happened. When she returned, she said, "I have an idea."

"What?"

"Why don't you meet with Senator Fairchild or at the very least someone from her office? She'd welcome a visit from one of the investigators on the case and may give you more insight into the political angle. I consider her legislative director, Landon Phillips, a friend. Back in the day, we worked together on some campaigns. I can call him with an introduction, if you'd like."

Jade thought about it for less than a second. She didn't need a friend of Zoe's to introduce her; her credentials ensured immediate attention from any senator. But letting Zoe introduce her to Senator Fairchild's legislative director might be a better, less official approach.

"I'd like."

CHAPTER THIRTY-SIX

Washington, DC

THE YOUNG MAN, who had introduced himself as Sean, stepped aside and indicated for Jade to enter.

Senator Whitney Fairchild rose from her chair and walked around her large mahogany desk. Jade's first thought was the camera did not do this woman justice. Despite the touch of sadness in her eyes, she was more beautiful in person than on television and carried herself like royalty. This initial impression was enhanced by the sound of classical music.

Senator Fairchild extended her hand. "Agent Harrington."

"Thank you for seeing me, Senator." Jade paused and listened. "Liszt?"

The senator studied her, surprised. "You're familiar with Franz Liszt?"

"Of course. This must be one of his symphonic poems, *From . . .*"

"*Von der Wiege bis zum Grabe.*"

"Right," Jade said. "*From the Cradle to the Grave.*"

The senator's smile broadened as she guided Jade to one of the guest chairs. "Please have a seat. Would you like anything to drink?"

"No, thank you, Senator. I'm fine." Jade retrieved a notepad and pen, putting her briefcase down on the floor next to her seat.

Seated, the Senator looked into her eyes. "Being an African-American female FBI agent cannot be easy."

Jade tensed, but did not react. How to answer. Somehow Jade knew this wasn't a woman who would accept the company line. That the Bureau was one big, happy family, where everyone was treated fairly regardless of the color of her skin. Yes, there was discrimination within the Bureau. She had to be twice as good as a white man to succeed. Jade held her gaze.

"Some days are more challenging than others."

Senator Whitney Fairchild crossed her legs. "I see. I am impressed by those who make things seem easy. I suspect you are one of those individuals, but believe me, I know what it feels like to be marginalized. Only twenty out of one hundred senators are women, while we make up more than fifty percent of the populace. 'We've come a long way, baby,' but we still need to fight the battle every day."

"Yes, we do."

"And, sometimes," the senator continued, "it is not the men who give us the most trouble, but other women. We always seem to be tearing each other down when we should be building each other up."

Jade liked this woman.

"Besides classical music, what are your other interests?"

"I read. Play basketball. I'm a fourth-degree black belt in Tae Kwon Do and speak fluent Japanese, a language much more helpful in the eighties than it is now. I should have studied Chinese or Arabic." She didn't tell Senator Fairchild about the haiku; her poetry hobby was hers and hers alone.

"You never know. Japan may make a comeback, yet. Nevertheless, I've done my research. Your background is impressive. Perhaps, you'll come work for me someday." At the knock, the senator glanced toward the door. "Ah, there you are. Come in."

Jade turned. A tall, slender, handsome man strode over to her. He extended his hand and smiled. "Hi. I'm Landon Phillips, the Senator's legislative director."

"Special Agent Jade Harrington." She rose; his handshake was warm, firm. Her eyes traveled from his green eyes to his straight white teeth. She remembered her mother's long-ago advice to always date a boy with perfect teeth. "If he takes care of his teeth, he'll take care of you," she would say.

Jade brushed away the thoughts of her mother's romantic guidance and sat down. The senator's eyes shifted from Landon to Jade, a mischievous grin starting to form. Jade needed to start this meeting before the junior senator from Missouri started playing matchmaker. Landon sat in the adjoining guest chair and crossed his long legs in front of him. An electronic tablet rested on his lap.

Jade glanced down at her well-used spiral notepad, the perforations beginning to shoot up through the wire. She had no qualms about doing things old school.

"Landon is being modest," the senator said. "He is my acting chief of staff and will be my liaison with your office. He speaks for me. What can you tell me about the investigation so far?"

Not much. Jade hesitated. She shifted in her chair. "We have composed a pretty good profile of the killer. We believe he is responsible for at least four murders. All the victims have been killed in a similar manner."

"Which was?" Landon asked.

"Some kind of blunt instrument. There is circumstantial evidence linking the cases." The severed tongues were more than circumstantial evidence, but no need to go into that now.

"What kind of circumstantial evidence?" Landon asked.

"I'm not at liberty to say at this time. Senator, what do you think would motivate a person to kill conservative media personalities?"

The senator brought a finger to her lips and removed it.

"As Albert Camus once said, 'There are causes worth dying for, but none worth killing for.' I don't understand why anyone would take the life of someone else for any reason, especially political ideology." The senator glanced down at her watch and back up at Jade. "I'm sorry. I have another appointment. Perhaps, the two of you can continue this conversation. I am sure Landon can give you a lot of good ideas. Excuse me."

The senator grabbed her purse, came around her desk, and shook Jade's hand. "It was a pleasure meeting you. Please keep me posted on your progress." She gave Jade's hand a brief squeeze and smiled. "And keep up the fight."

She left.

Stunned, Jade glanced toward the door and back at Landon. *What was that all about?*

The silence grew between them.

"Perhaps, we can—" Landon's hopeful expression changed when he noticed the look on Jade's face.

CHAPTER THIRTY-SEVEN

Palo Alto, California

WHITNEY SCANNED THE faces of her audience in the elegant ballroom of the Four Seasons in Palo Alto, California. Fifteen hundred people had paid thirty-five thousand dollars each to meet her and listen to her speak. Fifty-two million, five hundred thousand dollars; not bad for a few hours' work. The audience—made up of Silicon Valley billionaires and their families—was still in a frenzy after Beyoncé had finished singing her latest number-one song.

Whitney grinned as she waited for the buzz to die down.

"I should have delivered my speech first."

The crowd laughed.

"Thank you for coming. I know all of you have busy lives and I appreciate your taking the time to join me tonight." She segued into her speech, targeted to this group of technology and social-media entrepreneurs.

Thirty minutes later, she began to wind up her speech. Smiling, she said, "Reducing regulation is not something you typically hear from a Democrat." Her voice softened. "But I believe a president should not be a Democratic president or a Republican president"—her voice rose—"but the president of the United States of America!"

Someone yelled from the audience. "Preach, Whitney!"

She chuckled and raised her arms to quiet the crowd. The applause was not quite as deafening as for the pop star, but close enough. She'd take it.

"I believe we need a candidate who appeals to the best in us, not the basest in us, if we are to return to our rightful place as the most powerful country in the world that every other country aspires to be."

Whitney glanced down at her notes and back up. She took a sip of water. The smile was gone.

"I would be remiss if I did not address something tonight. A sick individual declared that he or she will kill conservative radio talk-show hosts unless we enact certain legislation." She paused again, thoughtful. "This is not how we resolve differences in our country."

She surveyed the room.

"This nation was founded on the basis that all of us enjoy the right of freedom of speech, a right protected by the First Amendment of the United States Constitution. Even if the speech is racist, sexist, or hateful—distasteful as it may be—it's still protected by this wonderful document.

"As you know, Cole Brennan doesn't say many positive things about me." She smiled and paused. "But he has the *right* not to say positive things about me, and I will defend his right to do so. Evelyn Beatrice Hall once said, 'I disapprove of what you say, but I will defend to the death your right to say it.' As will I.

"Be that as it may, violence never solves anything. If you are displeased with what politicians are doing in Washington, use your voice." Whitney's voice rose as the applause increased in volume. "Use your feet! Use your vote!

"I want to thank you again for joining me tonight. God bless you, and God bless the United States of America."

Every person in the room stood in a rousing standing ovation. Whitney smiled and waved to every area of the room.

She walked across the stage and down the steps for a long night of smiling, shaking hands, small talk, and encouraging these donors to part with even more of their money for her campaign. She happened to glance up. Halfway down the crowded, massive ballroom, a young man in a dark suit and tie leaned against the wall, staring at her. He appeared familiar, but she couldn't recall where she had seen him before. The intensity of his gaze made her uneasy.

She shook the hand of the CEO of a social media company that recently went public, listening to his complaints about the long, arduous initial-public-offering process. While he was speaking, her eyes drifted back to where the young man had been standing.

He was gone.

CHAPTER THIRTY-EIGHT

Washington, DC

"BILL FROM PITTSBURGH is on the line. Go!"

"Hi, Cole. A few months ago, one of the up-and-coming stars of conservative radio was murdered here. Now, I hear there may be other victims, that other conservative commentators have been murdered. How do you feel about that? Are you afraid?"

"First of all, I'm not afraid. You can come after me like a modern-day Braveheart, with an army of dyke Femi-Commies behind you, and you won't shut me up. You can't shut up common sense. You will not shut up conservative talk radio. The movement is bigger than me or any of us good conservatives who spend our time on the radio.

"This is America. Hasn't this TSK ever heard of a thing called freedom of speech? What is he, a Communist? He can't silence everyone. People throughout this country are waking up to how the Socialists have taken over our schools, our government, and our country. We need to be able to speak our minds without watching what we say or worrying that the government is spying on us. Political correctness is polite crap to our political discourse. A person shouldn't be killed because he doesn't buy into the elitist, Orwellian school of thought. I'll bet you ten-to-one the killer is a graduate of one of our esteemed, liberal institutions in which all its students are taught the elitist code of what we should think and when we should think it. So, to answer your question, Bill from Pittsburgh, I'm not afraid of this liberal pansy hiding behind his email. He can only stop me from talking over my dead body."

His high-pitched giggle filled the air.

"Oops, I guess I shouldn't say that anymore, huh?"

Cole Brennan surveyed the dining room and his six children sitting at the oblong table: Cole Jr., Colleen, Madeline, Ryan, Kaitlin, and Ronnie, named after the greatest American president. He smiled to himself at their constant bickering, one-upmanship, and teasing. He had come from a family of six brothers and sisters as well. This was what it meant to be a family. Big families were the backbone of America and the only hope for its future. *We need more of them*, he thought. He should consider doing a show called *Making Babies*. The Femi-Nazis would come out of the woodwork. Cole laughed out loud.

Kaitlin, his eight-going-on-thirty daughter, shot him a stern look. "What's so funny, Dad?"

"Nothing, sweetheart. Thinking about work."

"It's family time, Dad," she said. "No more working."

He turned toward her. "Oops, you're right. How was your day? Let's go around the table."

As each of the kids gave detailed reports of their day of swimming at the pool and playing with their friends, he couldn't help noticing Kaitlin's eyes never left his face. Her expression of disappointment—or distrust?—was palpable.

His gaze moved to his namesake. "Cole Jr.?" Cole never addressed his eldest son as "CJ," the nickname Cole Jr.'s friends had given him.

"Hangin' out," he said, sliding a forkful of green beans into his mouth.

"Football season is almost here," Cole said. "Preseason will be starting soon. Are you ready?"

Cole Jr. put down his fork with too much grace and stole a glance at his mother before staring at the food on his plate.

Cole glanced at Ashley and then back at him. "What is it, son?"

"I don't think I'm going to play football this year."

"Why not?"

His son glanced toward his mother again. He hesitated. A calm expression came over him. He had come to a decision.

"I'm just not into it."

"Not into football?" Cole paused. "Well . . . , okay. You can try out for something else . . . like golf or tennis or lacrosse. I wouldn't even mind if you played soccer." Cole speared a forkful of steak and shoved the morsel into his mouth, proud of his restraint. The old Cole would have forced Junior to play football, a man's sport. An American sport.

"I've been thinking the same thing. Going out for something else, I mean," Cole Jr. said, finally looking at his father. "I want to try out for the glee club."

Cole spit his chewed steak back onto his plate. "What?"

"I can sing, Dad. I can really sing."

Cole glanced at his wife, Ashley. Her serene smile never changed. Cole forced himself to stay calm. *This is a disaster.* "Say, why don't we go out for a spin in the 'Vette? We can talk about this." Cole collected classic American cars, but his white, 1953 Chevrolet Corvette was his pride and joy.

"I can't, Dad. I'm going to the mall to hang out with my friends and maybe go see a movie."

Something told Cole even if Junior had no plans, he wouldn't want to go.

Cole realized something else. He pushed his plate away. He was no longer hungry. He looked at Ashley.

"Sweetheart, how about another drink?"

❋

Later in bed, Cole lay on his back with his hands under his head staring at the ceiling, thinking. Ashley sat up next to him, leaning back against her pillows, reading the latest Harlan Coben mystery novel. He couldn't remember the last time he read a book for pleasure. He couldn't remember the last time he had read a book, period.

"How's your book?"

"Hard to put down." She laid it on her nightstand, and rolled over and snuggled up close to him, her hand on his chest.

He was grateful to be lying down; it was the only time he didn't need to suck in his stomach. They lay in silence for a few minutes.

"What's wrong?"

He didn't answer.

She raised her head, lines creasing her forehead. "I know you. I know when something's bothering you."

He glanced at her and back up at the ceiling.

"When I was a kid, my mother sang 'I Fall to Pieces' to us when she was making dinner or trying to get us to fall asleep. She had a beautiful voice. Like an angel. Sounded like Patsy Cline. If I close my eyes and concentrate, I can still hear her." Cole paused. "Can he sing?"

"Like an angel," she answered. When he didn't respond, she continued, "Is it something else? Are you worried about this Talk Show Killer?"

"I thought about running."

"Oh?"

"I've been testing the waters. As a Republican and as a third-party candidate. My advisors say my fans are rabid, but my base is too narrow. I can't win. All I would be is a nuisance to Ellison and distract the party from keeping the White House."

"What else?"

Cole remained silent for a moment. He turned his head to her, his eyes moist.

"I don't want to lose what we have," he said, his voice quiet. "I'm afraid I'm losing my daughter. And my son."

CHAPTER THIRTY-NINE

Washington, DC

FOUR MONTHS AND no progress. Jade stood behind the guest chairs in Ethan Lawson's office, sweating through her white dress shirt because of the heat but trying not to show it. July in Washington, DC, could be brutal. The sweat began emanating from her pores as soon as she walked out of her front door this morning and hadn't stopped.

She wasn't surprised that Ethan asked her to his office first thing. The CART team got back to her with an initial analysis of TSK's email. They believed the sender used a type of software, called Tor, that routes internet traffic over a network of six thousand relays. The routing information for the email and its content were encrypted, preventing the linkage of the origin of the email to its final destination. It also made it difficult to trace a user's location. As a result, CART hadn't been able to tell her much. The FBI analyst promised he would keep trying. The killer's silence did not deceive Jade. He was out there. Plotting.

"What is it, Ethan?" she asked. "I'm late for my own briefing."

Ethan reclined in his chair. "This will only take a minute."

"I need more time."

"You don't even know why I called you in here."

"I know we haven't made a lot of progress, but—" She stopped to hear him out. "What?"

He leaned forward, twirling his wedding ring. His starched, white shirt unwrinkled. His eyes searched hers. "I wanted to tell you that I believe in you."

She had braced herself for a tirade, a rant, something else. When he did not continue, she squelched the gratitude threatening to overcome her. His attitude almost made the situation worse. Now, she couldn't fail.

A "thanks" was all she could manage as she strode out of the room.

❋

The other agents were seated around the table when she arrived for the morning briefing. She didn't apologize for being late, she wasn't much of an apologizer.

"Updates?"

No one spoke.

"Anyone?" she asked. "Christian?"

Her "rock" shook his head and crossed his arms over his chest. "Nothing."

"Pat?"

The older woman shook her head as well. "Still trying on the email. We're coming up empty."

Dante just stared at her.

"I'm sick of this case!" Austin said.

Everyone turned to the rookie agent.

"I've sat at my desk. Day after day. Listening to these stupid radio broadcasts, reading these stupid articles, and they say the same thing over and over again about the same topics. It's enough to drive me crazy."

"Look on the bright side," Dante said. "You might learn something while on the job."

Pat addressed Dante, still staring at her computer. "Oh, is that your secret? Education through talk radio?"

"You'll find something," Jade said to Austin. "You have to find something. All of us, we've got to work harder." An unintentional rise in her voice. "We're not working hard enough. We're not putting enough time in. While we're sitting around failing, he is out there plotting, planning to outsmart us."

Austin sank back in his chair, crossing his arms like Christian, his face flushed. Jade started to continue her pep talk when Max Stover interrupted her.

"Let's take a break, everyone. Except Jade. You stay here."

The rest of the agents shuffled out of the room. Christian, the last to leave, glanced back at her with a concerned expression before closing the door.

Jade stared at her mentor. "He's going to strike again. I can feel it."

Max nodded. "This guy is a bright one. He will kill again unless we stop him. But blaming your staff for the lull in progress isn't going to solve this case."

"I'm not blaming my staff. I was just giving them a pep talk."

Max eyed her. "Then sign me up for a different team."

"Okay . . . , I shouldn't have taken it out on them," she said. She stood and paced. "I've gone over all the evidence. Hundreds of times. We've followed up on every lead. But I'm missing something." She stopped and turned to him. "What am I missing?"

"Patience."

CHAPTER FORTY

Washington, DC

LEAVING THE ANTEROOM for a vote on the Hill, Whitney and Landon stopped in front of the television, which was tuned to MSNBC. The midday host's guests were a woman and a man. The man, Blake Haynes, was a young political analyst at a Rosslyn, Virginia-based progressive think tank and a frequent guest star on the network. The think tank, The American Progressive Council (APC), was a staunch supporter of Whitney's and a major contributor to her campaign and the political action committees that supported her.

Whitney had never met Haynes, but liked the young man's intelligence and prodigious memory, his short gelled hair, and the way he carried himself. She was reminded of the young man who stared at her at the Palo Alto fundraiser. She never found out who he was.

"Wait a minute," she said to Landon. "I want to hear this."

Landon turned up the volume.

"Why are the so-called patriots always the first ones who want to secede from the union?" Haynes asked, in response to the midday host's question. "They're like children who, when they don't get their way, end the game by taking their ball and going home."

Whitney laughed and clapped her hands. "He speaks his mind."

Haynes listened to the next question and glanced up before he spoke.

"As you know and I know, almost all scientists believe in climate change. The only people who refuse to believe it are the intellectual descendants of those who believed the world was flat."

Landon muted the television, as Whitney headed for the door to the hallway. She was still laughing.

❊

Later that evening, Ted Bowling sat across from Whitney in a conference room at her campaign headquarters.

The door to the outer office opened and closed. Landon entered, coatless, shirt unwrinkled, and still wearing his tie, appearing as if he had arrived for work in the morning rather than a late-night strategy meeting. He always wore blue ties, Bill Clinton's favorite color.

"Hello, Senator," he said. He nodded at Ted. "Ted."

Whitney had recognized Landon's gifts when, as a legislative assistant, he helped her finish a floor speech at the last minute. The speech was well-written and persuasive, and she promoted him on the spot. Since, he had made her work life easier. Some people believed making things appear hard to do made them look good. She knew the best athletes—Michael Jordan, Peyton Manning, pre-scandal Tiger Woods—made things appear easy. Their talent masked the tremendous hard work involved. Landon was like that. He had the ability to distill complex legislation down to an understandable paragraph.

Life as a staffer on the Hill was rarely permanent. Not only did the staffer deal with the uncertainty of a legislator's re-election, the long hours and low pay often led to burnout. Most staffers used these jobs as a stepping stone to political office or the private sector, becoming influential lawyers or lobbyists. Landon, though, was dedicated and loyal to her. She wanted to keep him around for as long as possible.

Landon shook off his black leather briefcase. He removed his electronic tablet and sat down.

To Landon, she said, "Ted and I have been discussing poll numbers—surprise!—and which states I should be spending my time in over the next month."

Ted coughed. "Ohio, Michigan, Indiana, North Carolina, Virginia, and Florida. We're finishing up the TV spots for Ohio and Michigan."

"The public continues to believe," Whitney said, "that our party is weak on certain issues. I want these ads to show I am not weak."

After a silence, Ted said, "I'm on it," confirming to Whitney that he needed to reshoot the ads.

Ted shifted in his chair. "What about the serial killings? Is there some way we can use them to our advantage?"

Landon stopped typing and contemplated Ted with distaste.

"I don't want to be seen as capitalizing on this situation," Whitney said. "Rather, we should focus on condemning violence, sympathizing with the victims' families, and reiterating that freedom of speech is one of the pillars on which our democracy is founded."

Ted raised both of his hands to ward off the vehemence of her reaction. "Okay, okay, I was just asking. I wouldn't be doing my job if I didn't."

"What else?"

"Nothing. That's it."

After a moment, Whitney said, "I made a decision."

The two men looked at her.

"I have chosen a running mate," she said, "and it's not Senator Paul Sampson."

Detroit, Michigan

A WEEK AFTER the Republicans monopolized the media and renominated President Richard Ellison in Columbus, Ohio, the Democrats descended on Detroit for their convention. The congregants took over the town: hotel rooms, restaurants, coffee shops, bars. Security was tight; a two-hour wait time—at least—preceded every event.

Inside Joe Louis Arena, the atmosphere was charged. Taking back the White House, a distant dream two years ago, was becoming a possibility. Earlier, Senator Sampson had stirred up the crowd by giving a good pro-Democrats speech, despite not being offered the vice presidency. He did not take the news well when Whitney called him last week. She smiled when his speech concluded, realizing he failed to mention her, the Democratic nominee for president. Touché.

Whitney waited in the wings as her future running mate concluded his speech and introduced her. When her name was called, she walked out and opened her arms to accept a hug from the Democratic vice-presidential candidate, Xavier "Xavi" Fernandez, the Independent governor from Florida. They stood together, facing the audience, one arm around the waist of the other. The other arm extended, each hand in a slow, royal wave. He gave her a slight kiss on the cheek and walked off the stage.

Whitney refrained from wiping her cheek, as she strode to the podium. She scanned the audience: different faces, different skin tones, different hairstyles, different modes of dress, different sexualities, different genders. America. The applause would not cease. She said thank you many times to quiet the crowd, a trick she learned from biographies about the Kennedys. The applause subsided.

She smiled.

"Is this a party or what?"

The wild cheers started up again and she clapped her hands once, laughing. She was enjoying this.

※

After Whitney accepted the Democratic nomination with humility and grace, her husband, Grayson, and their two children, Chandler and Emma, joined her on stage, along with Xavi, his wife, and their four children.

She had not forgiven Grayson. But for the sake of the election, she was "standing by her man." She focused on smiling instead of cringing, his hand on her hip an unwelcome weight instead of a comfort.

The crowd was a sea of American flags, Our America, Our Future signs, and tons of confetti. "Celebration" by Kool and the Gang blasted from the speakers. The candidates and their families moved and clapped to the music.

Back stage, television reporters interviewed past and current members of the Democratic Party: senators, representatives, cabinet members, mayors, governors. Whitney was surrounded by her Secret Service team, including her new shadow, Josh McPherson, his brown, bald dome glistening under the lights. She heard snippets of the interviews. Her party was staying on message for once.

As she passed a male reporter interviewing Ted, the reporter turned. He appeared stunned. Whitney slowed and stopped in front of him. He continued to stare. She had always wanted to meet him.

Whitney held out her hand. "Hello."

The television political analyst, Blake Haynes, stared at a spot up and to the right of her head. He stammered a "hello" and took her left hand in his, a belated gesture.

She smiled, trying to put the young man at ease. "I wanted to say how much I admire your work. I'm a big fan."

His eyes widened. "Thank you. I admire your work as well."

Whitney laughed with delight. The self-assured man she had seen on television had returned. He offered her a charming smile. "Seriously, I'm a huge supporter. Since we admire each other so much, perhaps you'll let me interview you on MSNBC. All softballs I promise."

"In that case, I am sure it can be arranged. Call my press secretary."

He extended his hand. "One day I hope to be an FOW."

She looked at him quizzically.

"Friend of Whitney," he said.

Whitney smiled and shook his hand. She left him, and moved on to shake the hands of supporters in a line that had formed in her path.

She attended the after-party at a popular restaurant in downtown Detroit, occasionally thinking about Blake Haynes and wondering why she had such a strong affinity for the young man.

CHAPTER FORTY-TWO

Washington, DC

THE PHONE RANG.

"Harrington."

"Uh . . . Agent Harrington. This is Landon Phillips from Senator Fairchild's office."

"Yes . . ."

"I was wondering if you'd like to go to dinner with me."

"Now's not a good time. I'm sort of . . . busy."

"I know. I thought you may need a break."

"I can't afford the time."

"We could discuss motives. I can provide a different perspective." She remained silent, so he continued. "You have to eat sometime, right?"

The offer was tempting. Perhaps talking to someone outside the case with a different perspective could generate new ideas.

"Right?" he asked, again.

She paused for another moment and then made a decision. "There's a restaurant across the street from my office called Social Revolution. I'll meet you at seven. I can give you a half an hour."

"I'll be there."

She hung up. She wondered whether having dinner with him was a good idea.

❋

Landon sat at a booth in the back of the walnut-paneled restaurant, away from the other patrons. The lights were dim. Jade strode in his direction and stood next to him. He looked up at her, a smile starting to form.

"Is this all right?" he asked.

She didn't move. "Do you mind?"

He gave her a blank stare before grinning. "Ah, I get it. I saw *The Godfather*." He got up and motioned for her to sit in the vacated seat. He sat across from her, his back to the front door. He surveyed the restaurant and then the menu. "'Bi-partisan burgers,' 'The Lobbyist,' 'The POTUS,' 'The Bail Out,' and my favorite, 'The Balanced Budget-Sorry, we couldn't agree on contents. Please build your own.' I love this place." He glanced over at her. "What do you usually eat here?"

She straightened her silverware. "The Laissez-Faire. A burger with smoked bacon, cheddar cheese, and barbecue sauce."

He closed his menu. "A philosophy I agree with fiscally, but not socially. I'll get it anyway."

A waitress came to the table to take their order.

Jade spoke first. "Two Laissez-Faires, a Pepsi, and he'll have a—" She eyed Landon.

Amused, he said, "One of your craft beers. Something dark." The waitress left. "I've never had a woman order for me before." He paused. "I think I like it."

She smiled, but said nothing.

After a few moments, Landon said, "My sister played basketball, too. Do you still play?"

"Was she any good?"

"Pretty good. She got a free ride to a D-One school. So, as far as my parents were concerned, good enough."

"Did you play?"

He looked at his beer with regret. "Nah." He smiled at her, sheepish. "I sucked."

"Did you always want a career in politics?"

"Pretty much. My father was CIA, so I always thought I would follow in his footsteps. After a former president—who shall remain nameless—stole the election, I decided to go into politics instead. At the time, I wanted to change the system that allowed that to happen."

"You said, 'at the time.' You no longer feel that way?"

"Most days, no, but I'm going to keep trying."

"So what do you do?"

"Ha! It may be easier to describe what I don't do. My title is legislative director, but I act as Senator Fairchild's chief of staff. I help set her legislative agenda and priorities, develop strategies to help them pass, and evaluate their political outcomes. I manage the staff of assistants and correspondents and work with counsel to draft bills."

"Sounds like a lot of work."

"It is, but I love it."

The waitress brought their food and they began to eat.

"What's up with the pink wristband?"

He set his burger down, fingering the band.

"It says 'Strength,' for breast cancer awareness." He extended his arm across the table to show her. "My mother had breast cancer when I was in college." He noticed her expression. "No . . . she survived, but I saw the courage and strength she demonstrated to beat the disease. I've worn this ever since."

"She must be quite a lady."

"She is. She's my hero. Her illness forced me to grow up fast." He took a bite of his burger and sipped his beer. "But we didn't meet here to talk about me. I've thought a lot about your case. Any leads?"

"Not many."

He clasped the beer mug in both hands. "Citizens on both ends of the political spectrum are upset about the direction of our country. The reason Senator Fairchild is so passionate about winning is she believes we must come together, if we want to remain a superpower. To quote Abraham Lincoln, 'A house divided against itself cannot stand.'" He chuckled.

"What's so funny?" Jade asked.

"I'm starting to sound like the senator. She's always quoting political figures. Anyway, I believe the two-party system has outlived its usefulness. It panders to the extremists in both parties and to special interests. Politicians no longer govern."

"What does this guy hope to accomplish?" she asked. "Does he really believe Congress will pass legislation to prevent further death?"

"He's delusional if he does. Then again, he may not want Congress to do anything. If he's true to his word, this will force him to continue killing conservative talk-show hosts. That may be what he wants. For him, it's a win-win."

"Good point," Jade said. "Why taunt us?"

Landon paused, trying to catch up with Jade's train of thought. "Ah . . . the email. Beats me. Death wish? Hates authority? Had a run in with the FBI? Thinks the FBI is out to get him?" He laughed. "Well, I guess the FBI is out to get him now. He also may be Machiavellian. The end justifies the means and all that."

"How so?"

"He'll do whatever it takes to save the country or save democracy or purify the country of those filled with hate or intolerance or all the above. He may believe he's the only one who can save us."

"That's a lot of responsibility for one person."

They fell silent. The waitress cleared their plates away, refilled Jade's Pepsi and brought Landon another beer.

"Given the killer's liberal politics," he said, "have you checked out blogs and op-ed pages written by liberal thinkers?"

"I hadn't thought of that." She made a mental note to check it out.

❊

Jade and Landon lingered in front of the restaurant. A man on the street corner played the drums on several plastic buckets and a big overturned trash can. They stood watching him, listening to the reggae and African mix.

"He's pretty good," Landon said.

"We owe him a dollar," Jade said.

"Owe him?"

"Yeah. If a street performer is good enough to make you stop, you at least owe him or her a dollar."

Landon extracted a bill from his pocket. A five.

"He must be worth it," he said. He sauntered the ten yards to the near-full jar and returned. "I guess a lot of people stopped."

"Do you play an instrument?" Jade asked.

"I play a little guitar."

She nodded her head to the beat. "His music reminds me of my best friend."

"Who's your best friend?"

"Zoe."

"Zoe? First name only? Like Beyoncé, Rihanna, and Adele? Zoe and I worked together on several of Senator Fairchild's campaigns. She's a trip."

Jade nodded. No need to mention she already knew that. Zoe had given her Landon's phone number, but she hadn't used it. She'd called Fairchild's office directly. "I need to go."

"I know."

"Thanks for dinner."

"You're welcome. Maybe I can play for you sometime."

She eyed him with a quizzical expression.

"The guitar."

"Oh. Maybe. Goodbye." She turned toward her building.

"Wait!" He touched her arm. "Let me walk you."

Jade scowled, feeling the strength of his grip on her forearm. "I'm an FBI agent. I can take care of myself. Besides, it's across the street." She pointed to the employee entrance.

"Well, I'm a legislative aide and I would like to accompany you across the street."

She smiled at the spark in his eye. He was charming. And handsome. She checked her watch. Their thirty-minute dinner had lasted two hours. He offered her his arm. She peered at it and back at him.

"Thanks, but I got it."

A shadow of disappointment passed over his face.

Not her problem.

She crossed Ninth Street without looking back.

CHAPTER FORTY-THREE

Washington, DC

JADE HARRINGTON ENTERED the conference room for the task force's morning briefing.

"Kramer is the best QB prospect since RG3," Austin Miller said. "He runs like a running back."

By the earnestness of his expression as he spoke, Jade surmised they could only be chattering about the Redskins.

Christian, seated across from Austin, crossed his arms. "He throws like Billy Kilmer." He would know. Christian was an amateur Redskins historian and knew everything about the 1970s quarterback who led the franchise to its first Super Bowl. He knew the team's history, even as far back as when it was called the Boston Braves. "Start him on your fantasy football team, if you're so confident about his ability. I'll gladly take your money."

Jade laid her folders on the table, but remained standing. "No one understands better than I the importance of the Redskins and winning our fantasy football league, but I need to interrupt this discussion for something of equal importance. I received a phone call from the Pittsburgh PD."

She had their attention. Christian, Austin, Max, Pat, and Dante stared at her, tense and expectant. Dante lowered the front two legs of his chair to the floor.

"We have a match. The hair located at the scene in Pittsburgh where Randy Sells was murdered matches the hair found on Taylor LeBlanc, the victim in Baton Rouge. Neither hair belonged to the victim."

Christian and Austin pumped their fists and said "Yes!" The same reaction Jade had made at her desk, when she heard the news a few minutes ago. They now had conclusive evidence two of the cases were connected. A small moment of triumph.

It didn't last.

There was a knock on the door. A male agent poked his head in and pointed at the blank projection screen. "Turn it on. Shakespeare struck again."

❊

One advantage of having a rookie on her task force: Jade had someone to go out and get lunch for her. The half-eaten Italian sub heaped with meat Austin had brought her lay next to her keyboard. Normally a bottomless pit, she was so pumped up now she couldn't eat. Almost. She sipped a Pepsi through a straw as she stared at her computer monitor, the latest email from TSK taking up the entire screen.

To Whom It May Concern,

I am disappointed. In my last email, I had asked politely for new legislation to address the monopoly of conservative talk radio in this country. To fill the airwaves with an equal share of inclusiveness and tolerance and equality, not hate. An ideology of tolerance that brings us together, not divides us. I want to be a part of an ideology that is greater than the sum of its parts rather than one of divisiveness. How about you?

Perhaps not. I have seen no evidence of pending legislation or discussions taking place within Congress regarding the issue of balance and fairness on the airwaves. Our government is not taking me seriously, so, as the old saying goes, if you want something done right, you must do it yourself.

There will be another murder.

To my clueless friends at the FBI, I shall give you a clue this time. Just one. Within the next week, a conservative talk-show host on the West Coast will be killed.

My hope is that this death will bring the much-needed attention to the issue of fairness, and facilitate discussion in our august halls of Congress to help us build a bridge to a better, more balanced dissemination of information in the future.

Sincerely,

TSK

P.S. FBI, I may bump into you on the West Coast. Catch me, if you can.

She wondered about a person driven to kill because of ideology. An ideology of tolerance. How much sense did that make? She would have laughed at the hypocrisy, if the stakes weren't so high.

Jade's mood darkened.

What does he gain from taunting us? More exposure? Does he want to be caught? Is he one of us?

Why did she just think that?

She read the email again and sat back in her chair to think.

The tingle along her arms compelled her to look up from her monitor. Austin stood in her office doorway, his eyes shining.

"What is it?" Jade asked.

Although he seemed ready to burst if he didn't tell her, instead, he said, "You're going to want to listen to this."

❁

The CONFAB task force was back in the conference room. The group waited, restless, as Austin hooked up a laptop to two speakers.

"I've listened to hundreds of recordings." He glanced over at Jade. "I'm not sure what I ever did to you, but this was the worst assignment you could've ever given me."

Jade smiled, but said nothing, not bothering to hide her impatience.

"After a while," Austin continued, "I recognized a pattern by one caller whose vocabulary and speech were similar to TSK's writings." He paused. "And the same caller's voice talked to more than one of the victims."

The other agents glanced at each other, the tension in the room building the longer they waited.

Jade started to pace. "Get on with it, Austin."

Austin paused one more time for dramatic effect. "I heard the same voice today."

Christian sat forward in his seat. Austin began the recording and adjusted the volume.

"The Fairness Doctrine . . . are you kidding me?" asked a deep voice, born for radio.

"Yes. Why not?" asked the caller.

"Because we don't need it, you moron. If someone wants to listen to the other side, he can change the channel. I will never talk about liberalism on my show. My listeners don't want to hear about fantasy land. They want to hear about the real world. And this . . . TSK . . . wants minorities and women to own more broadcasting licenses? Haven't we done the affirmative-action thing? Haven't grievances been redressed enough? Minorities are already given too many breaks."

Silence, then: "You have no clue, you ignorant bigot, and no idea what it's like to be a minority in this country. You deserve to die."

Jade tensed and glanced at Austin. He was not trying to suppress the smile on his face.

"Oh, yeah? Am I talking to TSK? Hello? Hello?" The commentator's voice seemed to move away from the microphone. "Did we lose him?" A pause. "I guess we lost him. Shit. I hope I'm not next." The commentator laughed. A nervous laugh. He spoke into the microphone. "Well, uh, we're going to take a commercial break. Be right back."

Austin clicked off the recording. The room was silent.

"Could he be a minority?" Jade questioned Max, doubt evident in her voice.

"He doesn't sound black," Dante said.

"What does that mean?" Jade asked.

"You know . . ."

"No, I don't."

"It would be an unusual profile for this type of case," Max said, breaking the tension, "but, at this point, we can't afford to rule anything out."

"What station?" Jade asked.

"KSFC in San Francisco," Austin replied.

She turned to him. "This is good work."

He beamed.

Dante threw a sidelong glance at Jade. "West Coast."

She read a printed copy of the email again and sat up straighter.

"Last line . . . 'Build a bridge?' Could he be talking about the Bay Bridge?" She turned to Max. "Could it be that easy?"

Max shook his head. "I believe our UNSUB is too intelligent for that."

Christian shrugged. "I think we should check it out."

Jade turned to Dante. "Any luck with the yearbook photo?"

Dante's cheeks reddened. He shook his head. Under his breath, he said, "I think it's a dead end."

Jade wondered how hard he had tried.

Pat said, under her breath, "So's your love life, but you keep trying, don't you?"

"We don't have any other leads," Christian said. "Let's go for it. What do we have to lose?"

CHAPTER FORTY-FOUR

San Francisco, California

THE KSFC OFFICES were located in a gleaming glass skyscraper in the high-rent district of San Francisco. It was night. Jade, Christian, Max, Pat, Austin, and Dante were crowded in a van parked a block down the street, a computer repair company logo on its outside paneling. Monitors displayed multiple views of the intersecting streets in front of the building, the parking garage, and different areas of the radio station.

Arriving two nights ago, they had met with a team from the San Francisco Police Department. Men and women from the department were all around them outside now, dressed as businesspeople, tourists, and the homeless. Jade couldn't distinguish the cops from the civilians.

She had interviewed—twice—the radio commentator, Billy Stone, whose voice she had listened to on the audio recording. Although shaken, he agreed to continue his normal daily routine in the hope the killer would make an attempt on his life.

So far, nothing had happened.

MSNBC had not received another email from TSK.

Jade peered at her oversized, platinum watch. The talk-show host was wrapping up his broadcast. She scanned the monitors again. Nothing. Several people walked down the street, but they all seemed purposeful, with somewhere to go. More important, they strode by or away from the building.

"I don't like this," Max said, glancing at Jade. "I think he's sent us on a wild-goose chase."

Before Jade could respond, her radio crackled.

"I may have something. Parking garage. Second floor." Silence for a few minutes. "Our man just came out the door. Another man is walking toward him. I'm on it."

More silence. A grunt. Then, "Got him."

Jade, Christian, Austin, and Dante jumped out of the computer repair van, running, their FBI jackets flapping behind them with the wind. Passersby stopped and stared.

The team flashed their badges to the security guard in the lobby as they ran toward the stairs.

Jade's stomach clenched, uneasy. "I think Max is right. Something's wrong."

Right behind her, Christian said, "What?"

"Every crime, so far, has been in a different location: parking lot, alley, bedroom, parking garage. This one is like Houston."

From behind both of them, Dante said, "You're overthinking it. Sometimes, it is what it is."

Jade didn't turn around but kept running.

"With this guy?" Jade asked. "I don't think so."

They burst through a door to the garage's second floor, guns drawn but lowered as they ran. A cop squatted with his knee on the back of a prone man, struggling to handcuff him. A few police officers surrounded him, guns leveled on the suspect. Jade, Dante, Austin, and Christian rushed up to them.

Jade stopped a couple of feet away, the officer subduing the man at last.

The suspect peered up at her and grinned.

Her shoulders dropped. "Shit."

This kid appeared too young to be the mastermind of the TSK killings. Jade would go through the interrogation process, but she knew what they would determine.

They had the wrong man.

CHAPTER FORTY-FIVE

Washington, DC

HIS PRODUCER INDICATED the "Go" signal.

"Well, well, well . . . I would like to introduce to my audience my special guest: the Democratic nominee for the presidency of the United States, Senator Whitney Fairchild. Whitney, welcome."

"Thank you, Cole, it's good to be here, and, please, call me 'Senator' or 'Senator Fairchild.'"

"I stand corrected. Now, I must tell you, little lady, I do respect the fact that you crossed enemy lines for this interview."

"Well, Cole, presidential elections are important and I believe in fairness. Your listeners have the right to hear both sides of the issues in order to make better and informed decisions."

"Ouch. Nice plug for the Fairness Doctrine, but many conservatives would argue the mainstream media is already too liberal."

Senator Fairchild smiled. "Whom did we blame everything on before the media? Do you remember?"

Cole understood why women loved her. Men, too. She was more attractive in person. So much class. Aristocratic. Cole would play up her elitism. His audience hated that.

"Now you're the confirmed nominee, how does that change your campaign?"

"It doesn't. Our focus has always been on the economy, education, and equal rights for women."

"Whitney, come on now. Haven't you won equal rights, already? Isn't that what the Title IX business was all about?"

"You would think. But we still do not have a federal law providing equal rights for women. And, now, women are re-fighting the battles we won forty years ago. Unlike other civil rights—for example, gay rights—women's rights are regressing instead of progressing. And, Cole, please call me 'Senator Fairchild.'"

"You're talking about abortion."

"Over the last decade, the opposing party proposed numerous bills that blocked funding for critical women's reproductive health, particularly for low-income women. A woman's access to a safe abortion should not depend on her ZIP code. But the issue is not only about a woman's right to choose, but equal pay, economic and educational opportunities for poor women and women of color, and protection against gender-based violence. But, yes, more women need to be in the room when women's health issues are discussed."

"We aren't going to agree on this one. I'm not qualified to discuss women's health issues with you, so I won't even try."

Senator Whitney Fairchild smiled. "Exactly."

Cole realized—too late—he lost the point. He needed to be more careful with this woman. "Let's move on to China."

The senator nodded. "As you wish."

"China slowed down on the amount of our debt it's buying. Are you concerned, and, if so, what should we do about it?"

"'China is a sleeping lion. Let her sleep, for when she wakes she will shake the world.'"

Cole stared at her, perplexed. "Huh?"

"Napoleon said that." She smiled. "Of course, I am concerned. China had been a net buyer of US treasuries for a long time and is a significant and important trading partner of the United States. We're fortunate other countries took up the purchasing slack—namely, Japan—but the current situation is a warning about something we all realize. We must become more self-reliant."

"Finally, something we can agree on, my friend." Cole decided to switch topics, a tactic he used to rattle his interviewees. "Whit— Senator, tell me about your husband's affair."

The senator shook her head, pursed her lips, and wagged her index finger at him. "My husband made a mistake. And I don't believe we are friends, Cole."

"And a neighbor, of all people. Gives new meaning to the phrase 'borrowing a cup of sugar.'"

Senator Fairchild threw her head back and laughed. She had a pleasant laugh. "That's a good one."

"Uh, yeah." This woman couldn't be rattled. "You went to one of those liberal, Eastern schools—"

"I attended Northwestern undergrad and Harvard Law School, yes."

"—and you and your husband are extremely wealthy. How can you possibly identify with the struggles of the middle class in this country?"

"Because I know what's it's like to struggle. I grew up in a middle-class family in a small town in Missouri. My father was an insurance agent who owned his own small business; my mom was his office manager. They struggled to make ends meet for my two brothers and me. What I love about my party, Cole, is we are always fighting for the middle class and our ability to empathize. I don't need to be poor to want to raise the minimum wage to give people the opportunity to live a better life."

Walked into that one. Cole decided to change tack again. "What are your thoughts on TSK, the Talk Show Killer?"

"I think his actions are deplorable."

"Even though he seems to spout the same liberal B.S. you do?"

"I wouldn't describe my beliefs as B.S., but his acts are deplorable just the same and stem from the mind of a sick individual. Fairness on the airwaves and social equity are important issues and ones I care deeply about, but instead of killing conservative talk-show hosts, I ran for president."

Good answer. The interview ran for ten more minutes. After he signed off, he leaned back, tired, like a boxer who had been pummeled into the ropes for fifteen rounds. Still standing but barely. He smiled at her in spite of himself.

"I'm still going to do everything in my power to defeat your candidacy."

The senator smiled back. "And I am still going to do everything in my power to not let you."

The Democratic nominee picked up her purse and left the studio. Cole hesitated before turning to glance over his shoulder out the studio window into the hallway.

To his dismay, his smiling employees were lining up to shake her hand and take selfies with her.

CHAPTER FORTY-SIX

San Francisco, California

JADE SAT NEXT to Christian in an interrogation room at the local FBI office. Dante, Pat, Max, and Austin observed them through the one-way mirror. After confirming that the suspect in custody was not TSK, Jade had sent local agents to the home of Billy Stone, the San Francisco talk-show host, to make sure the incident in the garage hadn't been a diversion.

The man sitting across from them did not seem nervous.

She stated the date, case number, and her identification information. "Please state your name for the record."

"Kevin. Kevin Burke."

"So, Kevin, tell me, what were you doing in that garage?"

Kevin slouched in his chair, his arms folded across his slender chest. Dressed in all black down to his Chuck Taylor sneakers, he stared at her, but said nothing.

A criminal background check hadn't revealed much. Kevin was arrested six years ago for shoplifting a six-pack of Red Bull.

"Kevin, you could be in a lot of trouble unless you tell us what you know."

Kevin shrugged. "Walking."

She started to rise.

Christian stopped taking notes of the interview and put a hand on her arm. He asked, "Why did you happen to be walking in that garage at that particular time of night?"

"I was hoping to bump into the radio guy."

"Why?" Jade asked.

"I don't know."

"What do you mean you don't know?"

"I was supposed to bump into him."

"And then what?"

Kevin sat up. "Okay. Look. This guy I met on the street gave me fifty bucks to wait for the radio guy to get off work. All right? He told me to bump into him literally—the guy said he would be watching me—and afterward, we were to meet at the Starbucks on the corner and he would give me another fifty." Kevin slouched again. "Man . . . I guess this means I won't be getting the rest of my money."

"Which Starbucks?" Jade asked, knowing with a sinking feeling that there was one on every corner in San Francisco. Sometimes two.

Kevin told them.

Without a word from her, Christian left the room to send someone to check out the Starbucks. It was pointless. If TSK had ever been there, he was long gone. "What did the guy look like?"

Kevin surveyed the bare conference-room walls. Finding nowhere else to rest his eyes, he stared at Jade. "What's in it for me?"

"Reduced jail time. What did he look like?"

"I can go to jail for this?"

Jade said nothing. The silence stretched for a few minutes. She had learned over the years that sometimes silence was the best way to make someone talk. A lot of people hated silence. She did not.

Her patience was rewarded.

"White guy. Blond, brown hair, but I'm not sure. He was wearing a baseball hat. Sunglasses even though it was starting to get dark."

"Big guy? Little guy?"

"He was taller than me."

"I want you to work with a sketch artist to come up with a facial composite of him."

"If I help you, will you help me stay out of jail?"

Jade stood. "We'll see."

Kevin laughed.

This guy bugged her. "What's so amusing?"

"He told me I might get a visit from you, but he said not to sweat it. The FBI doesn't have a clue."

❋

Two agents led Kevin away. Dante, Christian, and the rest of the task force came into the room, along with some local agents. Jade leaned back in her chair staring at the ceiling. She had been wearing the same gray pantsuit for two days. She craved a shower, and they needed to head to the airport soon. But she didn't want to get up from this chair. She was drained: from the interrogation, from this case, from failing.

She lifted her head and turned to Max. "Well?"

Before Max had a chance to answer, Dante said, "You're not ready, yet. You don't have the experience to run a major investigation like this."

Jade counted to ten.

Before she finished counting, Dante continued, "You're always so damn impulsive. When are you going to start thinking before you act?"

Christian slashed his forearm down like a traffic cop.

"That's enough, Dante."

"Why can't she defend herself?" Dante said. "Because she's a woman?"

Jade banged both hands on the table.

Everyone froze.

The rage, building within her for months, exploded. "I'm impulsive? Weren't you the one to suggest the West Coast? What is it with you? Is this all because I wouldn't go out with you when I first arrived at the Bureau? Is it because others are starting to realize you don't have what it takes?"

His eyes hardened. "Well, at least I didn't need affirmative action to get into the Bureau."

That was a lie. At the FBI Academy in Quantico, Jade recorded some of the highest scores ever for a woman. Her proficiency levels for firearms broke Academy records for both genders. A rare breed at the FBI—women accounted for nineteen percent of special agents, black women, a paltry one percent—everything she had accomplished, she had earned.

Her face burned. She didn't hesitate. She took two quick steps toward Dante and punched him in the face. The pain in her hand barely registered as Dante went down hard. He touched his nose and stared at the blood on his fingers. He popped back up and came after her. Christian sliced between them, his body as immovable as an oak tree. The other agents, taken aback at first, recovered and grabbed Dante. Breathing hard, Jade and Dante glared at each other.

"Shit, you two," Christian said. "Let's tone it down."

Jade would have smiled if she weren't enraged. Christian never cussed.

Christian faced her. "We're all frustrated."

Still pushing against Christian, she lifted a finger and pointed at Dante. "You crossed a line. You were wrong for that."

Dante's face was flushed, more from embarrassment at being decked by a woman in front of his peers than exertion. A smile played at his lips.

"Have you ever thought, Ms. Thing, that *you're* wrong for this?" He raised his arms to take in the interrogation room, the building, the Bureau. Her life.

Washington, DC

BACK IN HER office after the August recess, Whitney paused from catching up on her paperwork to enjoy the view outside her window. Hill staffers strode along the sidewalk to and from the Capitol. The tree leaves were still in full bloom.

She turned at the knock on her door.

Landon stood in the doorway.

"Yes, Landon?"

"I have something for you."

He crossed the room and handed her a slim, gift-wrapped package. He cocked his head, smiled. "Happy Birthday."

"You remembered."

"Of course. It's a little late, though."

She started to open it.

He raised his hand. "Wait! You can't open it until after the election."

"Then wouldn't it be an election present?"

She flipped the package back and forth, eyeing the note stating what he had just said. By the weight and feel of it, she could tell it was a book.

"I'm intrigued," she said and placed the book at the corner of the desk. "Sit down. We need to start prepping for the debate."

Arlington, Virginia

JADE STEADIED HER hand and sighted her target, the outline of a man fifty yards away. She slowed her breathing. A calmness came over her. She stopped breathing and fired. She exhaled.

Fall was her favorite time of the year in Virginia. The days of ninety-degree-plus temperatures had finally abated. In college, however, she dreaded fall and the onset of pre-season, when all her basketball team did was run sprints and long distances in preparation for the upcoming season. She could run all day on the court, but believed running should be a means to an end and not an end unto itself. Like shopping.

A tingling sensation slinked down the back of her neck. Someone was watching her. She turned. Max. She removed her earplugs.

He gave her what she took for a smile.

"When you weren't at the basketball court or the dojang, I thought I might find you here."

"You should have been a detective."

"Must have missed my calling. Nice shot."

She glanced at the target and shrugged. She put the earplugs back in, set herself, and went through her breathing ritual again. She fired five more times.

Max pushed off the wall he had been leaning against and moved toward her. He stepped across her to tap the SmartPad. She lifted her safety goggles, removed her earplugs again, and shook out her hair.

The target stopped about fifteen feet away. Six shots. All through the heart.

Max smile-grimaced again.

"Remind me never to make you mad."

She tried not to smile but failed. "I'll try."

He waited.

She scowled and gazed down at her .40 Glock 23, running her hand along the barrel. "I lost it."

"Yep."

"I let him get to me," she said, smoothing the top of her hair. "I'm so sick of his little comments."

"Dante takes pleasure in getting to you. You played right into his hands. But that's not where you lost it."

Jade avoided Max's eyes and said nothing. She knew what was coming.

"That interview. It wasn't like you. You didn't even try to build a rapport with the subject."

"The killer is going to strike again. Soon."

"Which is why you need to get your act together. Forget about Dante and focus on what's most important. The case. You don't always need to be in 'prove' mode. You don't need to prove yourself anymore. To anyone. Just because you ask for help, doesn't mean you're not in control. You're the best. Act like you've been there before."

"My college coach used to say that all the time."

"You're the only person I know who doesn't root for the underdog. You always want the best team to win."

"I like to win. What more can I say?" She glanced around the range and back at Max. "This guy is always one step ahead of me."

"He's one step ahead of *us.*"

Max touched her chin, forcing her eyes to meet his. "Jade, you're a beautiful, strong, intelligent, and amazing woman."

She tried to move her head, but he held firm.

He continued, his voice soft. "You're no longer the bullied, overweight kid with glasses."

After a moment, he let go of her chin. She stepped back from him and pushed the button to send the target back out.

Max started to walk away, but stopped and turned. "Leave some targets for the other shooters, okay?"

He hesitated, and left. She didn't watch him go.

Her phone vibrated against her hip. She answered.

"You can't let Dante bother you," Ethan said, without preamble.

"What is it, Dante Day?"

"What?"

"Never mind. Ethan, I can't work with him."

"He's off the task force."

"He undermines my authority. He creates dissension. I don't trust . . . Wait . . . What did you say?"

"He's off. I've re-assigned him."

"Just like that?"

"Just like that," he said. "Now, there's something I want you to do for me."

Wary, Jade said, "What?"

"Relax." He hung up.

She reinserted the earplugs and pushed the goggles back down.

Jade sighted the target, telling herself it was wrong to pretend it was Dante. She held her breath and fired. She kept firing until the chamber was empty.

She didn't need to bring the target closer. All the shots went straight through the heart.

This was how she relaxed.

Arlington, Virginia

EARLY ON A Saturday morning, Jade and Landon strolled through the park near her house. She realized others had had the same idea. With the high humidity of summer finally breaking, the distinct sound of basketballs dancing on the pavement reached them. She loved that sound. It was music.

They arrived at the refurbished basketball court, the white lines painted fresh, the new rims and nets, a gift from a current Wizards player who grew up in the neighborhood.

Landon, wearing a t-shirt and baggy gym shorts, stopped a few yards behind the backboard and started stretching. Jade, in black sports tights and a sleeveless white Adidas shirt, dribbled onto the court and nodded at some guys on the adjacent court with whom she played occasional pick-up games.

She began shooting close to the basket to warm up. She went into the same shooting routine she had used since she was a young girl: shoot a couple of bank shots on each side, a couple of shots straight on, and then back up a few feet and do it again. She kept doing this until she was a foot behind the three-point line. She didn't miss many. After she had warmed up, she didn't miss any. When she was finished, she walked off the court to stretch, flipping the ball to Landon as he came toward her. He didn't catch it cleanly.

He gestured to the three-point line with his chin.

"Not bad."

She smiled, amused, and began stretching while he warmed up. His form was not good, his elbow at a twenty-degree angle to his body.

This should be easy. "I'm glad you called yesterday. This was a great idea."

"You were so reluctant," he said. "Thought you were scared."

She gave him a look in lieu of a response.

He shot the ball and missed. "How's your case going?"

"It's going."

He ran to retrieve the rebound. "Did you check out those liberal blogs I told you about?"

No. "Yeah."

"Did you find anything helpful?"

"Not yet."

He continued to shoot.

Jade stretched her hamstrings and looked down to the other end of the court. Some kids were playing three-on-three half-court. She loved listening to their laughter, the unadulterated joy of playing the game: no fans, no lights, no coaches, no refs, no money, no pressure. Just players, a hoop, and a ball. The way it should be. She lifted an eyebrow to Landon.

"Are you ready?"

"Bring it on."

"Okay."

She strode to the top of the key and he gave her the ball. She bounced it back to him to check. He twirled it in his hands, uncertainly, and then bounced it back to her. He positioned himself at the free-throw line.

She stared into his eyes. "Really?"

"What?"

Shaking her head once, she eyed the rim and shot the ball. Swish. Nothing but net. He retrieved the ball and bounce passed it to her again. He moved in a couple of steps closer.

She gave him an angelic smile. "Are you sure?"

He nodded his head, and raised his arms into a rigid, classic defensive position, one arm straight up to distract the shot, the other to protect against the drive. She pursed her lips and shot over his outstretched arm. Swish. Again.

He ran after the ball, handed it to her, and moved as close to her as he could.

"Now, you're learning." She faked a shot this time and blew by him for a layup.

"Damn it," he said.

After pulling out to a nine-zero lead, she finally missed a shot and Landon grabbed the rebound.

With the score at ten to three in her favor, he ball faked to the left and drove hard to the basket. Out of position, she ran at an angle toward the spot where he was going to be. He went up for a layup. She stepped into his path, crossing both arms over her chest to take the charge. His body plowed into hers.

She grunted and fell backward, using her arms to cushion her fall.

Landon scrambled up, the ball under one arm. He extended his other hand down to her. "Jade! What're you doing? Are you crazy?"

She grimaced. "Charge."

He pulled her up. "Are you all right?" He gazed into her eyes. "Your eyes are so beautiful."

Before she could react, he leaned down and kissed her.

His lips were soft. She responded.

The applause snapped her out of it.

She jerked her head back.

What was she doing?

She pushed him away and glanced over at the other side of the court. The six kids were lined up near half-court watching them. Clapping.

"Great defense, lady!" a girl yelled.

"Nice kiss, man!" shouted one of the boys. He pretended to kiss another boy and was pushed away for his efforts. The kids laughed and went back to their game.

Jade's face was hot. She grabbed the ball.

"Personal foul. My ball."

She dribbled to the top of the key, slapped the ball, and threw it back to him, harder than necessary. "Check."

"Jade, what's wrong?"

"I don't know. Just give me the damn ball. Game point."

Seattle, Washington

I HAD BEEN observing him for a couple of days, his routine always the same. At the appointed hour, I pressed the down button for the elevator. It stopped on the sixth floor—the one on which I was standing—a few times. A quick, cursory glance inside.

Empty.

I let the doors close and pushed the down button again. While I waited, I thought about Houston, Texas and my encounter with Pete Paxson. When he walked into the parking garage, I had been marveling at his BMW, wondering how much the vehicle cost and how many starving children in Africa—or in the United States, for that matter—it could have fed instead.

Shane Tallent was different than Paxson. He walked to work, minimizing his ecological footprint. At least he had one thing going for him. But it wasn't enough.

The elevator dinged open bringing me back to the present.

At last, the doors opened to a handsome man with dark hair and a high-wattage smile leaning against a corner.

My prey.

I avoided looking at him as I stepped in and moved to the other side. The man pressed the button for the lobby a couple of times and grinned at me, apologetic. "My son plays youth football. He's got a game tonight. I'm running late."

"No problem," I said.

His grin turned into an odd facial expression. The doors closed.

I did a double take, not quite meeting his eyes. "Hey, you are . . ."

The man grinned. "Afraid so."

"Wow. I love your show, man. I listen to it all the time."

"Thanks, I appreciate it."

I took a quick step forward and stabbed him in the stomach. I withdrew the blade and stabbed him again.

"Tallent cannot be your real name . . . right? Is it one of those stage names? You should have selected one more fitting."

Shane Tallent stared at me, uncomprehending. "Huh?"

I turned and pushed the button to stop the elevator. When I turned back to him, he was staring at his wounds, holding in his intestines with his hands. He started to slide down the wall. He reached the floor and stared up at me. "Why?"

I cannot be one hundred percent sure that is what he said. The word came out gurgled, as blood filled his mouth and began trickling down his chin. Articulation can be difficult after you've been stabbed.

It didn't matter.

She thinks I'm sick.

I pushed thoughts of her out of my mind. I bent down and stabbed him a few more times. It may have been more. I lost count. I did not like using a knife. Too messy. Too risky. It was not as fun for me. I missed my baseball bat. I was glad I would not be around to clean up this mess.

It took a while to remove his tongue. Stubborn.

Out of my backpack, I grabbed my charcoal gray hoodie and put it on and zipped it up, pulling the hood over my head. I would fit right in walking the streets of downtown Seattle. I placed the knife and tongue in separate plastic bags and placed them in my backpack. The blood on my black jeans was visible to me, but probably not to someone else at a distance.

I pressed the button to restart the elevator.

Prior to the door opening, I knelt by the slumped body. Shane Tallent seemed so peaceful. And, once and for all, silent.

"By the way, I lied. I hated your show."

CHAPTER FIFTY-ONE

Washington, DC

JADE ARRIVED HOME from work Wednesday night, trying not to trip over Card as she walked to the kitchen.

She foraged in the bare refrigerator trying to scrounge up enough food from different leftovers to make a meal. As the food warmed in the microwave, she thought about playing ball with Landon last weekend.

While eating at her small kitchen table, she kicked herself mentally for allowing him to kiss her.

After dinner, she grabbed her journal from the wall. She settled into a corner of the couch and began writing phrases. After a few minutes, she had written:

Senator Fairchild

The next US president

My own match.com

Horrible. She read the poem again. She would never be published or win any prizes, which was okay. She wrote for herself.

Her cell phone rang. She swept it off the coffee table and eyed the display. Ethan. Ten-thirty p.m. Not good.

She answered. "Harrington."

"He struck again."

"Where?"

"Seattle."

"When?"

"About seven p.m. Pacific. The body was found about fifteen minutes later. I've booked you and your team out of Dulles. Your flight leaves in two hours."

❄

A subset of the CONFAB team drove away from Sea-Tac airport onto I-5 North toward Seattle. With Max in the back seat and Christian driving, Jade surveyed the beautiful juxtaposition of the Olympic Mountains and the Cascades with the Puget Sound. Mount Rainier decided to make an appearance today. The rain did not. They stalled in traffic behind a blue minivan with a family decal on the rear window showing a stick figure of a daddy, mommy, three kids, and a dog. Jade shook her head; she believed those decals were road maps for predators.

Christian double-parked in front of an office building on Madison Street in downtown Seattle. Blue "12" flags—a tribute to the Seattle Seahawks' fans—were everywhere. They hung from poles, covered office windows, flapped on car antennas. Several police and unmarked vehicles were parked near the building's entrance, their lights and sirens off. On the sidewalk, a homeless man, his entire belongings wrapped up in a sleeping bag nearby, hopped past them, playing a game of hopscotch with imaginary lines.

A uniformed police officer met them inside the carousel doors and led them past a long marble desk manned by a security guard and through a modern lobby toward the back of the building. One of the four elevators gaped open, yellow crime scene tape draped across it.

A young man with shoulder-length hair came up to them and offered his hand.

"Agent Harrington? I'm Detective Kurt McClaine. I spoke to you on the phone."

He resembled Kurt Cobain—former lead singer of the famous Seattle rock band, Nirvana—and Jade almost did a double take. McClaine, with his slight frame and sporting a dangling gold earring in one ear and a tattoo snaking up his neck, appeared more like a rocker than a detective. Despite the crisp September day, he wore a black t-shirt with Don't Kill My Vibe in white letters on the front.

He shook her hand. "Yeah, I was named after him. My parents were into the grunge scene." He laughed. "They still are." He shook the rest of the agents' hands and said, "Good to meet you, man." Jade always thought the term "man" between men who were strangers brought an immediate intimacy and bond lacking in any expressions women used. McClaine gestured toward the elevators. "This way."

As they walked, Detective McClaine continued, "The victim, Shane Tallent, worked on the thirty-third floor."

McClaine pointed at the corner of the elevator. "He was found and killed here." Massive amounts of dried blood had congealed on the floor. "The UNSUB got on the elevator at the sixth floor."

"Camera?" Jade asked.

"He knew where it was. He averted his face."

Jade examined the blood spatter on the walls and the few drops on the ceiling. "The UNSUB must have got blood on him."

"Probably."

"No one saw anything? No witnesses?"

"No. It was after work hours, and the security in this building is pretty lax. We interviewed the guard on duty. He was reading a book at the time, but he remembered someone wearing a dark hoodie leaving around the time of the murder. He couldn't be sure whether it was a man or a woman, but thought the former. The camera by the guard's desk confirmed his account. We haven't determined, yet, when the perp entered the building."

"How many stab wounds?" Christian asked.

"Twelve."

Christian whistled.

McClaine nodded. "The perp obliterated the vic's internal organs—arteries, major muscles. The guy was butchered."

She glanced down at the bloodstain on the floor and then at Max. She murmured, "This isn't his usual MO."

Max nodded, apparently lost in thought.

McClaine's eyes shifted from Max to Jade. "What do you see?"

"Nothing. It's just—"

The detective's phone rang. "Yeah." He listened. He glanced at Jade. "We'll be right there."

❋

The agents followed Detective McClaine down a wide alley two blocks away from Shane Tallent's office building. Evidence of America's number-one "green" city, according to Jade's brief research on Seattle she conducted on the flight, was absent: dirty food wrappers, bottles, napkins, soft-drink cups, and Styrofoam containers littered the alley. The stench was overpowering.

A police officer walked up to them. "Over here, Detective."

The officer guided them down the alley. "The owner of a Chinese restaurant," the officer continued, pointing to a black door with peeling paint, "witnessed a man throwing something in her dumpster."

Jade's pulse accelerated. "Did she get a good look at him?"

The composite they had received based on the information provided by the San Francisco witness, Kevin Burke, turned out to be garbage. She hadn't bothered to send it out to anyone.

The officer shook his head. "Unfortunately, no. The establishments around here have an understanding they don't use each other's dumpsters. She was ticked off and dug through the trash, coming up with this bag. She decided to open it."

They all leaned in to peer inside the bag. A knife greeted them, coated with a massive amount of blood. It appeared to be eight inches long, and thick. A blanket and a few other items lay underneath.

Detective McClaine surveyed the alley. "The perp didn't try very hard to hide the evidence, if this belonged to him." He paused. "It better belong to him. Otherwise, I have two major crimes on my hands instead of one." He laughed without humor. "There are a million places in this city to hide this bag and it would've never been found."

Christian stood with his hands on his hips. "Maybe he was in a hurry."

A quiet interjection from Max: "Or maybe he wanted it to be found."

McClaine glanced at Max and then stared at the bag, unconvinced. The three agents—Jade, Christian, and Max—McClaine, and the police officer continued to stare at the bag, as if it would divulge the answers if only they were patient.

Finally, the officer cleared his throat. "That's not all." He guided them to the back door of the Chinese restaurant, bent down, and—with latex gloves—opened a carton of takeout Chinese food. With uncomfortable closeness, everyone again bent over to peer inside the small carton.

A coiled tongue lay within.

Christian stepped back. "Jesus."

The officer tilted the carton at a forty-five-degree angle. *Tongue Lo Mein to go* was scrawled in black magic marker on the side of the carton.

"I presume that's not on the menu," Jade said.

"The UNSUB has a sense of humor," Max said, "and he left us a calling card."

❁

Despite it being midweek and late at night, the Sea-Tac airport was crowded. Jade, Christian, and Max sat next to each other, seats far away from the gate, each deep in thought as they waited for their red-eye flight back to DC to be announced.

Jade leaned back in her chair with her eyes closed.

"What about the switch of MO? A blunt object in the first four killings, which he either took with him or disposed of. In this one, a knife. A knife he left for us to find."

Christian, seated across from her, bent forward to rest his arms on his thighs. "Copycat killing?"

Next to her, Max stirred. He hadn't been sleeping, but thinking. Always processing. "Not necessarily. It's not unusual for a serial killer to change his modus operandi. In the seventies, Gary Taylor started off by hitting women over the head with a wrench at bus stops before moving on to shooting them. He then moved on to machetes."

"Nice," Christian said.

Jade, eyes still closed, grimaced. "Max, maybe you do need a hobby."

Max continued, as if they hadn't said anything. "This killer studies his victims and their habits. He does his homework."

"He seems to be able to travel wherever and whenever he wants," Christian said.

"Which leads me to believe he has means and a flexible occupation," Max said. "He also diverted us with the San Francisco incident."

Jade yawned, but cut it short as her phone vibrated. "Harrington."

It was McClaine. "We got a hit on the knife. It was purchased two days ago from a Federal Army and Navy Surplus store on First Avenue. The knife is a Columbia River eleven-twenty-one Elishewitz Anubis."

Jade balled her hand into a fist. "Any description on the perp?"

"The owner remembers the buyer well: He was wearing a hoodie, but the owner observed he had short, light brown or dark blond hair. Here's the interesting part. The guy wasn't a local. He had an accent. The owner couldn't place it, but guessed East Coast. The buyer told him he was going camping and purchased the knife, blanket, a flashlight, and a few other items."

"Were all those items found in the bag?"

"Yes. All unused. Except for the knife, of course. The owner is coming in tomorrow to ID the items and to assist us with a facial composite."

"Thank you, Detective. Feel free to call me anytime."

"You're welcome. Good night and have a nice flight."

She called the local FBI office in Seattle, conveying the information to the special agent in charge with follow-up instructions. Jade hung up, as their flight to DC was called.

Was the UNSUB getting sloppy or playing games with them? And, if the latter, why?

CHAPTER FIFTY-TWO

New York, New York

THE MODERATOR STARED into the camera.

"Good evening. This is Blaine Jones and welcome to Radio City Musical Hall in New York City. The candidates have agreed to new rules for this election. Tonight will be the first, last, and only presidential debate between the Democratic nominee, Senator Whitney Fairchild of Missouri"—Whitney smiled for the camera while Jones paused for the applause—"and the president of the United States, Richard Ellison."

While the camera stayed on Ellison, Whitney admired the grandeur of the historic hall built in the 1930s and its art deco interior. Ted had created a similar setting yesterday for her debate prep, but the imitation was nothing like reality. She and Ellison stood at separate, stainless-steel podiums each with a thin free-standing microphone. They each had a glass of water, notepad, and pens.

Jones continued. "Since this is the only debate, we're going to make this an open forum. I may ask a question regarding any issue to one of the candidates, who then has three minutes to answer. The other candidate can respond. If the second candidate mentions the other candidate, the first candidate may have an additional one-minute rebuttal." Jones eyed both of the candidates in turn to make sure they understood.

"The first question pertains to unemployment. Five percent is considered the normal unemployment rate. The current rate stands at six percent. Some would argue the real unemployment rate, though, is twice that, if you include those who want and are able to work, but have become discouraged from looking. How would you reduce the real unemployment rate further? Mr. President?"

Ellison wrote as the moderator spoke. Whitney wondered what he could be writing already. The president put down his pen and stared at Blaine Jones.

"It's not the government's role to create jobs. The only action we can take is to create an environment in which business owners can be successful by eliminating onerous regulations and decreasing taxes so more money is pumped into the economy. Lower taxes give people the incentive to work harder, save, and invest, which improves living standards for all. We must continue to reduce the size of government and the role it plays in our lives. The free-market system works."

"Senator Fairchild?" the moderator asked.

Whitney faced Ellison. "When?"

Some members in the audience chuckled. After a few moments, Ellison shifted on his feet. When she realized he wasn't going to respond, Whitney turned back to the moderator. "I believe in capitalism as well, but the free-market approach in itself is not working and hasn't worked for many years. Businesses exist to make money for their owners. That's why, despite the turn-around in our economy, the pay for the average worker has remained flat.

"My goal is to spur economic and employment growth. One of my first initiatives after I am elected president will be to enact a significant training tax credit to businesses. There are millions of jobs available, but workers aren't trained to do them. In my first year of office, I will also propose a National Infrastructure Bank. The bank would work with local, state, and federal entities to provide financing and grants to build and repair roads and bridges, create rapid inner-city rail in all major cities, and modernize our air-traffic-control system. This proposal would put even more Americans back to work and increase worker productivity. Delays from congestion and damaged roads will cost two hundred and ten billion dollars over the next five years. There is nothing fiscally responsible about deferring maintenance of our crumbling infrastructure to future generations."

Whitney paused while the audience clapped.

Ellison shook his head. "How will you pay for that?"

Whitney faced him. "By ending tax subsidies for big businesses." Turning back to the camera, she continued. "We don't need to shrink the government. We need to modernize it. A limited government made sense when we were an agrarian society back in the days of Thomas Jefferson. People were self-sufficient. Today we are interdependent. Our government must change as our society changes. We have done this before. In the nineteenth century, we changed from an agrarian society to an industrial one. We became a superpower in the twentieth. The question is, 'What do we want to be in the twenty-first century?'"

"Time," Jones said.

"We can, however, streamline our government," Whitney continued, ignoring Jones. "The financial industry has proven time and time again that it is incapable of regulating itself. Bernie Madoff bilked investors for sixty-eight *billion* dollars. I plan to consolidate all of our financial agencies into one agency, the Federal Financial Regulatory Authority, making it more efficient and more effective in enforcing the law and protecting investors and consumers.

"I will propose a committee to review all current regulations: to revise those that do not make sense, to eliminate those we no longer need, and to create regulation that protects our citizens while encouraging innovation. Your party, Mr. President, transformed regulation into a dirty word. It is not. Regulation protects consumers: from the foods we eat, to the water we drink, to the drugs we take, to the safety of our highways."

"Can I talk?" Ellison asked.

The audience clapped, many of them laughing. Whitney joined in the laughter. The moderator waited for the clapping to subside. "Senator, may I remind you to limit your responses to three minutes?"

"Yes, you may."

Blaine Jones hesitated before realizing she was teasing him. Charmed, his cheeks reddened.

"Senator Fairchild, can you outline your tax plan for the audience?"

"Sure, Blaine. We must decrease income taxes for the middle class. For American couples making less than one hundred thousand dollars, I am proposing a flat fifteen-percent tax and elimination of all loopholes, exemptions, and deductions. This plan will lower the tax burden for most taxpayers and simplify tax preparation. I want to eliminate special tax breaks. To that end, I intend to raise rates for taxpayers making over one million dollars per year to the same levels as the Bill Clinton administration, aligning our tax system to better serve our economy and our planet."

"Mr. President?" Jones asked.

Ellison screwed up his face. "Your party, Senator, always wants to engage in class warfare, pitting the wealthy against everyone else. They forget who creates the jobs and the opportunities in this country. My plan calls for a flat ten percent tax for everyone. Further—"

"Your plan," Whitney said, "would not raise sufficient revenue to offset current spending."

"According to the reports I've received, it will."

"Well, as Hillary Clinton once said, 'I think the reports you provide us really require a willing suspension of disbelief.'"

Scattered laughter filled the hall like wind chimes.

Jones waited for the laughter to subside. "Mr. President, when you were elected, you promised to build a fence between our country and Mexico. Why haven't you done so?"

"These things take time, Blaine. I'm more committed than ever to building a fence to protect our borders. We spent a few years conducting feasibility studies on the terrain that can't be fenced easily. Once those studies are completed, the fence will be built."

"Senator?" Jones asked.

"Blaine, twelve million so-called illegals live in this country. Every year, five hundred thousand more cross the border. Instead of wasting our time discussing a fence that will never be built, we should devote our energies to a solution in keeping with a nation *founded* by immigrants and created by the rule of law."

"The next question is for the president." Blaine Jones looked up from the paper in front of him. "Your campaign promised four years ago to repeal health-care reform, which you've not done. If you're re-elected and repeal of the entire act is not possible, what parts would you repeal?"

Ellison stared into the camera and ticked off the points on his finger. "First, I'd do away with the individual mandate; a person shouldn't be forced to buy health insurance. Second, I'd lower the age that children could remain on their parents' insurance to eighteen. Third, I'd eliminate the penalties on companies who don't insure all of their employees."

The last statement was met with polite applause. The moderator turned to Whitney. "Senator?"

"First, as for the individual mandate, who pays when the uninsured go to the hospital? The insured. Why not put the burden on the individuals who use it? Isn't that what the free-market system is all about? Second, I would resurrect an idea proposed by the president's party"—she gestured at Ellison—"an eventual complete transition away from employer-provided health insurance. Why should companies be involved? Employer-provided health insurance began as a response to World War II wage and price controls, giving employees greater benefits and a sense of security. This made sense when employees stayed with a company for forty years, but how much sense does it make now when the average employee's tenure is three years? Exchanges or portable health insurance allow employees to change jobs without worrying. This will provide individuals with greater choice, and employers, as President Ellison always says, can then concentrate on their businesses.

"Third, President Ellison knows as well as I, health-care reform prevented many families from going bankrupt and children and young adults from joining the uninsured. These same children cannot find good-paying jobs. Throughout this campaign, I have talked with many college graduates—Michael in North Carolina, Jessica in Ohio, Matthew in Florida, bright and intelligent young men and women—who are working in fast-food establishments. I have two college-aged children. Is this any way to take care of our children? I don't think so. This is America. We are better than this!"

The audience rose to a standing ovation.

When the applause subsided, the moderator turned to Ellison.

"Mr. President, your turn to respond."

"Children? A twenty-six-year-old is not a child. Our young adults must start taking personal responsibility for their own care and learn early in life the government can't solve all of their problems. Third parties make costs go up. To bring down the cost of health care, we need to eliminate the middlemen. Health care should be between a doctor and his patient. If you break your leg, you should be informed of how much it's going to cost to fix it. This cost should not be disclosed to you for the first time when you open the bill."

Tepid applause followed.

Whitney scanned the audience and smiled. President Ellison's face was flushed and he gripped the podium as if he were holding on for dear life. Whitney understood if she did not make any major gaffes the rest of the debate, the night was hers. She focused on the moderator, Blaine Jones.

He looked at both candidates with a grave expression. "Let's talk about China."

CHAPTER FIFTY-THREE

Washington, DC

JADE STARED AT the blank wall on the opposite side of her office. She was back at the Bureau, two days after returning from Seattle.

The owner of the Federal Army and Navy Surplus store had provided a good description of the man who bought the knife. So far, nothing had come back from showing the composite to every airport, train station, bus terminal, hotel, rental car agency, and bed and breakfast within one hundred miles of Seattle. The facial composite had also been sent to every known victim's employer. No one remembered seeing the suspect. Her team had checked out every lead provided by the public. None credible. Austin called MSNBC and no one fitting the description had ever worked there. No one fitting that description had ever worked at the Bureau. Dead end after dead end.

She had been avoiding Ethan. Although he was still supportive, he was under pressure, too. She had grown up with demanding parents who only wanted to hear good news. She didn't want to see Ethan until she had something positive to report.

She started aligning the items on her desk. After she finished aligning her files, she selected one to review. Her phone rang again. "Harrington."

"Agent Harrington, Detective McClaine, Seattle PD. I wanted to let you know the evidence reports came back. I'm sending them over to you now."

"Hair?"

"No, but we found carpet fibers. We checked the victim's residence and car, and they don't belong to him."

Jade had opened his email during the conversation and scanned the report. Now, off the phone, she read it in detail. Jade started rifling through the files on her desk, grateful that she had just organized them in alphabetical order. She located the correct folder and flipped pages until she found the fiber-analysis report. Carpet fibers were also found at the LeBlanc scene in Baton Rouge and the Paxson scene in Houston. Unlike DNA and fingerprints, a national database didn't exist for fibers.

The color, diameter, shape, dye content, and chemical composition of the carpet found at the LeBlanc and Tallent scenes—as analysts would say—were consistent with each other.

Jade would say it was a match. She did a fist pump.

Yes!

The fibers were not consistent, however, with those found at the Paxson scene. Why not? The killer must have brought the fibers with him from his house or car. Perhaps he moved to a new residence between the Houston and Baton Rouge murders. Maybe he had bought a new car. No hair samples this time. Why not? Why did he switch modus operandi? How was he selecting his victims? Questions, questions, and more questions.

CHAPTER FIFTY-FOUR

Washington, DC

IN HER OFFICE the next day, Jade clicked open the PDF on her computer. A composite of a young white man with short-cropped hair and nondescript face stared back at her. The face of a killer.

MSNBC had received another email from TSK. She printed out several copies and called her team together for an emergency task force meeting. A few minutes later they were all assembled in the conference room.

Jade passed around the copies.

To Whom It May Concern,

Or should I ask, does it concern anyone? I told the world what would happen if my demands were not met. They should not even be called demands, because balance and fairness on the airwaves is what we deserve. What we should all want. The left and moderate views must be heard. How many more people are going to die before you start taking me seriously?

I gave the FBI a clue last time, albeit with some misdirection. This time, the Bureau will need to figure it out on its own.

I hope the death of poor Mr. (lack of) Tallent will propel our members of Congress to act. If not, you will be hearing from me again soon.

Sincerely,

TSK

Christian dropped the paper on the table. "Motive, means, and opportunity." Jade slipped a yellow peanut M&M into her mouth.

"Any hits on the sketch?" Christian asked.

Jade shook her head. "Nada. We sent the facial composite to every radio and TV station and all transportation possibilities in the victims' cities."

"The UNSUB's like a ghost," Austin said.

Jade turned to Pat, clicking away at her laptop. "Circulate the facial composite to former students, teachers, radio station employees, student housing, and restaurants in Chattenham. And send it to OPA"—Office of Public Affairs—"to add him to the Most Wanted list."

Pat nodded her assent without ceasing her typing.

"Christian, have someone from our Baton Rouge office interview the girlfriend of LeBlanc again. Ask her if she recognizes the sketch. Perhaps her memory can be jarred further."

"Got it."

"And run the facial composite through the database again."

Christian flashed a look at her.

"Do it again," she said. She turned to Max. "Thoughts?"

Max cleared his throat. "I studied every photo, autopsy, police report, witness statement, and pattern of the offenses again. The perpetrator is under a lot of stress and will become more frustrated and angry by the growing media attention and lack of action by Congress on his demands, evidenced by the overkill and concentrated knife wounds in the Tallent killing.

"He is trying to save our country and society isn't listening to him or giving him the respect he deserves. He'll start to believe the situation is hopeless. At the same time, he receives intellectual satisfaction from outsmarting the FBI and local law enforcement. It's a game. The inadequate part of him wars with the superior, grandiose side."

The other agents stared at him. Pat stopped typing. They had never heard Max say so much in one breath. He was in the zone.

He pushed his glasses up farther on his nose. "This guy isn't going to stop on his own."

CHAPTER FIFTY-FIVE

Washington, DC

A MONTH BEFORE the presidential election, Senator Whitney Fairchild worked at her desk in the Russell Senate Office Building. She had finally succumbed to Landon's suggestion of installing a TV in her office to keep up with current events. She glanced at the flat-panel television hanging on the wall across from her. The portrait of Eleanor Roosevelt had been relegated to storage.

Another Breaking News flash filled the bottom of the screen. News today, for the most part, was neither "breaking" nor even news, but this time, a TSK logo popped up in the top right corner. As time went on, the logo had become more elaborate. A facial composite of the killer was lodged in the bottom of the screen.

She came around her desk for a closer inspection. She wondered how someone could kill another person, especially over politics. What must be going through his mind? The face seemed familiar. Something in her stirred. She dismissed the feeling. The guy looked like a lot of young men today who wore hoodies. She turned up the volume.

"Moments ago, this network received what TSK is calling his *Manifesto for America,* a hundred-page document detailing his solutions to our country's problems. He demanded we post a link and the document itself on our website. We understand similar demands were made to the print and online departments of *The Washington Post* and *The New York Times.* Executives for MSNBC are not commenting whether they will honor the request. We have also been unable to reach the Director of the FBI or the Attorney General. We will continue to keep you updated on any further developments."

The talking head went on, "What has Kim Kardashian been up to and what is happening with her latest marriage? You'll find out after—"

Whitney muted the volume and returned to her desk. She pressed a button on her phone. "Landon, I need a copy of the TSK manifesto."

"What manifesto?"

"Turn on the news." She hung up.

Westchester County, New York

THE WOMAN WAS late for work. At fifty years old, she believed she was too old to have just picked up her child from an elementary school and taken her home. Hence, why she was late for work. She brushed back her hair as she yelled out the window at her ten-year-old.

"Daddy will be home soon. You can watch TV after you've done your homework. Listen to Isabella. I love you!" She blew her daughter a kiss as their au pair, Isabella, opened the door, allowing the woman's daughter to pass under her arm. Isabella waved. The woman waved back and put the car into drive.

The woman was Liz Holder. A former lawyer, she was now the most powerful woman in conservative politics. Born and raised in New York City, Elizabeth Holder, née Dolan, grew up in a Democratic household. She embarked on the typical liberal route, attending Brown University for undergrad and the University of Pennsylvania for law school. During her college years, she fell in love with the cheery optimism of Ronald Reagan and became a Reagan Democrat. She felt chills when Reagan told Gorbachev to "tear down that wall." Now, the lone Republican in her extended Democratic family, she was hardly tolerated by them. She didn't care.

After law school, she clerked for a forgettable federal judge in New York City, and then went to Washington for many years to work as a legal aide for a senator from New York. During the presidency of George W. Bush, she wrote a book defending his decision to invade Iraq. The book was a surprising best seller for a first-time author. She quit her day job, moved back to Westchester County, New York, and became an author full time. She began to receive numerous offers for guest appearances on all the cable-news networks. The networks loved her because she was smart, attractive, and controversial. When Liz Dolan spoke, ratings went up. After years of guest appearances, Patriot

News created a show for her. They allowed her to broadcast from a satellite studio not far from her home.

She was hated by Democrats and liberals across the country, and even some conservative politicians distanced themselves from her. Nevertheless, people read her books and tuned in to her show. She was second only to Cole Brennan in influencing conservative thought and ideals.

Still single into her late thirties and needing to quiet the budding lesbian rumors, she married Adam Holder, a partner with a New York City law firm. Theirs was a marriage of mutual respect and companionship, not love. Thus, while she was at the age she should have been traveling or enjoying her grand-children, she was instead dropping off her young daughter at home after elementary school.

She pushed the speed dial on her Jeep's phone.

Without preamble, she said, "I'm running late, but I should be there before the show starts."

"Hurry," her producer, Aaron, said. "By the way, we lost another advertiser."

"Who?"

"GE."

"I wonder why."

"You know why."

"I'm not going to apologize for saying what I think. I'm not going to be politically correct. I never claimed to be impartial, fair, and balanced. I only claimed to be right."

"Well," Aaron said, "some of their customers complained about your comment last week that if the Nazis had exterminated six million liberals instead of Jews, the world would be a better place. The comment about putting a numbered tattoo on liberals' arms in the event we wanted to round them up later didn't help. Oh . . . and what you said about white liberals being only slightly better than minority liberals put them over the top."

"I've not kept it a secret I hate liberals. They're Godless and moral-less. They won't be happy until the queers and minorities take over this country, which will be sooner than you think. Whites in the Sixties made up ninety percent of the population. By the year 2050, we will be the minority. Am I sup-posed to sit around and let them extinguish our race as we did to the Indians?"

Aaron ignored her rhetorical question. "Remember, President Ellison will be on the show tonight. Please try to control yourself. And get here."

"Are you afraid I'm going to endorse Whitney? Wouldn't that be a hoot? That would shake up Ellison's pseudo-conservative ass. I still think I should have convinced Cole Brennan or another true conservative to run against him in the Republican primary. Aaron, hold on a minute."

She pressed a button and her window lowered.

"Welcome to Starbucks. What can I get started for you?" came the tinny voice from the drive-thru microphone.

"I'll take a venti low-fat caramel macchiato."

"Will that be all for you today?"

"Yes."

"Please drive around. I'll have your total for you at the window."

An uncharacteristic foreboding preceded the shadow reflecting off the Starbucks menu.

Before she had time to press the button to slide up the Jeep's window, a flash of black—a coat sleeve?—and a glint from an object slipped through.

An excruciating pain began at the base of her throat. She reached up and touched her neck. She pulled her hand away. It was bright red. She thought of her daughter. She tried to turn her head to face the person who had done this to her, but her head fell forward and landed on the horn of her steering wheel.

In the passenger seat next to her, Aaron's voice was yelling from the cellphone she had dropped. "Liz, what's going on? What's happening?" Pause. "Are you all right? Liz!"

Through the drive-thru microphone, the Starbucks employee said, "Ma'am, would you like to order anything else? If not, please proceed to the window."

After that, she didn't hear anything at all.

CHAPTER FIFTY-SEVEN

Washington, DC

"WELCOME BACK. I'VE saved the worst for last. Now, we're going to talk about this so-called *Manifesto for America* written by the Talk Show Killer, aka TSK, which he sent to MSNBC. Yes, the executive folks over at MSNBC, after two minutes of intense deliberations, decided to post the document on its website. You can now find it on mine as well at www.theconservative-voiceonline.com.

"I read all one hundred pages of this liberal, Socialist crap and I can tell you all I want to do now is throw up. The killer doesn't even need to try to kill me. Just make me read this sh— stuff again and again and I'll kill myself. Folks, if you want to understand why our country is going to hell, read this thing. Why do these Commiecrats write these manifestos anyway? Who cares? Who does this guy think he is? The Unabomber?

"All right. Let's get to it. He starts off by writing about regulation and how we need big government to protect us from the greed of big, bad businesses. Have you been to a DMV lately, TSK? Who is it protecting you from? Getting a license? Keeping you off the road for a few hours?

"He writes about our efforts to abolish abortion in this country. The only lives we care about are the unborn. What about the women who bear them? What about a woman's freedom of choice of what to do with her own body? All that Seventies feminist crap. He states a fetus isn't a human life, yet, so it shouldn't be granted separate and individual rights. Wrong! Life begins at conception, folks, and abortion is murder.

"He complains the federal government slashed programs that helped lower-income young mothers care for their children. So, we force these women to bear children, who then die of malnutrition. Well, I can turn this argument around, Mr. TSK. Why do all of you liberals support children's health, nutrition, and education programs, but support the abortion of these future children? He doesn't understand why our party is pro-life and pro-death penalty. 'Is that not a contradiction in terms?' Yes, folks, that's how he writes. Probably went to an Ivy League school. He ends this section by arguing the abortion debate would be different if men instead of women were the ones who got pregnant. I don't even know how to respond to that.

"He opposes the death penalty, calling it unjust, inhumane, and cruel and unusual punishment. With every execution, the government takes a chance of killing an innocent person. The United States is one of the top five countries in executions along with China, Iran, North Korea, and Yemen. Okay, not good company, but executing a murderer for taking an innocent life is still okay in my book.

"I'll skip the part about the Fairness Doctrine and income inequality, since we've discussed them ad nauseam on this show. The killer condemns capitalism. Calls it evil. How did he type this manifesto? I would guess with a computer. How was the computer created? By the computer fairy? These Socialists complain about capitalism, but they don't mind using the products of capitalism.

"He yawns on about increasing the safety net for the poor and the elderly. Where is the money going to come from, big guy? One solution, of course, is to increase taxes on oil companies and the rich. On the one hand, we encourage entrepreneurship in this country. On the other hand, as soon as you become successful, we want to tax and regulate the hell out of you.

"Next, illegal immigrants should be granted amnesty and bestowed the same rights as American citizens. They should be given driver's licenses and their kids should be allowed to go to college at in-state tuition rates. I disagree. I think they should be paying out-of-country rates. He believes in the Dream Act, allowing illegals to attain permanent residency if they demonstrate good character—according to whom?—and get a college degree or serve two years in the military. The Dream Act is a nightmare, folks. We are a nation of laws and should only accept legal immigration. Let's secure our borders, President Ellison, by building that fence!

"Mr. TSK believes America needs to stop being so nationalistic and take a more global view. We are citizens of the world and through tolerance, diplomacy, and disarmament, we can achieve global peace in our lifetime. He wants to re-establish foreign aid to previous levels to help educate citizens in other countries on the virtues of democracy. If citizens of other countries understood democracy and became less hostile, they will be less likely to attack us.

"What friggin' planet does this guy live on? Does he want us all to gather around a global campfire and sing Kumbaya?"

Cole dropped the hundred-page manifesto on the table.

"Folks, that's about all I can stomach for today. There is a lot more in here—affirmative action, global warming, gay marriage, welfare—it's all in here. If you're suffering from constipation, grab this manifesto, and head to the toilet. I guarantee you'll feel better fast."

Cole signed off.

Washington, DC

JADE TURNED THE final page of TSK's *Manifesto for America*. She leaned back in her office chair and rubbed her eyes. She had read the document all the way through three times. The killer's writings didn't seem crazy to her. This was not the work of a raving lunatic. The writing style was coherent, methodical, and logical. What kind of person were they dealing with? What was driving him to kill? How did he continue to elude them? Who was he going to strike next? *How can I get there first?*

She must have gone into a trance, because her phone was ringing. Normally, she picked up on the first ring.

"Harrington."

"Hey you. It's your best friend, Zoe. Remember me?"

"What's up?"

"Do you need me to swing by and take care of Card?"

"Yes, thank you. I don't think I'll make it home tonight."

"Anything else? I can bring dinner."

"No, I'll pick something up." She paused. She could tell Zoe, couldn't she? "By the way, I've been sort of hanging out with your friend, Landon Phillips."

"Sort of hanging out . . ."

"Yeah. During my meeting with Senator Fairchild, she sort of set us up."

"Huh," Zoe said. "And?"

"We had dinner. Played a little ball."

"How romantic."

"You didn't tell me he was so handsome."

"I didn't? Hmph. I mean, he's okay . . . for a guy."

"Listen, I gotta go. My other line is ringing."

Jade punched the lighted button on her phone. "Harrington."

A pause. "Jade, this is Landon."

"Landon." She was caught off guard. He must be telepathic. "Hi."

"I'm calling to apologize."

She stayed silent.

"For the kiss. I'm not sure what came over me. Well, I know what came over me. You did. But, still, it was out of line."

"I kissed you back."

"Yeah, there's that."

After a few moments of silence, he asked, "I'm also calling for the Senator. Any update? On the case?"

She hesitated. "Did you read the manifesto?"

"Sure. No real surprises. No new solutions. Solid liberal positions. As a Democrat, I can't disagree with a lot of them, although in practice I'm more of a progressive than a liberal."

"What's your distinction?"

"Some say there isn't one. Some liberals call themselves progressives, because Republicans have painted 'liberal' as a dirty word. If I had to distinguish between the two, I'd say a liberal is someone who uses taxpayer money to help society—improving health care and giving subsidies to help people—whereas a progressive uses the power of the government to make large institutions and individuals play by the rules. Both believe in using the government for social change, such as improving food safety, instituting minimum wage and labor laws, and creating financial rules to make sure corporations don't hurt workers or consumers in their pursuit of profit."

He waited. When she didn't say anything, he went on.

"Progressives created the FBI. During the Progressive Era in the early twentieth century, Attorney General Charles Bonaparte formed the FBI from a force of special agents under Teddy Roosevelt's administration. Bonaparte believed government intervention was necessary to provide justice in an industrial society. The FBI also had a major role in integration and giving African-Americans the right to vote. Its investigation into the murder of three voter registration workers in Philadelphia, Mississippi was a key turning point in the civil rights movement."

"Thanks for the history lesson."

"You're welcome," he said, his tone embarrassed. "I guess you know all that, working for them and all."

"Listen, Landon, I need to go. 'And miles to go before I sleep.'"

"'The woods are lovely, dark and deep. But I have promises to keep.' Frost is one of my favorites. Maybe we can get together . . ."

"Landon, I need to go."

During her conversation with Landon, she had been turning the pages of the manifesto. Midway through the document, the killer had drawn a caricature of congressmen and congresswomen standing on the Capitol Hill steps. She traced the drawing with her finger. It spoke to her. And seemed familiar. Had she seen it before?

She opened up her web browser and entered "Congress standing on Capitol Hill steps" into the search bar to find the image online. She came up empty. She typed variations of the phrase. Still nothing.

She rolled her shoulders and moved her neck to loosen them up. She clicked on the television and turned to MSNBC. A four-person panel discussed the manifesto, all the panelists young, attractive, and dressed in the latest style. The most stylish was the handsome Blake Haynes. He was smooth. She loved to hear him talk; she could listen to him all day.

She remembered telling Landon she had checked out liberal bloggers as he suggested. She might as well do that now, in case he asked her again. Maybe she would find one that had the same writing style as TSK. With reluctance, Jade turned her attention from the TV screen to her computer and typed "liberal bloggers" into the search bar.

She began to read.

❈

After two hours of reading liberal blogs, Jade was no closer to finding a writing style that matched the manifesto's. She pushed back her chair and bent over, her head in her hands. She breathed in and out slowly for a few minutes before lifting her head, her heart rate steady. She needed to work out before she hurt someone. Something blinked red out of the corner of her eye. She gazed at the television, her stomach dropping at the sight of the now-familiar TSK logo and the breaking-news bulletin. *What now?* She turned up the sound.

A pretty Asian-American stared into the camera. "That's right, Joe. An anonymous source within the Seattle Police Department confirmed that radio host Shane Tallent's tongue had been severed."

"Was the tongue found?" asked Joe, the show's host.

"Yes. The tongue was found a short distance away from the scene of the crime in an alley behind a restaurant in downtown Seattle. The source didn't divulge the name of the restaurant. But Joe . . . there's more. Another source told me this isn't the first time. All the victims had their tongue removed."

The host thanked the on-the-scene reporter and the panelists in the studio began giving their thoughtful, compelling analysis of the significance of this new evidence. Their chatter, though, had an underlying tinge of nervousness.

Jade turned off the television and started to pace. *Shit!* The leak of the severed tongues was going to cause a media frenzy. She needed to brief Ethan.

She headed toward his office, dialing McClaine's number on the way to find out what the hell was going on in his police department. She realized, though, she had a leak at her end as well. McClaine didn't know about the other victims' tongues.

When she entered, Ethan hung up the phone.

"You saved me a call."

"What?"

Ethan only looked at her.

Her shoulders dropped. "Again?"

Westchester County, New York

CHRISTIAN, MAX, AND Jade drove in silence from the airport. The Starbucks was easy to spot long before they saw its sign. Yellow Police Line Do Not Cross tape encircled the parking lot entrance, the drive-thru lane exit, and the perimeter of the store. Christian parked the car, and they exited the vehicle. A huge man left the others he was speaking to and walked over.

"Agent Harrington?"

Jade nodded.

"John O'Shaunessy. I spoke to you on the phone."

As they shook hands, Jade gave him the once-over. This man had played professional football, or at least tried.

He acknowledged her appraisal. "Yep. Spent five years in the league. Defensive tackle for the Eagles."

"I thought so!" Christian said.

By the extended belly and the broken capillaries on his nose, Jade guessed he spent more time these days chasing pints of Guinness with shots than chasing running backs. She introduced Christian and Max.

Detective O'Shaunessy led them over to the drive-thru microphone. "The victim ordered her drink right before it happened. The employee who took her order asked her to come to the window a few times. When the victim didn't respond or move, the employee told his manager. The manager had already received complaints from drive-thru customers who had come inside the store to order. Other customers came inside when the victim's horn went off. None of the customers in line bothered to check out what was going on in her car. They needed their caffeine, I guess. The manager came out and found the victim's head on the steering wheel. The horn, still blaring. She saw blood everywhere and ran back into the store to call us."

Jade scanned the surroundings. "This happened at what time?"

"About four-thirty p.m."

"So, it was still daylight," Jade said. "With no trees or anything else around, how come no one saw the UNSUB?"

"The teenage girl in the car behind the victim observed her ordering, but began texting with a friend and stopped paying attention. She looked up when the horn started going off. She thought she saw a guy walking away, but couldn't be sure. There were cars behind her so she couldn't back up. She began taking selfies and Snapchatting her story that she was stuck in a line at Starbucks, but didn't think to get out of the car to find out why."

"No one else in line witnessed anything?" Jade asked.

"They were all on their cell phones," O'Shaunessy said.

"Unbelievable," Christian said.

"Not really," O'Shaunessy said. "How many times do you go to a restaurant and most of the customers are staring at their phones? Bus stops? Coffee shops? People would rather communicate with anyone else besides the people they're with."

"How did the UNSUB know Holder would be here?" Jade asked.

"The victim came to this Starbucks every day at about the same time. Ordered the same thing. She was running a little late yesterday, though."

"Any evidence?" Christian asked.

"We lifted a shoeprint over there," O'Shaunessy said, pointing toward a grassy median that separated the Starbucks from a nearby Wendy's. They walked over to where he had pointed.

Jade crouched for a closer view. "Pretty big feet. He was walking away from the car. Someone must have seen him at the Wendy's. Any results back, yet, on the shoeprint?"

O'Shaunessy shook his head. "Seen enough?"

Jade glanced at Christian and Max. Max held her gaze, but said nothing.

As he walked them back toward the car, Jade asked, "Have you interviewed her co-workers? Any enemies? Any threats?"

O'Shaunessy nodded. "We're in the process of doing that now."

"And?"

"Our problem isn't determining whether she had any enemies. It's narrowing down the list."

CHAPTER SIXTY

Bethesda, Maryland

COLE BRENNAN RELAXED with his wife and six children in their family room. He loved the term "family room." How appropriate.

He took a sip of his drink. Cole was stressed. Between the election next week, Liz Holder's murder, and someone wanting him dead, he had about all the anxiety he could take. Not to mention trying to save this damn country from the Socialists.

Was it worth it? Was saving the country worth risking his life? Maybe he should give the Democrats what they want. *Atlas Shrugged* them. When the nation drowned from runaway debt, twenty-five percent unemployment, loss of morals, and lost its superpower status, would the liberals be happy? The US would become the Great Britain of the twenty-first century—the former superpower of the eighteenth and nineteenth centuries, now reduced to being the obedient lap dog of the United States. The US, however, would be licking Chinese boots. Boots Made in China.

He laughed out loud.

His daughter, Kaitlin, raised an eyebrow. "What's so funny, Dad?"

"Nothing, sweetheart."

"You're doing it again, Dad. This is supposed to be family time."

He smiled at her. "You're right. I'm sorry."

His son, Ryan, came to stand before him. "Dad, guess what!"

"What, Sport?"

"I scored today!"

"You did? Wow! I wish I could've been there. I had to work late. That's awesome. High-five!" Cole reached his arm out to his son.

Cole Jr. groaned. "Dad, high-fiving is so out."

Cole retracted his arm. "Oh?"

"Try a fist bump," Cole Jr. suggested.

"That's okay, Dad," Ryan said. "Wait! I forgot to show you something!" He sprinted out of the room.

The running and yelling would annoy a lesser man, but Cole loved it. He wasn't a lesser man.

Ryan returned carrying a soccer ball.

Cole gazed into his son's beaming face. This face was what he was fighting for. "What do you have there, Sport?"

Ryan offered the ball to him, as if it were a Fabergé egg. "One of the dads gave this to me for scoring a goal!"

"Wow! That was nice of him."

Cole spun the blue and white soccer ball in his hands. In one of the white panels, the letters "TSK" were scrawled in black magic marker.

Pain tore through his stomach and his hands started to shake.

Cole dropped the ball.

CHAPTER SIXTY-ONE

Arlington, Virginia

JADE ENTERED WON Ho's Tae Kwon Do Academy, which was located a few miles from her house. She was dressed in a gray sleeveless sweatshirt and black workout tights. Master Ho had given her a key.

The place was empty at this time of night, as it should have been. She went through the small lobby and performed a slight bow before entering the dojang (school), not caring whether anyone else was present to ensure she obeyed the rules. She placed her gear bag against the wall and ran some laps and stretched to warm up.

Master Ho entered the dojang and walked over to her. She jumped to her feet, and they bowed to each other. Bowing in Tae Kwon Do was a sign of respect. She bowed to show respect for her instructor, the art, and herself.

"Good to see you, Ms. Harrington. It's been a long time."

"I've been a little busy, sir. I didn't think anyone would be here."

He shook his head. "Paperwork. Always paperwork."

"Do you mind if I work out?"

"Not at all. I'll come out and spar with you in a little while."

Jade gazed down on his short-cropped silver hair. As a fourth-degree black belt, she didn't require an instructor to work out with her.

"You don't have to, sir. I know it's late."

He shot her a look and left.

She started off doing *poomsae* (forms). She loved performing the pre-determined patterns of movement, kicks, punches, and blocks, and the concentration, strength, coordination, and flexibility required to do them well. She tried to execute the form for her rank better each time, competing with no one but herself.

Master Ho returned twenty minutes later in his sparring gear. She ran to her bag and put on her gear and moved to the middle of the mat. They bowed to each other again.

She went into her sparring stance and—

He kicked her in the head with a round kick.

Although over sixty years old, Master Ho had the physique of a man twenty years younger. He could still fight. Despite the headgear, the kick stung. A lot. While her head rang, she spun and landed a side kick in his kidney. He grunted and nodded, pleased. Counterattacking was the key to being a good fighter.

They exchanged punches and kicks until Jade punched him, hard. But missed.

"Damn it!" She took off her headgear and slammed it to the mat. The gear rolled away from them.

Master Ho walked over, picked it up, and returned it to her. He stared into her eyes.

"A good fighter never loses control. You cannot control every situation, but you can always control your body and your mind." He pointed to his temple. "The circumstance is not of consequence, but how you react to it is. Being still and doing nothing are two very different things."

She nodded her head, then stopped. "Wait . . . isn't that a line from *The Karate Kid*?"

The lines around his eyes twinkled. "No one can be endowed with all wisdom." He stared into her eyes, as if trying to see into her soul. "Ms. Harrington, trust your training."

"Yes, sir. Thank you, sir." She bowed.

Master Ho bowed. He hesitated before touching her shoulder, a brief yet comforting gesture. He nodded and left.

Jade had never noticed physical affection from him to her or any of his students. She stood there for a moment, assuring herself it had happened before splaying out on the floor and removing her gear. She stuffed all of it into her bag. Crossing her legs Indian-style, she closed her eyes.

For years, Zoe had tried to interest her in Zen Buddhism and meditation. At first, Jade didn't care much for the meditational aspect of Tae Kwon Do. She would rather hit people.

She focused her mind on her breathing. In, out. In, out. In, out. As often happened when her mind was quiet and her body stilled, thoughts of the past came forward unbeckoned. Growing up as an Army brat, the only mixed-race kid in her neighborhood, and a bullying victim made for a lonely childhood. She had thought then she was the only person in the world who lived like that. Besides Zoe, she had never had any friends. What was the point when her family could move away at any time? She felt disconnected from others. No one *got* her. Or she didn't get them. Now, she preferred to be alone. She had a greater connection to athletes or actors on television than people in the real world.

Jade had no time or need for romance. Never did. After three years of playing professionally in the WNBA and overseas in Japan, she started later than other agents at the Academy. She not only had to catch up, but she had to be better. Her work was her love. Being the best, her mission.

She did not have time for Landon Phillips.

Several thoughts swirled around in her head at once: the killer, the leaks, the slow progress of the investigation, all interwoven with pictures of the victims adorning the walls of the conference room at the Bureau.

After fifteen minutes, she gave up, realizing the meditation had failed to calm her mind. Or, maybe, she failed to let it. She opened her eyes and studied herself in the full-length wall mirror. She looked away.

She toweled off her face, stood, and started to zip her bag. Her phone indicated she had received a text message. She snatched it out of the bag.

Christian had texted an address and told her to meet him first thing in the morning.

TSK had sent Cole Brennan a gift.

❖

Early the next morning, Jade knocked on a massive red door. She had already rung the bell. The door swung open to the big man himself.

"Mr. Brennan, I'm Special Agent Jade Harrington and this is Special Agent Christian Merritt. We'd like to talk to you about the soccer ball your son received. May we come in?"

Cole Brennan's eyes did a quick survey of her body before moving aside. "Come on in."

She stepped into the foyer and marveled at the two curved staircases with black iron railing that led upstairs. Brennan led them toward the back of the house. She stopped at the door to a large room. Inside, chaos. She had heard he had six kids, but now she *knew* it. A woman sat on the sofa, her smile vacant, the skin around her eyes tight.

"This is my wife, Ashley. Ash, this is Agent Merritt and Jade."

"Agent Harrington," Jade corrected, shaking Ashley's hand.

Brennan addressed the room at large.

"Kids, these are our friends. We're going to go chat with them."

The younger children paid little attention and continued to play. Not fooled, the teenagers eyed Jade and Christian from their spots on the floor in front of the TV.

"Follow me," Brennan said.

He led them to a room off the great room. His home office. He waved for them to sit as he settled into a leather chair behind the grand desk. He nodded to his wife to close the door. She came up and stood beside him, placing her hand on his shoulder.

Brennan's demeanor changed as soon as the door closed, his face darkening.

"What are you doing to catch this liberal freak? He talked to my son!"

Ashley pressed down on his shoulder. "Keep your voice down, sweetheart."

Brennan ignored her. To Christian, "Are you any closer to catching this guy?"

Jade stared at Brennan waiting for him to turn to her. He didn't.

"Mr. Brennan," Jade said. "First, we need to make sure it's him. We're pursuing several leads. We had the soccer ball dusted for prints. The only prints on it were yours and your son's."

Brennan addressed Christian.

"Of course, it's him. TSK. The other parents don't hate me enough to play a joke like that." He paused. "I don't think. What are you doing to protect my family?"

Christian pointed at Jade, his eyes not leaving Brennan's.

"She's the boss, sir."

Brennan sighed and faced her as if it were painful.

"Your house is under surveillance," Jade said, "and agents are covering your office building. We're shadowing all of you to the best of our ability with the limited resources we have."

"Typical. The FBI is a stupid and useless government agency that should be eliminated."

Jade stood. "Then, we should be going. I trust you can find someone else to protect you and your family and to catch this killer. Good day."

She eyed Christian and they both moved toward the door.

"Wait! Come back!"

Jade paused.

Brennan gestured to the chair. "Sorry. Please sit. I'm just stressed out."

After Jade resettled in her seat, she looked past him. "Mrs. Brennan, may we talk to your son?"

Cole Brennan, stunned at the rebuff, glanced over his shoulder at his wife. She gazed at him. He nodded absently and she left.

"Mr. Brennan, have you received any suspicious calls lately? At work or home?"

"I don't think so. Socialists know better than to call me."

Jade eyed Christian again, willing herself not to roll her eyes.

Ashley came in with a young boy. Christian stood and moved to the credenza underneath the window, leaning against it. Jade smiled at the boy, patting the chair Christian vacated.

"Hi, there. Why don't you sit next to me?"

The child looked at his mother and she nodded. He sat.

"What's your name?" Jade asked.

"Ryan!"

"How old are you, Ryan?"

"I just turned seven!"

"So, you like soccer?"

Ryan's face broke out into a grin. "Yeah!"

Jade flinched, not sure why he was yelling. She glanced at Christian, who was trying not to laugh.

"I played soccer, too."

"It's so much fun!"

"I think so, too." She leaned forward, elbows on her knees. In a soothing voice, she said, "Tell me about the man who gave you the soccer ball."

"After the game, he told me 'Awesome goal!' and he said, 'Here's a present for scoring.'"

"Can you tell me what he looked like?"

Ryan thought for a moment.

"He was tall."

"Do you remember anything else, Ryan? Anything at all?"

Ryan scrunched up his face, deep in thought. "No, that's it." After another moment, "Wait!"

"What? What do you remember?"

Ryan tilted his head to the side. "He was skinny. Not fat, like my daddy."

❄

The October air was cool, the leaves beginning to change color. After the interview, they had spoken to the agent in charge of Cole Brennan's security detail. Now, Jade and Christian walked the perimeter of his home, checking on security.

Christian surveyed the property as they walked. "Did you check out the wife?"

"Yes."

"She was creepy. With that plastic smile and those glassy eyes, and how she stared straight ahead, it was almost as if she were—"

"A Stepford wife."

"Yes!"

The leaves crunched underneath their feet.

Christian smiled at her. "He sure doesn't hold back, does he? Everyone's a Socialist. He wants to eliminate the FBI."

Jade shook her head. "It's no wonder someone wants to kill him."

CHAPTER SIXTY-TWO

Philadelphia, Pennsylvania

COLE BRENNAN STOOD at the podium. He scanned the auditorium audience, the place packed, expectant faces waiting for him to begin. Wearing a white dress shirt opened at the collar and tan slacks, he was sweating under the lights. It didn't help that the shirt felt a little snug after fitting only a few months ago.

He didn't feel right being here. He should have stayed home, to be there for his family. But he had made a commitment. And this election was too important.

Cole began to speak.

"We had our only presidential debate last week. Today, I want to provide answers to our most pressing problems for which there is no debate. You see, politicians tend to fill their speeches with highfalutin ideas and beautiful prose. I want to talk about the specific common-sense things I would do if I were president of this great country." He paused and smiled. "But don't get any ideas, folks!" He waited for the laughter to die down.

"No, I'm not running for president, but I do love my country. At the rate we're going, though, the debts of the Greatest Generation, the Baby Boomers, and Generation X will be repaid by the Millennials and the next generation. And because of that, those generations will not have a chance at the American Dream as we had, unless we do something about it now.

"We need to eliminate federal agencies by privatizing or moving their functions to the states, or relying on private businesses or charities to perform them. I volunteer a lot of my time to raise money for learning-disabled children. I choose to donate my hard-earned money to people less fortunate than me. To me, that is much better than the government giving it to low-income folks to pay for their flat-screen televisions.

"All right. Do you want specifics on how we can reduce the deficit?"

"Yes!" the audience yelled.

"First, we need to eliminate the Department of Energy. We don't need a national plan to address our energy needs. We possess plenty of good sources of energy right here: oil, gas, and coal. The DOE—it should be D-I-E—has been poorly managed and wasteful from the get-go. It is counterproductive to fund wrong or inefficient energy companies. Let the private sector fund research into alternative energy. We need to shut down the DOE!

"During the first half of the last decade, we gave one-point-two billion dollars to farmers who no longer farm and a bunch of money to large farming companies who don't need it. Agriculture subsidies never made sense and they don't make sense now. Shut it down!

"Fraught with scandals since it came into existence, the Department of Housing and Urban Development should be eliminated. Understand this folks, federal subsidies help people buy homes they can't afford. Federal rent subsidies make people reliant on the government to pay for something that is their responsibility. Shut it down!

"As for the Department of Labor, unemployment insurance should be the responsibility of the states and OSHA downsized. Eliminate the federal minimum wage and job training . . . what in the world does the government know about training? Have you called the IRS lately? Shut it down!

"We need to privatize air traffic control. Canada created a private nonprofit organization to manage its air traffic. Our Federal Aviation Administration is poorly funded and has no idea how to innovate. Let's be more like Canada, eh? Shut it down!"

On a roll, the sweat poured down Cole's face, but he didn't care. He didn't wipe it away. Some members of the audience were standing up now and shouting "Shut it down!" with him, transforming the auditorium into an evangelical experience. The Department of Commerce, Federal Transit Administration, Federal Highway Administration, Department of Transportation, and Amtrak were all on his chopping block. Cole decided to wind down his speech. He could talk about this stuff forever.

"Assistance for needy families, children's health insurance, and Head Start can all be provided by the states or funded privately. We don't need the federal government to do these things."

By now, every single person in the audience was standing and applauding and cheering. The crowd flowed out into the aisles. He took a deep breath. He finally wiped his forehead with a hand towel and placed it back down on the podium.

"The federal government can slash the deficit if it has the will to do so." He paused. "If it has the will to do so." He repeated. "This is what's at stake in this election. A feminist Socialist who hasn't done much in the Senate is trying to unseat President Richard Ellison, a strong, conservative Republican and a good family man. Don't be fooled by Whitney's new moderate attitude. Once she's elected, she'll pull out Karl Marx's Communist Manifesto and turn America into twentieth-century Russia. If you don't believe me, folks, go back and read the papers she wrote in college. You'll receive a Socialist education. For your convenience, we've posted all of her undergraduate and graduate papers on my website, www.theconservativevoiceonline.com.

"Now, Richard Ellison is a man we can trust. Didn't he re-enact 'Don't Ask, Don't Tell, Don't Worry?' He's done more for America's families than any president since the late, great, President Ronald Reagan. Have you seen Whitney's family? She lives in Washington, DC. Her husband lives in Missouri in a very friendly neighborhood. What kind of marriage is that? Do we want a long-distance, open marriage in the White House? What kind of example does that set for our kids? Also, if she's that hands-off in representing her constituents in Missouri, what will happen if she becomes the president of the good ol' US of A?

"Whitney Fairchild is untested, untried, and unfit to be our president.

"I want my posse to get out and vote and get your neighbors out to vote. We can't leave this election to chance. We can't allow the Commiecrats back in office. Your children's future depends on it. Help me to re-elect President Richard Ellison, who has the will to give our children a future of prosperity and freedom rather than one of paying off the previous generations' debts.

"Thank you for having me tonight. God bless you and God bless the United States of America."

The applause was deafening.

Cole had given it his best shot. The rest was up to Ellison.

CHAPTER SIXTY-THREE

St. Louis, Missouri

YESTERDAY, WHITNEY, TED, and the road show flew across the country for last-minute campaigning, chasing the sun from east to west. She arrived home from California late last night. It had been a while since Whitney had been home. Her real home. She rose at six a.m., as if it were any other day. Grayson slept.

She pumped away at the elliptical machine in their home gym in St. Louis while watching a simulated bike ride through the mountains on a massive projection screen. She pushed herself hard, not sure when she would be able to work out again. Forty minutes later, she went back to their bedroom.

She watched him sleep for a few moments.

After learning about the affair five months ago, she still felt like crying every time she looked at him. She had thought long and hard about him, their marriage, his mistake. When she transcended the most difficult part of the pain, she thought about the role she had played in what happened. She hadn't been there for him or her family. In some ways, she still wasn't. She wasn't excusing what he did, but she believed she had to own her part of it. Grayson was human, and that's why she ultimately decided to forgive him.

She woke him. Head on the pillow, his hair grazing his forehead, he gazed up at her and smiled. The same smile that made her fall in love with him all those years ago.

He searched her eyes. "Is it time?"

"It's time."

"Okay, I'll get up."

He pushed up on one elbow, and she took his face in her hands. "Let's take a shower."

"Together?"

She nodded. They hadn't made love since she found out.

"Are you sure?" Grayson asked. "Do we have time?"

Whitney took his hand and helped him to his feet.

✺

Afterward, she walked down the hall to the children's rooms. Emma's room was white: white bed, white dresser, white walls. Posters of the singers Adele and Bruno Mars adorned her walls. Whitney touched her daughter's shoulder.

"Are you ready?"

Emma sprang up and gave her mother a hug. "I love you, Momma. I'm so proud of you."

Whitney, surprised at her own tears, hugged her back, tight.

She didn't go into Chandler's room. When he turned fourteen, his room began to take on a locker-room odor that nauseated her. She knocked several times, before he grumbled, "I'm up!"

"Are you ready?"

"I will be."

She went back to her bedroom. She sat in front of her vanity mirror in the sitting area adjacent to the bathroom to apply her makeup—not too much—before moving to her dressing room to put on a new suit designed by the up-and-coming female American designer Ashley Smith. She admired herself in the full-length standalone mirror and nodded.

Grayson sat on the off-white upholstered chestnut bench at the foot of the bed. Dressed in a dark blue three-piece suit, white shirt with a spread collar, light blue tie, and polished black dress shoes, he had his coat draped over one arm. He held a fedora hat in his other hand. She loved fedora hats.

"You look nice."

He gave her a smile, tinged with regret. "And you look beautiful, darling. Oh, and presidential."

She peered down at her suit in the same shade of blue as his, wiping away imaginary lint. She took a deep breath, exhaled, and held out her hand. "I'm ready."

He rose and took her hand in his strong, firm one. He squeezed. It did not give her the feeling of comfort, of safety, that it once did. Forgiving and forgetting were two different things.

They walked down the stairs. At the bottom, her children, dressed up, smiled as they looked up at their parents. Sarah, her body woman, and a few other members of her staff and Secret Service agents waited with them. As she reached the bottom stair, Josh McPherson, her lead Secret Service agent, slid in beside her.

"Are you ready, ma'am?"

She nodded.

He brought his wrist to his mouth. "Twilight is ready to move."

"Twilight?"

"I noticed that you read young-adult novels when you think no one is around."

Whitney laughed. "I like it."

Whitney and Grayson stepped onto the porch. A large crowd had assembled beyond the wrought-iron gate of their front yard. They gave each other much-practiced smiles, as the cameras clicked, turned to the crowd and waved.

It was a beautiful, crisp Tuesday in November.

Election Day had arrived.

❀

Whitney turned to her husband. "I forgot something."

She came out a few minutes later carrying a box.

Grayson shook his head, mystified. "Sweetie, what are you doing? Do you need some help with that?"

To Josh, she said, "Come with me. And bring some of your friends."

"Where are you going?" Grayson asked.

As Whitney headed out the gate enveloped by Secret Service agents, the crowd parted and then followed behind her. She strode to the front door of the house and knocked. A minute later, her neighbor answered the door. Although it had been two years since Whitney had seen her, the woman had aged ten. *That's what being hounded by the paparazzi will do to you.* When once Whitney regarded her as Midwestern cute, now she only looked plain.

The neighbor peered around Whitney at the large men in suits and sunglasses and the crowd beyond. She shrank away from Whitney's gaze. "What do you want?"

"You left these dishes at my house. Your services are no longer required."

❀

Standing with her hands on the railing, craving a cigar, Whitney admired the spectacular view from the luxury suite's balcony at the Ritz Carlton in Clayton, a suburb of St. Louis. She welcomed the cool night air on her face after being surrounded by people all day. She and Grayson had voted early in the morning and spent the rest of the day crisscrossing the state, shaking hands at as many polling places as possible.

Competing with the election coverage on television and social media, was Whitney's visit to her neighbor. Not only the television cameras, but many of the people in the crowd caught the exchange on video for posterity. #NeighborBoom was the number-one trending topic on Twitter for most of the day.

She drifted back into the living room. Ted, Landon, Grayson, Sarah, vice presidential candidate Xavi Fernandez and his family, friends, and others sat or stood near the television, their eyes fixed on the electoral map on the screen.

The returns had started to come in.

Maine, New Hampshire, New York, and all the northeastern states had gone to her. Georgia, South Carolina, Alabama, and the rest of the Southern states went to Ellison. No surprises, yet.

They split two of the battleground states. Ellison won North Carolina. She smiled to herself. She had eaten all that barbecue and potato salad for nothing.

Whitney took Virginia.

Thank you, high school kids.

The Midwestern states started coming in for the president: Nebraska, Kansas, Oklahoma, and—no surprise—Texas with its thirty-eight electoral votes. She picked up the key states of Michigan and, of course, her home state, Missouri.

The lead changed hands all night. And, then, she won Ohio.

As Ohio goes, so does the nation. She turned and gazed into Grayson's eyes.

Are we really going to do this?

He patted her hand, but didn't say a word.

They had never discussed what they were going to do if she won the presidency. Would he relinquish the CEO position to one of his brothers? Would he take a leave of absence? Or would he continue to work? Had a president ever had a long-distance marriage? Not in recent history. She had not wanted to jinx her chances by speaking to him about it.

A couple of her staffers shushed the others.

Someone turned the volume up on the television.

Blaine Jones, who had moderated the presidential debate, anchored the election coverage for CNN. He stared into the camera, and Breaking Results flashed at the bottom of the screen. A picture of Whitney popped up next to a picture of Florida. A big, blue check mark next to her face.

"This just in, CNN is now projecting that the state of Florida will go to Senator Whitney Fairchild."

The gathering in the room erupted in cheers. With the explosion of

Florida's population over the past sixty-five years, its importance in presidential elections had grown. The sunshine state not only had the third-largest number of electoral votes, but also its diverse population represented a microcosm of the United States. Whitney was glad Florida now had its voting act together. The people should decide elections, not the Supreme Court.

She eyed Xavi Fernandez, the governor of Florida, from across the room, and nodded her thanks. He smiled and raised his glass of champagne to her. Adding him to the ticket had paid off, but she wondered at what cost. He wanted to be president. Now. Not eight years from now. She would need to watch her back.

Whitney grabbed Grayson's hand while continuing to stare at the television.

One more.

She needed one more.

California.

Several minutes passed with no results. The staff parked in front of the television became antsy and started moving around the room.

Whitney did not move. The polls for California closed at 10 p.m. Central. The time was now 10:05.

CNN cut from a commercial.

She glanced at the Breaking Results at the bottom of the screen and at Blaine's face. He had a slight twinkle in his eye.

And she knew.

Her face appeared on the screen next to her name. Underneath her picture were the words Elected President. The living room was quiet for the first time that evening, except for the tinkling of ice in someone's glass.

"CNN has projected the states of California, Oregon, Washington, and Hawaii for Senator Whitney Fairchild. Whitney Fairchild, the Democratic Senator from Missouri, will be the next—and the first woman—president of the United States."

All around her, friends and campaign staff jumped up and down while trying to hug each other. Some cried. CNN cut to different cities across the country and around the world where crowds celebrated her victory.

She stared at the screen, hand over her mouth, in shock. Ted had told her the polls indicated it would be close, but she should win. She had found it hard to believe him. She faced Grayson. He smiled and held his arms wide. She fell into them.

He whispered into her hair. "I love you. I have always loved only you. I'm so proud of you, darling."

She clung to him, but did not respond. After a while, the others gathered around her, waiting. She stood to make it easier for them to hug her. She raised both arms.

"We did it!"

Everyone started cheering. She accepted the hugs from her family, staff, and members of the road show who had been with her every step of the way during the last two years. All of them felt like family. And this would be the last night they would all be together. Some of them would join her transition team and the administration. Most would not.

Whitney gazed out the window at the Gateway Arch, a monument to westward expansion and now a milestone in the country's history.

In a few minutes, she would be leaving for the Arch to deliver her acceptance speech as the first female president-elect of the United States of America.

CHAPTER SIXTY-FOUR

Bethesda, Maryland

A COMMENTATOR FOR the Patriot News television network insisted that all the votes weren't in for Ohio. But with the loss of California, it didn't matter. It was over.

Cole Brennan stared in disbelief at the television in his family room.

This did *not* just happen.

His wife, Ashley, patted his back and said soothing words to him he couldn't, wouldn't hear.

The tall, lanky, former cowboy—and soon-to-be former president—stood with his wife and two children on a stage somewhere in Wyoming and spoke about what he had accomplished over the last four years. That this wasn't the end, but only a setback. The beginning of the next phase of the journey. Their party was stronger than ever and its ideals would endure.

The son of a bitch doesn't even appear upset that he lost.

Cole dropped his head into his hands. He felt sick to his stomach. When he looked up, the scene on the television screen changed to the imposing Gateway Arch. The camera cut to Whitney's beaming face.

Cole couldn't take it anymore. He swept the remote off the coffee table and pressed the power button.

He got up and left the room to go to bed without a word to Ashley.

CHAPTER SIXTY-FIVE

St. Louis, Missouri

IT HAD BEEN a long night. I finally got back to the hotel and now sat on the room's couch, my eyes rarely moving from the television screen. A bottle of Ketel One kept me company on the side table. The hotel room was dark except for the light from the TV. The election coverage had been on nonstop; I even had a chance to watch the best parts again: Ohio, Florida, California. I poured a generous portion of vodka into a glass and placed my stockinged feet on the ottoman. As always, I had removed my shoes at the door. I do not like elements from the outside world contaminating my home or anywhere I slept.

An estimated one million people witnessed President-Elect Whitney Fairchild's election speech in person. The place was electric. Spectators in the crowd interviewed by on-the-scene reporters provided a consistent response; they were blessed to be given a once-in-a-lifetime opportunity to witness history.

The network was broadcasting her speech again.

The camera angle descended from the Gateway Arch to a close-up of Whitney's face. Her shoulder-length, light brown hair, with a tint of auburn, stirred in the wind. She gave her speech without notes or a teleprompter. Although she had a speechwriter, it was public knowledge that she wrote the major revisions herself.

Whitney scanned the crowd. "I am standing here, in my home state of Missouri, the geographic center and heart of the United States. Missouri is called the 'Show Me' state for a reason. Our residents are hardworking, independent, stubborn, conservative, and prudent. Like me . . . well, except for the conservative part." She smiled, as the audience laughed.

I did not.

"America was once a great country," the president-elect continued. "A place where you could raise a family, get a good job, enjoy your civil liberties, and retire after many years of service. A country you could be proud of, respected around the world for its leadership, diplomacy, innovation, and economic might."

President-Elect Whitney Fairchild fell silent.

"I promise you. We will make America great once again."

The crowd went wild. After a few seconds, Fairchild held up her hand for silence.

"America will once again be a place where individuals of all faiths, all races, and all walks of life can live together, work together, and use our differences to make us stronger rather than to divide us. We need to stop the discrimination against our Muslim-American brothers and sisters. We should not judge them by the acts of a few terrorists, as all Christians would not want to be judged by the acts of Timothy McVeigh.

"We must find a balance between safety and liberty. A liberty that allows fairness and unity. A former president once said, 'Tyranny is no match for liberty.' For those who want to cause harm to the United States, please listen and understand. We will continue to fight and defeat terrorism wherever we may find it. I warn you not to mistake our diplomacy for weakness.

"The United States, however, is not united now. We are a house divided. Our Pledge of Allegiance asserts we are 'One nation, under God, indivisible.'" She scanned the crowd. "Indivisible." She repeated.

"Today our country is like a large family with a big inheritance and our politicians are its children fighting between themselves to squander our money, our prosperity, and our liberty. So, what can we do about it?" She paused and pointed to the crowd. "We write the politicians out of the will!" She waited for the shouts of agreement to subside. "We need politicians who will work together, not at odds with each other. After this Congress and I take our oaths of office, we must put partisan politics aside and do what is best for this nation. Compromise is not a dirty word, but a necessity to govern." She paused for a few moments to gather herself for her concluding remarks. She scanned the crowd again and smiled.

I loved that smile.

Our next president did not mention me. With less opposition in the media—thanks to me—the divide should close and the country will become great once again.

Whitney continued. "During a campaign, politicians talk about everything they are going to do on 'day one.' But there are not enough hours in one day to resolve all the problems in this country. Our problems were not created in a day, and they will not be solved in a day. The solutions will take time, and they will not be easy. I remember hearing the stories from my parents about the race riots in the Sixties, and how they chose to be involved and fight for what is right and what is fair, even though their lives would have been much easier if they had stayed silent and lived a peaceful middle-class existence in the suburbs. Like my parents, I refuse to stay silent.

"I stand before you humbled and honored by your faith in me to lead this nation. Yes, we have a lot of work to do, but on this night, let us take a moment to celebrate and rejoice. I believe in this country. I believe in you. We can do this together. God bless you and God bless the United States of America!"

The crowd erupted again. Fireworks went off, lighting up the midnight sky. Everyone was so happy. Some people had tears streaming down their faces. It was as if Jesus Christ himself had been elected our Lord and Savior. I hugged the near-empty glass of vodka to my heart.

Whitney Fairchild summoned her husband and their two handsome grown children next to her behind the transparent, two-inch thick, bulletproof glass. They had their arms around each other's waists and bore huge smiles as they waved to the audience.

Using the remote, I froze the picture.

I walked around the ottoman and stood in front of the television, holding my glass. I traced each of their faces from their foreheads to their noses to their chins. I touched their cheeks. It was not lost on me that I had traced the sign of the cross over each of them.

I started to return to my chair and stopped. I finished my drink.

And I threw the glass at the television screen as hard as I could.

Nothing happened at first. And then a tiny crack formed. The crack made a slow, formal march downward.

I unpaused the screen. Whitney's family continued to wave and smile, now with a jagged line dividing them. How fitting.

Why is no one listening to me? Why am I not being taken seriously? Do they not realize who I am? Why am I not receiving the credit I deserve?

She ignored me. Congress ignored my demands. I must not be doing enough to get their attention. To get her attention.

After the long wave session, the network commentators began analyzing the president-elect's speech. This blather would take hours. The program cut to a commercial. Cole Brennan filled my screen holding his latest book.

That was the last straw.

I turned off the television, poured myself another drink, and walked over to the desk. I settled in the chair and took a sip of my drink, setting the replacement glass next to my laptop as I tapped the space bar. Good thing the hotel provided four glasses.

I leaned back, hands in my lap, closed my eyes, and exhaled a cleansing breath.

I opened my eyes and sat up, staring at the monitor. "Cole Brennan" was already typed into the browser's search bar.

I pushed Enter.

CHAPTER SIXTY-SIX

Washington, DC

SINCE THE SHANE Tallent killing in Seattle, the CONFAB task force had moved to a major-case room at FBI HQ to signify the importance of the case and to accommodate the team's growing number of members. The space resembled a war room, with photographs, maps, sketches, and notations plastering the walls.

Jade faced the team from the front of the room, pictures of each of the known victims of TSK, in life and in death, on the large flat-panel screens behind her. Liz Holder's publicity photo was the latest addition. The agents sat in chairs spread out before her. Ethan stood by the door.

She gave him a slight nod. He nodded in return. His faith in her unwavering. Still.

She held up her hands. "Let's get started."

The room quieted. Jade outlined the security measures taken at Cole Brennan's home and office. Agents posed as employees at his employer, Patriot News.

"What do you have for me?"

Christian waved his hand.

"Using the facial composite, we were able to trace the UNSUB's flight to Seattle. It originated in DC. He flew under the name Michael Brown."

Jade looked at Max, surprised. "This couldn't have anything to do with Ferguson could it?"

Max shrugged. "Who knows at this point? Maybe."

Jade turned back to Christian. "Connecting flight?"

Christian shook his head. "Not as far as we know."

Did the killer live here?

Other agents had minor information to report.

"I have something else," Jade said, nodding to an agent at the back of the room. The lights dimmed. "CNN sent us this iReport." Jade pressed a button on the remote and an image filled the large projection screen beside her. The picture was moving from side to side, as if the person holding the camera had Parkinson's disease or was striving for *The Blair Witch Project* effect. The camera's holder approached a parked car beside a drive-thru menu with a microphone in front of it. The camera turned. Inside the car, a woman with long, blonde hair was facing straight ahead, talking animatedly. As she turned toward the camera, something black filled the screen. A glint of metal flashed in the sunlight. The woman's head fell forward onto the steering wheel. The picture faded.

Jade glanced toward the back and waved her finger for the agent to turn on the lights.

Most of the agents' mouths were open.

"Man, that's sick!" Austin said, shaking his head back and forth.

"Was there audio? Did he send a note?" This from Christian.

"No," Jade said. She let the silence linger for a few moments. "Max?"

Max pushed up his glasses. "The murders are not only accelerating, but he is becoming bolder with each one."

"Do you think Brennan's next?" Austin asked.

"There's no doubt in my mind Cole Brennan is his next potential victim," Max said. "Every victim is more famous than the last." He paused. "But I want you to understand something. This guy won't go out in a blaze of glory, wanting the police to kill him after a standoff. No. He will kill Brennan and expect to get away with it. He believes he is doing the world a favor by eliminating their damaging rhetoric from our political discourse. Once Brennan is dead, his job is done. He wins. Liberals win. The country wins. He'll ride off into the sunset, finally attaining the respect he deserves."

Christian leaned forward to look at him. "So, what you're saying is he may knock off Brennan, go back to his life or leave the country, and we'll never find him."

Max nodded. "That's what I'm saying."

Jade glanced around the room.

"Everyone hang here for a few minutes while I give you your assignments. You may want to go home tonight and give your families a quick kiss, because you may not see them for a while."

The next day, Jade reviewed interview reports from the Holder killing in her office at the Bureau. A witness reported he had been filling up his gas tank across the street from the Starbucks when he saw a man walking away from the scene with what he had described as a knife dripping with blood. She grabbed a photo showing a wide-angle shot of the crime scene and shook her head. Given the distance, a defense attorney would argue the witness wouldn't have been able to tell if the substance was blood or some other liquid—or whether he was holding a knife, for that matter.

Since the knife-wielding man seemed to be headed for the gas station, the witness got into his car and drove away, but not before seeing the man hop into what appeared to be a Ford Focus parked at the Wendy's. He was too far away to see the license plate number. After seeing the iReport of the killing on the news, the witness decided to perform his civic duty and report what he saw despite, he said, his feelings about the victim.

The Focus was traced to a Dollar Rent-A-Car located at the Westchester County airport. The car was rented by Eddie Cullen, who flew from DC on a direct flight from National Airport. Jade had sent a team of agents to interview the ticket agents and flight attendants for Cullen's flight and contacted the FBI New York Division to cover the rental car agency.

She presumed the name used for the Seattle flight, Michael Brown, and the name Eddie Cullen, were aliases. What was their significance? Jade racked her brain, but came up empty.

She set the reports aside and brought up some liberal blog sites. She had narrowed down the group of bloggers to ten. Some of them worked at MSNBC. Emulating the talking heads on television or online was easy enough. *We've become a society of talking points.*

A few hours later, Jade journeyed to the break room to refill her coffee. The sludge at the bottom of the pot looked uninviting and undrinkable. She poured the liquid to the brim of her cup and took a sip. *Nasty.*

She returned to her office, full cup in hand, and surveyed the organized stacks of paper on her desk. She kept TSK's manifesto on the corner of it, always within arm's reach. As she sat down, the document fell from the desk. Jade reacted without thinking and caught it without spilling her coffee. She smiled at her athleticism.

I've still got it.

She set the cup down and opened the manifesto to where her thumb held it. It was at the page of the drawing she had noticed before. Like before, she traced the caricature of congressmen and congresswomen standing on the Capitol Hill steps.

Her finger stopped.

Her pulse quickened. She had seen this drawing style before.

She called the main number for Chattenham College. After several transfers, someone answered, "WCCO."

"This is Special Agent Jade Harrington with the FBI. I visited your radio station five months ago and there was a mural on the station wall. Do you know who drew it?"

"No."

Jade waited for the person to continue. When he didn't, she snapped, "Can you find out?"

"Yeah. Hold on."

The student on the other end dropped the receiver without bothering to put her on hold. Jade monitored her breathing to give her something to do while she waited. In, out. In, out. After several excruciating minutes, the receiver was picked up.

"Ma'am?"

Jade exhaled a breath she didn't realize she was holding. *When did I become a ma'am?* "Yes, I'm here."

"His name was Hewitt. Caleb Hewitt."

"Thanks." Jade hung up.

Caleb Hewitt. The "C" in Kyle Williams's journal?

❋

Jade didn't think she would ever visit Chattenham, Pennsylvania again in her lifetime.

Six hours had passed since she'd heard the name Caleb Hewitt for the first time, and now she and Max sat on a 1960s sofa covered in plastic in Hewitt's parents' living room. She wondered if Mrs. Hewitt knew this sofa was in style again. The Hewitts sat across from them on a matching sofa. Christian stood, arms crossed, near the window behind Jade.

Caleb no longer lived here.

After pleasantries and making the Hewitts feel at ease the FBI was in their home, Jade started the interview.

"When was the last time you saw your son?"

Mrs. Hewitt clasped her hands in her lap. She opened her mouth to answer, but closed it.

Mr. Hewitt had his arm around his wife, but not in a protective or comforting way. More as if he were playing a role in a performance.

"He left home about ten years ago," the father said. "After he graduated from college. We haven't seen or heard from him since."

Jade tried to hide her surprise. "Why?"

The mother examined her hands.

The father shrugged. "We don't know."

"What do you do, Mrs. Hewitt?"

"I'm the dean of the college."

Jade knew this. She had researched the Hewitts before she left DC. She turned to Mr. Hewitt.

"I'm a professor at the college," he said.

"He spends most of his time at the lab," Mrs. Hewitt added.

Mr. Hewitt glanced at his wife. His eyes narrowed and his jaw clenched. You didn't need to spend much time with this couple to realize that his time in the lab was a constant source of irritation in their marriage.

"I'm a scientist," Mr. Hewitt explained to Jade.

"Let's talk about Caleb."

The couple exchanged glances, but said nothing.

"What did he major in?"

"Philosophy." This from the husband.

"Did he participate in any extracurricular activities? Sports? Clubs?"

"The college radio station."

"Go on. What did he do there?"

"He was a disc jockey or commentator, whatever you call them. He had a weekly show in which he talked about politics."

"I saw a picture of the students who worked at the radio station. Your son wasn't in the photograph."

Mr. Hewitt glanced at his wife again. "That's because he . . . quit. After Hurricane Katrina and the federal government's reaction to the crisis, he sort of . . . lost it . . . on the air."

Caleb's mother looked up from her hands. "He was asked to leave the station."

No one spoke. The house was quiet, eerie. Jade wondered why Dante hadn't discovered all this during his investigation of the college yearbook. She knew the answer to her own question. He hadn't conducted an investigation. *Did he purposefully set her up for failure?*

Max spoke for the first time in his quiet way. "Mrs. Hewitt, do you know where your son is now?"

The woman's back straightened for the first time. "No, I don't."

✽

Jade stood and headed for the fireplace toward her left instead of the archway leading to the foyer on her right. Numerous pictures of a smiling, blond boy with a Beatles haircut dotted the mantle and a side table.

She picked one up and turned to Mrs. Hewitt. "Caleb seemed to be a happy boy."

For a brief, fleeting second, Mrs. Hewitt's eyes lit up. The Hewitts shared another look. Mrs. Hewitt wrung her hands. She opened her mouth to say something but nothing came out.

Mr. Hewitt hesitated, and said, "That's not Caleb."

"Oh?"

"That's our older son, James."

"Where is he now?"

"He . . . uh . . . died. When he was thirteen. A bicycle accident."

Jade replaced the frame on the mantel.

"Do you have any pictures of Caleb?"

Mrs. Hewitt nodded toward the pictures. "Such a happy boy, wasn't he? And he was smart and talented. An excellent athlete."

"What about Caleb, Mrs. Hewitt?" Max asked.

"Caleb was smart, too," Mrs. Hewitt said, "but he was quiet. Kept to himself. Spent a lot of time alone in his room. He didn't like sports much. He'd rather listen to the news." She gave Jade a feeble smile. "He was always . . . different."

Christian straightened from where he had been leaning against the window frame. "May we see his room?"

"You may," Mrs. Hewitt said, "but you won't find anything. I turned it into an office as soon as he left. My home office."

To prevent herself from pacing, Jade returned to the sofa and sat down. At her full height, she could be intimidating.

"Mrs. Hewitt, do you have any photographs of Caleb?"

The woman inspected her hands again. "I may. I'll need to check in the basement."

Jade stared into her eyes. "We'll wait."

✽

Mrs. Hewitt returned with a photograph of Caleb with four other boys and two girls. The boys wore ill-fitting business suits, the girls, shirts and skirts.

Caleb stood at the end. Long blond hair, a darker shade than his older brother's, leaning away from the others. Caleb appeared to be about fourteen.

This Career Day photograph was the most recent one Mrs. Hewitt had of her younger son.

The agents said good-bye to the Hewitts and walked toward their car parallel parked on the tree-lined street.

"Did you see how the mother's eyes lit up when she talked about her other son, James?" Christian said in a low voice.

"She couldn't wait to turn Caleb's room into an office for herself," Max added.

Jade pulled on the handle of the front door on the passenger side and looked across the top of the car at them.

"No wonder Caleb left and never came back."

CHAPTER SIXTY-SEVEN

Washington, DC

JADE SPENT THE next afternoon at the Bureau entering Christian's notes from the interview with the Hewitts into the database. She finished polishing off an Italiano sandwich from the Cosi across the street. At noon, swarms of agents left HQ for lunch at the many surrounding restaurants like kids sprinting out of an elementary school for recess. She avoided the rush by eating late.

She had given the photograph of Caleb Hewitt to Pat to analyze against the millions of faces kept on file and on the Internet. A nose, the width between the eyes, the chin, any aspect of the face could be matched and lead them to the suspect. Nothing had come back, yet. She also hadn't received any confirmed hits on the facial composite of the UNSUB.

Michael Brown.

Michael Brown, the name the UNSUB flew under from DC to Seattle.

Mrs. Hewitt had said Caleb had freaked out at the federal government's response to Hurricane Katrina. The person in charge of that operation worked for the Emergency Preparedness and Response division of Homeland Security. His name was Michael Brown.

Coincidence?

Jade didn't believe in coincidences.

She stood, stretched, and paced her office before sitting back down again. Sometimes, when she wasn't making progress with a case, she started from the beginning. Jade pulled out a folder from the bottom of the stack containing the emails from TSK. She read the first one and leaned back in her chair.

Something about the first email bothered her. *What was it?*

She closed her eyes.

Something involving Zoe. She thought back to the time when she had been working at home and Zoe dropped by with dinner. They had talked about the Fairness Doctrine and the haves and have-nots. Zoe mentioned the online chat room and how its members discussed the email from TSK.

Something about that remark.

And it came to her.

Zoe's group had been discussing the email *before* it was released to the public.

She grabbed her cell phone, touched a button, and stood.

"Hey, you. Long time, no—"

"The guy in the chat room . . . what was his name?"

"You're not going to bother to say 'hello?'"

"Zoe, I don't have time. The guy."

"Which guy?"

"We were at my house. The chat room. Where you talk with like-minded individuals. You told me once about a guy in that room. You said he was intense. We talked about the TSK email. What was his name?"

"Oh. Him. He uses the name Oedipus."

"But what's his real name?"

"I don't remember. Hold on, hold on. You're making me nervous. Let me think."

Jade tightened the grip on her phone.

After a while, Zoe said, "Caleb. His real name is Caleb. I'm not supposed to know that, but he let it slip one—"

Jade hung up.

❈

She put out an APB for Caleb Hewitt.

While waiting and without anything better to do, she reached over to a stack on her desk to pick up another report. Reading was more productive than pacing. The phone rang.

"Harrington."

Static. "Jade, it's Austin."

"What's up?"

"I may have something."

She sat up at the excitement in his voice. "What is it?"

More static.

"From the . . . three identical . . . voice—"

"What? You're breaking up. What about the three identical voices? Austin, are you there?"

"I'm going to move." He said nothing for thirty seconds. "Can you hear me—?"

The line went dead.

Jade speed-dialed Austin's number. The phone rang and rang and rang. She disconnected and tried again. And again.

Her calls kept going to his voicemail.

She tossed the phone on her desk and sat back hard. She got up and started to pace and waited for Austin to call her back.

❋

Jade placed her hand on the door handle.

Christian, a step behind her, said, "Where's Austin?"

"Not sure. He called me earlier and said he may have something. I haven't heard from him since. I've been trying to reach him all afternoon."

They walked in. Jade had had a liberal blogger named Evan Stevens brought in for questioning. Even though Caleb Hewitt was now the prime suspect, she decided not to cancel the interview.

Inside, sat a man, his posture excellent. He wore jeans and a button-down, black collared shirt. His hair was medium length and styled with gel, his short beard trimmed to perfection. His lawyer sat next to him, bent over a legal pad. Although the lawyer was in a suit, Evan Stevens appeared the better dressed of the two.

Jade went through the preliminaries of an interrogation.

"Tell me about your blogs."

"Have you read them?"

Jade didn't answer.

"What's there to tell? I write about injustice. Unfairness. Inequality."

"Is Evan Stevens your given name?"

"Yes."

She threw TSK's manifesto on the table. The document landed with a thud. Evan jumped.

"Did you write this?"

Evan leaned forward, peered at the cover. "No." He shifted his eyes to his lawyer and back at Jade, his eyes boring into hers. "I discuss ideas. I don't need to kill anyone to get my point across."

"Your writing style is similar."

"A lot of people believe in an equitable and tolerant society."

Jade hesitated. This wasn't going well. She wished she could see Max's face through the interrogation window. She was wasting her time.

A knock on the door. Her boss, Ethan Lawson, leaned his head around the door frame.

What was he doing here?

"I need to talk to you," Ethan said. "Both of you."

Jade and Christian glanced at each other, and followed him out.

From behind her, Evan asked, "What about me?"

"I'll be back," Jade said, over her shoulder and shut the door.

Max and Pat were standing in the hallway.

"Ethan, I'm busy. What's up?"

The somberness on Ethan's face surprised her. She had never seen this expression on his face before.

"What happened?" Jade asked. "Another killing?"

He spun his wedding ring. Once. Twice. "Yes."

"Dammit!" Jade slapped the wall. "Brennan?"

"No," he said. "It wasn't Brennan."

"No? Who else could it be?"

"Jade," Ethan said, placing his hands on her shoulders. His eyes searched hers. "It was Austin."

A knot started to form in her stomach. "What about Austin?"

"He's dead, Jade."

Her legs failed her. She sagged against the wall, as if someone had punched her. Christian's strong hand gripped the back of her upper arm holding her up.

Jade took two dribbles to the right, stopped on a dime, and went into her fluid shooting motion. The ball swished through the basket eighteen feet away, nothing but net.

Ordinarily, there was no sweeter sound.

Austin had discovered something and decided to check out his own lead. She still didn't know what he had found out.

His body was found by a couple of kids on an outdoor basketball court in Springfield, Virginia. Austin had stab wounds on the right side of his body. His tongue was left intact.

Austin wasn't a talk-show host.

After the crime-scene technicians had finished yesterday, she pushed her way through two agents as she used to bust through double picks during her basketball career. Despite the protests, she cradled Austin's head in her lap. Surrounded by agents, police officers, techs, photographers, and reporters, she held her rookie agent. *Her* rookie agent. She gazed at him. He appeared peaceful. She took in the freckles from the bridge of his nose to his cheeks.

A note was pinned to the lapel on his suit jacket.

Dear Special Agent Jade Harrington,

I'm sorry about this. It was an accident. He was in the wrong place at the wrong time. He seemed like a nice kid. My battle is not with him. Or you.

I have a job to do. Let me do it.

Your Friend,

TSK

P.S. I thought this would be an appropriate place to leave him.

After slicing through the net, the ball hit the ground and spun back toward her. The sign of an excellent shooter was one who didn't need a rebounder. She dribbled back to her original spot and took the same shot going to her left. She shot like a machine for a half an hour. She rarely missed.

She continued to shoot and think about Austin. How he balked at the beginning of his assignment to listen to the radio broadcasts. How he didn't quit. His passion. His enthusiasm. How his freckles seemed to multiply when he became excited.

No one had protected her when she was a kid. And, now, she had failed to protect Austin. She should have tried harder to call him back.

She shot an air ball.

The ball sailed out of bounds and rolled to a stop under a tree.

She thought about LaKeisha, the middle-school basketball player she had coached last year. LaKeisha told her life was hard, but with Jade she felt safe.

Jade sank slowly, ignoring the pain as her knees hit the asphalt. She looked up to the sky searching for a God she never thought much about and yelled.

"Why?"

After several minutes and hearing no answer from above, she started to cry. And cry. Her head fell to the ground with the weight of her tears.

She didn't know how long she lay there, but eventually felt a hand of comfort and strength on her shoulder. She looked up, expecting to see either Max or Christian.

"He was a good kid," Dante said.

Part III

Arlington, Virginia

"HOW LONG WERE you standing there?"

"A while."

Jade never wanted anyone to see her cry. Ever. Especially Dante. She shifted in her seat, uncomfortable.

"My father played professional basketball," he said.

Jade took a sip of her latte and swallowed. "I know who your father is."

Marco Carlucci was a long-time professional Italian basketball player who spent his twilight years in the NBA.

"You have no idea what it was like."

Jade glanced around the near-empty coffee shop. "Tell me."

"I was tall," Dante said, a bashful, charming smile spread across his face, "and I was awful. My dad put a ball in my hands when I was three years old. I couldn't hang on to it to save my life. I was so uncoordinated. I thought it would kill my father." He sipped his espresso. "Later, I tried soccer. To placate him." He laughed. "I couldn't play that either."

Jade sipped her latte, watching him over the rim of her cup.

"My whole life. Everyone told me how great my dad was." He pitched his voice an octave higher. "'Are you going to be a baller like your dad?' I got so sick of being compared to him. I still am. I joined the FBI over his objections. I did pretty well at the Academy. My first few years here were going well. I thought I would be promoted." He looked across at her. "And then you came along. You were great. You are great. At everything. People talk about you all the time. You have no clue how you come across. Like you're better than us. Better than me." He looked down into his cup. "You remind me of him."

They each sipped their coffee, lost in their own thoughts.

"There's more to life than basketball," Jade said. "No matter how great of an athlete you are, it ends someday, and most of your life is spent doing something else." She set her cup down. "What's your passion? Outside of work."

He gave her an embarrassed smile. "Cooking."

"Italian?"

A shake of the head. "French."

"I read in a book once," Jade said, "that athletes grow up later in life than everyone else."

"That makes two of us."

They eyed each other, before they both burst out laughing.

※

A few days after Austin's funeral, Jade sat at her desk at the Bureau staring—unseeing—at the 302 form for the aborted Evan Stevens interview. She dropped the document on her desk. She couldn't concentrate. Besides, she had a hard time deciphering Christian's handwriting on a good day.

The funeral had been a solemn affair with over a thousand people in attendance: FBI agents, police officers from Maryland, DC, and Virginia, Austin's family, as well as President-Elect Whitney Fairchild. She exchanged nods with Fairchild, but did not have a chance to speak with her.

When Jade's turn came to offer condolences to Austin's mother, Jade had trouble looking her in the eye. What do you say to a mother who has to bury her youngest son a week before Thanksgiving?

While she mourned her agent, TSK always seemed to be one step ahead of them. Jade was sick of waiting and reacting.

Enough!

She typed "Cole Brennan" into her browser. Millions of hits came up. She did a quick scan of his Wikipedia page. Most of the information she already knew. She clicked the link for his radio show's website. No, she didn't want to order his latest book or a t-shirt, thank you very much. After rifling through a few pages, she stopped at a link midway down the page of Upcoming Events. It read American Values Conference.

She clicked on the link and the screen filled with the conference's home page. The annual American Values Conference brought together conservative luminaries from across the country. The conference promised speeches on traditional family values, pro-life, gun rights, and protecting Americans from their government and illegal immigrants.

Cole Brennan was the keynote speaker.

Jade's pulse accelerated. She scrolled down to the bottom of the page to find out where and when the conference would take place. Three days from now at The Washington Convention Center.

Here.

What better place for TSK to strike?

✤

The task force gathered in the conference room, but the mood today was different. Earlier, she had met with Christian, Max, and Pat to go over her idea. If they were surprised at Dante's presence in the room now, they didn't show it. She outlined her plan to them, and they went over the logistics.

This time they would be preemptive.

She scanned the room and stopped at the empty chair. Austin's chair. Jade walked over and stood behind it, facing Dante sitting up straight in his chair instead of the usual slouch.

He searched her face, uncertain.

"Welcome back to the task force. I want you to finish what Austin started. Find out why he died."

CHAPTER SIXTY-NINE

Bethesda, Maryland

COLE BRENNAN OPENED the front door to his home. The younger kids ran past him and down the hall toward the family room. He and Ashley and the older kids followed. Everyone, except for Kaitlin and Cole Jr., was stoked; an animated conversation ensued throughout the ride home from the conference. His speech was a big hit, and TSK didn't appear. The younger children didn't realize how many people loved their daddy, outside the Beltway anyway.

Cole Jr. turned on the TV set, as Cole sat on the sofa. Ashley left and returned with cognac. He smiled and held his hand out, accepting the drink. He patted the seat next to him. She laid her head on his shoulder. The family viewed sound bites of his speech on the news.

Cole beamed. "Daddy looks good!"

The doorbell rang.

Cole Jr. left to answer it. A few moments later, he reappeared with one of the FBI agents wearing the regulation blue jacket and sunglasses. Cole let out a breath, relieved. But his relief soon turned to anger. He hated feeling afraid in his own home.

The agent looked at him. "I wanted to make sure everything was okay in here."

"Never better. In fact, if you've got a little time, sit down. I'm on TV."

The agent shook his head. "No, thank you." He did not turn to leave, but instead removed his glasses. He stared out the large window and scanned the room's interior, taking in each of the children. His eyes rested on Ryan. He smiled the indulgent smile that adults tended to give children. Cole's attention drifted back toward the television.

Ryan smiled back at the agent. "Thanks for my soccer ball."

Cole froze. The glass slipped from his hand, as if in slow motion, the thick carpet muffling its landing. The amber liquid spread, seeping into the beige carpet.

The agent whipped a gun out from under his FBI coat. "Everyone freeze. Do not scream or I will start shooting."

Three of the kids started crying. The others appeared confused, not sure whether this was for real or they were being punked on a reality-TV show.

The agent pointed to another couch.

"Kids, I want you to go sit over there." He jerked his head at Ashley. "You, too."

"I'm not leaving my husband," Ashley said, her tears not masking her resolve.

"Madam, this is between your husband and me. I don't want to hurt you. Your children will need you."

Ashley, puzzled at first, understood. She glanced at Cole. He nodded. She kissed him on the cheek and moved toward her children. She opened her arms and held as many of them as she could.

Cole's initial fear was gone. He was angry. "You come into my house and scare my family—" He started to rise.

The agent waved Cole down with his gun. "Sit down, old man. As always, you talk a good game, but you never *do* anything. I know you. I know everything about you."

"You don't know me. Why don't we go into my office? We can talk in there. Man to man."

"I know this is your favorite room in the house. So, I think I want to sit right here. I have some things to say to you and I wouldn't mind an audience."

CHAPTER SEVENTY

Bethesda, Maryland

CHRISTIAN PARKED THE car at the curb.

Jade glanced at him. "I feel like I need to take a shower."

"Come on, now, it wasn't that bad."

She threw him a look and moved her hand to the door handle. "We don't need waterboarding. Let's force terrorists to listen to Cole Brennan for a few hours. They'll talk."

Christian laughed. They got out and strolled down the street toward the agent in charge standing near a Suburban SUV parked in front of Cole Brennan's house. Christian and Jade had come here to conduct a routine check on the surveillance.

Jade surveyed Brennan's expansive lawn, stopping at the red front door in the distance. She eyed the agent. "Anything?"

The special agent in charge said, "Nah, it's been quiet," he hesitated, "but—"

Christian stepped forward, invading his space. "But what?"

"After the family returned from the conference, an agent told me he was going to check on them. I was on the phone with HQ, not paying attention. I didn't even see who it was. That was twenty minutes ago."

"And he hasn't come back out," Christian said.

The agent shook his head.

Jade gazed up at the red door again. "He's here."

CHAPTER SEVENTY-ONE

Bethesda, Maryland

THE FAKE FBI agent sat in a chair opposite Cole. Legs crossed, his pants were creased in the right places. With one hand, he smoothed a nonexistent wrinkle. The gun rested on his leg, the finger in the trigger, a casual gesture. If not for the weapon, an outside observer would surmise the two of them were having a normal conversation. Cole couldn't ignore the queasiness in his stomach. He shouldn't have goaded this killer into coming into his home and terrorizing his family.

The agent bestowed on him a condescending smile. "Do you believe all the shit that you say?"

"Yes, I do," Cole said. "And watch your language."

The agent raised an eyebrow, surprised. "My language? Do you realize how many hurtful things you say on any given day?"

"It's the truth. If some people find it hurtful, they have the right to listen to another station."

"You talk about circumstances about which you know nothing. You do not understand what it is like to be a minority or a pregnant woman or gay."

Cole laughed, a harsh sound. "And you do?"

"At least, I can empathize with them. Try to put myself in their place. Would you oppose marriage equality if you were gay?"

"Gay marriage has nothing to do with equality. Two people of the same sex shouldn't be together. It's in the Bible. That's just another politically correct term dreamed up by liberals to get public acceptance."

The agent ran his fingers through his hair. "Will you please answer the question?"

"What was the question again?"

"Would you oppose gay marriage if you were gay?"

"But I'm not."

"But what if you were?"

"I wouldn't be."

"So, you think your sexual orientation is a choice."

"Yes."

"And you choose to be heterosexual?"

Cole wanted to wipe that smile off his face. "No! It's what I am!"

The agent considered Cole, disdain written all over his face, as if Cole weren't his intellectual equal.

"You proved my point. Gays do not have a choice, either, and should have the same rights we do."

"Marriage is between a man and a woman."

"I guess if you repeat that often enough, it must be true."

The smugness of this guy wore on Cole's nerves. He couldn't stand these intellectual-elite types, always trying to show off how smart they were. Cole took in the agent's good looks. Something about him seemed familiar. Was he in the business? "Do I know you?"

From the couch, a male voice, which only a couple of years ago was one octave higher, spoke up.

"I don't think there's anything wrong with gay marriage."

Cole forgot about the killer sitting across from him for the moment and flashed a look at his namesake. "What's that, son?"

Cole Jr. regarded him. His hair, longer than it should be, brushed his shoulders.

"Why shouldn't gays be allowed to marry whom they love? How does that hurt you, Dad?"

Cole's emotions, shaken by the presence of a killer in his home, now roiled with the realization his son might be a liberal. Or worse. *Please, God, don't let him be gay.* He shook his head, exasperated. "Please tell me this isn't happening."

The agent laughed at Cole's discomfort.

Cole wanted to kill him.

After a beat, the agent stared up at the ceiling. "Are you willing to die for your country?"

A few of the kids began bawling.

Cole glanced over at his children. At Ashley.

The agent turned toward the kids. "Shut up!"

Cole started to rise. "This is my home. Don't you dare talk—"

The agent waved his gun again for Cole to stay seated. "Answer the question."

"Yes," Cole said. He studied his large hands. "No." He didn't care he was crying in front of his children and his wife or that snot was running over his lips or he was about to plead for his life to a liberal madman. "Man, I just want to be with my family."

The agent leaned forward. He smiled at Cole, his eyes fixed, unblinking. "Then, don't speak."

"What?"

"Don't speak."

"What do you mean? Now? I don't get it."

"I will let you live if you promise to cancel your show and stop writing your incendiary books."

CHAPTER SEVENTY-TWO

Bethesda, Maryland

JADE STOOD WITH the members of CIRG—the FBI's Critical Incident Response Group—as they congregated around a Suburban, an architectural layout of Cole Brennan's home and its surroundings on its hood. After several minutes of quiet discussion, the CIRG team broke off running toward the radio host's house in different choreographed directions. She started to follow.

Christian put a hand on her forearm. "They've got this."

She tensed at his firm touch, ready to argue. This was her case. Her perp. Her agent. This was for Austin. She wanted to be the one to bring this guy down. She glanced at Christian and stared at his hand on her arm. She gave him a crisp nod. He removed his hand.

Another agent handed her a headset so she could listen to the CIRG leader.

She heard nothing for a few minutes. Then, a hushed voice said, "The family is in the great room. I have a visual on our suspect. He's sitting on a chair across from them. Armed. Handgun. They seem to be"—the CIRG leader's voice ringed with amazement—"having a conversation." Silence. More minutes passed. "Brennan appears as if he's trying to stand up. The UNSUB's waving the gun around." Silence. "Our sniper has a clear shot."

Jade didn't hesitate. "Go."

A minute later, breaking glass.

And another shot.

Jade threw her headset on the ground. She, Christian, and the rest of the agents ran toward the back of the house. Jade arrived first. The large bay window overlooking the back yard now had a big, jagged hole in it. Jade jumped from the lawn to the brick patio and through the window, ignoring the shards of glass stuck to her clothing. She took in the situation. Brennan's kids were screaming. Cole Brennan and his wife held one of their daughters, tears streaming down their faces.

Brennan didn't take his eyes off his daughter. "He missed." He was crying. "He missed her by inches."

Ashley peeked up at Jade. "When the window exploded, the man's hand jerked and his gun went off."

Jade crouched next to them. She reached her hand out toward the girl but placed it on her own lap instead. She whispered to no one in particular. "Where did he go?"

Brennan cocked his head to the left but continued to stare at his daughter. "There's a side door off the kitchen. He went that way."

"Radio an ambulance," Jade said to Christian. She sprinted in the direction of the kitchen.

Christian called after her. "Jade, wait!"

The door had been left open. She didn't break stride as she went out the door and back into the night.

✻

For once, Jade was grateful for the big yellow FBI lettering on the back of their jackets. It made following him easier. TSK sprinted toward the woods bordering Cole Brennan's large backyard. Jade figured he had a hundred yards on her.

As she entered the forest, she slowed down, fearful she would sprain an ankle on a tree root or the uneven terrain. She didn't want to risk losing him, though.

The killer didn't slow down. He had been here before.

After what seemed like a mile, the woods gave way to grass and, beyond, the parking lot of a sizable, suburban shopping center.

She was gaining on him.

Signs for Macy's, Nordstrom, and Bloomingdale's were alight in large letters. The shopping center was closed at this time of night. Her suspect sprinted up the outside stairs to the second floor and jumped with ease over the sagging, useless chain at the top of the stairs.

She followed.

She ended up on the wide terrace of a restaurant. Tables, with chairs stacked on them, were pushed against the wall. The commingled aromas of steak, chicken, and fish permeated the air.

He was waiting for her.

He stood in the shadows, leaning against a table, his hands clasped in front of him. He had removed the FBI jacket. It lay on the floor nearby. Dressed in all black, he now wore a balaclava with only his eyes and mouth showing.

"Hello, Jade," said a soft, familiar voice, but she couldn't place it.

Jade said nothing.

After all the long months, thinking about this guy and talking about this guy and visualizing catching this guy, it felt surreal coming face to face with him.

"You are wondering why I did it," he said.

"I know why."

"Oh, you do? Sometimes, there is more to a situation than what meets the eye."

"I'm listening."

"Those conservatives were such horrible human beings."

"Does that mean they had to die?"

He smiled. "Yes . . . and no."

He lifted a Glock 23 in front of him with the barrel pointed up at a ninety-degree angle. FBI-issued. One of theirs. He caught her staring at it.

"A gift," he said, "from Austin."

The blood rushed through her veins. She took a step toward him, gun or no gun.

He held his hand up. "Don't. I don't want to shoot you, but I will."

She stopped.

He paused, and then placed the gun on the table next to him. He strode toward Jade and started circling her.

She still did not move.

"They were despicable creatures and our country is better off without them. You cannot disagree with me on that."

"If I disagreed with their points of view, it wouldn't mean I would want them to die. What about freedom of speech?"

"Ah . . . but what choice did I have? Their vitriol gets worse every year. You cannot debate someone who argues only with emotion, irrationality, or outright lies."

"You can use your vote."

"Yes, but you know as well as I that the Super PACS and corporations control elections today. No"—he tilted his head, a brief thought—"this was the only way. Besides, don't you want a woman president?"

"Not at any cost." She paused. "Is that what this is all about?"

After he completed his 360-degree examination, he stopped in front of her. The Brennan boy was right. He was tall. She continued to stare at the killer.

He crouched into a martial-arts sparring stance.

Jade hid her surprise. *Does he want to fight me?*

His eyes bored into hers. "I like this. Mano y womano. This is how it should be. Come now, Agent Harrington. You have trained and competed in tournaments for all these years. It is time to fight for real."

How did he know? Max's assessment came back to her. *The UNSUB is a planner. He studies his victims' daily patterns and knows when they'll be alone. He has some degree of superior intelligence.*

Why wouldn't he have studied her as well?

She didn't see the round kick coming.

Too late, she lifted her forearm to block it. His foot grazed up her arm and landed on her temple. She stumbled, before dropping to the designer concrete floor, dazed. On instinct, she shot back up on her feet.

She tried to steady her breathing, while calculating if she could draw her weapon before he neutralized her.

She went into her sparring stance.

He smiled again. A hideous smile, made more so by the balaclava. "You are not the only one with martial arts skills. Fifth degree. Jiu-Jitsu."

Her instinct to get off the ground had been correct. Jiu-Jitsu was a grappling martial art.

They circled each other.

He moved in to tackle her. She lifted her leg straight up for an inside crescent kick, bringing it down on his collarbone. In the still of the night, the crack of the bone was audible.

He bent over, holding his shoulder. He gritted his teeth. "Very good."

She stood over him, reaching for her handcuffs.

He shot up, still grabbing his shoulder, and punched her in the nose.

As her head popped back, he tackled her, knocking the wind out of her.

The pressure increased as he straddled her chest with all his weight.

Groggy from the kick and the punch, blood poured from her nose. The killer loomed over her. His face came into focus, tinged with pity.

"I know you're only trying to do the right thing. 'Fidelity, Bravery, Integrity,' and all that. But I'm sorry, Agent Jade Harrington. Despite your athletic exploits, your life will be a footnote in history. A casualty of freedom."

Jade spit out the blood that had seeped into her mouth. She held his eyes with hers. "You've got one thing right. You will be sorry."

He laughed. "I like you. And I love your confidence."

He encircled her neck with his hands, cringing as if he did not like her blood touching his skin. He squeezed.

She couldn't breathe.

Pinpricks of light darted behind her eyelids. Her brain was going to explode. *Where was Christian? The rest of CIRG?*

No one was there for her. Again.

Darkness started to descend. She thought of Austin. Zoe. Card. Max. Her parents.

The hand on the side of his body with the broken collarbone struggled to maintain its grip.

A calmness came over her, overriding the strong beating of her heart and her need for oxygen.

She had one chance.

Jade summoned all of her energy and lifted up her chest as high as she could. She slithered her arms through the opening of his legs, clasped her hands together, and brought them down on his injured shoulder.

He screamed in pain as he fell off her.

Jade scrambled away, coughing and holding her throat with one hand. They stared at each other, she clutching her throat, he clutching his shoulder.

They both rose and faced each other.

She relaxed every muscle as Master Ho had taught her. Control. *Trust your training.*

Jade struck him with a left knife-hand strike to his right temple, followed by a right knife-hand strike to his left temple. Before he reacted, her body coiled, twisted, and lifted higher and higher into a spinning hook kick. She hit his left temple again with her left heel, the same kick she had used at her fourth-degree black belt testing a lifetime ago.

The killer staggered backward, his lower back hitting the railing. He tumbled over it, out of sight. Jade clutched the railing with one hand, her throat with the other, and peered down.

The man was sprawled on the asphalt, his body positioned like an old police chalk outline. Light from the tall parking lot pole illuminated the dark liquid seeping from his head.

Jade ran down the stairs and over to the stilled form. She stood over the body. His neck was tilted at an unnatural angle.

He stared up at her, eyes unseeing through the mask.

Christian rushed up to her, followed by other agents, Glocks drawn.

She didn't bother to look at him. "You're late."

Christian said nothing.

Jade touched her nose. It still hurt, but the bleeding had stopped, and it didn't feel broken. She dropped her hand and kneeled next to the body.

She glanced at Christian once more before removing the balaclava.

Staring back at her were the lifeless eyes of Landon Phillips.

CHAPTER SEVENTY-THREE

Crystal City, Virginia

THE NEXT DAY dawned cold and quiet.

Jade and Christian, in their dark blue FBI coats, braced themselves on either side of the front door to an apartment in a high-rise building in Crystal City. She had called earlier and no one had answered.

She knocked.

No answer.

She eyed Christian. He had his game face on. He nodded. She moved to allow Dante to insert a key obtained from the building's management company. Dante opened the door and stepped back as well. Bomb-sniffing dogs entered first to make sure Landon Phillips's apartment wasn't booby-trapped. Members of the Critical Incident Response Group followed the dogs.

After five minutes, "Clear" came from someone inside.

Jade, Christian, and Dante entered. The vast apartment seemed larger with floor-to-ceiling windows on two sides. The sleek, modern furniture appeared brand new.

She peeked into the apartment's sole bedroom off the kitchen. Queen-size bed, a dresser, and a nightstand with a lamp on one side and a pile of books on the other. The walls were devoid of pictures and there was no television. Landon Phillips had not spent much time here.

It was weird being inside his home. His room. That he had never invited her over was not lost on her. She felt sick to her stomach that she allowed him to kiss her.

She checked out the closet, small for an apartment of this size. Pulling on gloves, she knelt and examined the bottom of a pair of hiking boots. They had been cleaned, but she bet the tread would match the shoeprint found at the

Liz Holder crime scene. She searched the rest of the closet, but didn't uncover any obvious evidence. She returned to the living room.

A team of forensic analysts collected fingerprints. One analyst began vacuuming. Another cut out a small section of the carpet to take back to the lab to compare with the trace evidence collected from the crime scenes.

She mentioned the boots to an analyst and walked over to a bookcase bulging with books. She peered closer. The books, arranged in alphabetical order, aligned with the edge of the shelf as in a library. Like hers at home. *OCD.*

That's why we got along so well.

Most of the books were political or philosophical: Hitler, Churchill, Roosevelt, Marx, Machiavelli, Locke, Sartre, Nietzsche. True crime and a few novels, predominately thrillers, also graced the shelves. Jade no longer read thrillers.

She lived them.

She pulled out one of Nietzsche's books, *Thus Spoke Zarathustra.* A hole gaped in the center of the cover, made by a knife or a pair of scissors. Landon probably hadn't recommended this one on Goodreads.

An electric guitar stood on a stand in the corner.

She walked to where Christian and Dante stood by a wall covered with pictures and newspaper articles, presumably of the victims and Landon's exploits.

As she got closer, Dante and Christian exchanged a look before parting for her. Puzzled, she glanced at each of them and then at the wall.

Her lips parted.

The entire wall was a shrine to President-Elect Whitney Fairchild.

At all stages of her life. The newspaper article of her wedding announcement to Grayson Fairchild. The birth of her two children. The announcements for her candidacy for the House, Senate, and presidency. Campaigning.

She looked at Christian, unbelieving, and back to the wall. She leaned forward, scrutinizing a sketch of the president-elect, the likeness unmistakable. The signature was in charcoal. *Landon Phillips.*

Confused, she glanced over her shoulder at Christian. "What the hell?"

Christian, arms crossed in front of his chest, scanned the wall. "Maybe he was in love with his boss. What if these murders were all for her?"

"Like John Hinckley and Jodie Foster?" Dante asked, laughing. "Isn't she a little old for him?"

Christian shrugged his shoulders. "Maybe it's a cougar thing."

"Or to help her get elected," Jade said.

After surveying the wall for several minutes, they ambled over to the corner of the living room set up as an office. Three flat-screen monitors connected to a laptop still nestled in its docking station. A forensic examiner from the FBI's Computer Analysis and Response Team worked on the laptop.

Dante gestured toward the large flat-screen television and the computers. He whistled. "Nice setup."

"I wonder why he didn't take the laptop," Christian said.

The technician tapped the touch pad. "I'm not sure, but lucky for us he didn't." All three monitors sprang to life. The technician glanced back at them. "He also never set up a password. Guess living alone, he thought he didn't need to. Today must be our lucky day."

Jade, Christian, and Dante peered over the technician's shoulder. One screen was filled with numerous Internet pages about Cole Brennan: his politics, his life story, and even an *Architectural Digest* article on his home. On another monitor appeared to be a transcript of a conversation or a chat. The last screen displayed the website for the American Values Conference. *Had Landon been there?*

Jade, Christian, and Dante left to allow the technician to finish his work. As they walked down the hallway toward the elevator, she stopped. "Wait."

She sprinted back to the apartment and straight to the desk. She stared at the screen with the transcript. Something about it nagged at her. She bent closer to read it. The technician got up from the chair without a word so she could sit down.

> ***SusanB:*** *It's another example of big corporations squeezing out the little guy.*
>
> ***PittFan:*** *Fuck yeah. The only welfare that matters is corporate welfare.*
>
> ***Oedipus:*** *'Corporations are people, too, my friend.'*
>
> ***SusanB:*** *<Groan.> Caleb, please don't start with the Mitt Romney quotes.*
>
> ***Oedipus:*** *Please call me Oedipus.*
>
> ***JoanofArc:*** *Did you all catch any of Cole's show tonight? Scary. And I'm not talking about the Talk Show Killer.*
>
> ***PittFan:*** *Cole's a fucking idiot.*
>
> ***AlextheGreat:*** *Guys, we listen to him so that we know what we're up against.*
>
> ***Oedipus:*** *I went to Cole's speech in Philadelphia last month. It was*

horrible. He wants to eliminate all federal agencies and move their functions to the states or privatize them.

SusanB: *The other party isn't going to be happy until all minorities and poor people die or go away. I wouldn't put it past them to be behind the killings.*

JoanofArc: *Why would they do that?*

SusanB: *To gain sympathy to win the election.*

JoanofArc: *That sounds a little farfetched. And we're the ones always blaming them for concocting conspiracy theories.*

PittFan: *The killer deserves a goddamn medal if you ask me.*

AlextheGreat: *Violence isn't the answer, PittFan.*

Oedipus: *Maybe for Cole Brennan it is.*

Jade stopped reading. No question Landon was Oedipus. The cursor blinked next to "Oedipus" at the bottom of the screen. She remembered Zoe was SusanB.

Jade's blood ran cold.

Did Zoe know Caleb was a killer? Did Zoe know Landon was Caleb?

CHAPTER SEVENTY-FOUR

Washington, DC

IN THE SENATE Radio-Television Gallery room in the US Capitol, President-Elect Whitney Fairchild stood alone at the podium. She scanned the audience of reporters. She glanced at her notes and took a deep breath.

"Ladies and gentlemen of the press and everyone else who may be watching, through the efforts of law enforcement in several jurisdictions, but especially our Federal Bureau of Investigation, the perpetrator of the heinous crimes attributed to the TSK killer is now dead.

"Nothing can bring comfort to the families of the victims at this time, but I hope Landon Phillips's death will provide them with at least a sense of justice and some measure of peace. I shall continue to keep these families in my thoughts and prayers and I ask all of you to do the same."

She peered down at the papers on the podium without seeing them. All she wanted to do was cry, but she would not. Female politicians could not cry. A crying male politician displayed his sensitivity. A crying female politician revealed her weakness. A president—even a future president—could not be weak.

"How does it feel knowing that you've been working side by side with a killer for years?" a voice shouted from the back of the room.

"Devastating. Landon was hardworking, intelligent, and loyal. He would be the last person I would think capable of committing these heinous crimes."

"A little too loyal, if you ask me," a reporter commented. This elicited some nervous laughs.

"Why do you think he did it?" cried out another reporter.

"Who knows why? Who knows what demons he faced? Perhaps, in some misguided way, he believed he was helping me or the causes of our party by silencing the opposition, but that is not the way to prevail. We win by the validity and effectiveness of our ideals, ideas, and implementation of our policies. As a country, we win when two sides oppose each other, find common ground, and come up with the best solution.

"I, too, have many questions. Could these senseless deaths have been prevented? Is there any way I could have stopped them? How can we prevent this situation from happening again? But today is not the day for questions. Today is a day for healing. I will not take any more questions. Thank you."

She picked up her notes and walked briskly off the stage, leaving behind an unusually quiet press corps.

CHAPTER SEVENTY-FIVE

Washington, DC

DANTE PUSHED ASIDE piles of transcripts stacked on the conference-room table at the Bureau. He placed a laptop in front of him and connected tiny speakers.

"I backtracked what Austin did. I listened to these recordings for weeks. Listen to this. Here's a call to the victim—Sells—in Pittsburgh." He clicked the play button.

". . . Income and wealth inequality have increased significantly over the last thirty-five years. What do you propose we do about it?" came a voice from the speakers.

He stopped the recording, clicked on another audio file, and pressed play. "Tallent in Seattle."

"Income and wealth inequality have increased significantly over the last thirty-five years. What do you propose we do about it?" said the same voice.

He pressed another. "Holder in New York." The same sentence was asked word for word. Dante pushed stop, an expectant expression on his face.

Jade thought for a moment. "Sounds like the same voice. From the Northeast. Like the witness from Seattle said. I'd say Philadelphia. I had a teammate in college from Philly and she had that same distinct accent."

"Confirmed by Linguistics. It's definitely a Philadelphian dialect and it belongs to Landon Phillips."

Jade looked doubtful. "He didn't sound like that in person."

Dante shrugged. "Maybe he disguised his voice. All three calls originated from Phillips's cell phone number." He hesitated. "This is what Austin discovered. This is why he died."

A quietness descended around the table. Pat stopped clicking. Max stared at the wall. Christian's head was bowed, as if in prayer.

Jade allowed the silence to continue for a few moments. "Good work, Dante. Okay. We're not done. Talk to me about Phillips."

Pat brought up a file on her computer. "Adopted by Addison and Maddy Hewitt when he was a baby, who christened him Caleb. Birth name, birthplace, and birth parents are all still unknown. We're working on it. The Hewitts had a biological son named James, who died at thirteen. He was killed while riding a bicycle on a street near his home. The Hewitts adopted Caleb shortly thereafter. They had no other children."

Max appeared thoughtful. "The Hewitts adopted Caleb to replace their dead child. You saw their living room. No wonder Caleb never measured up."

Jade recalled the photographs of James Hewitt scattered throughout the living room. Not one picture of Caleb. The mother had to hunt around in the basement for a picture of him.

Christian stood and turned his chair around. He placed his forearms on the top of the chair. "Probably didn't help the kid's confidence growing up."

Jade said to Christian, "The house was so quiet, remember? The dead son was still present."

Max pushed up his glasses. "And Caleb was waiting in that house, year after year, for his birth parents to come back for him."

"Sad," Pat said. The way she always hunched over her computer reminded Jade of Schroeder from the old *Peanuts* cartoon hunched over his piano.

Dante leaned his chair back. "Why did he do this? To get his parents' attention?"

"Maybe to hurt them," Max said.

He lied about having a sister. He lied to my face about his mother's bout with cancer, what his parents did for a living. He lied about everything. Except the guitar.

"He probably didn't even like craft beer," she said.

"Craft beer?" Dante asked, bewildered.

"Never mind," Jade said. She shook her head, disgusted with herself. She thought back to the Holder murder. Phillips had called her the day after. She shivered. *What kind of FBI agent am I?*

"Are you all right?" Christian asked.

"Yeah. Just felt a chill."

Pat continued her briefing. "Caleb Hewitt, a bright and gifted child, finished in the top of his class in high school. Family, friends, and neighbors described Hewitt as friendly but quiet. He preferred being alone with his books and his ideas.

"He was also a page for Representative Fairchild when he was a junior in high school," she added. "I wonder if Fairchild remembered him from back then."

"I wonder if his fascination with her started then," Max said. He made a note.

Some people that knew Caleb said the US invasion of Iraq infuriated him and propelled him into politics. He attended Chattenham College, which boasted a history of political activism. He also worked at the college radio station. This morning, Jade had spoken to the station manager during that time who told her Caleb was unhappy when the station launched a conservative program and confirmed that Caleb knew the first known TSK victim, the student conservative talk-show host Kyle Williams.

Cole Brennan was an on-air personality in Philadelphia at the time. The task force presumed Hewitt had listened to Cole's broadcasts, which would have enraged him further.

Caleb Hewitt received his BA in philosophy from Chattenham. He left the school and the town and was never heard from again.

"Over ten years ago," Christian said. "Maybe that's why he lost his accent or pretended to anyway."

A gap existed in Hewitt's history until three years later, when Landon Phillips joined Representative Whitney Fairchild's staff. Gone were the long, shaggy blond locks, jeans, and t-shirts. They were replaced by business suits, contacts that changed his brown eyes to green, nose job, and age-darkened light brown hair. He looked like a different person. Because he was.

The Hewitts had no idea their son worked for the woman who would one day become president. They wouldn't have recognized him anyway.

❋

Evidence proving that Caleb Hewitt, aka Landon Phillips, committed the murders began to come together. Analysts confirmed the carpet fibers found at the Taylor LeBlanc (Baton Rouge) and Shane Tallent (Seattle) scenes matched the carpet in Phillips's apartment. The carpet fibers found in the Pete Paxson (Houston) scene did not match. Pat found out Phillips had moved into his apartment after the Paxson murder. A baseball bat hidden underneath a floorboard in the living room was determined to be the murder weapon of his earlier victims. The bat had been wiped clean, but Forensics matched the blood residue, invisible to the naked eye, to the victims. So far, they hadn't discovered any more victims.

And, of course, Phillips wasn't talking.

"Oh," Dante said, "and the reports came back on the contents of his medicine cabinet. Guess what they found?" He smiled at her. "Rohypnol."

Her brow furrowed. "The date-rape drug used in the LeBlanc killing?"

"Yeah! The drug can also be taken to treat anxiety and insomnia. Phillips suffered from insomnia big time. We're still trying to track down how he got it."

She thought for a long moment. "Nate, the security guard at the college, told me they had had huge problems with date rape at the time Kyle Williams was killed. Dante, call him. Find out if any of the victims can identify Caleb Hewitt. Perhaps, we can provide them some closure."

Dante nodded. No smirk this time.

She squinted her eyes at him, but said nothing.

Christian examined a file. "Living in Crystal City was convenient. He could walk to Reagan National airport."

"Fairchild was traveling so often," Jade said, "she may not have noticed his personal side trips. We need to check out his travel records."

"On it," Pat said.

"By the way," Christian said, "they found detailed dossiers on his computer on all of his victims, plus the top fifty broadcasters in the country."

"Insomnia can be a blessing for a workaholic," Pat said. "He should have worked for us."

Christian continued. "There was also a dossier on Fairchild." He hesitated, and turned to Jade. "And you."

I'll bet.

She thought about their dinner together. Playing basketball. That kiss. She tried not to shiver.

"Also, CART found a list," Christian said.

"Of potential victims?" Max asked.

"No. It appears to be a list of everyone who had ever offended him or hurt him in his life. It's a long list. A lot of names I don't recognize, but his parents are on the list. Some famous people, too, including our future president." He looked at Jade. "And you again."

Because I wouldn't let him walk me back to the office? Because I stopped seeing him? Stop! Focus!

Dante shook his head. "Fairchild? She gave him a great opportunity. He worked for the soon-to-be most powerful person in the world. Crazy."

Jade looked at Max. "What about the shrine to her we found in his apartment?"

Max paused. "Hard to say. Could be an obsession, like Hinckley." He nodded at Dante. "Could be something else. We haven't uncovered any romantic correspondence to her, but it is certainly something we should look into."

"Perhaps, we should ask her," Pat said.

"But what about the Oedipus nickname?" Christian asked. "Was he in love with his mother? And, if so, why didn't he visit her after all this time?"

"I guess this means we need to pay the Hewitts another visit," Jade said. Christian groaned. "Do we have to?"

"We have to go to Chattenham anyway," Jade said. "I made a promise." She hadn't forgotten the promise she made to Kyle Williams's mother to bring home her son's journal and college yearbook.

Christian closed the file he had been reading. "CART found the manifesto and hundreds of articles written by Phillips on his computer. They also found a cryptic note. Almost like a suicide note, but no mention of suicide. He ended it with 'She never mentioned me.' No signature."

Dante dropped his chair on its front two legs. "Probably his mother."

"Or maybe Fairchild," Christian said. "Maybe he was pissed that she didn't thank him in her acceptance speech or something."

"Interesting ideas," Max said. "Worth pursuing."

Jade was still kicking herself that she hadn't matched Phillips's online articles with the manifesto. He had even suggested that she do so. She felt like an idiot.

A silence fell over the group. One by one each head turned to Austin's empty chair.

Dante interrupted the silence. "How's the kid?"

"Kaitlin's going to be fine," Christian said. "She was shaken up, but Brennan says she's almost back to normal. She started questioning his conservative politics again."

Jade joined in the laughter. It felt good.

CHAPTER SEVENTY-SIX

Washington, DC

COLE BRENNAN BEGAN his first broadcast after his encounter with the Talk Show Killer.

He boomed into the microphone. "'Free at last! Free at last! Thank God, Almighty, I'm free at last!' Never thought I would be quoting Martin Luther King. Yes, I'm back, folks. Safe and sound after staring down my would-be murderer. Before I forget, I owe a lot of thanks to a little lady from the FBI."

He wiped his brow. Despite the freezing cold December day, he was sweating. Maybe this attempt on his life was a wake-up call from God to start losing weight.

"Yes, folks, I had a scare, but that won't stop me. No one can stop the truth. And I am the truth! But enough about me. Let's take some calls. Josh from Arkansas. Go!"

"Hey, Cole. Love your show. I'm glad you're all right. Me and the Mrs. have been praying for you, man."

"Thank you, thank you. What's your question?"

"Next month, we'll have our first lady president ever. How will she change the office?"

"Besides painting the Oval Office pink, you mean? Ha! Well, my hope is she and this divided Congress will work on a plan for serious budget deficit reduction, but I also hope Marilyn Monroe comes back to life and asks me to be her fourth husband. Just kidding, Ashley! What I'm saying is, it's not going to happen, Josh. My guess is the first piece of legislation coming out of this Congress and this president will be an amendment for gay marriage and any other kind of marriage you can think of: man and beast; woman and beast; beast and beast; woman, man, and beast. The possibilities are endless!"

"That's scary, man."

"You're telling me. Mark my words . . ." Cole stopped. What was he saying? Sometimes, he lost track. He said the same things over and over without thinking. He thought of his son, Cole Jr. What if he turned out to be gay? Would that change how Cole felt about him? It didn't take long for him to answer the question.

No. He loved his son.

What had Landon Phillips asked him?

Do you believe all the shit that you say?

He had lost his train of thought. He stared at the monitor, trying to locate the caller's name.

"Thanks for calling . . . Josh. Next caller, Michelle from Iowa."

"Thanks for taking my call, Cole. I've been praying for you and your family ever since this tragedy happened. That girl didn't save you. God saved you."

"That may be true, Michelle, but I was there. She helped a lot. How can I help you?"

"What do you think is going to happen to the pro-life movement under this woman's presidency?"

"Good question. The liberals here in Washington are going to try to push back the term in which a woman can kill her baby. The number of abortions will go up. We'll probably see burning bras again as well. Morality will go in the toilet. Soon, we'll be back to LSD and free love, man!"

"Say it isn't so, Cole. What about illegal immigration?"

"The Commiecrats will open up the borders and illegals will scatter all over the place. You'd better learn Spanish, Michelle!" Cole started to continue and then stopped. "Wait a minute . . . ."

He had put his family in jeopardy by his egomania and stubborn hubris. He thought about his daughter, Kaitlin, and her disapproving glances and challenging questions about his politics. Despite them, he loved her for it. He was blessed and grateful she was still alive.

His heart wasn't in it tonight.

Do you believe all the shit that you say?

Cole breathed, a deep, cleansing breath.

"Hold on, folks. I want to say something."

His producer waved at him, indicating a new caller was on the line. Cole ignored him.

"Listen to me. Even though I don't agree with most of her political positions and I fought with all the strength I had to re-elect President Ellison"—he hesitated—"I ask you, my listeners, to come together as Americans and support our new leader, President Whitney Fairchild."

"Cole, you don't mean it."

"Yes, I do." Cole smiled. He hung up on Michelle from Iowa. "Yes, I do. This is Cole Brennan for life, liberty, and the pursuit of happiness. Come back after the break for more of 'The Conservative Voice.'"

Cole pushed a button and took off his headphones. He sat for a moment thinking about what he had said. His listeners and sponsors wouldn't be happy.

For once, Cole Brennan didn't care.

✳

After the show, Cole returned to his office and sank into the comfortable leather executive chair behind his desk.

The phone rang.

Uh, oh . . . it's starting already.

His assistant's voice came through the speakerphone. "Mr. Brennan, the president of the United States is on the line."

Cole, surprised, picked up the handset. He hadn't spoken to Richard Ellison in several weeks. And the president never called him.

"Yes, Mr. President."

"I listened to your broadcast. I'm calling to congratulate you. That took courage."

"Thank you, Mr. President."

"If you move toward the center, you could have greater influence. A positive one for the whole country."

"I'm not sure I want to go *that* far."

"Anyway, I haven't always agreed with your views, but I do want to thank you for your support over the years."

Cole waited for the president's usual snide comment. After a few seconds, he realized none was forthcoming.

"Thank you, sir. What's next for you?"

"Not sure, yet. I do know there's a lot of open land and clear blue skies in my immediate future. What about you?"

"I'm not sure either, but tonight I'll be going to a musical recital." Cole's chest swelled with pride. "My son's in the glee club. He's pretty good."

"That's nice."

The president sounded genuine. Cole again waited for a sarcastic follow-up. None came. "Good luck in Wyoming, sir. I wish you well in private life."

"I'm glad your little girl's okay. Take care of yourself, Cole."

CHAPTER SEVENTY-SEVEN

Washington, DC

JADE SURVEYED THE beer mugs raised in front of her and the faces of the individuals around the table holding them: Ethan, Christian, Dante, Pat, Max, and even Detective Miles Thomas from Baton Rouge. He was in DC to provide testimony to Congress supporting the Fairness Doctrine, the last act of legislation sponsored by Senator—now President-Elect—Whitney Fairchild.

"I want to thank everyone for all of your hard work," Jade said. "I wasn't always easy on you, and there were many nights away from your families, but—"

"Chief, can you hurry up? My arm's getting tired," said Dante. Everyone laughed.

"Anyway, thanks. To the good guys!"

"To the good guys!" the group responded.

The agents and Thomas clinked glasses all around and took long swigs of their beers. They sat at two tables pushed together at a sports bar across the street from the Bureau. The place was empty, a weeknight without the Redskins, Caps, or Wizards playing.

She hesitated and raised her mug again. Her breath caught. "To Austin."

A subdued cheer this time. "To Austin!"

She set her beer down. Everyone became quiet, as they thought about the freckle-faced kid who had grown up with the dream of being an FBI agent.

One mug still hung in the air. She peeked at its holder, surprised. Dante smiled at her. "You did good, Chief."

"Hear, hear!" The group yelled and clinked glasses again.

Two servers arrived and passed out their orders of burgers, wings, and French fries. Jade was glad Zoe couldn't make it. No healthy eating tonight. She eyed the waitress and twirled her finger for another round of beers. Everyone attacked their food.

"Miles," Christian said, in between bites of his burger. "You should have been here, man. She's tough. She kicked Phillips's butt. I'm sorry we got there too late to witness it."

"Oh, yeah? She's not that tough. I couldn't get her to eat alligator when she came to Baton Rouge."

Dante was stunned. "You eat alligator?"

Inevitably, talk turned to the case. They discussed the long hours, the ups and downs, the funny moments.

Christian tapped his fingers against his temple several times. "Did he really think he was going to get away with it? Silencing everyone?"

Max nodded. "Yes, he did."

Jade remained silent. Talking about him still hurt. No one, except Zoe, had found out about her budding relationship with Phillips. She wanted to keep it that way.

Dante leaned back in his chair. "Yeah, Landon Phillips had it all. Great job, great apartment, the women all probably thought he was so smart and handsome." He eyed Christian. "He was a goody-goody like you. Well, except for the fact he killed people."

Christian frowned. "I'm not a goody-goody."

"Yeah, right. Prove it."

Christian hesitated. "Okay." He drained his beer. He grabbed the mug off the serving tray the waitress had brought and downed that one, too. He got up and shot Dante a look, popping his shirt cuffs as he went.

Jade called after him. "Christian, what are you doing? Don't listen to him."

Christian stepped on a chair and onto a table next to theirs. He began to gyrate his hips, unbuttoning his shirt, stripping to his waist. Flexing his pectoral muscles back and forth, he never took his eyes off Dante. The group started hollering and catcalling.

Jade's lips parted, not believing what she was seeing. After a while, she started hollering, catcalling, and laughing with the rest of them.

She called out, "Christian, get down!"

Pat Turner, their surrogate mother, yelled out: "How much do you charge by the hour?"

Christian gyrated once more, raised his arms in victory, bowed, and jumped off the table.

"Where did you learn to do that?" Jade asked him.

Christian shrugged. "I had to pay for college somehow."

Dante threw a dollar at Christian. "You win."

The group broke up into laughter.

Max leaned over to her. "I need to go."

"I'll walk you out."

The frigid night was refreshing after the overpowering scent of fried food and beer.

"Thanks for everything," Jade said.

Max stood before her, his hands in the front pockets of his slacks.

"Like Dante said . . . you've done well, Harrington."

He lied to me. He lied to my face. "I missed so much."

Max peered at her over his glasses.

"Will you ever learn to take a compliment and just say 'thank you?' You just met up with a formidable opponent this time. It won't be your last." He took her chin in his hand. "You're a great FBI agent. One of the best we have. And notice I didn't use the adjective 'female.'"

He leaned in as if to give her a hug, but decided against it. Instead, he gave her chin a soft squeeze and walked away.

"Thank you," she said to his retreating back.

He didn't hear her.

CHAPTER SEVENTY-EIGHT

Washington, DC

JADE WAS ACCUSTOMED to the extremes of the DC-area weather. Last Wednesday, it snowed, accompanied by cold, unbearable temperatures. Today dawned sunny and a record-breaking seventy-five degrees. Global warming had its advantages.

She strode down the sidewalk alongside Independence Avenue in Southwest Washington, DC. She turned left into the entrance of the Martin Luther King Jr. Memorial. She spotted Zoe among the sightseers, staring up at the statue of the great man himself.

Zoe turned at Jade's footsteps. "Hey, you. Great news about the ERA, huh?"

Congress finally repealed the deadline. Soon thereafter, Florida, Virginia, and Missouri ratified the Equal Rights Amendment.

"Yeah. Great news."

"Huh! I thought you would be more excited."

Jade gazed at the statue for a moment. It never failed to give her strength, a sense of purpose. She cocked her head for Zoe to follow her away from the small crowd. They sauntered along the memorial stopping on occasion to read the inscriptions on the granite wall.

When they reached the end of the wall, Zoe stopped and faced her. "What's wrong with you? You're not one to take an afternoon off to go sightseeing."

"It's about Caleb."

Zoe's eyes widened, but she said nothing.

Jade handed her a sheet of paper.

Zoe read the document, her eyes blinking faster as she read. "I can explain."

"Then explain. I have all afternoon."

She examined the sheet again—a transcript of one of their chat conversations—and handed it back to Jade.

"It started out as something to do. I liked talking to other liberals without being careful of what I said. It was fun and totally anonymous." She shook her head. "Or so I thought. We were only chatting." She stared at Jade. "I had no idea he was going to *do* anything."

"You gave me a clue without realizing it," Jade said. "The night you came over to my house, and I was working. You brought dinner. You mentioned the first TSK email before he had sent it to the network."

"He must have told us about it in the chat room. I thought the whole thing was intense, but harmless. Those guys display such bravado. I call them ATNA—All Talk, No Action."

"And it never crossed your mind to talk to me about it? The lead investigator on the case?"

Zoe walked a few paces away. She sighed. "I fucked up. I didn't realize the significance of the email."

"He was killing people, for God's sakes!"

Zoe turned, her eyes blazed, her chest heaving. "Do you think I knew that? Do you think I would continue chatting with him and not tell you? Give me some credit. Fuck!"

Jade peered out over the Tidal Basin at the Thomas Jefferson Memorial. She was silent for several minutes. The nearby sightseers, who had stopped reading the inscriptions to eavesdrop, lost interest.

"Say something," Zoe said. "I hate when you get angry. You shut down. Yell at me or something."

"Did you know Phillips had a website? At aliberaltruth.com? He had about ten thousand followers."

"I didn't realize it was Landon's, but sure, I visited the site." Zoe paused. "I loved his blogs."

Jade whispered, almost to herself. "I read his blogs, too. I should have realized the similarities with the manifesto and the emails."

Zoe closed the distance between them. "It's not your fault. A lot of people missed it. You don't always need to be perfect, you know."

Jade continued to stare across the water, her arms crossed, protecting herself from the cooling late afternoon.

"I remember in college, you slept with one arm across your eyes, always protecting yourself."

Jade smiled. "Still do."

Zoe came and stood in front of Jade. "For a psych major, you have never taken the time to analyze yourself. Is that why you're always trying to solve other people's problems?"

Jade shrugged.

"Do you remember the first time we met?" Zoe asked.

Jade hesitated, and then nodded.

"When I realized you were sitting across the table from me in the campus library, I had to introduce myself. Did you really think my pen stopped working so I had to borrow one of yours? I had thrown it under the table, giving me an excuse to meet you. You introduced yourself as if I didn't know you were the best point guard in Stanford history since Jennifer Azzi."

Jade's face grew hot, embarrassed. She remained silent. She had no idea where this was going.

"Do you know why I did that?"

Jade shook her head, a slow, cautious movement.

"Because I knew underneath that tough-jock exterior, you needed me."

She reached up with her right hand and caressed Jade's cheek. The display of physical affection made Jade uncomfortable. She wasn't the touchy-feely type. Zoe, her beautiful best friend for the last ten years, knew this.

Zoe reached up with her other hand, cradling Jade's face. "I'm sorry. I should've suspected him. And I should have told you."

Before Jade could react, Zoe planted an exaggerated loud kiss on her lips.

Jade wiped her mouth. "Shit!" She cast a glance at the sightseers staring over at them again, amused smiles on their faces. Through clenched teeth, she said, "What're you doing?"

"Begging for forgiveness. You solved your case. Let's go celebrate it and the historic passage of the ERA. I know the perfect place in Dupont Circle."

The White House, Washington, DC

AFTER EIGHT INAUGURAL balls, President Whitney Fairchild stepped into the Oval Office, alone, and kicked off her high heels. *My feet hurt. And, besides, who's going to stop me?* In her stockings, she padded around the room, gazing at the wall paintings. She allowed her hand to trail along the softness of the sofas and chairs as she made her way to the most famous desk in the world, the nineteenth-century *Resolute* desk, a gift from Queen Victoria to President Rutherford B. Hayes in 1880. President John F. Kennedy was the first to use the desk in the Oval Office, as had many of the presidents since. She sat in the presidential chair and placed both hands on the top of the desk.

She thought about the swearing-in ceremony earlier that day at noon on the west steps of the US Capitol, when she tried to keep the dignified smile on her face despite the biting, freezing cold of Washington, DC, in January. The proud faces of her husband, Grayson, her two children, and her parents as they stood by her side. She was grateful to all of them for their support and sacrifices over the years. With her hand gracing the same Bible used in Abraham Lincoln's inauguration in 1861, she scanned the crowd on the Mall, the largest ever to witness the swearing in of a US president.

Next, the drive down Pennsylvania Avenue. The consternation of her advisors and the Secret Service when she and Grayson got out of the bulletproof Lincoln Town Car and walked hand in hand down the street waving to the massive crowd. She had lunch with her former colleagues in the Senate and House and attended meetings and briefings the rest of the afternoon, because the president never had a day off. The amount of information was overwhelming. For all the consideration she'd given it, she still had managed to underestimate the awesome responsibility she had assumed until she read her first President's Daily Brief.

She thought again of the balls earlier that evening and hoped she didn't appear too foolish dancing. She had practiced during the last few weeks, but it had been years since she and Grayson had gone dancing. She cringed now, thinking about some of their more awkward dance moves.

She had run into Blake Haynes at one of the balls. Her interview with him last week had been such a success that MSNBC had given him his own show. Needless to say, he was happy to see her. FOW indeed.

Leaning back in her—*her!*—chair, she reflected on the campaign and all the people she had talked to, the hands she had shaken, the late-night strategy sessions, and trying to find healthy food in some of the towns she had visited.

She thought of Ted and everyone on her legislative and campaign staffs. She remembered the scandals with her husband's company and his mistake with their neighbor. She was fortunate these scandals had not derailed her campaign. The other side had tried and failed. She let out a contented sigh. She was blessed.

When she and Grayson toasted, "To us!" with champagne in the private residence earlier in the evening, it felt like a new beginning. Not only for her term as president, but for their relationship as well.

An envelope addressed to her was positioned in the center of the desk. She recognized Richard Ellison's large, sloping scrawl. She opened it.

Dear Whitney,

By the time you read this, you will be president. Although our interactions going forward will be few, please know I'm rooting for you.

Respectfully,

Richard

Whitney smiled, touched, even though she knew Reagan had started the tradition with H.W. Every president since had left a note for his successor.

A gift sat on the corner of the desk. It was in the shape of a book. At first, she guessed that it, too, was from the former president, but now remembered it was a gift from Landon. In the confusion of the transition, she had never opened it. She hesitated, wondering whether she should do so now.

Whitney read the note scribbled on the decorative paper. *Please don't open until after the election.*

She opened it.

In her hand, she held a first edition of Louisa May Alcott's *Little Women*. The brown and white cover was well preserved. She flipped through the pages; none seemed to be missing or damaged. The book appeared as if it had never been read. A page of expensive beige parchment paper was tucked inside the front book cover.

Dear Senator,

I'm sure you already own this classic, but this volume is in pristine condition and, I am told, one of a kind. I've enjoyed our reading challenge, and since I'm so far ahead, I wanted to give you a chance to catch up.

Seriously, I want to thank you for the opportunity to work for you and alongside you all these years. Every day has been a joy.

I am proud of what we've accomplished and look forward to what we'll accomplish over the next eight years (yes, I said eight!). I know you will win.

I want to have one of our talks after you read this. I believe we'll have much to say to each other.

You have no idea how much I love you.

Your son,

Landon

The End

AFTERWORD

The Equal Rights Amendment was introduced into Congress in 1923, passed both houses in 1972, and was ratified by thirty-five states that same year. It failed to become law by just three states. The amendment has been reintroduced in every Congress since 1982.

J. L. BROWN

RULE OF LAW

A JADE HARRINGTON NOVEL

For Audi.

And for victims of bullying everywhere.

You are not alone.

There is a feeling among the masses generally that something is radically wrong. They are despairing of political action. They say the only thing you do in Washington is to take money from the pockets of the poor and put it into the pockets of the rich. They say that this Government is a conspiracy against the common people to enrich the already rich. I hear such remarks every day.

— Oscar Ameringer, 1932

If people throw stones at you, build something.

— Unknown

Washington, DC – One Month Ago

SHE SHOULD HAVE thrown the letter away.

Or shredded it.

She knelt before the altar of the small, quaint Presbyterian church near the White House. The nave was empty. Easter services had just ended. Her husband, Grayson, and the children waited outside. Lead Secret Service agent, Josh McPherson, stood alone by the entryway at the front of the church.

Although her hands were clasped together and relaxed, her head bowed in supplication, President Whitney Fairchild was not praying.

Instead, she was reading.

The expensive parchment paper, creased horizontally into two sections, lay on the raised carpeted step, worn from her reading it every day since her inauguration two months ago when she had first opened the envelope.

She needn't have bothered.

She had memorized every word.

Dear Senator,

I'm sure you already own this classic, but this volume is in pristine condition and, I am told, one of a kind. I've enjoyed our reading challenge, and since I'm so far ahead, I wanted to give you a chance to catch up.

Seriously, I want to thank you for the opportunity to work for you and alongside you all these years. Every day has been a joy.

I am proud of what we've accomplished and look forward to what we'll accomplish over the next eight years (yes, I said eight!). I know you will win.

I want to have one of our talks after you read this. I believe we'll have much to say to each other.

You have no idea how much I love you.

Your son,

Landon

Despite his sins, she still missed Landon Phillips.

"Mom?"

Whitney started at the sound of her son's voice.

Snatching the letter with reflexes she didn't realize she possessed, she stuffed it back into her purse.

Her son, Chandler, stood beside her, wearing a jacket, shirt, and slacks.

"What are you doing?" he asked.

"Working."

"Working and praying at the same time?"

She rose. "In this job, I do that often."

"Dad sent me in to get you. He's hungry."

She brushed the bangs off his forehead. His face was like looking at a mirror. "Dad, huh?" She looped her arm through his. "Did I tell you how handsome you look today, my favorite son?"

He grinned. "I'm your only son, Mom."

Whitney's smile faltered. "That is true."

They walked down the aisle past the stained-glass windows to the front of the church. As he chatted about the action movie they had watched last night in the theater room in the White House, her thoughts wandered.

She chastised herself for being careless. She was not ready to share the truth about Landon with anyone yet. Particularly her husband and her children.

That was close. I need to be more careful.

PART I

CHAPTER ONE

Fairfax, Virginia

YOU HEARD THE breathing first.

Heavy breathing from one. Quick breaths through the nose from the one accustomed to fighting.

Next, you heard the whack, whack, whack as gloves met flesh.

Then, the smell: the overwhelming musk of teenage sweat.

There were no lights.

The "spectators" used the flashlights on their iPhones to illuminate the area. Some shone real ones.

The two boys in the cage wore MMA gloves, but no headgear or pads. No shirts. No shoes. But—oddly—they both wore baseball pants. One was in pro-style knickers.

Those were the rules.

Blood speckled the fighter's knickers like an impressionist painting.

Not his blood.

Watching the fight, a boy clung to the netting outside the cage. He held it tight to hold himself up. His knuckles stuck out like small stones in the dark.

Every punch made him sick.

He didn't want to be here. If it were up to him, he would rather be anywhere else. Even home, doing homework. Or at the dentist, having a cavity filled.

But he had no choice. Attendance was required.

The fight would be over soon. The boy in the regular baseball pants was pinned against one of the poles. Each time he slipped off the pole from the sweat on his back and fell against the netting, the guy in the knickers would grab him, right him in front of the pole again, and pummel him some more. In the face. In the stomach. In the ribs.

In between punches and exhalations, the guy in the knickers shouted, "That's poppin'! That's poppin'!"

The spectators—also shirtless and in baseball pants—wore baseball caps. They chanted: *"Poppin'! Poppin'! Poppin'! Poppin'! Poppin'! Poppin'! Poppin'! Poppin'! Poppin'!"*

The gladiatorial dogfight atmosphere intensified as the fight went on. The punches landed harder. The cheering louder. The sweat shinier.

When the fighter against the pole finally faltered, the boy in the knickers threw him down and then lifted him by both ears and slammed his head to the turf.

No one made a move to help the loser.

Knickers started kicking him with the instep of his foot. "That's hot!"

The spectators chanted: *"Hot! Hot! Hot! Hot! Hot! Hot! Hot! Hot! Hot!"*

The presumptive victor mounted the prone boy, pummeling his head with vicious punches: his left ear, then right.

"Loser!" he screamed.

A regulation fight would have been declared over.

"Loser! Loser! Loser! Loser! Loser! Loser! Loser! Loser! Loser!"

"Tap out, man!" yelled one of the spectators.

"Yeah!" said another.

"Do it!" said an opposing voice.

"Fuck him up!"

"Queer bait!"

"Kill him!"

"Let him die!"

The victor's arm rose high in the air to deliver the coup de grâce, the ensuing punch anticlimactic. Blood flew from the nose and mouth of the boy on the ground, drops spraying those who were watching.

The vanquished fighter stopped moving, his long legs still. His arms extended perpendicular to his body. A crucifix without the cross. Even in the artificial light, the boy outside the cage saw the blood running freely from the prone boy's nose and mouth. Both of his eyes, blackening.

He looked dead.

The boy outside still clung to the netting. His arms shook.

He couldn't hold it in any longer.

A grumbling roiled in the pit of his stomach. The bile rose.

Leaning forward, his head between his arms, he threw up on the ground. Teammates near him jumped out of the way.

"Gross!"

"That shit better not be on my pants, man!"

"Wimp!"

"Idiot!"

"Faggot!"

The name calling hurt the boy, although he should be used to it. He battled the tears trying to escape his eyes.

He lost the fight.

He wiped his mouth with the back of his hand. Made sure his baseball cap was on tight.

And then he ran.

❊

With his arms around their shoulders, to an observer, he appeared drunk. Good friends were helping him get home safely. The illusion ended when they dumped him on the front lawn of his parents' home, his head barely missing the sidewalk.

"That'll teach you," one boy said, kicking him.

"Warriors don't run," said the other.

The two ran back to the car, their sneakers loud in the quiet of the neighborhood.

Every bone and muscle in his body ached. He scarcely registered the squeal of the tires as their car sped away.

His chest rose and fell as he breathed. The only movement he was capable of.

The stars burned bright against the black sky. The Little Dipper. The Big Dipper. Perseus—or was it Gemini? He had learned about constellations during a class field trip to a planetarium three years ago. Life had been great then. When he was young.

Running away had been stupid. Where could he hide? He saw these guys every day. Two of them had grabbed him before he made it off campus. Tossing him into a car like a crumpled piece of paper, they had driven to a three-sided section of the main building. Back in the day, it had served as the student smoking lounge, if you could believe that. Now, just an area the high overhead night-lights and security cameras missed.

Two other guys had joined them—one, the fighter in the knickers—and beaten the shit out of him until he passed out.

Dew began to soak through his shirt. He wasn't sure how long he'd been lying here. The grass, mowed to the perfection of a baseball field, smelled as the boy imagined heaven would. His dad took enormous pride in his lawn.

He could lie here forever.

Turning his head, he spotted it in the moonlight. "I thought I'd lost you."

He pushed himself up, picked up his cap, placed it on his head, and gingerly made his way to the front door. Pain shot through his hand as he extracted the key from his back pocket.

Inside, quietly and painfully, he climbed the stairs. The noise of a television behind his parents' closed bedroom door masked his footsteps as he tiptoed by. Some reality show that offered a different reality than their own.

The boy entered his room at the end of the hall. Not bothering to pull off his pants or brush his teeth, he crawled into bed.

An hour later, sleep still eluded him. He reached for his nightstand and removed a bottle of pain-relief pills hidden in the drawer.

He'd taken a lot of them over the past two years.

Shaking out four pills, he swallowed them dry and lay down and waited for them to work.

As he drifted off to sleep, he remembered the name of the constellation.

Perseus. The hero.

CHAPTER TWO

Fairfax, Virginia

WHY IS IT quiet upstairs?

Jenny Thompson's two youngest children, seven-year-old Mia and five-year-old Matt Jr., sat at the kitchen table, slurping cereal while playing games on their electronic tablets. Learning to multitask early. She often wondered whether her kids would be able to function, if forced to focus on one thing.

"Don't make so much noise," she said. "It's bad manners."

Both cut their eyes at her, briefly, and turned back to their tablets. And their slurping.

Her husband, Matt, had left for the Mercedes dealership in Fairfax City, a short distance from their home. She'd packed his lunch, attaching a Post-it note to the plastic bag safeguarding his sandwich:

I love you! See you tonight! Love, Jenny

The *i* in tonight was a heart instead of a dot.

As the general sales manager, Matt needed to be in the office early, most days arriving at 6 a.m. From the beginning of their marriage, they had decided that she would be responsible for waking, feeding, and sending the kids out the door for school in the morning. Yes, she was a stay-at-home mom—and proud of it—but that didn't mean her days weren't stressful.

Like today.

Jenny called up to her oldest son. Again. "Tyler, come on! You're going to be late!"

Her fourteen-year-old son used to be prompt and look forward to going to school. But when he hit his teen years, he became infected with the tardiness bug pandemic to most teenagers.

Removing the stainless-steel skillet from the stove, she scooped the scrambled eggs onto a plate next to the bacon. She placed it in front of Tyler's seat at the table. She poured him a glass of orange juice and texted him to hurry up.

Her younger two children chewed their food, their intense gazes never leaving their screens. Despite their ignorance of her presence, a surge of love for them swept through her. They were growing up before her eyes. She could admire them all day, but she had her priorities.

"Tyler, I'm not kidding!"

After a last glance at Mia and Matt Jr. and double checking that the stove burners were off, she said, "I'll be right back. Don't move."

Like I have to worry.

Making her way toward the front of their Colonial home, she climbed the stairs to the second floor. As she reached the top, she paused, her hand still on the wooden rail in need of refinishing. The smell of bacon permeated all the way up here.

But something was off. It was too quiet.

She shivered.

After a few moments, she realized what was wrong. She didn't hear music. Tyler always listened to music, mostly rap. Her Caucasian offspring from the suburbs couldn't read, watch TV, or sleep without it. His favorite t-shirt sported YOLO—You Only Live Once—in gigantic yellow letters, lyrics of a song by his favorite artist, Drake. He wore the shirt so often that it had faded from its original black to a dull gray.

Jenny shook off the bad thoughts and walked—conscious of each step— down the carpeted hallway to his bedroom, stopping at the door to listen.

Nothing.

She frowned. A gnawing started in the pit of her stomach, spreading through her body and into her fingertips. She placed her palm flat on his door, before slowly balling her hand into a fist. She knocked.

No response.

She knocked again, more insistently.

Still nothing.

"Tyler, open the door."

Her hand drifted to the knob, encircling it. She squeezed and turned. But the door did not open.

It was locked, which wasn't unusual.

When he was eight years old, Tyler saw the movie *The Haunting in Connecticut* at a sleepover with friends. Ever since, he'd been locking his door before he went to bed.

Jenny backtracked to her bedroom near the top of the stairs and through to the bathroom. She grabbed the bobby pin in a drawer of the vanity, kept easily accessible for just this purpose, and returned to Tyler's door. She inserted the already straightened pin into the hole in the doorknob.

A click. Success.

Jenny inched the door open to ensure that she didn't see anything she didn't want to see. Tyler told her he had started sleeping in the nude about a year ago. When he hit puberty, he strutted around the house without a shirt, his underdeveloped chest impressive only to himself. Every real and imagined chin hair pointed out for her inspection.

Yep. He still lay in bed, shirtless, the sheet thankfully covering the lower half of his body. She pushed the door open all the way.

"Tyler, wake up, now! I mean it!"

Stomping over to the bed, she stopped short.

His face, swollen and covered with bruises, sported a black eye. The inside of his nose and the corner of his lips were crusted with blood. Her eyes scanned his torso, the bruises forming an intricate tattoo.

What the hell had happened to her son?

She grabbed his shoulder and shook him—

And pulled her hand back as if scalded. Not because he was hot. Or warm. Just the opposite. Her son was cold. His shoulder barely moved.

She cradled her son's face in both of her hands. His eyes were closed. His face cold. An angel.

A bruised and battered angel.

Sleeping.

No. This can't be.

"Tyler, baby, please! Wake up! Please, baby. Please."

She bent and placed her ear to his chest and then over his mouth.

Nothing.

She initiated CPR. Never trained, she imitated what she'd seen on a hospital reality TV show. She put her hands together and, using the pads of her palm, pressed repeatedly against his heart. She tried mouth-to-mouth resuscitation.

Still nothing.

After a few minutes, she stopped. Her efforts fruitless.

Whispering in his ear over and over, "Wake up, baby," she closed her eyes, the warm tears cascading down her cheeks and onto his.

Still cheek to cheek, her eyes moved from his headboard to the lamp on his nightstand, to his cell phone streaming with texts until she spotted the medicine bottle laying on its side next to the phone. She reached for it.

Turning the bottle around, she read the label.

It belonged to her. A long-standing OxyContin prescription she used for knee pain, a constant reminder of her high school and college playing days.

The bottle was empty.

Only then did she start to scream. And couldn't stop.

Mia and Matt Jr. burst through the open door.

"Mom! What's wrong?"

"What's happening?"

They stood next to the bed.

"Why are you crying?" Mia asked.

"Why are you in bed with Tyler?" Matt Jr. said. He pushed his older brother with both hands. "Wake up!" He recoiled and looked at her. "Why is he cold?"

"I'm calling Dad!" Her daughter grabbed Tyler's cell phone off the nightstand.

Her children's voices reached her through a thick fog. She didn't register what they were saying.

Matt and the paramedics arrived at nearly the same time ten minutes later. Her husband must have called 911. Jenny was still crying and screaming. By that time, her two youngest children had joined her.

CHAPTER THREE

Arlington, Virginia

JADE HARRINGTON HOLSTERED her Glock on her hip and sipped the remains of her morning coffee as she looked out at the small backyard of her townhouse. The melting snow from last week's storm, unusual for April, exposed to the world her poor yard-work skills. Brown grass surrounded the concrete patio, the only furniture a rusted wrought-iron table and chairs. She couldn't remember the last time she had sat out there.

She glanced down at her cocoa-colored cat, Card, who stared up at her, a face of unmasked devotion.

"What?"

The cat continued to stare, a slight twitch of his ears the only evidence that he'd heard her. Placing the cup in the sink, she swooped Card up to cradle him like a baby and deposited a kiss on his forehead.

"Love you. Gotta go."

The smartphone in the pocket of her gray dress pants buzzed. She shifted the cat to one arm as she fished it out. Christian. She answered. "Hey, you."

"Hey," he said, his tone somber. Unusual for him.

While FBI agents don't have partners, she worked with Special Agent Christian Merritt more than any other agent. She wouldn't want it any other way.

Depositing Card on the floor, she placed her hand on her hip, ready, bracing for the bad news sure to follow.

"What?"

"My nephew . . . my wife's sister's son . . . he, uh, died of an apparent suicide. Last night. They . . . she found him this morning." Silence. "Do you think—"

Jade had started for the front door while he spoke. Grabbing her suit jacket off the back of a chair, she scooped up her briefcase and keys from a table in the foyer.

"On my way. What's the address?"

CHAPTER FOUR

The White House, Washington, DC

SHE LOOKED ACROSS the desk at her Chief of Staff, Sasha Scott. "Ninety days."

President Whitney Fairchild sat behind the *Resolute* desk, a gift from Queen Victoria to President Rutherford B. Hayes in 1880. President John F. Kennedy was the first to use the desk in the Oval Office, as had many presidents since.

She glanced around her office: the beige carpet with the presidential seal, the plush sofas and chairs, paintings of Lincoln, Washington, Franklin D. Roosevelt, and Susan B. Anthony—she could never exclude the famous suffragette.

"It hasn't gone as I had hoped," Whitney continued.

Sasha shifted in her chair. "You haven't accomplished anything."

Whitney proffered a wry smile. "Tell me how you really feel."

With both houses of Congress controlled by the other party, resisting— she preferred "obstructing"—every issue on her legislative agenda, her first ninety days in office had not gone well. Certainly not according to plan. This Congress allowed all legislation, even measures that had been supported by Republicans in the past, to languish or die.

"Every president since FDR," Whitney said, "has been judged on his accomplishments within his first hundred days. I only have ten left."

"But that Congress gave FDR everything he asked for," Sasha pointed out.

"Resulting in the highest GDP growth in history."

"I wish time travel existed. Like in all those books you read. We could swap this Congress for that one. So, what are you going to do?"

"That is the question. Isn't it?" Whitney held out her hand. "What's on the agenda for today?"

Sasha handed her several briefing books. "You're meeting with the Gang of Twenty on comprehensive immigration reform."

"Eight. Twelve. Twenty. No matter how many members of Congress work on it, they cannot seem to come to an agreement."

"A few freshmen congressmen requested a meeting about paving the way for another pipeline through the Midwest."

Whitney didn't bother to respond.

"And the president of the National Education Association wants to hear your ideas for education in the twenty-first century."

"I'm not ready."

Sasha nodded toward one of the books. "Just repeat what's in there." She settled back in the guest chair. "Did you see Maddow?"

"About Cole's son?"

She nodded. "Should be some show today. Cole's show, I mean."

Cole Brennan, the top-rated conservative radio talk-show host in the country, was Whitney's loudest and most vocal critic. His pledge during the campaign to support her had lasted exactly one day. Inauguration Day. Since then, he had criticized her every move, every decision, every outfit, every hairstyle. He even criticized her weight. His ratings had never been higher.

This morning his eighteen-year-old son announced he was gay—and worse, a liberal—on a special edition of Rachel Maddow's show on MSNBC. That he would do so on the liberal news commentator's television show must have been a staggering blow to Cole.

"Wish I had time to listen to it. Poor kid." Whitney crossed her legs, her left index finger resting on her lips. Her thinking position.

"What's on your mind, Madam President?"

"I'm worried. When was the last time you visited a truly diverse community? People live among other people who think like them, look like them, vote like them, and pray—or not—like them."

Sasha remained silent. She had heard all this before.

"Dual economies," Whitney said. "Different classes of people living side by side."

"The difference in income between the haves and have-nots," Sasha said, "continues to grow."

"The wealthy continue to earn the majority of income, but middle- to lower-class wages stay the same."

"And it's only gotten worse since you've been in office."

Whitney frowned. "Thanks." Leaning her head back against the chair, she stared at the ceiling. "Nineteen eighty-two began the start of gated-community construction. The year of the Great Divide. Today, seventeen percent of all new homes over five hundred thousand dollars are built in gated communities."

"It's no coincidence that 'segregate' contains the word 'gate.'"

Whitney smiled. "Ooh . . . I might need to use that."

"The question is: are the gates to keep people out or to keep people in?"

Whitney thought about it. "Both." She sighed and sat up. "I'm supposed to be the president who changes this. Reverses the trend."

"It's still early, yet," Sasha said, her pen ready. "What do you need?"

Whitney gestured at the briefing books stacked on her desk. "These aren't my legacy. Inequality is at its highest level in more than a century." She brought her fist down, tapping the table. "Income *equality* is the issue I want to solve. That is my legacy. I need you to come up with a plan. A brilliant plan that will stimulate the economy, inspire the American people, and ensure that everyone shares in the benefit. Not just the one-percenters. But, most important—"

"—will get buy-in on the Hill," Sasha finished for her.

"Work with—" She almost said "Landon." It had taken her more time than it should to name his replacement for director of legislative affairs. "—Rick."

"When do you need it?"

"Yesterday."

CHAPTER FIVE

Fairfax, Virginia

JADE PARALLEL PARKED her old Audi A4 behind the car in front of a traditional Colonial home. It wasn't one of the McMansions that had sprouted like weeds in the DC metropolitan area in the 1990s and the first two decades of this century.

Christian leaned against the trunk of a Bureau car, his arms crossed over his massive chest. His cropped blond hair stood at attention. He watched her approach.

She gave him a brief hug. It was like embracing a mountain. Pulling back to look him in the eyes, she brought her hand to his cheek. After a moment, she said, "Let's go."

A kid's bicycle lay across the walkway that bisected the well-maintained yard. They stepped around it.

He led her through the front door. A man the same size as Christian, but not as muscular, met them in the foyer. Christian gestured to Jade. "This is Special Agent Jade Harrington."

"Matt Thompson," he said, subdued, extending his hand. He showed them to the living room, one step down off the foyer to their right.

"Be right back," Matt said, turning toward the hallway that led to the back of the house.

Jade took in the immaculate room. A massive Matisse reproduction adorned one wall over the sofa, and a hodgepodge of framed photographs rested on an end table. She picked one up of Matt with a pretty, athletic woman and three kids, all smiling, their brown hair kissed by the sun. An orange promotional lifesaver ring with Carnival Dream in black lettering hung behind them. Matt's wife resembled her sister—Christian's wife, Amanda— but Amanda was blonde like her husband. Jade stared at the children's faces.

The silence in the house was deafening.

A soft voice. "Hello?"

Jade turned. Matt held his wife with both arms. She wore a pink bathrobe. Once fuzzy, it was now worn in several places. Enormous slippers in the shape of Goofy, the Disney character, adorned her feet.

Jade placed the photograph back where she found it.

"Honey, this is Agent . . . uh," Matt looked at her, apologetic.

"Jade. Jade Harrington."

"This is my wife, Jenny."

Her bloodshot eyes fluttered to Jade and widened. "Jade Harrington! The agent from the TSK case?"

Jade had solved the Talk Show Killer—TSK—case four months ago, becoming a sudden and unwilling celebrity.

Jenny knelt before Jade and hugged her legs. Crying. "I'm glad you're here. I don't understand. Why would my baby commit suicide? We were happy. We loved him so much."

Embarrassed, Jade didn't move. She looked at Christian. Matt pried his wife from Jade's legs, and guided Jenny to the sofa facing the hallway. Jade and Christian moved to chairs opposite them.

"Ma'am. I'm not here in an official capacity. Christian and I work together. I'm just here for support."

He meant more to her than that, but didn't think the situation warranted further explanation. She also didn't say she was sorry for their loss. She knew loss. No words from a stranger could comfort them.

To Jade, Jenny Thompson said: "The police just left. They took my boy."

"The coroner," Matt murmured.

"Tell me about your son," Jade said, in the soothing voice she reserved for victims' families.

"He loves rap music. Plays it morning and night. Do you like rap music?"

"This isn't really about me."

"Baseball. He loves baseball. He was proud of his cap. He wore it everywhere." Jenny smiled. "I remember when his coach gave it to him, he couldn't wait to put his initials inside it." She stopped smiling. "But he's lost interest."

Jade couldn't stop herself. "Were there any signs he was suicidal?"

Matt stiffened next to his wife. "No."

After a pause, Jenny said, "Well . . ."

Jade leaned forward, ignoring Christian's glare. "What? What is it?"

Jenny glanced at her husband. "Tyler seems different. He isn't eating as much as he normally does. And he complains a lot about stomachaches and headaches." Jenny spoke of her son in the present tense. As if he were still alive.

"Anything else different about him? How was he doing in school?"

"He used to be an A-B student. Lately, it's been Cs and Ds."

"Was he sleeping?"

Jenny shook her head, her body crumpling. She leaned against her husband, whose arms enveloped her.

Christian stood. "I'm going to check on Amanda."

"She's upstairs with the children," Matt said.

Christian shot Jade a warning look before he left.

If he didn't want me asking questions, he shouldn't have brought me. Or left me alone with them.

Jade waited for his footsteps to fade. "Did Tyler leave a note? An email? A text?"

Matt shook his head.

Jenny's head popped up from his shoulder.

"How would we know? They . . . the police . . . took everything. His laptop, his tablet, his phone." She didn't wipe away her tears. "Can you find out for us, Agent Harrington?"

CHAPTER SIX

Washington, DC

"NINETY DAYS AND nothing," he said into the microphone, shifting his bulk in the chair. "I hate to say 'I told you so,' but I told you this would happen if *those* people elected Whitney president. So, even though I hate to do it . . . I told you so!"

Cole Brennan laughed, a high-pitched giggle that seemed incongruous coming from a man of his size.

"Our new president has accomplished absolutely nothing in her first ninety days in office. Just like every Commiecrat before her. It's a disgrace."

He glanced at the TVs mounted on the yellow and orange wall, each tuned to a different network: FOX, MSNBC, CNN, ABC, and CBS. No breaking news.

"Let's try to help her out, shall we? What should she be doing? I'll take your calls now. Go!"

He gazed at the computer screen with the list of actives. "What do you think, Jonah from Oklahoma?"

"Cole Brennan! Wow, man! It's an honor to talk to you."

"I know. What's on your mind?"

"What you've been preaching for years, man. We need to stop all these illegal aliens from entering our country."

"Couldn't agree more. Our former president—God bless that ol' cowboy— reneged on his promise to build a fence. A fence is too easy to circumvent, anyway. What we need is a wall to keep them out. A great big wall. The Great Wall of the USA. Bigger than the Great Wall of China. And we need a true visionary—a man—to build it and get the Mexican government to pay for it. A win-win."

"A great wall that's free. Great idea, Cole. My town hasn't been the same since the damn aliens took all our jobs. Anything you could do to keep them out—better yet, send them back—would be appreciated."

"Don't think that'll happen during Whitney's only term, but I'll do my best. Probably going to be the opposite. Next caller. Mason from Alabama. Go!"

"Hey, Cole, love your show. How about keeping the Muslims out of our country? London elected one as their mayor, and now the mayor of New York City is one, too. They're taking over the world! What are we going to do to prevent that from happening?"

He took a sip of his ever-present sweet iced tea. "Well, she's going to let everybody in. Even radical Islamic terrorists. It's going to be like Motel 6. 'We'll leave the light on for you.' But not all Muslims are bad, Mason. There are good Muslims. We just need a stricter process to keep the bad ones out. Wouldn't you agree?"

"You can keep 'em all out, as far as I'm concerned."

"The Statue of Liberty says something like 'give me your tired, poor, et cetera, et cetera,' but it doesn't say anything about 'give me your filthy, your Islamist, your terrorist.'"

"You got that right, Cole."

He took several more calls in the same vein before wrapping up the segment. "Where is the candidate that represents our views? A real honest-to-God conservative who will make America great like it used to be. Is anybody out there? Hello? Hello?"

He sighed. "Well, everyone, we've run out of time. This is Cole Brennan protecting your life, liberty, and pursuit of happiness. Join us again tomorrow for 'The Conservative Voice.'"

CHAPTER SEVEN

Washington, DC

CHRISTIAN LEANED INTO her fourth-floor office at the Federal Bureau of Investigation headquarters, a hand on each side of the door frame. "Got a minute?"

The question that wasted her time more than any other.

Jade looked up from a case file. She glanced at the numerous files stacked neatly on her desk and back at him. "Not really."

"Tough. We have a visitor downstairs."

They navigated through the throng of agents traversing the lobby in all directions. Jenny Thompson sat on a low couch, her hands resting on her lap. She didn't rise as they approached.

Jade sat next to her. "Mrs. Thompson."

Christian remained standing next to Jade.

"I didn't tell you about the bruises. The scratches."

"On Tyler?" Jade said.

"His arms. His legs. Chest. Back. Face. Especially his face."

Jade's gut told her what had been happening to Jenny's son. Softening her voice, she said, "At your house, you mentioned some of your son's symptoms. Do you think he was being bullied?"

Jenny shook her head. "I told Matt that Tyler was going through teenage stuff. Girl problems. Teachers. Homework. Parents."

Jade waited, expecting Jenny to fill the silence. She didn't disappoint.

Jenny scrunched up her face. "If he was being bullied, I would've known."

The likelihood of Tyler telling his mother he'd been bullied was low. Not something a lot of kids—especially teenage boys—would discuss with their parents.

Jade would know.

Jenny hesitated. "They found pictures."

"Who?"

Jenny's jaw set. Voice clipped, she said, "The police found . . . pictures of him on the Internet. Naked pictures. Buck naked."

Jade glanced up at Christian.

He stared at his sister-in-law. "Tyler?"

"The police said . . ." She fell silent for a moment. "Someone took pictures of my son in the shower at school. In the locker room."

Jade started to take Jenny's hand and then thought better of it. "Is that why they think—?"

"There's a Twitter account," Jenny said, tears flowing down her cheeks. "Dedicated to my boy. A 'fan'"—she made air quotes—"account, and it has the vilest, nastiest tweets about my son. That he was gay and had a small penis and that he liked his baseball teammates a little too much. Someone tweeted: 'Nobody loves you.' It received over a hundred 'likes.'"

"Jesus," Christian said.

Jenny's voice rose, her breathing heavy. "People shouldn't be allowed to say whatever they want on the Internet, right? And take your picture without permission? They can't get away with this. Can you do something?"

Other agents glanced at them as they passed by.

Jade said, "There's nothing we—the FBI—can do. Maybe the county police can trace who created the account."

"They said it was created from a public computer, and they're having a hard time tracing it. I want answers! I need to know who did this to my son!"

"Mrs. Thompson, you're going through a horrible time, but I must ask you to calm down."

"Calm down? Calm down? I don't want to fucking calm down. My son is dead!"

She started to rise, but Christian grasped her in a one-armed bear hug and returned her to the couch. "Jenny, if we're going to help you, you must get ahold of yourself."

She waved at Jade. "But she said there's nothing you can do. You can't fucking help me. Can you bring my son back? Can you find out who did this to him?"

Christian and Jade looked at each other, but didn't respond.

After a few moments, Jenny's breathing steadied.

Jade ventured another question. "What else did the police say?"

"They're worthless. They can't help me. No one did anything to help my son. Not even me. Tyler was smart. Cute. Almost beautiful." Jenny Thompson gave her a defiant look. "But one thing I know for sure. I know my son. And he wasn't gay."

"How can you be sure?" Jade said.

"They won't leave us alone," Jenny said, ignoring Jade's question.

Jade glanced at Christian bewildered and back to Jenny. "Who?"

"Reporters. Camped outside our house. Fire questions at us as we try to get in our car. Follow my kids to school and Matt to work. I can't watch the news."

She put her hands over her ears and bent at the waist.

Someone in the Fairfax County police department had allegedly leaked to the media that Tyler Thompson had been cyberbullied. You couldn't turn on the TV without seeing the elaborate "Bullycide" logo next to Tyler's adorable high-school yearbook picture with the faux forest behind him.

Jenny sat up. "There's more."

What now?

Christian tensed.

"The police also discovered that Tyler exchanged texts with a girl at school. I didn't know her. He never talked about her. Never showed me her picture. But from the texts I could tell he really liked her."

"Who was it?" Christian asked.

The infinitesimal smile that appeared on Jenny's face at the thought of her son's happiness disappeared quickly. "I don't know. Turns out the girl played a joke on my son. All those fucking kids ganged up on him. That bitch never cared for him. The bullying wasn't what got to him." Jenny looked at Jade. "When Tyler found out that girl was laughing at him behind his back, that's what did it.

"That's why he took his own life, Agent Harrington."

The White House, Washington, DC

WHITNEY PACKED THE stack of briefing materials into her case and made her way up to the residence. It was only seven p.m., but she needed a break.

She had the rest of the evening to herself. Grayson was in Missouri running the family firm, Fairchild Industries, and her children were off at school: Chandler was a senior at the University of Missouri, and her daughter, Emma, a sophomore at Princeton. Whitney had not seen them since Easter.

She was alone. Well, alone if you didn't count the Secret Service. Or the White House staff. Or the residence staff. Or the military staff.

Setting the briefcase on a stand by the front door, she walked to the wine refrigerator in the living area and selected a bottle of 1997 Opus One. On the sofa, she tucked her legs under her. Holding the wine glass in one hand, and the remote in the other, she flipped through the channels on the flat-screen stopping on MSNBC. Another rally in progress.

Over the last week, rallies—protests?—had broken out in several major cities across the country, the one televised now in Philadelphia. The protesters seemed to come from all walks of life. Different races. Different ages. Different genders. Different religions.

Whitney turned up the sound.

"What we're seeing now is different from the Occupy Wall Street movement of years ago," said the red-headed male MSNBC commentator in front of a fake vista of the Liberty Bell. "These protests are more urgent, more desperate, and they don't seem to be going away anytime soon."

She sipped her wine. *Because the problem isn't going away anytime soon.*

"What do they want?" the anchor in the studio asked.

"To close the gap. According to the nonpartisan Congressional Budget Office, wealth for the rich has increased two hundred and seventy-five percent while increasing only forty percent for the middle class. For the poor, twenty. The top twenty percent own sixty percent of the wealth in this country."

More like eighty-five percent. The American people underestimated the share of wealth owned by the wealthiest individuals. But people were waking up. Reports had come in that income inequality protests were not only happening in front of businesses and banks, but also gated and other exclusive communities. Protesters had barred residents from entering their own homes. Fights had broken out in airports over first-class upgrades. In airplanes over the use of the bathroom in the forward section by coach passengers unwilling to wait with the four hundred other passengers for the three restrooms in the rear.

After a commercial break, the studio anchor introduced Evan Stevens, an influential liberal blogger. Handsome, with a short, trimmed beard and dark hair combed into the latest style, Stevens was a fastidious dresser. Everything about him seemed to be studied perfection. He railed against income inequality, an issue he had been battling for a long time.

People were starting to listen.

After several minutes, she muted the television and glanced at the stand in the foyer. The briefing books awaited her. Although she had a spacious office next door in the Treaty Room, usually, when she worked from "home," rather, upstairs, she ended up here. On the sofa.

Whitney closed her eyes, trying to forget—temporarily—this issue that had concerned her for years. The issue that could undermine not just her presidency, but her country.

Income inequality.

The outside wants in.

CHAPTER NINE

Fairfax, Virginia

STILL PUMPED UP, literally, from lifting free weights after practice, Zach Rawlins guided his BMW around the final curve before the entrance to his parents' subdivision. Since his father purchased the car and made the payments, the Beemer didn't really belong to him. A technicality his father reminded him of often.

Wending his way through the neighborhood, he needed to hurry. His father didn't like for him to be out late on a school night, especially when he had the car. Zach's mind drifted to his conversation with Kaylee after third period. She was captain of the junior varsity cheerleading squad for football, basketball, and baseball; he was captain of the JV baseball team. Handsome—everyone had told him so since he was a kid—a good student, and a jock. What's not to like?

They were perfect for each other.

Brianna, also a cheerleader, wanted to go out with him—she hinted she wanted a lot more than that—but he never settled. He wanted only the best. The best car. The best girl. He lived in the largest house in the neighborhood. If you didn't want the best, why bother?

After all, he was his father's son.

Zach slowed to turn into his driveway. For such a well-to-do neighborhood, the developers had skimped on lighting and neglected to install enough street lamps. The yard was shrouded in darkness. He looked up at the house. Most of the lights were turned off, his mother no doubt in the living room drinking a highball and watching *The Real Housewives* of some American city. He didn't understand how she could watch those shows all the time. They were stupid. All the drama.

His father probably wasn't home yet, working late at the office again. Good. No rush.

He parked twenty feet away from the garage, the inside of which was reserved for his parents' cars. Grabbing his backpack from the passenger seat, he opened the car door. Before he could slam the door closed, he heard a soft scraping sound in an otherwise still night.

What was that?

Zach turned his head to check out the yard on the side of the house where the noise came from.

Something hard hit him in the head.

"Fuck!" he screamed.

A baton? A pipe? A baseball bat? Whatever it was, it hurt like hell.

Dropping his bag, he clutched his head with both hands. He pulled his hands away, his left saturated with a dark liquid. Blood. His blood.

"I'm going to kick your ass, motherfucker."

As the anger surged through him, he cocked his arm back to deliver a Hail Mary punch. He caught a glimpse of his assailant. And paused. Surprised.

His hesitation cost him his life.

The person hit him in the head again.

"Damn it!"

A long-ball hitter, quickness was never Zach's strength. He didn't raise his forearms in time. The assailant hit him in the exact same spot. Now that fucking hurt. He yelped and grabbed his head again, which made him unprepared for the blow to his kidney. The pain cut to his core. The air left him. He doubled over.

The next blow came to the side of his leg, followed by two more in quick succession. Something popped in his knee.

Shit, I'm going to miss the rest of the season. Need to start fighting back.

But the blows kept coming.

His mind lost track of which part of his body was experiencing which pain. He couldn't get up.

He never had the chance to fight back.

His last thought was not of his parents or his friends or his teammates. His last thought was of Kaylee. She wouldn't go out with him with his face looking like this.

Before he drifted off into eternal darkness, his head was lifted by his hair. The roots tugged at his scalp. Zach had no energy left to scream.

Before his eyes, a photograph. Before he had time to formulate a name, his face was smashed into the ground.

And then, he felt nothing at all.

CHAPTER TEN

The White House, Washington, DC

WHITNEY TURNED OFF the television. She didn't want to be, but she was right about this issue. Things were going to get worse before they got better. The quality of life must be improved for all Americans, not just the ones at the top. If people revolted, the impact would spread beyond businesses and the boycotting of their products. The republic itself could be at stake.

She hit the remote for the stereo. The Four Seasons, op. 8 by Antonio Vivaldi was already loaded in the CD player.

She closed her eyes for a moment, a deep breath drawing the music in to soothe her. Unbidden, thoughts of Grayson arose—or as the mainstream media had dubbed him, "The First First Man." Some in the alternative media called him "The First Dude."

Whitney had never asked her husband during or after the election to turn over the reins of Fairchild Industries to one of his brothers or a professional CEO. During the transition, the Right had had an apoplectic fit, clamoring for him to place the business in a blind trust. Grayson never considered it. Since she wasn't a director or shareholder, and thus neither exercised any influence nor received any direct benefit from the business, she had hoped to assuage the public's conflict of interest concerns. The conservative media still wasn't buying it.

She hadn't asked Grayson to lead a pet cause like prior presidential spouses: the war against drugs, mental health, or supporting veterans. One of his unofficial responsibilities, to be a senior counselor to her and attend select cabinet meetings, would have bored him to tears. He hadn't made any appearances on her behalf, much less visited the poor and disenfranchised in other countries or helped to shape citizens' perception of her initiatives.

He wasn't much of a First Gentleman.

But that was fine with her. She didn't need the distraction.

His current job was important. As the CEO of a multi-billion-dollar agriculture and biotechnology conglomerate, his employees and customers and stockholders depended on him. He tried to live a normal life, despite the ever-present press corps and the small Secret Service detail shadowing him. He had resisted even that, until he realized they were going to follow him around anyway.

The media, of course, was having a field day. Grayson was not only neglecting his duties as the First Gentleman, but shirking an honor and a tradition and a privilege—although not constitutionally mandated—entrusted to him by the American people.

And the American people didn't like it.

The media speculated about their long-distance marriage.

Ted Bowling, her campaign manager, had told her that a recent poll had ranked her in the bottom twentieth percentile for "family values" out of all US presidents, a ghastly result considering the competition and unwelcome news, particularly for a female politician.

She and Grayson had lived separate lives for such a long time, while she was a representative and then as a senator in Congress. Back then, they would see each other once a month. Either she would go to him or he to her. It worked for them.

Now, he always came to her.

At times like this, she missed Landon, her congressional legislative aide. Their debates about politics. Late-night strategy sessions. Reading contests. The comfort of being able to discuss almost anything with him. He would have flourished in the White House, relishing the challenge of working with an obstructionist Congress.

For the last few months, those on the Right had tried to make more of what happened. The "TSKgate" scandal had overshadowed her presidential transition. Allegations had swirled about her complicity or knowledge of Landon's crimes. And that she hadn't done anything to stop him. FOX News had accused her of being the mastermind, an accusation repeated so often that, by some, it was now considered fact. FOX would continue to fuel the conspiracy until the next scandal erupted. Created by the network, if necessary.

She glanced at her watch. Seven p.m. in Missouri. He would still be at work.

He picked up on the first ring.

"Hello, darling," Grayson said.

"Still at the office?"

"Acquiring a biotech company in California." He sounded upbeat. "How was your day?"

"Unproductive," she said.

"Why is that?"

"Most of my legislative agenda has been stonewalled. These protests across the country concern me."

"Anything I can do?"

"Run for Congress?"

"No thanks. After this acquisition, why don't I come and spend some time with you? I can make some appearances. Join you at some events."

"Excellent idea." She glanced at her briefing books again. "Darling, I must run. Work is calling. I'll call you tomorrow. Love you."

"I love you—"

Whitney hung up.

CHAPTER ELEVEN

Washington, DC

"ASK ME WHAT I did this weekend."

She studied her colleague Special Agent Dante Carlucci. He dressed for work as if he were going out. Jade never understood how he could afford such expensive suits on his salary. His features independently—dark brown curly hair, long nose, and one ear slightly higher than the other—appeared out of sync, but together, they complemented each other. Handsome, and he knew it, Dante never passed a mirror he didn't like.

Even though they'd had run-ins in the past, the status of their relationship was one of détente. They didn't entirely trust each other, maybe didn't even like each other, but over the last year they'd developed a grudging mutual respect. It didn't mean she couldn't give him shit when warranted.

"I don't care."

"It's not like that. I met someone. Her name's Laurie. I cooked dinner for her. French, my specialty."

"And?"

"We watched a movie, and I took her home."

His cologne wasn't as overpowering as usual. Perhaps this woman was a good influence on him. Maybe now Jade would be able to work near him without gagging.

"Sounds as if you have a girlfriend."

"I think I do."

"I'm happy for you. Bye."

"What about you?"

She tore her eyes away from the file she wanted to return to reading. "What about me?"

"Don't you ever go on dates . . . with anyone?"

"I don't date."

"You should. It might take the edge off."

"Take the edge off what?" Christian said, filling up the doorway to her office.

"Nothing." Jade, in resignation, set the file down. "How was it?"

Christian had spent the morning attending his nephew's funeral. He shook his head.

Jade's desk phone rang.

The receptionist: "A Lieutenant John Briggs with the US Park Police is on the line."

"Lieutenant," Jade said. "What can I do for you?"

"I saw you on the news. The Talk Show Killer. Great work."

"Thanks." She didn't take compliments well. She straightened the items on her desk while she waited him out.

"Anyway," he said, "I caught a case you may be interested in."

"I'm listening."

"There's been a murder here. In Gravelly Point Park." He paused. "It's bad."

Gravelly Point Park was located just north of Reagan National Airport. *Oops. Zoe would kill me.*

Zoe, her best friend, believed it was blasphemy to call the Washington, DC airport by any other name than its original: National Airport. A true-blue liberal Democrat, Zoe might have been a little biased.

The park, a few hundred feet from one of the runways, was considered one of the best places in the United States for aircraft spotting—the hobby of watching airplanes take off and land. The site attracted all kinds of people: casual observers, aviation buffs, locals, and tourists. Jurisdiction over Gravelly Point Park fell to the US Park Police.

Why was he calling her?

Jade received calls like this often. Local police from all over the country requested her involvement in their cases. She should tell Lt. John Briggs that she was busy.

"How so?" she replied.

"The vic was a boy," he said. "Between fourteen and seventeen."

"With all due respect, Lieutenant, I still don't understand why you're calling me."

"The manner in which he died made me think of you. Well, TSK. Beat his vics with a blunt instrument, right? A baseball bat?"

Jade's heart beat faster, as she glanced over at Christian and Dante. "Are you saying this victim suffered similar injuries?"

"Did you hear about the murder of the high-school kid a few nights ago? The one killed in his parents' front yard? Next to their BMW?"

"Sure. What about it?"

"I called the cop who caught that case, and she's on her way over."

"You think they're related?"

"I think you might want to have a look, too."

Jade took one last glance at the neglected file. "We'll be right there."

CHAPTER TWELVE

Seattle, Washington

"DAYDREAMING AGAIN?"

Yes.

He glanced at his father standing in the hallway just outside his office. Although in his early sixties, he was still tall and fit, except for a small belly increasing in size in direct proportion to the number of craft breweries opening around Seattle. Noah was built like him.

Noah Blakeley, the chief operating officer of his family's international shipping firm and scion of one of the first families of Seattle, had been watching the local news on the TV in his office in the Pioneer Square neighborhood near downtown. Protests across the country dominated the noon broadcast.

Income inequality was a major problem. Not only in this city and in the US, but in countries around the world. A huge supporter of the president, he was skeptical of the federal government's ability to find a solution given the current dysfunctional Congress. Raising the minimum wage would be a start, but not a panacea. He had done his part. The lowest-level employees in his firm earned twice the state minimum wage. And Washington had one of the highest minimum wages in the country.

He'd met President Whitney Fairchild before, once, during her campaign, hosting the future president and most of Seattle's wealthiest Democratic contributors in his home in Madison Park, an affluent neighborhood in Seattle.

He wondered if she remembered him.

Given the net worth of his father's company, one would think Noah's office would be nicer. His television was the opposite of flat: the silver, boxy thirty-four-inch, early 2000s model sat atop a metal filing cabinet, threatening to squash it at any moment. The TV weighed over a hundred pounds.

Good luck hanging that on the wall.

His oak desk, purchased at a secondhand store, rested on a threadbare carpet, which had been traversed many miles before its installation.

Noah wasn't much better than his father. His clothes displayed his own frugality: frayed pants, partially untucked shirt, and scruffy brown shoes. People who passed him on the street would never guess he was a multi-millionaire. Like a lot of wealthy people in Seattle.

The most valuable thing in his office was the view. He gazed across Puget Sound to the hills of West Seattle. In the distance, low-hanging clouds surrounded the lofty snowcapped Olympic mountains.

Lofty. Like Noah's dreams.

He wanted to change the world. Make it a better place. Make a difference.

His father, however, dismissed his dreams, believing Noah had bought into all that talk about "white privilege" and was suffering from some kind of guilt over it. He didn't feel guilty about being Caucasian and wealthy, he just didn't think it was fair that some people were fortunate to be born white or in an environment with all the advantages.

Income inequality plagued him.

"Just thinking . . . ," Noah finally answered. He hesitated, knowing it was a waste of time. "About the foundation."

A few years ago, Noah's family had formed a philanthropic foundation, which now contributed generously to many causes. Not just in the greater Seattle area, but across the country.

"I want to run it, Dad," he said, trying to keep the desperation out of his voice. "I'd be good at it. It's a better fit for my skills and passions. I can make a difference. A real difference."

His father remained silent.

Noah rushed on. "August should run the business. He's a better businessman than I am. We should switch places. How could it hurt to try?" When he wasn't running the foundation, his older brother, August, spent most of his time sailing on Puget Sound. Noah often wondered when he stared out the window at the Sound, if his brother was staring back at him from his boat, cocktail glass raised. Laughing at him.

His father glanced out the window. "I want a detailed report of container shipments by country for the last month. Bring it to my office in fifteen minutes. And be prepared to discuss it."

He cast one last look at his son and left.

Noah unclenched his fist and grabbed the worry beads next to his desktop computer. Sitting back, he closed his eyes, and breathed deeply as he shifted each bead from his left hand to his right.

When he completed the circle, no less worried than when he started, he faced his computer and called up the operations software to produce the report his father wanted.

As he waited for it to print, he realized that even though the worry beads hadn't fully relaxed him or relieved his stress, they had worked. Grabbing the papers off the printer, he hurried to his father's office.

They had calmed him down enough to face him again.

CHAPTER THIRTEEN

Arlington, Virginia

CHRISTIAN CROSSED THE Memorial Bridge and, one hand on top of the steering wheel, guided the Bureau car south on the George Washington Parkway. Jade preferred driving her own car rather than checking one out of the motor pool.

Located in Arlington, Virginia, Gravelly Point Park was separated from DC by the Potomac River. Riding shotgun, she gazed out the passenger window, ignoring the dirty water, and choosing to stare instead at the monuments of the capital city. Dante lounged in the backseat.

There was no question as to where the body had been found. Lights flashing, US Park, Arlington County, and Fairfax County police cars were parked everywhere in a haphazard, Matchbox-cars-like fashion. Christian pulled into the parking lot.

Before she could completely exit the vehicle, a man rushed up to her.

"Agent Harrington? Lieutenant Briggs."

Jade introduced him to Christian and Dante. They followed Briggs as he sliced through a group of officers standing around the body. The officers parted. No one asked to see her badge.

Everyone knew who she was.

Briggs nodded to a forensic tech to open the body bag. The surrounding officers quieted. Other than the chirping of a nearby bird, the opening of the zipper was the only sound in the tranquil morning.

Pulling on nitrile gloves, Jade bent next to the corpse. She winced at the sight of him. So young. The injuries were similar to TSK's victims all right, except for one thing.

"This perp's right-handed," she said.

The left side of the kid's face was damaged. Beaten beyond recognition.

She inspected the length of the body, but stopped at the massive quantity of blood in the genital area of the victim's jeans.

"I hope he was already dead," Dante said.

Briggs jerked his head toward the coroner's van. "It's over there."

"Jesus!" Christian said.

"We'll need to see it," Jade said, ignoring the sick expressions on Christian's and Dante's faces.

She pointed with her pinkie. "Check out the scratches and bruises." To Briggs. "Has he been ID'ed, yet?"

He shook his head.

She scanned the faces of the men and one woman standing around her. "You're from Fairfax?"

The woman stepped forward. "Detective Chutimant."

"Similar to your vic?"

The detective nodded. "The injuries are almost identical. My vic's were worse, though, if you can imagine that."

Jade could. She'd witnessed the worst man could do to his fellow man. Woman, too. Evil was not a trait attributed to only one gender.

Standing, she glanced around the parking lot. "Who found the body?"

"A cyclist," Briggs said. "He does a twenty-mile ride every day before work. Got a flat tire and pulled off the trail to fix it. Spotted what he thought was a gym bag. When he came closer, he saw the body and the blood and called us from his cell phone." To Jade's unanswered question: "Clothes, fingernails were clean. No blood on him. All the cars registered to him are in his driveway."

From Christian: "You think the vic was killed somewhere else?"

"Believe he was dumped here, yeah," Briggs said, "but don't know for sure, yet."

"Could've rented a car," Dante said.

The ringing of a cell phone pierced the stillness of the morning. Everyone present with the same ringtone checked their phones. Each of them shook their heads, as they realized it wasn't their phone.

The ringing continued.

The officers looked at each other and then one by one down at the body.

"Ignore it," Briggs said.

"Answer it," Jade said.

A crime-scene technician knelt and removed the phone from the victim's pocket, handing it to Briggs.

"This is Lieutenant Briggs, US Park Police. Who's this? . . . Hello?"

Jade walked away from the group. Christian and Dante followed.

"The Talk Show Killer is dead," Christian said.

She waited for the plane overhead to pass. All three of them swiveled their heads to watch it land.

"Maybe someone wants us to think he's still alive," she said. "Let's go check out his—"

Dante grimaced. "Do we have to?"

Jade was already heading to the coroner's van.

CHAPTER FOURTEEN

Washington, DC

"THE WIZARDS ARE going to win it all this year."

"You're delusional."

Christian wiped his mouth with the napkin clenched in his fist, chewing hurriedly to make his point. "We have a true point guard who can also score, and a big man who can carry twenty points, ten rebounds every night. Two pieces of the puzzle we've been missing."

Perched on stools at the counter of a small sandwich shop near the Bureau, they were enjoying a late lunch, the shop empty except for them. Jade and Christian weren't regulars, but came often enough that the proprietor pounding a slab of meat behind the counter recognized their faces. After viewing the victim's severed penis, Dante begged off lunch and headed back to the office, declaring a loss of appetite.

She lowered her voice. "I've been meaning to talk to you." She scouted the restaurant to make sure she wouldn't be overheard. "I own some Anacostia swamp land. Can sell it to you real cheap. Great for condos."

He chomped, confidently, and swallowed. "You'll see."

Her phone vibrated. She didn't recognize the number.

"Harrington."

"Agent Harrington, Lieutenant Briggs again. We got a positive ID on the vic. Name's Nicholas Campbell."

"Hold on." Jade snatched the pen Christian held out to her. She grabbed the first piece of paper she saw. The one her sandwich was wrapped in ten minutes ago. "Go on."

"Age: sixteen," Briggs continued. "A sophomore at William Randolph Secondary School in Fairfax. Parents said he never came home last night."

"Did they report him missing?"

"No."

"Why not?"

"Because they knew from TV the police didn't start searching for missing persons for at least forty-eight hours."

She stopped writing. "Seriously?"

"Uh . . . yeah. I'm on my way to interview the parents now."

"Thanks for the update."

"No problem."

Jade clicked off.

Christian took a bite of his second sandwich. "What'd he say?"

She relayed Briggs's side of the conversation. Christian's chewing slowed. He swallowed hard.

"My son, Mark, goes to Randolph."

"Huh."

"So did my nephew, Tyler."

Washington, DC

WHITNEY WRAPPED UP her speech to over fifty local business leaders in a meeting room at the National Press Club. When she finished, the applause was polite and respectful, but unenthusiastic.

Because they realize what's coming.

During the campaign, she had promised to fix the nation's crumbling infrastructure, which would cost money. These businesspeople knew where that money would have to come from.

The response to her recent speeches was different from the frenzied, rock-star-like reception she had garnered as a candidate. She felt like a bride who, after a fairy-tale wedding and an idyllic honeymoon, learned that marriage was work and harder than anticipated. Lingering at the podium, she answered a few questions from the reporters in the audience.

"Judy," she pointed at the auburn-haired, middle-aged reporter who had accompanied her on the presidential campaign trail. A year ago, Judy had broken the news—to her and to the world—about Grayson's indiscretion. She had long since forgiven Judy, an old-school journalist doing her job. She wasn't the one who'd had an affair. Whitney had forgiven Grayson, too, although she hadn't forgotten. She stayed with him not for what he'd done wrong, but for all the things during their long marriage he had done right.

"Madam President, your one hundredth day in office is tomorrow. How would you grade your performance so far?"

"I'm glad someone is keeping track. Thanks, Judy." She waited for the laughter to subside. "We haven't accomplished as much as I would have liked. I didn't expect a Congress so . . . uncooperative. I would give myself a C. But I was a good student, and never settled for anything less than straight As. I won't settle as president either."

She answered a few questions from other reporters when her eyes alighted on Blake Haynes. She couldn't help smiling. "Mr. Haynes?"

"Madam President, does the federal government plan to respond to the protests occurring throughout the country?"

"We are monitoring the situation carefully and will plan our response accordingly."

After several more questions, she let Josh McPherson usher her toward a side door.

"Madam President."

She turned to see Blake Haynes standing there, a huge smile on his charming face. Josh's muscular body closed almost inconspicuously toward Whitney's, his eyes cutting from Blake to her.

"It's all right, Josh. Give us a moment." The Secret Service agent moved a few paces away, standing under a ceiling light that highlighted his brown pate.

Blake approached her. He offered her his left hand. She shook it.

"Ah. A lefty."

"Us lefties—literally and figuratively—must stick together," he said. "It's been a while. Since the inaugural ball. I never got a chance to thank you."

"For what?"

"For my show. The network gave it to me based on our interview."

"Glad to be of help."

"Perhaps, we can help each other."

She tilted her head.

"I was there," he continued. "In Palo Alto. Watching you speak to a bunch of Silicon Valley execs. After Beyoncé's performance, you had me at 'I should have delivered my speech first.'"

"Shouldn't that be 'you had me at hello'?"

"I like to be different. In any case, I want to return the favor. Another interview. Now that you're president. All softballs. Promise. Just like last time."

"But can I trust you?" she teased.

"Of course you can. I'm a good ol' Catholic boy. Cross my heart and hope to die." He made the sign on his chest.

She needed some favorable publicity. She glanced over at Josh. She would be late for her next appointment. Every hour of her day was scheduled. Every minute.

Holding out her hand, she said, "I need to run, but I'm sure that can be arranged."

He held her hand. "Income equality."

"Excuse me?"

"Income equality. That is your legacy." He stared into her eyes. "Let me help you."

Whitney masked her surprise as she turned away.

How did he know?

CHAPTER SIXTEEN

Fairfax, Virginia

THEY STRODE UP to the predominately brick Fairfax County police station. Christian hustled to the glass door first and opened it for Jade.

"We're here to see Lieutenant Chutimant," she said to the officer sitting at the front desk.

As they waited, she glanced around the gleaming lobby. No prostitutes or drunks sat waiting in chairs, pleading their case to anyone who would listen. The atmosphere was quiet, purposeful, almost businesslike.

The detective strode toward them in an off-the-rack blue business suit.

"Right this way," she said.

They followed her through the metal detectors down a hallway of modern décor.

In her office, she waved to the guest chairs in front of her desk. "I'm not much for small talk."

"Neither am I," Jade said.

"I am," Christian said. Jade shot him a look.

Chutimant typed several strokes on her keyboard before turning the computer monitor to face them.

"I'd like to introduce you to Zach Rawlins."

The crime-scene photo showed a massive quantity of blood pooled beneath the boy's head. Like Nicholas Campbell, the boy found in Gravelly Point, Zach Rawlins had suffered extensive damage to the left side of his face. Jade let out a breath. TSK was dead. His involvement in this crime, impossible. Still, it was unsettling. The two boys' injuries were similar to the injuries inflicted on TSK's victims.

"Vicious," Christian said.

Jade continued to survey the photograph. "Severed penis?"

Chutimant nodded. Christian grimaced.

"Look at his face," Jade said. "Bruises and scratches just like Nicholas Campbell."

"And Tyler," Christian said, his voice soft.

"Who's Tyler?" asked Chutimant.

"My nephew. He also went to Randolph." He swallowed. "He . . . died . . . recently."

"Oh. He's your nephew." An expression, sympathetic and fleeting, passed over Chutimant's face. She wrote something down.

Christian blew out a breath. "Three deaths at one school in such a short time. It can't be a coincidence."

"It's not," the women said at the same time. Jade didn't believe in coincidences.

Chutimant continued, "Zach and Nicholas played on the baseball team."

"What!" Christian glanced at Jade.

"So did Tyler," Jade said to Chutimant.

A moment of silence hung over them.

"What else?" Jade said.

"Not much. Zach was sixteen. Worked out in the weight room that night with some of his teammates after practice. We interviewed them. The last one left at eight p.m. that night. Zach was still there. The coroner estimated TOD between seven and ten. The father arrived home from work at around ten. Found his son in the grass near a BMW. The kid's car. Driver's door open. Overhead light off. The mother was in the living room watching TV. If she'd only looked out the window, she might have seen who did this to her son."

"Or prevented his death," Jade said.

"She wasn't worried he hadn't come home from school, yet?" asked Christian.

"Apparently not. Zach sometimes stayed out until eleven. His curfew on school nights."

"Weapon?" Jade asked.

"A blunt instrument," Chutimant said. "Could've been a baseball bat."

Jade pointed at the computer. "Can you enlarge it?"

Chutimant hit a few keys. Jade leaned in to view the autopsy photo. "Any signs of struggle?"

The lieutenant shook her head. "Nothing under the fingernails, except boy dirt—"

"Hey!" Christian said, in mock indignation.

The detective smiled before sobering. "No defensive wounds on his arms—"

"He was ambushed," Jade said.

"Pretty much," Chutimant said. "The coroner believes the bruising and scratches on Rawlins's face pre-existed the murder."

Jade sat back in her chair. "Would you mind if we talked to the parents?"

Chutimant handed Jade a slip of paper before she'd finished the sentence. "I thought you might ask. I'll email the case file to you as well."

Jade looked down at the address.

CHAPTER SEVENTEEN

Fairfax, Virginia

CHRISTIAN WHISTLED. "NICE . . ."

She agreed. The subdivision's long, winding roads were laid out like lazy ribbons. The meandering journey through Zach Rawlins's parents' neighborhood felt like a nostalgic Sunday drive.

Expansive yards separated McMansion-huge houses. Jade could never afford a house like this on her government salary, even if—when—she became the first female director of the FBI. But that was okay. Money wasn't her thing.

They pulled to a stop in front of the garage. Unsullied, the yard displayed no signs of police tape, investigation trash, or trampled grass. Not even a makeshift memorial honoring the victim. You wouldn't have known a murder of one of the home's occupants had occurred here a week ago.

She scanned the surrounding neighborhood. "Not many streetlights."

"Probably gets real dark here at night," he said.

She knelt in the yard, and ran her hand in an arc over the grass. *A person lost his life here. A child.*

She stood and walked with Christian to the front door. He rang the doorbell. A man of medium height and weight opened the door. A former athlete, by the way he carried himself.

"Mr. Rawlins, we're Special Agents—"

"Come in." Turning, he walked deeper into the house. Christian looked at Jade and shrugged. They followed Zach's father past a staircase leading to the second floor and down a hallway into a spacious room. Broad windows afforded a view of the backyard with a swimming pool and tennis court. She also spotted a batting cage. A weak evening sun tried to force its way into the room.

"I'm George. My wife will be down in a minute. Drink?"

"No, thank you," she said.

"Sit," he said, pointing to the sofa.

A visceral reaction exploded within her. "We're not dogs, Mr. Rawlins. We'll stand." Christian smirked, and moved to lean against the wall near the window.

Rawlins raised his hands in mea culpa. "I apologize." He motioned his hand to the sofa. "Please."

She glanced at the overstuffed sofa and chose a modern chair instead. "What do you do for a living, Mr. Rawlins?"

"I'm the vice president of logistics for the Visix Corporation, headquartered in Reston. We're one of the world's biggest shippers and distributors of petroleum products."

"I believe," she said, "you generated one billion dollars in revenue last year and earned the largest profits in corporate history."

Rawlins blinked and then nodded. "You do your homework."

A slender, light-brown-haired woman glided into the room. Her pointed chin, elevated at a thirty-degree angle, was preceded by her arm, extended as she walked toward them.

"Hello. I'm Vanessa Rawlins."

The couple sat apart on the sofa, just out of reach of each other.

"Mrs. Rawlins," she said, "I appreciate your taking the time to meet with us. We're here to ask you some questions about your son."

"Zach was a good boy. He did well enough in school. In baseball. At least, he was popular."

"He didn't work hard enough, if you ask me," George Rawlins cut in. "Could've started on varsity as a freshman last year. I started as a freshman in high school. It's not that hard. You just need to put in the work."

Christian sat in the matching chair to Jade's. "Was your son having any problems? Maybe, at school? Teachers? Girlfriends?"

Mrs. Rawlins shook her head before he could finish. "No, everyone liked Zach. He was handsome and outgoing."

"A lot like me." Mr. Rawlins's laugh came out like a bark.

"What about friends?" Jade said. "Teammates?"

"He got along with everyone," Mrs. Rawlins said. "Teachers, administrators, friends, teammates. He didn't have an enemy in the world."

He must have had one. Jade kept that thought to herself.

Mr. Rawlins looked at his wife. "Which means he wasn't trying hard enough. When you're the best, you're going to pick up enemies along the way."

"If he didn't have any enemies," Jade said, slowing her cadence, "who do you think did this to him?"

Vanessa Rawlins opened her mouth to answer and then closed it. After a moment, George Rawlins said, "Random. Must've been a random killing. My son was in the right place at the wrong time."

"What about security? Do you have cameras?"

"Been meaning to tighten security. Infrared cameras. An invisible fence. Maybe a couple of pit bulls. I just never got around to it."

"Did your son get along with Nicholas Campbell and Tyler Thompson?"

"Nicholas was his buddy," George Rawlins said. "They all played JV baseball together. Zach and Nicholas started. Tyler sat on the bench. He was enthusiastic, but didn't have any skills." His eyes watered. "It's not fair. Zach had so much potential, while that loser Tyler—"

Christian clenched and unclenched his fist, slowly. Jade raised her hand from her lap, palm down, signaling him not to react.

"Nicholas's family belonged to the club," Mrs. Rawlins said. She lowered her voice, as if to confide in them. "The country club we belong to. But Tyler's family didn't run in the same . . . circles. A different stratum of society, if you know what I mean. Nice family, though. Wholesome."

Jade let the last word hang, the Rawlinses unaware of Christian's relationship with the Thompsons. Or if they did know, they didn't care.

Or maybe they just didn't want to live long.

"What about you, Mrs. Rawlins?" she said. "What do you do for a living?"

"I'm an executive's wife. I plan our social calendar. Entertain George's business guests. I volunteer. Serve on a few charity boards."

"It doesn't sound like much," Mr. Rawlins added, "but it's a full-time job."

Jade stared at him a beat too long. "Can you think of anything else that can help us figure out who did this to your son?"

The murdered boy's parents looked at each other before shaking their heads.

Jade cast a glance at Christian, "Anything?"

He turned to a clean page in his small spiral notebook. His words came out terse. "We're going to need the names of everyone Zach encountered that day."

After the interview, Jade strode to the car, Christian close behind her. She opened the driver's side door. "I'm driving. What did you think of the Rawlinses?"

He looked at her over the top of the car. "He's an ass."

"So is she. Don't let what she said get to you."

As she shifted into drive, his phone rang. "Yeah? . . . Are they sure? . . . Okay, I'll be there as soon as I can." He disconnected.

At the next stop sign, Jade turned, raising an eyebrow. Christian looked shell-shocked. "That was Matt. It turns out Tyler didn't commit suicide after all. The coroner said he died from blunt force trauma to the head."

The questions swirled in Jade's mind like a programmer's computer code scrolling out of control. She pressed the gas pedal as the light changed. "Tyler was murdered. Is that what these other murders are all about?"

Christian nodded absently, staring out the windshield. "He's ruled it a homicide."

PART II

The White House, Washington, DC

"EMMA."

"Mom!"

Her daughter's unwavering enthusiasm for life never failed to bring a smile to Whitney's face.

"I've been trying to get in touch with you," Whitney said. "How's school?"

"I know. I'm sorry. I've been sooooo busy. Finals are coming up in a couple of weeks."

"I miss our talks every day."

"Well, Mom, you're a little busy, too. Running a country and all."

She could imagine Emma now, lying on her stomach on her dorm room bed twirling her long straight hair with her finger. Her lower legs sticking up, scissoring back and forth.

"Besides studying, what else have you been up to?"

"Not much."

"Met any interesting young men?"

"Sure, Mom. With my Secret Service escort shadowing me wherever I go? Not exactly a come-hither signal, you know? No, I haven't met anyone, and even if I had, it wouldn't be serious enough to talk to you about it."

Her daughter dated. Or did before Whitney became president. It was rare for Emma to introduce her boyfriends to her parents. Perhaps, Whitney and Grayson were too intimidating. Just a little.

"But I have been . . ."

Staring out at the Rose Garden from her chair in the Oval Office, the sound of her daughter's voice jolted her. A tone she had not heard before.

"What?"

Emma didn't answer right away. "Do you remember that income-inequality rally in Philadelphia a few weeks ago?"

"I saw it on the news."

"I was there!"

"You. Were. There."

"Yes!"

"Doing what, exactly? Watching from the sidewalk?"

"No, Mom, I was participating! I marched along with everyone else."

She tried to absorb her daughter's words. The political implications. Her safety.

The order of Whitney's thoughts was not lost on her. Why hadn't someone in the Secret Service told her? She made a mental note to follow up with the director.

"Sweetheart, are you sure that was a safe thing to do? Remember who you are now."

Whitney was referring to Emma's status as the First Daughter, neglecting to mention that as a member of the Fairchild family, Emma belonged to the very class of people the protesters were rallying against.

"It was amazing! Sitting here in my dorm room, I realized I could no longer stand by and do nothing. During the march, I felt like I was *doing* something. People are working two jobs—sometimes three—and still unable to make ends meet. I talked to this one woman who works full-time without benefits and needs—but can't find—a second job. She has no savings. What if she gets sick or loses her job?

"I have a wonderful life. I never worry about anything. Where I'm going to sleep. What I'm going to eat."

"I know, darling, but—"

"I don't need to worry about finding a job when I graduate. Do I?"

She was right. Whitney remained silent.

"Mom, we're on the verge of a revolution. We're going to take the power away from the wealthy and the corporations and give it back to the people. I have a voice. And a platform. I want to speak for those who can't."

When did Emma start using words like "platform"?

"How did you get away from the Secret Service?"

"I can't tell you all my secrets."

"Tell me."

"I went into a friend's room. I put on one of her wigs, and just walked out with another friend."

"Don't do that again. I can't lose you."

A pause. "I'm sorry, Mom. I get it."

"Did you tell your father about the protest?"

"He's going to freak. I thought maybe you could tell him."

Some revolutionist.

After the call, Whitney speed-dialed the director of the United States Secret Service.

"You need to fire the detail assigned to my daughter the day of the Philadelphia protest and replace them with your best team."

CHAPTER NINETEEN

Fairfax, Virginia

"ETHAN'S GOING TO kill us," Christian said the next day, as he parked the car. "Coming out here. Without official jurisdiction."

Jade placed her hand on the door latch. "You worry too much. Besides, he can't kill us if he doesn't know where we are."

"Seems like career-limiting logic to me," he said, getting out of the car.

"Bosses love employees who take risks."

"Said no boss ever who really meant it."

She waited for him on the other side. "We'll be back in the office in a couple hours. Thanks for arranging this."

"You're the one doing me a favor."

He held open one of the many blue doors to the William Randolph Secondary School. They immediately faced a massive, glass-covered trophy case filled to capacity. State championship trophies in golf, soccer (girls), football, basketball (boys and girls), cross-country, wrestling, baseball, softball, intermingled with pictures of the school's All-Americans.

A huge banner dominated the wall next to it: Home of the Warriors

This was a powerhouse sports school.

Christian led her to the administrative offices. "And, no," he said, "I don't know my way around in here because Mark is called into the principal's office a lot."

"Of course not."

"I've talked to the kids here a few times about staying in school and what can happen to them if they do stupid stuff."

A woman sat at a desk, a sign displayed on its front: All Visitors Must Sign in Here. She proffered a bright smile. "Can I help you?"

"We're here to see Mr. Trussell," Christian said.

"Is he expecting you?"

He nodded. Waving her hand at the clipboard with a sign-in sheet, she picked up the phone.

A minute later a man with a brown, buzzed haircut and a slight tan—unusual for Virginia in April—came out to meet them. He smiled and offered his hand. "Bobby Trussell. You must be Jade Harrington. Good to see you again, Merritt. Y'all come on back. We've set up a room for you."

Trussell led them down a short hallway and entered a conference room. Standard school chairs were pushed in around the exterior of four tables arranged in a square.

Jade walked to the other end of the room and sat in a chair facing the door. Trussell pulled out a chair and parked next to her. Christian leaned into a corner, crossing his arms.

"Thanks for allowing us to use this room," she said.

"So, what are y'all trying to accomplish here, exactly?"

"We want to talk to the teammates of Tyler Thompson, Zach Rawlins, and Nicholas Campbell. And, possibly, some of the other students."

"But that's not telling me what you hope to accomplish."

"Aren't you concerned that three of your students have died in the last few weeks? Three players on the same team? Seems like a lot. Even for a school of this size."

Trussell sat back. "Of course, I'm concerned. Do you think I *like* all the media attention? The police presence? I can't wait for things to get back to normal. It's been difficult for the team. For all the students. We've brought in grief counselors on a full-time basis. What a tragic set of coincidences."

"Coincidences?" she asked, disbelieving.

"Look. We're a big school, with the largest student population in Virginia. At least one of our students dies every year."

"And now a baseball player has died every week for the last three weeks. All murdered."

He flinched. "Tyler, too?"

She nodded. "What's going on with your baseball team?"

"Heck if I know."

"Can I speak to the coach?"

"He's not here. At a coaches' conference. Down in Richmond. He'll be back tomorrow."

Christian sat on the other side of Trussell and pulled out his notebook. "What's his name?"

"Daniel. Lane Daniel."

"Tell me," Jade said, "do you think bullying is a problem here?"

Trussell flinched again at the shift in topics. Holding the lapels of his suit jacket, he glanced at Christian for help. Christian offered none.

"Not more than any other school. Kids will be kids. Some kids think it's fun to torture other kids. Some may not realize it's bullying." He spread his hands. "I know. Doesn't make it right. Anti-bullying policies are in place. But as I said, this is a big school. A lot of places to hide here. Lots of nooks and crannies. We can't cover the entire building. Even with cameras. And that doesn't address the verbal bullying that goes on, or anything that takes place beyond these walls. Or on the Internet."

Trussell's face, flushed, looked as if it would burst if Jade poked it with a pin.

Christian gestured with his pen. "Nice ring."

Trussell stared proudly at the Harley-Davidson ring on his right hand. "Try to ride every weekend. Helps me get away from it all." He stood. "I'll go tell the assistant coach that you're ready. We sequestered the team in the locker room. Okay if I bring them in a few at a time? Otherwise, you'll be here all day."

Jade would have preferred to interview the boys individually, but he was right. They didn't have all day. Technically, she and Christian weren't here. "That's fine."

Trussell closed the door behind him.

"He's a pretty good principal," Christian said. "The kids love him."

"He can't be happy with all the negative publicity."

"This is a great public school. Not only in sports, but academically. That's why Mark goes here. Why all my children will go here."

"He's pretty protective of his school." Jade stood and stretched. "Maybe there's a reason."

❋

Three athletic boys entered the room. Each reacted differently when he saw her: one's eyes widened, one's mouth opened, and one's face flushed crimson. She ignored their reactions.

From the second boy: "You're Jade Harrington! Are you really with the FBI? Like on TV?"

"Well, TV is supposed to be like us," she said. "Although they don't always get it right."

From the third boy: "Can we see your gun?"

"Maybe another time."

Second boy: "Can we take a selfie with you?"

The first boy didn't ask her any questions. He just stared at her.

"This isn't a social visit," she said. "We're here to talk to you about Tyler, Zach, and Nicholas."

Her words sucked the air out of the room. The boys glanced at each other and sat down across from them. Two of them sported scratches and bruises on their faces just like the victims, the silent boy's face unblemished. The third had a faded black eye. Either this was one unlucky group of athletes, or something else was going on here.

"Let's start with your names."

The first boy pointed to himself. "I'm William Chaney-Frost."

"Do you go by Will or Billy?" Christian asked.

"Neither. It's William." He smiled, looking at Jade. "With a hyphenated name, what do you expect?" He pointed a thumb to the second boy. "This is Joshua Stewart. And this is Andrew Huffman."

"Tell me about your relationship with Tyler, Zach, and Nicholas."

William glanced at the other two. Was it a signal to let him do the talking?

"We all played freshman baseball together last year," he said. "Won districts. We all got along. We're all on JV this year. Tyler, too. He was okay."

"As a baseball player," she finished for him.

"He wasn't very good."

"Everyone on the team got along? No arguments? No fights ever broke out?"

Joshua's face twitched. "Fights?"

William shot him a look before turning to her. "Not really."

"Who bullied Tyler?"

"The cops asked us the same thing. Tyler was such a nerd. Easy to pick on. But I wouldn't call it bullying."

"What would you call it?" she asked.

"Just messin' around."

"Tell me about Zach."

"Z was cool. Funny. A good athlete, although not as good as he thought he was. Always trying to live up to his old man."

"Any of them have girlfriends?"

William laughed. "Tyler? No." An exaggerated shake of his head. "Nicholas liked to flirt with all the girls. But Zach only had eyes for one."

"Who?"

"Kaylee Taylor."

This kid was smart and observant. And handsome in a teen-heartthrob sort of way. She questioned them for another fifteen minutes, including their whereabouts on the nights of the murders, but didn't learn anything else. The other two boys didn't say much, only speaking when addressed directly. And not much even then. They stole looks at William Chaney-Frost for confirmation or approval of their answers.

She stood, walked over to them, and handed each of them her FBI-emblazoned business card. "Three of your teammates were murdered. That should make you nervous."

"Tyler committed suicide," William said.

Jade shook her head. "No, he didn't. Any idea who killed him?"

She got the reaction she wanted. The boys exchanged furtive glances. Only William's eye contact remained unbroken.

She waited to see if one of the other two would talk. They stared at the table. They looked scared. She needed to come back and speak to them one at a time.

"How did he die?" asked William.

As if she just thought of it, Jade asked, "Who created the 'TylerThompsonFan' Twitter account?"

Head shakes and shrugs. She wouldn't get anything more from these kids today.

"If you remember anything later," she said, "anything at all, don't hesitate to call me."

William examined her business card, and then held her gaze, as his thumb slowly caressed the raised FBI logo.

✻

After interviewing the entire baseball team, the woman manning the visitors sign ushered two girls into the room. Although Jade presumed the girls would be around fifteen or sixteen years old, they could have passed for twenty-one. The first girl strode into the room in black leggings, a pullover top, and a light cardigan sweater. A touch of lip gloss her only makeup.

The girl trailing behind her wore too much makeup, in an inverse relationship to the length of her dress. The dress seemed not only inappropriate for school, but inappropriate for the cool weather outside.

The girls sat across from them.

After Jade introduced Christian, she said, "Thanks for coming to talk to us. What are your names?"

"I'm Grace," said the girl in the dress, her eyes on Christian.

"What's your last name, Grace?" Jade said.

"Angleton."

Jade looked at the other girl. "And you?"

"Kaylee Taylor."

"We want to ask you a few questions. Were you friends with Tyler, Zach, and Nicholas?"

Grace laughed.

Jade tilted her head. "Why is that funny?"

"We were cool with Nicholas and Zach, of course." Grace glanced coyly at Kaylee and back at Jade. "You could say one of us was more than friends with Zach. But I'm single." She checked out Christian and waited for him to look up from his notes. He didn't. She turned back to Jade. "We weren't *friends* with Tyler. He was a geek."

"We only knew him because we're cheerleaders," Kaylee agreed.

"And you were more than friends with Zach?"

Kaylee glared at her friend and back at Jade. "Zach and I were cool."

"You were dating?" Jade asked.

"We were *aware* of each other," Kaylee said.

"Aware."

"She was playing hard to get," Grace said.

"Shut up!" Kaylee said, lightly tapping Grace on the arm. Her smile belied her words.

"Tell me more about your relationship with Zach," Jade asked.

"We didn't have a *relationship*. He played sports. I cheered. We had a lot in common."

"Like what?"

Kaylee seemed puzzled by the question. "Like I said, he played sports and I cheered."

Jade nodded. "Got it. How are you coping since he died?"

Kaylee hesitated. "I miss him of course."

"What about Nicholas?"

"What about him?"

"Were you close?"

"Not very. He was cute. A little too short for my taste. But he had nice muscles."

"I thought he was hot," Grace said.

Jade rejoiced she wasn't still in high school. "Is there anything more you can tell me about him that isn't physical?"

Kaylee thought for a moment. "Not really. We all hung out together. The athletes and the cheer squad. I'd see him at parties and stuff."

To Grace: "You?"

"Same."

"Are you both on Facebook?"

"Facebook's lame," Kaylee said. "It's for old people."

"People your age," Grace added, helpfully.

Jade let that slide. "What about Twitter?"

They nodded.

"Would you know anything about the 'TylerThompsonFan' account?"

The two girls shared a look.

"Heard about it," Grace said.

Kaylee could not quite meet Jade's eyes. "What about it?"

"Pretty horrible stuff, wouldn't you say?" Jade said. "If someone wrote those things about you?"

"I guess," Kaylee said.

"Did either of you ever exchange texts with Tyler?"

"Never!" Grace said.

"No," Kaylee said.

"Are you sure?"

"Why would we text *him*?" Grace asked.

Jade focused on Kaylee. "And you never texted Tyler? Not once?"

Kaylee shook her head.

Jade held her gaze for a moment, then let it go. "Last question. Is there a lot of bullying in your school?"

"No," Grace said.

Kaylee shrugged. "Is that why you think Tyler committed suicide?"

It was Jade's turn to shrug.

She didn't bother to correct Kaylee about Tyler's manner of death. She would find out soon enough.

CHAPTER TWENTY

Washington, DC

BACK AT THE Bureau, they exited the elevator on the fourth floor. As they walked down the hall, Dante strode toward them, his expression a warning as he passed by. "Ethan wants to see you. Both of you."

Jade and Christian glanced at each other, but said nothing.

Dropping off her briefcase in her office, she joined him in front of her boss's door. She knocked.

From inside: "Come in."

They entered and sat in the chairs across the desk from Supervisory Special Agent Ethan Lawson. He continued to scribble something on a legal pad. A display of the FBI's motto "Fidelity - Bravery - Integrity." hung behind him. White shirt, starched and pressed, his slacks held up by black suspenders, Ethan was a dapper throwback to a bygone era.

Setting down his pen, he turned his attention to them. "What've you two been up to?"

Jade looked at Christian—who stared at the floor—and back at Ethan.

"Research," she said.

"Hmmm . . . On what?"

"A case we're working on."

Ethan gave her a familiar look. "And which case is that, pray tell?"

"Three boys died—were murdered—at Randolph Secondary School in Fairfax in the last three weeks."

Ethan rifled through a stack of files on his desk. "I can't find that file." He threw up his hands. "Oh, wait. Now I remember. It's not our case."

"Yet."

"These were tragic murders, yes . . ." He glanced at Christian. "And I understand your personal interest, but we have our own cases to solve. Let the local police handle it."

Christian looked up at Ethan. "Hell no."

Ethan blinked. "Excuse me?"

She understood why Ethan was surprised. Christian never contradicted him. Or cursed.

"Tyler is family," Christian said.

"All the more reason why you shouldn't be involved," said Ethan.

Jade, her sleeves rolled up, leaned forward and rested her forearms on her thighs, as if about to enter a basketball game. "We're not letting it go, Ethan. Besides, I have a feeling about this."

"You and your feelings." He sighed, tearing his eyes away from Christian. "Okay. What do you have?"

"Tyler Thompson died as the result of blunt force trauma to the head. He had been bullied. Zach Rawlins was murdered with a blunt instrument a couple of weeks later. The following week, Nicholas Campbell was murdered in the same manner. Zach's and Nicholas's genitals had been mutilated. All three boys went to the same high school and played on the baseball team. All had scratches and bruising on their faces and bodies that predated their deaths. As if they fought a lot."

Ethan spun his wedding ring once. Twice. Three times.

Jade continued. "There are more deaths to come. Something's going on here. We have a serial killer on our hands. I know it."

He stopped spinning his ring. "Three murders don't equate to a serial killer. But, I'll give you two a little rope on this." He sat up, his eyes back to the work on his desk. "Don't hang yourselves."

❈

In her office, she focused on some of her cases. Her assigned cases. Her attention, though, kept drifting back to the interviews that morning.

This case tugged at Jade. A psych major in college, it wasn't too difficult to figure out why. Bullied as a teenager herself, one day she decided she'd had enough. She promised herself from that day forward she would never be bullied again. And now bullying in any form, especially of women and children, compelled her to act.

Her cell phone rang. Area code 703. Virginia. She didn't recognize the number.

350

"Agent, uh, Harrington. This is William. From the interview today. At the school."

That didn't take long. "I remember."

"Listen . . . there's something we didn't . . . I didn't . . . say. That I should have."

"I'm listening."

"Z . . ."

"What about Zach?"

"It was Z."

She let the silence linger.

He continued. "Zach bullied T—Tyler. Well, he wasn't the only one, but he was the leader. Z was always the leader."

"Go on."

"Like I told you today. T was easy to pick on. A dweeb, kind of nerdy. Read books in public. In places where people could see him. Told people he liked math. Watched the news. Sh—stuff like that. Z liked to mess with him in the locker room. He would steal his clothes, so he had nothing to wear after he took a shower. He made fun of T's . . . uh . . ."

Jade let him hang for a moment. "Private parts?"

"Yeah."

"Do you know that someone took naked pictures of Tyler and posted them on the Internet?"

Silence. After a few beats, he said, "I knew. Everyone knew. It sucked. I'm not really proud of my classmates."

"Who killed Zach, Nicholas, and Tyler?"

"One time, T fell asleep in class, and Z taped his head to the desk. T almost started crying, asking for help. Everyone in class just sat there and laughed. The teacher finally cut him out. Z did stupid stuff like that. I guess you would call Z a bully. I didn't think of it as bullying at the time. It was funny."

Hysterical. "What about Nicholas?"

"Nic would do anything Z said. Zach would goad him into stuff."

"Why didn't you say something earlier?"

The boy hesitated. "Sometimes it's easier not to get involved. So, I say nothing."

"You didn't answer my question."

"What question was that?"

"Do you know who killed Zach or Nicholas or Tyler?"

"I have no idea."

She thanked him and hung up.

Jade was not surprised by what William had told her about Zach. She thought back to the interview with his parents. Although Zach's father lamented that his son wasn't like him, Zach had followed in his father's footsteps.

He was a bully. Just like his father.

She wondered why William had called her. To manipulate the investigation? To manipulate her?

And, if so, to what end?

CHAPTER TWENTY-ONE

The White House, Washington, DC

SASHA SAT ACROSS from Whitney in the Oval Office and handed her a briefing book. "My proposal to address income inequality."

Whitney accepted it and opened it to the first page.

"It's based on the same three Rs as the New Deal: relief, recovery, and reform," Sasha said. "Relief for the unemployed poor, recovery of the economic system, and the reform of the financial system. My proposal is the same, but with a twist. This New New Deal will be based on relief for the unemployed and underemployed poor and middle class, the recovery of the American Dream, and reform of the financial system and the national infrastructure."

Whitney nodded, pleased so far. "Go on."

"The relief program will consist of training the unemployed, expanding the earned-income and child tax credits, and raising the federal minimum wage to twelve dollars an hour." She smiled. "I'm also proposing a thirty-five-hour work week, which will increase the demand for workers and improve work-life balance for everyone."

"That should be popular," Whitney said. "Does it apply to presidents as well?"

"Presidents are exempt."

"Pity."

To the media pundits, Sasha Scott, the black congresswoman from Texas, had been a surprising selection for chief of staff. Whitney had not known her well when they both served in Congress, but when they did work together, the woman's intelligence, strength, fortitude, devotion to her cultural roots, and passion for diversity and inclusion had impressed Whitney. Sasha was respected on both sides of the aisle, even when her direct—some would say "blunt"—communication style left some hurt feelings along the way. Strategic use of her Southern charm, however, always seemed to assuage those feelings after the fact.

Whitney's choice had been the right one. Gatekeeper, personnel manager, CEO, and fixer, the chief of staff's responsibility was to keep Whitney focused on the principal event of the day and to remove all distractions. Sasha turned out to be perfect for the job.

They didn't agree on every issue. Sasha, a devout Catholic, supported a woman's right to choose politically, but Whitney believed she struggled with the issue on a personal level.

Sasha turned the page. "The premise for the recovery program is the importance of education to social mobility. It consists of universal preschool, a cap on college tuition, and allowing students to repay student loans based on a percentage of post-graduate income."

"What about universal college education?"

"We couldn't get that through this Congress. Now, to reform. Instead of resurrecting the WPA, the Department of Commerce will oversee the building and repairing of highways, bridges, low-income housing, and parks."

"Twenty percent of our bridges are impaired and half of our highways—"

"—are not fit to drive on."

"How will we fund this?"

"Small- and mid-sized businesses will be given incentives to bid on these projects. The DOC will administer them."

"Ooh . . . I like that, too." Whitney thought a moment. "Although I'm in favor of universal pre-K, I need something that will impact the economy now. Like high-speed and inner-city rail. Or water systems."

Sasha shook her head. "According to the ASCE"— American Society of Civil Engineers—"it will cost three-point-six trillion dollars to fix this country's water and sewer systems."

"Trillion."

"Trillion," Sasha repeated. "Look at how much it cost to repair Flint."

"It was worth every penny."

"We don't have the revenue to approach it nationally in a significant way this time around."

Whitney crossed her legs. "Now, the sixty-four-thousand-dollar question: How will we pay for this proposal?"

"Increased tax rates, a limit on CEO pay, limits on tax deductions and loopholes. And eliminating pork."

She flipped through the proposal on her lap as Sasha spoke. After she fell silent, Whitney kept reading. After several minutes, she said, "This is good work. Thank you. Treasury won't be happy with all the changes to the tax code. But too bad. Leave it with me. I'll mark it up tonight, and give it back to you tomorrow. I'll want you to float it by Hampton and Bell."

Sasha scrunched up her face. "The 'Young Guns' on the Hill?"

"Who, by the way, are not so young anymore."

"I heard that one time Hampton spoke for ten hours on the Senate floor."

"He did," Whitney said. "I was there."

Sasha shook her head. "How could you stand it? It's hard for me to listen to that whiny voice for ten minutes." Sasha closed her briefing book. "It must be nice to be Senator Eric Hampton. I wish I had the privilege of always being so . . ."

"Certain?"

Sasha nodded. "They'll kill this before it has a chance to be debated."

Whitney smiled. "Then you may want to persuade them with sugar instead of your usual hot sauce. We need their buy-in, Sasha. It won't get through otherwise."

"But do you trust them?"

Whitney had battled Hampton before on previous bills. Last year, they came to an agreement on a major piece of legislation. Just before it went to vote, he added an amendment that was anathema to Whitney's principles and one she could never support.

But she needed him this time. She had no choice. As senate majority leader, he was her best chance of selling the proposal to others in his party.

Whitney laid the briefing book on her desk. "No. No, I don't."

Fairfax, Virginia

SHE STARED THROUGH the one-way mirror at Matt Thompson. Hands clasped on the table, he listened to instructions from his attorney sitting next to him. From his suit, the attorney didn't look like a high-priced one to Jade, but he wasn't a public defender either.

Thompson looked much better than the last time she had seen him. The reality, if not the acceptance, of his son's death had sunk in. Christian stood next to her, the anguish of seeing his brother-in-law in that room plain on his face.

Detective Chutimant had decided to bring Thompson in for questioning. She had invited Jade and Christian to observe.

She had also sent Jade the results of Tyler's autopsy report. The coroner ruled out the use of a blunt instrument. He didn't find any fingerprints on the body. This didn't surprise Jade. If Tyler was sweaty from baseball practice or struggled during the altercation, any fingerprints would have been damaged or lost. He could have unintentionally rubbed them off.

The coroner did find grass, glass, rocks, dirt, and fragments from fast-food wrappers on Tyler's skin. But no hair fibers.

Not much to go on.

The detective glanced at her now and nodded before opening the door to the interrogation room, followed by another detective from the county. The door clicked closed behind them, the sound loud in the observation room. By his slight head movement, Thompson acknowledged the detectives' entrance but didn't look at them.

Chutimant went through the interview preliminaries and then asked Thompson about his whereabouts the night Zach Rawlins was murdered.

He glanced at his attorney. The attorney nodded. Thompson cleared his throat and looked at Chutimant. "I was home. I left the dealership around eight p.m. and went straight there. My wife and I watched television until we went to bed."

"Was your wife with you the entire time?"

"Yes. Even before Tyler . . ." He looked away from Chutimant. "With two young children, we don't go out much."

"What about the night Nicholas died?"

"What night was that?"

"April twenty-seventh of this year."

Thompson cleared his throat again. "That would've been a Thursday. Same thing. Work and then home. We're basic. We lead a boring life."

The detective, her tone sharp and accusatory: "Did you kill Zach Rawlins and Nicholas Campbell?"

"No, I did not," he said.

After an hour of questioning, Christian said to her, "They don't have any evidence against him."

"Except motive." Jade stared at Thompson. "Or other suspects. Let's go talk to his wife."

❋

"This is a bad idea."

"It'll take some time to release him," Jade said.

The bicycle now lay in the grass.

Christian knocked. "House is quiet. Maybe she's not here."

"Let's wait," she said.

After a couple of minutes, they turned to leave.

The door opened. Jenny, her bathrobe cinched at her chest, said, "Sorry, I was in the shower. Come on in."

They headed without invitation to the living room. Jenny stopped at the stairs, her hand on the railing. She looked down the front of her robe and over to them. "I'm going to change. Be right back."

She trudged upstairs.

Jade said to Christian, "Her hair's not wet."

He nodded, distracted. "I don't think she's washed that robe in a while."

She glanced around the living room. It appeared as it had the first time she was here. Immaculate.

"I still think this is a bad idea," he said.

"I want to see if their stories match."

Jenny returned wearing a light-blue t-shirt and jeans. "I need to pick up the kids from school soon."

Christian cut his eyes at Jade before turning to Jenny. "We came by to check on you."

"We just left the police station," Jade said. "We saw Matt."

"They're wasting their time. Matt wouldn't hurt a fly."

"They asked him where he was the night Zach Rawlins was killed."

"I could've saved them the trouble. He was here with me. Watching TV."

"How do you remember which night it was?" Jade asked.

"Because it's what we do every night. We're not the most exciting couple in the world. No one would ever create a reality show about us."

"What about the night Nicholas Campbell died?"

"Same."

"And you're sure he was with you the entire time?" Jade pressed. "Both nights?"

"Yes."

"Do you believe Matt is capable of murder?"

"No, I don't. He's a big teddy bear." She gestured to Christian. "Like him."

CHAPTER TWENTY-THREE

Washington, DC

"JADE, COME IN."

"I wanted to update you on—" She stopped in the doorway of Ethan's office. He wasn't alone. "I can come back later."

Before she turned, his guest stood.

She processed several observations about him at once.

He wore an FBI-issued badge on a lanyard around his neck. Tall, the same height as she, his biceps filled out his suit jacket. His skin was the color of light mocha. The absence of a wedding ring.

He returned her stare, his eyes, gray and mesmerizing.

"I can come back," she repeated.

"No," Ethan said, "I want you to meet Micah Alexander."

She shook his hand. "Jade Harrington."

"I know who you are," he said through straight white teeth. A slight British accent tinted his words. They held each other's gaze until a throat cleared. She looked over at Ethan.

"Micah just graduated from the academy," he said. "Today's his first day. He just joined the department."

Jade turned back to the new agent. "Welcome."

"Thank you."

"Ethan, I'll catch you later."

She turned to leave.

"Wait a minute," he said. "Take Micah with you. I've assigned him to your team."

CHAPTER TWENTY-FOUR

Seattle, Washington

CHIEF FINANCIAL OFFICER David Smith rushed from the CEO's office of the technology company at which he worked and down the hall to his own corner office. His employees were accustomed to seeing him hustling up and down the corridors.

He strode straight to his chair and dropped his writing pad on the desk. He spun the chair to the credenza behind him and logged onto his laptop. Checking the time in the bottom-right corner of the computer screen, he opened the browser. He navigated to the Pacific Coast Bank website, where his company kept its operating and payroll checking accounts.

He glanced at the time again. Ten minutes to make the train to Sea-Tac for his four o'clock flight. The train wasn't always on time. He may have an extra two minutes. Worst-case scenario he could call a cab, but like any good CFO, he would rather spend $2.50 than $45 of the company's money for the same service. Plus, it was faster these days to travel by train than car with Seattle's worsening traffic.

He clicked Transfer Money, selected From the Operating Account, and typed in *1,000,000*. He clicked To the Payroll Account. It wasn't the exact amount of payroll, but enough to cover it. He could transfer the excess back later after his payroll accountant finished reconciling all the adjustments.

Spinning the chair back to his desk, he removed the security token from the center drawer. He pressed the blue button. A six-digit access code appeared in the digital display. He punched the code on the laptop's keyboard and hit Enter. The Transfer Successfully Completed page displayed on the computer screen. He emailed this page to his controller.

With care, he logged out of the bank's website and closed the browser. Tapping the Windows button and the letter L on the keyboard to lock his computer, he swept the laptop off the docking station. He stuffed it into the bag, and shoved it down the handle of his suitcase.

He grabbed his suit jacket off the hook on the back of his office door with one hand and breezed out the door with the suitcase and laptop in the other.

Thank God, transferring significant sums of money was easy and fast these days.

He would make the train.

✻

As David Smith hurried to the University Street train station, the million dollars he just transferred was not deposited in the company's payroll account at Pacific Coast Bank.

Instead, the funds jetted to Switzerland, then the Cayman Islands, London, and four other locations before ending up in a different Seattle bank.

CHAPTER TWENTY-FIVE

Quantico, Virginia

IT HAD BEEN over a year since Jade had visited Behavioral Analysis Unit 4 of the National Center for the Analysis of Violent Crime in Quantico.

Standing in the doorway of Max Stover's office, she watched him work. His hair was thinning, with only faint blond wisps remaining on top. Max was a supervisory special agent. Most people would call him a profiler. One of the agency's best. He was also Jade's mentor and godfather.

Without looking up, he said, "Are you going to stand there all day or are you going to sit down and tell me why you're here?"

Jade entered his office and removed a stack of papers and folders from the solitary guest chair, glancing around to figure out where to put it. He waved at the floor.

"How did you know it was me?"

He pointed to his ear. "I could tell by the sound of your walk. No one walks like you."

"I'll take that as a compliment."

Max stopped writing and placed the pen on his pad of paper. He pushed his glasses farther up on the bridge of his nose and looked at her. "To what do I owe this honor?"

"You look pale."

"I'm always pale."

"Paler than usual. You need to get out more."

"Now that that's cleared up, why are you here?"

"What do you know about bullying?"

Max shrugged. "Bullies are insecure. Bullying gives them power over someone or a group of people. A power they lack in other aspects of their lives. Sometimes, a bully has been bullied, and often models what has been done to him or what he sees others doing."

"Or her."

As a bullied kid, she never realized her attackers could have been victims, too. At the time, she hadn't thought much about them at all, except hoping they would all go away or die. She didn't tell Max any of this. He knew her history.

He nodded. "Women, too. If we're talking about kids, sometimes the victim's friends—or frenemies—are the meanest bullies of all."

"And with the Internet and smartphones, bullying is a twenty-four/seven endeavor."

"Your home is no longer a sanctuary. There is no safe place."

"You heard about Christian's nephew."

Max nodded.

During the conversation, she had straightened all the items closest to her on Max's gray metal desk.

"They posted photos," she said, "on the Internet of him in the locker room shower." She told him about the Twitter account, and the texts from the girl who played a joke on him.

Max watched her straighten, a smile-grimace etched on his face. "Bullying is different now than when I was growing up. Than when you were growing up. It's more psychological and socially cruel. Bullies target vulnerable groups like special-needs kids or LGBTQ kids or weak kids. And they keep coming up with creative ways to bully. It's more commonplace. Some of our politicians are the worst bullies of all."

Last year, a billionaire businesswoman threatened to oppose the incumbent president in the Republican primary. According to her, everyone in the GOP establishment was either a liar, a cheater, stupid, or out to get her. No segment of the population—except for Caucasians—escaped her wrath.

"Entertainment," Jade added.

"And games. Bullying behaviors in games are explained away as trash-talking. All these things desensitize kids—heck, all of us—to violence. By the time a child reaches eighteen years of age, she or he has watched two hundred thousand acts of violence."

"What can we do about it?"

"Adults could set a better example. Better enforcement of school policies. Tougher laws. There's no federal law against bullying. But at the micro level, victims need to tell someone and not stay silent. So they know they're not alone. And parents, teachers, and bystanders need to say something when they see it."

Jade aligned files she'd already straightened. "I wish bullies could channel that creativity and energy into something useful. More productive. Like becoming an FBI agent." She stopped and admired her handiwork.

Max glanced at his files. "Are you finished?"

She pulled her hands away. "Yes."

He removed his glasses to polish them and squinted at her. "You shouldn't take this case personally."

She examined her hands, her complexion the product of a black father and Japanese mother. The physical scars had long since healed. Her parents never knew about the bullying. Now that they were dead, they never would.

"I was a mixed-race Army brat. Always the new kid on the block. Always an outsider. It's hard to forget."

"What do they know about the perp?"

She relayed the skimpy information they had obtained so far. The killer, most likely right-handed, used a blunt instrument to murder his victims, and then severed their genitals.

"That wasn't in the paper."

"Two victims, Zach and Nicholas, both bullied Tyler Thompson, Christian's nephew."

"I like that you still use the victims' names like I taught you. It humanizes them."

"They were human beings. With lives. With hopes and dreams. What else would I call them? What do you make of the mutilations?"

Max didn't react to the shift in topics. He picked up his pen and started gently tapping it on his notepad. "We could hypothesize about that one all day. The obvious reason is the perpetrator is exacting revenge. Could these boys have raped Tyler? But it sounds as if most of the bullying wasn't physical. Maybe it has something to do with the baseball team. Any signs of resistance?"

Jade shook her head. She then described the scratches and bruises inflicted on all three victims before their deaths.

"Antemortem?" he asked, surprised.

She nodded. "I've seen them on other members of the baseball team, too. The living members. I believe that other kids are involved. And that they may be in danger."

"Not much to go on," Max said.

"Not much is right. Christian and I interviewed the parents of Zach Rawlins. His mother is a perfectionist, and his father is a bully."

"Dangerous combination. Zach most likely never felt comfortable in his own skin. Since he wasn't perfect, his parents couldn't see him for the person he actually was. Always judging him."

Jade looked away. *Like I judge myself.*

After a moment, she cocked her chin toward the paperwork on his desk. "What are you working on?"

"Serial-killer case in Wisconsin. Someone is kidnapping, raping, and killing girls from trailer-park homes spanning a three-county area."

Jade's stomach clenched. "Get him."

"I will." He paused. "Everything else all right?"

"Great." She got up to leave.

"How's Micah doing?"

"You know him?"

He nodded. "I trained him."

"Hmph."

"He's going to be good, Jade."

"As good as I am?"

"No one's that good." He smiled. "But I wouldn't sleep on him, though."

"You don't even know what that means," she said.

"I still teach, remember?"

She stood. "I need to go."

"A piece of advice. Forget the victims were bullies. You've got a killer to catch. Get. Him."

"I will."

She nodded and moved toward the door.

"Jade," he said. She turned to look at him. "Thanks for straightening my desk."

Over her shoulder, she said, "You're welcome," and strode out the door.

Halfway down the hallway, she heard Max shout from his office: "I was kidding!"

CHAPTER TWENTY-SIX

The White House, Washington, DC

IN THE OVAL Office, Whitney reviewed her chief of staff's proposal one last time. She crossed out the sections that would hurt middle-class families, including the elimination of the mortgage-interest deduction for homes under one million dollars. She made her final changes in the margin of the document.

To be palatable to the other party, distribution of income must benefit the wealthy in some way. With her revisions, she thought the proposal would be amenable to Hampton. Bell didn't matter as much.

Sean, her secretary, buzzed her. "Madam President? Ashley Brennan is here to see you."

"Who?"

"Cole Brennan's wife."

"Oh, yes. Send her in." Whitney had not seen or heard from Cole since she had appeared on his radio show late last summer. She had never met the wife of the radio talk-show host, and had been surprised by her request for a meeting.

"Mrs. Brennan."

"Whitney . . . Madam President, thanks for taking the time to see me."

Whitney gestured toward the sofa, as she sat in a nearby chair. Ashley Brennan, blonde and beautiful and a decade younger than her husband, carried herself like the model she once had been. In an Hermès dress, she perched near the edge of the sofa, her legs crossed at the ankle, à la Jackie Kennedy.

"What can I do for you?" asked Whitney.

"My husband hasn't been kind to you on the show these last few months . . . well, ever, but I've always admired you from afar. That you stand for what you believe in. I voted for you." A small smile. "Cole doesn't know that, of course."

Whitney crossed her legs. "I'm surprised, but flattered."

"You shouldn't be. As Madeline Albright said, 'There is a special place in hell for women who do not help other women.' I still believe that." She paused. "I'm here about our son. Cole Jr. CJ. You may have heard that he came out. That he's gay."

"I did."

Ashley hesitated. "He . . . was beaten up. Badly. Yesterday. By a bunch of boys at his school."

"Oh, Ashley, I'm sorry." She placed her hand over the woman's hands. "Is he all right?"

A shrug. "He'll be all right. Nothing broken. Doctors said the bruises on his face will heal. He'll still be handsome. He's strong. Stands up for what he believes in." Ashley glanced at Whitney. "Like his dad." That smile again. "But opposite."

"What can I do for you?" When someone called or visited her, the person wanted something.

"CJ is a good kid. Never hurt anyone. Bullying has to stop. Not just for my child, but for all children."

Whitney retracted her hand. "It is a problem, the pervasiveness of bullying in our schools. In our workplaces. In our politics." She bit her lip, but said it anyway. "On the radio."

Ashley didn't respond. The silence lengthened. Whitney thought she had gone too far.

"I don't always agree with what my husband says. But he is my husband. And I support him. Always. He's devastated by what's happened. But he feels helpless. He doesn't know what he can do about it." Her eyes, vacant and sad, implored Whitney nevertheless. "Is there something that you can do? Can you strengthen federal laws to stop bullying?"

Whitney bit back her comment this time, choosing to ignore the irony that Ashley—like many Republicans—opposed the federal government's intervention in the lives of US citizens in almost everything, except for women's reproductive rights. And when they needed something.

"There is no federal law against bullying."

"Can you create one?"

"This Congress would be an obstacle. I may need your husband's help."

Ashley Brennan's back straightened with resolve. Whitney suspected that many people underestimated this woman.

"You'll have it."

"But there may be something I'll need in return."

"To make this work, we need to align our interest groups. Just like the New Deal Coalition. Labor, minorities, intellectuals, liberals, and small businesses. We must be the party of prosperity. Like back in the Thirties."

Whitney pumped hard on the elliptical in the gym in the White House residence as she spoke. She glanced at the electronic dashboard. Fifteen minutes to go.

Sasha shifted on the bench she had pulled up close to the machine earlier. "No luck with Hampton or Bell, so far."

This didn't surprise Whitney. In addition to the inherent intransigence of the two congressmen, Sasha's direct approach rubbed some people the wrong way. Particularly men.

Whitney smiled. "I guess you didn't take my advice and feed them a spoonful of sugar."

"I always did prefer hot sauce."

"I tried to tell you."

"I was never a great listener, either."

Whitney's legs continued to pump. "At the end of the nineteenth century, the economic inequality prevalent throughout Europe at that time almost caused a socialist revolution."

"Met with them and their LDs a few times."

"The gap in wealth has not been this wide in the United States since the Great Depression."

"I'll keep trying," Sasha said.

"Poverty is at its highest level since 1993. It's harder for the poor to climb out of poverty. It matters more than ever that you were born to the right parents." She stopped exercising. "Seven percent of the people who work are poor. *Who work.*"

"We can take on Social Security and Medicare."

"Not until my second term." She realized her response came out sharper than intended. She softened her tone. "We'll fix them on our way out."

Sasha remained silent, realizing she was supposed to shut up and listen.

Whitney resumed her pedaling. "It's going to get worse. If the American Dream dies, chaos will reign. An economist on *Meet the Press* said that if we do not address income inequality, it will create a crisis of legitimacy for the republic." Wiping her face with a towel, she threw it on the floor. She stared at her chief of staff. "Not on my watch."

"Understood, Madam President."

"'When there is no vision, the people perish,'" she said. She pursed her lips, imitating the expression Sasha often gave her. "Don't look surprised. I read the Bible, too." Whitney started pumping faster. "How many do I need?"

Sasha calculated the votes in her head. "At least ten, maybe two more from our side."

"Bell is not intellectually curious. He just parrots whatever his constituents want him to say. Offer him some tickets to my box at the Kennedy Center. Sampson, too. He'll drink everything in the fridge, so make sure it's stocked."

Democratic Senator Paul Sampson was known for two things: his love of the University of Nebraska Cornhuskers football team and his love of drink.

"What about Hampton?"

"Off camera," Whitney said, "he has an open mind. More than others in his party. I think he could be persuaded."

"If something's in it for him," Sasha said.

"Be that as it may, schedule a meeting for me to meet with the three of them. Tomorrow."

"That's a mistake."

"Duly noted. Do it anyway."

Sasha nodded, rising from the chair. "Yes, Madam President."

"Is there a problem?"

"No, ma'am. I serve at the pleasure of the president."

Whitney searched Sasha's face for sarcasm. And found none.

CHAPTER TWENTY-SEVEN

Seattle, Washington

NOAH BLAKELEY LIFTED a champagne flute from the tray of a passing server. He sipped the cool liquid, the bubbles just right, as he scanned the room over the lip of the glass. Standing in a ballroom in the Grand Hyatt Hotel on Pine Street downtown, the muted light from the gigantic chandelier above allowed him to observe his fellow guests without appearing as if he were doing so.

He wondered whether other cities had as many fundraisers. He could attend a different one every night, if he desired. Seattle was not known for its pretentiousness like other cities such as New York or Washington, DC, but Noah knew that was a lie. Some pretentious Seattleites just hid behind their outdoorsy Pacific Northwest façade. The same people who excluded him from their cliques. His wife, Diane, never attended these events with him. After having accompanied him to a few functions right after their wedding, she now refused.

Never one to stand still, he began to stroll around the room. He squeezed by a woman and a man in animated conversation. The woman, wearing a tight dark-blue dress with a hint of gold at her neck, whispered to her companion in a fierce undertone. He caught the words "hacker" and "stole" and "cyber." He wanted to stop and listen, but didn't want to be conspicuous. Other snippets of conversation reached him: "money" and "million" and "IT consultants" and "beefed-up security."

What's going on?

He drained his glass. He needed something stronger than champagne and headed toward one of the bars set up in the ballroom.

A woman dressed in a black pantsuit and an expensive white shirt stood at the back of the line at the bar. Her smile always looked like a smirk to him.

He looked down at his own tan slacks and mismatched brown jacket. "Kyle. Hello."

"Good evening, Noah." She waved her hand, indicating he should cut in front of her. "Feel free. You seem to need a drink more than I do."

Kyle Madison was the founder and managing director of a powerful venture-capital firm.

He squeezed between her and the woman in front of her. "Thanks."

They stood. The silence uncomfortable. Noah hated silence. "How've you been?"

"Well, thank you."

She didn't bother asking how he was, but instead scanned the room. As if searching for someone more interesting. He had always sensed that she didn't like him.

"And business?" he said.

"Never better."

"Have you heard about something going on?"

She looked at him, her dark hair cascading like waves. Like one of those shampoo commercials. He wanted to reach out and touch it but knew she wouldn't appreciate that. Her beauty intimidated him.

"What do you mean?"

He shoved his hand in his pocket. "Just hearing things. About hackers. Stealing money."

"Sounds like a bunch of rumors to me." She spotted someone in the crowd. Or pretended to. "I see someone I need to speak to. If you'll excuse me."

Placing her glass on the tray of a passing server, she moved away from him. *Guess she didn't want another drink after all.*

But he knew it was him. He had that effect on people.

Noah inspected his jacket. He pulled a loose thread at the bottom, wrapping it around his finger. And kept pulling. The thread seemed endless. *Shit!* The woman in front of him glanced down at his engorged finger, and then abruptly faced the bar. He stuffed his hand in his jacket pocket.

He did not speak to Kyle Madison for the rest of the evening.

CHAPTER TWENTY-EIGHT

The White House, Washington, DC

SARAH, HER BODY woman, poked her head into the Oval Office. "Excuse me, Madam President. Senators Hampton and Sampson and Representative Bell are here."

"Send them in. And ask Sasha to join us, please."

Whitney rose, smoothed her skirt, and came around her desk, arm extended. "Gentlemen. How good of you to come."

"Madam President," Hampton and Bell said.

Sampson said nothing.

Her eyes narrowed. "Excuse me, Paul; I didn't hear you."

"Madam President."

She indicated for them to sit on the two sofas facing each other, while she sat on a Queen Anne chair, her back to the window. Sasha entered and sat in the matching chair.

"I won't mince words." Whitney looked at Hampton and Bell. "I understand the two of you met with Sasha. What are your thoughts about the proposal?"

Hampton adjusted his black-framed glasses. "We don't need another 'Soak the Rich' proposal. If you want our support, focus on growing the economic pie rather than wealth distribution."

"Income inequality isn't the issue," said Bell. "Economic opportunity is."

"'The fact is that income inequality is real; it's been rising for more than twenty-five years.'" She waited.

The men looked at each other.

"George W. Bush," she said. "Early 2000s. The gap has widened since then. We have less economic mobility in America today than in class-conscious Europe."

"You make income inequality sound like a bad thing," Hampton said. "Howard's right. The issue is making sure that everyone has the opportunity for a better life. What they do with that opportunity is up to them."

Senator Paul Sampson rested his hands on top of his belly. "Some income inequality is beneficial. It creates an incentive for people to be productive, innovate, and create wealth."

Whitney glanced at him. *Aren't you a Democrat?* "But too much impedes economic growth and marginalizes the people at the bottom, leaving them feeling disenfranchised."

"That's not the problem," said Bell. "The quality of life for everyone is improving. Even if you're poor today, you're likely to own a smartphone, the latest Nikes, a flat-screen TV—"

Sasha sat up. "Excuse me?"

"What Howard is saying," Hampton cut in, "is that the government shouldn't be in the business of altering economic outcomes, but should instead focus on creating opportunities."

"All right," Whitney said. "Give me an example."

Hampton and Bell glanced at each other.

Bell spoke up. "Didn't you see on the news about those two guys on food stamps who became billionaires overnight by inventing a smartphone app?"

She held up a hand, signaling Sasha to stop laughing. Turning to Bell, she didn't even try to mask the incredulity in her voice. "You're kidding, right?" He wasn't. "How often is that going to happen? Really, Howard. That's not real life."

"You make it seem as if being born poor is a life sentence," Sampson said. "My daddy was a farmer." He spread his arms. "Now, look at me."

"Yes," Whitney said. "Look at you."

He dropped his arms.

"Social mobility isn't dead," Hampton said. "The people with vision and drive, who are willing to work hard and take risks, will be rewarded."

"An economist once said that 'it's harder to climb our social ladder when the rungs are further apart.'"

He leaned forward. "For argument's sake, let's say we enact what you propose. How do you intend to pay for it? Taxing the rich is a nonstarter. There's no way we're going to sign on for any of the usual class warfare championed by you and your party."

"My party? Do you think if you say 'class warfare' enough, constituents in *your* party will forget that they are part of that middle or lower class that is falling behind, too?"

"They have so far," Sasha quipped.

Hampton's cool demeanor dissipated. "Instead of demotivating the rich with new taxes, how about easing their tax burden by eliminating the corporate tax? They'll work harder, be more productive, create more jobs, and expand the economy."

"Come on! Historical evidence proves that higher taxes don't demotivate people. Between nineteen forty-seven and nineteen seventy-seven, income taxes were high and GDP grew by almost four percent. The top one percent owned sixteen percent of the wealth versus eighty-five today. That's why Americans remember those times fondly. It was the golden age of the middle class."

"And what are *we* going to do with all those tax dollars?" Hampton said. "Our government has a propensity to be inefficient and waste resources."

"I still don't understand why so many in your party bash the federal government, when they themselves are the ones making the decisions. That has never made sense to me."

Hampton glanced at the other two men. "How about this? Instead of the American people funding social programs through the government, what if we allow them to 'self-tax' by giving directly to the charities of their choice?"

Sasha sighed, shooting a meaningful glance at Whitney.

Whitney did not try to hide her frustration. "That won't work. Not all needs can be met by established nonprofits. Poor, minority women would be forgotten. I want to return to Clinton-era tax rates, which will increase revenues by seventy-six billion dollars a year. With just that much, we're talking about improving a significant number of people's lives at a small cost to the wealthiest Americans."

Hampton had started shaking his head when she mentioned the former president from Arkansas. "No way. I can't even bring that to the caucus with a straight face. The one percent will migrate to Galt's Gulch."

"I wish we could discuss income inequality without your party resurrecting Ayn Rand."

"She has her uses," he smiled. "The one percent start companies, employ millions of people, pay their benefits, create products. Let's make it easier for them to provide that. What we really need to do is help them compete in the world marketplace so they can generate that wealth for their workers. Streamline regulations. Reduce their taxes."

"Or we can increase social benefits," Whitney countered, "such as food stamps and unemployment. History has shown that benefits stimulate the economy four to five times more than tax cuts."

Hampton shook his head again, knowing he didn't need to respond.

"A columnist once said that the rising tide is not lifting all boats, only the yachts." She decided to change course. "Minimum wage?"

Hampton smoothed his tie. "Historically, minimum-wage increases have been ineffective at improving standards of living."

She looked at him. "How would you know? Reagan and H. W. kept the minimum wage fixed for nine years, and based on real buying power, it hit a fifty-one-year low during W.'s administration."

Bell snorted. "It's easy to raise the federal minimum wage when the federal government doesn't have to pay for it. Let the states decide."

"Higher pay increases autonomy, personal freedom, and responsibility," Whitney said. She turned to Hampton. "Bottom line, it increases their buying power. Conservative principles, Eric. Ones you profess to believe in. Or used to anyway."

"You're forgetting the negative consequences. Inflation, higher prices, and layoffs in businesses that can't afford the new wage."

"With all due respect, Madam President," Bell said, "there will always be poor people. Your party has to get over it. That's what charities are for."

Before Sasha could react, Whitney said, "Adam Smith said, 'No society can surely be flourishing and happy, of which the far greater part of the members are poor and miserable.'"

Hampton raised his hand. "Before you quote someone else, I'll concede to raising the minimum to ten-fifty. But that's it. That will lift nine hundred thousand people out of poverty."

Bell protested. "But that will cost five hundred thousand jobs."

Whitney considered it. Improving the lives of only a million people wasn't enough for her. She wasn't getting anywhere with them. She rose to signal the end of the meeting. The three men and Sasha stood, too, Sampson faster than the rest.

"We like the EITC and child-tax credit expansions," Hampton said. "We can work together on repairing bridges, roads, and schools, and modernizing our shipping ports and airports. We might even give you high-speed and inner-city rail, but we want to privatize Amtrak." Whitney shook her head. He tilted his head and offered his charming smile. "Come on. Give us something."

She said nothing.

Hampton extended his hand. "Eliminate the new tax brackets. I'll float the Clinton-era rates. No promises, though. Good day, Madam President."

CHAPTER TWENTY-NINE

Washington, DC

ETHAN LAWSON LEANED into her office. "My office. Five minutes." He left before she could respond. She mentally reviewed her active cases in preparation for whatever he might ask and grabbed her notebook.

He was hanging up his suit jacket on the mahogany coat rack in the corner as she entered. Over his shoulder, he said, "What's up?"

Jade sat in the guest chair. "Preparing to testify in the Morales case tomorrow. Merritt and I are interviewing a source in the Blanchett case later today."

"What else?"

"That's about it."

"I heard a rumor."

She gave him a blank look.

"Don't you want to know what it is?" Ethan asked.

"Not really."

He leaned back in his chair, one hand on his desk. "This is an interesting one, though. It involves you."

Jade feigned ignorance.

"Rumor has it," he continued, "that you and Merritt not only have an interest in the deaths of those three teenage boys, but you have an unofficial investigation going. An administrator for the Fairfax County school system told me that you interviewed students at one of his esteemed institutions of secondary education. I also heard you interviewed the parents of one of the victims of this case-that-isn't-ours. Observed an interview of an alleged suspect, for that same case. Any of that ring a bell?"

He didn't seem to know about their visit with Jenny Thompson.

Jade tilted her head and shrugged. "Maybe. Who did you hear that from?"

He ignored the question. "You shouldn't be involved."

"Why not?"

Ethan raised his hands in exasperation. "It's not our case!"

"More kids are going to die."

"Jade . . ."

"More. Kids. Are. Going. To. Die."

He sank into his chair. "There are rules for a reason." He twirled his wedding ring, then sighed. "Until this is officially our case . . . if you continue to pursue it, I'll place you on administrative leave."

Jade's heart beat faster. Her cheeks flushed. She shot Ethan a look and headed for the door. Holding the door open, she turned, staring at him for a moment.

"Then place me on leave."

She made sure to slam the door as hard as she could on her way out.

CHAPTER THIRTY

Columbus, Ohio

"WHERE IS THE crowd?" she asked, as she accepted a bottled water from Sarah and took a quick sip.

Sasha shrugged. "Things change when you go from candidate to president."

What a difference six months make.

Sarah held the daily schedule and the ever-present stack of briefing books. Scanning the invited guests sitting in the three rows of bleachers behind the podium, she said, "Don't bother to thank Senator Harris in your remarks. He didn't show."

"Asshole," Sasha said.

As Whitney's body woman, Sarah was on call twenty-four/seven and accompanied her almost everywhere. She didn't have time for a private life, so Whitney never bothered to ask her about it. A specific document, a Sharpie for autographs, a breath mint, snacks, a messenger, her cell phone, or a sounding board, Sarah anticipated and catered to Whitney's every need. She even worked out with Whitney sometimes.

Whitney glanced up at the bleachers, a quarter of them still empty. They were both right. The senior Democratic senator from Ohio was not in attendance, which was bad form and showed a lack of respect for a sitting president. And he was an asshole.

This was the first stop on a road trip through the Midwest to get her message out about the New New Deal. In the wings of a makeshift stage at Ohio State University's St. John Arena, she waited for the governor to wrap up his introduction. She took deep, relaxing breaths until her name was announced.

"Let's do this." Handing the bottle back to Sarah, she adjusted the specially-made Kevlar vest under her suit and walked into the basketball arena.

She smiled and waved at the crowd. At the podium, she shook hands with the governor. "Thanks, Bill." She turned back toward the crowd. "How are you, Columbus?"

A lukewarm response greeted her. She didn't take it personally. She was a politician, after all.

"I'm here today to talk to you about the New New Deal Coalition legislation. Franklin D. Roosevelt once said, 'Throughout the nation men and women . . . look to us here for guidance and for more equitable opportunity to share in the distribution of national wealth . . . I pledge myself to a new deal for the American people. This is more than a political campaign. It is a call to arms.'

"No words are more true today.

"The New Deal reduced income inequality by putting eight point five million people to work, built six hundred and fifty thousand miles of highways, and one hundred and twenty-five thousand buildings. The Lincoln Tunnel, LaGuardia Airport, and the San Francisco Bay Bridge were all built during this glorious period of American achievement.

"But the legislation wasn't only about what it built. The New Deal represented what was best about our country. It was about coming together, making real change, caring about the American worker, and providing security and a sense of purpose.

"Income inequality is the defining issue of our time. Five years ago, the three hundred and eighty-eight richest people in the world were more wealthy than the poorest three-point-five billion combined. Three years ago, it was the top eighty-five people. Now, it's eight people. Eight."

She paused, allowing that number to hang in the air.

"The concentration of wealth is accelerating. No other economic system in the history of the world has ever had the concentration of untaxed wealth that we do now. This deprives the government of much-needed resources for public services and erodes trust that there is a level playing field of equal opportunity. For everyone.

"In the nineteen forties and fifties, the gap between the rich and everyone else was small. In the eighties, with technological advances, deregulation, and tax cuts for the wealthiest Americans, fortunes began to diverge; the rich got richer, but everyone else stayed about the same. I call this time the 'Great Divide.'

"Although we saw some improvement in the nineties during the economic boom and with the increasing of the highest marginal tax rate, it got dramatically worse during the first decade of this century when that administration slashed taxes, cut social services, and deregulated industries. And it has worsened ever since.

"In 1980, a CEO made about forty-two times the average worker. With the decreasing influence of unions and changing societal norms, CEO pay has climbed to over three hundred and eighty times worker pay." Whitney spread her arms wide. "Has the productivity of CEOs increased that much compared with yours?"

She waited for the shouts of "No!"

Instead, she received a low grumble of disagreement.

She'd take it.

"A CEO of a software company has a net worth of twenty-seven *billion* dollars and could spend three hundred thousand dollars an hour every *hour* until he died, and still not make a dent in his net worth.

"On the other side of the Great Divide, there are two-income families who still need government assistance to make ends meet. Who's fighting for these families?

"We even have some teenagers who must work to feed their families. Who's fighting for these teenagers?

"Twenty-five percent of the children in the United States live in poverty. That is one out of every four. In the United States! Who's fighting for our children?

"Our middle class is shrinking. Historically, the prosperity of this country flowed from the middle class. Who's fighting for our middle class?"

Whitney scanned the arena, letting the last statement sink in, gauging their response. This audience, predominately middle-class and white, must identify with this statement or her message was dead. Her historic legislation was dead.

"And everyone knows that women make only seventy-seven percent of what a man makes for the same work. Everyone *knows* this. Who's fighting for our women?

"If we do not act now, our country will continue to grow evermore divided. We can do better. The Great Divide does not need to be the status quo. My New New Deal Coalition legislation will not eliminate income inequality—a problem that has been over three decades in the making—but it will put us in a position to start closing that gap and realize our true wealth by making a significant investment in the American people.

"And I'll make that investment any day."

Whitney outlined the plan. She did not mention the changes that

Hampton sent to her after their meeting. She would allow him to take credit for them with his constituents.

She wrapped up her speech, surprised at the tepid applause. Surprised because this audience would benefit the most from her plan. Pasting on a smile, she waved and met Sasha and Sarah backstage.

"You wrote an incredible speech," Sasha said.

Whitney accepted a fresh bottle of water from Sarah. "Doesn't matter if no one listens."

CHAPTER THIRTY-ONE

Washington, DC

"BOY, HAVE TIMES changed. Remember when her acolytes treated her like Jesus? And the crowds gathered forth? Like some young, talentless pop star. Now, you can't pay people to attend her speeches. And, yes, I'm talking about the president of the United States.

"This morning a paltry one thousand people showed up to hear Whitney peddling her liberal snake oil message at Ohio State University, one of several stops in the Midwest. And a waste of taxpayers' money, if you ask me.

"Let's talk about this New Old Deal, shall we?

"Are we really going back to the nineteen thirties to help solve today's problems? Can't you be more original, Ma-DAMN President?

"The New Deal built miles of highways—Cha-ching!—thousands of buildings—Cha-ching!—airports, tunnels, bridges—Cha-ching, Cha-ching, Chaaa-ching. All I hear is cash registers, folks!"

Cole was on a roll. He leaned into the studio microphone. "Income inequality is not the defining issue of our time. What is the defining issue of our time, you ask? Well, I'll tell you. It's the disappearance of manufacturing jobs. Back in the day, people didn't need to go to college and earn fancy degrees to carve out a decent living for themselves and their families. The 'Great Divide,' my ass. It's the 'Trade Divide,' people! Eliminate those trade deals and bring those jobs back home to the good ol' US of A. Who's fighting for these workers? I am.

"And regarding CEOs, they make the big money because they make the tough decisions. Like in *Atlas Shrugged*. Anyone can dig, but we need someone to tell us where. That's what CEOs do.

"By the way, that's one book I did read. If you've never read it, I suggest you do. Along with my book, *Communism in Russia is Dead, but Alive and*

Well in the USA. I wrote it almost a year ago, but it's still true today. Maybe more so. Can I get an amen?

"We have the greatest economic system in the world. Capitalism worked just fine until our federal government started tinkering with it."

Cole grabbed a hand towel to dab his forehead. "We have to take a break here to pay the bills. After the break, a special guest will be joining us. Don't go away."

CHAPTER THIRTY-TWO

Seattle, Washington

NOAH BLAKELEY BIT into the sesame-seed ciabatta smothered with cream cheese that he'd picked up at the Specialty's bakery on the way to the office. This was his favorite part of the day: sitting at his desk, eating breakfast, drinking his first cup of coffee, and reading the *Seattle Times.*

He opened the paper. President Whitney Fairchild had just completed a tour of Ohio, Michigan, Indiana, Illinois, and Missouri. Noah always read the editorial section of the paper first. Today's editorial was supportive of her latest speech, describing it as one of the most important presidential speeches of the twenty-first century so far. The editorialist believed it was a moral imperative for the country to address income inequality and its dire consequences before it was too late.

He agreed.

The Associated Press news article on the first page covering her speeches wasn't as positive. The correspondent reported on the unreceptive audiences, even in the president's home state of Missouri. Noah couldn't understand why. Her legislation would create jobs. Employment cured many ills.

He finished the ciabatta and sipped his coffee, wondering how he could help the president.

He turned to the business section of the paper. He slowly placed the to-go cup on his desk.

The rumors he'd heard at the Grand Hyatt fundraiser were now fact.

Several major corporations in the Seattle area had fallen victim to cybertheft. Hackers, using dummy bank sites, had siphoned off millions of dollars. One controller, acting on an email from his CEO about a secret acquisition, transferred a million dollars to a bank account via a link in the email.

The email turned out to be fake. The CEO hadn't sent it. The police had not located the money.

He let the paper drop and speed-dialed his chief financial officer whose office was on the other side of the building.

"Check our bank account."

"Why?"

"Just do it."

He listened as the CFO tapped on his keyboard.

"Hurry up," Noah said.

After a moment, the CFO said, "This can't be."

Noah felt the first stirrings of fear developing in his stomach. "What is it?"

"The balance in the account is about a million dollars lower than it should be."

"Call the bank. I'll wait."

The CFO did as instructed. Through the CFO's speakerphone, Noah heard the message: "Thank you for calling Pacific Coast Bank. All customer-service agents are busy now. Please leave a message or try your call again later."

He slowly replaced the handset.

His father was going to have a fit.

CHAPTER THIRTY-THREE

The White House, Washington, DC

BACK IN THE Oval Office the day after returning from her trip to the Midwest, Whitney reviewed the daily presidential briefing books. Although available in electronic tablet form, she still preferred to read the print version. The weight of the document in her hand reinforced the weight of the issues it represented.

Included in today's report—along with scores of terrorist threats, terrorist cell movements, a potential terrorist attack on a Planned Parenthood building in Idaho, and US and euro currency manipulations by the Chinese government—was an item about network security breaches involving substantial sums of money at several companies in Seattle. The report speculated Chinese government involvement.

The Chinese had been suspected of various attacks on US corporate and military computer networks for years, including theft of medical data, Social Security numbers, and classified information. Whitney's national security team believed that most of the attacks were government-sanctioned. What they didn't have was proof.

She called Sasha into the Oval Office. Within a minute, Sasha stood in front of her desk.

She held up the briefing book. "The Chinese?"

Sasha shrugged. "Why not? We blame them for everything else."

Whitney smiled. "Like the Japanese in the Eighties? Call ODNI"—the Office of the Director of National Intelligence—"and find out who's handling this."

Sasha made a note.

"And can you turn on the radio? Cole's on."

Sasha's neck twitched, the way it did every time she thought Whitney was doing something foolish. "Why do you want to listen to him?"

Whitney thought of Ashley Brennan. "I have my reasons."

Sasha moved to a table against the wall and turned on the radio. She settled into the chair across from Whitney.

At the end of a commercial, Cole said, "Welcome back. I'd like to introduce my special guest, Paul Sampson, the Democratic senator from Nebraska. Welcome, Senator." Whitney and Sasha shared a glance. Foreboding pressed against Whitney's chest. "What's all this I've been hearing about income inequality?"

"Income inequality isn't a bad thing," Sampson said. "It creates an incentive for people to be productive, innovate, and create wealth. Besides, the quality of life for everyone is improving. Even if you're poor today, you're likely to own a smartphone, the latest Nikes, a flat-screen TV—"

"Sounds familiar," Whitney murmured.

"Bunch of BS," Sasha said.

"But don't you think this legislation will pit Americans against each other?" Cole asked. "Don't you think it's just another attempt by you and your Commiecrat comrades to engage in class warfare?"

"The president mentioned you in a meeting recently," Sampson said. "We were discussing increasing taxes on the rich and distributing the wealth."

Whitney burned, listening. How dare he talk publicly about a private meeting.

Cole laughed. "At least she's thinking about me." He sobered. "No more taxes, Senator. Please! Americans are taxed enough."

"I agree, Cole," Sampson said. "We need to streamline regulations and reduce taxes for everyone."

Sasha's mouth opened. "What is he saying?"

Whitney held her hand up for silence.

"Switching gears," Cole said. "What are your thoughts about these protests?"

"I don't think they're helpful."

"Me neither. Instead of protesting, I think they all should be working. Don't you? Put that energy to good use. Well, I'd like to thank you for coming on the show today. Is there anything else you want to say?"

"Well, I have a lot to say, Cole, but first I want to tell you that today I burned my Democratic voter-registration card. And I registered as a Republican. I am now a proud member of the GOP, and I'm ready to take my country back."

Cole's high-pitched giggle filled the airwaves. "God Almighty, you've seen the light!"

Whitney visualized Cole with his hands raised in a televangelist pose.

"Yes, I have, Cole," Sampson said. "And my first order of business will be immigration. We're going to build that wall that Ellison was too scared to start, and we're going to place a moratorium on all non-Christian immigration to this country."

"Jesus H. Christ," Sasha said.

"I'm not sure even He can help us," Whitney said. She made a shooing motion with her hand. "Turn that off."

Sasha complied. "Without him, it will be harder to get our agenda through."

Whitney willed herself to calm down. She couldn't do anything about Sampson now. "I didn't call you in here for that. Set up a meeting with Jade Harrington."

Sasha didn't hide her surprise. "The FBI agent from the TSK case?"

"One and the same."

"What has that got to do with Sampson?"

"Nothing."

Sasha hesitated, waiting for Whitney to elaborate further on the purpose of the meeting. She didn't.

"Yes, Madam President." She turned to go, but then stopped. "This may be a little unprofessional . . . but can you introduce me to her? I'm a huge fan."

"You don't strike me as a person who gets star-struck."

"I'm not," Sasha said. "It's the magic."

"Magic?"

She winked. "Black-girl magic."

❅

Later that afternoon, Sarah escorted FBI Special Agent Jade Harrington into the Oval Office. The agent strode toward Whitney with the confidence evident in current and former athletes. Whitney had forgotten how tall Jade was. And striking. The most intriguing part was that Jade didn't seem to realize it.

Whitney rose to greet her in the middle of the room. She covered the agent's proffered hand in both of hers. "Agent Harrington. I hope you've been well."

"Yes, Madam President. It's been quite a year."

"Yes, it has. Please have a seat."

Jade sat on the sofa, as if she were invited to the Oval Office every day.

Not in a disrespectful manner, but as someone comfortable in her own skin. Whitney moved to her favorite chair. She hadn't spoken to the agent since they had met in her Senate office. "I never thanked you for solving the TSK case."

The agent hesitated. "I'm sure its resolution was bittersweet for you."

Whitney gasped, but recovered quickly. She had not told anyone about Landon's letter. And the devastating secret it contained.

"Bittersweet?"

"He'd created a shrine."

"Pardon me?"

"In his apartment. We didn't disclose this to the press. He had this wall covered with pictures of you. Articles about you. From your campaigns, your marriage announcement, the births of your children."

Whitney breathed, realizing she had overreacted. "How disturbing."

"He drew this picture of you," the agent said, shaking her head. "It was amazing. The likeness, uncanny."

Whitney paused a moment, taking it all in. "I guess no matter how close you are to someone, you can never really know him. Or her."

"That's the truth," Jade said, a slight color rising to her cheeks. Whitney wondered why.

Jade pulled out a ragged notebook. If Whitney wasn't mistaken, it was the same one Jade had used to interview her last year. *Was the FBI's budget that tight?*

"Why am I here?" Jade asked.

No small talk for this one. "I have a proposition for you. What do you know about the cyberthefts occurring in Seattle?"

"Only what I read in the papers."

Whitney filled her in on the contents of that morning's PDB, which wasn't much more than what was reported in the newspapers.

"Any evidence that the Chinese are involved?" asked Jade.

"Just suspicions. Suppositions. Rumors."

"I'm still not sure why I'm here."

"I want you to be the liaison between the Secret Service and the FBI on this."

Most people were familiar with the Secret Service's responsibility of protecting the president and other high-placed government officials, but the Service also had jurisdiction over other domains, including cybercrime. As did the FBI.

Jade shifted, uncomfortable. "This isn't my area of expertise. Shouldn't you be asking someone from our cyber division?"

"I've talked to your boss," Whitney said. "Ethan Lawson, isn't it? He's approved this assignment." She smiled at the scowl crossing Jade's face. "Is something wrong?"

Jade glanced out the window. "He wants to distract me from the bullying case."

"Bullying case?"

"Never mind."

"There's something else."

Jade remained silent, probably thinking about what she would say to her boss next time she saw him. Whitney didn't envy him.

"I'm sure you're aware of the income-inequality protests taking place across the country," Whitney said.

Jade turned back to her. "Sure."

"Evan Stevens. A liberal blogger. Smart. Irreverent. Heard of him?"

"I've met him. We interviewed him about the TSK case."

"What did you discover?"

"Not much. I read a lot of his blogs. He's passionate about the causes he believes in. He turned out to be clean."

Whitney crossed her legs and smoothed her skirt. "It may be more than that. He seems to be . . . stirring up the masses. I believe he is one of the reasons these protests are having such a long shelf life. I am contemplating inviting him here. To talk to him."

"Sounds like a good idea, but I don't understand why you're telling me."

"I want you to look into his background."

Jade's eyes narrowed. "Don't you have people for that?"

"Yes, but I want you to do it. I trust you." Whitney stood, ending the meeting. She bit back a smile. "Oh . . . and Agent Lawson said it was okay."

CHAPTER THIRTY-FOUR

Washington, DC

SHE WAITED IN the queue at Peet's Coffee & Tea near FBI HQ. She thought about her conversation with the president and what she'd said about Landon. That you can never really know someone. Fairchild didn't know about her relationship with him, unless he told her, which Jade doubted. No one knew, except Zoe. And it was going to stay that way.

Her phone rang. She wanted to ignore it. She needed her coffee. Badly. She glanced at the display. A 206 number. Seattle.

Stepping outside the shop, she scanned the surrounding area. "Agent Harrington."

"Harrington, it's your favorite detective in Seattle."

"I only know one detective in Seattle."

She had worked with Detective Kurt McClaine on the TSK case.

He waited a beat. "And I'm still not your favorite? Ouch." A smile in his voice. "I need your help."

"Another murder?"

"No. Not a murder this time. It's about money. Someone or some organization or a sovereign nation that starts with a 'C' is stealing a lot of money from the good people of Seattle."

"I heard."

"I know. From the president."

She frowned. "How do you know that?"

"I'm who you're liaising with on the local level. I need you to come to Seattle. I was informed the president cleared it with your boss."

She looked at the phone, wanting to throw it. She brought it back to her ear. "When?"

"You're booked on a flight early this afternoon your time. I emailed the details."

On the sidewalk, people walked around her on either side. Some of them slowed, their eyes widening when they recognized her. A woman with Asian features took her picture.

"I suggest you pack for a few days," he said.

Jade glanced back at Peet's. "Damn. It looks like I won't get my coffee."

"We have plenty of coffee in Seattle. I'll pick you up at the airport."

CHAPTER THIRTY-FIVE

The White House, Washington, DC

WHITNEY SWUNG HER legs onto the sofa and picked up the glass of red wine from the coffee table in front of her. A healthy pour.

Is there any other kind?

A biography about Victoria Woodhull, who, in 1872, was the first female candidate to run for president of the United States—before women had the right to vote—lay beside her. She took a sip of wine, rolling it around on her tongue. Savoring it. She reflected on her conversation with Jade Harrington.

I'm sure its resolution was bittersweet for you.

Whitney was concerned. If Landon's secret got out, her presidency would be destroyed. Or, at least, it would give the other party and the political pundits fodder to talk about for a long time. It would impact her family.

She thought about Jade. Her intelligence. Her confidence. Her swagger. She had "It." There was something about the agent that Whitney was drawn to. A kinship.

The initial melody of Chopin's Nocturne in E-flat Major, op. 55, no. 2 trilled from her cell phone. Chandler.

"This is a nice surprise."

"Hey, Mom. What's up?"

She envisioned her son sitting, one leg bobbing up and down with nervous energy. His bangs flopping down on his forehead.

Whitney glanced at the briefing books stacked on the end table, untouched, and then back at her glass. "Taking a break from work. And you?"

"I have some good news, and some bad news. Which do you want first?"

Gripping the phone tighter, she tried to remain calm. "Bad."

"I'm not graduating until September. I can't get all my credits in without summer school."

Whitney exhaled. "That's not bad. I think it takes six years now for the average student to graduate, so you're still ahead of your peers."

"I didn't know it was a competition, Mom."

"It's always a competition. What's the good news?"

"I've decided to work for Dad after graduation."

She smiled. "That's wonderful! He's going to be happy."

"He is. I told him."

"I'm proud of you. What made you choose the family business?"

"I couldn't get a job anywhere else." Before she could respond, he said, "Just kidding. It seemed like a good way to learn how to run a big business. Besides, I don't want to end up like those protesters."

"What protesters?"

"The ones on TV. Protesting that income-inequality bullsh—stuff. I want to make my own money. Someday own my own business. Be in charge of my own destiny."

She placed her glass on the table. "Sometimes being in charge of your own destiny is not enough, son."

"Sorry, Mom, I just don't buy that. You and Dad always taught us that if we worked hard, good things would happen. To not wait for anything to be handed to us. To go after what we want."

Whitney chose her words carefully. "I still believe that, but there's more to it. Some people are born into a bad situation that is difficult to rise above. Others encounter bad luck: financially, a health crisis, the unexpected death of a provider. There are systemic issues within our economy that allow the wealthy to become wealthier, and everyone else to stay the same."

"The wealthy get a bad rap. It's not their fault they're rich. I can't wait to be one of them."

"Well—"

"Mom, I need to go. I'll call you again soon. Love you."

"I love you, too."

She looked at the phone display. Chandler was gone. She placed it on the sofa and picked up her glass. The person on the phone did not sound like her son. Their normal playful banter, absent. He sounded like a damn Republican.

She finished the rest of the wine in one gulp. The president of the United States crossed the room to the refrigerator to retrieve another bottle.

CHAPTER THIRTY-SIX

Seattle, Washington

DECLINING THE RECEPTIONIST'S offers for a seat or coffee or water, Jade and Detective Kurt McClaine stood off to the side of the sleek, gray front desk. McClaine, with his blond, unkempt hair, gold earring, cheap suit jacket, jeans, and a tattoo on his neck peeking out of his customary t-shirt, looked more like a handsome rock star than a detective.

"You brought the sun," he said. "That doesn't happen too often in May."

"I don't think I had anything to do with it," Jade said.

"I wouldn't be so sure," said the tall woman walking toward them. "It's rained for three weeks straight. And, please, forgive the good detective. Talking about the weather is what we Seattleites do best." She extended her hand to McClaine. "Good to see you again." Her green eyes focused on Jade. Extending her hand, she said, "Kyle Madison."

Her grip was firm. Jade held her gaze. "Special Agent Jade Harrington."

The woman turned. "Follow me," she said over her shoulder. She didn't wait to see if they complied.

Jade liked that.

Something flickered in McClaine's eye as he gestured for Jade to walk ahead of him. She followed Kyle down a long hallway, taking in the shimmering medium-length black hair, the expensive, fitted dark suit, and the high heels. She noticed everything, except the sway of Ms. Madison's hips.

Kyle's office, in the same décor as the reception area, was gray and white and black, save a red rose in the slim vase on her desk. Elegant, but impersonal. No pictures. No knickknacks. No plants. Nothing to reveal more about the woman.

Except the rose.

After they were seated, McClaine said, "Ms. Madison, can you—"

"Hold that thought," the executive said, as she pushed a button on the phone on her desk. "Kevin, can you bring in some tea, please?" She turned to McClaine. "You want me to tell Agent Harrington what happened."

He nodded.

Kyle leaned back in her chair. "I manage a venture-capital firm. We help social media entrepreneurs turn their dreams into reality by providing Series A financing so they can reach more customers, increase revenues, and grow their businesses. We're selective in the companies in which we choose to invest. You've heard of most of them. Our approach is different. We invest in the people, not the—"

Jade interrupted the sales pitch. "Where are your tombstones?"

A discreet knock on the door postponed the answer. The receptionist entered and placed the tea service on the desk.

"Thank you, Kevin," Kyle said.

He left. She lifted the silver-plated tea pot that appeared as if it cost more than Jade's monthly mortgage payment. Kyle looked at them. "Tea?"

They both shook their heads.

She poured a cup for herself. "To answer your question, I don't need to be surrounded by visual reminders of my successes. It keeps me hungry."

"How big is your typical fund?"

"Our last one was one billion."

McClaine whistled.

"Tell me what happened," Jade said.

"Obviously, a lot of money flows through here. In. And out. My CFO discovered that our account reconciliations had been slightly off consistently for months. Not by enough to cause alarm, so he didn't think it necessary to inform me. It's crazy around here. All the time. The companies, investors, entrepreneurs in residence. He chalked it up to minor errors by his staff. Rounding. A few days ago, he realized they weren't errors."

Jade leaned in. "How much was stolen?"

"One million dollars."

She glanced at McClaine and then back at Kyle. "They were testing your internal control systems to see if any red flags would be raised. When there weren't, they struck."

Kyle nodded. "That's what my CFO said."

"We'll need to talk to him."

"Certainly."

Jade turned to McClaine. "Any luck tracing the money?"

"Your local brethren are working on it. Nothing, yet."

To Kyle, Jade said: "Talk to me about your systems."

"I'll have you speak with my IT director. He will be able to help you much better than I could."

Do only men work for you?

"Agent Harrington," Kyle said, "as I told the detective," nodding at McClaine, "it's imperative that we keep this quiet. I don't want to spook our investors. We're about to embark on raising our largest fund ever. In my business, trust is everything."

"I understand."

Kyle rose, a signal for them to leave.

Jade stayed seated. "I wasn't finished."

Kyle hesitated before returning to her chair.

"We need a copy of your financial records for the last year. And I want to interview everyone in your accounting department."

"That can be arranged."

"I'll also need copies of your personal financial records during that period."

For the first time, the confident smile faltered, hardened. "I'm the victim here."

"Standard procedure," McClaine reassured her.

"To rule me out. I get it. Are we finished?"

Jade stood. "Now, I'm finished."

"*Now* . . . I'll show you out." Kyle strode toward the door, again not waiting to see if they followed.

Back out front, she spoke to the receptionist, and turned back to them. "Kevin will make arrangements for you to talk to everyone." She shook their hands again. "I would appreciate your locating my clients' money as soon as possible, and bringing the criminals to justice."

"We'll do our best," McClaine said.

Kyle turned toward her office and then back as if realizing something. "Agent Harrington, when are you going back to DC?"

"Tomorrow. Why?"

"Would the two of you like to join me tonight for a Storm game?"

"We don't have time," Jade said.

From McClaine: "What time's the game?"

"Seven."

"We should be finished with our interviews by then," he said.

"Perfect."

"But I can't make it," he said.

Jade gave him a sharp glance.

Kyle's penetrating gaze turned to Jade. "When was the last time you took in a WNBA game?"

When I was in the league. "It's been a while."

"Splendid. Then, you must come."

She didn't particularly like how McClaine set her up. Or the look that passed between him and Kyle. Jade should spend the evening drafting interview reports and preparing for her early-morning flight tomorrow.

"Sure," she said. "Why not?"

CHAPTER THIRTY-SEVEN

Fairfax, Virginia

MARK MERRITT WAS late. Since running in the hallways was forbidden, he half-ran, half-walked down the empty school corridor, headed to his last class of the day. His homework was unfinished, but he'd worry about that when he got there. He couldn't be late. For every minute late, the teacher forced you to write a one-page essay. Mark didn't like to write. There was little he liked about school lately.

Almost there. His class was on the second floor, first classroom on the right.

He was going to make it.

As he passed by the stairwell, with his foot almost on the first step, the top of his t-shirt sliced against his throat. He couldn't swallow. The person who'd grabbed him from behind pulled him backward. He tripped over an outstretched foot, his feet leaving the floor. He heard laughter. His head banged against the linoleum, an instantaneous explosion of pain followed by tiny stars.

That hurt.

He was dragged under the stairs.

Touching the back of his head, he felt a bump forming. He opened his eyes and saw three people. They looked like boys, but their heads blocked out the overhead lighting so he couldn't see their faces. It was dark. Without warning, he felt an intense pain in his side. He cried out.

Someone kicked him again. "Shut up!"

The now-familiar pain inflicted on his other side.

Something wet and unpleasant hit him in the face and started trailing down his cheek. He hoped it wasn't spit.

"You're so lame."

"Dork."

"Fag."

Each utterance, followed by a kick, composed an off-beat rhythm to their attack. The boys continued to converse.

He was not invited to participate.

"Retard."

"You take up space."

"Wasted oxygen."

"Everybody hates you."

"Everyone wishes you were dead."

"Why don't you go choke on some pills like your cousin?"

Someone crouched beside him. "Your dad should mind his own business." Mark thought he recognized the voice. Losing consciousness, he couldn't process it.

He was punched in the face.

Whimpering, he tasted something like metal. Blood. His tongue touched the top of a tooth where it met his gums. It was loose.

He tried to raise his arms, but to no avail. The punching and kicking continued. He gave up. He lay still, praying it would end soon.

I wonder how many pages Mrs. Johnson will make me write?

And then, mercifully, darkness.

CHAPTER THIRTY-EIGHT

Seattle, Washington

JADE HAD NEVER watched a WNBA game from a courtside seat. During her playing days, she hadn't spent much time on the bench. Located in the Uptown—or as the locals called it, Lower Queen Anne—neighborhood just north of downtown, the antiquated Key Arena was packed for the first basketball game of the season. The Seattle Storm were hosting the Los Angeles Sparks.

The environment evoked a small rush of emotion within her: the squeak of the sneakers on the court, the thump as the basketballs bounced off the floor, the high fives, the half hugs. This was the game she'd loved and had spent a significant portion of her life playing. Just a small rush. That part of her life was over.

She didn't live in the past.

Many fans shook Kyle's hand as they walked by. Others called out to her from the seats behind them.

Storm players nodded and smiled at Kyle during warmups. Star player Sky Williams jogged over, a basketball under her arm. "Hey, Kyle." She stopped in front of Jade and held out her hand. Jade shook it.

"I'm a big fan of yours," the player said. "You're the reason why I went to Stanford." She pointed to her jersey. "And the reason why I've worn number twenty-two since middle school. Thanks for coming." Sky pivoted and dribbled away.

Middle school.

For the first time, Jade felt old. She looked at Kyle. "I give. Are you famous or something?"

Kyle smiled. "Or something."

"Hey, you."

The voice was out of place. Like way out of place. Like the wrong coast or the distance of a continent out of place. *Zoe?* Jade turned in her seat, puzzled. "What are you doing here?"

Zoe pointed at the back of Sky Williams. "Let's just say, I'm a fan."

"You're dating her?"

"'Dating' might be a little strong. We met at a party last year. In DC. After a Storm-Mystics game."

Jade shouldn't have been shocked. She had long since lost track of Zoe's copious number of exes. Jade just hadn't realized until now how geographically dispersed they were.

Zoe glanced at Kyle before asking Jade: "What are you doing here?"

Good question.

"She's with me," Kyle said, reaching across Jade to shake Zoe's hand. "Kyle Madison."

Zoe hesitated. "Zoe." They shook, their eyes held each other's gaze.

"How do you two know each other?" Zoe asked.

Jade was curious about the look they shared. Had they hooked up in the past, or were they attracted to each other now?

Neither Jade nor Kyle responded to Zoe's question.

Zoe fidgeted. After a while, she said, "I see. Well, we're going to a party after, if you want to join us."

"We have plans," Kyle said.

Jade glanced at Kyle, but said nothing.

Zoe looked at Jade. "When are you going home?"

"Tomorrow."

"Who's taking care of Card?"

"I got a neighbor to check on him. Since you weren't around."

Zoe shrugged and looked out on the court. "I had plans." She winked. "I need to get back to my seat."

More fans stopped by to say hello before the game started. Mostly for Kyle, but some acknowledged Jade as well. She was rarely recognized anymore for her basketball exploits. And she was okay with that.

Her phone vibrated. A text. From Zoe. Are you dating her?

Jade laughed.

"What is it?" Kyle asked.

"Nothing," she said. She texted back: Mind your business.

You're my BFF. You are my business.

The first half, an exciting one with a lot of fast breaks and even a dunk by Seattle's six-foot-eight center, ended. At halftime, Kyle excused herself, and Jade trekked to the concession stand for popcorn. She resettled in her seat and scanned the crowd for danger. Professional habit. The arena didn't have much of a security presence. She worried about a major terrorist attack targeting a US sporting event, and was surprised there hadn't been one yet.

When she looked back toward the court, Kyle stood at the half-court line next to two other people and a cardboard check. Jade stopped chewing the stale, salty popcorn.

Into a microphone, Kyle said, "On behalf of the entire Seattle Storm organization, I present this check for ten thousand dollars to the Make-A-Wish Foundation."

Seizing the program on the seat next to her, Jade flipped through it until she came to a profile of Kyle with a quarter-page picture of her. Kyle was a minority owner of the Storm.

Kyle waved to the crowd and strolled back to her seat, a mischievous smile forming as she caught Jade watching her.

Kyle grabbed a handful of popcorn out of Jade's bag. "I've been a PAC-Ten, Twelve, whatever, fan all of my life."

"You knew who I was," Jade said.

"Of course I did."

❊

"I would've been okay," Jade said. "I think I can take care of myself."

Kyle adjusted her hair under the hood of her North Face jacket. "I'm sure you can. But this is my town. I don't mind walking you."

"Where'd you park?"

"I didn't. This is a city for walking."

The night air had turned chilly since they'd entered the arena. A light drizzle fell as they strolled the twelve-block walk to Jade's hotel downtown.

"I enjoyed the game. Thanks for inviting me."

"My pleasure," Kyle said. "Do you ever miss it?"

"Some parts I miss. There are few things in life that compare to hitting a shot at the buzzer to win a big game or threading the needle with a perfect, no-look pass. But what I miss most is the time that I spent with my team-mates off the court. The bus trips. Airplane rides. Team meals. Hanging out in the hotel."

"I wish we could have won for you tonight."

"LA is always tough. You know a lot about the game. Did you play?"

"No. I've always been more of an outdoor enthusiast: skier, hiker, cyclist."

"Not much of a team player, are you?"

This made Kyle smile. "I guess not."

In front of the hotel, Jade stopped. "Well, thanks again. I'll be in touch with you about the case." She yawned. "Time difference." She extended her hand. Instead of a firm handshake this time, Kyle simply held it. Her hand, soft.

Kyle gazed at her.

Those eyes.

"I travel to DC on occasion. I'll look you up next time I'm there. To check out the status of my case in person." A slight tilt of the head. "Perhaps we can have dinner."

Anything related to the case could be discussed over the phone. Before Jade could voice this, Kyle gave her hand a light squeeze and turned and walked away.

She didn't look back.

CHAPTER THIRTY-NINE

The White House, Washington, DC

"HOW MANY?"

"Maybe ten," responded her chief of staff.

"Still?" Ten out of a hundred senators. Whitney looked at Sasha, who sat across from her in the Oval Office. "We have a long way to go, don't we?"

"For so many things. But you're right. We need Hampton."

"That will make him happy."

"And maybe Sampson."

Whitney held up her hand like a crossing guard. "Let's try to do this without him."

"I do have some good news. Gas prices are at a three-year low."

"Why are presidents blamed when gas prices go up, but receive none of the credit when they go down?"

"Politics 101. Bad news is always the president's fault. Judy from ABC called me."

"Nice segue."

"She wants to interview you. About your childhood. Teenage years. Confirmation on some details. A fluff piece. I think it's a good idea."

"I think we should focus on the legislation, not me." Whitney's phone buzzed. She pressed the blinking line. "Yes?"

"The First Gentleman's assistant, Madam President," Sean, her secretary said.

Sasha rose, but hesitated. Whitney waved her to stay.

She leaned back in her chair, waiting for Grayson's assistant to connect them. "Yes, darling."

"What's this I hear about this new legislation?"

"Which one? There are many."

"This New Deal Coalition. Tell me about it."

"The New New Deal Coalition." She summarized the bill for him.

"I see," Grayson said. "What businesses will be regulated by it?"

There it is. The real reason for his call.

"Almost every business in the United States will be touched by it. And, yes, agribusiness is included."

Silence. Then softly, he said, "Touched."

"Businesses must pay their fair share. Even your business."

"This bill will hurt businesses. Our business. Have you thought about the unintended consequences?"

"Don't talk to me as if I'm an idiot. This legislation will right a wrong. It will bring a measure of fairness and equity into the economic system."

"I provide thousands of jobs. Treat my employees well. Pay them fairly. I don't need interference from the government. Let me do my job. Let me run my business."

Whitney felt her blood pressure start to rise. "This country is my business, and I must do what is right for the country, not Fairchild Industries."

"You should've talked to me about this first. Don't do this."

"Darling, I don't need to run my decisions by you. That's not how this works."

She hung up.

Sasha was nodding, a hint of a smile on her face.

Whitney forced thoughts of Grayson from her mind. "Where were we?"

"What do you want me to tell Judy?"

"Put her off."

CHAPTER FORTY

Fairfax, Virginia

JADE DRUMMED HER fingers on the steering wheel. She drove faster than normal.

When she had returned to her hotel room last night after the game, she finally checked her smartphone. Christian had texted her. Multiple times.

His son Mark had been rushed to the hospital. The final tally: two black eyes, a few broken ribs, and bruising all over his face. Luckily, there was no internal bleeding or liver damage. Released, he was home, resting.

Instead of taking the morning flight as planned, she had taken the last flight out and was now driving straight to Christian's house from National Airport.

He answered the doorbell.

She entered without being asked. "How is he?"

She turned when he didn't respond. His eyes were hard, his jaw flexing. "The doctor said he's going to be okay." He lifted his chin. "He's in his room."

"Did he say anything?"

"I tried to talk to him about it, just like I tried to talk to him after what happened to Tyler. He didn't say much. He's afraid of something."

"Or someone."

Jade headed up the stairs, Christian's soft footsteps behind her. She knocked at the closed door on the second floor.

A weak "yeah" in response.

Opening the door, slow and cautious, she poked her head inside. Mark lay on his bed. The TV off. She didn't see a cell phone, electronic tablet, or game console.

What had he been doing? "Hey, guy."

"Hey, Mrs. Harrington."

Jade didn't correct the boy's inaccurate characterization of her marital status. "Can we come in?"

He shrugged. She sat on the bed, careful not to jar him. His face and arms sported bruises, some more purple than others. He looked bad. She noted the absence of faded cuts or scratches.

Mark didn't play on the baseball team.

She tried to quell the rage building inside her. He was a good kid. Polite. Respectful.

Christian didn't enter the room. Instead, he leaned against the door frame, his hands clasped in front of him. His head down.

"I'd hate to see the other guy," Jade said.

The boy gave her a weak smile. "It hurts to laugh."

"You're lucky then. Because I'm not that funny."

This time he did laugh, stopping as suddenly as he started. He winced and touched a rib. "My dad said you were in Seattle. Did you catch the bad guys?"

Instead of cyber perpetrators, his question conjured up thoughts of Kyle. "Something like that. Do you want to tell me what happened?"

A brief shadow of fear crossed the boy's face.

"You can trust me," she said.

The boy looked from her to his dad and back to her. "I was getting ready to take the stairs to my sixth period, when someone grabbed me. Tripped me. They dragged me under the stairs and beat the crap out of me."

"Did you see who it was?"

"No."

"How many were there?"

"Three or four," he said.

"All boys?"

"I think so. It happened so fast, I didn't see their faces. It was dark under there."

"Did you recognize any of their voices?"

The boy's eyes shifted infinitesimally to the left. He swallowed. "No."

"Are you sure, Mark?"

"Yeah, I'm sure." He grimaced, and held his side.

"Why you? Why did they choose you?"

He glanced at his father and then back at Jade. He shrugged.

The kid was hiding something from his father. Or did it have something to do with Christian? Was that possible?

"What about Tyler? Do you know what happened to him?"

He slid farther down into the comfort of his bed. He closed his eyes. "I'm tired."

"Can you tell me anything else about the attack? We want to find the kids who did this to you."

He opened his eyes. "I thought I was going to die."

Mark's eyes closed again. Jade turned to glance at Christian, his face a dark mask. She'd never seen him this angry. She felt pity for what he and his family were going through.

She also pitied whoever had done this to his son, oblivious to what they had unleashed.

CHAPTER FORTY-ONE

The White House, Washington, DC

"MAYBE WE SHOULD change the name."

Whitney shook her head. "Nonnegotiable. The New New Deal Coalition represents our future, and serves as a reminder of a time in our history when we came together to change the course of this country."

Sasha nodded. "That's good."

As they walked down a hall in the West Wing, Whitney and Sasha continued to debate strategies for selling the legislation to Congress and the American people.

Sasha stopped.

"What is it?" Whitney asked.

Her chief of staff glanced up and down the hallway and lowered her voice. "I had lunch at the Four Seasons today."

"When did I start giving you time off to eat?"

"Sampson, Hampton, and Bell were having lunch with Xavi."

Xavier "Xavi" Fernandez, the former Independent governor of Florida, was now the vice president of the United States.

"Brutus isn't trying too hard to hide his plot against me, I see."

"The conversation seemed pretty intense. Hampton did most of the talking."

Sampson's presence didn't surprise Whitney. He had never forgiven her for breaking her implicit promise to name him as her vice president after he dropped out of the closely contested Democratic primary in exchange for her support for a bill that he'd sponsored. He still blamed her for his unnecessary sacrifice. This was one of the reasons he had switched parties. Maybe the only reason. "See if you can find out the purpose of the meeting."

"Yes, Madam President." They resumed walking. "What do you want to do about the situation in Colorado?"

A dozen armed ranchers, calling themselves The Last Patriots, were squatting on federal property in Colorado protesting the federal government's decision—her decision—to designate more land as national parks. They threatened to annex the land and secede from the union. The FBI had surrounded the ranchers, but had been instructed to wait it out. No shots had been fired, yet.

"Let them secede?" Whitney joked.

"I wonder what the Second Amendment crowd would say if it were a bunch of African Americans with assault rifles squatting on federal property?"

She didn't bother to answer Sasha's question. She knew white privilege existed. "Our Founding Fathers gave us the right to bear arms, not arsenals."

"Tell that to the militia."

"Let's not move in, yet," Whitney said. "But keep me posted."

"Did you see Sampson's press conference in support of the 'patriots'?"

"Contrary to what they profess, Republicans—even newly declared ones—do not have a monopoly on patriotism."

Descending the steps to the basement, they continued walking until they arrived at an unassuming door. Josh McPherson opened the door that led into the Sit Room. The Situation Room.

Although she had selected Xavi as her running mate to attract the Hispanic and independent vote, she had never trusted her ambitious vice president. On Election Night, after the results were in, she reminded him that Hispanics were not the only minority in this country. She envisioned providing opportunities for all minorities. He responded that Hispanics were the only minority that mattered.

And now that man stood to her left at the table dominating the diminutive room. With dark hair and eyes and a trim build, Xavi's smile never quite reached his eyes.

What are you up to, Xavi?

"Good afternoon," she said. "Ladies and gentlemen, shall we begin? Please be seated."

CHAPTER FORTY-TWO

Fairfax, Virginia

"IT'S TEN O'CLOCK in the morning," Christian said.

"So?" Jade pushed open the door to The Stratford Arms, a bar a few miles from Christian's house. Near a strip mall, the English-style pub was a stand-alone building surrounded by its own parking lot.

The inside was dark. Pictures of current and former members of the royal family, prime ministers, English celebrities, pennants of all the English Premier League teams, and English quotes and slogans covered almost every inch of the dark brown, wood-paneled walls.

Christian cocked his head. "Please, don't tell me it's five o'clock somewhere."

"Then pretend we're in Prague."

He shrugged. "Never been. As good a place as any, though."

The place was understandably empty, since most normal people were at work. With no one behind the bar, she called out, "Hello?"

A female bartender slammed through the swinging saloon doors, wiping her hands with a white towel. "May I help you?"

Jade pointed to the tap, as she and Christian grabbed stools at the bar. "Two Guinnesses."

"And a shot," he added.

"You came around quickly." Jade signaled a peace sign to the bartender. "Two shots. Of whiskey."

The bartender set her palms on the bar, taking in the two of them. "Rough day already?"

"Something like that," Christian mumbled.

"Then, I'll make it a double." She pushed away from the bar. "If you're going to do it, do it right."

"My kind of woman," Jade said, turning to Christian. "I thought it was too early."

"Well . . . since we're here."

The bartender placed their drinks in front of them. Jade picked up her pint-size glass and motioned for Christian to do the same. "To Mark."

Christian's jaw tensed. He looked down for a moment and back at her. "To Mark."

They clinked glasses, and each took a gulp. They picked up their shot glasses and drained the whiskey.

She grimaced at the bitter, unfamiliar burn. "This was not a good idea."

"Actually," he said, "it's the best idea you've had this year."

"Thanks a lot," she said, punching his shoulder harder than intended.

"Ouch."

The bartender stood a few feet away, wiping pint glasses. Christian twirled his finger for another round.

They sipped their beers in silence, as the bartender placed another beer and shot in front of them.

In a quiet voice, he said, "I want to kill them."

She placed her hand on his arm, and stared into his anguished, angry eyes. "We'll find out who did this."

"I'm an FBI agent," he said, "sworn to protect and defend the United States of America." He rubbed his eyes, hard, as if he no longer wanted to see. "And I can't even protect my own son." He stared at his glass. "Amanda told me that when Mark gets home from school, he runs to the bathroom. Do you know why?"

She shook her head.

"Because he holds in his pee all day long, too afraid to use the bathrooms at school." He took another sip of beer. "He flinches every time he receives a text message."

"He's lying about not knowing who did this to him." She gulped another swig of beer. "I think it has something to do with you."

"He's afraid I'll kick their asses if I find out their names. It's not like back in the day. If another student hit you, you'd hit him back. Today, you'd get in trouble for that. Suspended, because you're trying to defend yourself. Ridiculous." He drained the second beer and signaled for a third. "How was Seattle?"

Jade filled him in on the electronic theft at Kyle's company. She didn't mention the Storm game. Or the walk back to the hotel.

"Could it have been an inside job?"

"Not sure yet. We interviewed the accounting staff and those with access and authorization to make a transfer of that amount: the CFO, CTO, and Ky—the managing director. Could another insider have done it? Maybe. Haven't had a chance to send my report to Cyber."

"Funny how you keep getting drawn back to Seattle. Ethan was in a funk while you were gone."

"I wonder why."

"Maybe it had something to do with your threatening to leave the Bureau. Or your slamming the door on him."

Or maybe it had something to do with receiving a call from POTUS requesting my services by name.

"Well," she hiccupped, "he had it coming. I'm hungry. We should order some fish and chips or something."

"Going all-in on this English thing, eh?"

She called their order down to the bartender, now at the end of the bar making calculations on a pad of paper.

The bartender stopped writing. "We're not serving lunch yet."

Jade leaned over the bar to look at her. The bartender hesitated and then put the pad down. She went into the kitchen, the doors swinging behind her.

"Case in point," Christian said. "Because you're Jade Harrington, you don't need to say a word for someone to do your bidding. You're already a legend at the Bureau. Ethan doesn't want to lose you. No matter what." He motioned for her to pick up her refilled shot glass. "To the good guys!"

"We usually save that toast for when we win a case."

"We're going to win both of these."

Jade belched. "Excuse me." She picked up her glass. "Both? Ethan says the bullying case isn't our case."

"It is now."

"In that case . . ." She twirled her finger for another round, as the bartender came back out to retrieve her writing pad. "Make it shots two," she said to the bartender, holding up three fingers. "I mean two shots."

She snatched the first shot glass before the bartender placed it on the bar. Jade downed it, loving the burn as it went down. She grabbed the second shot glass and nodded at Christian's first.

"Catch up."

CHAPTER FORTY-THREE

The White House, Washington, DC

"MADAM PRESIDENT, YOU might want to turn on the news," Sasha said.

Whitney gave her a questioning look, before turning on the television on the credenza in her study right off the Oval Office. Although the internal TV system in the White House showed CNN Headline News day and night, the TV in the study was normally tuned to MSNBC.

"ABC," Sasha said.

On the screen, Judy Porter stood in front of an older house, one somehow familiar to Whitney. She moved closer to the TV.

"Yes, Glenn, ABC News has been working on a feature about the president's early years. We've been focusing on her aunt, Mary Churchill. President Fairchild has never spoken publicly about their relationship, or why she lived with her for a year during high school."

My God. That's my aunt's house.

The reporter continued. "Churchill died at the age of forty-one, a year before the president was elected to her first term in the US House of Representatives."

Whitney stared at the house behind the reporter. The memories of her nine months there—repressed since her stay—assailed her in a way that was almost physical. Her aunt had been good to her. And there for her when her parents were not.

"Interesting," said Glenn, the anchorman.

"It is, Glenn. We will continue to delve into this relationship and its impact on the president's life."

"Thanks, Judy. And now to Robert in Glendale, Missouri."

The TV screen switched to a man in shirtsleeves standing on a road in a wooded area holding a microphone with ABC in big letters. "And that's not the only mystery we're trying to solve tonight, Glenn. Through our intensive investigative efforts, ABC News now believes that the death of US Representative Steven Barrett wasn't an accident.

"To remind our viewers, Congressman Barrett died in a one-car collision late one night on this road"—he gestured behind him with his other arm—"in 2005. Soon thereafter, Missouri State Representative Whitney Fairchild ran in, and then won, the special election to replace him."

"Can you give us any details of what brought you to that conclusion?"

"Not at this time, Glenn. We've turned over our investigative documents to the local police. We believe they will reopen the investigation into his death, and change the cause of death from an accident to murder."

"Thanks, Robert," Glenn said. His expression turned serious. "It sounds as if anyone who stood in President Whitney Fairchild's way didn't have much time left in this world. Was it luck that propelled a state senator—and former housewife—to the highest office in the land? Or something else? We'll talk about it after the break. Don't go away."

Without turning around, Whitney waved her hand at Sasha. "Change it."

Whitney tried to still her heart. *What was going on?* She didn't trust herself to move for fear her legs would fail her.

Sasha tried to laugh it off. "There is no end to the media's conspiracy theories." When she didn't respond, Sasha's laugh subsided. "Madam President, is there something I should know?"

Whitney still did not turn around. "Find Agent Harrington. I need to talk to her. Now."

CHAPTER FORTY-FOUR

Arlington, Virginia

CHRISTIAN LUMBERED UP the walkway to his house. His wife, Amanda, would not be happy. Jade watched and waited for him to open his front door before indicating that they could go.

In the driver's seat, Zoe was leaning forward watching him, too. "I know I'm not supposed to ask any questions, but why were the two of you getting drunk on a Wednesday morning? And, most importantly, why didn't you call me to join you?"

Jade turned to her. The best decision she had made this morning—contrary to what Christian had said—was realizing that she was too drunk to drive. She had called Zoe to come pick them up at the pub.

Jade burped. "I'm. Not. Sure."

Zoe laughed and put the car in drive. The acceleration caught Jade by surprise. The back of her head bounced off the headrest. She cracked up laughing. Zoe glanced over at her before turning her attention back to the road.

Mesmerized by the numerous colorful bracelets on Zoe's arm, Jade stole a glance at her friend. Zoe's hair stuck up all over the place. On purpose. Stopping at a traffic light, Zoe turned to her and smiled, brightening up the car's interior.

"You're beautiful," Jade said.

Her best friend in college—and since—shook her head and laughed again. She turned on the radio.

Jade started moving her head to the beat of the music. "Uh, uh." She sang the first line of the song.

Zoe stared at Jade, her mouth open. "You must be drunk."

"I. Think. You're. Right."

As the Nelly song, "Hot In Herre" played, Jade sang and danced and tried to take her shirt off. Zoe laughed until she cried, trying to keep Jade's shirt on with one hand while driving with the other. Eventually, after Jade promised not to undress, Zoe joined in.

Windows down, they sang classic R&B songs at the top of their lungs and chair-danced, just like they did in college. Their own version of car karaoke.

※

Parked in front of the townhouse, Zoe glanced at Jade's door. "I'm not carrying you in there."

Zoe, at five three, weighed no more than one-ten. At slightly over six feet, one hundred and sixty pounds, Jade towered over her.

She uncharacteristically put an arm around Zoe, and they zigzagged into the house. Jade zeroed in on the Japanese journal on the sofa, open to the latest haiku she'd written. She grabbed it before Zoe could notice it and stuffed it under a cushion, before stumbling onto the couch, willing herself not to throw up.

She hadn't told Zoe about her poetry hobby.

Zoe left and returned with a thin, worn blanket from the upstairs hall closet. When she bent over to lay the cover on her, Jade glimpsed a tattoo on Zoe's chest.

進捗

"What's that?"

Zoe glanced to where Jade pointed. "Oh. I got a new tattoo."

Jade peered closer, but the design became less focused rather than more. "It doesn't look new."

"Because you're drunk. Be right back."

She left again and came back with three Advil tablets and a glass of water. "Swallow."

"Thank. You."

Zoe strolled over to Jade's bookcase. The books were arranged in alphabetical order and aligned at the edge, library style. "Next time you're out of town, I'm going to rearrange these."

"Where's my phone?" Jade had not checked her voicemail messages in Seattle. She wouldn't make the same mistake again.

Zoe dug through Jade's jacket, thrown in a heap in the foyer. She brought the phone to her.

"I'm going to go," Zoe said. "I need to get back to work. Eat something when you wake up. Call if you need me."

She headed for the front door.

"Okay." Jade navigated to her voicemail messages, an almost insurmountable task in her condition. She checked the screen. Ethan. Ethan. Ethan. She couldn't talk to him drunk. She'd call him later.

She frowned at a 206 number she didn't recognize.

It wasn't McClaine. She didn't think so, anyway. Pressing the voicemail icon and speakerphone, she placed the phone on the hardwood floor.

"Hi. This is Kyle." Jade's eyes popped open. Too late to grab the phone to click it off. "I'm calling to make sure you arrived safely back in Washington, and to tell you how much I enjoyed last night. I'll see you again soon."

She stared at the ceiling. Waiting. The front door had not opened. A creak from one of the wood panels on the floor in the foyer. The jangling of Zoe's bracelets slowly drew closer, and then her face filled Jade's line of vision.

"Why is Kyle calling you?"

CHAPTER FORTY-FIVE

Fairfax, Virginia

"MAN, I GOTTA go," Joshua Stewart said.

"We just tapped a new keg," said the boy hosting the party who had been talking to Kaylee Taylor. "Come on, man. One more beer."

"Nah. I can't. I'm leaving with my parents to go visit my aunt and uncle in Bel Air tomorrow morning. Early."

"Okay. Hold up. I'll walk you out." To Kaylee, he said, "Be right back."

The living room looked nothing like it did when Joshua arrived. All the furniture was pushed against the walls, including a lamp without its lampshade. The plush white carpet was now spotted with yellow splotches of draft beer.

William Chaney-Frost surveyed the damage. "My parents are going to kill me."

"Yep."

Outside, they crossed the front porch and bounded down the stairs, stopping at the end of the walkway that bisected the yard.

"Great party, man," Joshua said, although he hadn't had a good time at all. Same shit, same people. Staring down at the sidewalk, he kicked at a small rock wedged between the cracks. "Do you ever . . . think about T?"

William glanced around the deserted suburban street. "Yeah. All the time."

"He wasn't a bad guy."

"No."

"Sometimes, I can't sleep. I have nightmares."

"Easy. It wasn't your fault."

"Of course it was. I—"

"It was an accident."

"I think about what happened to Z and Nic . . . Aren't you scared?"

William put his hand on Joshua's shoulder and squeezed. Comforting at first. Until it hurt. "No. It's just a coincidence. Our boys were in the wrong place at the wrong time. No one's coming after us. Take it easy." He gave Joshua the killer smile that drove the girls at school crazy. William could have any girl he wanted. Must be nice. Another squeeze of his shoulder commanded Joshua's attention. "Got it?"

Joshua shrugged him away. "I got it. What about that kid?"

"He's young. He'll get over it."

"That lady FBI agent made me nervous."

"She made me hot." William patted Joshua's shoulder. "Everything's going to be okay. Trust me. Go have fun with your family. I'll catch ya on Monday."

"Okay. Later."

Joshua ambled down the sidewalk in the direction of his house.

"Hey!" William shouted. Joshua stopped and turned. "The cage is a go next weekend."

Joshua nodded without enthusiasm and resumed walking. He popped an Altoids mint in his mouth to cover up the beer smell in case his parents were still up. They usually didn't wait up for him.

The conversation with William hadn't made him feel better. He'd been T's best friend on the team, though that wasn't saying much. They hadn't been that close. But still. Joshua's face grew warm remembering the shame he felt when he saw the pictures of T circulating on the Internet. Tyler didn't deserve to be treated like that. No one did.

A car started up behind him, but Joshua paid no attention to it. Probably one of his classmates who shouldn't be driving. They had all seen the don't-drink-and-drive videos.

He didn't agree with what his teammates had done to T. What he had done to T.

I should've spoken up. Should've stopped it.

Now, instead of the quasi-friendship with T, shame was his constant companion.

He passed the last house on William's street and kept walking. In the new subdivision, Joshua's parents had built a house one street over on Cedarbrook Way, the lone house on the street so far. He stepped off the curb to cross. Still lost in his thoughts, he didn't bother to look both ways.

He didn't hear the car coming.

And then he did.

It accelerated toward him, its headlights blinding.

Joshua froze in the intense light.

The driver saw him. Right? "Stop! You drunk ass!"

He realized—too late—the car was not stopping and not going to swerve around him. The automobile hit him. As he propelled upward on impact, his coat caught on the emblem of the car's hood. The coat ripped away. He continued to roll over the hood and up the windshield. And then he was airborne. His head smacked the asphalt. Every bone in his body felt broken. And he had a massive headache. A pool of liquid spread under his head, seeping into his shirt. He felt all these things, which meant—

—he was still alive.

Maybe after realizing he accidentally hit someone, the drunk driver would help him. Or maybe someone heard the impact, although it had happened down the street from the last house on the block. Maybe William was still outside.

Help me!

Losing consciousness, the cry for help heard only in his mind.

The car idled.

No sound of a car door opening.

He called out again, but still no sound came. He tried to lift his hand, but it wouldn't budge.

Don't leave me.

The engine revved.

Please, don't go.

The tires squealed.

Help me.

He exhaled, his hopes fading.

But wait. Something wasn't right.

The car sounded as if . . . as if . . . it was getting closer.

That can't be.

The car accelerated backward. Joshua felt the heat of the exhaust burning his face, right before the back tires ran over it.

I'm sorry, T.

And then he felt nothing at all.

CHAPTER FORTY-SIX

Washington, DC

THE BOOKSTORE ON Connecticut Avenue was empty. Whitney stopped to scan the biography section before choosing a book on Franklin D. Roosevelt she had not read. If she were going to resurrect him now, it behooved her to learn everything about him.

The Secret Service had cleared the store of patrons and staff before her arrival, except for one employee. An avid reader, Whitney visited one of the local independent bookstores at least once a month, schedule permitting.

She moved on to the glass case where they kept the first editions. Collecting them was her hobby. She pointed to and examined and returned several books to the employee before selecting a first edition of *Emma* by Jane Austen.

The book was in good condition. Touching the slightly worn cover, she thought about her son, who seemed to be getting his act together; her activist daughter whose name in script she stared at on the cover; and the media who had seemed out to get her ever since she declared her candidacy for the presidency.

Family came first. Perhaps, it was time they all got together. She made a mental note to tell Sean to schedule it.

Her thoughts turned to her vice president, Xavi Fernandez. What was he up to? Whatever it was, it wasn't good. Was it the New New Deal legislation? Or something more sinister? She could ask him directly; he would just lie about it. She shouldn't have to deal with this now.

Trust between a president and vice president was vital and the only way they could work together. He should have been her partner, as Al Gore was to Bill Clinton. Then again, if she wanted a partner, she should have selected someone else. But she had gotten greedy.

She wanted Florida.

Since the inauguration, she had continued to meet with Xavi every Tuesday for lunch. No minutes were kept. Not much was accomplished. But she liked to keep her friends close and her enemies closer.

Which was Xavi?

Conflict in the workplace didn't bother her. A difference of opinion was a good thing. Healthy. It improved decision-making. As long as the conflict stayed within the White House. Beyond, the two of them needed to present a united front.

Moving to the young adult section, she smiled as she passed the *Twilight* books. "Twilight" was the Secret Service agents' code name for her, because of her weakness for young-adult fiction. She spotted Josh near the front door and winked. The agent returned the wink with a smile. She stopped when she saw an interesting book cover: *The Running Dream* by Wendelin Van Draanen. She grabbed it.

She headed down an aisle toward the cash register, where the employee stood, waiting for her. Whitney handed her the book to add to the almost-filled white bag with the bookstore's green logo, and strolled around the store one final time.

As she passed the politics section, a title caught her eye.

Why not?

She selected a recent edition of *The Prince* by Niccolo Machiavelli and smiled. She had read the political treatise many times. If Xavi Fernandez were present to witness her smile, he would be concerned.

And nervous. Maybe even afraid.

"Madam President?" Josh called out to her, still near the door. She turned to see the tall woman nod at him, the look that passed between law enforcement officers that were good at their jobs. "Agent Harrington is here."

Washington, DC

"THANK YOU FOR coming."

"Sorry, I couldn't make it yesterday. I was . . . uh . . . busy."

"I understand."

I don't think you do.

Jade glanced around the store, gingerly, her head still pounding from the whiskey. "It must be nice to have a bookstore to yourself."

The president smiled. "The presidency has its privileges." Her expression changed to concern. "Are you all right?"

They sat in two overused comfortable chairs in the center of the store, the bag of books next to Fairchild's feet.

"Never better." Jade raised her chin at the bag. "You had a successful day."

The president glanced at the books and back at her. "Agent Harrington, I need your help."

"Did you already talk to my boss?"

Fairchild shook her head, laughing. "I apologize for that. I guess that was cheating, but I don't like to be told no. I'm sure you can understand that."

Jade conceded the point. "We checked out Stevens. He's been arrested several times for disturbing the peace. Protests. Sit-ins."

The president seemed distracted. "Good." She paused. "Have you been watching the news? About me? My aunt? The congressman?"

"No, ma'am."

The president hesitated. "I may be opening Pandora's box here, but I need to know."

Jade waited.

"ABC News is reporting that my aunt and my predecessor in Congress died under mysterious circumstances."

"Did they?"

"Aunt Mary died a year before I was elected to Congress. She lived in a suburb outside of Chicago. My parents told me at the time she died from natural causes. Congressman Barrett died in a one-car accident in Missouri. I know that stretch of road. It's curvy and dangerous. Especially at night."

"And ABC is insinuating that you had something to do with their deaths. That you profited in some way?"

"My aunt was a widow, who took me in when I needed her. That's not common knowledge, by the way. I had nothing to gain from her passing. The rep's death gave me the opportunity to run in the special election to replace him. But I was not thinking of running for national office when he died. I was happy working for the state government."

"Why did she take you in? Your aunt."

"Let's just say I needed time away from my parents."

Jade believed there was more to the story. She let it go for now.

"Why are you telling me this?"

"I need you to find out what ABC has. They claim to have investigative materials on Congressman Barrett's death, which they turned over to the local police. I want to be informed of everything they have before it becomes public."

What am I? J. Edgar Hoover?

"You have people who can take care of this for you. Why me?"

"Because I trust you," said the most powerful person in the world. "And in this job, I can't say that about too many people."

❁

After leaving the bookstore, she returned to the Bureau. The conversation with the president had unsettled her. She stopped by Pat Turner's cubicle. "I need to talk to you."

She headed to her office.

Jade sat behind her desk. "Shut the door and have a seat."

Pat cocked her head, but did as she was told. Jade told her about the meeting with President Fairchild and the president's request for her help.

Pat processed the information in silence and then said, "Do you think this has something to do with the TSK case?"

Jade had wondered the same thing.

"I don't know."

CHAPTER FORTY-EIGHT

Washington, DC

"JADE, COME TO my office. Bring Merritt."

She had just booted up her computer. Frowning, she locked the system and left her office. She pointed at Christian sitting in his cubicle and pointed toward Ethan's office, as if she were still a point guard directing a play on the basketball court. She knocked once on Ethan's door and strolled in, Christian right behind her.

She sat in one of the guest chairs.

In a wry tone, Ethan said, "Come in."

She gave him an unapologetic smile. They waited for Christian to settle in the chair next to her.

"What's wrong with you two?" Ethan asked.

"Nothing," Christian said.

"I need more coffee," she said.

"I don't think that's it." He scrutinized them. "Are you hungover?"

"No," said Christian.

"Not really," Jade added.

"I need you to sober up," Ethan said, a sad look crossing his face. "A teenage boy was murdered late last night. Hit-and-run."

She sat up. "Where?"

"Virginia. Fairfax."

Christian leaned in. "Did he go to Randolph?"

"Yes."

Christian pounded his fist on the armrest.

Jade felt sadness for the murdered boy's parents. And then, just as quickly, anger at whoever took these young persons' lives.

She stared at Ethan, as her pulse quickened, knowing what was coming. "And?"

"Fairfax County police have requested our assistance." He handed her a thin folder. "It's your case now."

CHAPTER FORTY-NINE

Fairfax, Virginia

JADE DROVE THROUGH the new subdivision, Dante in the passenger seat beside her, Micah in back. Christian had taken personal leave for the afternoon to attend a conference with a school guidance counselor about his son, Mark.

Joshua Stewart's parents lived in an upper-middle-class neighborhood with ample yards, but the houses in this neighborhood were not as big as the ones in the Rawlins's neighborhood. Sod had not been laid yet in some of the lots. Empty lots separated homes at various stages of construction. They wouldn't be empty for long. The real-estate market in the DC area, especially at the upper end of the market, was hot.

She drove down Meadowbrook Drive, but slowed when she saw a familiar figure washing a car. Shirtless and barefooted, he wore baseball pants.

She lowered the window. "I didn't know you lived in this neighborhood."

William Chaney-Frost walked toward them, stopping at the curb. "That surprises me, Agent Harrington. I thought you knew everything."

"Not everything." She looked up at the gathering clouds. "It's going to rain."

He followed her gaze. "My dad doesn't care." He waved the sponge at the car behind him. "His new wheels. He's trying to keep me busy. I'm grounded indefinitely. 'Cause of the party." He inched up his chin. "Going to the Stewarts?"

"Mind if I look?"

"At what? The car?"

She nodded.

He squinted at her. "Never seen a Porsche up close before?"

"Something like that."

She didn't have a warrant, but she interpreted his question as an invitation. She hopped out of the car and started walking to the front of the Porsche. Another car door opened and closed behind her.

She squatted and examined the bumper, Micah next to her. He looked at her and at the bumper but said nothing.

No dents. No chipped paint. This wasn't the car that hit Joshua Stewart.

"Nice, huh?" William said.

"What about you? Where's your car?"

"Don't have one. Not sixteen yet."

Jade headed back to her car.

"Agent Harrington?"

She turned.

William glanced down the street and back at her. "I hope you catch who did it. J-man was my friend."

❈

"Anything we need to know?" Micah asked from the back seat.

"Not sure yet."

She turned right onto Cedarbrook Way.

"These street names are peaceful," she said.

"Makes you want to puke," Dante replied.

She glanced at him. "Lovely."

Dante's left hand was resting on the dashboard. His fingers were long, his hands graceful. She hadn't noticed this about him before.

"I think the names are quite lovely," Micah said from behind them.

She could listen to his accent all day.

Dante turned in his seat. "What are you, queer?"

"Shut up, Dante," she said.

"You don't have to be gay to like nice things," Micah said, in a quiet voice, his eyes meeting Jade's in the rearview mirror.

She cut her eyes back to the road.

She parked at the curb in front of the lone house, midway down the street.

The door opened to a slender man with glasses.

"Mr. Stewart? I spoke to your wife earlier. May we come in and talk to you about your son?"

The man exhaled. "Sure."

Stepping aside, he led them into a generous living room. A leather sectional sofa took up most of the room, facing a flat-screen TV that hung on the wall over the fireplace.

"My wife will be down soon."

Situated, she said, "Mr. Stewart, can you tell us what happened?"

"Please, call me Joe."

He repeated what she had already learned from Det. Chutimant on the phone that morning. That Joshua went to a party and never came home. A parent's worst nightmare. He didn't mention that his son was struck by a hit-and-run driver, or rather, a hit-and-hit-and-run driver. Per Chutimant, the driver had been going over forty miles an hour. She also mentioned that Joshua still possessed his private parts.

"The time of death was close to midnight," Jade said. "Weren't you concerned that he was out late?"

"Not really. He was just down the street. Wasn't driving. Joshua never gave us any trouble."

"Did your son have any enemies?"

Before he could answer, a woman descended the staircase and entered the living room. She didn't bother to shake their hands. She sat near her husband.

Jade repeated her question.

"Well—" Joe Stewart said.

"Of course not," his wife said. "He was a good kid, a baseball player. Smart. He planned to go to UVA or William and Mary."

"Mr. Stewart?"

He glanced at his wife, then back at Jade. "Sometimes I noticed bruises and scratches. On his arm and—"

"That's from playing sports. Everyone who plays a contact sport gets bruises."

"Baseball isn't really a contact sport," Joe Stewart replied. "He had this cut on his forehead. We had to take him to the doctor. I asked Joshua how he got it. He said he ran into a door."

"See!" his wife said.

"He didn't run into a door, Cindy," Stewart said. He looked at Jade. "Lately, he had become withdrawn, thoughtful, more"—he paused, searching for the right word—"*introspective* over the last year."

"He was finally growing up," his wife said.

Joe Stewart continued to stare at Jade. "No, I don't think that's it. I think he was being bullied."

"By whom?"

"If I had to guess, I would say Zach Rawlins."

A pinch came to Cindy Stewart's lips. "Zach . . . He never lived up to his mother's high standards . . . until he died. And then he became the perfect son." She confided to Jade. "His parents pressured him to succeed at sports."

Joe Stewart scoffed. "His mother wasn't the problem. It was his father. Always yelling at his son. The refs. Coaches. Players. Even other parents. He acted as if they were playing in the World Series instead of a JV game."

"He was just passionate," his wife said. "She, on the other hand, bullied her son with silence."

The agents' heads swiveled like at a tennis match. Jade was okay with that. She let them speak. You learned more by listening than speaking.

"I never liked the way he spoke to Joshua," Joe Stewart said.

"Zach?" Jade asked.

"The father."

From Dante: "Was your son a bully?"

"This is ridiculous," Cindy Stewart said. "It's just a bunch of boys being boys. You're too sensitive, Joe, really."

"I may be sensitive, but I'll tell you one thing. I'll bet Zach Rawlins had something to do with Tyler Thompson's death. And my son's."

"Why is that?" asked Micah.

"That boy was trouble."

CHAPTER FIFTY

The White House, Washington, DC

WHITNEY DROPPED THE *Los Angeles Times* on the table, among the other newspapers she perused every morning with her breakfast in the residence kitchen: the *New York Times*, the *Wall Street Journal*, the *Washington Post*, the *Chicago Tribune*, and the *Guardian*.

She refilled her coffee, inhaling the rich aroma before taking a sip.

The lead story in every paper was the same: income-inequality protests in its own city and other major cities. The number of people participating increased with each successive protest. And the tenor was changing. She felt it.

Violence was coming.

She muted the television.

ABC News's stories about the deaths of her aunt and the congressman had not been reported widely by the rest of the media. The story wasn't dead. Judy would never let it go.

Whitney wanted to chastise the veteran reporter. In public. Hold a press conference. There were more important things going on in this country than digging into her past: homelessness, economic insecurity, inequity, racial injustice.

Judy knew that. A competent reporter, she was well-respected in the journalistic and political community.

Judy could become a problem.

Meanwhile, the numerous protests across the country were still not enough to convince Congress to consider, much less pass, Whitney's legislation.

Frustrated, Whitney needed a Plan B.

She called Sean, already at the office. "Schedule a meeting with Evan Stevens. Today."

❊

"Thanks for coming."

"Did I have the option to refuse?"

"Of course. This isn't Communist Russia or Nazi Germany."

"Sometimes, I'm not so sure."

Evan Stevens glanced down at the badge sporting a red-letter A clipped to his black turtleneck shirt. "*The Scarlet Letter?*"

"That depends. Have you sinned?"

"The day's still early."

Sarah placed a tea service on the coffee table.

"Thank you, Sarah," Whitney said.

Sarah poured tea for them and left.

Evan picked up his cup. "You called this meeting."

"These protests," she said. "What are your thoughts about them?"

Evan sipped his tea and then placed the cup and saucer on the thigh of his jeans, his legs crossed. "People are frustrated, Madam President. Wealth is concentrated at the top. The rest of us are working harder for the same or less money. The cost of living is far outpacing wages. Since the founding of this country, the American Dream was never as attainable as the American people were led to believe, and now, even less so."

"What's the solution?"

"I've read your New New Deal plan. I like it. I think it will help. Do I think it will be enough? No."

"What would you do differently?"

"Are you familiar with the works of Thomas Paine?"

She smiled and nodded at the rhetorical question.

"Paine advocated that citizens should receive a basic income whether they work or not. Some of our manufacturing jobs are never coming back. They've been automated. A universal basic income would remove the stigma of welfare for the long-term unemployed and combat poverty and social inequality."

"That's fair."

"For Paine, it wasn't about fairness. It was about equality. Natural rights."

"I stand corrected. Please continue."

"I would also peg CEO compensation to a multiple of the lowest-earning employees' wages, remove the cap on the Social Security tax, and provide universal childcare and pre-K so that parents can work, and tuition-free college so that our children can enter adulthood debt-free."

"I see you haven't thought about this." Whitney sipped her tea. "A lot of those reforms won't be popular. CEOs aren't going to go along quietly."

"Corporate profits are at an all-time high. The ratio of wages to profits is at its lowest level in over fifty years. It's not sustainable. The workers will revolt."

"And you're going to help them?"

Evan set his cup and saucer on the table. "I'm just a blogger."

Whitney smiled. "And I'm just a bureaucrat. The cost for universal college education alone would be upwards of sixty billion dollars. How would I ever get that through Congress?"

"We spend sixty-nine billion on subsidies. Universal college may be a bargain." He leaned forward in earnest. "Only thirty percent of students enrolled in college today will graduate. How many more would graduate in four years—instead of the current average of six—if they didn't need to work?

"Unemployment would be reduced, state funding could be used for other pressing needs, and there would be fewer people on public assistance." Evan's eyes shone with an intensity that bordered on the maniacal. "Students who graduate from college, on average, make more than a million dollars over their lifetimes than those who don't. Highly educated people are happier and healthier. It's harder for our students to compete with those countries who offer free education, like Germany, Finland, and Norway. Some US states spend more money funding their prison system than education."

She and Sasha had discussed and dismissed universal college education, but his unwavering passion stirred something within her. She recognized it. The same passion that had driven her to enter politics in the first place. Back then, she was going to change the world. Start a revolution. Like Emma.

"The other party will say that students should have some skin in the game. I am inclined to agree with them. Those students would benefit the most from a free education."

Evan waved away this detail. "I'm not just talking about a more educated workforce, but an educated citizenry. So, that when we discuss issues like climate change there will no longer be a debate about whether it exists, but the more important question: what are we going to do about it?"

"Spending all that money on education, during a time of pervasive homelessness and a crumbling infrastructure . . . That's a tough sell."

Evan's eyes blazed. "I don't think you're listening, Madam President. Outstanding student loans total over one-point-four *trillion* dollars. A higher education is almost out of reach for the poor and now some of the middle class. We *must* do this." Abruptly, Evan relaxed and offered her a sheepish smile. "I'm sorry. I get worked up about this stuff. Look. Almost half of the members of Congress are millionaires. They're out of touch with the rest of us. They don't know what it's like to struggle. To live paycheck to paycheck. There's other alter-natives. We could tax pollution. Carbon emissions. Raise taxes on the wealthy."

"That too should go over well," Whitney said.

Evan's eyes flared again. "There's a benefit from being born in this country. Taxation is a responsibility and a privilege of citizenship."

"I don't think a lot of people see it that way."

"Well, they should."

They discussed his ideas for another ten minutes. She placed her cup on the table. "If we don't pass my legislation or implement your ideas, what do you think will happen?"

"Capitalism leads to greater and greater levels of income inequality. The United States has reached a level at which soon it will be unable to function. Historically, when inequality increases unabated, something horrible happens. The Great Depression. The Great Recession." Evan stared at her, unblinking. "This time, I predict there will be a Civil War. But it will not be a war between the states. Between the North and the South.

"No. It will be a war between the wealthy and everyone else."

CHAPTER FIFTY-ONE

Arlington, Virginia

AFTER DROPPING DANTE and Micah off at the Bureau, Jade drove home. Her phone rang. Christian.

"How's Mark?"

"He's okay. The ribs are healing. He goes back to school tomorrow. They're beefing up student patrols in the hallways. Not sure how much good it'll do. How did the interview go?"

"The dad believes the son was bullied. The mother doesn't believe it or doesn't want to believe it."

"Well, if their son was a bully, then he got what he deserved."

"Christian," Jade said. A warning.

"I'm serious. This has got to stop."

"We don't know if it was the same killer. Different MO."

"What I said still stands."

"Justice isn't served by some vigilante knocking off teenage bullies. There's the rule of law. Our job is to uphold it, by the way."

"At this point, I don't care how it's upheld."

Jade understood why someone would want to take the law into his own hands. It's how she would feel if someone hurt someone she loved. But the legal system of this country was built on the rule of law principle. That we are a nation governed by laws, not the arbitrary decisions of individuals. Vigilantes assumed the role of police officer, judge, jury, and in this case, executioner. She believed vigilantism had no place in a civilized society.

"You don't mean that."

"An eye for an eye. It's in the Bible."

She closed her eyes at his words. "Then we'd all be blind."

Parked in front of her townhouse for the last few minutes of their conversation, Jade watched her neighbors arrive home from work and enter their houses, oblivious to the turmoil roiling inside the car. Inside her.

He had lost all objectivity.

"Christian?"

"Yeah?"

With reluctance, she said, "You're off the case."

※

Jade returned to the living room of her townhouse with a bag. Eating the delivered pad thai straight from the carton, she chased it with a Tsingtao, the cold beer refreshing after the day she'd had. The week. The month. She was frustrated with her lack of progress on the bullying case, even though officially, she'd only been on it for a day. No progress on the cybertheft case, either, for that matter.

Oh-for-two.

She spent some time connecting the PlayStation to the television. At her request, Christian had brought in the system earlier that day. She hoped Mark could live without it for one night. Slipping in the disc, she settled back into the sofa.

She couldn't think about Christian now.

The game's logo, *Bully*, filled her screen. Never much of a video-game player, like some of her teammates back in college, it took her some time to figure out the instructions and how to navigate the controls to do what she wanted.

The name of the game brought back memories. Childhood memories she would rather forget.

Her phone rang.

Pat spoke without preamble. "The death of Rep. Steven Barrett wasn't an accident. Someone tampered with his brakes. He didn't stand a chance going around that curve."

"Why didn't the detectives discover this at the time?"

"They should've."

"Anything else? Anything on the aunt?"

"Not yet."

"Thanks." Jade hung up.

Who would gain from Barrett's death? Fairchild wasn't assured of winning the election for the seat to replace him. Maybe it didn't have anything to do with Fairchild. It could've been Barrett's wife, a disgruntled husband, or an unhappy constituent. She made a mental note to call the local detective on the case tomorrow.

Glancing around her living room, the word "minimalist" sprang to mind. She had remarked that Kyle's office was bereft of tombstones, but Jade's home, too, displayed no evidence of her past glories.

Back to the game. The objective was for a teenager, involuntarily enrolled in a boarding school filled with bullies, to bring peace to the school and the town. Who would want to play this game for fun?

Based on her research of the game's sales, a lot of people.

An hour in, she was hooked.

The still half-full carton of Thai food rested on the wooden coffee table, ignored, as she negotiated teenage cliques, completed missions, attended classes, and used a wide variety of weapons to vanquish her opponents. She wondered, briefly, whether William Chaney-Frost was like the protagonist or one of the bullies.

She played until well past midnight. Being as competitive as she was, by the end of the night, she had become quite good at *Bully*. She didn't know if that was good or bad.

She did, though, have trouble falling asleep that night.

CHAPTER FIFTY-TWO

Fairfax, Virginia

THERE IS NOTHING sadder than the funeral of a child.

Jade stood with Dante and Micah, away from the grieving family and friends, as Joshua Stewart was laid to rest at Fairfax Memorial Park. Earlier, the clouds, dark and ominous, threatened the gathered mourners with a thunderstorm, but a light rain had fallen instead during the service. Now, as if cognizant of the occasion, the sky cleared and the sun appeared, as the procession made its way to the cemetery. The park, with its rolling hills and impeccable landscaping, was peaceful. It turned out to be a beautiful day.

Most of the mourners had journeyed here from the church. A dozen teenage boys stood together, wearing their best black suits. Suits that were getting a lot of wear lately. A few of them were pallbearers, including William Chaney-Frost. Jade recognized some of them from interviews at the school.

From behind dark oversized sunglasses, she catalogued each of the attendees in her mind. After offering her condolences to Joshua's parents, she inclined her head to the car, signaling to Dante and Micah that it was time to go.

"Agent Harrington!"

She turned, expecting William, but it was one of the other boys she had interviewed. She allowed her mental Rolodex to come up with his name. "Andrew."

"Yeah."

The boy was larger than his teammates. He glimpsed over his shoulder at the still-gathered mourners. "There's something we—I—didn't tell you."

She waited.

"Something's going on with our team." He looked over his shoulder again. "It's gotten out of hand."

"What is it?"

"One of our best players, Sam, is going to quit because of it."

"Tell me what's going on."

William called out to him.

Andrew's eyes widened. "I gotta go."

"Andrew, how did you get those scratches on your face?"

Although Joshua's casket was closed, Jade read in his autopsy report that he'd had stitches removed over one eyebrow. The injury his mother said he received from colliding with a door.

Andrew mumbled something, eyes imploring her of—something—before he took off running up the hill.

William seemed to chew him out before smiling and waving at her.

She didn't wave back.

"What did Andrew say?" Dante asked.

"Not sure. It sounded like 'age,'" she said.

"That kid was scared to death," said Micah.

"I think we need to take a closer look at Mr. William Chaney-Frost," she said. She turned to Micah. "You game?"

The White House, Washington, DC

SHE GLANCED AT the stack of bios of congressmen and congresswomen she needed to convince to support the New New Deal Coalition legislation. Picking up the phone, she started to dial the first name on the list.

"Do you have a minute?" Sasha asked.

Whitney hung up and beckoned her in. "Good. You saved me from making these dreaded calls."

Sasha sat in the chair across from her. "I found out what Xavi is up to. He's shopping his own proposal. A competing income-equality plan."

"I'm surrounded by Judases. What's in it?"

Sasha shook her head. "Don't know yet. I'm meeting someone later this afternoon to find out."

Whitney didn't bother to ask from whom. If Sasha wanted her to know, she would tell her.

"He's receiving some support from the Republicans," Sasha said. "Hampton, Bell." She hesitated. "Sampson."

"What do they want in return?"

Always quid pro quo in this political game they played.

"My source tells me that Xavi promised to work with them on comprehensive illegal-immigration reform,"—Sasha hesitated—"when he becomes president. He's willing to compromise on some points Hispanics have demanded in the past."

Whitney smiled without mirth. "That makes a lot of sense. I don't think that will be popular with his Hispanic brothers and sisters."

Sasha pursed her lips. "I don't think he worries too much about the welfare of his brothers and sisters. The only person Xavi worries about is Xavi. Are you going to confront him?"

Whitney knew Xavi's goal wasn't to be president eight years from now. Or four years from now. He wanted her job now.

"Judas Iscariot purportedly committed suicide. Xavi may do the same."

Sasha gave her a questioning look.

Whitney picked up the phone again to call the first congressman on the list. Before dialing, she said, "Political suicide, of course. What were you thinking?"

CHAPTER FIFTY-FOUR

Fairfax, Virginia

BASEBALL PLAYERS STREAMED out of the gate that separated the outdoor athletic complex from the school parking lot.

In ones, twos, and threes, they slowed and gawked at each other at the sight of Jade perched on the front end of her car, one foot on the ground. Micah leaned against the car next to her, looking like a model in his fitted suit and Ray-Ban sunglasses.

At the end of the pack was William, who broke into a cocky smile. He sauntered over to her. "You two look like a GQ ad for FBI agents. Where's Howie Long?"

She couldn't help smiling. Christian *did* look like the Hall of Fame defensive end for the Oakland Raiders and NFL commentator.

"He wishes he could be here."

"I bet. He seems to be MIA lately."

She didn't explain it was probably for the best that Christian wasn't here. She glanced over at the players who were huddled halfway between them and the school. "Nothing to see here!"

She waited until she saw their backs before turning to William. His uniform was filthy. His face streaked with dirt. His blue and gold baseball cap looked brand new compared to the rest of his uniform. "FC" was written in black magic marker just over the bill.

"Shouldn't that be 'CF' for Chaney-Frost?"

"I really need to catch up with my team," he said.

"How do you do it?"

"Do what?"

"Keep your face so smooth, while your teammates' faces are scratched and bruised?"

He stroked his chin and perched his cleat on her bumper, resting his arms on his thigh. "They're clumsy?"

She glanced down at the dusty cleat.

He hesitated and then removed it.

"What position do you play?" Micah asked.

"Why? Are you planning on coming to a game?"

"Answer the question, William," Jade said.

"Shortstop."

"Tell me about your teammates who died," Jade said.

"Haven't we gone over this?"

She had debated whether to bring him down to FBI HQ to shake him up a bit, but decided it was premature. "I want to go over it again."

"Zach was a bully, you know that. Nic, too, but . . ."

She waited him out.

" . . . he was bullied as well. By Z." He kicked at an imaginary rock on the asphalt. "Joshman was weak, but a bully, too. He would do whatever Z said."

"Sounds like a team full of bullies."

"Are you one?" Micah asked.

"Do I look like a bully?"

Jade thought back to their original interview and Andrew Huffman's reaction after the funeral.

"Yes."

※

"It's late."

"Thanks for seeing us."

Jade sat in an institutional-gray chair across from Coach Lane Daniel in his cramped office on a lower floor near the gymnasium. Micah stood next to her, the room not large enough for another chair.

Daniel was barrel-chested, a former athlete who still ate—but didn't exercise—like one. He was dressed in the same uniform as his players. Jade always wondered why baseball was the only sport in which that happened.

He observed her taking in his office. "Yeah. It'd be bigger if I coached football."

"We won't take up a lot of your time. We'd like to ask you a few questions."

"Saw you talking to Chaney-Frost. Did he say anything that could help you?"

"What do you think is going on with your baseball team?"

The big man leaned back in his chair. "Hell, if I know. I told the police it must be a rival team. No one likes to see a successful man."

"You think this is about you?"

"I didn't say that. Someone's just out to get us. Since this is my team, it means they're out to get me."

"Do your players get along?"

"As well as any team. It's not peaches and cream all the time. These guys want to win. They won't hesitate to get in each other's faces, if necessary. But off the field everything's forgotten."

"Is that why so many of your players have bruises and scratches on their faces? Black eyes?"

"Baseball is a tough sport. We play hard every day. Doesn't matter if it's practice or game day."

"Seems like it's more than that." She paused to see if he would respond. He didn't. "Do you think there's bullying going on? Hazing? Anything like that?"

"Missy," he said, "I'm trying to raise men here, not pu— pansies."

"It's Agent Harrington."

"What?"

"My name is not 'Missy.' It's Agent Harrington."

She asked him his whereabouts the nights of the four murders. The coach leaned forward and paged through an opened school calendar on his desk. "The first night I was at a coaches' meeting." Licking his finger, he paged to the next date. She tried not to grimace. His hands were still dirty from practice. "Here." He showed her the date. "My daughter's soccer game. These other two nights aren't marked, so I was probably at home. In my home office. I'm pretty much all-in during the season. Watching tape. Working on practice plans."

"Do you think someone on your team could be killing his teammates?"

Daniel looked at her, incredulous. "The teams at this school are expected to win. Every player knows that when he signs up. To be a part of that tradition. That would be self-defeating, wouldn't it?"

"What do you think of Chaney-Frost?"

"Solid player. He's gotten some PT—playing time—as a sophomore on varsity, too. Better with the bat than in the field. Better talker than doer."

"What about as a person?" Micah asked.

"He's bought into the program. That's all I care about."

CHAPTER FIFTY-FIVE

Washington, DC

COLE BRENNAN SAUNTERED past the crowded bar to a table around the corner, where Republican Senator Paul Sampson sat nursing a drink. Judging from the redness of his face, it wasn't his first of the evening.

Cole's drink waited for him at the table. Most nights, he rushed home from the studio to be with his family, but on occasion he held business meetings at the Capital Grille on Pennsylvania Avenue near the Newseum.

Sampson looked up. "What do you want to talk about?"

"Can't a man sit down first?"

Cole made a show of scanning the menu, even though he had ordered ahead. He didn't like to wait. "Try the porterhouse. Amazing."

The waiter materialized and took Sampson's order.

"Can we talk now?"

Cole glanced around to see if anybody else was here. Anybody who was somebody. Politicians frequented this place. A congressman or one of his staffers could be sitting next to you. Yeah, yeah, congresswomen, too.

"Look here," Cole said, "if you're going to be 'my guy,' you've got to become a populist."

"Okay . . ."

Cole paused as the waiter set down his food.

The aroma of his steak compelled him to take a bite.

"Don't wait for me," Sampson said, his tone sarcastic.

Cole ignored him. "If you want to be president you need to become folksier. More likable by the people."

"How do I do that?"

"You say what they want to hear. Anything against Muslims or minorities or illegal immigrants is usually a winner."

"Got it. What else?"

"Intellectuals, the media, and women are all good targets."

"Women?"

"September twenty-first, nineteen eighty-one. The beginning of the end."

"What're you talking about? What happened on that date?"

"Sandra Day O'Connor was nominated to the Supreme Court."

Sampson appeared baffled.

"And if you really want to endear yourself to the good folks on the right," Cole continued, "just mention abortion. They'll love you. Even better, all the Feminazis will come out of the woodwork. That's always fun."

The waiter set down Sampson's plate and withdrew.

"What about the gays?"

Cole thought about his son. "Them, too."

"What about Hampton? Why aren't you backing him?"

Cole waved his fork, dismissing the suggestion. "He's too uptight. Too full of himself. He's also an intellectual. No one likes an intellectual."

Stabbing another piece of steak, he pointed at Sampson's plate. "Good, huh?" He stuffed the morsel in his mouth.

Sampson scanned the restaurant. "I've been here before, Cole."

"Yeah, but not with me."

The waiter asked how their steaks were. "Great," Cole said, pointing to his drink. "Bring us another round."

He had heard the rumors that Sampson was a lush. He didn't mind. In fact, it would make it easier to control him.

"Now, where were we?" Cole said. "Disagree with everything the president says. Everything. Even, if you agree with her. Especially anything about raising the minimum wage or government intervention. Your constituency will be with you, even though she wants to give them a raise. It doesn't make sense, but that's okay. It helps us. Also, it doesn't matter if what you say is the truth or not. You can say one thing one day and the complete opposite the next day, and your followers won't care. They don't care about the truth. They want to be with you. They want—no, they need—to believe in someone. To believe in something. Again. Like Reagan."

Sampson was nodding at everything he said. Cole had him.

"You should declare your candidacy about a year from now," Cole said. "The people must be on your side by then."

Sampson looked doubtful. "I don't know if I can make people love me like that."

Cole bestowed a broad smile. "You're probably right. But I can. Now, how about a cognac?"

CHAPTER FIFTY-SIX

Washington, DC

JADE BLEW HER whistle from the sideline. All ten players on the court stopped running and turned to her.

She addressed her point guard. "LaKeisha, I want ten passes before a shot is taken."

LaKeisha flashed her a questioning look. "Ten passes, Coach? That's a lifetime."

"Just do it, LaKeisha. I know we can score. I want to see you run the offense."

LaKeisha grinned at her and bounced the ball in place. "You got it, Coach." Facing her teammates, she held up her fist. "Stanford!"

The team ran their flex offense, named after Jade's alma mater. Last year, LaKeisha played on Jade's team of middle-school girls. She'd had a good freshman year, averaging ten points a game, leading her team to the city championship, and earning the *Washington Post's* third-team All-Met honors. Jade now coached the high school's spring-league team.

After practice, Jade stuffed basketballs into a bag, LaKeisha lingering nearby.

"How's school?"

LaKeisha untied her low-tops. The mini-twist hairstyle of last year had grown out to dreadlocks. Her hair now hid her face. "It's okay."

Jade set the bag aside and sat on the bench next to her. "Let me ask you something."

LaKeisha tensed, still fiddling with her laces.

"Is bullying prevalent in your school?" LaKeisha relaxed. "I mean, is there a lot of it?"

LaKeisha sat up and shrugged, flipping the hair off her face. "I guess so."

"Have you ever been bullied?"

"Nah. No one messes with me. I'd fuck them up." She glanced at Jade. "Sorry, Coach."

"Ever witness someone else being victimized?"

LaKeisha hesitated, knowing what Jade did for a living. "I won't testify to anything, but yeah. It's everywhere. In the halls. In the locker rooms. In class. Online."

"And I suppose the school's anti-bullying policies don't help."

LaKeisha gaped at her. "There's policies against it?"

CHAPTER FIFTY-SEVEN

The White House, Washington, DC

THE NEXT AFTERNOON, Whitney disembarked from Marine One onto the helipad on the South Lawn. Sasha and Sarah came down the stairs behind her. As she walked toward the White House, Sean hurried toward her.

Unusual.

"Madam President, something is happening in Seattle."

Whitney glanced at Sasha before hurrying after him.

The television was on in her study off the Oval Office, the screen filled with police officers in riot gear shooting pepper spray at protesters on a city street. The protesters threw rocks and cans and other objects at the officers. A bottle shattered against an officer's helmet. At the bottom of the screen, the caption read Seattle Protest Turns Deadly.

Whitney motioned for Sean to turn up the volume.

"If you're just tuning in," said the voiceover, "we are looking at Pine Street in downtown Seattle, witnessing what at one time had been a peaceful march against income inequality. In the last hour, however, the march has spiraled into a deadly protest. At least three people are confirmed dead after being trampled in the crowd." A gasp from Sarah behind her. "Seven more have been injured."

"Damn!" Sasha said.

The announcer continued. "Those numbers may escalate. The mayor has called for a peaceful resolution and cautioned the police to respect the rights of protesters—"

"What about the rights of police officers?" Whitney murmured.

Although Whitney's attention didn't waver from the screen, she could feel the intensity of Sasha's glare. "Police officers' rights are protected well enough. Don't you think?"

"Not now, Sasha."

Sasha put her hands on her hips. "When then? When is a good time to talk about police brutality? I think now is as good a time as any."

"The coverage is everywhere," Sean said, oblivious to the growing tension between the two women. "Twitter's blowing up and—"

"Thank you, Sean," Whitney said, interrupting and dismissing him at the same time. "That will be all, Sarah."

After they left, Whitney shook her head, sickened by what she was witnessing on the screen. She held Sasha's gaze. "I want you to stay on top of this and keep me updated."

"Black lives matter."

"I know."

"It's happening every week now."

The week before, three black women, college students, were critically injured on a Mississippi university campus at a police brutality protest. A protest that went horribly wrong.

"We'll address it," Whitney said.

Sasha pursed her lips and crossed her arms. "Hmph. When?"

"In this term. I promise." She pointed at the screen. "But first we must address this. Perhaps, this will finally get Congress's attention."

"It hasn't yet," Sasha said, still staring at the television.

Whitney's intercom buzzed.

"Madam President," Sean said. "Senator Hampton is on the line for you."

CHAPTER FIFTY-EIGHT

Washington, DC

"WELL, ISN'T THIS a nice surprise!"

Jade turned to find Cole Brennan standing near her, his arms wide ready to envelop her in a hug. She braced herself and held her glass high in the air, as he hugged her.

They had not seen each other since the night TSK had paid him a visit, with almost tragic consequences for his family. The animosity he had shown toward her during that case had vanished. If she wasn't mistaken, he was now looking at her with respect. Possibly affection.

"Mr. Brennan. Mrs. Brennan."

His wife reached out and touched Jade's arm. "It's good to see you."

"How's Kaitlin?" Jade asked.

The woman gave her a vacant smile. "You remember her name . . . She's back to normal. As if it never happened. We'll never forget what you did."

"Hmph!" Cole said. "You're a hero to my kids. But things aren't back to normal. My oldest son, CJ, and Kaitlin are liberals. That ain't normal."

He guffawed. Despite herself, Jade joined in his laughter.

"Well, I'm glad she's okay. It was good seeing you both."

She moved off to a space near a large window to watch people arrive at the Washington Hilton on Connecticut Avenue. The White House Correspondents' Dinner had transformed into a red-carpet event, with more celebrities—actors, athletes, performing artists—in attendance than reporters.

Wearing a gray suit, crisp white shirt, and black shoes, Jade enjoyed watching other people garner the attention for a change.

She sipped her beer. She'd never been invited to this dinner before. But this year, her invitation had come from the top.

"First time?"

Turning from the window, she scrutinized the gentleman next to her. Attractive, with short, sandy, gelled hair, he wore designer glasses and a well-cut suit.

He held out his hand. "Jade Harrington, it's an honor."

"Thank you, Mr. Haynes." They shook. "I watch you sometimes on MSNBC."

He smiled. "Sometimes?"

"I don't watch much TV."

"Do you follow politics?"

"Some," she said. "My best friend is into it."

"Who's that?"

"Zoe."

He sipped his drink. "I know her. We worked together occasionally when I lived in DC."

"I should ask 'Who hasn't worked with Zoe?'"

"May save you some time. Me, too, by the way."

"Me, too, what?"

"This is my first time." He waved his glass at the photographers and the famous attendees posing on the red carpet. "Quite a spectacle."

"Not really my thing."

"Mine either."

They stood comfortably next to each other, observing others.

"What do you think about the protests?" he asked.

"They're intensifying."

He nodded. "The deaths were inevitable. The rhetoric is getting out of hand. I'd be surprised if we didn't see more violence."

"If anyone can bring this country together, Fairchild can."

"You sound like an 'FOW.'"

"FOW?"

"Friend of Whitney. I am by the way."

Since my invitation came from her, I guess, I am, too. That and her personal FBI agent.

She kept these thoughts to herself.

"We better go in." He tilted his head toward the ballroom where the other attendees had started to migrate. "What are you doing later? There's an afterparty at a bar down the street."

"I can't. Early day tomorrow."

"That's too bad."

Before they parted to go to their assigned tables, he said, "It's been a pleasure. I hope to—"

She held out her hand. "Me, too."

She turned to head toward her table, and then back to him. "What's the name of the bar?"

He told her.

After President Whitney Fairchild roasted herself, the current male host of a late-night TV show began the traditional roast of the president. She sat next to the podium with a tense smile on her face, as if bracing for the onslaught.

"Now," the comedian said, "thanks to President Fairchild, and passage of the ERA amendment, women are entitled to the same rights as men. Thank God. Now, my wife can have an erection lasting four hours . . ."

CHAPTER FIFTY-NINE

Washington, DC

"... TWENTY-EIGHT, TWENTY-NINE, THIRTY."

She released the chin-up bar and dropped to the mat.

The Bureau gym, after lunch, was nearly empty. Jade liked it that way. She didn't like to wait on machines. She didn't like to wait for anything. Period.

She grabbed a towel to blot the sweat on her face and neck and under her ponytail. She was working hard, punishing herself for staying out late. She ended up joining Blake Haynes at the bar for a drink. One drink. Charming, intelligent, well-read, she enjoyed his company. And did she say he was attractive?

"Not bad," came a voice from behind her.

She turned. "And you can do better?"

Micah grinned. Pulling off his gray FBI t-shirt, he jumped and grasped the bar, his hands facing him. As he pulled himself up and started to count, the muscles in his arms, chest, and back rippled. His body, a work of art. He passed fifty with ease.

"Showoff," she said, throwing her towel at him.

She headed toward the leg-press machine.

After their workout, she sat on a bench up against the wall. Micah sat next to her on the matted floor, his back leaning against the bench.

She capped her Gatorade. "You don't say much during interviews. You know you have the green light, right?"

"I'll ask a question when I want to know something."

She nodded, pleased. "Anything on Chaney-Frost?"

"We've been trailing the kid every night for the last two weeks. His parents must have him on lockdown."

She had assigned a veteran agent to accompany him. Still, she couldn't resist needling him. "And you're sure he hasn't given you the slip?"

Micah gave her a look.

She believed William was involved somehow. "Okay. Let's give it another week."

❋

"I need to ask you something," Jade said, leaning against Pat's cubicle.

Special Agent Pat Turner turned away from her computer. "Sure, boss, what's up?"

Although Pat appeared older than her fifty-one years, and most of the staff treated her like a favorite grandmother, she had a sharp mind and an unwavering tenacity to complete any project she was assigned. Possessing a vast knowledge of the Bureau's history, she knew its policies and procedures and the way the place worked better than anyone. She could run the Bureau, in Jade's opinion.

Her only weakness was that Pat didn't want to supervise people, a career-limiting predilection at the FBI. She would rather spend her day hunched over her computer, as she had been doing before Jade had interrupted her.

Jade pulled up a chair just outside the cubicle, her arms on her thighs. She felt refreshed after her workout and recovered from her late night with Blake. She scanned pictures of characters from the *Star Trek, Twilight Zone*, and *The Big Bang Theory* TV series, pinned to the cubicle's three walls.

"You've read what we have on the cybertheft case. How do you think they're doing it?"

Pat thought for a moment. "About a decade ago, a Trojan horse malware package called Zeus was used to steal banking information through keystroke logging and form grabbing."

"What's form grabbing?"

"Appropriating the authorization and log-in credentials before they reach a secure server to avoid HTTPS encryption. It can be more effective than keystroke logging, because it can capture copy-and-paste or auto-fill entries."

"How was it installed?"

Pat shrugged. "A download. Or phishing email. After the software installed itself on the victim's computer, it captured passwords, account numbers, and any other information needed to access online banking sites."

"And then the perp could transfer the money to his or her own account?"

"Pretty much. Before his arrest, the person who created Zeus sold his code to a Russian national who created its successor, SpyEye. It targeted financial institutions, and used a form-grabbing technique while the victims conducted banking business online. The victim was on the bank's website, but some of the fields were fake. The malware was difficult to detect."

"What about antivirus and other security software?"

Pat shook her head. "Nothing could detect it. Caught the perpetrator a couple of years ago when he tried to sell one of his kits to an undercover agent."

"I believe our perp is using something similar. Whoever it is has a high level of technical skills."

"Could be one of the employees of the victim organizations, a hacker acting alone, or a foreign agent: Russian mafia, European criminal outfit, China."

"Is that your short list?" Jade said, wryly, rising.

"Wait. I have something for you, too." Pat handed her a file. "Haven't had a chance to review it in detail."

"What is it?"

"The autopsy report on Mary Churchill. The president's aunt."

CHAPTER SIXTY

Washington, DC

IN THE BACK seats of the presidential limousine—"The Beast," as the Secret Service called it—Whitney and Sasha conversed in low tones. Sarah reviewed their daily schedule on the adjacent sofa seat. En route to the Holocaust Museum, Whitney planned to give a major speech on the future of Palestinian and Jewish relations.

Her phone buzzed. Her daughter.

After their usual chitchat about school and friends, she asked Emma if she had talked to her brother.

Silence greeted her on the other end.

"Emma, what is it?"

"Nothing, Mom."

"Obviously, it's something."

"You're busy. It can wait."

"Tell me."

"Chandler's . . . changing."

"In what way?"

"He's not . . . nice! He's dismissive when I talk to him about my participation in the protests. Actually, 'condescending' might be a better word."

"That doesn't sound like him."

"That's why I said he's changing."

"When was the last time you spoke to him?"

"It's been a while," Emma said. "When's the last time *you* spoke to him?"

"Two weeks ago."

"And you didn't notice anything?"

Her son *was* different. He wasn't his usual jovial self. More serious. She had hoped that he was maturing. "Perhaps."

"To be honest, Mom, I'm not speaking to him."

"You're always honest, Emma. You don't need to use that phrase."

"Mom! I'm having a serious conversation with you. I don't need a lecture on word choice."

She smoothed the leather on the seat's armrest. "You're right. Why aren't you speaking to each other?"

"He called minorities, 'those people.'"

She sat up. "What!"

"He's going to these crazy meetings. The Young Conservatives or something like that. The words that come out of his mouth are outrageous. Every time we talk, we fight. I don't enjoy talking to him anymore. I'm supposed to go home next week, and I'm not looking forward to it. I don't want to go."

Prior to his political awakening, Chandler never cared about anything except girls, skateboarding, and video games.

"I'll talk to him."

"I don't think it'll help."

"We need to get together as a family soon." Whitney sighed. "I meant to have Sean schedule something."

"What did we do before we had Sean to schedule our lives? I need to go study, Mom. Love you!"

"Love you, too."

Whitney stared at the phone a moment, pressing End before handing it to Sarah. She turned to gaze out the window at the Smithsonian National Museum of Natural History, Emma's question hurting her more than her daughter probably had intended.

How will I bring this country together if I can't do the same for my own family?

CHAPTER SIXTY-ONE

Washington, DC

SHE IGNORED THE knock at her office door.

Sheepish, Christian said, "You got a minute?"

She continued to ignore him. When he didn't leave, she gestured to the lone guest chair in the office. "What's up?"

He sat. "What's the latest with the bullying case?"

Jade said nothing.

"Look," he said. "I lost it after what happened to Mark. He's my son. My job is to protect him and the rest of my family. I felt . . . helpless."

She slipped a red peanut M&M in her mouth from the large bag she kept in the center drawer of her desk. She was not going to make this easy for him. "Our core values include respect for the dignity of all those we protect and uncompromising personal integrity. That's nonnegotiable with me."

The anguish was evident on his face. "I'm sorry. Okay? Rule of law and all that. I get it. It won't happen again."

She looked at him for several moments. "Apology accepted."

Christian seemed to be waiting. "Aren't you going to ask me something?"

"Like what?"

Exasperated, he said, "The case. Aren't you going to welcome me back to the team?"

"Oh." She wasn't going to make it *that* easy.

"Lawson has me working on a lot of BS stuff. Filing. Follow-ups. I want to catch the person who is killing these kids. Even if they deserved it." He waved his hands. "Not deserved to be killed, but deserved to be taught a lesson."

"I don't know . . . Dante is turning out to be a pleasure to work with. And Micah's learning quickly."

"Sometimes, I wonder how Dante got in. Must've been a tough recruiting year."

"He has his useful qualities." *Isn't that what Ethan said last year?*

"Like what?"

She frowned. "Still haven't figured that out yet."

They laughed and gave each other an exploding fist bump.

Jade picked up some files from her desk and handed them to him. "Welcome back."

CHAPTER SIXTY-TWO

The White House, Washington, DC

"WELCOME BACK. MADAM President, during the presidential election, different solutions were proposed for dealing with illegal immigration. What are your thoughts on building a one-thousand, nine-hundred-and-fifty-four-mile wall or fence?"

"Well, Blake, it's impractical, and doesn't address the root cause of immigration. A wall won't stop someone who is desperate to feed his or her family. Increasing the number of Border Patrol agents and erecting more barriers will only result in more people dying trying to cross over into this country with the hope of attaining a better life."

"And setting up an operation to deport eleven million people?"

Whitney crossed her legs. "That will turn us into a society we probably don't want to live in."

The interview was being aired live on MSNBC. They sat in two chairs facing each other in front of the unlit fireplace in the White House Library. Portraits of Franklin D. Roosevelt and Woodrow Wilson adorned the walls. During the transition, she had retrieved Eleanor Roosevelt's portrait from storage in the basement of her Senate office building. It now hung in the place of prominence over the mantle. And rightfully so.

"How do you feel your first year in office is going?"

"We're not accomplishing as much as I'd hoped, but I'm excited as people become familiar with and understand the New New Deal, and what it will mean for jobs, improving the economy, rebuilding our infrastructure, and expanding access to education. We'll be able to help millions of people."

"I don't doubt you. You're a fighter. You never give up."

"This is true."

"Any surprises so far? About the job?"

"No one can know what the job is like, until you sit in that chair in the Oval Office."

She didn't mention how scary the view of the world was from that chair.

Blake steepled his fingers against his lips while she spoke. He removed them. "By sitting in that chair, you have shattered the glass ceiling. How does that make you feel?"

"Wonderful, of course. But it was never about me, Blake. It's about all the girls out there who can now grow up believing that, if they work hard, they can be whatever they want to be."

"Switching topics. What are your thoughts on Senator Sampson switching parties?"

"I'm sure children are watching this broadcast. Next question."

He laughed. "Okay . . ."

He asked her several questions about the specifics of the New New Deal Coalition legislation. Whitney presented her plan, but not its tepid reception so far, by Congress or the American people.

Five minutes before the top of the hour, Blake wrapped up the interview. "Madam President, it was a delight having you on the show today. I hope we can do it again soon."

"I believe that can be arranged, Blake."

He turned and faced the camera. "This is Blake Haynes with *The Haynes Report*. Good night, everyone."

The interview had gone well. They had an easy rapport with each other that she believed would come across well on camera.

He did not push back on the lukewarm response to her legislation. Or bring up that another two protesters in Seattle had died from their injuries. He also didn't mention the speculation around why she had lived with her aunt for a year or her aunt's subsequent death. Or the mysterious death of the congressman from her district on a dark and winding road near her home in Missouri.

Blake had promised a softball interview.

He had kept his word.

And could be useful to her in the future.

CHAPTER SIXTY-THREE

The White House, Washington, DC

"WHAT ARE YOU doing here?"

"I could ask you the same thing."

He hooked his thumb over his shoulder. "Interviewing the president."

"How did it go?"

"Wonderfully," said Whitney Fairchild from behind him. She glanced at both of them. "I did not know the two of you knew each other."

"We don't," Jade said.

"We do," Blake Haynes said.

The president smiled. "Which is it?"

Jade willed herself to stop blushing. "We met at the Correspondents' dinner, but we don't *know* each other."

"I see. That's what that dinner is all about. Bringing people together. Well, I'll leave you two to continue your conversation."

She handed the president a file, detailing Cyber's analysis on the cyberthefts. Their report was conjecture at this point. "This is for you. The documents you requested."

Fairchild held her gaze. "Thank you. Stop by my office when you're finished here."

"Yes, Madam President."

Blake nodded toward the receding back of Fairchild. "I guess that's what you're doing here. How close are the two of you anyway?"

She reminded herself that he was a reporter. "She's the boss."

"What are you doing after you meet with the president? My flight back to New York doesn't take off for several hours."

"I have plans." She didn't, but she didn't want to give him the wrong idea.

They'd had a drink together. A quiet conversation in a noisy bar. She wanted to leave it at that.

His eyes twinkled behind his glasses. "I don't give up easily."

Jade started to walk away. "Neither do I."

CHAPTER SIXTY-FOUR

The White House, Washington, DC

AFTER THE INTERVIEW, Whitney returned to her study next to the Oval Office. The television was on, the volume low. She grabbed the top one off the ever-present stack of briefing books, and began to read it in more detail.

Something on the TV captured her attention. The banner on the lower part of the screen said State Legislator Pushes for Investigation.

Her breath caught.

With a shaking hand, she turned up the volume with the remote.

The mid-day news anchor spoke into the camera. In the box next to him, a handsome, middle-aged man addressed a crowd of reporters.

"Cameron Kelly," said the anchor, "a Missouri representative from the Eighty-Seventh District, is advocating for an investigation by the FBI into the mysterious death of United States Representative Steven Barrett. Let's listen in."

The legislator was the picture of a hard-working politician fighting for the people he represented. He wore a white shirt with the sleeves rolled up, red tie, and dark slacks.

"Congressman Barrett was a Missouri son," Kelly said. "He was born here. Raised here. And represented our district and our state admirably for most of his adult life. He deserves better than this. He deserves justice. And I won't rest until he gets it."

Whitney stared at the screen, her hand over her mouth. She resisted the urge to scream.

She knew Cameron Kelly well. He had been a classmate of hers in high school.

He had been her boyfriend.

He was also a monster.

She didn't hear the knock.

"You wanted to see me, Madam President?" Agent Harrington looked at her expression and then at the television. "What happened?"

Seattle, Washington

HE OPENED THE front door of his home in Madison Park to Blayze Tishman, recently retired CEO of the number-three software company in the Fortune 500, now searching for a professional football team to buy.

Noah waved him in.

Tishman had been there before. He headed down the hall to the rear of the house before Noah had closed the door and followed him.

Pausing at the entrance to the great room, Noah admired the panoramic view of Lake Washington through the floor-to-ceiling windows. That view never got old.

The temporary bartender served Tishman a whiskey sour from the permanent bar in the corner. Noah clapped his hands once. "Let's get started."

"What are we, at camp?" Tishman chortled, gazing around at the others.

No one else laughed.

Noah scanned the faces of the men and one woman sitting on the sofas and chairs. In addition to Tishman, in attendance was a real estate developer who had built more than one million square feet of office space in the city; the CEO of the online conglomerate which handled transactions for almost every individual and business in the world and was—as of this morning—the second most valued company on the New York Stock Exchange; the mayor of Seattle; and Kyle Madison. The combined net worth of the people sitting in Noah's living room was somewhere north of a hundred billion dollars.

"Welcome," Noah said. "You all know why you're here today. Our president needs us. Our country needs us—"

"Aren't you being a little melodramatic, Blakeley?" Tishman interrupted.

"No, I'm not. We're facing an issue that can tear this country apart. How can we help her fight income inequality?"

"Seattle has led the way on income inequality," the mayor said. "We were the first city to raise the minimum wage to fifteen dollars an hour. And now all the other major cities are following suit."

"We don't need a stump speech, man," Tishman said, as he struggled up from the couch to fetch another drink. "All you politicians do is talk. It's time to *do*."

"I've *done* a lot," the mayor retorted. "You're just not paying attention." He paused. "I'm getting ready to launch an extensive initiative around equity. I'd like for all of you to be a part of it."

"We must figure out how to stop these protests, before they impact businesses and tourism," the real-estate developer said, "in *your* city."

"*Our* city," the mayor said. "My point is that we need to show America the way again. We can enact progressive measures here in Seattle that will demonstrate to other areas of the country that they work."

The developer shook his head. "But that will take time. Anything like that won't be felt for years."

"Are the protests such a bad thing?" the CEO of the online conglomerate asked. "They're keeping the issue in the public eye."

The wealthy progressives debated for over an hour. Noah listened to the powerful people around him. He noticed Kyle Madison didn't say much either, her eyes on him for most of the evening. She didn't bother disguising her distaste. Or was he imagining it? She wore a smart black business suit and matching Gucci shoes. His wife had a pair just like them.

After a time, they quieted, the conversation exhausted. A rare time when this group had nothing to say.

Finally, Kyle spoke into the void. "Have any of you heard of the Equality One Foundation?"

CHAPTER SIXTY-SIX

Washington, DC

"THIS IS NOT a good idea," Sasha said.

"Getting out and walking or going to see Hampton?"

"Both. The former makes us look stupid. The latter makes you look weak."

Her driver let them out at the corner of Louisiana and Constitution Avenues in Northwest Washington. Whitney had insisted it would be fine if they walked the rest of the way. Imploring her to reconsider, Josh McPherson argued that she was making a mistake and taking an unnecessary security risk. The look of consternation on his face made her almost laugh out loud. Josh and the Secret Service agents scrambled at the change of plans.

Whitney and Sasha passed through the ninety-foot atrium, which afforded an abundance of natural light into the building. The Hart Senate Office Building was the most contemporary of the three Senate buildings. Whitney, however, preferred the neoclassical architectural style of her former workplace, the Russell Senate Office Building.

The two of them were ushered into Senator Hampton's office on the seventh floor. His staff formed a line and stood respectfully to shake her hand. It was not often that a sitting president visited the Hill except for the annual State of the Union address.

The senator rose as she entered, arm extended. "Madam President."

"Senator."

Representative Howard Bell and Senator Paul Sampson sat in chairs opposite the desk. Bell rose, slow and reticent, to shake her hand, as did Sampson. Hampton returned to the chair behind his desk. A power move.

Bell and Sampson glanced at each other.

"I'm the senator," Sampson said.

Bell stared at him for a beat, and then scanned the room for another chair. A quick-thinking staffer brought him one.

Sasha continued to stand, staring at Hampton. He hesitated and then plastered a smile on his face. "Madam President. Please." A chivalrous gesture toward his desk chair. He settled in the chair next to Sampson. Sasha moved to a sofa behind them.

Whitney wasted no time. "Something needs to be done."

Hampton tilted his head back, the ever-present smirk on his face. "To what are you referring?"

"The unrest in this country," she said. "Nine people lost their lives in Seattle. The widening gap of income and wealth among our citizens. Take your pick."

"What are you suggesting?"

"Pass the legislation I put before your chamber."

"Isn't it our job to create legislation?"

"It used to be. How many bills have you passed this year?"

"Now, see here—" Bell said.

Hampton waved him to keep quiet. "Instead of always penalizing the people who reach the top, why don't we find ways to empower those at the bottom. Provide opportunity. And help people rise up out of poverty."

"Save it for your constituents. You don't really believe that anyway."

"My anti-poverty initiative is starting to gain some traction."

"But how long will it take before we'll see the impact? What about the middle class?" Whitney looked at Hampton. Although the Speaker of the House had the most power over legislation—arguably more than the president—Eric Hampton was the leader of the Republican Party, since former President Richard Ellison left office. "It's a good bill, Eric."

He held her eyes for a beat. She rarely used his first name. He leaned back in the chair, smoothing his tie. "I concede that there is an inequality of *opportunity*. Let's work on the portions of your bill that address that. But, let's get down to it, shall we? What's in it for us?"

Meaning, what's in it for *him*. He wanted her to betray one of the values she had built her career on. Campaigning against pork. "What do you want?"

Hampton stared off into some middle distance, and then turned around in his chair. To his staff: "Leave the room."

They quickly shuffled out of the office. He turned to Sasha.

"She stays," Whitney said.

He hesitated and then nodded. He gestured toward Bell and Sampson. "Our districts and states need infrastructural improvements. With interest rates at historic lows, now is the time to invest. I get that. If you could see your way to allocate a significant portion of federal funds to us, we can make this happen."

She glanced at Sampson, wondering what had happened to him. Their political stances used to be more alike than different. He shrugged, his hands in their customary position on top of his stomach. "You owe me."

"Paul, I owe you nothing."

Whitney looked back at Hampton. She would need to amend the proposal just enough so that he would receive some of the credit. Still, she hesitated. He had reneged on deals with her before. Unfortunately, she didn't have a choice. He was her only option.

"A senator once said, 'There are two things that are important in politics. The first is money, and I can't remember what the second one is.'" She came around Hampton's desk to shake his hand, aware that she was making a pact with the devil. "You have a deal."

She pivoted to leave, staring straight ahead. Ignoring Sasha, still seated, whose head shook vigorously in dissent.

CHAPTER SIXTY-SEVEN

Arlington, Virginia

CHRISTIAN SHIFTED IN the passenger seat and glimpsed back at his son. "Excited?"

Jade glanced up at the rearview mirror. Mark shrugged, but didn't respond. He continued to stare out the window. She looked over at Christian and mouthed, "Chill."

Parking at a strip mall near her home, she strode toward a nondescript storefront with a faded Won Ho Tae Kwon Do Academy stenciled in the glass. Christian and Mark ambled behind her.

They were greeted in the lobby by a diminutive, athletic man with short-cropped gray hair in his mid-sixties wearing the blue *dobak* (uniform) of the school. His black belt sported six thin gold stripes at the end of the right side of the belt, his full name in cursive stitched on the left.

Jade bowed, barely bending. She straightened. "Master Ho, I would like to introduce you to Mark."

Mark Merritt extended his hand dutifully for a handshake. Master Ho ignored the hand and gave Mark a slight bow. "I bow to show my respect to you and to our art. You should do the same."

Mark imitated him. His arms flat against his sides, his hands pointing down.

"Very good." Master Ho looked at Jade. "Excellent timing. I have time before my next class. He'll be done in a half hour."

Jade's instructor pointed at a small room, the interior of which could be seen through a square window from the lobby. Mark glanced up at his dad, reluctant.

Christian touched his shoulder. "Go on."

The boy followed the older man through the door, glancing back at his dad before entering the room. Christian started for the window.

Jade reached out and grabbed his wrist, tugging him in the opposite direction. Toward the front door.

"I want to stay," he said.

"That's why we need to leave," she said, smiling. "He'll be okay, Dad."

He appeared unconvinced.

She let go of his wrist. "Come on. I'll buy you a cup of coffee next door."

CHAPTER SIXTY-EIGHT

Washington, DC

AFTER DROPPING MARK off at home, Jade and Christian returned to the Bureau. In her office, she went over the police reports from the three murdered bullies. She had lost count of how many times she'd reviewed the case files, hoping to find something she had missed. The cases were linked, but she needed evidence. The last few weeks had offered none. Her office phone rang.

"Agent Harrington."

"Good afternoon, Agent Harrington," came the smooth, confident female voice.

A stirring in her stomach.

The voice continued. "This is Kyle Madison."

Jade aligned the five pens on her desk in perfect formation. "Ms. Madison, how can I help you?"

"We enjoyed a wonderful evening together. I think you can call me Kyle."

"Okay, Kyle. What can I do for you?"

"So formal. Okay. I'm in town on business. Did you receive my message?"

That would be the message Zoe overheard the day Christian and Jade got drunk. She hadn't returned the call.

"I did."

"I'm staying at the Hay-Adams hotel. I was hoping you could meet me for dinner tonight."

"Tonight . . ."

"We could discuss the case."

"Do you have additional information pertinent to your case?"

"I may."

"Ms. Madison—Kyle—if you have information material to your case, tell me now."

"Ms. Harrington—Jade—I'll meet you at the restaurant in the lobby of the hotel at seven. Don't be late."

"Kyle—"

Jade looked at her phone. Call Ended.

The White House, Washington, DC

SASHA GLANCED OVER at her, as if to say something, but remained silent.

"What's on your mind?" said Whitney.

"What's wrong with you? Is everything all right?"

"Why do you ask?"

After enjoying a working dinner in the residence, the two women sat on matching sofas in the sitting area. The window allowed an unobstructed view of the Washington Monument and the National Mall. A bottle of wine rested on the glass table between them.

"You're more pensive than usual," Sasha said. "Notwithstanding the weight of the world on your shoulders, I think it's something else. Xavi?"

Whitney flicked her hand as if shooing a gnat. "I wouldn't waste my time."

She couldn't tell Sasha the truth. That Cameron Kelly, the state representative fighting for justice for a murdered congressman, was a rapist. And the father of the baby she gave up for adoption.

Instead, she said, "My kids. They're not speaking to each other."

"Is that all? I don't always speak to my siblings, either. They get on my nerves."

"No. It's more than that. They have always been close. I think politics, of all things, is getting between them. Emma is becoming more liberal every day, and Chandler is heading in the opposite direction. Any day now, I expect to hear him call into Cole's radio show. If he does, I'll disown him."

Whitney smiled to indicate she was kidding.

"It may be just part of growing up. Trying to find their own way. Striving to find their own identities, separate from yours. And the First Gentleman's."

Whitney stared out at the Monument. Constructed in two phases, pre- and post-Civil War, the structure was built with marble from three different quarries. The spotlights now made the bottom third of the structure appear pure white against the purple sky. "Perhaps. Sometimes, it feels as if I am losing my son. As if I have to choose between him and the presidency."

"If you were a man, you wouldn't need to make a choice. We wouldn't even be having this conversation."

"Maybe. But I feel this way just the same. My family means everything to me. I don't want my legacy to be that 'she was a great president, but a lousy mother.'"

"When was the last time you saw them?"

Whitney opened her mouth and then closed it. "I don't know. Easter? I've been meaning to . . ." She shook her head. "They're busy now. Chandler's in summer school, and Emma's in New York interning for a nonprofit that focuses on income equality."

"Madam President, you're an amazing mother, and a role model that both of your children are trying to emulate. They want to leave their mark on the world. Not sit around and rest on *your* laurels. You should be proud of them."

Surprised by the tears pressing against her eyelids, Whitney had never cried in front of Sasha or any of her staff. She was not about to start now. She did not speak, afraid her voice would betray her.

Sasha reached out and took her hand and stared deep into her eyes. "Remember why you entered politics in the first place. To help people. And you've done that. You continue to do that. You have many things you want to accomplish. I believe in you. Many Americans believe in you. You need to finish what you started." Sasha released her hand. "Be more gangsta."

"Gangsta? What? Are you going all 'Sasha Fierce' on me now?"

"What do you know about 'Sasha Fierce'?" Sasha stopped smiling. "This New New Deal legislation is your legacy. You can't beg for it. You must *take* it."

Whitney understood, with a deep certainty, that Sasha was right.

"Eisenhower said that 'every president needs an SOB.'" She smiled at Sasha. "I guess you're mine."

"I would be honored. You can start calling me 'Fierce,' if you'd like." She winked.

Whitney smiled. After a moment, she said, "As the first woman president, I can't fail. I would be crippling every woman who tried to run after me."

"Then, we just can't let that happen, can we?"

Whitney held up her glass. "No, we can't. Now, how about some more wine . . . Fierce?"

CHAPTER SEVENTY

Washington, DC

"TO WHAT DO I owe this visit, now that you're famous?"

"I was in the neighborhood?"

"Yeah, right," Zoe said, opening the front door wider to let Jade by. The explosion of colors in Zoe's Adams Morgan apartment never ceased to overwhelm Jade's senses at first, and then the colorful ambiance embraced and drew her in. The walls displayed framed posters from various local and national political campaigns she had worked on: marriage equality, taxation without representation of DC citizens, and the Equal Rights Amendment that passed six months ago.

The bookshelves reflected her fascination with all things African: Nigerian statues, Ghanaian mementos from Zoe's time with the Peace Corps, and Ivory Coast knickknacks, including swaths of Kente cloth.

Jade moved to the sofa. A big round orange throw pillow rested in its corner. She held it under one arm like a basketball.

"One day, I'm going to get rid of that thing," Zoe said. "Beer?"

Jade nodded, throwing her suit jacket on a chair. After Zoe left the room, she lay down and started shooting the pillow straight up in the air to herself.

Zoe returned. "I knew it. Here." Jade sat up and took a sip of the India pale ale.

Zoe flopped onto a cushioned circular wicker chair. "By the way, I 'liked' your fan page on Facebook."

Jade thought about the high school girls' comments about Facebook. "It's all so ridiculous. I'm not even on Facebook."

"You're famous, your Highn-ass."

"Nice . . ."

"You have a following. Get over it. You're a verb. A guy at work the other day said he 'Jaded' a presentation."

Jade set down the beer, lay back, and resumed shooting. She changed the subject. "What've you been up to?"

"Enough."

Jade cocked an eyebrow.

"Enough gun violence. Our goal is to reduce the number of mass shootings. Create a national database, implement universal background checks, and resurrect the assault weapons ban."

Zoe worked for a nonprofit organization that advocated for pro-choice, Democratic female federal and state candidates.

Still shooting the pillow, Jade looked at Zoe. "Why will it be different this time?"

Zoe stared at her for a moment. "How do you do that? Anyway, after that lone, white gunman gunned down over one hundred elementary-school kids playing at recess, even some Republicans have had enough. We'll get it this time. You'll see."

Jade stopped shooting, raising her hands in surrender. "I hope you're right."

The best friends lapsed into a shared silence. Comfortable. Unhurried.

"What about you? What's happenin'?"

"I'm working on two major cases. Both stalled."

"Can I help you this time?"

Jade sat up again for another sip of beer. "Maybe. You were clutch on the TSK case."

Zoe beamed. Jade gave her a brief description of both cases without revealing any confidential information.

"And you have no idea who could be behind the cyberthefts?"

Jade shook her head.

"Have you spoken to Kyle?" Zoe drew Kyle's name out. A smile, mischievous and deadly, spread across her face.

"Only about the case."

"Huh."

"Why 'huh'?" Jade paused, then, "She did ask me out to dinner tonight."

Zoe's smile disappeared. "Oh?" She frowned. "She's here?"

"On business."

"She must have had a lot of information about the case to take up an entire dinner."

"I didn't show."

"Why not?"

"Let's just say I don't like being told what to do."

"I Googled her, by the way. Your Kyle gets around."

"She's not mine." Jade placed her beer carefully on the table. "What do you mean?"

"Not like that. She attends fundraisers and other events in Seattle. Sometimes with an attractive man—or woman—on her arm. Most often alone." Zoe swigged her beer, eyeing Jade. "Is she gay?"

A question lobbed casually with the explosive weight of a grenade.

"I wouldn't know."

"Are you?"

Jade flashed her a warning look.

"I'm your best friend. You can tell me."

Instead, Jade swiped her bottle off the table and held out her hand. "Finish."

Zoe drained the last of her beer. Jade went to the kitchen to retrieve a fresh round. She selected a couple of German hefeweizens this time. She handed one to Zoe and returned to the sofa. After a moment, "Why did you research Kyle?"

"I was bored."

"Yeah, right. You didn't need to do that. We checked her out when we first took on the case." She picked lint off the pillow, not looking at Zoe. "What else did you find out?"

"I knew it!"

Zoe regaled Jade with Kyle's family history and her successful business exploits.

When she finished, Jade said, "How did you find out some of that information?"

"You know I have skillz," Zoe grinned.

"You're still doing that?"

"Not really. I couldn't find where she's been romantically linked with anyone. I don't think she's ever been married."

"Huh," Jade said, not sure why this pleased her.

"But there's a problem."

"What's that?"

"You know how many people in DC act as if they're in the one percent and they're not?"

"Sure."

"And that most one-percenters are men."

"If you say so."

"And that you and I are proud card-carrying members of the ninety-nine percent?"

"Get to the point, Zoe."

"Your Kyle Madison is not like us. She is definitely in the one percent."

CHAPTER SEVENTY-ONE

Washington, DC

JADE SPENT THE following day in her office, reviewing both the murdered bullies and the cybertheft cases. As she told Zoe, the bully case had stalled. There hadn't been another death for weeks, but there hadn't been any new clues either as to who was killing suburban teenage boys.

Two of the murders were linked. That the wounds in two of them were consistent with damage caused by a blunt instrument had been released to the media. The severing of the baseball players' penises had not. What was the significance of that?

On the other hand, there had been movement in the cyberthefts case. In the wrong direction. Not only had three more significant thefts occurred in the Emerald City—an online retail company, a real estate developer, and a Fortune 500 software company—but also, the crimes were no longer isolated to Seattle. They had spread to other cities. Incidents of significant unauthorized bank transfers had been reported in Oklahoma City, Anaheim, Omaha, and San Antonio.

What was the motive here? Was it one of the crime syndicates from the Ukraine? Russia? A political statement from the Chinese? Simple greed? Or something else?

Although she had initially explored whether one of the employees of a Seattle organization could be responsible, she had eliminated them as suspects. They had investigated the CFO, CIO, accounting, and IT personnel of every firm where a theft had occurred. All of them clean.

These were not inside jobs.

Mid-morning, McClaine called, asking her to return to Seattle to interview additional victims.

Leaning back in her chair, she rubbed her eyes. When she opened them, her gaze fell on the Churchill file, kept separate from the other files on her desk. She hadn't had a chance to review it. What the hell? She wasn't making any progress on her cases. She might as well be useful to the president.

Jade took her time studying the case file, starting with the autopsy report. Cause of death was a heart attack, not natural causes as Fairchild was led to believe. Pretty straight forward.

A co-worker had found Mary Churchill—concerned when she didn't show up for her job three days in a row as head librarian at the public library—dead in her bed. She was forty-one years old.

Jade reviewed the toxicology report. Halfway down the page, she stopped. *Oleander*.

She read the word again, thinking she misread it. Four grams of oleander were found among the contents of Churchill's stomach. She needed to be sure. She fired up her computer. All parts of the shrub—the flowers, leaves, stem, roots—were poisonous, and could be found in an ordinary garden. Ingesting honey created by bees that consume the nectar from oleander plants could also be toxic. When a chemical in the plant, oleandrin, was absorbed into the blood stream, it could cause irregular heartbeats or stop the heart from beating altogether. Jade scanned the autopsy report for Churchill's weight. 105 pounds. It wouldn't take a large dose of oleander to be fatal for a woman of her size.

Did Mary Churchill, the president's aunt, commit suicide? Was it an accidental poisoning? Or was she murdered?

She picked up the handset to call the local police department in the Chicago suburb, and then replaced the receiver in the cradle without dialing.

She left her office and paced up and down the hallway. Other agents—used to Jade's habits—ignored her. She thought about what she'd discovered, and what she was going to do about it.

Back in her office, she picked up the handset again. What she was about to do went against her grain as a sworn agent of the Federal Bureau of Investigation of the United States of America.

She dialed.

"This is Agent Harrington. I need to speak to the president."

❈

After she hung up with the president, she called the local police department in the Chicago suburb. She relayed her discovery to the officer in charge of the case.

She had a feeling that Churchill had not committed suicide. The president didn't believe it when she told her. She said her aunt always had a positive outlook. Jade put Pat to work, scouring the manifests of flights and train schedules into and out of Chicago and hotel registrations in the surrounding suburbs around the time of the president's aunt's death in 2001.

While she waited for an update from Pat, Jade checked her email inbox. Earlier in the day, Pat had sent a list of the latest victims in the cyber case:

Capstone Energy Partners, Oklahoma City, OK, $1,500,000

BMR Aviation, San Antonio, TX, $1,250,000

TVX Corporation, Anaheim, CA, $10,000,000

Third Data Corp., Omaha, NE, $1,125,000

What was the significance of the amounts, if any? She opened a spreadsheet on her computer and entered the four companies' names, locations, and amounts. She then entered Kyle's—Ms. Madison's—organization, Madison Ventures, Seattle, WA, $1,000,000 and the other Seattle organizations that had been victimized. She stared at the numbers, then opened her web browser to further research each company.

Her cell phone vibrated on her desk. A text message.

This is Kyle. I missed you the other night.

Jade typed back: Too busy. Then. And now.

I'll let you go then. Until next time.

She stared at Kyle's last text for a minute. And then two.

Don't do it. Don't do it.

She didn't like anyone telling her what to do. Even herself.

Jade texted: I'll be in Seattle the day after tomorrow.

I'll see you then.

Her face flushed. She looked up at the knock on her door. Christian leaned against the door frame, staring at her.

"What's up with you?" He peered at her strangely. "Are you . . . blushing?"

CHAPTER SEVENTY-TWO

The White House, Washington, DC

"I UNDERSTAND, GOVERNOR."

My aunt died from poisoning?

Into the phone, she said, "Yes. You will have the full support of the federal government behind you." Whitney spotted Sasha standing at a door to the Oval Office, an anxious expression on her face. The Republican governor of Alabama thanked her for her help in dealing with its latest hurricane and the flooding aftermath. "You're welcome. Good day."

She waved Sasha in.

"Are you okay, Madam President?"

"I'm fine. What's wrong?"

Sasha remained standing in front of her desk. "I have some bad news."

"What is it now?"

"It's Emma."

Whitney froze. She had witnessed and read about many atrocities in this office, but when it came to the well-being of her own children, the world stopped.

"Is she all right?"

"I'm not sure."

"What do you mean? Spit it out, Sasha."

"She's been arrested."

"Arrested!"

"She was picked up at an income-equality rally in New York City. She and about fifteen thousand other people. The largest mass arrest in US history, by the way. The media will find out about Emma shortly. We need to prepare a response for Lena."

Lena was the White House Press Secretary.

"I don't give a shit about the media right now." She pressed the button to call Sean. "Get Mayor Nasir on the phone. Now!"

"Do you think that's a good idea?"

"What?" Whitney snapped.

"Emma wouldn't want to be treated differently than any of the other protesters."

"I don't care—"

Whitney stopped and thought about it. Sasha was right. Into the phone, she said, "Sean, hold off on that call for now." She said to Sasha. "I need to call Gray—The First Gentleman."

CHAPTER SEVENTY-THREE

Washington, DC

"IT TOOK YOU long enough to say 'yes.'"

"I've been busy," she said. "I can't tell you the last time I was in a museum."

"I wanted to do something different."

Blake Haynes didn't know that Jade didn't date much. So, this was different.

Strolling through the National Gallery of Art at Sixth and Constitution, they stopped to gaze at a huge painting of Phillip II of Spain—his face replaced by the face of pop star Michael Jackson—clothed in 16th-century battle gear, sword and all, astride a gigantic horse. Two cherubs hovered over his head.

"This is dope," she said.

"The colors are vibrant," he agreed.

He waited for her to finish reading the museum label. They moved to the next painting in Kehinde Wiley's collection, a black woman in a black dress with an exaggerated bouffant hairstyle, shrouded in flowers.

"He should paint you," he said.

"He'd have to lose the flowers."

"I envision a royal officer headed into battle."

Me, too. "How often do you come to DC?"

"Not often," he said, still staring at the painting. "But that could change."

Jade's face grew warm. Without waiting for him, she moved on to *Bound*, a sculpture of three black women bound together by their interlocking braids.

He joined her. "Okay . . . let's not be different. How about dinner?"

Jade hesitated. "Sure. Give me a call next time you're in town."

"I was thinking we could go now."

CHAPTER SEVENTY-FOUR

Arlington, Virginia

STILL THINKING ABOUT her dinner with Blake, she stopped short. "You shouldn't be here."

That smile. "I missed you."

She continued walking toward her townhouse, car keys in her left hand, stopping several yards away. Her right hand was at her side, loose, not too far from the gun in her holster. "What are you doing here, William?"

"I have some information."

"You could have called me."

"Aren't you happy to see me?"

"I guess I don't have to ask how you know where I live."

"Same way you have pretty boy following me around." Sitting on the top step to her front porch, he scooted over. "Want to sit?"

I guess Micah isn't that good, Max. But then again maybe I'm not either.

"I'm fine right here."

He glanced around. "It must suck for you to live in this area. Most of your victims and—what do you call them?—perpetrators make more money than you do."

"Including you?"

He shook his head. "I was lucky to be the offspring of a couple of high-priced lawyers, who married later in life. The DC way."

Jade had checked into William's background. His father was a corporate attorney at a prestigious law firm in DC. His mother was the top defense attorney in the Northern Virginia area.

"It's late. What do you need to tell me?"

He stared at a long blade of grass in his hand, an unwitting reminder that she needed to mow. "It's about Tyler."

The Thompson case was still with Fairfax PD. With Chutimant. And, as far as Jade knew, growing colder by the day. "What about him?"

"There's a reason why Zach bullied him. Why others bullied him." William placed the grass between his thumbs and blew until it made a musical note. "He was queer."

"How do you know that?"

He flicked the grass away and stood. "Because he was sleeping with my best friend." He started to walk past her. "He and Joshua had a"—he whispered in her ear—"thing." He kept walking. "Goodnight, Agent Harrington."

CHAPTER SEVENTY-FIVE

Bellevue, Washington

THE NEXT MORNING, Jade breezed by the airline ticket counters at National Airport. She didn't check a bag. She wouldn't be in Seattle that long. She was glad she didn't have to wait. The queue for the main-cabin service was long. There was no line for first-class customers.

At the gate, first class was called to board, followed by Platinum and MVP passengers.

If you ever want to feel like a second-class citizen, travel by air.

Six hours later, the plane descended into a blanket of clouds. McClaine picked her up from Sea-Tac airport and headed north on I-5. The sleepy, cloudy, overcast day seemed conducive to curling up in a chair with a cup of hot chocolate and a good book.

She turned from the window. "What do we have?"

"A CFO named David Smith called us," he said. "He was fired from his job for embezzlement. Swears he's innocent."

"How much?"

"One million. Even."

"Where are we headed?"

"To his house."

Forty minutes later, they arrived at the Seattle suburb of Bellevue. Smith's neighborhood was a study in contrasting styles. Time periods. Big houses, like Smith's, towered next to small houses that appeared over a century old.

"This used to be a small ranch house like the others. Throughout the Seattle area, but especially here on the Eastside, they're tearing down all the little old houses and building tall boxy new ones."

"Sounds as if you don't approve."

McClaine shrugged. "Seattle is destroying its history. One house at a time."

A thin man in his mid-fifties, wearing blue track-suit bottoms and a Seahawks t-shirt, greeted them at the door. He showed them to the living room, his movements slow and measured.

After initial pleasantries and their denial of refreshments, McClaine said, "Mr. Smith, tell us about the money."

Smith scratched the stubble on his cheek. "I was in my office. Downtown. And in a hurry. A plane to catch. I opened the browser on my computer and clicked on the website for our bank—"

"Was the website saved in your browser?" asked Jade.

"Yes."

From McClaine: "Which bank?"

"Pacific Coast Bank. The company maintains both of their checking accounts there: operating and payroll."

"Go on," McClaine said.

"I transferred a million dollars from the operating to the payroll account. I used to transfer payroll every two weeks."

"Anyone else authorized to make transfers?" Jade asked.

"Only my controller, but she needed a dual authorization from me."

"What was the company's revenue last year?"

"About seventy million."

"And payroll?"

"About seven hundred thousand a pay period. I transferred additional funds because I was going out of town, and I wanted to make sure taxes were covered. Planned to transfer the excess back when I returned from my trip."

"Where did you go?" McClaine asked.

"Chicago. Where the parent company is."

Jade pressed. "Did you need to enter an additional password or use a security token? Anything like that?"

"The bank provided a security token. It displayed a six-digit authentication code prior to transfer."

"Where did you keep it?"

"In the center drawer of my desk at work."

McClaine and Jade shared a glance.

From McClaine: "Who had access to your office?"

Smith shrugged. "A lot of people. I had an open-door policy. Kept it locked at night, though. And when I was away on travel."

"Anyone have a master key?" McClaine asked.

"The office manager. My controller. The rest of the exec team. The cleaning staff."

"Who knew that you kept the token in the drawer of your desk?"

"My controller, for sure. No one else, unless they went through my things."

"Anything else, Mr. Smith?" she asked.

"I logged out of the bank's website and closed the browser. I always do. I take security very seriously."

"Was it a laptop?" This from Jade.

"Yes."

"Did you take it with you?"

"Yes. I took it home every night. The day after, I had meetings all day in Chicago."

"Who did you meet with?"

"CFOs of all the subsidiaries. I couldn't check our accounts until that evening. We weren't allowed to bring cell phones into the meeting." He turned his dead eyes to Jade. "One million dollars had been deducted from the checking account. The payroll account had a zero balance. When I got out of the meeting, I had received over a hundred text messages from my office."

"I don't understand," Jade said. "If you were at corporate, why didn't your office try to reach you there?"

"They did. They were told I couldn't be disturbed." He hacked out a laugh. "Well, I'm disturbed now."

"If you didn't embezzle the money, who did?" McClaine asked.

David Smith glanced around the room, his eyes tearing. "I have no idea. Wish I knew. I've lost everything. My job. No one will hire me. I'm not sure how long I can keep this house. What's going to happen to me and my family? Whoever did this ruined me."

❋

"Harrington."

"What time will you be finished?"

"Why?"

Jade gazed out the passenger window at the pedestrians striding down Fifth Avenue. She and McClaine had just wrapped up interviewing David Smith's former co-workers at the technology company and were headed back to the police station.

"I'm picking you up from your hotel in an hour," Kyle said.

"For what? And how do you know where I'm staying?"

"I'm taking you to a fundraiser. For our mayor's equity initiative."

"But I didn't bring anything to wear."

"This is Seattle. It doesn't matter what you wear." Kyle hung up.

Jade waited a beat before looking over at McClaine.

He was grinning. "I think we're done for today."

"What are you talking about? We have interview reports to finish and—"

"It can wait until tomorrow. I'll drop you off at your hotel."

Air Force One

"HOW'S EMMA?" SASHA asked.

Her chief of staff sat across from Whitney's desk in her spacious office in the presidential suite. The 747-200B airplane was en route to the West Coast for a three-day trip where Whitney would speak about income equality in Seattle, Portland, San Francisco, Sacramento, San Jose, Los Angeles, and San Diego. They had just wrapped up her daily briefing.

"None the worse for wear."

"And the experience of getting arrested?"

"She said the police treated them decently throughout the entire process."

"The protesters must've all been white."

"Sasha . . ."

"I'm just saying . . ." Quietly, she said, "Regardless, getting arrested is never easy."

Whitney masked her feelings. It sounded as if Sasha were speaking from experience.

"Yes, me, too," Sasha said. "I was the cool kid with the Walkman at the University of Texas, participating in a sit-in in front of The Tower."

"Against what?"

"The lack of faculty diversity. We overstayed our welcome and spent a night in jail." Sasha shrugged. "Glad it wasn't another part of Texas. Could've ended up like Sandra Bland."

During the last few years, reports of healthy black women dying under mysterious circumstances in Texas jails had reached the national news. Bland, arrested for a minor traffic violation, allegedly committed suicide in her jail cell.

Sasha still didn't rise to leave.

"What is it now?"

"Xavi."

Whitney threw her hands into the air. "It's like *Peyton Place* around here."

"He's making quiet innuendos, suggestions," Sasha said, "that given your daughter's arrest . . . it's your duty, as a mother, to step down and take care of her and your family."

Whitney's face got hot. "His concern for my family is touching, and I'm sure, genuine."

If Xavi believed this would make her second-guess herself about her purpose—her destiny—he was wrong. His actions were having the opposite effect. Her pity party was over. She could take care of her family. And her country.

"And one more thing."

Whitney pinched the bridge of her nose. "What is it?"

Sasha gestured with her thumb toward the back of the plane. Toward the press. "FOX is running another story about the year you spent with your aunt. There's a lot of speculation out there. Not only on FOX. But on Twitter. Facebook." When Whitney didn't say anything, Sasha continued. "They've also interviewed some of your classmates who recalled that you were shy and kept to yourself. That you didn't make any friends during your year there."

"Really. Don't they have anything more important to report on? They're on Air Force One, for God's sake." Whitney leaned back in her chair and closed her eyes. After a moment, she opened one eye. "Anything else?"

Sasha shook her head.

Whitney closed the eye again. "Then I'm hitting the gym."

The gym on Air Force One was quickly becoming her go-to refuge.

Sasha hesitated. "Is there something you need to tell me about your aunt?"

CHAPTER SEVENTY-SEVEN

Seattle, Washington

NOAH STOOD AT a window overlooking Eighth Avenue in a ballroom at the sleek and modern Hyatt Olive 8 hotel downtown. As he sipped white wine, he surveyed the crowd over the lip of his glass.

He swallowed hard as he saw Kyle Madison snake her way through the room. People parted for her like the Red Sea did for Moses. In her wake was a tall woman, beautiful in her own right, mocha-skinned, medium-length light brown hair, wearing a black business suit. She strode with confidence. Her eyes took in her surroundings, missing nothing.

Noah wasn't the only one staring at them.

After Kyle introduced the woman to the mayor, they waited in line at the bar for several minutes talking to each other, as if no one else were in the room. After receiving their drinks, Kyle began to work the room, introducing her companion along the way.

She looked familiar, but Noah couldn't quite place her.

Finally, Kyle stood before him. "Noah."

"Kyle."

"This is Jade."

"How do you do?" he asked, shaking her hand. "What do you do on weekends?"

She appeared puzzled by the question.

"It's different here than on the East Coast," Kyle explained. "Where your first question upon meeting strangers is 'What do you do?' Here, our hobbies are more important than our occupations."

Someone struck a spoon against a glass several times.

At the front of the room, the mayor spoke into a microphone. "You may have wondered about the extra security tonight. It's not for me." He paused as the crowd laughed. "But for a special guest who's here to help me introduce the Seattle Progressive Equity Initiative. Someone who is rectifying inequities across this country. Ladies and Gentleman, the president of the United States of America."

The three of them were as surprised as everyone else. After a moment of silence, the attendees applauded.

As President Whitney Fairchild navigated through the ballroom surrounded by a large coterie of Secret Service agents, conversation ceased.

"Agent Harrington," the president said when she arrived at the threesome. "What a pleasant surprise."

"The surprise is mine, Madam President."

"I'm sorry I was rude the last time we saw each other. I had just received some bad news."

"No apology necessary."

The president took both of Kyle's hands in hers. "Kyle Madison. Good to see you again. Thank you for your considerable support during the campaign."

"My pleasure."

President Fairchild turned to him. "And you are?"

Noah's face burned. "Noah Blakeley."

The president didn't react.

"I had a fundraiser for you at my house," he said. "During the campaign."

"Of course. My apologies. Thanks for your support."

The president moved on quickly to shake other hands.

"You all right there, Noah?" Kyle asked.

His face felt warm. "I'm fine." He gawked at the FBI agent. "*You're* Jade Harrington?"

She nodded, her smile modest.

"Noah's the president of AMB International," Kyle said.

He continued to stare at Jade. "Why are you here?"

"Don't be rude, Noah," Kyle said.

Puzzled, the agent said, "For a good cause?"

"No. I mean why are you here in Seattle?"

"She's looking into some thefts," Kyle said. "Cyberthefts. Come to think of it . . . weren't you asking—"

He barely registered the angry look the agent gave Kyle. "How much money?"

"Millions," Kyle said.

Jade looked at her sharply. "That's enough."

The ballroom seemed warm. He wiped his brow and murmured, "I wasn't the only one."

"What are you talking about, Mr. Blakeley?" the agent asked.

"We had a problem, too. My firm. Money stolen, I mean."

"Did you report it?"

"No."

She stepped closer, invading his space. "When did this happen?"

"I don't know. A couple months ago."

"Why didn't you report it?"

His eyes darted around the room, as if someone would throw him a lifeline. "I . . . uh . . ."

"How much was stolen—"

"Excuse me, I need to go to the restroom."

Noah walked away. He placed his half-full glass on a tray table near the wall and headed toward the stairs down to the main lobby. He didn't bother to retrieve his black North Face jacket from the coat check. He had an old one just like it at home.

He struggled through the revolving door and motioned for one of the valets to flag down a taxi. He didn't want to wait for a Lyft.

His father was going to kill him. He didn't like negative publicity concerning the family firm. Much less attention from law enforcement.

Why hadn't he kept his big mouth shut?

CHAPTER SEVENTY-EIGHT

Seattle, Washington

"HOW BORING WAS it?"

"It was okay."

"Liar."

Jade smiled. "I did like the basketball game better."

"How do you know the president?"

"She's my boss."

"Right," Kyle said.

"What about you?"

"What about me?"

"How do you know the president?"

Kyle waved her hand. "Connected her with some donors here in Seattle."

"I have a feeling you weren't one of the millions of small-dollar contributors."

Kyle smiled, but said nothing.

They strolled down Olive Way in silence. The June evening air was cool, the street empty of traffic. Few pedestrians walked the sidewalks. This part of downtown was not a happening place. The night was quiet, save the click, click, click of Kyle's heels.

"The guy we met at the beginning," Jade said. "What's his story? The one who admitted to the theft at his company."

"Noah? He comes from one of the first families, too. Our families probably knew each other, but there haven't been any intermarriages. Thank God! Any that I'm aware of anyway. Noah's not much of a businessman, but supports a lot of causes. An odd bird."

"How so?"

Kyle laced the fingers of both hands behind her back. "Noah dresses as if he's homeless instead of a multimillionaire. Maybe billionaire. He keeps one hand in his pocket. I've always wondered what the hell he's doing down there."

Jade made a face. "Nice . . ."

"He's just odd. He's one of those guys that if you found out he was a serial killer, you wouldn't be surprised."

Jade stopped walking and glanced at her.

Kyle looped her arm through Jade's. "Oops, forgot who I was talking to."

They continued walking.

"What's AMB International?"

"Transportation. Shipping. His father is Augustus Mathias Blakeley, the CEO. Noah has an older brother Augustus Jr.—they call him August—who is the opposite of Noah. Handsome, self-assured, a good business mind. August oversees the family foundation, and Noah runs the family business." Kyle shook her head. "It should be the other way around."

"Maybe Noah is easier to control."

"Good point. Augustus Sr. is private. Very private. Almost Howard Hughes-like."

They passed a local credit union with an odd juxtaposition of large vases filled with colorful artificial carnations protected by security bars.

There was a loud cry.

Jade flinched and swiveled her head.

A black woman of indeterminate age—she could have been forty or seventy—shuffled toward them, her dark clothes tattered. Tears flowed down her face. Jade could not understand what she was saying.

The woman's hand was out, palm up, begging for money.

"Please help me. Please help me. Please help me."

The woman reached out and touched Jade's arm. Jade backed up, arms raised, per her Tae Kwon Do training. The gesture meant that she didn't mean any harm, but she could quickly get into sparring position, if necessary.

Jade dropped her arms. She was being ridiculous. This woman wasn't going to hurt her. Or anyone else. She was the one who had been hurt. She stared at the woman, almost paralyzed by her pain.

She felt a tug on her sleeve.

Kyle whispered, "Let's go."

She put her arm around Jade's waist and led her away.

After a few steps, Jade said, "Wait."

She jogged back to the woman. She pulled a twenty-dollar bill out of her pocket. "Here. Get yourself something to eat." Jade searched her eyes. "Take care."

The woman stopped crying and gave her a grateful nod. "Bless you."

In those eyes was the belief in something, or someone, Jade didn't understand.

Disquieted, she rejoined Kyle.

A block away, Jade glanced over her shoulder. "So much homelessness. How can you stand it?"

Kyle hesitated. "It's difficult. I'm sad for that woman. Heartbroken for her, really. I help where I can. But I can't help them all."

"What's the solution?"

Kyle sighed. "Jade Harrington, you like to solve things. The more unsolvable, the better. Probably why you're good at your job. I'm not sure what the answer is. There are organizations that help fund education and job opportunities. Provide mental-health services. Drug treatment. New construction in Seattle requires inclusion of affordable housing. But, at times, the problem seems insurmountable." Kyle stopped. "I see some beggars in the same place every morning at the same time without fail. They're more punctual than some of the people who work for me."

They stood in front of a white building, the word Escala displayed in large, black cursive letters near the entrance.

Jade noted the name and looked back at Kyle. "Isn't this where that movie took place? *Fifty Shades of Gray?*"

"Where it was set. Yes."

"And you live here?"

"I lived here long before that foolishness came out. And don't worry. I don't have a red room of pain."

"I'll take your word for it." Jade gazed up at the building, and then back down the street from which they came. "Such vastly different ways of life, only a block away from each other."

Kyle stared at her, her green eyes piercing. "Jade, I won't apologize for who I am, what I do, or how much money I make. I had a lot of advantages because of who my parents are, but I've worked hard my entire life and earned everything that I own."

"The one percent. The protests. That woman." Jade raised her hands. "People like you living like this. Worth millions. Sometimes it's hard for me to see where it will all end."

She was still unsettled by the homeless woman, alone, crying on a sidewalk in prosperous, downtown Seattle. This was why people were protesting across the country. Against a system that favored the one percent.

That favored people like Kyle.

"How would you know how much I'm worth?"

Jade glanced away briefly and back at her. "What?"

Kyle stepped back. "Have you been looking into my background?"

Jade remained silent.

"Why?" Kyle asked. "Am I a suspect?"

Jade hesitated. She'd ruled Kyle out, but something prevented her from revealing that to her now.

Kyle's eyes narrowed. "Do you think I stole the money from *myself*? To what end?" She backed away, and then hurried to the front door of her building.

Jade made no attempt to stop her. She watched Kyle enter, and then turned and headed south down Fourth Avenue toward her hotel, her heart heavy and troubled.

She wasn't thinking about Kyle. She couldn't stop thinking about that homeless woman and her river of tears.

She had cried like that once. In middle school, after she was bullied for the last time. Even when she received the phone call in her Stanford dorm room from Max, when he told her that her parents had been killed by a drunk driver, she hadn't shed a tear.

It wasn't until she had lost an agent during the TSK case that she had learned how to cry again.

Air Force One

"WHAT IS IT now?"

She peered at Sasha over her recently prescribed "progressive" glasses. The term "progressive" had replaced trifocals. All Whitney knew was that her eyesight was getting progressively worse.

"It's Xavi again. There's a situation."

"There always seems to be a situation with Xavi." Whitney glanced at how far she had cycled: 1.2 miles. "Not much of a workout."

She climbed off the stationary bike and followed Sasha back to her office.

They were headed home. The trip had surpassed expectations. Not wildly enthusiastic crowds, but they had listened.

Still in her workout tights, she sat behind her desk. "What is it?"

Sasha remained standing. "A satellite picked up troop movements into Iran. Speculation is that they're Russian. Xavi and the JCs are in the Situation Room waiting for your call."

"Xavi and the JCs. Sounds like a singing group."

"Not one I'd want to hear."

"Me, neither. I guess I don't need to ask what this is about."

"What else? Oil."

"Put me through."

While Sasha placed the call, Whitney thought about her vice president. Three days. She had only been gone three days and now faced a global crisis.

Over the last several years, Russia had been quietly building a significant military presence in Europe and the Middle East. A Russian strategic document surfaced last year purporting the United States' role in NATO threatened Russian national security. US-Russia relations had been deteriorating ever since. The Pentagon hadn't worried much about Russia since the Cold War ended in 1991, but had begun to develop a contingency plan if Russia decided to turn back the clock.

Her vice president came on the line. "Madam President, I understand you've been apprised of the situation."

"I have."

"I recommend that we prepare a military response," Xavi said.

"Frances," Whitney said, into the phone, "what do you recommend?"

General Frances Wilkerson, chairwoman of the Joint Chiefs of Staff, and the first woman to hold the title, possessed a high standard of integrity and guided the US military with restraint. Wilkerson despised partisan politics and believed it had no place in governance. Whitney trusted her implicitly.

The general hesitated. "Madam President, I would wait until we receive better intel to assess the situation. Confirm that those are, in fact, troop movements."

Xavi's frustration was evident through the phone. "What else could they be? Cows? No, we need to be prepared in case the situation on the ground escalates."

Whitney considered. "I'm with Frances on this one. Let's stand down and see what happens."

"Madam President, I respectfully disagree with your decision."

"Mr. Vice President, my decision respectfully stands."

She disconnected.

"Boom!" Sasha said and laughed. Whitney broke out into a smile as well. Sasha extended her fist. They fist bumped.

Whitney spoke into the speakerphone. "Sarah, get Andrei on the phone." Sean had stayed behind in DC.

She stared at Sasha as the call went through to the president of the Russian Federation.

Sarah's voice came over the line. "Madam President, I have President Andrei Tamirov."

She picked up the handset. "Andrei, what the hell are you doing in Iran?"

CHAPTER EIGHTY

Seattle, Washington

IN THE CONFERENCE room she had been using as an office at the local FBI field office, Jade logged onto her laptop and opened the spreadsheet she had created in DC. She tapped into the Securities and Exchange Commission (SEC) database and brought up the 10-K for Capstone Energy Partners, the Oklahoma City victim of cybertheft.

She navigated through the company's annual report until she came to the financial statements. The company had earned $150 million in revenue last year on assets of $356 million. She typed those numbers into her spreadsheet. The San Antonio firm, BMR Aviation, had earned $125 million on $274 million. TVX Corporation, the Anaheim firm, $1 billion in revenue. Third Data Corp., $112.5 million in revenue.

It didn't take long for her to see a pattern. Under the column Amount Stolen, Jade had entered $1.5 million for Capstone Energy Partners, $1.25 million for BMR Aviation, $10 million for TVX, and $1.125 million for Third Data.

She added a column to the far right, titling it % of Revenue. She divided the data in the Amount Stolen column by the Total Revenue figure. The number in the % of Revenue column was the same for every company.

One percent.

One percent of last year's revenues had been stolen from the bank account of each firm.

She and McClaine still believed the rash of cybercrimes had started in Seattle. Those firms were all private, their financial information not available in the SEC database. How would the perpetrators find out the organizations' revenues? It wasn't impossible. A lot of private and confidential information could be found on the Internet.

Maybe I should ask Zoe. Or there's always the old-fashioned way.

She went online to find the phone number of AMB International.

"Noah Blakeley, please," she said, when the receptionist answered.

"May I ask who's calling?"

Jade told her and waited. And waited.

After a long silence, the receptionist returned. "Mr. Blakeley is not available. May I take a message?"

"Please tell him I called." She gave the receptionist her cell phone number and the number of the Seattle FBI field office.

She held the phone in her lap. She navigated to the Recent Calls screen and hesitated, her thumb poised. She pressed on the name.

The number rang and rang. Jade started to think she wouldn't answer. Then, "I don't want to talk to you."

"This is business."

Kyle's voice was cool. "What can I do for you, Agent Harrington?"

"How much in revenue did your firm earn last year?"

"That's none of your business."

"Actually, it is. I can subpoena the information."

Kyle exhaled, irritated. "About a hundred million."

The perpetrator had stolen one million dollars.

One percent.

"That's all I needed. Thank you."

Before she pressed End—

"Wait a minute," Kyle said.

She brought the phone back to her ear, but Kyle didn't say anything.

"Kyle, I was just doing my job."

"I know. I just felt . . . invaded. You don't need to check me out. Or run a background check on me. Just ask me what you want to know."

"Okay."

The silence lingered. Jade said, "Well, I should go."

"What are you doing later?"

"I have a meeting."

"After your meeting."

"Getting ready for my flight back."

"I want to take you somewhere."

"Where?"

"Volunteer Park. There's a Tai Chi class there this evening."

Jade did not bother to hide her disappointment. "Tai Chi."

"It'll be good for you. Relaxing. You'll stretch your mind and your body."

Zoe had tried and failed numerous times to get her hooked on meditation. "Don't you have a dojang around here?"

"A what?"

"A dojang. A Tae Kwon Do school. I'd rather spar with someone. Work out. Hit people. Work on protecting myself."

"You don't need to protect yourself from me."

Au contraire.

Even so, she was tempted. "I can't. I have a lot of work to do. Rain check?"

"As you wish, Agent Harrington."

CHAPTER EIGHTY-ONE

Casper, Wyoming

AIR FORCE ONE landed.

She scanned the near-empty tarmac. There was no crowd. No local officials to welcome her. No band. No cheerleaders. No banners. Good. It's what she wanted. No one knew about this last-minute, unscheduled visit.

The seven-car motorcade left Casper-Natrona County International Airport and drove east on US 26 before exiting south on a one-lane road. The landscape was dotted for miles with occasional cottonwood trees, ranches, and farms. The press and her staff, including Sasha, had been shuttled onto buses and taken into Casper, the nearest town, for lunch and an afternoon off.

Whitney didn't want an audience for this visit.

Twenty minutes after leaving the airport, the limousine pulled into a gravel driveway, which stretched a hundred yards to the ranch house in the distance.

A slender man dressed in jeans, a t-shirt, and cowboy boots stood on the front porch.

"Madam President," the former president of the United States, Richard Ellison, called out to her. "Welcome to Wyoming." He opened the screen door. "Come on in."

❋

The Presidents Club started with the 34th president, Dwight D. Eisenhower, and solidified under his successor, John F. Kennedy. Ever since, the former living presidents of the United States had formed the most exclusive club in the world. It currently had three members. This was the first time she had called on one of them.

The club had an unspoken rule of not badmouthing the sitting president. During Whitney's first six months in office—despite the beating she had endured from the press, by the other party, and on social media—Ellison had remained mute.

Maybe he'd felt he didn't need to speak out. He had plenty of others to do it for him.

Ellison handed her a glass of iced tea, and sat next to her in the matching rocking chair on the back porch. He pointed. "That's Casper Mountain over there."

"Are you sure your wife doesn't mind?"

He laughed. "She's grateful for your visit. Now that my term's over, we spend a lot more time together. Too much, if you ask her. She's fine."

"It's peaceful here," she said. "No wonder you love this place. How's private life treating you?"

"I can sleep at night. And sleep through the whole night."

She took a sip of her drink. "Do you ever think about the decisions that you made? The ones you were unsure of?"

"Sure. But not much. Presidents need to take the long view."

She surveyed his property. There was land as far as she could see. "How so?"

"The pundits and the American people all have an opinion about you and your decisions. None of them are in the arena with you. The future will be the best judge."

She stared down at her glass, thinking about what he said.

Ellison leaned back to start the motion of his rocking chair. "Whitney, what's bothering you?"

She looked up at him. "The New New Deal. My legacy legislation. It would help so many people and move this country forward. I can't let it fail."

"Then, don't." He inclined his head. "Do you know what our state's nickname is?"

She smiled. "I'm going to go out on a limb here . . . the Cowboy State?"

"That's one of them. But the one I'm thinking of is The Equality State."

She gave him a questioning look.

"Our motto is 'Equal Rights.' Wyoming was the first state in the nation to give women the right to vote, to serve on juries, and to hold public office. In 1924, Mrs. Nellie Tayloe Ross was the first woman to be elected governor of a US state."

"I didn't know that."

"She was a Democrat, by the way."

"Even better."

"We haven't voted for a Democratic president since 1964. Our state was somewhat supportive of your work on women's rights, but this New New

Deal." He shook his head. "Our unemployment rate is four percent. We don't need it."

"It's about more than creating jobs. It's about rebuilding America. Aspiring for something greater than ourselves. Making us respected around the world again." She glanced at him. "No offense."

"None taken."

The global reputation of the United States had plummeted during the Ellison Administration. His neoconservative foreign policies, resurrected from the George W. Bush era, had become passé for the times.

"Sometimes . . . I feel all alone. Did you ever feel that way?"

"The loneliness of being president can kill you, if you let it. The buck really does stop with you." He stood. "I'll be right back."

The screen door slammed shut, as he went inside.

Just talking to Richard helped. He understood. There was strength in the club, and she wouldn't be afraid to rely on it in the future. The members were the only people in the world who had walked in her shoes.

He returned and handed her a glass. "I thought we could use something stronger."

The first sip of whiskey burned Whitney's throat.

"How did you feel when the first revelations about your past came out?"

He shook his head. "It was a dumb, youthful mistake. Whoever said, 'Youth is wasted on the young' had it right. I should've come forward, but I'd forgotten all about it."

Numerous scandals—about them both—had surfaced during the campaign. Although Whitney trusted Richard to a certain extent, she knew it would be political suicide to tell him her teenage secret. It had not come up last year, and she would do everything in her power to prevent it from coming out now. FOX be damned. She did not plan to tell him about her problems with Xavi either. She could handle Xavier Fernandez.

Richard left again and brought out a pitcher of beer, a shot of whiskey for each of them, and two bowls of chili.

"This should warm you up. Sorry, no wine. Not any that I could give you in good conscience anyway. Be right back."

He returned with a Native American blanket for her, and a light jacket for him, to ward off the encroaching evening chill.

After they ate, she and Richard spent another two hours on the back porch. The former president and his successor rocked in their chairs, as the sun set on the land of the free, drinking beer and talking about everything and nothing.

Finally, Whitney said, "Enough about me. What have you been up to?"

"Fly fishing. Walking around my property. Writing my memoirs. Planning my library." He leaned over putting his forearm on his leg propped up on a wooden box. "I have an idea. Will you come to the library opening next year? Perhaps, make the opening remarks?"

Whitney smiled at him. "I wouldn't miss it."

CHAPTER EIGHTY-TWO

Fairfax, Virginia

THE FOLLOWING DAY, Jade pulled into the Kamp Washington Shopping Center parking lot on Fairfax Boulevard. "I'm hungry."

Christian smiled as he exited the car. "Multitasking. I love it."

The heavenly aroma of freshly baked bread enveloped them as they entered the Jimmy John's.

They ordered, but instead of moving away from the counter, she moved to stand in front of one of the employees making sandwiches.

It took a moment for the boy to raise his head from his work.

"What are you doing here?"

"We want to have a chat with you."

He glanced over his shoulder and back at her. "I'm working."

She pointed at a table. "You have until the time we finish eating to take a break. Ten minutes." She looked at Christian and back to the young man. "Maybe five. He eats fast."

Andrew Huffman nodded and turned his attention back to making her late lunch.

She'd been spending the last couple of weeks on the cybertheft case, not so much on the bullying case. She had decided to follow up with the players individually. Starting with Andrew.

She had just finished her sandwich when Andrew stood at the empty chair at their table. He hesitated, then sat.

She balled up the paper the sandwich had been wrapped in. "How do you like working here?"

"It's a job. I get a discount on food."

"It must be tough going to school, playing sports, and working."

He shrugged. "I wouldn't be a sandwich maker, if I didn't have to be. I don't have a choice. We're not rich like some of my classmates."

"Like William?"

He lowered his eyes and stared at the table.

"What were you going to tell me? At Joshua's funeral?"

He shrugged his big shoulders. "That was a month ago. I don't remember."

"What happened to Tyler, Andrew? Did William have something to do with his death? Did you?"

He lifted his head. "Do you ever feel a part of something and not a part of it at the same time?"

She thought about it. "Sure."

"I'm a part of something that I can't get out of. I'm sorry I can't help you."

"Andrew, we can help you."

He glanced out the window and stood suddenly, knocking the chair to the floor. He looked back at Jade, and said, "Warriors don't run. I need to get back to work."

He righted the chair and hustled back behind the counter. She looked out the window.

William stared back at her. He raised his hand and waved.

CHAPTER EIGHTY-THREE

Arlington, Virginia

SHE COULDN'T BREATHE.

Jade's eyes popped open. Her cell phone was vibrating on the table. Card, her cat, had lately taken to sleeping on her neck. He had no concept of personal space. She gently pushed him off.

She grabbed the phone. Two missed calls. Ethan.

"Your vigilante struck again."

"Where?" she croaked.

"Not too far from you. A 7-Eleven in Arlington. I'll text you the address. The rest of your team is on their way."

She dropped the phone on the table among the files she'd been studying prior to nodding off on her living room couch last night.

It was ironic that it was just this afternoon she had turned her focus back to the bullying case. There hadn't been any reason to. There hadn't been any new leads. Or nothing new happening.

Until now.

✳

Jade parked the Audi down the street from the 7-Eleven store, which was a mile from her house. She could have walked.

The night was lit up like day. She had no trouble spotting Christian among the police officers and detectives.

"You got here fast," she said.

Before he could answer, Dante and Micah came up to them. She rolled the sleeves of her shirt up her forearm. "What do we have?"

"I'll show you," Christian mumbled.

They followed him around the store to the small parking lot in back.

Christian flashed the badge on a lanyard around his neck to a police officer, and slipped it back into his shirt pocket.

Two crime-scene technicians in protective gear bent over the body. Several others searched for evidence nearby. The crime scene photographer shot pictures of everything.

The condition of the corpse was like the other victims. Bruises and welts down the left side. The head, a bloody mess. The crotch area appeared worse.

Her eyes closed. A brief bow of her head. "Damn."

"Who is he?" Micah asked.

"Andrew Huffman," Christian said, quietly. "We just interviewed him today." He inclined his head toward the Arlington County police officers. "They notified his parents. They're on their way."

"Fairfax is pretty far from here," Jade said.

"There's a popular spot nearby where the Randolph kids hang out sometimes. Frankie's. Games. Pool. Heard of it?"

She nodded. "Did it happen here?"

Christian flicked his thumb at the techs. "They think so. It doesn't look like he was dumped."

She raised an eyebrow. "You think William's good for it?"

"What's his motive?"

"Not sure." She looked down at the body again. "But this warrior won't be running anymore."

CHAPTER EIGHTY-FOUR

Washington, DC

JADE POKED HER head into her boss's door. "You wanted to see me?"

Ethan Lawson looked up from the newspaper spread out on his desk. He showed her the front page. She walked in and sat across from him. The headline blared The Bully Killer Strikes Again; underneath, smaller type: Randolph High School Parents Frantic.

"Haven't had a chance to read it today," she said, taking it from him. She skimmed the article.

"Press office says its phones have been ringing off the hook," Ethan said. "Local media. National media. The local police. Parents of the students."

She gestured at the paper. "These headlines don't help."

"They've beefed up security around the school. Some of the parents of the baseball team are homeschooling their kids until this is over. The season has been suspended." He waited for her to finish reading. "What's the latest on your end?"

She updated him on the investigation into the murder of Andrew Huffman. "We're headed over to the school now. To interview the students again."

"We need to solve this."

Jade returned his stare. "You sure have changed your tune."

"All right. You were right." He leaned back in his chair, twirling his ring. "How many bullies can there be in one school?"

"Looks like a lot. Are you asking me if there will be more deaths?"

He stared at her, waiting for an answer.

She put her hands on her thighs and pushed herself up from the chair. "If we don't catch him . . . yes."

CHAPTER EIGHTY-FIVE

Fairfax, Virginia

CHRISTIAN SQUATTED IN a chair much too small for him and glanced around the room. "Déjà vu."

They then spent most of the afternoon in a conference room off Randolph Secondary School's main office, individually interviewing the same students they had talked to in groups two months ago. The students who were still alive anyway. The nonchalance that Jade and Christian had endured at those prior interviews had transformed into something else.

Fear.

Dante and Micah were in the other room also conducting interviews. Despite their intense questioning, they were no closer to discovering whether any other students were involved in bullying Tyler Thompson or who could be killing the boys who bullied him.

The final interview of the day was with William Chaney-Frost.

He strode into the room. "Howie's back!"

Most of the kids she'd interviewed earlier were visibly shaken. Not this one.

Jade ignored Christian's puzzled look. After William situated himself, she said, "Talk to me about Tyler."

He sighed and pulled a folded piece of paper out of his pocket. "I'm a year older." He created a paper football as he talked. "We didn't run in the same crowd."

She pointed. "I haven't seen one of those in a while."

The boy glanced at it. "My Dad showed me. He used to make them when he was in school. Now, I have everybody doing it. We have tournaments and stuff during class."

"Where were you last night?"

"Home. My parents are keeping me on a short leash these days."

"What were you doing at Jimmy John's?"

"Meeting up with Drew."

"I thought you were on a short leash."

"My parents were at work. I got home before they did."

"Who bullied Tyler Thompson?"

"I don't know."

"I think you do."

"It could've been a lot of people."

"Was it you?"

"I bet it was Zach and Andrew, but I don't know that for sure. Like I told you, they had a problem with Tyler being gay."

Christian looked up from his notebook, but didn't react. Jade had already told him about William's claim.

"Did you?" she said.

"No."

"That just doesn't sound like Andrew to me," she said. "And I can't ask either of them, because they're dead. I can only take your word for it." William gave her an exaggerated shrug. "Any idea who might be killing your teammates?"

"We won states last year and the year before that. We were projected to go again this year. Maybe a rival team? There are a lot of haters out there. You know what that's like."

"What do you mean?"

He gave her a shy, charming smile. "You're a badass, and you're beautiful. If you don't have haters, you ain't poppin'."

Badass enough to be inured to your charms.

Jade did know about haters. As an All-American basketball player at Stanford and a former WNBA player, a lot of people wanted to be her friend on the way up. The same people who couldn't wait to watch her fall. Some of those people tried to get back in touch with her after the notoriety of the TSK case. She hadn't returned any of their calls or texts.

"Your teammates are dying. How does that make you feel?"

The lingering smile evaporated. The bravado gone. "Scared."

"You don't look scared."

He put the football in his pocket. "I am. On the inside."

Jade stood, hands braced on the table, leaning toward him. "You don't seem too anxious to find out who's killing your teammates. Aren't you afraid this person will come after you?"

The kid slouched in his chair. "I shouldn't be. I didn't bully T. I haven't bullied anyone. I tried to get close to him. Become his friend."

"Why is that?"

He glanced over at Christian. "Because of his mom, man. She's fine."

Jade had heard this from some of the other male students, particularly the athletes. "Why would that make you want to be his friend?"

"So, he'd invite me to his house." He glanced over at Christian again, giving him a man-to-man look. "Because she's a MILF."

Mom I'd Like to Fuck.

"You know what that means, right Howie?"

Jade reached over and caught Christian's forearm in a firm grip before he began to rise. If he could murder with his eyes, William Chaney-Frost would be dead.

Perhaps, the kid didn't realize he had just insulted the sister-in-law of a federal agent.

She looked at him. "I just saved your life." She rose. "I'm going to get some water. You want some?"

The teenager sat up. His eyes round, unblinking. "You're not leaving me alone with him. Are you?"

She walked toward the door. "I'll be right back."

Christian stood. The closer he came to William's chair, the more the boy leaned back in his seat, until he was almost horizontal. Christian stopped at the chair, raised his fists, and then flinched. "Boo!"

William recoiled.

Christian smiled before preceding Jade out the door.

She took one last look behind her.

William finally looked scared.

CHAPTER EIGHTY-SIX

Washington, DC

LATER THAT AFTERNOON, she and Pat Turner sat alone in a conference room at the Bureau. As Pat fiddled with a VCR playback recorder, Jade thought about William and the bullying case, trying to tease out how he was involved. After the interviews, Dante and Micah had interviewed William's parents. They vouched that he was home with them all night.

Pat finished setting up and put the first tape in. "I can't believe businesses still use this technology."

Jade slipped a small plastic yellow bag out of her pants pocket, and selected a red M&M. She returned the bag. "Start it at eight p.m."

A call mid-morning from the coroner had pegged Andrew Huffman's time of death between nine p.m. and midnight.

Pat fast-forwarded until the time stamp in the lower-right corner of the screen showed 20:00, and then pushed play. The view, from the ceiling, covered the 7-Eleven's entrance and the ATM just inside the store.

"Forward until you see movement."

At 20:11, a man walked in, his image grainy, his movements jerky because of the tape's low-quality. The picture was the opposite of hi-def.

"Stop," Jade said. She scrutinized the face, but didn't recognize him. "Mark the time. Go on."

They continued to watch the tape in this way, stopping and examining everyone who came in, fast-forwarding when the store was presumably empty.

At 22:50 on the time stamp, Jade sat up. Huffman entered wearing a t-shirt and ripped designer jeans. The same clothes he had worn when she viewed his body in the parking lot. He was out of the picture for a few minutes, but returned drinking a large Slurpee through a straw. Before he reached the door, two men came in. One wore khakis and a polo shirt with a baseball cap pulled down low on his forehead. The other, dark slacks and a white dress shirt and tie, as if he had just gotten off work. Baseball Cap's face was averted from the camera.

Did he realize the camera was there?

Huffman and White Shirt had a conversation, before the boy smiled at him and left.

"Stop," Jade said. "Rewind. Pause."

She drew closer to the projection screen. Huffman had known him. Without looking at Pat, Jade said, "Can you zoom in on the guy's face?" She studied the image. Although it was blurry, she recognized him.

"That's Matt," she said, her pulse racing. "Zoom in on the other guy."

Only his chin, lips, and the bottom of his nose were visible. The hat bore an old Redskins logo.

Huffman left. The men followed him soon thereafter, Matt carrying a paper bag.

No one else of note came into the store from then until the time of death.

Jade returned to her seat. "We need to find out who that other guy was, and whether he's a part of this. Can you try to get a hit on the lower portion of his face?"

Pat nodded. Later, she would attempt to match it with the five hundred million photographs in the FBI's facial-recognition database. It had taken them an hour to watch the tape.

"What about after the attack?" Jade said.

"I already checked. Nothing. No surveillance camera covered the parking lot out back, either," Pat said, "but this came from a competing convenience store across the street." She grabbed another tape, but hesitated before sliding it into the VCR machine. "Do you need a break?"

Jade gave her a look.

They went through the same process as the previous tape, but now the view was of customers entering and leaving the store from the outside.

At 22:45, a woman walked out of the store, as Huffman walked in.

"I don't remember seeing her on the 7-Eleven tape," Jade murmured.

A knock on the door.

She didn't bother to answer it.

Dante opened the door, glanced at the two of them, and then at the screen. He took a seat at the table without being asked.

On the screen, Huffman held the door for the woman, admiring the view from behind as she strutted away. He entered the store. The two men walked toward the store, passing the woman, but not acknowledging her.

After they entered the store, there was no activity on camera, except an occasional passing car. Jade couldn't see into the store from this angle.

Huffman came out. The men walked out a few minutes later.

Pat stopped the tape without being asked. Jade moved closer to the screen. "Enlarge it."

She peered again at the nose, the chin, the jaw. If she didn't know better, he looked like—

Dante moved next to her. "What's he doing there?"

"Who?"

He pointed to the screen. "Christian."

CHAPTER EIGHTY-SEVEN

Washington, DC

"SHUT THE DOOR."

Christian complied and sat down.

"Why didn't you tell me?"

He shrugged. "I don't know."

"Trust is everything," she said. "To me."

A painful expression crossed his face, but he said nothing.

"What were you doing there?" Jade asked.

"We met for a drink after work. He needed someone to talk to. Jenny's driving him crazy."

"You're not answering the question."

"Jenny called him. Asked him to pick up a few things before coming home. We said goodnight, got in our separate cars, and left."

"It looks bad. You arrived at the scene before I did."

"Hadn't gone far when I got the call." He looked at her. "Jade, you know I didn't have anything to do with murdering that kid. Any of those kids."

She didn't think so. But she'd made up her mind.

"Dante's going in with me."

※

In an interrogation room at FBI HQ, she stared across the table at Matt Thompson and his lawyer. Dante sat next to her taking notes. Behind her, Christian, along with Pat, Max, and Micah, observed them through the one-way glass.

After dispensing with the preliminaries, Jade said, "Why were you in the 7-Eleven that night?"

"Like I told the police and you many times already, I was on my way home from the Mercedes dealership in Arlington."

"Why were you there?"

"I had a meeting with the GM. General Manager. We meet occasionally to discuss sales, promotional tactics. Inventory issues. I didn't feel like going straight home so I asked Christian to meet me for a drink."

"Can you state Christian's last name for the record?"

"Merritt."

Jade felt Christian's eyes boring into the back of her head. "And what is his relationship to you?"

"He's my brother-in-law. Anyway, my wife called and asked me to pick up a few things at the store."

"Like what?"

"Some chips, popcorn, a liter of soda." *Easy to check.* "We were going to watch a movie after we put the kids to bed. A date night. We haven't had many since . . ."

His voice trailed off. Jade let the silence hang for a moment.

"Did you know Andrew Huffman would be there?"

"I didn't know who he was until he started talking. I thought he could've been one of Tyler's teammates, but wasn't sure. A lot of those guys look alike."

"What did you talk about?"

"He asked me how I was," Thompson said. "That he was sorry again about Tyler. He hoped I would make it out to a game next year."

Jade switched topics. "Don't you find it strange that every murdered boy allegedly bullied your son?"

He glanced at his attorney. The attorney nodded. "Sure. I won't lie and say I didn't want to beat the crap out of them, but I didn't kill them. Hell, I didn't even know who all the bullies were."

"Do you think your wife did?"

Thompson shrugged. "Maybe. She went to all his games. Sometimes, I had to miss games because of work, especially the away games. My wife," he hesitated, "is not well."

"What do you mean?" Jade asked.

Thompson's eyes watered. "She"—he gulped—"won't leave the house. She rarely showers. Wears that ratty old bathrobe and slippers most of the time. Watches TV all day. Or sleeps. I want her to see someone. A psychiatrist. She won't go. The only place she *will* go is the cemetery. I take her sometimes. She lays on Tyler's grave. She can lay there for hours."

CHAPTER EIGHTY-EIGHT

Fairfax, Virginia

JADE EXITED THE car and strode up the sidewalk that bisected the yard. She knocked on the front door, turning to scope out the surrounding houses while she waited. They had been waiting in her car for over an hour. The neighborhood of Colonial homes—the keeper of lives and their secrets for longer than four decades—mostly quiet.

Now, at six a.m., the residents had started to stir. A few of the Thompsons' neighbors departed, commuters trying to beat Washington's insufferable early-morning traffic.

She knocked again. This time, Jenny Thompson answered the door. She stared at them vacantly, cinching the top of her bathrobe at the neck.

"Are you here to tell me who killed my son?"

Jade handed her the warrant. "Jennifer Thompson, we have a warrant to search your house and garage for the contents listed on that document."

Jade didn't wait for an invitation inside. She pushed past the dazed woman, followed by Dante and Micah and forensic techs. The techs dispersed throughout the house.

Jenny caught up to her and grabbed Jade's arm. "What is this? Where's Christian?"

Jade stared at Jenny's hand until she removed it. "Where's your husband?"

"He's at work. Why?"

Jade had seen him leave. Other agents were simultaneously serving him a warrant at his office at the dealership. "I suggest you gather your children and stay in one room. One of our agents will keep you company."

Jade left her and followed the techs into the living room. They knew what to search for: any evidence linking Matt Thompson to the four murdered William Randolph Secondary School students.

She turned to Micah and Dante. "I'm going upstairs."

"I'll go with you," Micah said.

Dante shook his head, smirking.

To Micah, she said, "Suit yourself."

They watched the techs process the master bedroom and the bedrooms of the two youngest children.

The technicians hesitated at the last bedroom. Everyone knew that the Fairfax County police had processed the room after Tyler's case was ruled a homicide.

"Do it anyway," Jade said.

She glanced at the twin-size bed, neatly made, the nightstand, the dresser. Everything seemed in its place.

But something was off. She couldn't put her finger on what.

She moved to the dresser against one wall. On top of it were a few trophies—one of the plaques said Most Improved, another Best Attitude—several text books, and his baseball cap.

A forensic analyst turned off the overhead light and began spraying Luminol on the walls, the carpet, and the bed.

Expecting to find nothing, Jade turned to leave.

A blue glow glimmered on the wall behind the bed, followed shortly by the bedspread and the carpet nearby. As the photographer clicked away, Jade stopped, her mouth slightly open as she took in the scene. She stared at the light for the entire thirty seconds it took to fade away, her mind churning.

A chemical in Luminol reacted to iron, which was found in hemoglobin.

Jade looked at the tech for confirmation. He nodded.

She said to Micah, "That means—"

"—there's trace amounts of blood present," he finished. "What's the big deal, though? The victim was beaten up before he died."

"Yeah. But he didn't lay on the wall."

CHAPTER EIGHTY-NINE

Seattle, Washington

NOAH ENJOYED A turkey sandwich at an organic deli near his office in Pioneer Square. He sat at the counter at the front of the restaurant, staring out the window at the activity taking place among the trees, tables, and black streetlamps in Occidental Park.

Pioneer Square had begun as the city's center. Noah's ancestors had settled there in 1852. Most of the original wooden buildings erected at that time had been destroyed in the Great Seattle Fire of 1889. The neighborhood's current brick and stone buildings replicated that original architecture.

The vibrant area consisted of art galleries, nightclubs, sports bars, restaurants, and bookstores. But the neighborhood had its dark side: vandalism, prostitution, drug dealing, and, sometimes, homicides. A large population of homeless people also called Pioneer Square home. The area was beautiful and primed for revival. The transition had been a struggle. Noah wasn't sure the neighborhood would make it. He didn't spend much time here after dark.

His phone vibrated.

He looked down to see a text from Jack, one of his running buddies. A text from him was rare, unless it was to schedule a run or a bike ride for the upcoming weekend.

I heard about what happened. Let me know if I can do anything.

Noah stared at the message, wondering what Jack meant. He shrugged and took another bite of his sandwich. Jack had probably intended to send it to someone else. As Noah sipped his bottled water through a straw, he received another text, this one from a fellow member of a nonprofit board on which he served.

Horrible news. I'm here for you.

Had something happened to his father? After a few more texts from well-wishers, he returned Jack's text.

What are you talking about?

He bussed his table and left the restaurant. Office workers walked to and fro or ate lunch at the outside tables, sharing the busy park with the homeless, beggars, a couple of street performers, joggers, and CrossFit members swinging kettlebells. He thought the latter activity should be illegal. Someone could get hurt. His phone vibrated in his pocket. He dug it out and stared at the message.

The money stolen from your firm.

He frowned and then texted Jack back.

How do you know about that?

He kept walking, staring at his phone, oblivious to everything going on around him. The wait seemed interminable, but may have been only seconds.

The Times just posted a link to an article on Twitter, man.

Noah stopped and navigated to the *Seattle Times* app. His father's face—his face!—was on the front page. The front page. Not the business section. For all the world to see. The article stated that one million dollars had been stolen. AMB International was listed with Kyle Madison's venture-capital firm, and other firms in Seattle and across the country, in a chart in the middle of the article.

Some people grumbled as they walked around him. He barely noticed. He fished his wallet out of his back pocket, and found the card the federal agent had given him at the fundraiser and dialed.

"Special Agent—"

"Did you tell the media?"

"Who is this?"

"Noah Blakeley."

"Took you long enough to return my call."

"I . . . uh . . . didn't get the message."

She paused. "Interesting . . ."

"You leaked it to the media. It's on the front page of the *Times*. Everyone's going to know now. Why did you do that? Because I didn't return your call?"

Noah could hear the hysteria in his own voice.

"Calm down, Mr. Blakeley. Why would I call you, if I already knew? Besides, I can assure you that no one from my office told anyone in the media about what happened at your firm."

Her politeness was increasing his blood pressure. "Who did?"

There was a moment of silence. "I don't know. This is the first I've heard of it. But I can try to find out."

"I don't believe you."

He pressed End. His hands shook. His father was going to kill him. He had to figure out a way to avoid him for the rest of the day.

His phone buzzed again. Another well-wisher? No. This text was from his father.

Come back to the office. Now!

He glanced around him. He must look wild. Crazy. He jammed the phone and the wallet into his back pockets, spun, and took off in the other direction, barely missing a hard body swinging a kettlebell. Perhaps he should have let the Amazonian woman hit him. It would have felt better than what his father was going to do to him.

Instead, he swerved around the woman and speed-walked. Away from the office.

And his father.

CHAPTER NINETY

Washington, DC

AFTER THE ABRUPT, strange phone call from Noah Blakeley, she returned to the spreadsheet she had worked on in Seattle. She was trying to keep busy, while she waited for the lab results on the Thompson case.

Pat had long since provided the rest of the financial information Jade needed on the victimized Seattle firms.

She stared at the completely filled-out spreadsheet: the list of firms, locations, total assets, total liabilities, cash balances, last year's revenue and net income amounts, and the amount stolen.

She sat back. Exactly one percent in each case.

Was this some kind of Robin Hood thing? Steal from the rich and give to the poor? She shook her head. Was she allowing Zoe's lectures on the evils of the one-percenters to influence her? But, most important, who would have the capability to pull off heists of this magnitude?

She continued to stare at the computer screen, as questions tumbled around in her brain and she tried to come up with logical answers.

Her cell phone vibrated. Kyle.

"I'm in the middle of something," Jade said. "Can I call you back?"

"I don't like this kind of publicity."

"I had nothing to do with the leak. I'm working on finding out who did."

"It's a little late now. My investors have been calling. They're spooked. And threatening to withdraw their money from our latest fund. I'm not happy."

"I'm sorry." Jade hung up.

She returned to examining her spreadsheet, but almost immediately her mind wandered back to Kyle.

Jade liked her. Enjoyed talking to her and spending time with her. Her feelings for Kyle were complicated, beyond professional. And wrong. Jade should have learned her lesson with Landon. She chastised herself. *Caleb Hewitt.*

She looked at the spreadsheet again.

She needed to stop seeing her, except for case-related business.

Or, at least, not until the perpetrator was caught.

Pat entered her office and sat down uninvited. "Michael Brown."

"What about him?"

Michael Brown had overseen the federal government's response to Hurricane Katrina. Hewitt had used the name as an alias during his killing spree.

"You asked me to look into transportation manifests in and out of Chicago around the time the president's aunt died. On a lark, I did a search on all of Hewitt's aliases: Michael Brown, Eddie Cullen, Caleb Hewitt, Landon Phillips, and any combinations thereof."

"And?"

"Nothing. There was an Eddie Brown, who flew from New Orleans to Chicago for a conference, but his whereabouts during that time are accounted for."

Jade's forearm tingled. "But you found something."

"Who did Caleb Hewitt hate more than anyone else?"

She thought back to the interview with Hewitt's parents. "George W. Bush. Caleb believed he stole the 2000 election."

Pat handed her a file. "Here is the manifest for a Southwest flight from Newark to Chicago Midway in 2001."

She stared at Pat an extra beat. She opened the file, her eyes scrolling down the list until she reached the name that Pat had highlighted. Her eyes widened, as a small fist formed in her gut, and started creeping its way upward.

She glanced at Pat, and back down at the list.

The highlighted name was Walker G. Bush.

She stared at the Pennsylvania driver's license photograph of Walker G. Bush. His hair was dirty blond and longish. The eyes brown. There was not a doubt in Jade's mind that she was looking at Caleb Hewitt before he had transformed into Landon Phillips.

"There's more." Pat handed her another file. "Given how Hewitt felt about Bush, I deduced he hated someone else just as much."

"The godfather of 'enhanced interrogation techniques'?"

Pat nodded. "Good guess."

"Or Sherlockian deduction."

"At any rate, you're right. Dick Cheney."

The folder contained an airline manifest from 2005 establishing that a

Rick Cheney flew from Philadelphia to St. Louis. The photo on this driver's license was taken five years after the Bush photo. The hair was shorter and light brown. The eyes were green. And the nose job was in place.

The face Jade knew as Landon Phillips.

The fact that Caleb Hewitt was in Clayton, Missouri at the same time Representative Barrett was killed couldn't have been a coincidence.

"What about hotels?" Jade asked.

"Once he arrived in St. Louis, the trail runs cold. No one by that name stayed at a hotel within a hundred and fifty miles of the city."

"And the Congressman's car is long gone, so we can't verify fingerprints."

"Since it was an accident, it wasn't retained as evidence. The family sold what was left of it to a mechanic. We followed up with him. He sold it for parts."

"Thanks, Pat," she said, wanting to be alone with the file.

This time, she didn't pace. As soon as Pat left, she picked up the handset. "This is Jade Harrington. I need to see the president."

CHAPTER NINETY-ONE

The White House, Washington, DC

"I HOPE YOU don't have any food restrictions."

"No, when it comes to food—just like anything else—I don't discriminate. My best friend, though, is always telling me that just because you look healthy doesn't mean you are."

"Good advice. And who is your best friend?"

"Her name is Zoe."

"Doesn't she have a last name?"

"She doesn't want anyone to know it." The agent shrugged. "Like Madonna, Cher, Beyoncé. You understand."

"I do."

"She does a lot of work for you, actually. Worked on many of your campaigns."

Jade told her the name of the organization Zoe worked for.

Whitney lifted her glass. "Then, here's to Zoe."

"To Zoe. She would love this by the way. The president of the United States toasting her."

They clinked glasses and drank. Hers was filled with wine. Agent Harrington's with sparkling water.

"I don't have dinner guests here often."

"I'm honored," Jade said.

Jade's eyes surveyed the beautiful place setting on the table in the President's Dining Room in the residence, the Sheraton chairs, the chandelier, the grandfather clock, the fireplace, and the painting over the mantle of a woman with a child sitting in her lap.

The young woman seemed to be waiting for her. Whitney picked up her knife and fork and began to eat.

"I wanted to give you an update on the case," Jade said.

Whitney held up her hand. "After dinner. I assume the news will not be pleasant, and I would like to enjoy this wonderful meal my cook prepared. Especially, if you're going to tell me this is my last."

"It's bad, Madam President, but not that bad. This pasta is delicious."

Whitney eyed her plate. "There's more, if you're hungry."

The agent reddened. "It's not often I eat a home-cooked meal. I'm not much of a cook."

"Last year, when we were together, you told me about your hobbies. If I remember correctly, you play basketball and practice Tae Kwon Do."

"Good memory. I'm afraid I haven't had much time for either."

"That's a shame. Hobbies are important."

"What's your hobby? Let me guess. Reading."

Whitney nodded. "First editions."

"Expensive hobby. I read through your New New Deal Coalition proposal."

"Then you must have a lot of free time. And?"

"I like the part about funding infrastructure projects. Can you add the Bureau to the mix?"

Whitney laughed. "I'll see what I can do."

It was no secret that FBI headquarters was falling apart. Literally. Netting had been installed along Ninth Street to prevent passersby from being hit by falling concrete. The interior was worse. The agency needed a new building to reflect and support its critical mission in the modern world. And to better protect the building and its employees from terrorism.

Despite the elephant in the room, Whitney tried to relax during dinner. They would talk about it soon enough.

Afterward, they retired to the living room. Jade sat in one of the two chairs facing the sofa. Whitney lifted the bottle of whiskey. "Drink?"

Jade held up a hand. "No, thank you."

"Come on. Let your guard down for a night."

"All right." Jade hesitated. "Do you have any beer?"

Whitney smiled. "I'm sure we can come up with something."

She called Jade's request down to the kitchen, and selected a tulip-shaped glass from a cart and returned to the sofa. She poured the whiskey and waited.

There was a discreet knock on the door.

"Come in," she said.

One of the butlers entered with a cart. On top of it sat an ice bucket with twelve different brands of beer nestled within. Jade selected one. The butler offered her a glass, but she waved it away.

After he left, Whitney raised her glass. "Now, we can have a proper toast."

"That's a lot of beer for one person."

"If you drink too much, I have plenty of bedrooms in which you can stay. Twenty, plus or minus."

"I don't think that will be necessary."

Whitney curled her legs under her on the sofa. "I guess we should get this over with. What did you discover?"

"We don't know for certain what happened to your aunt. We do know that Landon—Caleb Hewitt—was in the Chicago area at the time of her death."

Whitney set her glass down, horrified.

"He was also in Clayton, Missouri at the time of the Congressman's accident."

"That can't be a coincidence."

"We don't think so either," Jade said, quietly.

The agent filled in the details. As she spoke, Whitney thought about her Aunt Mary. She didn't deserve what had happened to her. She was sweet, and one of the most genuine people Whitney had ever met.

She moved to a table by the window and opened the humidor. She cut the cap of a cigar and grabbed a wooden match from a section of the humidor. She glanced over her shoulder at Jade. "Would you like one?"

The agent shook her head.

Whitney returned to her seat on the sofa. "Don't tell anyone."

"Your secrets are safe with me."

Whitney caught the full weight of her words.

Secrets. Plural.

"Landon worked for me for years," Whitney said. "He volunteered for my first congressional campaign, and eventually became indispensable. I thought of him as more than a staffer."

"He worked for you before that."

"What do you mean?"

"He paged for you when he was in high school."

Whitney's mind swirled with the implications of this information. She tried to fit it in with what she knew, some of which the agent did not. She picked up her glass and swallowed a large portion of her whiskey. She grimaced at the burning sensation in her throat. After a while, she said, "I didn't know."

"Are you sure?" the agent pressed. "He was fixated on you for a long time. Was he in love with you, Madam President?"

Whitney puffed on her cigar.

Your secrets are safe with me.

Could she trust her? She was going to find out. She exhaled. "In the second quarter of my junior year, my parents sent me to live with my aunt. She was a widow and worked as a librarian at the public library. She was always reading. The love of reading was something that we shared. Once a week, she volunteered as a librarian in a convent's library near her house. It was a cold winter. Have you ever been to Chicago in the winter?"

Jade nodded.

"I kept a coat on pretty much all the time. Even indoors."

"You were pregnant."

It wasn't a question.

Whitney nodded. "My aunt brought me to live in the convent under an assumed name. I stayed there for three months until the baby was born. I gave it up for adoption." She moved to a table against the wall and retrieved the letter from her purse. She walked over to the agent and handed it to her.

Jade's mouth parted as she read. She looked at Whitney. "Landon Phillips—I mean, Caleb Hewitt—was your biological son?"

"So he claimed. I prefer to call him Landon. Otherwise, I wouldn't be able to deal with this."

The agent drained the rest of her beer. She stared out the window at the Washington Monument in the distance. Almost to herself, she said, "Oedipus."

"What was that?"

"His alias—or handle—he used in a chat room we discovered. We thought he chose Oedipus to honor his adoptive mother, Maddy Hewitt." Jade's long arms reached for another beer in the bucket. She twisted off the cap and took a long swallow, wiping her lips with the back of her hand before turning to Whitney. "But we were wrong. He chose it because of you."

CHAPTER NINETY-TWO

Washington, DC

"LOOK WHO'S BACK," Dante said.

Christian entered the conference room at the Bureau and settled in the chair next to hers. At Jade's strong suggestion, he had taken a few days off.

Jade scanned the faces of her team around the table. On the wall, she had posted a photo of each of the victims in life and in death.

"Let's get started."

She pointed to the photos. "Zach Rawlins, Nicholas Campbell, Joshua Stewart, and Andrew Huffman. Four boys who will never get married, raise children, embark on a career, coach youth sports, or make their mark on the world.

She waved her hand behind her. "All students and baseball teammates at William Randolph Secondary School. All believed to have bullied Tyler Thompson, who died from blunt-force trauma."

From Micah, "Do you think there are other bullies?"

"Yes."

"How are we going to protect these kids anyway?" asked Christian. "There are still nineteen kids left on that team."

"Good thing they didn't play football," Dante cracked.

No one laughed.

"Get it? A football team has—"

"That's not funny, man," Micah said.

Dante allowed his chair to drop from its forty-five-degree angle without softening its impact. "Just trying to lighten it up in here . . . man."

Pat tore her eyes away from her computer to look at Jade, a historic event. "What positions did they play?"

"Good question," Jade said, rummaging through her files. She found the one she was looking for and glanced at a document inside. "Rawlins, third base; Campbell, second; Stewart, first; and Huffman was the catcher."

Her team digested this information for a moment.

Christian tapped his pen on his notebook. "What do we have left? Pitcher? Shortstop?"

"Outfield," Dante said.

"It seems as if the killer is starting with the infield and working his way out," Max murmured.

"The infield players will be our priority," Jade said. "Chaney-Frost is the shortstop. We need the names of the players for the other positions. Their backups, too." She dropped the file.

"On it," Pat said.

From Christian: "Any leads in Tyler's death?"

Jade shook her head. "I talked to Chutimant this morning. Nothing. Let's move on." She nodded at Pat. "We've mapped out the murders."

Pat tapped several keys on her keyboard. On the screen behind Jade, a map of Northern Virginia materialized with four dots glowing where each murder had taken place.

Jade pointed at each dot. "Rawlins was found outside his home in Fairfax. Campbell in Gravelly Point near National Airport."

"Reagan National Airport," corrected Dante.

"Stewart was also found in Fairfax a block away from his home. Huffman in Arlington behind a 7-Eleven."

Dante eyed Jade. "Don't you live in Arlington?"

Before she could answer, Christian said, "Campbell was the only one killed elsewhere and moved. I wonder why."

"My grandmother was an awesome cook," Dante said.

"Who cares?" Christian said.

"She told me that in the kitchen you 'waste nothing.'"

"What does that have to do with the price of eggs in China?" asked Christian.

Dante looked at him as if he were dense. "Because cooking is like an investigation. Don't waste information. You don't know where it may lead. In this case, the murders took place in different counties, which means more than one jurisdiction. Increasing the likelihood that we would be called in. I'm trying to tell you. Maybe, it has something to do with Jade."

"Not bad," said Max, nodding.

"Any results from the lab, yet, on the Thompson house?" asked Christian.

"Still waiting," Jade said. Besides the blood, the search warrant hadn't yielded anything else. "Zach, Nicholas, and Andrew were all bludgeoned by a blunt instrument predominately to the face, their penises severed." She turned to Max. "All of them had prior scratches and bruises on their bodies. Thoughts?"

"A lot going on here. Rage, revenge, envy. The severing of the penises is beyond extreme. Reminiscent of the Bobbitt case, but obviously the motive is different."

"Bobbitt case?" asked Micah.

When no one spoke up, Dante said, "Back in the Nineties, Lorena Bobbitt whacked off her husband's penis."

"After years of alleged domestic abuse," Pat added.

"The dude was asleep," Dante continued. "She took his member and threw it out her car window."

Micah looked uncomfortable. "What happened? Did the guy bleed out?"

"No, someone found it, and the doctors put Humpty Dumpty back together again."

Max tried to steer them back on track. "The penis removal could be a result of the bullying. Perhaps Tyler Thompson was sexually abused. This killer may be a vigilante administering his own form of justice. A vigilante with a God complex. Or it could have something to do with the baseball team itself. Was there a lot of dissension on the team?"

"Not that I'm aware of," Jade said. "The coach and the principal denied that there was." She recalled the first interview at the school, and the boy— Joshua Stewart—who had reacted when she asked about fights. "Although, I'm not sure."

Max pushed his glasses up farther on his nose. "It may have nothing to do with bullying or baseball."

"Then, there's Joshua—" Jade said.

"Roadkill," Dante said.

Micah scowled. "You're a wanker."

"A what?"

"The killer probably thought running him over was faster," Max said, ignoring the younger agents, "less risky than getting out of the car, killing him, disposing of the body—"

"And fleeing the scene without being seen," Jade finished for him.

He nodded. "That is, if it's the same killer."

"There's not a lot of evidence," Dante said. "Maybe it's someone who knows criminal procedure. Someone in law enforcement."

He looked at Christian.

Jade's cell phone buzzed. She swiped it off the table. "Harrington."

"Hi," a boy's voice said.

Jade held up her hand for silence. She placed the phone back on the table and pressed Speaker. "Who's this?"

"William. Chaney-Frost."

"What do you have for me, William?"

"Have you found anything yet? Any evidence?"

"Why do you ask?"

"There's something I haven't told you."

"What?"

"Someone else was bullying T. Tyler. No one's saying anything, 'cause no one likes him. They're probably hoping he gets whacked."

"What's his name?"

"Carter. Sam Carter. He's the pitcher on the team."

She wrote the name down. "Got it. Anything else?"

"Nah, that's it . . . and, uh, Agent Harrington?"

"Yes?"

"Sorry for being crude the other day. About T's mom. I'm not even like that. Not sure why I said it. Just upset, I guess. About what's going on. It's crazy that I'm never going to see my teammates again. My friends."

He sounded teary. Her job wasn't to comfort him. "Thanks for bringing this information to my attention. If you think of something else, call me."

"I will, Agent Harrington."

She pressed End.

"What did he say about Jenny Thompson?" Dante said.

She glanced at Christian. "Not now."

"Can we trust him?" asked Micah.

"I don't," Jade said. "He's a person of interest. I'm just not sure for what, yet. He's playing with us. With me." She thought for a moment. "Maybe we should shadow him again. And Carter."

"A waste of time," Dante said.

"Matt has motive," Christian agreed, quietly. "A huge motive."

"He's not the only one," Dante said.

Christian rose. "I'm sick of your insinuations."

Dante stood as well and stepped toward him. "Who's insinuating?"

The two men were the same height, but Christian had at least seventy-five pounds on him.

Micah grabbed Dante's arm. Dante shrugged him off.

"I don't think you should be here," Dante said. "You should be on leave until we know your involvement with this case."

"I'm trying to solve this case. That's my involvement. Why don't you butt out?"

Dante turned on her. "He's too close to this."

"And you're too close to me," Christian said. "Back off. It's not your call."

"It's mine," Jade said. The room felt smaller with the four of them standing. Pat and Max remained seated. Observing.

Anger surged through her. "These children are dead. And I have a team of grown men acting like children. It pisses me off. We don't have time for this."

She looked at the three men. "This is a team. I don't care if we like each other. But we're going to work together. Understood?"

"But he shouldn't be on this case," Dante said. "If he wasn't Robin to your Batman, you would've already reassigned him."

Christian's eyes narrowed. He shook his head at Jade. "This isn't right."

Her partner—her rock—opened the door and left the room.

The door clicked softly behind him.

After a moment, a quiet, British voice, said, "Some team."

CHAPTER NINETY-THREE

Arlington, Virginia

AFTER THE MEETING, Jade returned to her office, her adrenaline dissipated after the confrontation in the conference room. Her stomach growled. That was the fifth time in the last hour. She glanced at her watch. 8:30 p.m.

She needed to find something to eat.

She drove across the Memorial Bridge into Virginia. Instead of taking 395 South toward home, she headed south on GW Parkway. Shortly thereafter, she pulled in to the lot of a nearby park and got out. It was vacant.

The park was closed. Officially, she was trespassing. She sat on a stone bench, not too far away from where the second victim, Nicholas Campbell, had been found. She gazed up at the sky and waited. She didn't have to wait long.

A passenger jet roared overhead as it began its descent into National. As planes continued to land, she thought about how she would bring her team together.

She thought about Matt Thompson. Even if these boys bullied his son, was he capable of killing kids? What was he hoping to accomplish? These murders would not provide closure for him.

It seemed as if there had always been bullies—since the beginning of mankind—and there always would be. What could she, Jade Harrington, one FBI agent, do about it? Probably, not much.

She had not heard from Kyle since the story broke. Or Blake.

She thought about her conversation with the president. Did Caleb Hewitt clear her path to the presidency by methodically eliminating anyone who could say or do something damaging to her presidential aspirations? Or was he upset that Churchill allowed Fairchild to give her baby—him—up for adoption?

She had a lot of questions. But no answers.

Although watching the planes land was fascinating, she could no longer ignore the pains in her stomach. She headed back to her car.

Her phone buzzed in her pocket. A text from Pat.

I may have something. Talk to you tomorrow.

CHAPTER NINETY-FOUR

Arlington, Virginia

AT HOME THAT night, surrounded by folders, Jade reviewed rows upon rows of electronic funds transfers on her laptop. Prince's "Baby, I'm a Star" played at a low volume on her turntable.

A couple hours later, bleary-eyed, she set down her third cup of coffee. She checked the numbers again to be sure. All the cyberthefts, after flowing through many accounts in different countries, seemed to all end up in the same bank. In the same account. In the Cayman Islands. She wrote down her findings in an email and sent the records to Pat to find out who owned the account.

Jade's phone rang. A 206 number displayed on the caller ID. It wasn't Detective McClaine. And it wasn't Kyle.

"Agent Harrington, this is Iyanna Adey from KIRO 7. In Seattle."

"How did you get this number?"

"I'm calling for an update on the cybertheft case. I haven't heard anything lately."

"No comment at this time."

"That's a shame. Agent Lawson was so kind as to provide information on the Madison Ventures, AMB International, and other thefts. I thought you would be just as helpful. I promise not to attribute anything to you. Perhaps we can meet next time you're in Seattle."

She sat up. "Ethan Lawson?"

"He helped me out with the TSK case last year as well, and now he's always unavailable."

Jade tested pieces in different spaces of the mental puzzle. She tried to remember the chronology of the TSK case. She had suspected other people of leaking details of the investigation to the media. Ethan wasn't one of them.

The reporter was still talking. "I think he's avoiding me. Are you sure you don't have any information to share? Even off the record?"

Washington, DC

"DO YOU HAVE time now?"

Jade looked up from the computer in her office. She tore her eyes away from the same records she had worked on last night, the call from the Seattle reporter, Iyanna Adey, not far from her mind.

She followed Pat to her cubicle. Pat started typing on her keyboard before she sat down. Sometimes it was hard to tell where Pat's fingers ended and the keyboard began.

"I've been working with CART"—the FBI's Computer Analysis Response Team—"on the records you sent over last night." She pointed to the screen. "Most, but not all, of the victims share conservative political leanings."

Jade pondered this. "Most, but not all."

Pat clicked to different websites as she talked. "They donated to conservative Super PACs, candidates, foundations, organizations. We're still waiting on the registration papers for the bank account in the Cayman Islands."

Jade started to return to her office. "Okay, thanks."

Pat didn't bother to turn around. "That's not all." She brought up another screen. "The money didn't stay in the Cayman Islands. We traced it to its destination. The money ended up in one account. In Seattle."

Jade pulled up a chair. "Where?"

"The Puget Sound Bank. The account is registered to a nonprofit organization called The Equality One Foundation."

Pat brought up the foundation's home page, and then navigated to the About Us page. She clicked on the Board of Directors and pointed at the screen.

Jade leaned in and scanned the list of twelve names. Noah Blakeley was the chairman. David Smith, the CFO cybertheft victim, and Evan Stevens, the blogger, were on the board as well. The rest of the names she did not know, until she reached the bottom.

Her breath caught.

The last name on the list was Kyle Madison.

CHAPTER NINETY-SIX

The White House, Washington, DC

THE VICE PRESIDENT slowed when he saw Sasha sitting in a chair across from Whitney's desk in the Oval Office.

"I thought we were meeting alone."

"Xavi, have a seat," Whitney said, not bothering to rise. "Welcome back. How was China? Fruitful, I hope?"

He sat in the chair next to Sasha and crossed his legs. "Of course."

"And Lei Min?"

Min was the president of the People's Republic of China.

"He sends his regards. I laid the groundwork for a new trade deal and a bilateral agreement forbidding government-sanctioned cyberespionage. He understood our position."

Our. "Tell me about it."

"I'll draft up a memo for your review."

He didn't share any specifics. He never did. Whitney leaned back in her chair. "I've been sitting here thinking about where I've come from."

Her handsome vice president's smile did not quite reach his eyes. "You have time for that?"

"Sometimes, I like to think about where I've been, to know where I'm going."

Xavi nodded, a skeptical look on his face. "I like to look forward, not backward."

"I'm sure you do," Whitney said. "Let me tell you what I've been thinking about. I had a talk with Eric Hampton."

"Oh?"

"He told me about your willingness to work across the aisle on comprehensive illegal-immigration reform."

Humbled, he said, "I believe we can find common ground. Hispanics want reform just like everyone else. It's a matter of compromising. Like you're always saying."

"When is the last time you spoke to Eric, by the way?"

He examined his cuticles. "I can't recall."

Whitney leaned forward, her eyes hardening. "Compromise. Such as not allowing a pathway to legalization for undocumented immigrants? Agreeing with Sampson on building the wall? Placing a moratorium on all non-Christian immigration? You told him that Americans need to defend their country from Hispanics taking over. All those babies, you know. That we don't need any more 'Mexican'ts.' Shall I go on?"

Xavi's face stilled. "Is that why you sent me to China?"

"Our relationship with China is important. I needed you there."

"Bullshit."

Whitney stood and went to the window. She glanced out at the Rose Garden: the grandiflora, tea roses, white shrub roses, and seasonal flowers. She could stare at the beautiful colors all day, but only stayed in that position for a moment. She did not want her back to Xavi for too long.

She turned. "Washington is such an interesting place to work. Politics makes strange bedfellows. Eric and I are bedfellows. For now."

He dropped the respectful pretense. "What do you want?"

"When I added you to the ticket, I did so because of your compelling story. Both of your parents had escaped from the Castro regime by boat, traveling across treacherous waters. The boat sunk a few hundred yards off the coast of Key West, Florida. Your parents swam the rest of the way, eventually migrating to Miami. Your father found a job in construction. Your mother became a housekeeper. They built a life for you and your four brothers and sisters. Born in America, and therefore an American citizen, you were the first person in your family to graduate from high school, college, and graduate school. You became a self-made man in your own right. The epitome of the American Dream. Your story was inspirational. To millions of Hispanic-Americans and Americans in general. To me."

His eyes blazed with an undisguised hatred he'd never revealed before. He remained silent.

Whitney returned to her seat, and rested both of her arms on the desk, her hands clasped. "Under your 'compromise,' you would have been deported." She stared at Xavi so that there was no misunderstanding her intent. "I won't tell anyone that you want to prevent other immigrant families from attaining the success yours has had. That you have had. Or your true feelings about

Mexicans. In return, you will cease going behind my back to sabotage my legislative agenda. You will stop pushing your own. And, finally, you will support this legislation fully and unequivocally and with a smile on your face."

"And if I don't?"

"I will make your life so uncomfortable that you will resign the vice presidency and return to your insignificant life in disgrace."

"My children look up to me. I am a hero to my community and Hispanics everywhere. You captured the Hispanic vote because of me. You wouldn't do that."

She straightened. "Watch me."

Xavi stared at her.

Sasha stood, a smirk on her face. "I'll show you out, Mr. Vice President."

CHAPTER NINETY-SEVEN

Arlington, Virginia

IN HER BEDROOM a few days later, Jade packed for her evening flight to Seattle. She'd asked Christian to accompany her. He would be by soon to pick her up.

She stuffed the rest of her clothes into the open carry-on bag on her queen-size mission bed and allowed herself to think about Kyle Madison.

The two of them came from different worlds: Kyle went sailing and skiing, attended symphonies and the opera, was fluent in several languages, CEO of her own firm, owned a professional sports team and a second home in Palm Springs. Jade played pickup basketball, practiced Tae Kwon Do, listened to Seventies and Eighties music, and preferred a night out drinking beers with her fellow agents to going to a fancy gathering. The only property she owned was this small townhouse and her car. And even then, the bank still technically owned both of those.

She zipped up the bag and grabbed her phone. "Hey, you. I need a favor."

"And good evening to you, too," Zoe said. "I'm fine, by the way."

"I'm going to Seattle for a few days. Can you take care of Card?"

"Following up on a lead?"

"Something like that."

"Are you going to see your girlfriend?"

Jade snapped. "She's not my girlfriend."

Zoe paused. "The lady doth protest too much, methinks."

"Can you take care of Card or not?"

In her best *Downton Abbey* voice, Zoe said, "As you wish, my lady."

"Shut up."

Jade clicked off the phone, and allowed herself a small smile.

CHAPTER NINETY-EIGHT

Seattle, Washington

HE LOVED THIS time of the morning.

North of downtown, Green Lake was surrounded by a three-mile path. The air, crisp and cool at six a.m., caressed his face as he biked along the outer path for cyclists and runners. The inner lane was designated for walkers. The early hour allowed him to enjoy the relative quiet, and the space to maneuver.

He felt good.

He had told his father last night that he was retiring from the firm. He couldn't take another day working in a job for which he had no passion.

Besides, his nonprofit was keeping him busy.

His father had accepted his resignation, not even trying to hide his pleasure at the unexpected gift. He wasted no time appointing Noah's older brother, August, as president of the company, and hired an outsider to run the foundation. He never considered Noah for the foundation's executive director position. The position at one time Noah had coveted.

His father had never forgiven him for allowing the cybertheft to become public and bringing unwanted attention to the firm. He hadn't wanted the additional shame of firing his younger son. Now, he wouldn't need to.

It didn't matter now. Noah had been serving as the president of the Equality One Foundation, in addition to his role as chairman, and now would be able to do the job full time. He had been working out of his home, but recently found a suite of offices nearby. He planned to move the foundation's headquarters from New York to Seattle.

As he rounded a bend, he happened to notice the woman.

What is she doing here?

The FBI agent, Jade Harrington, stepped out from behind a copse of trees ten yards off the path, her badge held high in one hand. A gun was lowered to the ground in the other.

He almost lost control of his bike.

"Noah Blakeley, you're under arrest."

It took him a moment to stop the bike and another to realize she was talking to him. *Arrest?*

He tried to unclip his cycling shoes from the pedals, but it just wasn't happening. He braced himself as he hit the asphalt hard, still clipped in, the bicycle between his legs.

Someone laughed.

The agent approached. The heat rose in his face, as he gazed up at her. Not from exertion, but from embarrassment. He still couldn't clip out of the pedals.

Sweat started to trickle down his face, into his eyes. Other agents in blue FBI jackets came out from behind nearby trees. One guy, jacketless, wore a t-shirt and jeans. He looked like Kurt Cobain with a badge. Strange.

"Don't move," Agent Harrington said to him.

A big blond male agent moved next to her.

"Is that a joke?" Noah tried to appear dignified, despite the decidedly undignified position he was in. "What is this about?"

"Equality One."

"I don't understand."

"You're in violation of sections ten twenty-eight, ten twenty-nine, ten thirty, and thirteen forty-one of the US Code title eighteen."

He shook his head, hitting his temple on the bike path. "Ouch! Goddamnit! I still don't understand. What are all those numbers?"

"Your organization is a fraud. You've obtained funding illegally. Agent Merritt?"

The nonprofit? Could his dream of making the world a better place, including being his own man, be over already?

Noah allowed his head to hit the pavement again, not caring.

His life was over.

The blond man walked over and crouched next to him, handcuffing his arms behind him. "Before I read you your rights, you want some help getting out of those clips, buddy?"

CHAPTER NINETY-NINE

Seattle, Washington

JADE GOT TO the point. "Why did you steal the money?"

"Don't answer that," the attorney said. Noah's father had not hired him. Noah had had to retain one on his own.

"I didn't do what you're accusing me of."

"Then explain how these thefts were initiated from your computer."

"For the last time," he yelled. "I don't know!"

He seemed genuinely perplexed. Jade stood in the interrogation room of the Seattle FBI field office. She started to pace.

She needed to calm him down. She returned to her seat. "Okay. Let's start from the beginning. Tell me about Equality One."

He exhaled. "It's a nonprofit. Its purpose is to provide jobs and homes for the homeless, low- and middle-income families, and the long-term unemployed. We do a lot of good. A lot of good. I'm the president and chairman of the board."

"That must have pleased your father."

He stared at her, as if she were insane. "I failed PE in school. I could never please my father. No. He didn't know. He wouldn't have cared." He gazed through the observation glass. "My father had other plans for me."

"Like what?"

Noah gave Jade a rueful smile and shook his head, his eyes kept fluttering to the one-way mirror. "I still don't know. Surely, he didn't think I was the best person to take over the firm when he died." He noticed Jade's expression. "My great-great-grandfather started the business. My father would have never entrusted it to me."

"What about your mother?"

Noah looked down at the table. "After I was born, I'm not sure she knew I existed."

This guy is sad. She wanted to tell him to man up. "How is it funded? Equality One."

"May I have some water?"

Jade nodded.

Detective McClaine went to the door. After a moment, he returned with the glass, setting it down in front of Blakeley.

Noah took a sip. "Mostly through donations. We receive large gifts from progressives and liberals across the country, but primarily New York, DC, San Francisco, and here in Seattle."

Jade listened to the sound of Christian's pen scratching on his notepad, as she thought of her next question. "Why are you the only signatory on Equality One's bank account?"

Noah dropped one hand under the table. She remembered Kyle telling her he liked to keep it in his pocket.

"Because I oversaw the operations of the organization."

He told her that David Smith raised funds and attended board meetings, but wasn't heavily involved.

As evenly as she could, Jade said, "Tell me about Kyle Madison's involvement."

"She's an officer and contributes money," he said. He smiled ruefully. "In fact, she was the one who told me about Equality One in the first place."

"And Evan Stevens's?"

He shrugged. "The same."

She glanced at McClaine. "Anything?"

He shook his head.

"Okay. That's it for now."

Agents came into the room to take Noah away.

"Give me a minute," she said to Christian and McClaine.

After they left, she stared at the table. It was an enormous relief that Noah hadn't implicated Kyle.

She didn't ask herself what she would have done if he had.

Seattle, Washington

"I'M GETTING READY to head out."

She looked up from her paperwork and smiled.

Detective Kurt McClaine entered the conference room Jade had commandeered as an office. Still wearing the same jeans and Bumbershoot Festival 2014 t-shirt from that morning, he sat across from her at the table.

"You need to move to Seattle. You could solve all my cases."

"Then what would you do?"

"Good point." He glanced at her paperwork. "You guys taking the red-eye?"

"Christian is." Jade hesitated. "I'm leaving tomorrow."

McClaine rapped his knuckles on the table. He came around and stood in front of her. "Have fun your last night in Seattle. I enjoyed working with you again, Agent Harrington. Until next time."

"How do you know there'll be a next time?"

"I'm a detective." He waved off her outstretched hand, and gave her a brief hug.

When he got to the door, he turned, his hand on the knob. He gave her a slight smile. "Give my best to Ms. Madison."

❃

"I've never seen so many coffee shops in my life," Jade said.

"We do love our coffee in Seattle," Kyle said.

From their table next to the window, Jade glanced around the empty, independent café on Sixth Avenue.

"Tell me about Equality One."

"My mistake. I thought we were just having coffee."

"I don't like loose ends."

"Very well. As I told you before, I try to do what I can. Homelessness is pervasive here. The mission of Equality One is one in which I strongly believe."

"But not Noah. You don't seem to care for him much."

A slight move of her shoulders. "There was something about him." She shook her head. "And now he has used our organization to commit crimes."

"It's Raining Men" began to blare from the coffee shop's speakers. The lone barista pirouetted in cabaret fashion, eyes closed, as he sang the chorus of The Weather Girls' song at full volume into a long spoon to an imaginary audience.

"He actually has a good voice," Jade said.

"His dance moves aren't bad either."

They watched him in silence for a few minutes, the young man oblivious to them. A line of customers could have been waiting in front of him, and he wouldn't have known. Or cared. After the song, he lowered the music to a conversational level.

Kyle sipped her coffee, and then placed her cup on the table. "I can't get away from Eighties music when you're around."

"One of the reasons why I like Seattle."

Chin in hand, Kyle smiled. "I hope that's not the only reason."

Jade's cheeks warmed. She stared into her wide cup, the latte-art heart mocking her. She didn't trust herself enough to answer.

Her phone vibrated.

Saved by the buzz.

A text. From Blake.

In town. Can I see you tonight?

She texted him back. Out of town.

"Is everything all right?" Kyle asked.

Jade pocketed her phone. "Never better."

The White House, Washington, DC

IN THE EAST Room, Whitney listened as the prime minister of Thailand leaned toward her and told a joke in flawless English. She was enjoying herself. The prime minister and his wife had been in DC the last two days for a state visit, staying at the Blair House across the street. He was charismatic and funny; she was graceful and kind.

Attending the event were athletes, entertainers, diplomats, businessmen, and fellow politicians. After a four-course meal that showcased cuisine from different geographical regions of the United States, an up-and-coming band from Fairfax County, Virginia—which has a large Thai community—played a variety of Thai and American music. From her vantage point at the center of the raised table, Whitney enjoyed a decaf coffee as the prime minister rose to go dance with his wife.

She wished Grayson were here.

In this room, presidents such as Abraham Lincoln, Franklin D. Roosevelt, and John F. Kennedy had lain in repose, children of presidents had been married, and significant legislation such as the Civil Rights Act of 1964 had been signed. But when Whitney moved in, she thought this room would be perfect for dancing. She'd replaced the carpet installed by her predecessor with hardwood floors. The walls were repainted a stone color, the gold floor-to-ceiling draperies replaced with light blue ones. A gigantic mirror hung over the fireplace next to a portrait of Martha Washington.

Whitney spotted Senator Eric Hampton dancing stiffly with his wife. She had read once that how a man dances is how he made love. If that were so, she could only assume watching him make love would be a painful experience. During the planning for this event, she'd told Sasha to make sure that he and Xavi were seated at tables on opposite sides of the room.

Sasha walked over from her table on the outer edges, and bent down to whisper in Whitney's ear. "The poll's in."

"And?"

"Fifty-six percent in favor."

Whitney smiled and did a fist pump under the table, her actions obscured by the table cloth. A nationwide poll on her income-equality legislation taken today showed the public now favored it by a slight majority, a huge improvement over its polling in the high teens earlier this spring. The mood on the Hill had shifted dramatically as well. Xavi had lived up to his end of the bargain, crisscrossing the country touting the legislation as if he had drafted it himself.

More power to him.

If that's what it took to get it passed, then so be it. With passage more likely, the violent protests had subsided. And the media had moved on to other things.

The band segued into "Wobble" by V.I.C.

Whitney clapped. "I love this song. Let's dance."

Sasha looked out on the dance floor, and shook her head firmly. "I'm not dancing with you. Besides, there's something else I need to tell you."

"It can wait. Come on, it'll be fun." Whitney pulled her down the few stairs to join the front of the line dance.

Whitney hadn't danced since the Inaugural balls, but the rust wore off quickly. Next to her, Sasha dropped it down and wobbled lower than anyone else.

After the song, Sasha waited for Whitney to settle in her seat, and leaned down to whisper in her ear. "Now, I really need to tell you something."

Whitney reached for her glass of water. "What now?"

"FOX News is reporting that the reason you lived with your aunt for a year is because you were an unwed pregnant teenager and had a baby. No wonder you and the First Gentleman live apart. He's mad about your having a baby out of wedlock."

Whitney set the glass on the table with a slight tremor in her hand.

"Everyone wants to know, Madam President."

"Know what?"

"The number-one trending hashtag on Twitter. *#WheresTheBaby.*"

Washington, DC

ON THE WAY to work, Jade had stopped by the 7-Eleven where Andrew Huffman's body had been found to purchase a big bag of peanut M&Ms. The store had reopened the afternoon after the murder. Life goes on. She slipped an M&M into her mouth and stuffed the bag in her center drawer.

Mid-morning, she looked up from the file she was reviewing at Christian's knock.

"Hey," he said, as he leaned against the door frame. Since returning to the team, Christian had been working to the point of exhaustion.

"Get some sleep."

"I can't. I keep thinking about Andrew Huffman. That could've been Mark." She knew he didn't need comfort. He wanted to solve this case. "What's up?"

"I got a hit on the blood."

"Whose is it?"

"Nicholas Campbell."

It took a few seconds for the information to click into place. "The second victim?" Jade straightened in her chair. "What the—?"

He sat across from her. "Not just blood. Other bodily fluids were found on the sheets."

"Semen?"

Christian handed her a file. "Yes." He picked up a basketball paperweight on her desk. "And on the bedspread. On the carpet. The wall."

"On the wall?" She shook her head in disbelief or disgust. She wasn't sure which. Or both. "And they're sure it wasn't Tyler's?"

He nodded, averting his eyes.

She sat back. "You think he was raped."

He tossed the paperweight back and forth between his hands. "Or, maybe he was . . . gay."

She banged her palm on the table. "How did Fairfax miss this?"

Christian set the paperweight back on the desk. "I don't know. Chutimant seemed really sharp."

She leaned forward and moved the paperweight to its original position. "Let's have another talk with Matt."

❁

"Was Tyler close friends with anyone on the team? Did he have a best friend? Or a special friend?"

Matt Thompson scowled. "Special friend? What does that mean? I don't think he had a lot of friends. But Jenny would know better. He didn't talk about his teammates. At least, to me."

He sat across from Christian and her in the same interrogation room at the FBI. Same lawyer.

Thompson didn't seem to know what had occurred in his son's bedroom. She thought about how to broach the subject now.

"What about his room?"

"What about it?"

"You mentioned the last time we spoke that Jenny spent hours on his gravesite. Does she ever sit in there? In his room?"

A vigorous shake of the head. "Neither of us can go in there."

She began carefully. "Mr. Thompson, did Tyler ever have someone come over? Spend the night?"

"No. Like I said, I don't think he had a lot of friends. Why? Why do you keep asking about this?"

"We found semen in your son's bedroom."

He blinked. Thompson rose, making his chair tip to the floor. The impact was loud in the quiet room. "Wh— what did you say?"

"Please sit down, Mr. Thompson."

"I don't understand what you're saying."

Jade gestured to the space where his chair had been. "Please."

He retrieved the chair and sat.

"We believe your son had sexual intercourse in his room."

"And you're trying to find out—"

"The semen belonged to Nicholas Campbell."

He started to rise again, but his attorney placed a hand on Thompson's forearm, restraining him. "None of this is making sense. And what? Are you thinking he was gay?"

"Possibly," she said. More quietly, "Or raped."

Matt Thompson's eyes darted around the room with nowhere to land. She gave him a moment to process what he'd just heard. If he already knew this information about Tyler, he deserved an Academy award.

Christian looked up from his notebook, his eyes anguished. "Did you kill those kids, Matt?"

Thompson stared back at him, unflinching. "No, I did not." His eyes pleaded. "You know me, man."

"Mr. Thompson." Jade waited for him to look at her. "Would you be willing to take a polygraph test to prove it?"

Washington, DC

JADE, PAT, CHRISTIAN, Max, Dante, and Micah were back in the same conference room at the Bureau discussing a surveillance plan for William Chaney-Frost and Sam Carter.

They never had celebrated the resolution of the cybertheft case. There hadn't been time.

Max pushed up his glasses. "Are you more concerned that William will get killed or that he's the killer?"

Jade paused. "Either we're going to protect him or we're going to arrest him."

"Or both." Pat typed on her computer. "He doesn't seem too concerned about getting whacked himself."

"I still say this is a waste of time," Dante said.

"You're welcome to leave," Jade said.

Dante remained in his seat.

She rested her forearms on the table. "I believe this is what we need to do to catch this killer. Does anyone have a better idea?"

She looked at each of them in turn.

No one said anything.

"That's what I thought," she said. "Crickets."

"I think we should shadow Carter," Christian said.

"And William," said Micah.

The team spent the rest of the afternoon planning the Carter-Chaney operation.

At one point, Christian threw his pen onto his notebook. "Dante might be right for once. This could be a waste of time."

"I'll take that as a compliment," Dante said.

"I'd rather be safe than sorry," Jade said. "Especially with kids' lives at stake."

Christian shook his head. "You're right. But how long can we protect these kids, though?"

"As long as it takes."

"Or until Finance tells us to stop," Pat said, typing.

Max, always soft-spoken, said, "This vigilante will not stop until he has accomplished his mission." The other agents quieted and turned to him. "If there are any other bullies out there that victimized the Thompson boy, their lives are in danger."

"Then, we can't stop until we've accomplished *our* mission," Jade said. "Dante, you and Micah shadow William."

Dante stood and looked at Micah. "Let's go."

Micah remained seated. "I want to stay here with Jade."

Dante laughed. "What? You have a thing for the boss?"

"Shut up, Dante," Jade said.

"I just want to learn from the best," Micah said.

Dante stopped smiling, his expression almost hurt.

Micah was right. He was a junior agent assigned to her. She had an obligation to teach him all she could. She also thought it would be good for Christian and Dante to work together. She looked at Christian. "Go with Dante."

Christian's eyes questioned hers, as he pushed back from the table. "Sure."

Dante glanced at Micah as he followed Christian to the door, humming the chorus to "When a Man Loves a Woman."

Fairfax, Virginia

JADE DRUMMED HER fingers on top of the door near the driver's side-view mirror. Her open window let in the mild night air, the temperature breaking after another scorching summer day. "How long does an AAU basketball practice take?"

Micah glanced over at her. "I would think you should know."

"The time seemed to go faster when I played."

"Do you miss it?"

Jade shrugged. "Sometimes."

"What do you do to fill that void?"

Those eyes. "I work."

He got the hint. He scrunched down in his seat. "Thompson passed. What now?"

The results from Thompson's polygraph had come through that morning. Unless he was a gifted actor or found a way to cheat the test, Matt Thompson was innocent of the murders of Zach Rawlins, Nicholas Campbell, Joshua Stewart, and Andrew Huffman.

"Back to square one."

They returned their gaze to the building just as a bunch of tall boys walked out of the gym.

"I guess practice is over," Micah said. "Why didn't you want to shadow William?"

Jade wasn't sure herself. "Wanted to check this kid out myself."

One of the kids headed toward a used Volvo. He waved goodbye to his teammates, glanced around the parking lot, and then opened his car door. The boy was handsome. With a skin tone the color of sand, he could pass for Caucasian at this time of night and at this distance.

They were parked several rows away from the Volvo.

"That was odd," Micah said. "What was he looking for?"

The Volvo entered the line of cars to exit the parking lot. She put her car in reverse, and joined the line as well, several cars behind the Volvo.

From the lot, they followed Sam Carter at a discreet distance. The kid drove perfectly, using his turn signal when appropriate, stopping at every stop sign without rolling, demonstrating all the Virginia DMV rules to perfection. His driver's ed teacher would be proud.

He parked on the street in front of his parents' house. Jade parked two blocks away. The tall, lanky kid sauntered up the driveway and disappeared into the house.

Two hours later, he hadn't reappeared.

The White House, Washington, DC

SEAN BUZZED HER. "Madam President, someone is here to see you."

"Someone, Sean? Really!"

He had already hung up.

Whitney was surprised. Sean's professionalism was normally impeccable. She replaced the handset a little harder than necessary.

Before the interruption, she had been gloating. Privately. Earlier that day, she had invited a reticent Senator Eric Hampton to the Briefing Room as a sponsor of the New New Deal Coalition legislation. He wouldn't be able to resist a photo op with her. Or, more accurately, a photo op televised to a nationwide audience.

He hadn't disappointed her. He accepted.

One of the doors to the Oval Office opened. She started to rise, still not understanding—and disturbed—that Sean hadn't announced her guest according to protocol.

Wearing a gray business suit, white shirt with a spread collar, black silk tie, and carrying a matching gray fedora hat, her husband walked in with one arm behind his back.

"Grayson?" she asked, shocked.

She came around her desk and met him halfway. He whipped his arm in front of him. Flowers. Lilies. Her favorite.

She accepted the bouquet, breathing in the sweet, heavy aroma. "What is this? Why didn't you tell me you were coming? It's not on the schedule."

"Schedule, schmedule. We've been living according to schedules for too long, my darling. Surprise!"

He hugged her. She breathed in his familiar scent.

"I'm going to kill Sean." She pulled away slightly. "You're smiling, so the kids must be okay. Why are you here?"

"To see you. Can't I surprise my wife?"

"I have never known you to do anything without a reason. How long will you be visiting?"

"It's not a visit." He sat, crossed his legs, and draped both arms over the top of the sofa. "I'm here to stay."

"Stay?"

"I've heard about the rumors. About the baby. And your aunt."

Whitney's heart dropped. She was not ready to have this conversation. "I've been meaning—"

"I turned over the reins of Fairchild Industries to my younger brother for the duration of your presidency. Whether that's four years or eight. I realized that my family needs me. My immediate family. That you need me. You're more important to me than the business."

Whitney was still trying to comprehend this turn of events. "Are you sick?"

He laughed. "No. I'm in perfect health."

"But what are you going to *do*?"

"What the First Ladies did before me. Get involved in causes. Maybe take up golf."

"Golf?"

She was conflicted. The joy of him living with her was offset by the fact that they hadn't lived together for years, not since Whitney left Missouri to join the United States Congress.

She was used to living alone.

Sean entered carrying a vase, two glasses, and a bottle. "Trade."

He handed her the Taittinger and the glasses and took the flowers from her. He arranged them in the vase on an end table.

When he finished, he said, "I've cleared your schedule for the next hour."

He gave her a sly smile and left.

Grayson reached for the bottle.

"Wait," she said.

She sat next to him, took his hand, and stared into his eyes. "I need to tell you something."

He searched her face. "Aren't you happy?"

"I am," she said. "I'm glad you'll be here. In fact, I'll love it. To share this"—she motioned with her hand to take in the room, the Oval Office, her presidency—"with you. It's not about that. It's about Landon."

"Landon?"

"Open the champagne. This may take a while."

❀

Grayson spooned ice cream into her mouth. "You need to tell the kids at some point."

"I know."

Whitney tasted his strawberry ice cream, for once not caring about her weight or that she was eating after eight p.m. Food consumed after eight inevitably stuck to her hips forever.

It was now after nine.

She sat on a stool at a stainless-steel table in the kitchen on the lower level of the White House. She had dismissed the remaining kitchen staff. She didn't come down here often, the eeriness unsettling in such a large empty space late at night.

Grayson sat on a counter, his ankles crossed. He had changed into jeans and a t-shirt. His sandals lay stacked on the floor beneath him, where he had kicked them off earlier.

He finished the rest of the ice cream, jumped off the counter, and placed his bowl in the massive industrial sink.

Sitting on a stool beside her, he gently took the spoon from her hand. He scooped up the last of her mint chocolate chip ice cream and slipped it between her lips.

She swallowed. "I can't remember the last time you fed me. Are you sure you're not sick? Are you really Grayson Fairchild? What's your middle name?"

"Spencer."

An old joke between them.

He grabbed her chin and gazed into her eyes. His hands, soft. Gentle. Strong.

"Don't worry," he said. "Our children love you. They'll accept this. None of this is your fault."

"I still feel responsible."

"Because that's who you are. Does Kelly know that he's the father?"

She shook her head.

He came closer and licked just to the left of her lips. "Yum. That's good."

Whitney was shocked at Grayson's uncharacteristic displays of intimacy.

Grayson placed the spoon back in the bowl, giving her a mischievous smile. "And, no, I'm not having an affair. I just couldn't stand being away from you for another minute. I think you're finished with your ice cream. Let's go to bed. I want to show you how much I missed you."

As he leaned down to kiss her, she heard footsteps at the kitchen's entrance.

"Mom, I'm home!" yelled her daughter. She stopped short when she saw them. "Save room for Jesus, you two!"

Whitney and Grayson laughed. She shrugged at him with regret, and ran to kiss her baby.

Fairfax, Virginia

"I THINK I like soccer better. Baseball is so boring."

"I sort of miss Zach."

"And soccer players have great legs. Did you see—? Oh, there's my mom! I'll see you tomorrow!"

Grace ran to the car and jumped into the passenger seat.

Her mom leaned forward. "You need a ride?"

Kaylee knew she was just being nice. Taking her home would have been out of their way.

"That's okay, Mrs. Angleton. My mom will be here soon."

"I hate leaving you here alone."

"It's still light out. I'll be okay."

As the car pulled away, Grace quick-waved at Kaylee through the open window, and then went back to snapchatting on her smartphone.

Kaylee plopped down on the curb in front of the school's main entrance and shrugged off her backpack. She had a driver's license, but she was in the doghouse because of her grades last semester. The only reason her mom had allowed her to attend summer cheer camp was so Kaylee could try out next month for fall sports. Her mom, not used to picking her up anymore, was always late.

She wasn't kidding about Zach. Even though she had played hard to get—and he never "got"—she had liked him. And enjoyed their game of cat-and-mouse. Who knew? They might have become a couple. High school sweethearts. Maybe even married.

A car she recognized stopped in front of her. The window slid down. "Do you need a ride home?"

"My mom will be here soon."

"Hop in. I'll take you."

"You sure?"

"It's on my way."

This would save her mom a trip. She could text her from the car. "Okay."

She hopped in the front seat, dropping her backpack on the floor between her legs.

Kaylee, hands poised on her phone ready to text, said, "Thanks—"

The driver slapped metal handcuffs onto her wrists. Their grinding clicks a finality. The steel cold. Kaylee's phone was ripped out of her hands and thrown out the window.

"You're not going to need that."

Before Kaylee understood what was happening, a soft cloth covered her mouth. A sweet unfamiliar smell tingled her nose.

The window closed.

And then nothing.

PART III

The White House, Washington, DC

SHE LOOKED AT the phone display. Chandler.

"Mom!"

In the gym, she signaled the private yoga instructor to take a break.

Whitney was relieved. She had told Emma about Landon this past weekend during her visit. Emma was shocked, understandably, but hugged her and told Whitney she loved her. Afterward, Whitney had called Chandler. His reaction was different. He was distant, as if he thought it was her fault she had been raped and impregnated.

She had also talked to him about the use of the phrase, "those people." He had said he had been caught up in the excitement of the club. He had quit soon thereafter. She was glad.

Now, he sounded happy again, like the son she knew. She sat cross-legged on the mat.

"Are you at school?" she said into the phone.

"I'm on the downslide, Mom. One more week of summer school, then finals, and then I'm out of here."

"Your dad can't wait for you to join the firm. Are you taking some time off first? Because once you start working, you won't stop for a long time."

Her son was silent for a moment. "That's why I'm calling, Mom. So you'll hear it from me."

"Hear what from you?"

"I changed my mind. About working for Fairchild after I graduate."

"Oh? What did your father say?"

"I wanted to tell you first."

"He'll be disappointed, but I'm sure he'll be okay with your decision. You should tell him."

"It's not that . . ."

"He had to realize that you wouldn't necessarily follow in his footsteps. Are you joining another firm?"

"I decided to do something else. Go in a different direction."

Whitney couldn't suppress the sense of foreboding. She worried about his decision-making abilities. He made judgments based on the moment, instead of what was best for the long term. If she voiced disapproval or disagreed with his early career choices, however, she may lose him forever. She would give him her full support, no matter what. She smiled so that he could hear it in her voice.

"What did you decide? Who will be the lucky employer? Or will you take a year off to travel? Volunteer?"

"I decided to enter politics. I'm coming to Washington."

"Politics?" Except for dabbling with the group Emma had told her about, Chandler's interest in politics had been nonexistent, even though his mother had been a politician for most of his life.

She wasn't sure she wanted a political life for her children.

"I got a job as a legislative assistant," he said, hesitating. "I'm joining the staff of Senator Paul Sampson."

At first, she thought she'd misheard. She was silent for a few moments. She couldn't forbid him from working for Sampson.

Distracted, she said, "That's wonderful, son. I'll see you at graduation." She hung up without thinking.

She resumed the downward-facing dog pose, waiting for the instructor to return.

Instead of relaxing her mind, her thoughts wandered. Why did she beam with pride when Emma stood for what she believed in, but couldn't conjure up the same feelings for her son? Because his political views were different from hers? Was he getting back at her for some perceived slight?

Or was she upset because the media was going to have a field day over the career choice of the president's son?

Fairfax, Virginia

"THIS PERP IS sick," Christian said, his voice muffled by a handkerchief.

Jade, Dante, and Micah stood next to him, staring down at the body hidden under a fallen tree. Partially decomposed, the body had been discovered in the middle of Van Dyck Park. Kaylee Taylor had been missing for three days. She had been found by a dog with the Fairfax County canine unit. The temperature for those days had been over ninety degrees, the odor emanating from the corpse almost unbearable.

Jade's eyes watered from the smell. "What else do we know?"

Dante's eyes were watering, too. "That she smells."

Micah's eyes flashed above the protective mask he wore. "Your use of humor to compensate for your inadequacies is getting old."

"What? Are you vying for Max's job now?"

"Cut it out," Jade said.

"They found her phone in front of the school," Christian said. "Forensics is examining it now."

She pointed. "Check out the hands. Max'll have his work cut out for him with this one."

Dante laughed, but stopped when he realized she wasn't joking.

Like the other victims, all the damage had been inflicted on the left side of the girl's head. Her wounds appeared worse, if that were possible. Unlike the boys, however, Kaylee's genitals were intact. But her fingers were gone.

"Give me a minute," she said to them.

Jade crouched next to the body. The right side was free of bruises and scratches. She glanced briefly at the crime-scene techs ten yards away, waiting to finish their work.

"Speak to me, Kaylee," she said, her voice low. "Who did this to you?"

She stared at the young girl's once-pretty face. A face that would never wrinkle. Jade's eyes trailed down the decomposed body to the damaged hands. The missing fingers.

She stood. To Christian, she said, "I need to see her phone."

※

The data from Kaylee's phone was in her email inbox when she arrived at the office. She spent most of the day viewing what felt like millions of texts and photographs. A lot of pictures of Kaylee and Grace. Other cheerleaders. Friends. And, of course, boys. Lots of boys. But nothing helpful.

Jade started going through the saved Snapchats. Again, teenage stuff. Kaylee and Grace. Grace and Kaylee. She swiped through them quickly. Something caught her eye. She swiped in the other direction.

And stopped.

The school loomed in the background behind the two girls. Someone else was in the picture. Behind them. They may have not known he was there.

His face was partially cut off.

Jade smiled. "Thanks, Kaylee."

The White House, Washington, DC

WHITNEY AND GRAYSON had fallen into a daily routine. Every morning, they ate breakfast and read the newspapers before she headed down to the Oval Office. Living together every day had been an adjustment for them both, but they were getting used to it. He had even found a cause to lead: overseeing a major initiative to provide job and business training to the long-term unemployed.

He slipped a forkful of eggs into his mouth. "How are you feeling?"

"Now that my son is a Republican?"

"Yes."

"I keep asking myself, 'Where did we go wrong?'"

They shared a laugh.

"He's still young," Grayson said. "He may grow out of it." He picked up the *Washington Post* from the table. "How's Emma?"

"She says her activist days are over. For now."

"She seems more mature."

"Being arrested can do that to you."

He peered at her over the paper. He hesitated. He seemed to be trying to get the words just right. "Do you ever think about what might have been?"

He was referring to Landon. After the initial surprise at learning the truth, Grayson had taken her revelation about Landon in stride.

She pushed her fruit plate away. "In the beginning. Yes. But we raised two beautiful children that I love with every fiber of my being. They are enough for me."

She kissed him on the cheek and moved to the living area. Picking up her purse from the table, she opened it to retrieve her lipstick.

Her hand stilled, and then a frantic search. The lipstick forgotten.

Landon's letter was gone.

Fairfax, Virginia

NO ONE TALKS about the monotony of a stakeout. They don't show it on the cable TV shows or in the movies.

They had been shadowing Sam Carter for two weeks. Dante and Christian were surveilling William Chaney-Frost. She planned to confront William in the morning.

As they waited for practice to finish, Jade said, "What about you?"

"What about me?" Micah asked, surprised.

"What do you like to do? For fun."

"I'm a football fan. What you Yanks call soccer."

"Team?"

"Arsenal. Maybe we can catch a game together some time. There's an English pub by my house that shows all the EPL games."

Jade feared that she'd been to that pub before with Christian. "Maybe."

She put the car in drive and followed Carter, pulling over two blocks down from his parents' house. As they had done every night. They settled in for a long night.

Tonight, however, he stopped in front of the house, but the car was still idling.

Jade and Micah glanced at each other.

A minute later, the boy resumed driving. They followed.

Carter left the subdivision via a different exit. After a few miles on Jackson Parkway, he exited and took the first right into Oak Creek Park, a Fairfax County public park. Officially closed at dusk, lights illuminated a couple of soccer games still in play.

"What's this kid up to?"

Micah shook his head. "Nothing good."

Carter drove past the soccer fields and turned into one of the many small parking lots that dotted the park. She parked on the side of the road about thirty yards from the lot entrance. She looked at Micah and brought a finger to her lips. They gently eased the car doors shut but did not close them all the way. Just enough for the interior lights to go off.

They approached the entrance on foot. It was dark here. If there were lights, they hadn't come on yet.

She spotted the Volvo parked at the other end of the lot next to another car. She couldn't see the make and model. She debated whether to draw her weapon. The kid could be just meeting a girl here. Or a friend.

Better to be safe.

She drew her Glock, the weapon pointed at the ground. From the side, she peered into the backseat of the Volvo and then the front.

Empty.

The other car was an older Mercedes. Ducking between the cars, she peered into its back and front seats as well. Empty. She crouched as she walked to the front of the Mercedes and put her hand on the hood.

It was cold.

She scanned the area, but didn't see anyone. She glanced back at Micah and pointed to the woods with her index and middle fingers, indicating where she was headed. There was a break in the trees. Despite sticks and a few fallen leaves, they walked toward the opening as silently as they could.

In the center of a small clearing was a playground set with a slide, climbers, and swings. Carter was pressed against the beams supporting the slide, whoever was with him was barely visible, and at least a foot shorter than he was.

She felt stupid, but headed toward the couple anyway. They were kissing.

Jade shone her flashlight, stopping several yards away from them.

Carter swung around, his face pale with fear. He put his hand up to protect his eyes from the glare, while shielding the person behind him.

"Sam, my name is Special Agent Jade Harrington with the FBI. I need you to step away."

"FBI?"

"Sam, please step away."

"What do you want? I didn't do anything."

"Your teammates are being murdered. We're trying to protect you."

"I don't need protection."

"We think you do. Now, step away."

He glanced behind him at his companion and whispered something, before taking several steps away from the other person.

The girl glared at Jade. Rather, *woman.*

The last piece of the puzzle slid into place, as Jade stared not at the fearful, but the defiant expression on Jenny Thompson's face.

Fairfax, Virginia

"'THE FIRST RULE of fight club—"

"—is you do not talk about fight club,'" Micah finished. He explained to Jade. "It was popular in the UK, too."

Sam gave him a small smile. "Yeah, William saw that movie a thousand times. Ours is called the WRSS FC—William Randolph Secondary School Fight Club. 'FC' for short. Every fight night, he starts with, 'Welcome to fight club.' He has all these rules. None of them are written down. We can't post videos or anything on social media. New players on the team fight the first night. I went only once." He shrugged. "I broke all the rules. I was out."

The night had turned unseasonably cool.

"You sure you don't want to sit in the car?" Jade asked.

Jenny had been whisked away to the local FBI office in Fairfax. She would be transferred downtown tomorrow.

He glanced at the Audi. "No, thanks."

It was dark in this part of the park. She suspected the darkness made it more conducive for Sam to talk to them.

"All right," she said. "What did you see when you went?"

"William likes to wear old-school knickers. The rest of us wore baseball pants. We were allowed to use MMA gloves. Nothing else. He beat the crap out of Joshua, who's supposed to be his best friend. J-man held the netting like he was holding on for his life. Then, William threw him on the ground, and kept hitting him and hitting him. Supposed to be when you go limp, you tap out, and the round is over." He shook his head, an expression of incredulousness. "William wouldn't stop." Carter looked at her. "But what was worse was the chanting. 'Loser! Loser! Loser!' Like a cult. Tyler threw up and ran when he saw what happened to his friend. Big mistake."

"Why didn't someone tell the coach? Call the police?"

"Tell them what?"

"About what was happening."

Sam wagged his finger at her. "Remember the first rule. Besides, the coach . . . Let's just say, snitches get stitches. The thing is FC, for those who belong, helps the team form a closer bond. The club represents something bigger than themselves."

"More than a normal team."

"Yeah. William has his own army. Disciples. What do you call them?"

"Acolytes?" Micah offered.

"Yeah."

"How so?" Jade said.

"The guys in the club would do whatever he said. Batshit crazy stuff. Like the SS during the Third Reich. Some of the players really got off on it. If you aren't in, though, you're terrified. They can come after you. Your sisters. Your girlfriend. Your mother. Kids rat each other out. After I left the club, I couldn't eat. Couldn't sleep. I almost quit the team. And baseball's my life. You know what's funny? The guy in the movie? Brad Pitt? His name was Tyler. William hated that Tyler Thompson had the same name. The name William wanted."

"What about Jenny? Mrs. Thompson?"

Sam's face reddened, visible even in the dark. "She came on to me. What was I supposed to do?"

"Say 'no'?" Jade said.

"Easy for you to say. You're older. You're smart enough not to be tempted by someone who isn't good for you."

Well . . .

Sam explained that Jenny had started texting him. She was upset about losing her son, and needed someone to talk to who knew him.

"Did you know him well?" Jade asked.

"No. But hey . . ." He smiled, sheepish. "Anyway, tonight was going to be our first night together."

"And, maybe, your last. On earth."

Sam stopped smiling.

Fairfax, Virginia

CHRISTIAN SAT ON a big blue concrete ball, one of three in front of William Randolph Secondary School, which protected the building from someone trying to drive through the main entrance. Jade stood near him scanning the faces of the students as they hurried to their summer-school classes that morning. They had arrived early, but she had a feeling that the person they were waiting for was not an early bird. Her dress shirt stuck to her back, the humidity not taking a day off this summer.

Finally, William Chaney-Frost sauntered toward them. He had alighted from a new BMW M4. He slowed as he saw the agents. He glanced back at his car and back at her, his smile wide. "Agent Harrington! Howie! Nice, huh? Present for my sixteenth birthday."

She could never afford a car like that on her bureaucrat salary.

"It's Agent Merritt," Jade said. "We need to talk to you."

"Sure."

Instead of heading inside to the conference room with the little chairs, they led him to a backless steel bench away from the front entrance. She sat next to him. Christian stood beside her, arms crossed over his chest.

"What's up?" William asked.

"We need to ask you some more questions."

"I've told you everything I know."

"Not everything," she said. "Can you remove your sunglasses?"

"No, I'm good."

"That wasn't a request."

He hesitated, then did what he was told.

"Besides Grace and her mother, you were the last person to see Kaylee alive."

"How do you know that?"

"Did you kill her?"

"Of course not."

"What was she to you?"

"We were just friends."

"Just friends?"

"She was dating one of my teammates. I don't roll like that."

"But he's dead."

"Doesn't matter."

"Why didn't you come forward about being there?"

William's head drooped. "I was in shock. I thought you'd think I had something to do with it."

"Why were you at school?"

"Lifting."

"Anyone see you?"

"Yeah." He rattled off some names.

"I had a long talk with Sam Carter last night," she said.

A tightening of the eyes, but the boy's facial expression remained cool. "What did he say?"

"That he didn't bully Tyler. In fact, he said *you* were involved. Not only that, but you were the boss."

"He's lying."

"He told us something else."

William remained silent for as long as he could. "What?"

"About the fight club. The batting cages"—she pointed toward the baseball fields in the distance—"where you beat the crap out of each other. About how the teammates who didn't want to participate were bullied outside the club."

"We messed around. So what?"

"It looked like more than messing around to me. Sam showed us a video he took with his phone the night he was there."

"He recorded us?"

Jade nodded.

William swore, but regained his composure quickly. This was one cool kid. "Fighting's not illegal."

"Trespassing is."

"Our coach said . . ."

"What?"

"He said it was okay. If we used the cages at night to fight."

Christian stepped forward. "Sam also told us something else. You beat up my son. You and Andrew and Joshua."

Christian was acting and not well. He hadn't even been there last night to interview Carter. They had planned the bad cop/good cop routine earlier.

William's eyes widened. He glanced at her. "Isn't it a conflict of interest for him to be here?"

Christian inched closer. "Are you a lawyer now?"

"Do you know who my mother is?"

"I don't care who your mother is." He removed his badge and his gun and handed them to Jade. "You think you're tough. You've only been fighting boys in your little club. Why don't you fight a real man?"

William's eyes bulged. He turned to her, his eyes pleading. "Do something!"

She held up Christian's gun and badge. "He doesn't work for me anymore."

"Hey, man," William said. "I'm sorry."

The kid was shaking. Jade reached out and grasped Christian's wrist. "William, why don't you tell me everything from the beginning, and Agent Merritt will take a step back and let you."

Christian hesitated and then stepped back. She returned his badge and gun. And William started talking.

Washington, DC

JADE HAD JUST settled into her seat in an interrogation room at FBI HQ. Jenny needed no prompting.

"Zach was slow. I've been watching him play sports for years. I knew I could take him."

"Why is that?"

"You weren't the only one who played ball. I played softball in high school. A small town in Iowa. Catcher. Got a partial scholarship to GMU. I know how to handle my son's bat."

Technicians found a baseball bat with Jenny's fingerprints at the top of the slide at the park. On the bat, they found hair and fibers from Zach Rawlins, Nicholas Campbell, Andrew Huffman, and Kaylee Taylor. Jade and Micah had arrived in time, before Carter had become a statistic. And not of the baseball kind.

"Was it your Vicodin your son took?"

Jenny nodded, a sad look crossing her face. "Bad knees."

"Is that where you met Matt? At George Mason University?"

"Yeah. We got married right after I graduated, and I never went home."

"Tell us about Nicholas."

"He was easy. Tyler told me the guys on the team said I was a MILF. He was embarrassed." Christian paused in his writing. He stared at Jenny. "I asked Nicholas to come over and help me pack up Tyler's things. He got off on doing it in Tyler's room. I didn't care. It was a means to an end. While he was on top of me, I hit him on the head with the lamp."

No wonder Fairfax County PD didn't discover the blood and semen. Jenny had had sex with Nicholas after they had processed the scene.

She was still talking.

" . . . and then dragged him to my car and dumped him in the park by Reagan."

"By yourself?" Jade asked, doubtful.

"I'm stronger than I look. When someone messes with your kids, you develop a strength you can't even imagine. I suppose you wouldn't know about that."

Jade ignored the barb. "And you had no help from your husband?"

"Matt's weak. He isn't strong enough to protect our family. I'm the strong one. No one is going to fuck with my kids."

So, you fuck someone else's kids?

Jade recalled the gnawing feeling that something was off when she was standing in Tyler's bedroom. Now she knew what it was: the circle, absent of dust, on the nightstand. There was something else off in that room, as well. She had thought about it a lot. But try as she might, whatever it was remained elusive.

"What did you do with the lamp?"

"I cleaned it, and dropped it off at Goodwill. I support the causes I believe in."

She was serious.

"Why did you cut off the victims' penises?" Christian asked.

"They were not the victims here," Jenny snapped. "I didn't want them spawning demon seeds."

The chill in her voice produced goose bumps on Jade's arms.

"Tell us about Andrew Huffman," Jade said.

She shrugged. "I flirted with him like the others. I saw how they used to look at me. When I sat in the stands. I could see it in their eyes. All of them. They wanted to fuck me. I could've had them all."

This was one sick woman. "I'm sure you could have."

"Are you mocking me?"

Jade let the question hang in the air for a moment. "Finish telling me about Andrew."

"I arranged to meet him behind the 7-Eleven."

"What was your husband doing there?"

"I knew you suspected him. He was my . . . what do you call it? Red herring."

"You blame Matt for Tyler's death?"

"He should've taught Tyler to be tougher. To fight back. Like I said, he's weak. I made him think I was going crazy. Wearing a bathrobe all the time. Not showering. I was sleeping during the day. At night, I would follow those boys around. Watch them. Watch their stupid fight club. Learn their habits. And then I picked them off one by one."

Jenny spat on the floor.

Christian stared at his sister-in-law, as if she were an extraterrestrial being who just landed from outer space.

William had corroborated Sam Carter's story about the fight club and that he was its leader. He downplayed its viciousness.

"How did you find out which kids bullied Tyler?" Jade asked.

"The fight club. They did as much talking as fighting. I found out everything."

Not everything.

"How come Matt didn't recognize you at the 7-Eleven?"

"I was wearing a lot of makeup. And a wig."

"Why the 7-Eleven? There are lots of places closer to your house. To Huffman's house."

Jenny looked at her oddly. "Because it was closer to yours."

Dante was right.

Jade realized what Ethan had been trying to tell her about Dante. One of his useful qualities was his ability to take disparate information and make it fit together. Make something out of nothing. Like any good cook.

Christian stopped writing and stared at Jenny. "Explain."

"I wanted to make sure she noticed." She nodded at Jade. "The great Jade Harrington. Super FBI agent. I read everything about the TSK case. Where do you think I got the idea to use the bat? I wanted her to catch me. I wanted everyone to know. To read about it. Just like her TSK case. Now, Tyler will live forever."

"That doesn't make any sense, Jenny," Christian said, exasperated.

"Why did you kill Kaylee?" Jade asked.

"That bitch texted my son. Pretended to like him. I cut her fingers off so she would never be able to text anyone again. Even in the afterlife. I also found out she was the one who created that awful Twitter account. That whore got what she deserved."

She continued to talk, as if they weren't there. "I don't care what happens to me. I did the world a service. All those boys and that bitch who bullied my son will never hurt anyone again, and will not beget more bullies. I stopped the cycle."

Jade waited for Jenny's head to start spinning like the character in *The Exorcist.*

"Except one. We believe one other boy was involved in bullying your son."

Jenny snapped out of it. "Who?"

Jade stood, a sudden need to be out of Jenny's presence. "It wasn't Carter. You almost murdered an innocent kid."

Jenny digested this information. A manic expression returned to her face. She tried to stand, the manacles restraining her.

"Who? Who was it?"

Jade signaled to the window for Dante and Micah to remove Jenny.

"Answer me!" Jenny screamed.

They entered, each agent holding one of her arms. She fought them, as they pulled her toward the door.

"I won't be in jail forever," she said, her eyes never leaving Jade's. "I'll find out who it was! And when I do I'll—"

Mercifully, Micah closed the door behind them. Jade would never know what Jenny would do.

The White House, Washington, DC

"I DON'T THINK he's ready," Sasha said.

"Who could ever be ready for that job?"

"Lena is doing a good job. Why make a change? There are other unfilled positions that are a higher priority."

Whitney fiddled with the pen on her desk. "He thinks well on his feet. He's well-spoken, and he could sell ice cream to Eskimos. He has a prodigious memory, which will come in handy. He doesn't need to write anything down, so notes from our conversations would never be subpoenaed. He's perfect."

"Isn't it my responsibility to make hiring decisions?"

"My mind is made up."

"Do you really want a man speaking for you?"

"I am not going to dignify that question with a response." Her phone buzzed. "Yes, Sean."

"Madam President, Mr. Blake Haynes is here to see you."

Whitney looked at Sasha, as she spoke into the speakerphone. "Send him in."

A minute later, he crossed the room, taking in the Oval Office before he shook her hand.

"I wish I had seen your office when I was here for the interview." He glanced around again. "Amazing."

"Take a seat." She waited for him to sit in the chair next to Sasha. "Mr. Haynes, I have a proposition for you."

"Another interview?"

"Something like that."

He leaned forward. "I'm intrigued."

She glanced at Sasha, whose pursed lips were hard to ignore. Whitney turned back to Blake. "How would you like to be the White House Press Secretary?"

His mouth opened in surprise.

She would never forget the expression on his face as long as she lived. The young man with the gift of gab was speechless.

Washington, DC

"I NEED TO see you when you get in."

"I'm on my way."

Jade tapped the button near the car radio to end the call. What could Ethan want first thing in the morning?

When she arrived at the Bureau, she dropped her briefcase in her office.

She stood in his doorway for a moment watching him work. In a starched white shirt and maroon tie, he marked up a document, oblivious to her presence.

She had suspected Dante of leaking details about the TSK investigation to the media, but he'd been off the case at the time, and wouldn't have had access to the information. She never suspected her boss. A man she admired and respected for his work ethic, integrity, and loyalty to the agency.

She knocked.

He looked up from his writing. "Shut the door."

She sat across from him and began updating him on Jenny's interrogation.

He interrupted her. "That's not why I called you in here." He spun his wedding ring once. Twice. "I'm leaving the Bureau."

Jade opened her mouth and closed it. She had not expected this. At all. "What do you mean?"

"In all the years I've been here, I can count on one hand the number of times I've had dinner with my family."

"You're not answering my question."

"It's personal."

"Does it have anything to do with the leaks?"

"How did you find out?"

"So, it's not personal. A reporter called me. From Seattle."

Ethan, with an uncharacteristic display of anger, slammed his hand on the table, startling her.

"This is crazy," he said.

"She said that you provided her information about the TSK case."

"I didn't leak anything."

"You think someone set you up?" Jade asked, doubtful.

He let out a lungful of air. "Now, you think I'm crazy. Why would I leak it? I would be jeopardizing an operation. One of my agent's cases, which is a reflection on me. It doesn't make sense."

He had a point.

Realization dawned. "This isn't voluntary."

He didn't respond.

"Can we fight it?" she said.

He shook his head. "The decision's been made. I'm out of here."

She remained silent. She hadn't known an FBI without Senior Supervisory Special Agent Ethan Lawson. "I don't know what to say. Is this permanent or a leave of absence?"

"I don't know."

"When are you leaving?"

"Not sure yet. Probably in a few weeks."

Jade started to rise. "This is a lot to process." At the door, she thought of something. "Who's going to take your place?"

"You are."

The White House, Washington, DC

"CONGRATULATIONS," THE PRESIDENT said, as she walked around her desk, hand extended.

"Thank you."

"You're batting a thousand."

Jade shrugged. "I win more than I lose."

"And modest. Please have a seat. I was just about to have tea. Care to join me?"

"That would be nice."

President Fairchild placed the order and returned to the chair next to the sofa. A woman brought in the tea service and placed it on the table between them. She poured for both of them.

"Thank you, Sarah." The woman left. "And to you for solving the 'Robin Hood' case." The president lifted her cup and toasted Jade. "Well done."

The cups, fragile and expensive, displayed an exquisite design. Jade added a spoonful of sugar to hers before taking a sip.

"There is a reason why I asked for this private meeting with you," President Fairchild continued.

Jade wondered what it could be. With Ethan leaving, he couldn't have volunteered her services for another case.

Or could he?

"I haven't forgotten my promise to you," the president said.

"What promise?"

"The one I made to you over a year ago."

Puzzled, she said, "I apologize, Madam President. I don't remember."

"I told you that perhaps you would come work for me someday." The president replaced her cup in the saucer and placed it on the table. "That someday is today. I'd like for you to join my staff."

Jade glanced around the Oval Office. Not one to impress easily, she was impressed. The elegance. The power.

Work here?

"Why me?"

"As I said before, I trust you, and I need strong people around me. I have big plans for you, Jade Harrington."

Quantico, Virginia

"THANKS FOR COMING."

"Not often a beautiful woman asks me out to lunch."

She looked askance at Max. "But it does happen?"

"What a beautiful day," he said, ignoring her question. "The dog days of August are finally over."

They sat next to each other on a bench. He glanced around the small park she had chosen near the FBI Academy. At this hour, they were the only two people in the park, except for a young woman pushing a toddler on a swing. "This is nice. I didn't know this park existed."

"You need to get out more," she said.

"The day all the serial killers take a day off, is when I'll take a day off."

"You might need to take a day off before then." She handed him a sandwich she'd picked up at a deli down the street. "I wanted to talk to you about something."

She told him about her career choices: joining the president's staff as a special assistant or staying with the Bureau and filling in for Ethan while he was on leave.

Max chewed his egg-salad sandwich. "They both sound like great opportunities." He swallowed, thoughtful. "Aren't you forgetting one?"

She frowned. "No."

"What about moving to Seattle? We have a local office there."

Jade's cheeks grew warm. "Why would I do that?"

He shot her a look. "You forget I study human behavior for a living."

She bit into her Italian sandwich. Squeals of laughter emanated from the child on the swing. Jade never thought much about having children. A family. She hadn't thought about it at all.

"I don't know what you're talking about."

"Look at me," he said.

She stopped eating and complied.

"My wife left me after thirty years of marriage. Because I was committed to the job. My vows to the Bureau more important than my vows to her. Do I regret the choice I made? Sometimes." He gestured at the child. "But look at her. She doesn't have a care in the world. She's free. Safe. That's why I do what I do." He turned to her. "You've been chosen. To serve the president or the Bureau. You don't have a choice. You're made like me."

She balled up her sandwich wrapper and shot it at a nearby trash can. Good. "You're my godfather. You're supposed to guide me. Which position should I choose?"

"Duty is your only choice."

Washington, DC

TONIGHT, HE DINED alone at the Capital Grille. The crowd seemed light, even for a week night. He read the *Washington Times* as he ate. The only legitimate paper in DC. He stared at a photograph of the happy couple.

He glanced around. The restaurant was empty.

Odd.

"They say you shouldn't drink alone."

"They're probably right," Cole said, "but they never said anything about eating." He held up the newspaper. "Nice picture."

"Thank you," the president said. "May I sit down?"

"Knock yourself out." He circled his fork in the air. "I suppose you had something to do with this?"

"The Service takes my safety seriously."

He laid the paper on the table. "Well, I'm glad the Homo Erectus came home. Your daughter is an agitator with an arrest record. You had an illegitimate child who's gone missing. And your son has jumped ship to the good side. You need a man around the house."

"No one's here. You can drop the act."

"What act?"

"Do you really believe all the stuff that you say?"

He dropped his fork. "What did you say?"

"What's wrong? You look as if you've seen a ghost."

More like heard one.

Landon Phillips had said almost those exact words to him. Right before he shot Cole's daughter. He pushed his plate away. He was no longer hungry. He dabbed his mouth with a napkin and then wiped his forehead.

"Whitney, why are you here?"

"It's Madam President, Cole. Your wife came to visit me several months ago. Did she tell you?"

"Ashley? What for?"

"She told me about your son. CJ, isn't it?"

He nodded. "She didn't tell me."

"Your wife is a strong woman."

He had never thought of Ashley as strong. He remembered her bravery when their home was invaded by that monster. And how she was always there for him. And his family.

"What did she say?"

The president said, "She asked me whether I could put forth a federal anti-bullying law."

This was interesting. "Can you?"

"I can, but I'll need your help."

"I'm listening."

Washington, DC

"JADE, I THINK you're going to want to see this."

"I'll be right there."

Jade frowned as she replaced the handset. She locked her computer, left her office, and stopped at Pat's cubicle.

"What is it?"

Pat turned in her chair. "I know the Robin Hood case is closed, but something about it kept nagging at me. You might want to pull up a seat."

Jade looked around, but didn't see a vacant chair. She eyed the agent in the next cubicle.

He stood and grabbed his coffee mug. "I need a break anyway."

She scooted his chair next to Pat's. Pat's fingers flew across the keyboard at the speed of sound.

"The hack was sophisticated. The perpetrator created a malware program and sent it to potential donors in an email asking them for money."

"Wouldn't that be double-dipping?"

A slight smile from Pat. "Good one. He named it Astrea."

"Goddess of Justice."

"Correct. Astrea detected the passwords to the victims' banking sites stored on their computers." Pat stopped typing. "I watched a recording of your interview with Blakeley and, between that and what you told me, he just doesn't seem to possess the skills or background to pull off something like this."

"Noah didn't seem technically proficient to be the brainchild behind this," Jade conceded.

"I don't think he was. I've been working with CART on his computer. His password was 'equalityone.'"

"There's that."

"At first, we thought that since he was one of the victims, the likelihood of him being the perpetrator was small. Then, conveniently, all the evidence pointed to him. But now I think he was not only the victim of theft, but that he was set up to take the fall for a crime he didn't commit."

Jade sat back in her chair. "Why do you think that?"

"I believe someone hacked into Blakeley's computer a second time and installed a file that would make it appear as if all the transactions were conducted from his computer."

"Can you prove it?"

"Not yet."

"If it wasn't him, who was it?"

Pat's fingers stilled. "That, we don't know."

❀

Back in her office, Jade packed up her briefcase and thought about Noah Blakeley.

He had been charged with ninety-nine counts of wire, bank, and computer fraud; computer intrusion; aggravated identity theft; computer hacking; and violation of numerous other federal laws. If convicted, he would spend the rest of his life in prison.

If Pat were right, she could never live with herself. She had told Pat to quietly continue the investigation while she untangled all the "good" Equality One had done.

"Outta here?"

Micah joined her in the hallway as she headed for the elevator.

"Kind of late for you," she said.

He grinned. "Trying to impress the boss."

She pressed the down button. "I think you've already done that."

He looked at her. "Not him. You."

Her heart may have skipped a beat, but she ignored it.

They both stared at the numbers above the door, as the elevator descended. He smelled faintly of cologne. Micah wasn't encroaching on her personal space, but she was cognizant of his lean, muscular body just the same.

At the second level of the parking garage, he hesitated, allowing her to exit first.

"You parked on this level, too?"

"No," he said.

"I don't need you to walk me to my car."

He shrugged. "I'm not doing it for you. I'm doing it for my mum."

"Huh?"

"She raised me right." He smiled. "Isn't that what you Yanks say?"

She couldn't help smiling. "I guess."

"I've been meaning to tell you. Great work on the Robin Hood case."

He didn't know she had authorized Pat to continue working on it. "Thanks."

They stopped behind her car.

"On to the next one," he said, his look intense.

"Yep."

He cocked his head. "You mean it?"

"Sure."

"Good."

"Where's this coming from, Micah?"

"I just think you need to focus on your next case. Let Robin Hood go. Move on."

"Thanks for the advice."

"That's what I'm here for. Good night, Agent Harrington."

He strode toward the elevator. As he got on, he turned and held up a hand. He stared at her until the doors closed.

She felt an inexplicable chill, as she opened her car door.

Why did his advice feel more like a warning?

Arlington, Virginia

PRESIDENT WHITNEY FAIRCHILD said something to Senator Eric Hampton, who gave her a false smile.

"I wonder what she said?"

Zoe swallowed a sip of her beer from a microbrewery in nearby Burke. "Not sure. But he's not happy. The legislation had originally been a few votes shy. He was pressured into making it happen."

"By the president?"

Zoe shook her head. "Cole Brennan."

"Interesting."

The two friends were sprawled on Jade's living-room couch watching the news. After her weird run-in with Micah, she wanted some company. On the TV screen, the president moved to a table where a blue hardcover folio held the New New Deal Coalition Act.

"Hampton will smile to her face today, and be back at her throat tomorrow."

Jade took a pull of her beer. "Is he worse than Sampson?"

"Not even close. When we lie, we get fired. Since he switched parties, Sampson lies every time he opens his mouth. That's not just my opinion either. *Politico* recently ranked him one of the least honest politicians."

"That's saying something."

"He'll get his, though."

"Why do you say that?"

"Word on the street is that his farming corporation in Nebraska employs illegal workers."

"Mexicans?"

Zoe nodded. "Guess he didn't build that wall fast enough."

The president selected a pen, and smiled, as she signed the New New Deal Coalition Act, the most extensive—and expensive—economic legislation in this country's history. Standing behind her was former President Richard Ellison, who had flown in for the occasion.

"Ellison being there is huge," Zoe said. "Bipartisan cooperation. If only the rest of his party could follow suit."

Jade sipped her beer. With Zoe, she didn't need to say much.

"I guess she's not going to mention Xavi," Zoe said.

"Not today."

A competing story to the signing of the historic legislation was the announcement that the vice president of the United States, Xavi Fernandez, had resigned for personal reasons. This was only the third time a vice president had resigned in US history.

"I'm glad she finally stood up for herself and got rid of that misogynistic ass."

Jade glanced over at her friend. "It was forced?"

"That's what I hear. He's such a potato." She gave Zoe a questioning look. "Someone who has lost his heritage. Brown on the outside. White on the inside."

"Got it," Jade said. "Your 'word on the street' seems pretty informed. Anyway, I think Fairchild can take care of herself. Maybe she was waiting for the right time."

"I just wish she'd take a stand against special interests. Wall Street. Getting big money out of politics. Everyone needs to stand for something." She glanced at Jade. "Even you."

"What do you mean?"

"You can't be middle-of-the-road on everything. Are you a progressive? A liberal? Gay? Straight?"

Jade smiled. "Nice try. I don't do labels."

"But you must stand for something."

"I do. I stand for justice." She thought of her last conversation with Max. "Duty."

"Barf." Zoe made a gagging motion. "You're such a Bureau poster child." Zoe sat up, placing her beer on the table in front of them, and stared at Jade. "That's not good enough, though." She placed her hand over her own heart. "You have to stand for something that's personal. That matters. That hurts, if you don't say something."

"Why are you saying this?"

"Because we're family."

"We're not related, Zoe."

"Blood doesn't mean family. Blood is just blood. You're my chosen family, which means more to me."

Jade was touched. Besides Max, Zoe was the only family she had. She should respond in kind. Instead, she lifted Zoe's bottle and used a napkin to wipe the condensation off the table until it was spotless. She wiped the bottle's bottom before placing it on the napkin.

She was saved from responding by a knock on the door.

"You expecting someone?" asked Zoe.

Jade shook her head, as she moved to the door. She returned with a large box and set it on the hardwood living room floor.

The packing slip contained a note:

Jade,

Thank you for solving my case. I hope these remind you of Seattle.

Always,

Kyle

"Aren't you going to open it?" Zoe said, her tone, mischievous.

Jade had to be careful. Zoe knew her. If Zoe sensed that there was anything between Kyle and her, Zoe would tear her apart for information, like a starving Rottweiler left alone with a steak. She feigned nonchalance. "I'll open it later."

"Like hell you will."

Zoe started tearing off the packaging. Jade hesitated, and then knelt to help her.

"Wow," Zoe said.

Inside the box were dozens of original Motown albums from the Sixties through the Eighties. The sight brought an unusual pang to Jade's heart. She missed Seattle. Missed the attention.

Missed Kyle.

Jade didn't dare look at Zoe.

Zoe stared at the vinyls in disbelief or confusion. Jade couldn't tell which. She turned to Jade, her eyes huge. "Why is she sending you these?"

The White House, Washington, DC

WHITNEY GLANCED AROUND his office. "When are you going to settle in?"

Blake laughed. "I live here now."

In between the Press Briefing Room and the Oval Office were the White House Press Secretary's office and those of his large staff, which was appropriate since the press secretary served both the president and the press. Her official presidential portrait hung on one wall, as did the portraits of JFK and Bill Clinton. Another wall displayed a panoramic photograph of the pre-9/11 New York City skyline. Blake's desk was covered with briefing books, reports, transcripts, and a few bottles of water. Papers covered the entire surface of his desk, the round table he used for meetings, and his credenza. She also spotted a couple of gourmet-food magazines.

She inclined her head toward the skyline. "Do you miss it?"

"Sometimes. As a foodie, I miss the restaurants. But I like the West End. Everything is within walking distance, and I can walk to work. A lot of great places to run. Maybe we should run sometime."

"I'm sure Josh would love that. No, I prefer my elliptical. Less stress for all of us."

Whitney sat on the edge of his desk and crossed her legs. She checked the flat-screen TV. The CNN caption blared Killer Momma Arraignment at the bottom of the screen.

"How are you settling in at home?" she asked.

"Not as well as here. I'm never there."

"No social life?"

"As I said, I'm always here."

"Pity. I thought you and Ms. Harrington made a striking pair. How did the gaggle go this morning?"

The press gaggle was the daily briefing he gave from the desk in his office. The press gathered around him, as he took them through her schedule, measured their temperature about what stories they were following, which in turn helped him plan his day. Although what he said was on the record, these briefings—unlike in the Briefing Room—were not recorded or televised.

"It was fine. A lot of questions about Chandler's first day of work. I handled it."

"Good. I need you to do the talk-show circuit soon. Educate people on what they can expect from the New New Deal and our other legislative initiatives."

Blake smiled. "Got it, boss."

At the door, she turned. "I'm glad you're here. We're going to make a great team."

CHAPTER ONE HUNDRED TWENTY-TWO

Alexandria, Virginia

WEARING AN EXPENSIVE black suit, her makeup flawless, Rachel Chaney sat at the table across from her. Her hair was brown, cut just above the shoulders.

Like Jenny's.

Jenny had known William's mother of course. Had seen her at the baseball games dressed in her suits, just so. She had always showed up late—the fourth or fifth inning—when she bothered to show up at all.

The small room off the courtroom barely had enough space for the rectangular table and two chairs.

She rubbed her wrists, grateful that Rachel had asked for the handcuffs to be removed.

Rachel pulled out a legal pad and a fancy pen from her briefcase. She opened her mouth to tell Jenny about the process for her arraignment at the United States District Court for the Eastern District of Virginia.

Jenny didn't have much time. But she did have the element of surprise.

On the count of three to herself, she exploded from her chair and wrapped her hands around her attorney's neck in a vise grip. And squeezed.

Rachel Chaney's eyes bulged.

The rage coursing within Jenny threatened to explode. Everything her family had suffered. She had suffered.

Her little boy, her angel, had suffered.

The woman's body finally relaxed.

Jenny had to move quickly.

When Jade Harrington had told Jenny that her son's killer was still alive, she realized she needed an attorney after all. She had remembered William's mother from the games. That she was a defense attorney. That they looked alike. And were nearly the same height.

She switched clothes with her. The suit was loose, but fit well enough. She set the attorney upright, now with her back facing the door.

She left the pad of paper where it was. And the woman's briefcase. She adjusted the suit skirt, and slapped the door as she had seen on TV. The bailiff opened it, looking in on the defendant.

She breezed past him. "I need to use the bathroom. I'll be right back."

He closed the door behind her.

Jenny walked down the commodious hallway, her newly acquired high heels clicking on the floor. She passed benches where defendants and their lawyers waited. Passed courtrooms. She cruised on past the ladies' room.

And walked out of the courthouse into a beautiful autumn day.

Washington, DC

SHE FELT A presence.

Christian filled the door frame.

"What's up?"

"Did you see the news this morning?" he said.

Jade nodded. Jenny Thompson, now forevermore dubbed "Killer Momma," perp-walked into the US District Courthouse for her first court appearance. The video had been plastered on cable and local news and social media throughout the morning.

Half the public demonized her. The other half considered her a hero.

He sat in the only other chair in her office.

"Matt wants to take the kids and move to Minnesota."

"Minnesota?"

He shrugged. "He thinks they can live a normal life there."

"Maybe. Any family there?"

"Nope. But they could never return to a normal life here."

The "Killer Momma" stigma would probably follow Thompson and his kids around for some time. Maybe the rest of their lives.

"How's Amanda?"

"My wife is a strong woman. I think she's accepted what happened. That her sister could commit these murders. The statutory rapes."

"Matt say anything else?"

"Only that Jenny can rot in prison forever as far as he cares." Christian pushed off to leave. "He's already taken Mia and Matt Jr., and moved out of the house. They're living in a hotel now. Said he can't stand to be there."

"Because of Jenny?"

"Yeah. But Tyler, too. He can't even go into his room."

Dante entered her office without knocking, his face unusually pale. "You haven't heard."

Jade started to rise, a horrible premonition overcoming her. "What?"

"Jenny Thompson escaped."

Fairfax, Virginia

HE WIPED A tear from his eye. He and his mother hadn't been close. She was never around. Always working. His dad had told him the story multiple times that when his mother was pregnant with him, she took only one day off work for maternity leave. The day he was born.

Still. The thought of never seeing her again . . .

He parked the BMW near the gate in the vast, empty lot. Grabbing his cap and gloves, he exited the car and jogged toward the field in the distance.

Earlier, he had called the team—what was left of it—together for a fight night. He needed to work off the emotions from his mother's death. But it was more than that. She never saw him fight. And, now, she never would. He was good. Really good. This was a way, for him, to honor her.

He was early.

He stripped off his baseball shirt and shoved the cap back on his head. He donned the MMA gloves and removed his shoes.

He entered the cage.

In the fading light, he spotted an object in the middle of the turf.

It was a cap. He wondered which of his idiot teammates had left it. He picked it up.

And his hand began to shake.

The faded "FC" was written in black magic marker over the bill where he had written it before last season. Seven months ago. He turned it over. Inside the bill, written in the same magic marker, were his initials "WCF."

It was the cap he had lost the night they had beaten up Tyler.

"My son was wearing that when he died."

William spun, dropping the cap.

Mrs. Thompson stood in the darkness at the end of the cage. She held a baseball bat relaxed against her shoulder, as if she were on deck.

Before he could react, she took several quick steps toward him and swung the bat. He didn't get his arms up in time, and the bat smashed into his left temple.

"Fuck!" he yelled as he clutched his head.

"That was for Tyler."

He hit the turf. Head throbbing, the blood seeped through his hands. Another blow to the kidney.

"Ow!"

"You killed my baby!" Whack.

"You took my family away from me!" Whack.

"You even hit on me. You pig!" Whack.

Where's the damn FBI when you need them?

Whack.

Whack.

Whack.

Before the next blow came, a massive body flew over him and tackled Mrs. Thompson.

"Howie?" William whispered. "What took you so long?"

Arlington, Virginia

SATURDAY MORNING, SHE sat with Christian, his wife, Amanda, and three of their kids in the stands of the same arena where Jade had received her fourth-degree black belt two years ago. A lifetime ago. She should be testing for senior fourth-degree by now, but had scarcely trained.

The attention of the three adults was focused on a ring where twelve-year-old boy and girl blue belts competed in a *poomsae* (forms) and sparring tournament. Christian's son, Mark, had not done well in the *poomsae* competition. In fact, none of the boys had finished in the top three. The girls performed the patterns unerringly and with precision, in a way the boys hadn't yet mastered.

Mark competed against a much taller boy for the sparring championship. The score was two to one, in favor of the other boy.

Christian turned to Jade. "Tyler must've lost his cap running away from the cages, or when they beat him up afterward. William accidentally dropped his when he and Andrew dumped Tyler in the front yard."

"That's why William had a brand-new cap with 'FC' on it when Micah and I interviewed him."

He turned back to the match. Three to one. "Jenny figured it out in jail."

Jenny had told them that Tyler had been proud of his baseball cap and had worn it everywhere. That as soon as he'd gotten it, he'd put his initials on it. Though a meticulous housekeeper, in her grief, she hadn't realized it wasn't Tyler's cap on his dresser. Jail had given her plenty of time to remember.

"He almost committed the perfect crime," Christian said. "His fists were his instrument. He didn't leave fingerprints. The witnesses are dead." Three to two. "Way to go, Mark!"

"I wonder why William told me that Tyler and Joshua were gay."

"He was just trying to throw us off. Did you hear about Daniel?"

William wasn't the only one who wouldn't be returning to the team. Coach Lane Daniel had been placed on administrative leave pending an investigation. Based on information supplied by William and Sam and corroborated by their teammates, Daniel had encouraged an environment of hazing. Players had hurled racist, homophobic, and religious insults at each other. The coach had humiliated them for poor play and getting injured. It had become a game to see who could say the meanest, most hurtful things. Although the head coach and assistant coaches hadn't been present during the fight club sessions in the batting cages, they were being held liable because they'd known about them.

At a press conference yesterday, Mr. Trussell, the principal of William Randolph Secondary School, had renamed the baseball complex Tyler's Diamond. The team would play again next year, and he would expect nothing less than another state championship. He'd also announced his retirement from the county school system, effective immediately.

"Mark was afraid of William," Christian said.

"He wanted to send you a message through your son."

"After he gets out of the hospital, I don't think he's going to like prison much."

Four to two.

"I think you're right."

"He's going to be engaging in a whole new level of fight club in a different kind of cage."

Jade grimaced. "Ouch."

"Oh, and the handcuffs Jenny used. An old pair of mine. She must've lifted them from my house." Four to three. "Yes!"

Amanda leaned over. "Can you two stop talking shop for once?" Her smile gave away the fruitlessness of her request.

The judge happened to be Master Won Ho, Jade's instructor. He said, "*Sijak!*"

Mark rushed in and punched the other boy in the abdomen before he had a chance to react. Four to four.

The next point won.

Christian stood. "You got this, Mark!"

Jade grabbed his forearm and guided him down, knowing his muscular frame blocked the view of at least three spectators behind him.

Before Mark could rush in to surprise the boy again, the taller kid used his long leg to fire a side kick to Mark's abdomen. His body lifted in the air, and flew a few feet. His "Oof!" was audible to them in the stands. He fell on his back, clutching his stomach.

Christian started to rise again, and again she forced him to sit. "Like you said, he's got this."

Mark's opponent reached down with both hands to help him up. Mark tapped the boy on the shoulder, thanking him.

During the medal ceremony afterward, the Merritt family and Jade cheered wildly, as Mark bowed for the judge to put the ribbon attached to the silver medal around his neck. The boy's face, unhidden now by headgear, looked as if it would burst with pride.

As she clapped, Jade said to Christian, "I don't think you need to worry about him being bullied in the future. He can take care of himself."

"I didn't tell you what happened a few weeks ago. Mark was drinking from the water fountain, and a couple of guys were giving him a hard time. Mark, still drinking, mind you, lifted his leg and shot a back kick right into the privates of one of them. No one has bothered him since."

Jade nodded, still clapping. "A kid after my own heart."

The White House, Washington, DC

SHE STARED OUT at the array of flowers and the gathered reporters in front of them. She fingered the index cards in her hand. She had occasionally spoken to the press in her role at the FBI, but never to this many. The cameras shuttered, unceasing, like the sound of an old movie projector. Never in her wildest dreams did she think she would ever stand here. In the Rose Garden.

As she stood next to President Whitney Fairchild and the radio talk-show host, Cole Brennan, a young woman spoke from the podium. She had spent her high-school years bullied repeatedly because of her sexual orientation. She recounted the broken noses, the cracked ribs, the bruises, the fear, the anguish, the loneliness. Wanting to die.

Most of those years, she had spent hiding behind a book, a safe place where she could go anywhere she wanted, unmolested. Anywhere but school.

Her story had a happy ending. The girl had persevered through her time in high school, gone on to college, majored in sociology, and was now a counselor working with bullied youth.

The president spoke next.

"October is National Bullying Prevention Month. How appropriate and right that I will be signing legislation that will do just that on this glorious day." She raised her hands, taking in the seventy-five-degree weather. "But first, I want to say a few words and then introduce another special guest.

"Bullying is a major public-health issue. What at one time may have seemed innocuous or just part of growing up, has been proven to have long-term health consequences, such as headaches, stomachaches, sleep deficiencies, and academic failure.

"Thirteen million kids in America are bullied every year. One third of all children. Our children.

"Two hundred and eighty-two thousand kids are bullied each month. One hundred and sixty thousand kids skip school *every day* in this country for fear of being bullied. Ten percent of them drop out or change schools. The leading cause of death for kids under the age of fourteen is suicide.

"It doesn't have to be this way. And it's not a coincidence."

"Everything is connected. When the leaders and potential leaders of this country speak to each other and about each other with disrespect and vitriol, it trickles down through the populace. Civility matters.

"Until our leaders embrace tolerance and inclusion—no matter if you are LGBTQ, overweight, Muslim, physically challenged—none of us will be accepted as individuals. And bystanders do not receive a free pass. Silence equals acquiescence. When a bystander gets involved, bullying stops.

"Now, I would like to bring up a special guest. She is with the Federal Bureau of Investigation. She apprehended the Talk Show Killer, the modern-day Robin Hood, and Killer Momma. May I introduce Special Agent Jade Harrington?"

Fairchild turned to her and smiled, and beckoned her forward.

Jade stood at the podium as the president moved behind her. She placed the index cards with her remarks on the flat surface and raised the microphone.

She did not like to talk about herself, and now she was about to tell the entire world something she had never admitted in public—or private—to anyone but Max.

"Good afternoon. My name is Jade Harrington, and as President Fairchild said, I am an FBI agent." She stood proud and strong. "And I was bullied as a kid."

She relayed to the journalists present and to the nation the story of when she had been beaten up by three of her classmates and left alone in the woods. How a stranger had come by to help. And how she had learned to protect herself by participating in Tae Kwon Do.

"They say what doesn't kill you makes you stronger. If you were bullied as a child, you never forget it. Some of the physical scars may heal, but the emotional ones never do.

"Kids need our protection. I'm proud to be standing here today to witness President Whitney Fairchild's signing of the Federal Anti-Bullying Act, the toughest anti-bullying legislation ever created.

"This bill includes cyberbullying. And it not only protects kids. It will also be a federal crime to bully teachers.

"And to all the kids out there watching, ask for help if you need it. Check out stopbullying.gov. Accept who you are. Find a passion. Be confident. It's okay to be different.

"And, remember, you're not alone."

Jade stepped back from the podium, surprised and pleased at the applause. She joined the group standing behind the president, who moved to sit at a nearby table. She glanced at Cole Brennan next to her and smiled at him.

He leaned toward her. "How's my favorite FBI agent?"

"How's my favorite conservative talk-show host?"

He displayed mock surprise. "You have one?"

Jade smiled. "How's your son?"

"I'm proud of him. He's the lead in his school's musical."

She turned to the president who reached for one of the pens that her body woman, Sarah, had placed on the table.

After signing the document with a flourish, Fairchild beckoned Brennan, Jade, and the young woman who had spoken to join her. The president held out her hand, palm down, and looked at Jade. As a former athlete, Jade needed no instruction about what to do next. She placed her hand on top of the president's. The young woman placed her hand, the scars faint but still noticeable, on top of Jade's. Cole Brennan laid his beefy hand on top. The four of them held this position and smiled, as cameras from the White House press corps clicked away and saved the moment for posterity.

Afterward, Jade leaned close to the president. "May we talk privately? It's about the offer. I have an answer for you."

Washington, DC

OVER THE RAISED beer mugs, she scanned their faces: Christian, Amanda, Pat, Max, Micah, Blake, Dante, and his girlfriend, Laurie. Ethan couldn't make it. His leave had started last week.

"Although it was sometimes painful," Jade said, "we came together as a team and got it done. To the good guys!"

"To the good guys!" the agents in the group yelled.

Glasses clinked all around. At a sports bar across the street from the Bureau, they had annexed two long tables and pushed them together. The place was packed, the Wizards game on all the TVs.

On the screen, the Wizards' big man soared for an offensive rebound and dunked the ball before returning to the floor.

"Told ya!" Christian shouted to her from the other table.

"That condo is still for sale," she yelled back.

"Won't need it."

"No dancing on the table tonight, okay?"

He grinned. "I'll try to control myself."

As they waited for their food, the group sipped their beers and talked.

Blake leaned in to her. "I have to go out of town for a week or so. Business." He looked around at her rowdy crew. "Maybe, we can have a quiet dinner when I get back."

She had invited him to join them after the Rose Garden ceremony that afternoon. Now, she felt Micah, motionless, on the other side of her. Waiting for her answer.

"Maybe," she said.

When Blake turned to talk to Max, Micah lifted his chin toward Blake. "Why is he here?"

"He's a friend," she said.

"I wish I had friends who looked at me like that."

She was saved from responding, by Zoe walking through the front door. Jade smiled and waved her over.

She wasn't alone.

What the—

Behind her sashayed Kyle Madison, whose eyes never left Jade's.

"Look who I found standing in front of the Bureau!" Zoe raised her arms in a vee. "Surprise!"

Jade's mouth parted. And, for some reason, her eyes landed on Dante.

"I see you're taking the edge off just fine," he drawled, putting his arm around Laurie and looking from Micah to Blake to Zoe and, finally, to Kyle. He laughed. "Let me count the ways."

Washington, DC

SHE WOKE UP at her customary time of five a.m. and was at her desk by seven. A high-ranking analyst from the Office of the Director of National Intelligence had just left.

A door to the Oval Office opened. Whitney looked up, surprised that there had been no knock or warning from Sean.

She stood, a premonition, overwhelming her. "Sasha, what's wrong? Is it one of the children?"

She had left Grayson eating breakfast in the residence kitchen, so he was fine. She was scheduled to have lunch with Chandler today. Emma was back at Princeton for her junior year and studying for mid-terms.

Sasha shook her head and inclined her head toward the study. She grabbed the remote and hit the power button. The two women moved in front of the TV, although they both could have seen it perfectly from where they stood.

The channel was set to MSNBC. Rubble and smoke and ash filled the screen. The front of a building had been blown away.

"We're looking at a picture of 30 Rockefeller Plaza in Midtown Manhattan," said the voice-over. "Ten minutes ago, we received reports of a loud explosion. As you can see, it's utter chaos."

The camera cut to people running away from the building, most of them blanketed in gray ash. Some were limping. Some, bleeding. A mother ran with her daughter in her arms, the toddler's pink dress, a sharp contrast with the gray.

Whitney would not be having lunch with her son today.

"Why didn't we foresee this?" she said.

"I don't know."

Whitney moved to the desk and pressed the Intercom button on the phone. "Sean, get the ODNI guy back in here. Now!"

She disconnected and returned to stand next to Sasha. They watched the report in silence for several minutes.

"Sasha," she said, still looking at the television, "you asked me once whether I had something to tell you about the time I lived with my aunt."

"Yes, Madam President."

"I need to tell you something. About Landon Phillips."

Sarah materialized next to Sasha. She, too, stared at the screen in shock before addressing Whitney. "Madam President."

"Sarah, what is it? Sasha and I are in the middle of something."

"It's Blake."

"Tell him to come here ASAP. We should start working on a statement."

"I can't."

"For God's sakes, Sarah, get him in here. Now!"

"I can't, Madam President. He's not here."

"Where is he?" Whitney snapped.

Sarah's finger shook as she pointed at the screen. "He's there."

❋

"My fellow Americans, today was a dark day in our nation's history. In New York City, a suicide bomber walked into the Lower Plaza at the center of the Rockefeller complex and not only took his own life, but killed and injured dozens of innocent people.

"Twenty-seven people were killed and another forty-five injured, five of them in critical condition. This was a terrorist attack. And mark my words, I will use all the powers vested in me and the United States government to track down and bring to justice any other individuals responsible for this heinous attack.

"Members of the press, Blake Haynes, our White House press secretary, stands here every day informing you of events, answering your questions, and speaking for me." Whitney paused. "This morning, he was at MSNBC giving an interview on my behalf about the recent passage of historic legislation: The New New Deal Coalition Act and the Federal Anti-Bullying Act. Blake was critically injured in today's attack." She swallowed. "I ask you to pray for him, and for everyone else who was injured or who lost their lives today at Rockefeller Center Plaza. Pray for their families."

She blamed herself.

He was at the MSNBC studio because of her. His last smile haunted her. The one he gave her the last time she visited his office. She scanned the solemn faces of the reporters scribbling furiously, most of them—if not friends with Blake—at least, shared a common bond with him: love for this country, communicating what was happening within it, the need to perfect the story every day, and the jokes, pranks, and arguments along the way.

She stood at the famous podium in the James S. Brady Press Briefing Room, with the presidential seal and the mock columns behind her. She wrapped up her address to the White House press corps before her, and the nation and the rest of the world through the cameras present in the rear of the room. Another set of cameras to the right of her was aimed at the press, normally ready to capture an aggressive reporter who asked a tough question.

She had insisted that those cameras be turned off today.

She stepped down from the dais and headed toward the door.

Sasha joined her in the hallway.

"Madam President, I need a word."

"It's been a long day. I'm going back to the residence. Can it wait until tomorrow?"

"I don't think it can."

Whitney stopped. "What is it?"

Sasha touched her arm and guided her to an alcove.

"What were you going to tell me about Landon Phillips?"

"It can wait. What's so important?"

"It's Blake."

Whitney felt the blood drain from her face. "He's not—"

Sasha squeezed Whitney's hand, her grip strong and reassuring. "He's still alive, but he's in bad shape."

"I wish there were something I could do."

"Maybe, you can."

Whitney looked at her sharply. "What? Anything. My resources are at his disposal."

"Blake needs a blood transfusion."

"Okay."

"He has a rare blood type that is only shared by two percent of the Caucasian population." Sasha hesitated. "It doesn't match either of his parents' types or his siblings'."

"What can we do for him? Can we find a matching donor quickly?"

"We've located two people with a matching blood type."

"Sasha, what are you waiting for? We can fly one of them or his or her blood to New York. At my personal expense. Do whatever it takes." She exhaled, trying to calm herself. "Who are they?"

Her chief of staff stared into her eyes.

"One is a state legislator in Missouri. The other is you, Madam President."

Philadelphia, Pennsylvania
– One Month Later

"THESE ARE THE times that try men's souls."

Thus began the 240th meeting.

Those famous words kicked off every meeting. The Paine Society, or The Society, as most of its members called it, met in person once a year at an undisclosed location.

A US-based secret group of like-minded individuals, The Society was founded by Thomas Paine in 1776. A founding father and the author of *Common Sense* and *The Age of Reason*, Paine was also the intellectual forefather to liberals, feminists, and progressives. An offshoot of the Illuminati, it was rumored that the two groups had partnered together to start the French revolution.

The Society's mission was to create a progressive new order. Its current objectives, based on Paine's writings and beliefs, were to:

1. Remedy the evils of poverty, illiteracy, and unemployment
2. Provide education, a living wage, relief for the poor, pensions for the elderly, and work for the unemployed
3. Promote liberty, tolerance, community, and social progress

Like most secret organizations, The Society had its rituals, symbols, and passwords. Though every member used an alias, their true identities were not a secret from one another. The current leader glanced out at the ninety-eight members—and one other—seated in chairs throughout the great hall. In the front row sat Franklin, Jefferson (who hated the name, complaining "Might as well call me 'The Farmer.'"), Washington, and Hamilton, who oversaw The Society's finances. The leader also spotted Dickinson, Marshall, and Adams.

"First," Paine continued, "I wish to thank Adams for her service over the last year. Your plan was brilliant. Your execution flawless."

Adams raised a hand to her heart and bowed her head slightly at the praise. She would be quick to point out that her alias was based on Samuel, not John.

Although Adams had received a degree in poli sci at Stanford and a master's degree in public policy from Duke, she had also always loved to take things apart and put them back together. She had done that with her first computer in high school. Always up to mischief, she broke into her friends' AOL accounts and IM'ed crazy stuff to their girlfriends. A gifted hacker, she ventured on the dark side for a time, but then decided to use her skills for good. For social change. She referred to herself as a "white hat, with shades of gray."

It had been Adams's idea to form the Equality One Foundation. The mission of the organization was real: to provide jobs and homes for those who needed them. The source of revenue, donations and gifts from wealthy progressives and liberals, was real as well. The foundation was also used, however, as the vehicle to appropriate one percent of the revenues of conservative companies and foundations and those who supported them and redistribute that money to people in need. The targets each had more wealth than could be spent in a lifetime. It was money they wouldn't miss.

It was also her idea to initially steal from progressive Seattle corporations to throw off the scent for conservative conspiracy theorists.

Hamilton had suggested recruiting Noah Blakeley to be its chairman and then, eventually, president.

The leader thought of Noah Blakeley. While, regrettably, he would be spending the rest of his life in jail, sometimes a life had to be sacrificed for the greater good.

He wasn't, and wouldn't be, the only sacrifice.

Congressman Steven Barrett's death hadn't been an accident.

And Landon Phillips didn't kill him.

The airplane manifest had been altered. The driver's license fabricated to point law enforcement to the desired conclusion. Franklin had seen to it that the FBI's investigation into the death of Representative Barrett had been buried.

"But this was a team effort," the leader continued.

Supervisory Special Agent Ethan Lawson was a good man. His career wasn't over, just on hiatus. The leader nodded to Franklin, who had leaked the information on the TSK and cybertheft cases to Dickinson, the recipient of those leaks.

The leader stood and raised a chalice of wine to the group.

"To duty!"

"To duty!" ninety-eight voices responded.

"To preserve and protect our democracy."

"To preserve and protect our democracy," they repeated.

The leader took a sip of wine, and then beckoned to someone in the front row.

"And now, I'd like to welcome the newest member of The Paine Society. May I introduce Madison?"

As the other members clapped, the inductee stepped forward until he stood before her. Madison had been successful so far in deterring the FBI from pursuing the Noah Blakeley case any further.

The case needed to be closed.

The handsome man smiled, his mesmerizing gray eyes never leaving the leader's, as he slowly unbuttoned his shirt. He held it open to reveal the new tattoo he had received that morning, on the left side of his chiseled chest.

進捗

The End

THE
JADE HARRINGTON
NOVELS

DON'T SPEAK * RULE OF LAW * THE DIVIDE * FEW ARE CHOSEN

*To my mother, Julia, who raised me to be the best that I can be.
And I shall be forever grateful.*

Divide and rule, the politician cries; unite and lead,
is watchword of the wise.

—Johann Wolfgang von Goethe

One Week Ago

Philadelphia, Pennsylvania

THE FIRST ONE to leave the meeting, he jogged down the stone steps of the historic building, cinching the lapels of his coat to ward off the late-autumn chill.

Thanks to "Franklin," his sponsor, he had been inducted into the Paine Society, or the Society, as his fellow members called it. Membership lasted for life, either a member's natural-born life or otherwise. Standing before the ninety-nine other members, he pledged to preserve and protect the democracy of the United States.

How had he ended up in this predicament? Parliamentary government worked just fine, thank you very much. Was assigning him the name "Madison" someone's idea of a joke? The real James Madison, a founding father and the fourth US president, known primarily for his part in drafting the Constitution and the Bill of Rights, was less remembered for leading the fledgling country into war against the newly elected Society member's homeland in 1812.

The present-day "Madison" stopped and stared at his reflection in the window of a closed clothing store. His gray eyes stared back at him.

Under Franklin's direction, Madison had been covertly working for the Society, deterring his boss from pursuing the Robin Hood case and discovering the Society's role in it. His job was to ensure that the case remained closed. Permanently. The warning he issued to Jade Harrington a couple of months ago had not given him pleasure. Over the past year, working alongside her, he discovered that she was one of the good ones. Always trying to do the right thing. An agent he could learn from and aspire to be like someday.

But he had a higher calling, and as his dad used to say, one's calling wasn't a choice.

A SEPTA bus swooshed past. Glancing at his watch, he hurried toward the 30th Street Station to catch the 10:18 p.m. Amtrak to Washington, DC.

He had to report to work at the Federal Bureau of Investigation headquarters first thing tomorrow. And he couldn't be late.

PART I

@TheGodOfVeritas: While thousands of NYC citizens won't be eating dinner tonight, Sebastian Scofield is attending a $1000-a-plate dinner at the NYPL. #shame

Washington, DC

"WHAT DO YOU want to show me?"

Jade Harrington leaned forward, forearms on her thighs. Next to her, Pat Turner sat perched on a seat cushion, a sweater draped over the back of her chair. Photographs of TV characters from *Star Trek*, *The Twilight Zone*, and *The Big Bang Theory* covered the three walls of Pat's cubicle. A space heater under the desk blew hot air against Jade's legs.

The rest of the agents on the fourth floor had left for the night, their cubicles dark.

Pat, gray-haired and in her early fifties, had been with the bureau long enough to understand how to get things done within the bureaucracy. She knew where all the bodies were buried—Jimmy Hoffa's included, it was rumored.

She pointed at the monitor. "Read it for yourself."

After selecting a blue peanut M&M, Jade slipped the small bag back into her pants pocket while she read the text on the screen. It was a report from CART, the bureau's Computer Analysis Response Team.

"What the… ?" She looked at Pat. "This means…"

The other woman nodded. "He didn't do it."

Jade leaned back in the chair and briefly closed her eyes. Not in prayer, but in shame. "How could I make a mistake like this?"

Pat's shoulders sagged. "It wasn't just you. It was all of us."

"But the buck stops with me. Damn!"

She jumped out of the chair and paced back and forth a couple of times before returning to her seat.

"Explain," Jade said.

"We messed up. As I told you months ago, something about fingering Noah Blakeley always nagged at me. All the evidence pointed to him, but his technical skills lacked the proficiency to create a hack as sophisticated as Astrea."

"The Goddess of Justice."

"The perp used Tor to anonymously send malware via email asking for donations from prospective donors of Noah's nonprofit. The program stole the victims' passwords to their online banking sites and then drained their bank accounts. The hacking of Blakeley's computer made it seem like all the transactions originated from there."

"If it wasn't Noah, then who was behind the hack?"

Pat sighed. "*That* we're still working on."

Jade glanced down at her watch. "It's 6:00 p.m. there. I need to make a call." She looked the older woman in the eye. "Good work, Pat."

Popping out of the chair, Jade sprinted down the corridor between cubicles to her office.

CHAPTER TWO

Camp David, near Thurmont, Maryland

" WHY ARE WE here?"

Her younger son stood in a wide stance in the middle of the living room of the main house. Once his bangs had flopped on his forehead, but now his hair was cut close on the sides and in back, the hair on top a little longer. His hands were in the front pockets of his dark blue slacks, and his white shirt was open at the collar, the uniform of a young staffer on the Hill. His red tie was draped over the armrest of a chair.

"Mom," Chandler said, "I'm needed back in Washington. I have work to do."

"I can only imagine," she said. Chandler Fairchild was a legislative aide for Nebraska senator Paul Sampson.

"What's that supposed to mean?"

"Nothing. Although you might want to think about switching to a winning team."

Emma laughed from her chair adjacent to the fireplace.

"Shut up," he said, whirling on her.

"Don't talk to your sister that way," Whitney said.

"Yeah," Emma said. "Don't talk to me that way."

Whitney flashed her daughter a warning look. "Emma."

"He's so stupid, Mom," Emma said.

Grayson, Whitney's husband, sat next to her on the sofa.

"Don't call your brother stupid," he said.

"Well, he is. He doesn't believe half the things he says." She turned to face her brother. "They're using you to provoke Mom. That's the only reason Sampson hired you."

"You think?" Chandler asked.

Leaning toward him as if in confidence, she said, "It wasn't for your political mind."

"That's enough, Emma," said Grayson.

Chandler turned to Whitney. "Are you on the winning team, Mom?"

"History will reflect favorably on my legacy."

"Doesn't seem like you're winning. The New New will die die."

The New New Deal Coalition Act, a modern incarnation of the New Deal implemented by Franklin D. Roosevelt in the 1930s, rendered relief for the unemployed and underemployed poor and middle class, recovery of the American Dream through the provision of universal preschool and a cap on college tuition, and reform of the financial system and the national infrastructure, which would build and repair highways and bridges and provide low-income housing.

"What makes you say that?" Whitney said.

"No reason," he mumbled.

"Take a seat, son," Grayson told him, "and watch your mouth."

"Yeah!" Emma said. "When you hold a real political position, then you can talk. She's your mom and the president. You should respect both."

"Emma, I'm not going to tell you again," Grayson said.

Despite the chastisement, Emma appeared pleased with herself. Chandler, on the other hand, shot each of them a look before sitting in the chair on the other side of the fireplace.

Whitney clasped her hands in her lap. "We have something to tell you."

"You're getting a divorce," Chandler blurted.

This caught Whitney off guard. "What?"

Chandler's leg bobbed up and down with nervous energy. "What else could be important enough to drag us out here to the country? You told us about that psycho, Landon. There's not another sibling we don't know about, is there?" He barked out a laugh.

"Being a victim of rape isn't funny," she said. "You make it seem as if it was my fault."

Under her breath, Emma said, "I told you he was stupid."

Chandler's face softened. "Sorry, Mom."

She looked at her son. He had become a stranger to her. Though Emma, too, had changed. For both of them, Whitney suspected, it was more than the usual pangs of growing up. The pressure of being the president's children—not to mention the children of the first female US president—didn't help. The two siblings had been close until a couple of years ago. They rarely spoke to each other now. When they did, their words weren't kind.

Whitney glanced at her husband. "Landon Phillips," she said carefully, "believed he was my son."

"We know," Chandler said.

"It's not true," Whitney said.

Emma sat up. "What?"

"What's not true?" Chandler said.

Soldiering on, Whitney said, "For some reason, perhaps because of our mutual circumstances—coincidences—he conjured up this entire scenario that I gave him up at birth."

"Why would he do that?" Chandler asked.

"I don't know," Whitney said.

"Who's his biological mother?" Emma asked.

"I don't know that either."

"You don't have another son?" Chandler asked, hopeful.

She pondered, not for the first time, if this was the root cause of her son's drastic personality shift over the last year.

"That's not why you asked us here," Emma said. "There's something else."

"Yes." Another glance at her husband, who winked at her, bestowing a smile that nestled her in a warm blanket. He patted her hand.

"After the terrorist attack on Rockefeller Center," she said, "my press secretary needed a blood transfusion."

"Blake Haynes," Chandler said.

Whitney nodded.

"Wait a minute," he said, standing. "Haynes is your son? Is that what you're saying?"

"Yes."

"Are you sure this time?"

"Watch your tone. I've had enough of your attitude."

Chandler brushed back bangs no longer there. Was he analyzing the political implications as she had when she'd received the test results? Or were his calculations more personal?

"Yes, we're sure," Whitney continued. "DNA testing proved beyond a doubt that Blake is my son, and your half-brother."

"He's not my brother," Chandler said.

"Since his politics are more aligned with Mom's than yours are," Emma said, "maybe you're the one who's adopted."

"Emma!" Whitney said.

"Just kidding, Mom." Emma rose, crossed the room, and sat on the other side of her. Hugging Whitney tightly, she whispered in her ear, "I love you, Mom," before resting her head on Whitney's shoulder.

"I love you too." Whitney laid her cheek on her daughter's head and looked up at her son.

"Are you going public with this?" he asked.

"Not yet. This is between us for now. And Dr. Sangha." Dr. Sati Sangha was the physician to the president.

"Who's the father?" Chandler asked.

She and Grayson had agreed, for now, not to share the identity of the rapist with anyone. Another secret they wouldn't be able to keep for long.

"He wasn't a father," Emma said. "He was a rapist. You should be supporting *her*. Your mom is president of the United States!"

Chandler glared at her, grabbed his tie, and stomped out of the room. Grayson rose to go after him.

"Let him go," Whitney said. "It's a lot to absorb."

Since Chandler had discovered politics during his last year in college, a chasm had opened between Whitney and her son.

She needed to get him back.

CHAPTER THREE

Seattle, Washington

"WILL THE DEFENDANT please rise?"

From the back of the crowded courtroom of the US District Court on Stewart Street, Jade watched as a man at the defense table stood. In a mismatched tan jacket and brown slacks, he appeared bigger than the last time she had seen him, thanks to a prison weight room.

The Asian-American judge said in a soft voice simmering with anger, "Noah Blakeley, you have endured a gross miscarriage of justice." Through enormous owl-like glasses, she scanned the spectators from the dais, the polished wood gleaming. The United States and Washington State flags stood sentry. Jade could've sworn the judge's eyes paused when they landed on her.

Did she recognize Jade as the arresting agent?

The judge's gaze returned to the man before her. "On behalf of the federal government, I am ashamed and apologize for its actions. You are hereby exonerated from the ninety-nine counts of wire, bank, and computer fraud, computer intrusion, aggravated identity theft, and all other charges brought against you." She paused. "I am pleased to tell you, Mr. Blakeley, that you are free to go."

Slamming her gavel once, she gathered her black judicial robes and made a brisk exit through the door behind her.

Noah's legs buckled slightly. With a pained keen, he began to sob.

One of his hands flew to his mouth, while the other found purchase on the table, gripping the edge as if to prevent him from falling. His attorney belatedly moved in closer to hold him up. She handed him his cup of water, and he gulped it gratefully.

There was no one else to catch him. After his conviction, his wife, Diane, had left him. The couple had been childless. His brother, August, and his father, Augustus, weren't present.

Jade slipped out the door and stood across the hall from the courtroom door, waiting. Ten minutes later, Noah and his attorney came out. Up close, Jade saw stubble dotting his cheeks and chin.

This wasn't one of her better ideas. As Noah and his attorney started to walk past her and out the front door of the courthouse, she stepped forward.

"Noah."

He stopped. "Agent Harrington."

"I—"

Noah grabbed both of her hands, his eyes still moist. "I'm glad you're here. I wanted to thank you in person, and here you are."

"For what?" she said, incredulous.

"For never giving up on me. Without you, I would've rotted in that cell forever. I wouldn't have survived."

You were in that cell in the first place because of me.

Letting go of her hands, he hugged her. A desperate hug, like he was clinging to a life raft. Maybe he was.

She extricated herself gently. "What are your plans?"

Shrugging, he said, "Equality One is dead. The concept is still a great idea, but it'd be hard to raise money after what happened. I'm not sure my father will take me back." He hesitated. "Not sure I want him to anyway."

Just before his arrest, Noah had resigned as the chief operating officer of his family's international shipping firm to head up Equality One, a nonprofit that provided jobs and homes to people who needed them.

"You can start something else," she said.

A glance downward. "The stigma from this will follow me wherever I go. For the rest of my life. No matter what I do. But you may be right." He extended his hand. "Thanks again, Agent Harrington."

Jade hesitated and then shook it.

Noah's attorney led him out the front door, where a crowd of reporters and camera crews anxiously awaited his statement on the courthouse steps, and probably his plans to sue the Seattle Police, the City of Seattle, the Federal Bureau of Investigation, and Jade Harrington.

To avoid the crowd, Jade headed for a side door she'd spotted on her way in.

"Agent Harrington."

She turned. A woman she didn't recognize held out a smartphone, the red button indicating that it was recording.

Guarded, Jade said, "Yes?"

"My name is Iyanna Adey. I'm with KIRO7. We've spoken before, on the phone."

Jade remembered. The reporter had asked for a comment on the Robin Hood case. When Jade refused, the woman divulged that Jade's supervisor, Ethan Lawson, had been the source for details regarding that case. Soon thereafter, Ethan took a leave of absence from the bureau.

The black reporter wore expensive three-inch heels and a tight-fitting blue dress, despite the forty-degree weather outside.

Jade had never understood women who wore sleeveless dresses in the winter. Was it to show off their arms? It did appear that Adey worked out. Or was it more comparable to those football players who sported short sleeves in below-freezing temperatures? To prove... something.

Eyeing the phone, Jade said nothing.

Adey gazed through the glass doors at Noah, who spoke into a microphone on a makeshift podium. "Care to comment about Noah Blakeley's release?"

"No."

"You arrested an innocent man and were instrumental in his conviction. I'm giving you a chance to explain your side of the story. To set the record straight. The people have a right to know."

"No comment."

"Are you sure? I can portray you in a positive light."

Sure. Jade started to push past the reporter.

"Come on," Adey said. "We need to stick together. Won't you help a sistah out?"

"Excuse me?"

"It's hard for us to be assigned real stories."

"I can't help you."

"Can't or won't? I'm sure you feel guilty about what happened—"

Jade strode away down the long corridor, what she should have done when the reporter had first called her name.

From behind her, Adey said, "Lovely to finally meet you in person, Agent Harrington. I'm rooting for you."

What did Adey mean by that?

Jade kept walking. Before reaching the door, she glanced back.

Iyanna Adey had joined two people: Detective Kurt McClaine of the Seattle PD, whom Jade had worked with on the Robin Hood and TSK investigations, and Kyle Madison, the managing director of a venture capital firm, a victim in the former case, and someone Jade had become close to during the investigation.

Too close.

Out of the three of them, Kyle was doing most of the talking.

Jade watched them for a moment longer before turning, pressing the release bar to open the door, and stepping out into the misty morning.

CHAPTER FOUR

Washington, DC

THE WALLS OF the private room were painted gray—not an institutional shade but a modern one. Except for the medical equipment, it could have been mistaken for a hotel room.

A man was sitting up in the bed. Most of his face was covered in bandages, except for his eyes, which never left her face.

"Not bad for a hospital room," Whitney said.

"Most people would kill for this room," Blake said, "but I miss the office."

"Not home?"

"My office was my home."

They both pretended to watch the muted television on the wall near the foot of the bed.

The clear liquid in Blake's IV flowed to the needle inserted in the thin skin on the back of his hand.

"Sorry I haven't visited before now," she said.

"You're busy."

"Still."

She'd squeezed in this midday visit between meetings with the CEO of Goldman Sachs and the president of the Service Employees International Union.

"It's only been a couple of weeks," he said. "Any leads?"

Blake Haynes had been at New York City's Rockefeller Center, promoting the New New Deal and the Federal Anti-Bullying Act on MSNBC's morning show, when a suicide bomber blew himself up, killing twenty-seven people and injuring forty-five others. Five more subsequently died from their injuries.

Blake had needed multiple blood transfusions, leading Sasha, Whitney's chief of staff, to discover that he and Whitney shared the same rare blood type. DNA testing proved her maternity.

"No." She hesitated. "I guess we should talk about—"

"Not sure I'm ready," he said.

"I owe you an explanation."

"You don't."

"You deserve to know."

She described the circumstances of his birth. "Seventeen and still in school," she concluded, "I wasn't in a position to raise a child. I did what I thought was best for you."

She didn't mention that she'd wanted an abortion.

Blake listened without interrupting. "My parents were good to me. I never felt adopted." He hesitated. "Who was it? The rapist."

"I don't know," Whitney lied.

His bandaged left hand reached for hers. She slipped her left hand through the side rail, meeting him halfway, their hands resting on the thin bedspread. Their eyes met. For a few moments, they didn't speak. A bond had always connected them, even before she'd learned that he was her son. Now she understood why.

"Thank you," he said, "for donating the blood."

"Better than my liver."

His brow furrowed.

"I'm joking," she said. No need to mention the amount of wine she had consumed since the attack.

He released her hand. "It's going to take some time. To get used to."

"For me too."

"Does the First Gentleman know?"

She nodded.

"What about Chandler and Emma?" he asked.

"Yes."

"How did they take it?"

She made a face.

"That well?"

"They'll need time to adjust." *Especially Chandler.*

"How are things at the office?"

Whitney laughed. "That question is different for my job, isn't it?"

"Guess so," he said, chuckling. "How's Lena doing?"

Lena had been White House press secretary before Whitney poached Blake from his commentator job on a cable news channel. Lena left the administration to form her own public relations firm. When Whitney called after the tragedy to offer her the acting press secretary position, Lena accepted without hesitation.

Whitney wasn't sure she could be so forgiving. She looked at Blake. As either of them.

On the television screen, a reporter spoke outside the hospital. Judy Porter, middle-aged with auburn hair, had been in the press pool accompanying Whitney during the presidential campaign. In uncovering an explosive story about Grayson, her reporting led to the revelation that Whitney had given up a baby for adoption.

Whitney didn't bother turning up the sound on the TV. Judy wasn't finished digging into Whitney's past. And she never would be.

She turned back to Blake. "What's the prognosis?"

"I won't be running marathons anytime soon."

"Seriously."

"Healing."

"Well, that's great news."

"But not fast enough. My recovery will take months."

"Any friends been by?"

"A few."

"Jade?"

The bandages prevented her from seeing his face, but his eyes betrayed him. He shook his head.

Whitney frowned. "That's surprising."

"It's okay." He exhaled. "I can't face her."

"Why not?"

His eyes flashed. "I don't want her to see me like this!"

A knock at the door. Josh McPherson, Whitney's lead secret service special agent, poked his head in. The florescent light from the hallway shone on his bald ebony dome. "Is everything all right, Madam President?"

"I'm fine, Josh. Thank you."

He looked from her to Blake, then shut the door.

"I think you underestimate her." She paused. "I thought there was something between you two."

Shifting his gaze, he said, "So did I."

"She's a hard one to read, that one," Whitney said gently, "but I'm sure she's worth every word. I wouldn't give up just yet."

He didn't respond. He was still looking out the window when she left the room.

CHAPTER FIVE

Washington, DC

AT THE FEDERAL Bureau of Investigation, Acting Special Agent in Charge Jade Harrington was no longer in her old cramped office down the hall. She was now ensconced in Ethan Lawson's office, reviewing a report.

Jade couldn't stop thinking about Noah Blakeley and the part she played in his arrest and conviction. She hadn't forgiven herself. The details of the case replayed on an endless loop in her mind. What had she missed? She wasn't one to make mistakes. Jade was the type of person who could ignore everything she'd done right and focus on the one thing she'd done wrong. Since learning of Noah's innocence, she was figuratively sore from kicking herself.

Leaning back, she slowly spun around once in the high-backed chair. The old FBI emblem on the wall behind her, depicting the scales of justice and the motto Fidelity, Bravery, Integrity remained, as did the mahogany coatrack in the corner. Her former boss's diplomas, of which he was proud—especially the one from *the* George Washington University—were stored with his other personal effects in a cabinet in the credenza.

To an outsider, it appeared to be the temporary office that it was. No diplomas. No family pictures. Jade's only personal items were a basketball paperweight sitting on one of the stacks of files on the desk, a family-size yellow bag of peanut M&M's that she kept in the center drawer, and an old basketball she spun on her finger when she needed to think.

Jade was waiting for Ethan to return from a leave of absence that she didn't believe was voluntary. He couldn't be the source of the leaks on her last two major cases, as she'd been led to believe.

She missed him. His guidance and his unwavering support. Ethan had put her name forward to fill in for him. Jade had no idea when he'd be coming back. He hadn't called, and she suspected he didn't want her to call him.

Around the same time that Ethan left, President Whitney Fairchild had asked Jade to be a special assistant on her staff. Serving in the White House and for the person whose decisions impacted three hundred fifty million lives, even more when you counted the rest of the world, was an honor that Jade hadn't taken lightly. But it was also a temporary position lasting the remainder of Fairchild's presidency, whether that was three more years or seven.

Regardless, the FBI was in her blood now. It was her life. One day Director would be on the nameplate next to her door. Leaving the bureau, even temporarily, would put that aspiration in jeopardy. The decision had been a no-brainer; her eyes were on the prize.

"I don't pay you to daydream."

Jade started at the sound of his voice. "I was thinking," she said. "There's a difference."

Assistant Director, Criminal Investigative Division, Warren Barringer strolled into Ethan's office and heaved one of his haunches onto the desk. She cringed. He was white-haired and overweight, and Jade found it hard not to stare at his white bushy eyebrows.

"We need to talk," he said.

"Okay."

"About your cases…"

"What about them?"

"Solving them. Since you took over, the department's solve rate has decreased."

Jade offered no excuses. He was right.

Although she'd replaced Ethan, she hadn't found someone to replace her, because she'd been too busy doing both jobs. She didn't want to hire someone from the outside in case Ethan returned. Promoting someone on her team was an option, but Pat Turner didn't want to supervise people, Micah Alexander was too green, and neither Christian Merritt nor Dante Carlucci was ready.

Or she wasn't ready to let go. Jade wasn't much of a delegator.

"I hear you," she said.

"You'd better," Barringer said. "I'm not happy about the outcome of the cybertheft case."

Sitting up, she inclined her head, frowning. "But we sent an innocent man to prison."

"It was closed," Barringer said.

"You'd rather keep the wrong—"

"I can always bring Ethan back."

Jade shrugged. "Do it. That's what I want. Why is he on leave anyway?"

"Or install someone more… suitable."

Something within her ignited. Before counting to ten, she said, "What does that mean?"

"You know what I mean."

"I don't."

"This diversity stuff has gone too far."

What was he saying?

He slid off the desk and left, not bothering to shut the door.

Before this interim appointment, she hadn't worked much with Barringer. Clearly unenthused about her promotion, he'd been unnecessarily hard on her. Opening the desk's bottom drawer, she removed the furniture polish and a towel. As she rubbed out the moist spot he'd left, she concluded that the Robin Hood case was the real reason he'd come to her office. Even though truth had won, he wasn't happy with the outcome.

Why?

CHAPTER SIX

New York City, New York

SEBASTIAN SCOFIELD LAUGHED at Hasad Nasir's joke, although the city's mayor wasn't that funny. Earlier that evening, Sebastian had announced—to loud applause from the crowd of wealthy businesspeople, athletes, and entertainers—that he would make a significant donation to the sponsor of the fundraiser, a children's literacy foundation, and match all donations up to $25,000 per gift.

Laughing with Nasir now would make the ask easier later.

Sebastian loved the city. The lights. The people. The restaurants. The museums. Broadway. Times Square. The city that never slept, like him. Working almost one hundred hours a week at his day job as the founder and managing director of a hedge fund, Sebastian lived for the nights. For these dinners. He'd better, since he attended one almost every night. He loved the schmoozing, the clinking of glasses, turning on the charm, meeting new people, asking them for their money. His Rolodex, or, rather, the extensive contact list on his smartphone, contained the names of every influential person in the city, the cause or causes important to them, and what story would yield their maximum donation. Sebastian believed in the causes he supported, especially when they benefited him, his company, or his political beliefs.

But that was his secret.

Most of all, he enjoyed being seen. A picture of him sitting next to and laughing with the mayor would be on the front page of the *New York Times* style section tomorrow. Possibly the front page of the entire paper.

They would definitely make Page Six.

After a main course of filet mignon, curried potatoes, and asparagus, a chocolate hazelnut tart was served for dessert. He admired the building's architecture, including the thirty-foot-high glass and cast-iron dome above him.

The men—and some women—were in tuxes. Other women wore gowns and expensive jewelry. A chamber quartet played quietly in the corner. A server exchanged his empty champagne flute for a full one.

Over the floral centerpiece, he grinned at his wife, sitting across from him at the oblong white linen–covered table. Her black dress matched her hair. The sizable diamonds around her neck, in her earlobes, and on several of her fingers—including the rock on the ring finger of her left hand—sparkled in the light of the multitude of fixtures overhead. She gave him a crisp nod. She understood why he was laughing.

The program was wrapping up. After the host's closing remarks, Sebastian stood and clapped along with everyone else in the ballroom.

Outside, at the top of the steps near the entrance of the New York Public Library, he and his wife, who was bundled in a white fur coat, shook hands, air-kissed both cheeks, and said goodbye to the who's who of the city.

"Scofield!" someone called out to him. "You did well tonight!"

"Thank you!" he said. Someone had told him the event raised over four million dollars.

Touching his wife's back, he bent to whisper in her ear that it was time to go. As he did, a stab of pain spread through his lower back. Odd. In his mid-fifties and in excellent health, he had never suffered from back pains before.

"Excuse me," said a gentleman wearing a formal hat pulled down low over his forehead. He picked up an event program and handed it to Sebastian.

"You dropped this."

"No, I…"

Sebastian's fingers clutched a strange object protruding from his back. His coat was wet. When he brought his fingers in front of his face, they were covered with a dark liquid. If he wasn't mistaken, it looked like blood.

Mine?

Lightheaded, he started to fall. He reached out for his wife to steady himself, his hand leaving red prints on the sleeve of her white fur coat. When he hit the pavement, his wife's scream sounded far away. Footsteps rushed toward him. Images of people towering over him began to converge, then grew hazy. Fingers pressed against his throat, checking for a pulse.

Sebastian Scofield fell into a deep sleep from which he would never wake.

CHAPTER SEVEN

New York City, New York

ACTING LIKE ANY other successful businessman late for another appointment, Devon hurried down the steps, bumping into and apologizing to people. Some of them were on their cell phones and barely noticed. The first scream curdled as Dev ran down 42nd Street. Other screams joined in, as well as loud voices shouting commands. Her deed had been discovered.

She didn't stop running, and she didn't look back.

In the middle of the block, she cut through Bryant Park, her men's dress shoes tapping on the walkway that surrounded the lawn. She passed the fountain and emerged on 40th Street. Slowing her gait, she blended in with the other pedestrians on the crowded sidewalk: businesspeople headed home, theatergoers, shoppers carrying bags, people going out for food and drinks, residents walking their dogs, dog walkers walking other people's dogs.

Androgynous, Dev had always been able to blend in, passing for a man or a woman, white, Hispanic, Asian—even a light-skinned black person. An asset in her career.

Previous and current.

A homeless man covered with a blanket sat against a building, his legs spread in a *V*. Next to him, a trash bag was stuffed with clothes. He was reading a book in the light of a streetlamp. A John Grisham novel. *A Time to Kill.*

How appropriate.

The man met her eyes. Watchful. Wary. Knowing.

Dev stopped and took off the black coat she'd worn to the fundraiser. The victim's blood was most likely on it. Destroying the coat would be the smart thing to do. Instead she handed it down to the man, who gripped the coat in both hands in front of his chest. Jaws clenched, he nodded his head.

A careless act, but she didn't have the heart to burn it or throw it away. Not when he needed it.

While he struggled to his feet to try it on, she continued walking. After a couple more blocks, she hailed a yellow cab. Ten minutes later, she entered the revolving doors of a hotel in Chelsea.

Just inside, a uniformed doorman greeted her. "Welcome back, sir."

"Thank you."

He eyed her tuxedo jacket. "Bit nippy out."

Shrugging her shoulders almost apologetically and praying there wasn't blood on her pants, she said, "Thought I'd risk it." She pointed a thumb vaguely to the south. "Formal dinner in the financial district."

"Well, you're here now," he said. "Good night."

"It already has been."

"Oh… killer deal?"

Dev smiled. "Something like that."

CHAPTER EIGHT

Washington, DC

"YOU WANTED TO see me, boss?"

Jade looked up from the case file she was reading. A major difference in her new role was that she had to be aware of the facts of all the cases in the department, not just her own.

Special Agent Dante Carlucci poked his head into her office. His brown hair was cut short, all the curls gone. He looked handsome. And happy.

She didn't care for the new nickname, but it was better than chiefette or chief.

"Have a seat," she said.

In the guest chair across from her, he leaned back, spreading his long legs. "What's up?"

"Comfortable?"

"Yeah."

He'd missed the rebuke.

"Barringer came to see me," Jade said.

Dante raised an eyebrow but remained silent.

"He's not happy about our close rates. Since Ethan left."

"We're working as hard as we can."

"But not as smart as we can."

Frowning, he said, "What are you saying? You think it's my fault?"

Jade straightened the five pens in front of her into perfect formation. "I've been trying to run this office like Ethan did, but it's not working. There's someone missing."

"Who?"

"Me."

"You?" He shook his head. "I don't get it."

She stopped messing with the pens. "I need someone to replace me."

Dante scowled. "I get it. You're promoting Merritt." He started to rise. "Whatever."

"Sit down," she said, reaching into her center drawer and pulling out a small unopened bag of peanut M&M's. Jade threw it at him.

He caught it and looked at her questioningly. "I don't like M&M's. Or peanuts."

"It's a metaphor. Go put them in my desk."

His expression remained blank.

"Congratulations," she said. "While I'm acting as Ethan's replacement, you're acting as mine."

"Me?"

She nodded.

A grin, wide with wonder, crossed his face, then dissipated. "Is this a joke?"

"No," Jade said. "I think you're ready to take on more responsibility." She waved him away. "Now, go claim my office before I change my mind and give it to Merritt."

He hustled to the door.

"Hey!" she said.

He turned, his expression communicating that he was prepared for the punchline.

"This doesn't mean I like you now or anything."

Dante laughed. "I got it. Boss."

❉

Later that morning, during her team's weekly meeting, Jade listened as each of her staff presented updates on their current caseloads. Sitting around the oval table in the conference room were Christian, Pat, Micah, and Dante. Absent was Max Stover, a behavioral analyst out of Quantico, Virginia, who wasn't technically on the team but worked with them on high-profile serial killer cases.

Interrupting them occasionally to ask for more detail or suggest they pursue a different angle, Jade waited until the updates were finished before saying, "I have an announcement."

"A new case?" Micah asked, his slight British accent a feather against her skin.

"No," she said. "I've been trying to do my job and Ethan's job since he left. It's too much."

"Even for you?" Christian asked.

"I thought you could do everything," Micah said.

"Someone needs to take over my responsibilities," she said.

"Be in with a chance?" Micah asked.

From a chair leaned back at its customary forty-five-degree angle, Dante said, "What the hell does that mean? Can't you speak English?"

The second question was asked without irony.

Shaking his head, Micah stared at Dante. "Hopeless."

"Someday," she said to Micah. Glancing at the rest of the expectant faces, she steeled herself. Inclining her head toward Dante, she said, "Effectively immediately, Dante is your acting supervisor."

Pat stopped typing. She peered over her glasses at Jade and mouthed, "What the fuck?"

With a look of horror, Micah said, "Shite!"

Christian's face transformed from a look of horror to one of amusement. He laughed. "You got me."

Jade said to him, her tone soft, "There wasn't time to tell you."

Christian's laughter died as his eyes narrowed. "You're serious."

She gave a slight nod.

Dante smiled sweetly at Christian. "You may call me 'Daddy' if you'd like."

"Shut up, Dante," Jade said, glaring at him.

Pushing back his chair, Christian shot a look at Jade and walked out of the room without another word.

Micah watched him leave and turned back to Jade. "I feel as if I've seen this movie before."

He was referring to a time during the bullying case, when Christian had words with Dante and walked out of a team meeting.

"Me too," Dante said. "It's my favorite movie."

The White House, Washington, DC

FROM BEHIND THE nineteenth-century *Resolute* desk in the Oval Office, President Whitney Fairchild watched her chief of staff's mouth move, an actor in a silent movie. She was thinking about Blake.

Across from her, Sasha, a former Texas congresswoman, stopped talking, her lips pursed. Whitney prepared to hear it.

"Have you listened to a word I said?" asked Sasha, a look of annoyance on her dark-complexioned face.

"Pardon me?"

"I knew you weren't listening," Sasha said. "I told you that you're too thin, we might have a lead on the attack, and I'm concerned about the New New Deal."

"I missed all that?"

"Apparently. Do I need to tell my momma to bring you some real food? Put some meat on those bones?" Sasha slid her arms down the side of her body and shimmied. "These curves didn't come from eating kale."

Whitney held up her hand. "Stop shimmying."

Her appetite had suffered in the wake of the terrorist attack as she continued to have nothing substantive to report to the press. The guilt wasn't helping either. She still didn't know who was responsible, much less brought anyone to justice as she had promised the American people she would.

None of the usual suspects—ISIS, Al-Qaeda, the Taliban, Hamas, Hezbollah—had claimed responsibility.

Because she'd avoided the press's questions about Blake's condition, citing HIPAA concerns, reporters started calling her aloof. Unapproachable. Cold. Some nicknamed her the Steel Lady in an unflattering mimicry of the Iron Lady, the former prime minister of the United Kingdom, Margaret Thatcher.

Last week's State of the Union address—her first—hadn't gone well. Although the Democrats clapped at everything she said and stood at the scripted moments, the response was subdued. The Republicans hadn't bought what she was selling, and neither had her own party.

"Do you have something to tell me?" Sasha asked.

"As far as?"

"About Blake."

"He's in better spirits."

"That's not what I meant."

I know what you meant.

Not ready to confide in Sasha about Blake's parentage, she said, "'Not knowing when the dawn will come, I open every door.'"

"Who said that?"

"Emily Dickinson."

Hands on her hips, Sasha said, "Are you trying to tell me to not be so curious? To mind my own business? Because you are my business."

"That's the great thing about quotes," Whitney said, smiling. "You can interpret them however you wish. Now, tell me about this lead and why you're worried about the New New Deal."

Washington, DC

SHE'D PUT OFF this visit long enough.

Shifting the Audi to park, Jade exhaled and stared at herself in the rearview mirror, smoothing the top of her light-brown hair. She hadn't seen Blake Haynes since the terrorist attack over six weeks ago. They'd planned to meet up when he returned from New York.

She'd called to check on his condition a few times, but the hospital wouldn't release any information. She could have gained access through the president but didn't want to be obligated to her.

Jade didn't want to owe anyone anything.

The administration, through its acting deputy press secretary, Lena Smith, would not comment on Blake's condition.

Jade and Blake had seen each other before the attack. They weren't dating. Or friends. She wasn't sure what they were, but she enjoyed being with him. He was intelligent. And he made her laugh.

With her promotion, she hadn't had time to visit him until now. At least, that's what she told herself. In truth, she was reluctant to face him, and not because of the changes to his face and body. What was she afraid of? Although she'd been a psych major in college, she didn't spend much time analyzing herself.

She got out of the car and locked it, the beep loud in the silence of the underground parking garage. Her eyes lingered on each gray concrete pillar as she imagined the possibility of someone hiding behind it.

Professional habit.

Jade entered George Washington University Hospital and wended her way to the information desk. Clearing her throat, she waited for the nurse manning the station to look up.

"I'm looking for Blake Haynes."

"Your name?"

"Jade Harrington."

"Relationship to the patient?"

"Uh… friend."

"One moment please."

The young man tapped several computer keys and then spoke into his headset. Personnel were being paged over the intercom system and directed to various areas of the hospital. After a moment, he looked at her.

"What room is he in?" Jade asked.

The nurse searched her eyes. "I'm sorry. You're not on the approved visitor list."

"Can you double-check? I'm sure he wants to see me."

He sighed. "Mr. Haynes left specific instructions. He doesn't want to see you."

"There must be some mistake."

"Maybe so, but you're not seeing him today."

@TheGodOfVeritas: It's no secret that the Carr brothers and their Super PAC are behind the push to repeal the #NewNewDeal They should feel #shame

CHAPTER ELEVEN

The White House, Washington, DC

WHITNEY PICKED AT her Cobb salad.

"You're quiet," Grayson said.

Putting her fork down without eating, she took a sip of wine. "I'm sorry, darling. A lot on my mind. How was your day?"

Grayson sat across from her at the dining room table in the Residence, his light-brown hair grazing his forehead. A fire blazed in the fireplace, warding off the chill. One of her favorite paintings, a woman with a child sitting on her lap, hung over the mantel.

"We're finally making progress," he said. "I met with business leaders from across the Metro area again today, and we're close to finalizing the plan. I'll have something on your desk by the end of the month."

Grayson's cause as First Gentleman—or the First First Man, as the mainstream media called him, or the First Dude, as the alternative media called him—was to oversee a major initiative to provide job and business training to the long-term unemployed. Although initially averse to taking on his First Gentleman duties, he had since embraced them with the same fervor as his former position: CEO of Fairchild Industries, a family-owned global biotechnology company. He'd relinquished the job to one of his brothers so he could join Whitney in the White House.

Refilling her wine glass, she said, "You seem excited about it."

"I am." He reached across the table and touched her hand. His tone was gentle as he said, "Don't you think you should slow down?"

She glanced at the grandfather clock. "A president doesn't have the luxury of slowing down."

"I was talking about the wine."

There was a knock at the front door of the Residence.

Moments later, Sasha entered the dining room, her face strained.

"Madam President, I'm sorry to interrupt."

Whitney set her glass down. "It's fine, Sasha. What is it? The terrorist attack?"

"A false lead."

"Then what?"

"My source on the Hill says Hampton and Sampson secured enough votes to overturn the New New Deal."

Whitney's first thought was not of the time and energy and political capital they'd expended to pass the legislation, but rather of her son and his comment at Camp David.

The New New will die die.

Chandler had known.

CHAPTER TWELVE

Chicago, Illinois

IN A PRIVATE upstairs dining room of the Oak Club, Jared F. Carr Jr. looked across the table at his younger brother.

"Superb steak," Jared said, wiping his mouth with a white linen napkin.

"That stuff will kill you eventually."

"At least I'll die happy. Unlike you. Your dying wish will be for a juicy double cheeseburger. With cheese fries."

"I doubt that," Jason Carr said.

The Oak Club was founded over a century ago by Yale alumni living in Chicago. It provided a place for members and their guests to meet, dine, and socialize in a refined and exclusive atmosphere in the city's North End.

The server entered and cleared their dinner plates. The two men were silent as he returned carrying a tray containing two glasses of port and clipped cigars. After lighting the cigars, the server retreated. Technically it was a nonsmoking room, but the federal, state, city, and club regulations didn't apply to them.

Rules were for those without money.

Except for their expensive dress, the brothers were nothing alike. Jared was blond, portly, and a Yale alumnus, like their father and his father before him. Jason had dark hair and a runner's physique, and had graduated from the University of Illinois business school, to their parents' eternal regret. Jared, married with three children, lived in the Chicago suburb of Glencoe, while Jason, a lifelong bachelor, owned a penthouse condo overlooking Lake Michigan in Chicago's Lakeshore neighborhood. Often photographed with wealthy women—businesswomen, socialites, models, celebrities, athletes—Jason never managed to keep a relationship going more than a few months. The press constantly speculated on when he would settle down and who the lucky woman would be.

Whenever he read such speculation, Jared laughed. His brother would never settle down with any woman. Jason was gay. Although he wasn't out, he wasn't so deep in the closet that he would enter into a sham marriage. Jason's sexual orientation was ironic—their nonprofit organization, Freedom of America (FOA), financially backed the Defense of Marriage Act in the nineties.

At the time, Jason was too busy working for their father's real estate investment firm to date anyone. In correlation with the nation's grudging recognition of gay relationships and, finally, gay marriage, Jason began seeing men discreetly, but he still hadn't come out to his family, including his brother. Jared knew only because of reports submitted by private investigators. It wasn't personal. Jared investigated everyone. He could never possess too much information about someone, even his flesh and blood.

After battling the issue of gay marriage for decades, Jared realized that Jason's sexuality didn't matter to him. When Cole Brennan had tried to resurrect the Defense of Marriage Act II a couple of years ago, Jared quietly ordered that the topic be removed from FOA's website and all its promotional materials. It was a lost cause. He only spent his time and money on issues he could win. If Jason noticed the change, he never said anything.

Not even a thank you.

Admiring the cigar, Jared said, "A wonderful day."

"Yes, it was," Jason said.

"The free market reigns," said Jared, taking a slow, sensuous puff.

"Did you talk to Hampton?"

Jared exhaled. "I did. The Senate majority leader was a good solider on this one."

"The house we bought him on Hilton Head didn't hurt."

"True."

Jason eyed his brother. "What's next?"

"Not sure yet. I'm going to enjoy tonight and think about that tomorrow." After a while, he placed the cigar in the ashtray's stirrup. "I need to go." Jared didn't like to keep his wife, Lisa, waiting. He stood. "Are you coming?"

"No," Jason said. "I think I'll stay here and enjoy this." He held up his cigar. "Then go down to the bar."

From the door, Jared turned and gave his younger brother a pointed look. "Be careful."

Jason gave him a sad smile and saluted. "I always am."

Returning the salute, Jared thanked God again that he was straight. Living with an affliction like Jason's couldn't be easy.

Downstairs, he retrieved his coat, bracing himself before going out into the sub-zero temperature. As he waited for the valet to bring his car around, he thought about what his sources on the Hill had told him earlier about the overturning of the overreaching New New Deal Coalition Act.

They had the votes.

Although Jared was the brains behind the brothers, he and Jason had never received the credit they deserved for their influence on US conservative politics. But that was fine. They didn't do it for the glory but for love of their country.

He disdained both major US political parties. In truth, Jared was a Libertarian, believing government had no role in the lives of the American people—period. But to make his dreams a reality, he had to choose a side. Today's victory, one of many since his ideology supplanted that of his father's Republican Party, was only the beginning. Jared wouldn't stop until he'd amassed his fair share of the economic pie, which, to him, meant the whole pie.

A homeless man shuffled toward him, the bottom of his tattered pants dragging behind him on the sidewalk. He carried a cardboard sign painted in red letters: This is what invisible looks like. The doorman of the club started toward the man. Jared waved him off. "It's okay."

The doorman returned to his place by the front door.

The homeless man's eyes shone clear in his dirty face. He held his hand out. "I need to eat too."

"Get a job," Jared said, not unkindly. "Then you could buy food, and it will make you feel better about yourself. Give you confidence and self-esteem."

This surprised the homeless man. Perhaps no one had ever given him this advice.

The man tilted his head. "Why do you think I don't have a job?"

This brought Jared up short. While formulating a response to this improbable question, the man whipped out a knife from under his thin sweatshirt—unsuitable for the weather, Jared noted belatedly—and stabbed Jared in the chest three times in rapid succession.

Clutching the knife in both hands, Jared hit the pavement face-first, the blood flooding through his fingers as the knife burrowed further into his body.

"Hey!" the doorman yelled.

The homeless man flipped up the bottom of Jared's coat, ripped the wallet out of his back pocket, and took off at a run, the sound of his footsteps receding into the night.

Kneeling next to Jared, the doorman said into his cell phone, "A man's been stabbed. In front of the Oak Club. Hurry." He recited the address and hung up. "Mr. Carr, you're going to be all right. An ambulance is on its way."

It wasn't true.

Jared Carr had known he didn't have much time left. As the darkness descended for the final time, he mourned for himself. He would never seize the entire pie.

CHAPTER THIRTEEN

Chicago, Illinois

DEV RAN AWAY, knowing the doorman would choose to try to save the life of a coveted member of the club—and reap all the rewards that that would entail—rather than apprehend her. He wouldn't have caught her anyway. She kept herself in peak condition, not only for her work, but for herself, taking pride in her long, sinewy muscles. The absence of body fat.

Before crossing the street, she risked a brief glance over her shoulder. She'd been right. The doorman was bent over, attending to Carr.

Ignoring stoplights, she sprinted another four blocks before slowing down to a homeless-man shuffle. She passed a delivery van, then ducked into an alley that bisected the block between skyscraper office buildings. Littered with takeout cartons, crumpled candy wrappers, rotting garbage, and empty liquor bottles, the alley was shrouded in darkness, most of the lights extinguished on the lower floors.

The number of wailing sirens in the distance multiplied. Reaching behind a dumpster, Dev retrieved the bag she'd stashed there earlier. A car drove by the alley's entrance. She shed the homeless persona, donned a T-shirt over her chest-compression wrap, and slipped on an Under Armour tracksuit. As she changed, she ignored the pitter-patter of rats scurrying nearby. They were looking for food like everyone else.

Balling up the rags and tucking them under her arm like a football, she ran out of the alley and back into the icy wind.

Security gates protected the storefronts at this time of night. Every few blocks, she deposited an article of clothing into a trash can. Midblock, some homeless guys and one woman gathered around a blazing barrel drum.

Serendipity.

They stared but said nothing as she approached. Eying each of them, she threw the remainder of the clothes, including the sweatshirt, in the drum.

One man said, "Thanks."

A police car rushed past on its way to the crime scene. She followed it with her eyes before resuming her run in the opposite direction.

While she ran the remaining six blocks, she daydreamed about a woman.

How she would punish her when she saw her again.

The doorman of the hotel stood under the awning and opened the front door for Dev. "Evening, sir. How was your run?"

"Exhilarating," she said.

PART II

Washington, DC

"COME ON!" MICAH shouted down to her.

The Potomac River below her, Jade looked up at his backside, which was snug in running tights, five steps ahead of her on the Watergate Steps. This was their hundredth set.

He jogged in place at the top, waiting for her. "Slow poke."

"We're not done," she said.

Taking off at a sprint, she passed him, calling over her shoulder, "Last one to the memorial is a chump!"

"I presume that's not a good thing," he shouted back.

They ran along Lincoln Memorial Circle, avoiding the midday traffic, and ended up at the plaza at the bottom of the monument. It was nearly empty. Few tourists had braved the bitter January cold.

Micah and Jade shared a quick glance and, without a word, sprinted up the fifty-eight steps.

Jade arrived at the top first and shot both arms up like Rocky Balboa in the first *Rocky* movie, one of her father's favorites. She shuffled her feet and delivered some air punches at Micah as she hummed the movie's theme song.

He shook his head. "Gracious. You look like the female Creed."

At the reference to the main character and the name of one of the sequels, she stopped shuffling and bowed. "When you got it—"

"You did okay," Micah said, pausing, "for a girl."

He took off running—the man wasn't stupid—to the other side and hid behind one of the thirty-six Doric columns, each of which represented a state in the Union at the time of President Abraham Lincoln's death.

Jade laughed and jogged over to sit beside him on the top step. "Smart man."

He smiled, his white teeth bright against his mocha skin. "I inherited my brains from my mum."

Staring out at the reflecting pool, the World War II Memorial, and the Washington Monument, she said, "You don't talk much about your parents."

"Neither do you."

"Touché."

Her cell phone vibrated in her pocket, saving them both from a topic neither of them wished to discuss.

"What's up?" she said.

"A detective from Chicago PD called," Dante said, "asking for you. Lieutenant Tom Blanchard."

"What did he want?"

"He has a case that might interest you."

Jade had solved three high-profile cases over the last two years—well, two, if you didn't count the Robin Hood case. Consequently, members of law enforcement from all over the country called her office requesting her counsel. She removed her hair tie and shook out her shoulder-length hair.

"What is it?"

"He caught the Jared Carr case."

"And?"

"Blanchard just got off the phone with a detective in New York City."

This caught her attention. "New York?"

"The investment guy? Knifed outside the library? Sebastian—"

"Scofield."

"There are some similarities to their cases."

Rising, she stepped back up to the monument level and started pacing. "How so?"

"Both victims were stabbed. Knives left in the body. He said that his crime looked like a robbery."

Jade stopped pacing. "Looked like?"

"Yeah," Dante said. "He didn't think robbery had anything to do with it."

✼

Forty-five minutes after hanging up the phone with Dante, Jade stared at a photograph on her computer screen of the late Jared Carr. While she and Micah had sprinted from the memorial to the FBI gym to take (separate) showers, Lieutenant Tom Blanchard had emailed Dante part of the case file, which he'd forwarded to her.

Carr's body was pitched forward, face-first, on the sidewalk, a pool of blood in a semicircle beneath him. She clicked the arrow key for the next photograph. This angle was from behind him. The back of his coat was lifted, his pants pocket ripped, apparently empty. His clothes looked expensive, the bottom of his dress shoes barely worn. The autopsy photos revealed that he was obese. Wealth afforded him suits that masked his girth.

Carr had been stabbed three times in the chest. The medical examiner found evidence of prostate cancer, which had metastasized to other organs.

Had Carr known? Was that what had driven him? Impending death?

She called Dante and told him to come to her office.

"What did you think?" she asked after he was seated.

"He was stabbed in the aorta. The other two strikes were overkill. I called the Chicago ME, who said Carr would've bled out in two to thirty minutes from the first wound."

"Where did it happen?"

"The Oak Club. A membership club downtown."

"Any witnesses?"

"Only the doorman."

"Did he check out?"

"Said Carr was talking to a homeless guy, then said something that seemed to agitate the other man. The guy then took out a knife and stabbed Carr."

"Camera?"

"Yeah. Aimed at the front of the club. Corroborated everything he said."

She sat up. "And the perp?"

"Blanchard said you can see him shuffle into view, exchange words with Carr, and then stab the hell out of him."

"We need that recording."

Dante didn't move. "I'll get it, but Blanchard said you can't see anything. The perp's back is to the camera, and he's wearing a hoodie."

She sat back, momentarily deflated. "Any prints on the knife?"

Dante shook his head.

"We need the number of the detective in New York," Jade said.

Fishing something out of his pocket, he held up a slip of paper.

❋

Later, Jade poked her head into his office. "Busy?"

Dante looked up from his computer. "Nope."

She frowned. "You should be."

"I should've said, 'Not too busy for you.' What's up?"

"That's better," she said.

She settled into the only other chair in her old cramped office, which Dante had made his own. Photographs of him and his live-in girlfriend, Laurie, sat on top of his desk and the one filing cabinet. She was the reason he was so damn happy. Until he'd met her, Dante had hit on every woman under fifty. Including Jade. He hadn't appreciated her rebuff at the time, but he eventually got over it.

A photograph of his favorite chef, Eric Ripert, hung on the wall behind him—French cooking was Dante's hobby—as well as a poster of his father, Marco Carlucci, soaring for a jump shot in his Italian professional basketball league uniform. He'd played his twilight years in the NBA.

"Awesome," Jade said, admiring the poster. Turning to him, "Seen Christian?"

Dante averted his eyes. "He took the week off."

She waited for him to look at her. "We need to keep him. He's a key member of this team. I expect you to make that a priority."

"I got it."

She said, "Talk to me about Scofield."

"Talked to a Detective Katz, NYPD. Unlike with Carr, there were lots of witnesses, including Scofield's wife. She claimed a gentleman bumped into her husband seemingly by accident. Only after he fell and she saw the knife did she realize her husband had been stabbed in the back."

"Any visual on the perp?"

"No one got a decent look at his face. He was wearing a dark coat, slacks, and a hat. Might've attended the event."

"Katz doesn't know?"

"Not confirmed yet."

"Anyone see anything else?"

"No," he said.

They had watched the recording of Carr's murder earlier. As Blanchard had warned, it hadn't yielded much. The perp's back was turned the entire time. He appeared to be about five ten, medium build. The dark-gray hoodie didn't have any recognizable markings or logos. It was impossible to see in which direction he had run.

"So… one vic stabbed three times in the chest by a homeless guy. The other once in the back by a possible fundraiser attendee. I presume Scofield was also white and wealthy." Jade waited for him to nod. "Both of them probably attracted a lot of haters. Why does Blanchard think these cases are connected?"

"The knives were left in both victims," Dante said.

She shrugged. "Still."

"They were the same brand."

CHAPTER FIFTEEN

The White House, Washington, DC

THE FOLLOWING MORNING, Whitney and Sasha stood close together in front of the television on the credenza in Whitney's private study off the Oval Office. She did the majority of her work in this room, the Oval being reserved for meetings and photo ops.

On the TV, men and women of the US House of Representatives walked to and from the podium to cast their votes in a synchronized process. At the bottom of the screen, in a large archaic font reminiscent of the halftime score of a seventies college basketball game, were the words H-5861, Repeal of the New New Deal Coalition Act. Underneath, the count: Yeas 86, Nays 63, the numbers ticking up by the second.

The two women didn't speak, knowing what was at stake: Whitney's signature legislation that would define her presidency and preserve her legacy. Everything that Whitney, Sasha, and her entire team had worked for during the last year would be for naught. As would Blake's personal sacrifice.

"How's it going?"

An African-American woman wearing a black dress and a gold brooch stood at the door, her expression grim. Her straightened hair, high cheekbones, broad forehead, and strong physical features, coupled with her inner strength, gave her a presence. She was the kind of person who, when she walked into a room, everyone stopped talking. A woman not to be messed with.

Whitney waved her in.

After forcing Vice President Xavier Fernandez to resign, Whitney had nominated Josephine "Jo" Bates to replace him. In accordance with the 25th Amendment, a majority in both houses of Congress—despite Republican control—quickly confirmed Jo. Everyone involved realized the urgency of filling the role to ensure a smooth presidential succession.

A popular senator from California, Jo chaired the Congressional Black Caucus. She was a former lawyer and fierce advocate for gender equity. She and Whitney had cosponsored the Equal Rights Amendment, the watershed legislation that finally gave women equal rights in the United States. They had become close while working together on the ERA, and because of them, federal and state laws were changing to eliminate bias toward men.

Equal pay was now the law of the land.

Whitney chose Jo because of her qualifications, not her Northern California constituents. Their party had a lock on those. Jo was intelligent, a savvy negotiator, fearless, a smart political operative and insider, and she didn't hesitate to speak her mind. She also possessed a rare trait for a politician these days: integrity.

Now the first woman, the first *black* woman to hold the second-highest office in the federal government, Jo—like Whitney—understood that a lot rode on her performance. The same opportunity for all the women and women of color that came after her would depend on her success.

Crossing the room, Jo stood next to them. "This Congress didn't waste any time."

The Yeas maintained, then grew their lead.

The final vote count: 389 Yeas, 146 Nays.

"That's it then," Sasha said.

Whitney remained silent, afraid her voice would betray her roiling emotions.

"It still needs to pass the Senate," Jo said, always the fighter.

The camera cut to a man standing in a hallway of the Capitol, a Corinthian column behind him. Senator Eric Hampton, his slicked black hair parted on the side, wore a dark suit and his ever-present red tie.

Jo said, "He's smiling as if he won the lottery."

"He probably did," Sasha said.

"Turn up the sound," said Whitney.

Sasha grabbed the remote off a nearby table. "I can't stand his whiny voice."

"You and me both," said Jo.

In answer to the commentator's question, Hampton said, "This is a wonderful day for democracy, individual independence, and capitalism. Supply and demand should determine winners and losers in the marketplace—not the government."

"There shouldn't be winners and losers among the American people," Sasha said, her eyes not leaving the screen.

"Senator," the commentator said, "when will the bill be voted on by the Senate?"

Hampton smoothed his tie. "We've promised a swift vote all along. This will be on the docket tomorrow."

Whitney gasped. "Tomorrow!"

"He's not wasting any time either," Sasha said. "The little twit."

"Mute it, please, Sasha," Whitney said.

Sasha retracted her shoulders, preparing to strike.

"Not you," Whitney said, "the television." She moved to the chair behind her desk and sat heavily.

"I'm sorry, Madam President," said Sasha. "I know how much this legislation means to you."

Whitney picked up a letter opener made of wood and pewter and gently tapped it against her hand. "It's not about *me*. It's about all the people who would have been positively affected by this legislation."

Income inequality started increasing in the 1970s and had widened ever since. The disparity had grown to the point that her economic advisors reported to her on the performance of the economy for the wealthiest one percent of the population separately from everyone else. During the presidential campaign, Whitney had called the gap the "Great Divide."

Now there was nothing to stop the economic divide from continuing to grow unabated.

And becoming permanent.

Jo came to stand in front of Whitney's desk. "The New New Deal is a worthy piece of legislation."

"So I keep hearing," Whitney said.

"It's a good law," Jo said. "We need to fight for it. Even if the Senate repeals it. A lot of people supported this bill. Inside and outside the Beltway. We might not be able to resurrect it again in its entirety, but we can implement the parts that matter. I'm willing to do whatever I can to make that happen."

Sasha stood next to Jo. "Me too."

Whitney's pulse quickened as she observed the quiet confidence on the faces of her vice president and chief of staff. "Let's get to work."

CHAPTER SIXTEEN

Washington, DC

"HERE'S THE INFORMATION on Carr," Pat said.

"Have a seat," Jade said. "Should I bring Dante in?"

Pat settled in Jade's guest chair and said, "Updated him earlier."

"Go on then."

Pat opened her laptop. "Jared and Jason Carr own a real estate firm, estimated to be the fifth-largest private company worldwide. Their holdings span across the United States, with properties in Chicago, New York, DC, LA, San Francisco, and almost every major international city, including London, Berlin, Madrid, Rio de Janeiro, Johannesburg, and Singapore."

"Sounds like beaucoup bucks."

"Individually, they are the eleventh and twelfth wealthiest people in the world, worth roughly about forty-five *billion* dollars. Each. They're not in the one percent. We're talking about the point-oh-oh-one percent.

"They started a foundation called Freedom of America, a major GOP donor, that supports senatorial, house, gubernatorial, and a lot of down-ballot races: state, local, even school boards."

Jade considered this. "They don't leave anything to chance."

"I think that's the plan. The organization's operations are shrouded in secrecy, but I found out that they fund other foundations that support limited government, lower taxes, elimination of regulation, and eradication of services for the poor and needy. For all intents and purposes, Freedom of America *is* the Republican National Committee."

"Anything else?"

"They secretly fund grassroots protesters at events. Cyber believes they use Russian hackers to influence Americans on social media to support their causes."

"And they call themselves patriots," Jade said.

Pat clicked a few keys on her keyboard. "Jared Junior was an outspoken climate-change denier and a vocal opponent of the Department of Housing and Urban Development. During the sixties, HUD cited their father, Jared Senior, for housing discrimination against minorities who tried to rent apartments in buildings he owned in New York City. Senior fought the violations for years. The case wound up in the Supreme Court."

"What happened?"

"He lost. His firm shelled out millions of dollars in fines and reparations. The stress eventually killed him. Heart attack."

"And this initiated Junior's beliefs in limited government?"

"More than that," Pat said. "Junior never forgot what happened to his father, and he never forgave the US government."

CHAPTER SEVENTEEN

Chicago, Illinois

DANTE WHISTLED UNDER his breath. "Worth killing for?"

"People have killed for less," Jade said.

She hadn't comprehended real wealth until that moment. Standing in the foyer of the home of Jared Carr Jr., she gazed at the marble flooring, the two sitting areas, and the side table, over which hung an oval mirror in a gilded frame. A massive chandelier dangled overhead. Dual half-circle staircases with shiny banisters led to the second floor. The foyer alone was almost the same size as the first floor of Jade's townhouse.

The gray-haired African-American butler nodded at her before leading them to a spacious living room. Jade paused at the threshold.

An older woman with coiffed white hair and a plain but expensive red dress sat on a couch between a middle-aged man in a sweater, collared shirt, and slacks, and a middle-aged woman in black tights with a long, pale-blue sweater shirt. Her medium-length dyed-blonde hair was cut at a severe angle to her shoulders.

Beyond them, an expansive fireplace displayed family photos on the mantel. A grand piano occupied one corner. Heavy draperies covered the tall windows. There were two sets of French doors: one leading outside, the other to a sun room.

Jade felt as if she were on the set of *Downton Abbey*.

The man rose to greet them.

"Thank you, Charles," he said to the butler. To Jade and Dante, he said, "I'm Jason Carr."

His eyes met hers but didn't linger. Jade shook his hand and introduced them.

"Thanks for seeing us," she said.

"This is Jared's wife, Lisa, and my mother, Judith. Please," he said, gesturing to the chairs on either side of the glass coffee table, which had a ceramic vase in the middle. He returned to his seat. One glass, halfway full of amber liquid, rested on a coaster on the table. "We'll do whatever we can to help find Jared's killer. What would you like to know?"

"Tell us about what happened that night."

"He and I met at the club after work."

"Club?"

An indulgent smile. "Sorry. The Oak Club. Near our office. When we were both in town, we stopped by there a couple of times a week."

"To do what?" Dante asked.

Jason arched an eyebrow, as if he'd never been asked that question.

Many women would kill for those eyebrows.

"Our weekly dinner," Jason replied. "Sometimes lunch. Our lives are hectic; it was our time to catch up. Or unwind. To discuss business outside of the office and away from prying ears."

Jade frowned. "Your staff eavesdropped on your conversations?"

He crossed his legs. "Or competitors. You can never be too careful these days."

"Did you discuss business that night?"

"Yes."

"What did you talk about?" Dante asked.

"It has no bearing on what happened to Jared."

"Let us be the judge of that," Jade said.

Jason reached for his drink, took a sip, and replaced the glass. "We were celebrating."

"What?" Dante asked.

"The overturning of Whitney's Folly."

"The New New Deal?" Jade asked.

"There was nothing new about it."

"Why were you celebrating its repeal?"

"Because it righted a wrong."

"How so?"

"It was another example of government overreach being crammed down the throats of the American people. Never should've passed."

"And the overturning of it benefited your business."

"That too."

"So you celebrated," Dante said, waving his small notebook. "What happened after that?"

"Jared left to come home."

"What did you do?" Jade asked.

"Stayed for a drink at the bar."

"Were you meeting someone there?" Jade asked.

"My assistant stopped by to deliver some papers."

"How did you find out about your brother?"

"The doorman came running into the lobby screaming, 'He's dead!' I heard him all the way in the bar. I didn't think much of it at first. We have so many old members who, frankly, are dying off all the time."

"Did he come find you?"

Jason leaned forward, picked up his glass, and drained its contents. "He stood in front of me, covered in my brother's blood, and said, 'I tried.'" In a hushed voice, Jason said, "That's when I realized he was talking about Jared."

Lisa glanced down at the table.

Jade directed the next question at her. "Mrs. Carr, did your husband ever mention any enemies, competitors? Anything like that?"

"Why would you ask that?" she responded. "He was murdered by a homeless person."

"Please answer the question."

"Of course he did," Judith Carr interjected. "Every liberal in the country hated my son. Many in the GOP too. If it turns out to be premeditated, there would be a long list of suspects."

The older woman sat up straight, her hands clasped casually in her lap, her purse leaning against her hip.

"'Premeditated' isn't a word we often hear from civilians," Jade said.

"I watch all those shows on TV," Judith said, nodding with satisfaction. "Even the documentary about you, Ms. Harrington. What was it called?" She thought for a moment. "*Don't Speak*. Don't worry, I can speak your language."

Under different circumstances, Jade would have enjoyed this conversation with Judith Carr. "Do you think it was premeditated?"

"Who's to say? It could have been exactly as it appeared. A homeless man robbed my son for money. But it wasn't a secret that my boys frequented the club, as their father did before them. Jared took the same route to work every day."

"How do you know?"

"I'm a mother." She nodded at Jason. "I told them to vary their routes. Their routines. My sons say I'm paranoid from watching too many crime shows."

Jason sighed. "You were right, Mother."

Jade turned back to Jared's widow. "Mrs. Carr, do you know of anyone who wanted to hurt your husband?"

"He rubbed some people the wrong way," Lisa said. "You should speak with the head of security at the firm. Jared and I sent any threats we received to him."

Jason gave Dante the security head's name.

"What was Jared like, Mrs. Carr?" Jade asked.

The question was for Lisa, but Judith Carr answered.

"Disciplined," she said. "Methodical. Competitive. Jared hated to lose. Sore loser, that one."

"Mother…," said Jason.

"When he was ten, he lost his first race ever at a championship meet. Never swam again for the rest of his life." She touched her purse, as if to check that it was still there. "He was such an excellent swimmer."

"Did he ever get angry?" Dante asked. "As an adult? Lose his temper?"

"Sure. He had tantrums, but if you ignored him, he'd get over it. At least, that's what I did. You couldn't win an argument with him. No matter what. Not like Jason here, who you can reason with."

She patted her son's knee.

"Jason was the opposite," Judith continued. "Always sneaking off to be alone with his books. Jared always did what was expected of him. Jason was a little rebellious."

"Mother, that's enough. This isn't about me." Grabbing his glass, he walked over to the small bar between the French doors.

"You're right," Judith said. "This is about Jared." To Jade, "Will you find the man who killed my son?"

Did they know Jared had cancer and would have died soon anyway?

"We'll do our best. Is there anything else you can tell us?" Jade asked.

The two women seated on the sofa shook their heads.

"The answer appears to be no," Jason said. He drained his fresh drink and set the glass down too hard on the bar. "Charles will show you out."

❁

"What do you think?" Jade said, glancing at Dante as she fastened her seatbelt.

Although the plane was accelerating for takeoff, his seatbelt remained unfastened. "Seemed nervous."

"Like he was anxious to get rid of us."

Dante raised an eyebrow. "How would he tie in to the other murder, though?"

"Not sure. We need to check him out."

"Will do."

"His mom might be right."

"About what?"

"If they ate dinner there once a week, someone could've studied their patterns. Knew they were going to be there."

He closed his eyes. "If we're not careful, she might put us out of work."

She tapped him on the shoulder and waited for him to open his eyes before she glanced down at his seatbelt. "Are you going to buckle that?"

"Didn't know you cared."

"I don't," she said. "I'm asking for Christian."

@TheGodOfVeritas: Word on the street is that Finn Hurley is in secret meetings with Senator Hampton. I wonder what Congress will do next to boost her business. #shame

CHAPTER EIGHTEEN

Arlington, Virginia

FEW CYCLISTS BRAVED the cold. The odometer showed ten miles. Five to go before she arrived at her home in Old Town Alexandria. She picked up the pace as she headed south on the gravel path that paralleled GW Parkway, the mud-brown Potomac River on her left. Ordinarily, she rode ten miles every morning, but today she strove for fifteen. Because of her ever-rising stress level? Was she procrastinating going to work?

She pedaled harder.

The board of directors was unhappy with last quarter's financial performance: flat sales, escalating payroll costs, and a decline in earnings.

They're shortsighted.

She'd never understood why American markets focused only on a public company's last quarter. She had negotiated several new client contracts, increasing the backlog, which meant future revenues. One was a lucrative contract with the federal government. She ran her company for the long term, a perspective that was hard to keep in this market environment.

She wanted her "baby" to be around long after she was gone.

Six months ago, she increased her employees' pay. Not out of kindness, but to retain her top performers before they left to seek higher wages elsewhere. Was she rewarded for her efforts? No. Some of her best talent still left, and profits fell. To compensate, she'd need to increase her fees, which would alienate most of her clients. She couldn't win.

The one bright side: she was still running the company.

Her front tire hit a rock. In an attempt to control the bicycle, she overcorrected. As she fell, she clicked out of the pedals and landed on the grass adjacent to the path, the cycle still between her legs.

As dew seeped into her cycling clothes, she assessed the damage. She wasn't too worried. She wore a helmet. Nothing was broken or even scratched, the grass landing having softened the blow. Sitting up, she examined the bicycle. The front tire was whacked out of alignment, but otherwise things looked okay. Easy to fix.

She heard the clicking of an approaching bicycle.

It was one of those red bike-share bikes you saw everywhere these days. The rider stopped near her and disembarked. He was dressed in all black—cycling glasses, helmet, tights, and jacket—and toted a backpack.

"Are you all right?" he asked, concern etched on the visible lower half of his clean-shaven face. He had a strong jaw.

She liked that. "Yeah. It's no biggie. My ego is hurt more than anything else." She laughed. "I fall about once a week."

He joined in the laughter. "Here." He laid his bicycle next to hers and held out his hand. "Let me help you."

"How kind," she said.

Placing her gloved hand in his, she thought how refreshing it was to meet a friendly person. A friendly man. Men in DC were pretentious, unable to be involved in a real relationship with anyone but themselves. Her husband divorced her after becoming fed up with the hours she spent at work and client dinners. She hadn't met a considerate man in a long time. She laughed inwardly. There she went again. A glance at the gentleman's gloved left hand. He might not be single.

After he helped her up, she righted her bike, preparing to adjust the tire. She turned to thank him… and a burning sensation spread up her thigh. She saw the hilt before her brain registered that it was a knife.

Eyes wide, she looked at him. "What are you—?"

He stared at her, his face neutral, as she fell again. He didn't say a word while she lay there, her blood soaking the grass. She closed her eyes for the final time. Her last thought wasn't of her company. Or her accumulated wealth. Or her ex. Or the children she would never bear.

Instead, it was, *I guess he wasn't such a nice guy after all.*

Arlington, Virginia

DEV PEDALED AWAY.

She understood why the target chose to ride at this time of morning. It was quiet. Peaceful. Only a few other riders and runners were out.

The lack of nearby witnesses was advantageous.

But that's not why she had killed the cyclist here. She'd been given specific instructions, and Dev was a stickler about following orders.

But she had messed up once. Just once.

And here she was.

Following the path to Crystal City, Virginia, she reached Jefferson Davis Highway. She located an available bike-share dock on her phone and locked the bicycle, then walked back to her room at the Holiday Inn.

Showering hastily, she changed into a business suit. She hailed a taxi in front of the hotel, climbing into the well-worn back seat.

Entering the automatic sliding glass doors of Ronald Reagan National Airport, she averted her face from the surveillance camera, bypassed the check-in counters, and went straight to security. Patiently waiting in line, she smiled as she allowed a black woman with two young children to cut in front of her.

Retrieving her small carry-on and briefcase from the conveyor belt, Dev blended in with the rest of the early-morning business commuters as she headed to the gate, in time for the announcement of the 8:00 a.m. American Airlines flight to New York City.

CHAPTER TWENTY

Arlington, Virginia

BUSTING THROUGH THE circle of cops huddled around the victim, Jade was oblivious to their shouts of protest and dirty looks. Kneeling close to the body, she stared at the victim's face, placing her palm on his cheek, his freckles a galaxy of stars across his nose and upper cheeks.

"Wake up!" she said. Then, more urgently, "Austin, wake up!"

He didn't stir.

She shook him, but to no avail.

Special Agent Austin Miller was dead.

Jade sat up in bed, sweaty, her cotton T-shirt clinging to her back. Light filtered in under her bedroom blinds. The alarm clock on her nightstand displayed 7:00 a.m. in bright red numerals. The vibrating cell phone next to it had awakened her.

Lately, her fallen agent appeared recurrently in her dreams.

She allowed her head to clear for a moment before she picked up the phone.

"Harrington," she said.

"Agent Harrington. Lieutenant John Briggs. Remember me?"

"Of course."

Briggs had worked with Jade on the bullying case a year ago.

"I've got something for you," he said. "Again."

"Talk to me."

"A stabbing victim. A cyclist. I think there are some similarities to other cases I've been reading about. Want to check it out?"

"Where are you?" she asked.

"Not too far from Gravelly Point Park."

This stopped Jade short. "Really?"

"I know, right? What a coincidence."

Nicholas Campbell, one of the bullying victims, had been murdered and dumped in the same park. Jade didn't believe in coincidences.

She hopped out of bed. "I'm on my way."

❋

"Where's Christian?" Jade asked.

Dante shook his head.

She'd arrived to find him and Micah waiting for her. She'd called Dante earlier and asked him to meet her here. Both of them wore suits, although Micah looked like a *GQ* magazine model, while Dante looked like a character from *Miami Vice*. They stood apart from the other police personnel. Jade scanned the crowd for Briggs.

Briggs, medium-complexioned with the build of a middleweight mixed martial arts fighter, spotted her first and strode over to greet her.

"Good to see you again," he said. They shook hands. She introduced him to Micah and Dante.

The detective eyed Dante's suit. "I remember you."

Micah threw his head back and laughed.

Jade bit back a smile. To Briggs, she said, "What do we got?"

After checking in with the officer maintaining the sign-in sheet, they followed Briggs across the swath of grass to the bike path. Response techs in white space suits collected evidence. A photographer snapped pictures of the victim and the crime scene from every angle.

Looking down at the body, Jade said, "Who is she?"

Briggs shook his head. "No ID."

Jade took in the pocketless black bicycle tights and bright yellow reflective cycling coat with an open pocket in the back. "Maybe it fell out."

Dante stood next to her. "Or she didn't carry any, afraid it would fall out."

"Or the perp stole it," Micah said.

"There was a key in the small bike bag under the seat," Briggs said. "Looked like a house key."

"Who found her?" asked Jade.

"Two runners on their daily run."

"Did you eliminate them?"

He nodded. "A commuter saw the whole thing. Started recording after the stabbing and sent it to us." He pointed south. "The perp took off that way. We're canvassing Crystal City."

Jade waited for the technicians to finish their work.

They finally stood. Recognizing her, one of them nodded.

Snapping on a pair of blue nitrile gloves, Jade crouched next to the body and stared at the victim's face.

"The corpse whisperer," Dante whispered behind her.

"Why do you call her that?" Micah whispered back.

"Because they talk to her. Haven't you noticed?"

"What do they say?"

"I don't know," Dante whispered. "It's like telepathy or something."

"Incredible."

Still crouching, she pivoted to look up at them. "You know I can hear you, right?"

Dante said, "Not saying anything that isn't true." He pointed at the victim. "What's she saying?"

Jade ignored him and turned back to the body. The knife was still rammed in the victim's thigh. Her helmet was removed, and the vivid redness of her medium-length hair splayed across the grass. Her eyes were closed. Other than the stab wound, she appeared to be sleeping. A dark stain covered the ground around her body.

The bike, a few yards away, looked undamaged. Except for the front tire, which was askew.

"Did she fall?" Jade asked.

Briggs nodded toward the techs, who stood off to the side, chatting, waiting for Jade to complete her examination. "They think so."

"Forced off?"

"I would've expected more damage."

Jade scanned the area surrounding the body. "Lots of blood."

"She bled out," Briggs said. "It didn't take long."

Since she'd been wearing a helmet, the victim's face was unblemished. A plethora of freckles dotted her nose and cheeks. Jade thought of Austin.

"Who did this to you?" Jade whispered to her, wishing she knew the victim's name.

"See?" Dante said to Micah.

"When I die," Micah said, "I hope she talks to me like that."

"If you two don't shut up," Jade said, "that might be sooner than you think."

Dante was right. She did talk to her victims, and although they didn't talk back to her, they often led her in the right direction if she stilled herself long enough to listen. She continued to gaze at the dead woman.

Around her, the DC rush hour went on. Bumper-to-bumper commuter traffic crept along GW Parkway. In addition to the normal traffic, drivers squeezed into one lane due to the emergency vehicles blocking the other. The rubbernecking didn't help. Jade tried to ignore the excessive honking and occasional shouting.

She swiveled her head as a plane took off. She grinned despite herself, thinking of her friend Zoe, who would only call the airport by its former name: National. Zoe had a fit when Republicans introduced a bill last year to name this park after the former first lady Nancy Reagan.

Lieutenant Briggs stepped forward. "No ID, but we did find something."

Jade stood as he waved over one of the techs.

"Found this in her jacket pocket," Briggs said.

The female technician—the one who'd recognized Jade earlier—handed her a clear evidence bag with a sheet of beige paper inside. It was handwritten in tight block letters. Black ink. As she started to read, Dante and Micah moved in close—too close—to read over her shoulders.

> *But if thou live, remember'd not to be,*
> *Die single, and thine image dies with thee.*
>
> —Bard of Avon

"What the hell?" Dante said.

Micah shook his head. "The inadequacy of an American education."

"What?" asked Dante.

"The Bard of Avon," said Micah incredulously. "Shakespeare, man."

Jade thought back to a team meeting during the TSK case. After the killer sent an email to a cable news station, the agent who'd brought it to her team's attention said, "Shakespeare strikes again." This homicide couldn't be related to that case. TSK was dead. Jade knew because she had killed him. But somehow he seemed to reach from beyond the grave.

"Was it hers?" she said. "Or did the killer put it there?"

CHAPTER TWENTY-ONE

The White House, Washington, DC

THEY DID IT.

That morning, the United States Senate had repealed the New New Deal Coalition Act, the final vote along party lines. Soon, the measure would come to Whitney's desk. She would veto it, of course, but the House had secured enough votes to overturn it.

Sitting in the Oval Office, she read a letter from Joseph Babineaux, a worker from Pike County, Missouri. He'd received a call from a construction firm, rescinding an offer of employment on a crew replacing a crumbling bridge that spanned the Mississippi River. Almost a quarter of the bridges in Whitney's home state needed repair.

Placing the letter on her desk, she rubbed her eyes in frustration. It was one of many she'd received. Hundreds of thousands of emails opposing the repeal inundated the White House website, most of them from her base outside of Missouri. Thousands of people signed petitions on MoveOn.org and other political action sites.

Sometimes even *she,* the most powerful person in the world, felt helpless.

Her phone buzzed. It was Sean, her secretary, who sat in the Outer Oval, the office right outside of hers. She didn't want to talk to anyone, but as for any boss, that wasn't always an option. She pressed a button.

"Madam President," he said through the speaker. "Cole Brennan is on the line."

He couldn't be calling to gloat, since he was the one who'd strong-armed Senator Eric Hampton into sponsoring the bill, a major reason it had passed.

She would take the call.

Cole, the most popular conservative radio commentator in the country, was not one of Whitney's biggest fans. He constantly pilloried her legislative positions and accomplishments on his show. Her dress, relationships with her family and celebrities, even her hair—nothing was off-limits to his scrutiny.

Last year, after Cole's son, CJ, was bullied and savagely beaten, Cole's wife, Ashley, had visited her in the White House. As a result of that meeting, Whitney and Cole teamed up to pass the federal Anti-Bullying Act, the first national law protecting children and teachers from bullying.

"Cole," she said. "Is this a condolence call?"

"Madam President, I assure you I had nothing to do with it."

Whitney stayed silent. She believed him.

"I want to wring Hampton's scrawny little neck," he went on, "with one of his little red ties. He's behind this. And Sampson… Sampson is a two-faced little pri—piece of crap. He's crossed the wrong person."

Whitney said, "You needn't worry about him for long."

"Oh?" he said. "Something I need to know?"

"Perhaps."

"Sexual harassment? Sexting? Embezzlement?"

"You don't think too highly of the senator, do you?"

"I've been in this game for a while."

"How's CJ?" she asked, shifting to Cole's favorite subject.

"He's doing well in school. Even hosting his own show on the radio station at his college. One of those liberal shows, talking about issues that impact LBGT and all those other letters."

Pride in his voice.

"LGBTQIA," she said.

He sighed. "I can never keep up."

"Sounds as if he's following in his dad's footsteps."

"That he is. Well, Madam President, this isn't over. I don't care for your politics much, but I gave you my word, and I'm one of the few people left in this world whose word is his bond."

"I don't care for your politics much either, Cole, but that's kind of you to say."

"Kindness nothing. It's the principle of the thing."

"What are you suggesting?"

"Don't know yet, but I'll think of something." He paused. "In the meantime, is there anything you can do about deregulation? Good God, woman! You're strangling businesses out here!"

Whitney laughed. This was the Cole she knew and had started to respect. "I'll see what I can do."

"I'll be in touch," he said.

CHAPTER TWENTY-TWO

Washington, DC

JADE HIT A speed-dial button on her phone. "I need to see you."

A few moments later, Christian's bulky frame filled the doorway.

"Come in," she said, "and close the door."

She signed off on a report and set it aside. Christian sat in one of the chairs across from her. His blond hair, cut military short, stood at attention.

"Missed you this morning," she said.

"I was busy."

Jade mentally reviewed all his cases but didn't come up with anything pressing in his caseload. "Doing what?"

"This."

He handed her a sheet of paper.

A letter addressed to her. His resignation.

She tore it up without reading it in its entirety.

He scrunched up his face. "I could print out another one."

Leaning back in her chair, she said, "I guess the gesture isn't as dramatic as it once was."

This elicited a small smile from him. "No."

"You can't close cases if you don't show up."

Christian stared at a spot on the wall behind her. She followed his gaze to the FBI emblem and looked back at him.

"I no longer want to close cases here," he said.

"We need to talk about this."

"Rather late for that."

"I meant to talk to you beforehand. About my decision. Time got away from me."

He said nothing, his fist clenching and unclenching.

"I stand by my call." She paused. "Give him a chance."

"I. Can't." He stood and turned to leave.

"I wasn't finished," Jade said.

He hesitated before returning to his seat.

"Dante approaches things in a way I've come to appreciate."

Christian winced. "You don't need to explain this to me now."

"I want to."

"He's a hothead and he's lazy."

"He's overcome his anger issues," she said, "and he's not lazy. Rather… unchallenged. This situation won't last forever. Ethan will be back soon. I'll return to my job full time, and you'll report directly to me again. Roll with it for now. This team needs you." She locked eyes with him. "I need you. You're still my rock."

"I'm more experienced. Closed more cases. I'm the better person for the job."

"You're prepared. Smart. One of the best FBI agents I've ever worked with. You'll get your chance. I promise." She stood and extended her hand. "I don't make promises I can't keep."

He sat there, waiting so long she thought he'd leave her hanging. Finally, he grasped her hand.

"Let's go grab a sandwich," she said.

"I need to do something first."

❈

On their way back from lunch, Jade's phone vibrated. She swept it off her hip.

"Talk to me," she said.

"Got an ID back on the victim," Dante said. "Briggs called and said someone from his precinct recognized her photo."

"How?"

"Because she's a bigwig. Her name's Finn Hurley, CEO of Hurley Technologies, a cybersecurity firm headquartered in Crystal City, not too far from the Pentagon. I'm headed over there now to interview her employees."

"Sounds good. Take Micah with you."

"Already asked him."

"What do we know?"

"Divorced. No children. Lived in Old Town."

"Talked to the ex?"

"Still tracking him down. No prints came back on the bike, except for hers. Either the killer didn't touch it or he wore gloves."

"Makes sense, if he was riding a bike."

"And it was cold," he said. "You got jokes?"

"Excuse me?"

"Who hung the poster in my office?"

"What poster?"

"Those dudes from *Miami Vice*. The eighties version. Guys with their shirts open to their belly buttons, lots of chest hair, showing off their bling. Someone wrote 'Dante' and 'Micah' on their chests. You know anything about that?"

Jade stole a glance at Christian, who had found something interesting to admire in the sky.

"No," she said into the phone, "I don't. But you're an FBI agent. Figure it out."

She clicked off and looked at Christian. They both laughed.

Back in her office, Jade grabbed the file on top of a stack. Inside it, she located a phone number with a 312 area code.

"Lieutenant Blanchard."

"Lieutenant, this is Agent Harrington."

"What can I do for you?"

"Learn anything from the head of security at Carr Holdings?"

"He gave us a lot of leads. Too many. Still chasing them down."

"I have a weird question," she said. "Did you find a poem or a sonnet?"

"Not on the victim," he said.

Wishful thinking.

"But," he continued, "we found a poem on his computer. Didn't think much of it. It was sent via email. Just the poem. Nothing else. No subject. No greeting. No text. No signature. Thought it was spam. One of a thousand emails he'd received that day."

"Who sent it?"

"Need to double-check. I remember it, though, because I thought it was odd."

"How so?"

"Because it wasn't a modern poem. It was old. Like from Shakespeare's time."

Jade's heart quickened, as it did whenever she uncovered a lead. "Can you send it over?"

"Sure can."

Ten minutes after they hung up, an email arrived in her inbox.

So thou, thyself outgoing in thy noon,
Unlook'd on diest, unless thou get a son.

—Bard of Avon

Jade was as unfamiliar with this sonnet as the one found on Finn Hurley.

She entered the first line of the poem in the search bar and clicked on the first result. The sonnet sent to Jared Carr was the seventh one. These were its last two lines.

Jade hoped this wasn't the seventh killing.

Next she searched for Sonnet VII. The first link provided an analysis of the seventh sonnet. She read the poem again. It didn't yield any clues as to why Carr was killed.

But it linked the Chicago and Virginia murders. Why did the murderer leave a sonnet on Hurley's person but email one to Carr? Were the sonnets relevant to the victim? Or the killer?

Were there others?

She forwarded the email containing the sonnet to Dante and Pat with the message:

Dante and Pat,

The attached sonnet was found on Jared Carr's computer. Call the detective in New York and ask if they found a sonnet. Also, try to trace the origins of this email.

Jade

A few minutes later she received a reply from Dante.

I could've done that for you.

A minute later, a second email arrived from him:

Isn't this my case?

CHAPTER TWENTY-THREE

Washington, DC

"ACCORDING TO FINN Hurley's coworkers, she rode her bike every morning before work," Dante told Jade later that afternoon in her office. "Sometimes during lunch. Most weekends. She was always training for races, sometimes the distance was over 100 miles."

"They're called centuries," Jade said. "What else did they say?"

"As a boss, she was demanding but fair. Didn't take shit from anyone." Dante grinned. "Sounded like someone else I know."

From him, an unusual compliment.

"She spent most of her time with major clients out of the office," he continued. "Worked late. Competing demands on her time. Quarterly investor calls. Press requests. Information requests." He paused. "Seemed to be under a lot of pressure."

Looking across her desk at him, Jade said, "Customers?"

"Her assistant is sending over a client list with contacts, but the government made up the bulk of their business. Other Fortune 500 companies. Hurley's products and services don't come cheap."

"Could her death be related to her work?"

"Maybe. In the cybersecurity industry, she dealt not only with competitors and suppliers but also hostile agents: Russia, China, Ukraine, et cetera. Or it could have been an employee. They all knew her routine."

Jade frowned. "How does she fit with the other victims?"

"Don't know."

She aligned her basketball paperweight with the edge of the desk. "What happens to the firm now?"

"Although she founded it, it shouldn't die with her. The board will find a replacement."

"And its corporate life will go on. If the perp was a competitor, he bought some time at best. Who are her possible successors?"

"I don't know." He patted his pockets, then looked at her. "Can I borrow a piece of paper?"

Grabbing the legal pad on her desk, she tossed it to him. "You should always keep something to write on with you."

"I thought I was coming in here for a brief chat." He hesitated. "Can I borrow a pen too?"

She handed him one and opened her mouth to share further words of wisdom.

He held up the hand with the pen. "I got it, boss."

As he wrote, she asked, "Was she seeing anyone?"

Dante shook his head. "She didn't discuss her private life. Most of her employees assumed she didn't have one."

"Did you talk to her neighbors?"

"She lived on S. Lee Street, in one of those federal-style townhouses. Micah and I canvassed the neighborhood. It's a quiet one. Neighbors aren't very neighborly. They seldom saw her, except for her comings and goings on her bike. One neighbor resented that sometimes she left her trash and recycling bins out on the street for days after they were emptied."

"Did she entertain much?"

"No."

"Social media?"

"Pat's looking into it."

"Reviewed the autopsy report?"

"Haven't received it yet," he said.

"Anything back on the commuter's recording?"

"I watched it. It's from far away. Looks like a guy riding his bike before work, not like a guy who just stabbed someone. Forensics is going over it frame by frame."

"What about the ex?"

"Talked to him on the phone. He lives in Atlanta and was at the office at the time of the murder. He's an accountant. January is a busy month. Said the two of them barely spoke."

"Bad blood?"

"No. More like indifference."

"Remarried?"

"Live-in boyfriend," Dante said with distaste.

"Oh."

"The ex had no idea who would do this to her. Oh, one more thing: Pat said Hurley was a major contributor to Ellison during the last campaign."

Was that significant? After a moment, she said, "You're going to need a bigger team. A task force. Daily briefings."

"I agree. Is that your approval?"

She nodded. "We can't let the sonnets get out. The media will have a field day."

"Anything else?"

Jade rattled off next steps. "Got it?"

He waggled the legal pad next to his head. "I got it. Thanks."

CHAPTER TWENTY-FOUR

The White House, Washington, DC

WHITNEY PUMPED HARD on the elliptical in the Residence gym. The television atop the machine was on, but she wasn't paying much attention to it. She was thinking about how to resurrect her signature legislation.

A breaking news chyron scrolled across the bottom of the screen. The name Sampson snapped her out of her reverie. She pressed the up arrow on the display to increase the volume.

The red-headed male MSNBC commentator said, "This just in. Early this morning, ICE raided the offices of PS Corporation, which owns the farming operations of Republican Senator Paul Sampson and his family. You might remember that Sampson was a vocal proponent of building a wall between the United States and Mexico and a staunch opponent of illegal immigration ever since he switched parties after losing the Democratic nomination for president.

"According to our sources, the government agency searched for evidence that the corporation employs hundreds of illegal immigrants, the majority of whom are Mexican. Senator Sampson was unavailable for comment. After the break, Senator Maureen McAllister will join us to talk about this shocking development."

Whitney wasn't shocked. She wasn't even mildly surprised. She had ordered the raid based on evidence presented to her by the director of the agency. At one time, she would have been surprised by Sampson's hypocrisy. They'd worked together on progressive issues they both cared about. His views flipped 180 degrees when he thought they were his route to the highest office. She wondered how Sampson was handling the negative attention.

He loved his farm.

The screen filled with a headshot of Maureen McAllister. The senior senator from Mississippi stood somewhere in the august halls of the Capitol.

She was in her early sixties, her fashionably cut short blond hair interwoven with gray. Her outfit was stylish. It didn't take much of an imagination to understand that she'd been a beautiful woman once. Still was.

"Senator McAllister," the MSNBC commentator said from the studio, "what do you think of all this?"

The senator laughed. "My colleague wasn't thinking. He didn't think he'd get caught? It's like posting a crime that you committed on Facebook. I swear God wasted His time giving some people brains they don't use. I'm from the great state of Mississippi. I know something about farming. Agriculture employs almost thirty percent of our workforce—farmers who farm the right way."

"Should he resign?"

"Not sure if that's for me to say, but I will say that Senator Sampson should be ashamed of himself. Illegal immigration needs to be addressed, but participating in it and then talking out the other side of your mouth isn't the best way to do that. Shame on him."

"He's a rising star in your party, Senator. What happens now?"

"Look up in the sky, young man. You'll see a fallin' star. I hope one day he ends up having to work his farm himself."

When the interview concluded, Whitney muted the sound, pedaling in silence. After several minutes, she pressed a button on the equipment's console.

"Yes, Madam President," Sean said from the Outer Oval.

"Schedule a meeting with Senator Maureen McAllister," she said. "In the Oval."

CHAPTER TWENTY-FIVE

Washington, DC

MIDMORNING THE NEXT day, Jade made a trip to the break room for a refill. She could have had a coffee service installed in her office, but she liked how the break room offered chance meetings with her fellow agents. The only way to know how they were doing was to be with them.

On the way back to her office, she stopped in the doorway of Dante's office.

"What did the detective from New York say?"

"You were right," Dante said, looking up. "The perp handed Scofield a piece of paper with a sonnet written on it, tucked into the fundraiser program. NYPD thought it was part of the program, so they didn't think much of it."

"Scofield dropped it?"

"The wife couldn't remember. NYPD is reexamining the sonnet now. Dusting it for prints. I emailed you a copy."

"I don't want to wait. Bring it up."

While Dante searched for the document, she walked behind his desk, holding her recently refilled FBI mug. "Was it the perp's program? Did he attend the event?"

Dante's long, graceful hands typed on the keyboard. "Don't know. Might have slipped the sonnet into Scofield's program."

"But he'd have no guarantee that Scofield would keep it the entire time. Afterward?"

"Not enough time."

She sipped her coffee, avoiding the chip on the rim of the mug. Way past time to get a new one. "Cameras?"

"Front of the library. The detective said a hat obscured the perp's face."

"Unlucky."

"It was more than that. She said his head was tilted away, as if he knew about the camera. She offered to send us a copy of the recording."

"Get it. We need to interview Scofield's tablemates at the event. All the waitstaff."

Dante stared at his computer. "We," he mouthed.

"I saw that," she said.

He opened the email containing the sonnet and swiveled his monitor.

Pity the world, or else this glutton be,
To eat the world's due, by the grave and thee.

—Bard of Avon

"Which one is this?" she asked.

"Sonnet I."

"New York could have been a warm-up for Chicago."

"Or, since we found Sonnets I, III, and VII, there've been four other murders."

"I hope not," she said. "Any idea what it means? What the other two mean?"

"English was never my best subject."

She thought for a moment. "You should—"

"I put a call in to an English professor at GWU," he said. "My meeting with her is in"—he peeked at his watch—"forty-five minutes."

"Good idea. Mind if I tag along?"

"No."

"We should bring Micah."

"Whatever." Under his breath, he said, "The more the merrier."

"Don't hate," Jade said, draining the dregs of her coffee. "He might surprise you."

CHAPTER TWENTY-SIX

Washington, DC

THE PROFESSOR EXAMINED the three sheets of paper on a cleared spot on her cluttered desk. The teetering stacks of papers and files and books reminded Jade of Max's office.

Professor Alaia Bennett stared at the sonnets. She read one, then the second, then the third, then back to the second. She was slender, pretty, and dark skinned, her hair short and natural, shot through with gray. She wore bright red lipstick.

Jade, Dante, and Micah sat in silence, their chairs close together in the professor's cramped office in Rome Hall on the George Washington University campus.

Finally, the professor removed her reading glasses. "The Bard of Avon. Shakespeare. Sonnets I, III, and VII, which you've probably figured out."

"Are those numbers or those sonnets significant?" asked Jade.

"If the numbers are significant, it's not because of the sonnets. Shakespeare didn't number them."

"What do you mean?" asked Dante. "I remember the numbers from high school."

"He wrote the sonnets in the late fifteen hundreds, early sixteen hundreds," the professor said. "They weren't published until 1609, and it was by someone else, without Shakespeare's knowledge. The numbers are arbitrary. No one knows the exact order in which they were written."

"They were circulated among his friends before publication," Micah said.

Bennett appraised Micah. "That accent. And he knows Shakespeare. I think I'm in love."

To Bennett, Micah said, "Shall I compare thee to a summer's day?"

The professor pretended to swoon.

Jade cleared her throat. "You were saying…"

The professor tore her eyes away from Micah. "The sonnets were written at different times in his life, which might've explained the different themes: brevity of life, the transience of beauty, and the trappings of desire. Most were written about obsession and his overwhelming love for a young man, the Fair Youth. Over the centuries, there's been much speculation about whether he was Shakespeare's lover or if their relationship was an intense platonic friendship. Or whether they reflected the writer's personal feelings at all. Most of his work did not. So why would the sonnets?"

A slight head shake from Dante. "Wasn't he married?"

"He was married."

"Then why would he be writing love poems to a guy?"

Micah winked, then blew him a kiss.

Dante shifted uncomfortably in his chair.

It was Alaia Bennett's turn to keep the conversation on track. "Sometimes the men during that age developed strong platonic relationships with other men. For example, artists became attached to the patrons of their work."

Jade pointed at the papers on the desk. "Are these sonnets related?"

"The first seventeen focused on the brevity of life. Shakespeare argued that the way for his young friend's beauty to live forever was for him to beget children."

Dante shook his head. "Why would someone want to read about that?"

The professor stared at him. "Unfortunately, television hadn't been invented yet. Reality TV, a distant art form of the future. Sonnets were one of the few entertainment options at the time."

"What if," Jade said, "Shakespeare was thinking of his own mortality?"

Bennett turned to her. "Excellent."

Jade warmed with unexpected pride as if she were back in school. It had always been about achievement with her, although she refused to explore the issue too deeply. Probably something to do with wanting her father's approval.

"Later," the professor continued, "Shakespeare introduced a Rival Poet, who the Fair Youth ends up preferring."

"Shakespeare was one strange dude," Dante said.

"Didn't the young man reject the procreation argument, starting with sonnet eighteen?" Micah asked the professor.

"He did, but Shakespeare was consoled that the sonnets alone would preserve the young man's beauty forever. And he was right. We're still talking about it, analyzing it, over four hundred years later."

Dante looked at Micah with wonder. "Damn… where did you learn that?"

To Dante, Jade said, "Told you."

Micah grinned at him. "I'm not just a pretty face."

"I remember something about a lady," Jade said.

Bennett nodded. "The remaining sonnets were written about an affair with a woman. Some scholars call her the Dark Lady. Not because she was black, mind you, but because of her hair. I call her his Dark Bae."

Dante sat up. "I want to hear more about *her*. For investigative purposes."

Ignoring him, the professor peered out the window overlooking F Street before turning back. "I would presume your killer is obsessed with the brevity of life." Donning her reading glasses again, she picked up the first sonnet. "*Glutton* means excess." To Jade, "Was the victim rich?"

"Yes."

The professor returned her attention to the sheet of paper. "This sonnet is about selfishness, narcissism, obsession with appearance."

"Sounds like someone I know," Micah said, glancing at Dante.

To Jade, Bennett said, "Is this the best use of my tax dollars?"

"You can request a refund," Jade offered. "Please continue."

"This sonnet is also about usury," Bennett said. "Charging exorbitant interest on money. Commercial profit. Any of that ring true with regard to your victim?"

"He was an attractive hedge fund manager who paid a hundred million dollars to put his name on a building in New York City," Jade said.

"That seems to fit. Did the victim have children?"

"Yes," Dante said.

The professor frowned. "Then I'm not quite seeing the connection."

"Maybe there isn't one," he said.

They sat in silence for a moment. Jade pointed at the sonnet found on the third victim, Finn Hurley. "This one is straightforward. 'But if thou live, remember'd not to be, / Die single, and thine image dies with thee.' You die childless and your beauty dies with you."

"Correct," Bennett said. "The line before this is 'Despite of wrinkles, this thy golden time.' The young man could only experience a 'golden time' in his old age through his children."

"This victim was a divorced woman."

"She won't be having a 'golden time,'" said Dante.

The professor said, "Shakespeare implored his friend not to deny any woman the chance of becoming a mother and a vessel to pass on his beauty."

Dante sat up. "Now you're talking."

"Are you always a pig?" the professor asked him.

"Pretty much," Jade said.

The two women shared a smile.

Picking up the last sonnet, Bennett said, "Number seven. Now, this one is interesting."

Jade leaned forward, hands clasped, arms on her thighs. "How so?"

"In this one, Shakespeare compares the journey of human life to the passage of the sun. Once we reach the apex, like the sun, the only direction is down."

"How depressing," Micah said.

"When you reach 'feeble age,' as he called it," Bennett said, "not only your physical appearance deteriorates, but the people who used to gaze at your beauty with awe will 'look another way.' You will not be remembered."

"That is depressing," Dante said, stroking his chin. "Not much to look forward to."

"That's why," the professor concluded, "he should bear a son. This was the first time the poet specified the gender of the child."

Sitting up, Jade said, "Son. S-O-N. Sun. S-U-N."

"The two of you would receive an A in my class," the professor said to Jade and Micah. To Dante, "*You* need some work."

Jade turned to Dante. "Did Carr have a son?"

He nodded.

Alaia Bennett looked down at the sonnets again. "I wonder why the killer is only providing the last two lines?"

"How many lines are in a sonnet?" Jade asked.

"Fourteen," Micah said.

"Usually," the professor said, "but not always. The last two lines rhyme with each other, unlike the rest of the sonnet, where the rhyme alternates in a pattern. The couplet at the end sums up the previous twelve lines."

"Or provides a surprise ending," Micah added.

"Correct."

"The beginning of the sonnets could have been left with other victims," Jade said.

No one spoke for a moment as they weighed the meaning of that.

"Professor," Jade said, "we've taken up enough of your time. Is there anything else?"

Bennett steepled her fingers. "These sonnets have something in common, which you wouldn't know by looking at the couplet."

"What's that?" asked Dante.

"They all include the word *die*."

Dante said, "I hope he's not planning to kill someone for each sonnet."
"I hope you're right."
"How many sonnets are there?" he asked.
Alaia Bennett said, "A hundred and fifty-four."

The White House, Washington, DC

"SENATOR."

The bangles on Maureen McAllister's wrists chimed as she walked toward Whitney, her hand extended. "Madam President, your invitation is an honor and a privilege."

"The honor is mine," Whitney said, taking the other woman's hand in both of hers. She gestured to one of the two matching Queen Anne chairs in the Oval Office. "Please. May I offer you something to drink?"

"Is it too early for a martini?"

Whitney's mouth parted.

Mo rushed on. "I'm just messing with you. How about some sweet tea?"

Picking up the phone on the end table, Whitney placed the order. "The reason I asked you here, Senator—"

"Please call me Mo."

"The reason why I asked you here, Mo—"

Mo held up her hand. "I'm sorry to interrupt again, Madam President, but I do want to ask after your husband and children."

Whitney's smile faltered. One thing she didn't want to discuss with the senator—or anyone, for that matter—was her family. A butler with a gray bob entered carrying a tray with two glasses of iced tea and placed them on the coffee table. Whitney thanked her, and she left without a word.

Whitney handed a glass to Mo. "They're fine. And your family?"

Mo marveled at the glass. "This is how I prefer my tea. Sweatin'. Anyhow, they're fine, thanks for asking. My husband, Jimmy—we call him Nub—can't stand Washington and can't wait for my term to be over." She leaned toward Whitney and said, sotto voce, "He doesn't know I'm running again." She straightened. "Our daughter's fine. She's in Mississippi. Last year, she married one of her classmates from LSU. They just had a baby. He's a Cajun boy—the husband, not the baby—"

"Uh, Mo… unfortunately, I don't have a lot of time. Sean, my secretary, only scheduled us for 15 minutes, so I want to shift the conversation to the purpose of this meeting."

"Well, you asked, Madam President. I can't help myself. There's a difference between how you northern women and us southern women converse."

"Missouri isn't in the north—"

Mo raised and lowered her hand again. "I'm sorry I keep interrupting, Madam President, but this is important. A Yankee woman would say 'She put on her coat and went to the store.' Us *real* Southern women embellish and speak florally. We would say 'Before she went to the store, she put on her mink coat given to her by her third husband three days before he left her.'"

Whitney's laugh was spontaneous and light. While in the Senate, she hadn't worked much with Mo. Now, Whitney wished she had. "I wouldn't want you to go against your grain. Excuse me for a moment."

She picked up the receiver again and pressed a button. "Sean, please clear another fifteen minutes for the Senator."

"But you're meeting with—"

"It will need to be rescheduled." She hung up. "Where were we?"

Mo shifted her gaze from the phone to Whitney. "We were talking about grain, which would be impossible for me to go against, as I'm sure it is for you. Now." She patted her lap with both hands. "Why am I here?"

"I saw your interview about Paul Sampson's troubles."

"One of his troubles. Trying to be someone he isn't. Messing around with Cole Brennan." Mo shook her head. "Senator Sampson also drinks like a fish who hasn't seen water for five days."

Whitney raised her own hand before Mo continued embellishing and speaking florally. "Be that as it may, I think we may be able to help each other."

Mo sipped her tea. "I didn't know I was in need of help."

"This is Washington. We all need help occasionally."

"I'll bite. How can we help each other?"

Setting her glass down on the table, Whitney crossed her legs. "Your party leadership is in a precarious position. With Sampson out, that only leaves Hampton."

Mo made a noise. "Don't get me started about him. I know we're running out of time, but Lord, that man boils my water and chaps my ass."

Whitney leaned forward. "We need someone to lead your party into the next decade. A decade of almost certain turmoil and change."

"I wasn't aware of your concern for my party. I do say that warms my heart."

"Mo, we live in turbulent times. Geopolitical issues. Terrorism. The economy. Income inequality. Gun violence. Climate change. Women's rights. The list goes on. I need to be able to work with someone from across the aisle. To effect real change."

"You and I don't agree on a lot of these issues."

"But we agree on whether they exist. Which is a start. I don't think our positions are all that far apart. Our nation faces significant problems. Unless we work with people we disagree with, our country will be unable to govern itself. 'Alone we can do so little; together we can do so much.'"

"Helen Keller?"

Whitney nodded. "What do you say, Mo?"

"People always say 'Thank God for Mississippi,' but not as a compliment. They're grateful their state doesn't take the lowest ranking in every goddamn survey." Senator Maureen "Mo" McAllister took a final sip of her sweet tea and set her glass down next to Whitney's. "I always knew it would take our state and us women to save this damn country." She stood, holding out her hand. "Where would you like to start?"

CHAPTER TWENTY-EIGHT

Washington, DC

HER WARNING TO Dante about leaks was for naught.

"This just in. WTOP has learned that the murders of three wealthy and prominent individuals may be connected."

Jade turned up the volume on the car radio.

"Sebastian Scofield, founder and managing director of Scofield Asset Management and a New York philanthropist; Jared Carr Jr., co-CEO of Carr Holdings, Inc. and founder and CEO of conservative Super PAC Freedom of America; and Finn Hurley, CEO of cybersecurity firm Hurley Technologies in Crystal City, Virginia, all died of multiple stab wounds. Three similar murders in three different cities: New York, Chicago, and Arlington."

So far, so good.

"But what connects these murders isn't the victims' wealth. Or their method of death. No. What connects them is that the killer left a calling card: sonnets by William Shakespeare. We'll talk more about the Shakespeare Killer after the break."

Jade slammed her hand on the dashboard. "Goddamn it!"

She lowered the radio's volume and pressed a button, drumming her fingers on the steering wheel while she waited for Dante to pick up.

"Yes?" his voice drawled over her car's speakers.

"Who leaked?" she asked. "You or Micah?"

"What do you mean?"

"It's on the news. They're calling him the Shakespeare Killer."

"Damn! It didn't come from me. Micah?" He hesitated. "Or you."

Jade let the accusation slide. Was it Micah? Pat only knew about one sonnet. And Jade trusted Pat. Over the years they'd worked together, she'd proven her discretion.

"The professor?" she asked, doubtful.

"I wouldn't think so, but I'll ask her."

"Set up the task force. We'll need to come up with an action plan quickly before hysteria ensues."

"And before the copycat killers come out of the woodwork."

"That too."

She hung up and pressed another button.

"Yes, boss?" Micah answered.

"You've been hanging around Dante too long."

"Why do you—?"

"Never mind. Did you talk to anyone in the media about the Shakespeare case?"

"Of course not."

"Someone did."

"Wasn't me. But…"

"What?"

"Barringer asked for an update. But he's your boss. He wouldn't say anything to them… would he?"

Chapter Twenty-Nine

The White House, Washington, DC

"RAISE A STINK," Sasha said. "That's what I'd do."

On their way to the Cabinet Room, Sasha had stopped Whitney in the hallway outside of the Oval Office.

After three decades of stagnant growth, Japan had come roaring back. One of its major tech houses developed a significant breakthrough in artificial intelligence, resulting in less need for humans in economic production. Given the country's demographic crisis—a population shrinking at an alarming rate—the discovery was auspicious. Recently, Japan had joined the BRICS alliance: Brazil, Russia, India, China, and South America.

It was now JBRICS.

The rising sun had risen again.

Meanwhile, China had solved its debt problems, and its GDP growth was returning to double digits. And Russia had awakened from its hibernation, the black bear now a political force.

China, Japan, and Russia were increasingly considered the "Big Three."

This morning, the Netherlands, which experienced one of the lowest income inequality rates in the world at 12.4 percent, announced that it would be hosting a summit in three months' time to share the secrets of its success with the invited countries. Japan, China, and Russia were to give keynote addresses. The US was invited, but Whitney hadn't been asked to speak.

Income inequality was *her* issue. The issue she'd campaigned and won on, and the basis for her signature legislation, recently overturned by the US Congress.

How would Americans fare when their country was no longer a superpower? The United States, the world's longest-lasting democracy, was not any more immune to demise than the republics before it.

"Are you listening?" Sasha asked. "You'll be in the room. Speak."

"Don't worry, I will."

"Here's the information you requested." Sasha handed her a folder. "When are we going to start working on New Cubed?"

"New New New?"

"We can do it without Hampton."

Whitney's eyes narrowed. "He thinks I'm Charlie Brown to his Lucy. I will never let him pull the football away from me ever again."

"Hampton isn't the only senator. You should find a different teammate."

This gave Whitney pause. "Like Peppermint Patty?"

"If you want something done."

As they resumed walking, she told Sasha about her conversation with Mo. "Tell Sean to schedule a meeting for me with Senator McAllister and the vice president."

"Will do," Sasha said. "By the way, I have news. About Sampson."

"What did he do now?" Whitney asked.

"He's going to resign," Sasha said.

"How do you know?

"It's my job to know."

Sasha had her sources, and they were usually accurate.

"You're always ten steps ahead of everyone else," Whitney said.

"I know," Sasha said.

Whitney stopped before the Cabinet Room door. "Even me?"

Sasha pressed her lips together but said nothing.

She didn't have to.

Her look, inexplicably, gave Whitney chills.

Washington, DC

A PETITE WOMAN with funky hair and wearing a rainbow of colors wended her way through the throng of after-work patrons crowding the tables and booths at happy hour.

Taking her foot off the brass rail under the bar, Jade eased off her stool. "Hey, you."

She bent over to give her best friend a hug.

When they pulled apart, Zoe noticed the sleek glass filled with beer waiting for her on the bar top.

"To think people say you're a control freak. What are we drinking?"

"German. Hefe."

"Thank God!" Zoe said, climbing onto her seat. "I couldn't stand to drink a Russian beer today. Or China. They brew the worst beers. Japanese beers aren't bad."

Jade returned to her seat. "What are you talking about? We never drink Russian beer."

"The three superpowers. I refuse to drink their beer now. Germany and the US are on the outside looking in. The only beer I'll drink is our ally's."

"Anything for the cause," Jade said, raising her bottle of beer before taking a sip.

"Pretty soon those three countries will be pushing their beliefs on us—and their beers. As we used to do to other countries. We must take a stand."

"Why is it always about politics for you?"

"The same way it's always about 'winning' for you. What else is there?"

"True."

"I'm glad you called," Zoe said. "It's nice to get out. It's been a rough month."

"Besides what happened to New New... is it work?"

Zoe's nonprofit organization supported progressive issues and female candidates for all levels of political office.

"It's an uphill battle sometimes."

Jade worried the edge of the label on the bottle, wet with condensation. She'd turned down the bartender's offer of a glass. "I wouldn't count the US or Fairchild out."

"I don't." Zoe sipped her beer. "Enough about me. What've you been up to? Any exciting new cases?"

Zoe had been involved in two of Jade's major cases. Too involved. "Not really."

"Hmmm…" Zoe's brow furrowed. "The Shakespeare Killer case seems like something you would take on. I minored in English Literature."

"I remember," Jade said.

Zoe raised her hand to draw the attention of one of the bartenders. The female bartender, wearing a gray vest and a black tie, immediately cut off her conversation with another customer and stood in front of Zoe, who beamed her hundred-watt smile. "Do you have any Belgian beers?"

The bartender leaned in, placing her forearms on the bar. Behind her, a mirrored wall dazzled with strategically placed color-coded liquor bottles. Jade wondered how the bartenders found what they needed. It was comparable to those people who organized their books by color rather than in alphabetical order.

Holding Zoe's gaze, the woman said, "I'm sure I can find something you'd like."

"I'm sure you can too," Zoe said.

Jade imagined a dialogue bubble above her own head. *Puke!*

After the bartender moved away, Jade said, "Seriously?"

"She's cute, isn't she?"

"Do you flirt with every attractive woman you meet?"

Zoe pretended to think about it. "You should try it sometime." Then, slyly, "Maybe you already have."

Jade shot her a warning look.

Zoe's dating habits were legendary and geographically dispersed. If Jade met a lesbian on the other side of the country, there was a distinct possibility that she had dated Zoe. Jade sometimes tired of Zoe babbling about her exploits, although Jade couldn't talk. She ruminated about Blake. And Kyle. She didn't count Micah.

"Here you go," the bartender said, deftly pouring a beer into a Duvel-labeled tulip glass and placing it on the bar before Zoe. She set the other bottle in front of Jade, grabbed her empty, then discreetly laid a folded napkin next to Zoe's glass.

"Thank you," Zoe said, pocketing the napkin with a practiced motion.

The bartender stared at Zoe several seconds longer than necessary before returning to her long-ignored customer.

"Let the woman work," Jade said, taking a drink of her fresh beer.

"Are you jealous?" Zoe asked.

Jade shook her head. "You wish."

She'd never thought of Zoe that way. They were best friends and nothing more. At least from her perspective.

She glanced around the bar. Almost all the patrons were millennials or Generation Z. The few Generation Xers, the "invisible generation," stood out.

A voice rose above the chatter. The guy sitting on the stool next to her, trying to impress his companions.

Jade leaned in to Zoe so she wouldn't be overheard. "What if we were working on that case?"

"The Shakespeare Killer? Is this another hypothetical?"

"Maybe."

"What do you want to know?"

"Tell me about the sonnets."

"They were collected by a Mr. W. H. from private friends of Shakespeare, and published years later, most likely without Shakespeare's permission." Her face brightened. "May I see them? Do you have the evidence on you?"

"Of course not."

"Which sonnets?"

"I can't tell you."

"Ugh! You never let me have any fun."

"There's nothing fun about murder."

"You're right," Zoe said. "I'm sorry."

She proceeded to tell Jade about the sonnets. Much of it Jade had learned from Alaia Bennett, the GWU professor, and Micah.

When Zoe paused to take a breath, Jade asked, "Tell me about the Carr brothers."

Zoe made a face. "Their extremist views changed the direction of this country forever."

Another motive. "Extremist?"

"Some right wingnut philosophies are now considered legitimate schools of thought because of them. Twenty years ago, most Republicans believed that humans caused climate change. Those beliefs were inconvenient for the Carrs' business, so they set about changing them."

"How?"

"Advertising. Forming foundations and deputizing experts to bully and discredit scientists. It worked."

"Tell me more."

"Despite the Carrs claiming ad nauseam that they're for limited government, they have a history of using it to expand their businesses through tax breaks and regulation. Through their company and its subsidiaries, they form nonprofits, which they use to support their beliefs. They hide behind these organizations so they can spend massive amounts of money against their political opponents."

"To the outside world, their philanthropy appears generous."

"Right," Zoe said. "But the money they're giving away is used to manipulate American politics and further their business and private interests."

"And it's all legal," Jade said.

Zoe shrugged. "They're privileged. They can get away with murder."

Jade raised an eyebrow.

"Literally," Zoe said.

The two women drank in silence, and then Zoe leaned in. "Ever check out 'The God of Veritas'?"

"What do you mean?"

"On Twitter. Instagram."

"No."

"Your JadeHarringtonFans account has over two hundred thousand followers."

"Zoe…," Jade said, in a tone that conveyed her impatience. It was one Zoe was familiar with.

"All right, all right. The God of Veritas tweets a lot about the Carr brothers. I follow him on Twitter." She turned to smile at the bartender and held up her glass before turning back to Jade. "You want another one?"

Jade placed her hand over her bottle, still three-quarters full. "I'm fine."

"You should check him out."

After Zoe finished her third drink, the two friends headed to the door. Inclining her head back toward the bar, Jade said, "Aren't you going to say goodbye?"

Zoe didn't look back. "I've got her number."

❋

Leaving the bar, they emerged into the middle of the hustle and bustle of Georgetown's upscale businesses and specialty stores. The northwest neighborhood pulsed with activity, as it usually did this time of night. Diners and partygoers crowded the sidewalk, while drivers honked, protesting the traffic.

"How did you get here?" Jade asked.

Zoe pointed at the curb.

Jade's mouth gaped open. "You bought a motorcycle?" She examined the black and gray Honda sandwiched between two parked cars. "Nice."

"I like it," Zoe said, beaming. "It's a Rebel."

"How appropriate."

Stepping around Jade, she hopped onto the bike. "You wanna go for a ride? I don't have an extra helmet, but I promise to be careful."

Jade surveyed the small bike with its single seat and shook her head. "Nah. I'm good."

In truth, she wouldn't have accepted the offer even if Zoe had lent her an extra helmet and protective clothing, the bike had training wheels, and the streets were empty.

Zoe strapped on her helmet and revved the engine. As she did so, the sleeve of her leather jacket crept up her wrist, exposing a tattoo. Jade recalled the time she'd caught a glimpse of the new tattoo on Zoe's chest, right above her heart, exposed as she covered Jade with a blanket. Jade, in a drunken haze, had asked about it; Zoe claimed it wasn't new.

Now Jade peered closer. "New tat? I haven't seen that one before."

"There are a lot of areas on my body you haven't seen before."

"Stop," Jade said, feigning disgust. She paused. "Is that a tree? What does it represent?"

Zoe shrugged. "Nothing. I just like the way it looks."

Jade squinted at her. "You don't seem happy about it. It didn't come out the way you wanted?"

Glancing at the tattoo for a moment, Zoe readjusted her sleeve to cover it.

"It's what I wanted," Zoe muttered. "It's others who don't care for it."

"When did you start caring about what other people think?"

A faint smile. "You're right. I don't." She revved the engine. "I gotta go. Sure you don't want a ride?"

I prefer living.

Frowning, Jade said, "Zoe, what's going on?"

"Thanks for the drinks," Zoe said, brightening, her somber mood over.

Jade placed her hands on her hips. "It's funny how I always get stuck paying the check."

Zoe flashed her characteristic game show–host smile. "Didn't you just earn a promotion?"

As Zoe cut into traffic on M Street, Jade prayed for the other drivers. What was the deal with her friend's melancholy mood? It wasn't like her.

Not like her at all.

CHAPTER THIRTY-ONE

Arlington, Virginia

AS JADE LEFT the Chinese restaurant, she thought about what Zoe had said about China, Japan, and Russia taking over the world. Glancing at her takeout bag's greasy bottom, Jade figured she wasn't helping matters.

When she opened the door to her townhouse, her cat, Card, came running from whatever mischief he'd been up to. Scooping him up, she squeezed him and planted several kisses on his head. After ten seconds of bonding, he struggled to free himself and, once liberated, sprinted for the kitchen. After replenishing his water and food bowls on the tile floor, Jade picked up her briefcase and the takeout she'd left in the foyer and plopped cross-legged on the espresso-colored leather couch in her spartan living room. The scuffed hardwood floors needed buffing. Her bookshelves were filled with books and vinyl records, all in alphabetical order. Trophies and medals that she'd collected over the years were packed in cardboard boxes and stored in the basement.

With the case files for the Shakespeare Killer—they were probably stuck with the name now—spread out around her, she fired up her laptop. Using chopsticks, she scooped mouthfuls of the chow mein right out of the carton. She'd forgotten to eat breakfast and lunch. Again.

Jade reflected on her earlier conversation with Micah. Warren Barringer might not be a pleasure to work with, but she didn't want to believe that he'd leak sensitive details about such a high-profile case.

Putting thoughts of Barringer aside, she logged in to her rarely used Twitter account. Jade wasn't on social media much, both because of her job and because she wanted her private life to remain private.

She could've assigned Pat or Cyber to this task, but sometimes she preferred to conduct research herself. She found @TheGodOfVeritas easily. One hundred thousand followers—fewer than her fan account.

Veritas meant truth. The God of Truth.

His profile was bereft of description and location. He tweeted. A lot. Specifically about President Whitney Fairchild.

The more Jade read, the more concerned she became. His criticisms of the president were harsh, a recurring theme being that she was too conservative and not a real Democrat. A DINO—Democrat In Name Only.

Reading the replies to his tweets reinforced Jade's decision to avoid the platform. Had the human race always been so hateful, racist, and close-minded? Or did the anonymity of social media foster that behavior?

She kept reading, stopping short when her eyes landed on one particular tweet:

@TheGodOfVeritas: Word on the street is that Finn Hurley is in secret meetings with Senator Hampton. I wonder what Congress will do next to boost her business. #shame

Jade checked the date. About a week before Hurley was killed.

Thirty minutes later, she found another tweet of interest.

@TheGodOfVeritas: It's no secret that the Carr brothers and their Super PAC are behind the push to repeal the #NewNewDeal They should feel #shame

Tweeted a week before Carr was murdered.

The skin on Jade's forearms started to tingle.

Finally, after another hour, she came to:

@TheGodOfVeritas: While thousands of NYC citizens won't be eating dinner tonight, Sebastian Scofield is attending a $1000-a-plate dinner at the NYPL. #shame

Again, approximately a week before Scofield's death.

When she looked at the clock, it was 1:00 a.m. She'd been reviewing The God of Veritas's timeline for hours. The Chinese food was long gone, as were the two bottles of wheat beer from a microbrewery in California.

Card had fallen asleep next to her, his cocoa-colored head resting against her leg, snoring.

She wondered how long it would have taken the FBI to discover The God of Veritas's tweets if Zoe hadn't pointed her in this direction. The timing of the murders wasn't a coincidence. If his tweets signaled or were associated with the Shakespeare killings, what were the killer's plans for the president?

CHAPTER THIRTY-TWO

The White House, Washington, DC

"I APOLOGIZE FOR the late hour," Whitney said to the senator and the vice president, who shared the cream sofa under the elegant half-moon window in the West Sitting Hall off the Master Bedroom of the Residence. Whitney, sitting in a gray chair perpendicular to them, continued, "but I thought we'd be more comfortable here."

She waited as Senator Maureen McAllister took in the beige walls with landscape prints and white wainscot and chair rail. A bookcase leaned against one wall, filled with coffee table books interspersed with Fairchild family photos. Vice President Josephine Bates didn't need to behold the surroundings; she'd been here before.

"I don't mind," Mo said. "Those drapes! And the flowers are lovely." Mo's gaze returned to Whitney. "I do declare that I'm starting to enjoy visiting here."

"It can be habit-forming," Jo agreed.

"You're welcome anytime, Senator," said Whitney.

Mo sipped her hot tea before setting her cup on the square wooden coffee table. "I suppose you want to get down to business. Being from the North and West Coast and all."

Whitney asked, "What did you think about our proposal for New Cubed?"

"Why do y'all always go there?" Mo said.

"Pardon me?"

"Income redistribution. I don't believe in it, and it would be political suicide for me. I'd rather give people opportunity. Give them a fair shake."

Jo straightened her back. "Which 'people' are you talking about?"

"All the people who need it. Shoot, Jo, you know I don't care what color you are or whom you pray to."

To Mo, Whitney said, "Opportunity. I've heard that before—more suc-cinctly, by the way—from Senator Hampton."

Mo laughed. "Unlike my esteemed colleague from the Commonwealth of Virginia, I can find my backbone on an anatomical chart."

"Hampton is weak," Jo agreed.

"I believe in creating opportunities for *everyone*," Mo said, glancing at Jo, "especially those who've been left behind by technology or trade. We've been dealing with these issues in Mississippi for a long time."

"Same with California," Jo said.

"If you don't like my proposal," said Whitney, "do you have some-thing better?"

"Instead of free college and all that give-the-store-away foolishness, how about a national apprentice program? There are more jobs than available workers. Jobs that don't require a college degree. Employers want workers with experience. We can give it to them."

Whitney said, "I can support that."

"Me too," said Jo.

"What about providing capital to encourage the creation of small businesses?"

"We tried that with New New," Whitney reminded her.

"But that was the part of your legislation that I *liked*. That most of my party liked, before some of them lost their godforsaken minds. Some of my colleagues aren't *for* anything anymore. They just want to stop progress. Let's keep that part in."

"And increase the federal minimum wage," said Jo.

"To a living wage," Whitney agreed.

"We need to take care of our workers," Jo said. "Notably, workers of color."

Mo shook her head. "No can do. You start fiddling with the market, it gets all messed up."

There was a difference between compromising and, as Mo said, giving away the store. Increasing the minimum wage was important to Whitney's base. She wouldn't forget the people who had voted her into this office.

"What would you suggest?" Whitney asked.

Mo stared at her thoughtfully. "Do you mind if we liven things up in here?"

"In what way?"

The senator reached for her purse, perched next to the lamp on the round end table, and pulled out a flask covered in glitz and sparkle.

She held it up. "I always carry."

"I heard that about you people," Jo kidded.

Mo poured a small amount of the liquid into her tea. She held out the flask to Whitney.

"I'm too old to be drinking out of a flask," Whitney said to the older woman.

"Suit yourself," said fifty-five-year-old Jo, extending her cup. Mo poured a drop. Jo continued to hold out her cup.

"You don't need much," Mo said. "Trust me."

Jo took a sip and swallowed. Beads of sweat dotted her forehead. "She speaks the truth."

Whitney proffered her own cup. "I guess this is our version of breaking bread."

After Mo poured a drop for Whitney, the three women clinked cups. "Cheers," they said.

Whitney took a sip and coughed from the strong, bitter taste.

"What is this?" asked Whitney, still coughing.

"A little Mississippi moonshine."

"Is it legal?"

Mo winked. "Depends on which state you're in."

"Since we're not in a state," Whitney said, "we should be all right. Now, what were you suggesting before we… livened things up?"

Mo's response was measured. "I could tolerate regional minimum wage increases tied to the standard of living." She waved her hand. "We can let our staffs work out the nitty-gritty details."

"What do you think, Jo?" Whitney said.

"I think we can make that work."

Whitney took another sip of her moonshine-laced tea, this time without coughing. "Let's also help people save money so they'll be able to retire."

"We can privatize retirement," Mo said. "I could sell that to my colleagues."

"I'm sure you could," said Jo, between sips of tea.

Whitney waved her hand as if shooing a fly. "Now *you've* gone too far, Senator Mo. It won't work. Even if it did, it wouldn't work fast enough. What if we required employers to contribute a mandatory amount to retirement accounts? No matching required. That would go over well with the American people."

"I like the sound of that," Jo said.

Retrieving her flask, Mo poured more moonshine into her own cup. Jo held out hers for a refill. Whitney hesitated but did the same.

"I can't support that," Mo said. "My people want less government intervention, not more."

"Even if it's for their benefit?" Jo asked.

"That's a nonstarter, Madam President. Madam Vice President. Sorry."

Whitney gazed out the window at the West Colonnade, the West Wing, and beyond to the Eisenhower Executive Office Building. The retirement savings of baby boomers and Generation Xers had been depleted or wiped out by the Great Recession. She considered their retirements an impending crisis. It was one of the many worries that kept her up at night.

"I remember that time," Mo said to Whitney, "when you filibustered the Protection of Rights for All Citizens bill. The longer you talked, the more Senator Hampton's face scrunched up, as if he smelled something bad."

"I can top that," Jo said. "I remember when you"—she pointed at Mo—"filibustered a bill by reading *Gone with the Wind*. All one thousand pages of it. Your accent made it seem twice as long."

"You're not disparaging my floral ways, are you?" Mo said.

The three women laughed.

"Hampton was a young pup then," Jo continued, "and he kept interrupting you. And you kept talking over him. I thought you all were on the same side."

"We may be in the same political party," Mo said, wiping the tears of laughter from her eyes, "but that doesn't mean we're always on the same side." She turned to Jo. "Veep, I remember when you were a guest with him on *Meet the Press* while trying to pass the ERA. You told him, 'I'm a strong black woman, and I shall not be intimidated by anyone. Especially by a skinny, spineless little prick like you.' The network didn't beep you fast enough."

"I thought he was going to shit his pants," Jo said.

Mo fell against Jo with the weight of her laughter. Whitney bent over with hers.

Finally, Jo eased Mo off her shoulder, her expression turned serious.

"You'll need to hit the road," Jo said to Whitney. "Sell this thing."

"I can do that," Whitney said.

"I can too," Mo said. "There's only one problem remaining with our proposal."

"What's that?" Whitney said.

"There's no bad guy. If we work together, no one can blame either party. People need someone to blame."

Whitney drained the remainder of her tea. "I'm sure we can find someone for them to hate, Mo and Jo, because… I've got my mojo!"

The three women burst into hysterical laughter.

"Wait! Wait!" Mo said. She held out her cup. "A toast! To the resignation of Senator Paul Sampson!"

"Hear, hear!" said Whitney.

"To one fewer old, out-of-touch white guy making decisions for the rest of us," Jo said. She drank and reached for the flask on the table. "Still almost full. We're going to need some more tea."

Whitney reached for the phone. "I can take care of that."

"Now this," said Mo, spreading out her arms, "is a Tea Party."

CHAPTER THIRTY-THREE

Washington, DC

JADE CHECKED HER watch with its slim black band before glancing back at The Complete Works of William Shakespeare, perfectly aligned with the right corner of her desk. She lifted the hefty tome and opened it where she'd placed the first blue sticky note.

She checked the time again, then shut the book.

After the third murder, the newly formed Shakespeare Killer task force moved to a major-case room. The team was meeting there now, which was why she remained in her office—to prevent herself from hijacking Dante's meeting.

For a long time, Zoe had been nagging her to meditate, instructing Jade to clear her mind and count her breaths: "one" on the inhale, "two" on the exhale.

Jade closed her eyes and breathed in deeply. *One.* She needed to give Dante the space to do his job. Start over. *One.* She believed he could do it. *One.* She wondered what they were discussing. *One.* Had they thought about—

She popped out of her chair and left her office.

Jade stepped through the doorway into the crowded case room. Christian, Pat, Micah, and Max sat in chairs in the front row. Christian's seat was turned around, his forearms on the top of the chair's backrest. A score of other agents and representatives from other law enforcement jurisdictions were spread out behind them.

Dante, positioned at the front of the room, said, "All the victims were between the ages of thirty-five and fifty-five. Scofield, fifty-four. Carr, fifty-five. Hurley, thirty-five."

"The victims that we're aware of," said Pat. The clicking of her fingers on the keyboard was audible from the back of the room.

"Right," he said. "Pat, check out VICAP"—Violent Criminal Apprehension Program—"for cases with similar characteristics."

"Yes, boss," she said, her fingers tapping furiously.

He squinted at her, as if assessing whether she was making fun of him. After a moment, he seemed to conclude that she wasn't. "No hair, fiber, or other trace evidence was found on any of the victims," he said.

"Were they acquainted with each other?" Micah said.

Pat's eyes stayed glued to her computer. "I'll check that out too."

Glancing back down at his notes, where his index finger kept his place, Dante said, "Both males were married. Hurley, divorced. All three were white." He spotted Jade at the back of the room. "Can I help you, boss?"

Standing just inside the door, Jade shook her head.

"Like I was saying—" he said.

She raised her hand. "How are you doing with Twitter?"

Dante shook his head, smiling, and pointed. "Pat?"

Pat was the team's liaison with the FBI's Cyber Division.

She turned to face Jade. "The company refuses to release the identity of The God of Veritas. Legal is preparing a court order."

"The God of Veritas," Micah said. "Humble that one."

"What about Scofield's, Carr's, and Hurley's social media accounts?" asked Jade.

Pat read off her computer. "Carr and Hurley weren't on social media."

"Carr probably because he was secretive," Dante said. "Hurley, being in cybersecurity, didn't trust it."

"But Scofield lived on social media," Pat said. "He tweeted his every move, making it easy for anyone who wanted to hurt him."

Dante asked Jade. "Anything else?"

She waved her hand. "Carry on."

He turned his attention back to his team.

"As I was saying"—his eyes cut to Jade and then back to his notes—"all the victims came from similar socioeconomic backgrounds."

"They were rich," Christian said.

"More like wealthy," Micah said.

To Max, Dante said, "What are you thinking?"

Jade hadn't seen Max since they'd shared a quiet Christmas dinner at his house. She looked at him now. The faint wisps of blond hair on the top of his head had disappeared after his wife left him.

"Usually, the motive of a serial killer comes down to anger, financial gain, thrill, or attention seeking," Max said. "I can't narrow it down yet. Could be any of them or some combination. There's a lot of rage here. The victims suffered from deep, penetrating wounds through muscles, organs—even to the bone, in Finn Hurley's case. The killer is also organized."

"But an organized killer doesn't usually murder his victim in the same place where the body is found," Jade called out. "Usually, he'll move it and dump it somewhere."

Max pushed up his rimless glasses and then conceded the point. "He might be mixed. I would lean toward organized rather than disorganized. The murders were well planned."

"He seems to enjoy an audience," Dante said. "Scofield and Carr were murdered in front of witnesses, and Hurley's murder was witnessed by the entire GW Parkway's early-morning commuter traffic."

Christian glanced back at Jade. She gave him a look. *This is why I picked him.*

"Signature?" Jade asked, for the benefit of the others in the room.

"The sonnets, of course," Max said. "I'm not sure yet if they relate to the victim, a situation, the perp, or if he wants us to think he's smart. An intellectual."

"What do you make of the absence of defensive wounds on the arms and hands of the victims?" she said.

"You're getting ahead of us here," Dante said, checking his notes.

"Then catch up," she said to him. "Max?"

Max's lips twitched. "That's true. Either the victims knew and trusted the suspect, or the murderer caught all of them unawares."

"The perp possesses some knowledge of anatomy," Micah said thoughtfully. "He stabbed Carr in the aorta and Hurley in the femoral artery. If help didn't come immediately, death was all but certain."

Max looked pleased. "Very good."

Jade did a private eye roll at the teacher praising his favorite pupil.

"Why did he leave the knife in?" Christian asked.

"Good question," Max said. "Extracting the knives would've exacerbated the victims' injuries. Made them suffer."

"Which doesn't fit with the rage or anger motive," Christian pointed out, glancing at Jade as if to say, "You still should have picked me."

"You're right," said Max.

Micah said, "Or he's not totally heartless."

"What else, Max?" asked Dante.

"Serial killers were often abused as children: physically, emotionally, sexually. Usually by a family member."

"Here we go," Dante said sarcastically.

"There's been no evidence of sexual activity with any of the victims," Micah said.

"That doesn't mean he wasn't abused," said Pat.

"Let's move this along, Max," Dante said, "since *everyone's* been abused these days. Let's say he was abused in some way."

"What a twit," Micah whispered to Pat, in a voice that reached Jade in the back of the room.

"I heard that," said Dante.

"Many serial killers were bullied, rejected, and neglected as children," Max said, ignoring them both. "They grow up seeking approval from parents, sexual partners, friends, but they never receive it. Over time, the serial killer develops an inability to attach."

"Psychopathy," said Micah.

Dante said, "Same sad story."

"Unfortunately, it usually is the same sad story," Max said. "What's unusual in this case is the age of the victims. Your odds of being a victim of a serial killer significantly decrease after thirty."

"Thank God," Pat said as she continued to type.

Dante eyed her. "There are always exceptions."

Pat scratched the side of her head with her middle finger. Some of the other agents laughed. Even Dante cracked a smile.

"New York City, Chicago, and here," Christian said. "The perp has some means."

"He does his homework," Max said. "He studies his victims, learns their habits, where they'll be."

"Not a lot of time between the murders, though," Christian said.

"What if he planned them all beforehand, then struck?" Dante said.

No one had a response.

"Anything else?" Dante asked the group.

"Update them on our meeting with the professor," Jade called out to Dante.

He scowled but did as she said.

"Anything back on the paper the sonnets were written on?" Christian asked.

Pat stopped typing. "The same paper was used in the Scofield and Hurley murders. The analysts believe it was manufactured in England. Same paper used by the royal family."

"Makes sense," Dante said. "Shakespeare and all."

"The perp has fine taste," Micah said.

"What about the kids?" Jade called out.

Brow furrowed, Dante said, "Huh?"

"Shakespeare keeps telling his friend that he should bear children so his beauty can live on for eternity," Jade said. "Maybe this has something to do with the victims' kids."

Dante blinked at her before turning to Christian. "Why don't you take that on?"

Christian smirked. "You sure you're up to this supervising thing, compadre?"

Dante's eyes returned to his notes. "Just check it out, Merritt."

The team discussed next steps and batted ideas back and forth. After a time, no one seemed to remember that Jade was in the room.

As the discussion continued, she slipped out the door without anyone noticing.

❈

Later that afternoon, Dante burst into her office, his eyes alight with excitement.

Jade looked up from the email she was typing.

"We've got a lead," he said. "A solid one."

"What is it?"

"I'll tell you on the way."

"Where are we headed?"

"New York."

CHAPTER THIRTY-FOUR

The White House, Washington, DC

"MADAM PRESIDENT, LEI Min is on the line."

Whitney frowned. "Put him through," she told Sean through the speakerphone.

"This is a pleasant surprise," she said to the president of the People's Republic of China.

"You may not think so once I've told you why I've called," he said, his voice clipped. His English was flawless.

"Oh?"

"I want to forewarn you—or, as you Americans say, give you a heads-up."

A pressure in her chest, a foreboding.

"About what?" she said.

"My country signed a deal today," he said. "With Russia. The Sino-Russian Partnership Trade Agreement, or SRPTA."

Whitney almost gasped. This was bad. Why hadn't her team warned her?

Focused on domestic issues during her first year in office, her secretary of state, Charles Staunton, had kept a low profile, making only a few obligatory overseas trips. Except for a brief skirmish with Russia in the Middle East, things had been quiet on the international front. Whitney had encouraged Staunton to resign after the announcement of the income inequality summit.

And she hadn't replaced him yet.

Into the phone, she said, "Is it too late for the United States to come to the table?"

"That ship has sailed," he said. "We will shift some of our exports from the US to our friends in Russia. My staff will send over the details. I thought you should hear it from me. Goodbye."

As opposed to your new BFF leaking it to the media?

Pressing the intercom button on the telephone, she said, "Sean, ring Tamirov immediately."

As she waited for the call to go through, she spun her chair around to gaze out the window at the Rose Garden. The foliage was dusted with snow.

The goods trade deficit with China had grown to $500 billion; US companies liked employing cheap labor and materials to manufacture their products, and US consumers liked cheap Chinese imports—"Buy American" notwithstanding.

The US and China shared a strong relationship, an entangled one, based on trade. A trade war could result in their mutual economic destruction.

Russia and China supplied petroleum to the global economy. Perhaps this deal was about staving off the green-energy revolution for a while longer?

Both countries funded antidemocratic and anti-US countries with arms and currency while playing the peacemaker on the world stage. Whitney—and her foreign policy advisors—had considered them an "axis of convenience." An opportunistic relationship tainted with mistrust. It seemed to be something more now.

Apparently, Tamirov had forgotten his envy of China's sustained economic growth, or he was using Min in some way. Whitney would bet on the latter.

Recently, Russia had stepped up its government-sanctioned cybermeddling in US and European commerce and political elections, weakening the public's perception of institutions and democracy itself on both sides of the Atlantic. The Cold War of the eighties hadn't been resurrected; rather, a new one had been born: a cyberwar. No, this wasn't the same Russia, but this wasn't the same United States either. The US was more polarized. More fractured.

Divided.

Most of Tamirov's moves had heretofore been behind the scenes, but now he'd emerged from behind the Iron Curtain. With one ambition.

To be the only star on the world stage.

"Madam President," the Russian president's smooth, confident voice came over the line, with only a trace of an accent, "what a coincidence. I was just talking about you to our mutual friend, President Lei Min."

"What's going on?" she said, her voice hard.

"Ah," he said, "you heard."

"Tell me about the deal."

"China and Russia have a long history of mutual respect. An alignment of shared interests. Some might call it love."

"Love, Andrei?"

"I love the Chinese people. This Russian-Sino agreement will greatly benefit the citizens of both our great countries."

"I thought it was Sino-Russian."

"Semantics," he said dismissively.

"Oil for consumer products," she said.

"And natural gas and military hardware."

She thought for a moment. "Infrastructure."

He chuckled. "I don't care what your American press says. You are much smarter than your predecessor."

Whitney ignored the compliment, or the dig at former president Richard Ellison. "The United States—"

Tamirov cut her off. "The deal is done. Perhaps next time. Good day, Madam President."

She didn't care for being hung up on twice in the span of thirty minutes. This deal weakened her position. Weakened the United States. The entire premise of international trade was for countries to leverage each other's strengths and support each other's weaknesses, creating greater economic growth for all. Successful trade agreements were essential to the healthy functioning of the US economy. After listening to the dial tone for a few moments, she slowly replaced the receiver.

This would not stand.

She leaned back in her chair, the index finger of her left hand rising to her lips. Her thinking position.

After several minutes, she sat up and called Sean. "Hold my calls for the rest of the day and cancel all my meetings."

"Your afternoon is booked. At noon, you're meeting with the Joint Chiefs—"

"I don't care."

Whitney pressed the End button.

She opened a folio with a pad of paper inside and reached for a pen.

And she started to write.

CHAPTER THIRTY-FIVE

New York City, New York

JADE PACED AS she waited.

Dante stood by the one-way observation window, watching her, a bemused smile on his face. Detective Elaine Katz of the New York Police Department stood next to him.

"Picked him up on 40th, between 7th and 8th," Katz said. "He'd been wearing the coat for a while."

"Anything back on it?" Jade asked.

The detective shook her head. "Still working on it. A lot of fingerprints. Bodily fluids. Probably his." She pointed at the window as a uniformed officer brought the man into the interview room. "It was exposed to the elements for a while. Sorting it all out might take some time. We found blood on the coat."

Jade stopped pacing. "Scofield's?"

"Don't know yet."

"Let's see if he can help us," Jade said. "Shall we?"

She and Dante had taken a shuttle flight to LaGuardia and come straight to the Manhattan precinct from the airport. Detective Katz—short and solid, with a square face, dark eyes, and dark brown hair—led them into the room.

The pungent smell of body odor hit Jade as soon as she entered. She stilled her face and resisted the urge to cover her nose and mouth with her hand. Behind her, Dante gulped.

The man wore a tattered brown shirt and faded black pants. The toes of his black shoes were scuffed gray.

Jade sat in the chair between Dante and Katz. Thinking the witness might find Jade less threatening, Katz had suggested earlier that Jade conduct the interview.

Dante had leaned in to Jade, whispering, "If she only knew."

Sitting across from them, the man trembled.

Jade relaxed and tried to appear docile and nonthreatening. It was hard. She clasped her hands together on the table.

"You've met Detective Katz. My name is Special Agent in Charge Jade Harrington, and this is Assistant Special Agent in Charge Dante Carlucci. We're from the FBI, and we're here to ask you some questions. That's all, okay?"

He hesitated, then dipped his head.

"What's your name?"

"Ben."

"Ben what?"

"It's just Ben."

"What's your last name?" Dante asked.

"If Oprah's allowed to have only one name, why can't I?"

The two agents and the detective looked at each other. Dante shrugged.

"My mother named me after a damn mouse," Ben said. "Her favorite song."

Jade recognized the song, of course. She fought back memories of her parents slow dancing in the living room of their California home.

"When the police found you," she said, "you were wearing an attractive coat. Where did you get it?"

Ben fingered the frayed cuff of a shirtsleeve. "May I have some water?"

Katz stood and went to the door. She opened it and said something to someone on the other side. The observers watching through the window had heard Ben's request.

Soon after she was reseated, a police officer entered, placed a cup in front of Ben, and left.

Jade waited for Ben to take a sip. After he'd chugged the contents, she tried again. "Tell us about the coat."

A grin split Ben's gritty, grimy face. Some of his teeth were missing. The remaining ones were a dull brown. He'd been handsome once.

"Did you see it?" he said. "Wasn't it nice?"

"Who gave it to you?"

"Some guy."

"What did he look like?"

Ben shrugged. "Like all those guys, I suppose."

"Those guys?"

"A suit. Slicked hair. White guy. Money."

A faraway look in his eyes.

"What did you do before?" Jade said.

"Before what?"

"Before—" She faltered. "For work."

"I was a head trader at Lehman. Until 2008. Used to be one of them. One of those slick-haired guys in a suit."

"You haven't worked since?"

Ben shook his head and looked at the cup, as if debating whether to ask for something stronger. "There weren't any jobs after that. Lost the apartment on Park Avenue. Then the Porsche. The house upstate. My wife. Kids. Everything. Now these guys walk around like they're too good for me. Don't even see me."

"Why don't you get back in the game?"

He shook his head, more vigorously this time. "Too old."

"How old are you, Ben?"

Ben thought about it. "What's today?"

Jade told him.

"Thirty-nine."

Jade gasped. She couldn't help it. He looked fifty-nine. Or older. She recovered quickly. "Where were you when the guy gave you the coat?"

"My usual spot. The same place they found me today."

"They?"

"The police."

"Why do you think he gave it to you?"

"I caught him staring at me. Most people look through me, if they notice me at all. He just took it off and gave it to me. The nicest gift I've received in a long time."

"Then where did he go?"

"He kept going down 40th."

She made a mental note to ask Katz about cameras in the area. "Would you do something for me?"

The skin around Ben's eyes tightened, his suspicion returning. "What?"

"If you worked with a sketch artist, do you think you could describe the man?"

Ben considered her, calculating. "As long as you'll do something for me."

Jade was prepared to give him food, drink, and a warm shower, even help him find a place to stay for a short time. It wasn't much or a long-term solution, but it was the least she could do.

"Sure," she said. "What do you want?"

"May I have my coat back?" he asked.

CHAPTER THIRTY-SIX

Air Force One

"COME IN, SASHA."

As they soared above the clouds, Sasha crossed the spacious office of the presidential suite and sat in the chair next to the desk.

"Have a seat," Whitney said dryly. "Be with you in a moment."

Sasha waited while Whitney continued to write.

The Boeing 747-200B airplane was en route to the Midwest on a two-day trip to Michigan, Indiana, Ohio, Wisconsin, and Illinois, to sell the slimmed-down version of the New New Deal. Mo was headed to the South, and Jo to the West, to accomplish the same thing. Whitney would be visiting manufacturing plants, colleges, and town halls.

She finally set down her pen. "I've been working on something."

Sasha cocked her head, as she was wont to do. "You sure look proud of yourself."

"I guess I am."

Whitney perused the papers one more time before handing them over to Sasha.

"What's this?" asked Sasha.

Whitney settled back in her chair. "Reagan established the Reagan Doctrine. Truman, the Truman Doctrine. Nixon, the Nixon Doctrine. I can't sit by and watch Min and Tamirov divide up the world like seventeenth-century colonial powers. It's time the United States got back in the game."

"I agree. What are we going to do?"

"In your hands is our approach to foreign policy."

"We don't have a secretary of state," Sasha reminded her.

Waving off this detail as if it were insignificant, Whitney said, "Staunton's departure gives me the opportunity to appoint the best person to carry this out." She pointed at the document. "Someone who supports and shares my beliefs about our place in the world."

"Who?"

Whitney hesitated. "I haven't figured that out yet."

The two women laughed.

"And what is this"? Sasha asked.

"You hold in your hands the Fairchild Doctrine."

Sasha's mouth fell open. "Really!"

Whitney didn't blame Sasha for being surprised. She'd kept her foreign policy views private for the majority of her political career; most people thought Whitney was a pacifist.

For more than a century, the world had been in awe of America's military might. In recent times, public sentiment leaned toward the US focusing on its own problems and letting other countries deal with theirs. The difficulty with that approach was that other countries' problems eventually became America's problems.

Her problems.

While Sasha read through the document, Whitney watched the flat-screen TV on the opposite wall, red and green numbers crawling across the bottom of the screen. The Dow was down one hundred points.

Sasha looked up. "I noticed you didn't mention Russia or China by name."

Whitney returned her gaze to Sasha. "No need. Tamirov and Min will know."

"I love how it's based on *precedent*," Sasha said, "and *presidents*. Everyone's represented." She flipped through the pages. "Truman. Eisenhower. Kennedy. Nixon. Clinton."

"That's the whole idea," Whitney said. "My policy incorporates their legacies, honors tradition, shows continuity, and builds on them for the future."

Sasha handed the document back to her. "I like it."

"Wonderful. I'm going to run it by Jo and Mo."

Sasha cocked her head. "Mo?"

"Yes, Mo."

Affecting a pronounced Southern drawl, the former Texas congresswoman said, "Didn't realize y'all were so close."

Whitney pursed her own lips, imitating Sasha. "As if your accent is any better." She turned her attention to the briefing books on her desk.

Sasha started to rise. "What's next?"

"I need you to find a secretary of state."

CHAPTER THIRTY-SEVEN

Washington, DC

IN HER OFFICE the next morning, Jade stared at the sketch of the nondescript white man with medium-length brown hair. Pat had sent the image to FACE—Facial Analysis, Comparison, and Evaluation Services—which managed over thirty million mugshots and four hundred million images in its face-recognition database. Many of those images weren't of people who'd committed a crime, but citizens who'd applied for a passport or a driver's license and unwittingly provided law enforcement access to their likeness at any time.

Jade and Dante had reviewed the footage from the camera in front of the New York Public Library. Katz was right. The perp's face was not only obscured by the hat, but it was tilted away from the camera, as if he knew the facial recognition software didn't need much: the width between the eyes, the shape of a nose, the curvature of the lips.

Katz had gotten back to her on the coat. NYPD Forensics found Scofield's blood on it and lots of smudged fingerprints.

Ben had encouraged anyone he encountered to touch his new coat.

After vigorous reassurance, NYPD had obtained Ben's fingerprints. Although he'd already been ruled out as a suspect, his fingerprints would be on file if they showed up later in connection with the case. His name came back as Ben Havenstein. Arrested twice for trespassing. His address of record, a high-end apartment on Park Avenue.

The week of the murder, NYPD had gone door to door within a six-block radius of the library, but no one claimed to have seen the perpetrator/coat-giving Samaritan. After the interview yesterday, Jade and Dante canvassed the Meatpacking District neighborhood. They stopped by a Men's Wearhouse. She selected the item over Dante's protestations.

"I'm choosing it," she said. "I've seen the way you dress."

Later, they found Ben in his regular spot on 40th Street. She handed him his new coat. It wasn't the same one the police had confiscated, but he didn't seem to mind.

After struggling to his feet, Ben modeled it for her and Dante.

Stroking the sleeve, he said, "This coat fits even better."

CHAPTER THIRTY-EIGHT

Washington, DC

DANTE POPPED HIS head into Jade's office. "We're having a task force meeting. Wanna join us?"

She needed to prepare for afternoon meetings, take care of some bureaucratic details, and go over witness testimonies for other cases. Without answering him, she locked her computer and accompanied him to the major-case room.

It now resembled a war room, with maps, sketches, diagrams, and photographs plastering the walls. Dante had blown up pictures of the victims, in life and in death, and affixed them to the wall. As Jade did for her major cases.

The agents were assembled. Jade stood near the door again. Dante moved to the front of the room.

"What do we got?" he said. "Christian?"

"Why don't you go first?" Christian asked.

Dante's eyes widened, but he said nothing.

Christian gave Dante a look before pulling a small notebook out of his back pocket. "The first victim, Sebastian Scofield, had two kids. A boy and a girl, ages two and four. Jared Carr, three: two boys, seventeen and nine, and a girl, five. Finn Hurley was childless."

"Did you find out anything that made you think the murders involved the children?"

"Given my limited investigative experience," Christian said, "it's no surprise that I have not."

Dante scowled at him. "Grow up!" He turned to Pat. "Anything on the sketch?"

"No match."

"What about the cameras from 40th Street?" Jade asked.

Dante shook his head, frustrated. He scanned the room. "Does anyone have anything?"

Silence. Then Christian said, "I found the bike." He savored the moment of attention. "In Crystal City. It's one of those bike shares you see all over the city. Although the perp wiped it clean, forensics found blood."

"Whose?" asked Jade.

"Hurley's."

"Did you track down who rented it?"

"Nope. The perp reserved it online. His personal information was fake, the credit card stolen."

"Anything else?" Dante asked, his tone impatient. Jade eyed him. Leading a case could do that to you.

"Got Hurley's client list," Pat said. "Corporations, nonprofits, all levels of government, including the White House, the FBI. Cyber worked with her on the Robin Hood case."

Dante used his pen to scratch behind his ear. "Were the other two victims on the list?"

Pat shook her head. "Although Scofield's firm was private, we're trying to piece together its client list through SEC and other filings. So far, we've come up with wealthy individuals and pension fund managers. The Carrs' firm is private, too, but a lot more secretive. The surviving brother hasn't been cooperative."

"Let me know if you need help there," Jade said.

Dante held up his hand. "We got it." To Christian, "Anything on the knives?"

"All three were the same brand," Christian said. "Maxam hunting knives, which you can buy on Amazon in packs of eight. No prints were found on them. Forensics believes the unsub wore gloves."

"Why did he leave the knives in their bodies?" asked Jade from the back of the room.

Everyone turned to Max.

Max thought for a moment. "I don't think the knives mean anything to him. They're a tool. A means to an end. The weapon of choice might be more important. A knife can be quieter than a gun. It's more personal. If you want to make sure you don't miss, you need to be close."

"But messier," said Dante.

"What if each knife was meant for each victim?" Micah said. "Like the sonnets."

"That's good," Dante said.

Max nodded thoughtfully.

"Or he's trying to make a statement," Christian said.

Dante smirked. "I think we got the point."

Pat, known throughout the bureau for her inappropriate dark humor, said, "That's bad."

CHAPTER THIRTY-NINE

The White House, Washington, DC

"EVERYONE," WHITNEY SAID, "please be seated."

Always the last to enter the Cabinet Room, she strode past the fireplace with *The Declaration of Independence, July 4, 1776* hanging above the mantle, the busts of George Washington and Benjamin Franklin, and around the table to the late eighteenth-century replica chair situated in the middle. Affixed to the back of her chair, which was two inches higher than the other chairs, was a brass plate engraved simply with the words The President. The other members' positions were affixed to the backs of their chairs. The elliptical mahogany table was purchased by President Richard Nixon in 1970 with his personal funds. Glancing at the United States flag and the flag of the president behind her, Whitney was awed, not for the first time, by how appropriately the latter represented her position: an eagle clutching white arrows in one talon and an olive branch in the other.

Once everyone was seated, she said, "Shall we begin? Sasha?"

Over the past week, the two of them had refined the document that Whitney had shown Sasha on Air Force One. Sean had typed it up. Whitney had not run it by Mo. Or Jo. The circle—or triangle—of people who knew about its contents had been kept intentionally small.

In front of each member, Sasha placed a folder bearing the presidential seal on the cover.

Whitney looked around the table at the faces of her cabinet members, their deputies and aides sitting behind them in chairs against the walls.

"'Let every nation know,'" she began, "'whether it wishes us well or ill, that we shall pay any price, bear any burden, meet any hardship, support any friend, oppose any foe to assure the survival and the success of liberty.'"

"What?" asked Secretary of Labor Tucker Price, a quizzical expression on his face.

"Kennedy," Secretary of Education Pravir Ratta said out of the side of his mouth. "John," he clarified.

"That's right," Whitney said. "President John F. Kennedy said those words as part of his inaugural address on January 20, 1961. It would later form the basis of the Kennedy Doctrine. To that end, I present to you the Fairchild Doctrine."

The expressions on the members' faces ranged from questioning to shocked.

"The United States will no longer sit on the sidelines of global affairs," Whitney said. "We have a responsibility to be at the center of the international order. Only then will we enjoy global prosperity and international peace and security. At one time, we were the most respected, emulated, and revered country on earth. There is no reason we cannot achieve that again. Starting today, we will strengthen relationships with our key allies and strategic partners and regain their trust."

Price's chair creaked as he shifted. "How are we going to do that?"

She pointed to his folder. "Read."

As they opened their folders, Whitney reached for the delicate cup on the table and took a sip of tea.

Price looked up. "I thought we were focusing on domestic issues this year. Like homelessness."

"Minimum wage," Vice President Josephine Bates said.

"Infrastructure," said Julio Casillas and Ashton Crawford, the secretaries of transportation and commerce.

"What about police brutality?" Jo continued. "African-Americans are more than three times as likely to—"

Whitney held up her hand. "Jo, I'm not abandoning those issues. We will continue to address homelessness, raise the minimum wage, and invest in our crumbling infrastructure—"

"You forgot police brutality," Jo said.

"Things aren't always black and white," Whitney said.

"For some of us, they are."

"Hear, hear," Sasha said.

Whitney flashed Jo a warning. "You didn't let me finish. Those issues are important to me, and my commitment hasn't changed, but I also want to focus on issues that impact everyone, not just Americans."

"Like what?" said Price, doubtful. He scanned his colleagues' faces to ascertain who was with him. Several other cabinet members seemed to share his doubts.

"Create opportunities for women. Reduce income inequality. Provide an affordable quality education. Eliminate poverty. Combat climate change. Improve health outcomes. Ensure security by cracking down on cyberthreats." She nodded at Malachi Winters, chairman of US Cyber Command. "Private and government-sanctioned groups." A pause. "World peace."

She let the silence linger as they absorbed her words. Whitney gazed at each of their faces. "Franklin Roosevelt won World War I and created the international financial and diplomatic systems that we still use today. Kennedy dreamed about landing the first man on the moon. Johnson expanded civil and voting rights. Reagan helped end the Cold War." She pounded her fist on the table. "Name one watershed accomplishment over the last two decades."

Some of the members flinched. Whitney, typically not one to show emotion—especially anger—had their attention.

"We can no longer go it alone. We will no longer take our allies for granted."

"What about diminished wages and lost jobs in the US?" asked Ashton Crawford. The commerce secretary's hair, makeup, and nails were always flawless. Born in an old money New York family, she'd never had to worry about lost wages or jobs in her life, but Whitney had chosen her because she was smart and got things done.

"You'll be mindful of that in your trade negotiations," Whitney responded. To everyone, she said, "Unless we want to kowtow to authoritarianism or terrorism, we will engage in international diplomacy and continue to be a strong ally with NATO." She raised her hand toward Maricela Salcedo, the secretary of homeland security. "We will support those countries resisting outside agents and protect the territories and independence of such nations. And use military force, if necessary, to defend our economic and national interests."

She scanned the stunned faces of her cabinet.

Jo raised a quizzical eyebrow. "War... and peace?"

Titters from some of the members.

Whitney stood and glanced at the west wall across from her. Each president chose the paintings that hung there. Instead of paintings, she had chosen to hang three black-and-white photographs of suffragettes. Her favorite was one of women picketing in front of the White House.

To Jo, Whitney said, "You must fight for the things that matter."

Arlington, Virginia

JADE EXHALED AS she transitioned from the at-rest stance to the first move. Crossing her arms, she extended them to either side, her triceps perpendicular to the floor, her hands in fists, palms facing forward.

She stared into the intensity of her own light-brown eyes in the mirror, pretending she was her opponent. Fists to her hips, she extended her left arm, while her right fist came up in a slow-motion uppercut as she moved to a left front stance. She repeated the movement on the other side. She continued the movements of the *poomsae* against an imaginary opponent, her stances solid. No one could knock her off-balance. Her punches were sharp and swift. Her hands sliced through the air like horizontal guillotines.

When she completed the form, she sat cross-legged on the matted floor in the middle of the room, facing the wall-length mirror, which was split horizontally by a bar, like one found in a ballet studio. But no one performed ballet at Master Won Ho's Tae Kwon Do school, located at a strip mall within walking distance from her house.

Jade closed her eyes and rested the back of her hands on her knees. "One…"

As she tried to meditate, she thought about her team meeting. Well, Dante's team meeting. Dante had followed up with her later and reported that after she'd left it had continued for another hour without much progress. Despite his frustration with the lack of movement on the case, he seemed motivated since his promotion. He was one of the first agents in the office every morning and one of the last to leave every evening. No one could accuse him of being lazy anymore.

Although she dreamed of being the first black woman FBI director, Jade had never given much thought to how it would feel to attain that goal. She'd always spent the least amount of time behind her desk as possible. It was harder to do while her team pursued the case without her.

Oh… she forgot. She was meditating and wasn't supposed to be thinking about anything at all.

She inhaled. "One."

Her mind drifted to Ethan Lawson, his starched white shirts and suspenders a throwback to bureau agents of days gone by. She wondered if he was ever coming back and why he'd been forced out. She hadn't looked into it.

New cases had gotten in the way.

"One."

"I can tell you're not meditating," said a serene voice.

Jade opened one eye.

In the mirror, she saw a diminutive man with short-cropped silver hair. He was in his blue *dobok*, a white athletic shirt underneath, standing near the entrance behind her. One end of his black belt sported six thin stripes. The other, his name emblazoned in gold cursive writing.

"How?" she asked, opening her other eye.

His soft footsteps padded across the floor until he stood before her. He pointed down.

She looked at her hands. Instead of being relaxed, they were balled into fists. One tapped her knee. "This was never my strong suit," she said. A fourth-degree black belt, she should have mastered meditation by now.

"It's the most important aspect of your training," her long-time instructor said.

"I know," she said, unclenching her fists. "How's the hip?"

He sat next to her, which took a little more effort than normal. Master Ho, in his sixties, was still recovering from hip surgery he'd had this past summer. He was back to work full time but couldn't train. Still, she wouldn't bet against him in a sparring match.

"It feels good."

"Looks as if it still hurts."

"How you feel is a state of mind, grasshopper."

She smiled at his reference to *The Karate Kid*.

Jade envied her teacher's calmness. The peace that radiated within and exuded from him, no matter the situation.

She hadn't mastered that either.

"How have you been?" he said. "You haven't been to class much."

At her rank, Jade could work out by herself, but she needed to attend a certain number of classes before testing for fifth degree. Given her schedule, training was difficult to fit in.

"Been busy."

She never talked about work with him. He knew what she did. Who she was. He focused on helping her achieve her martial arts goals. His only concern was her well-being. Sitting with him helped relieve her stress.

"Care to spar?"

Surprised, she said, "With that hip?"

The corner of his eyes crinkled. "I possess other weapons."

"This I know."

The last time she'd sparred with him, his round kick almost knocked off her head gear—and her head along with it.

The vibration of her phone filled the silence. "Saved by the buzz, I guess."

"Or divine intervention."

They both placed a hand on the floor and stood, Jade in a fluid motion, Master Ho in a more labored one. "I'll leave you to it then." A slight bow. "Good night, Ms. Harrington."

She bowed in return. "Night, sir."

Jogging to her bag resting against the wall, she dug out her phone. A text from Dante.

Pat found The God of Veritas. We're flying out tonight.

Where to?

See for yourself. Meet you at Dulles.

CHAPTER FORTY-ONE

The White House, Washington, DC

A SCALED-DOWN VERSION of the New New Deal Coalition legislation, S.564—Put America Back to Work, sponsored by Senator Maureen McCallister, narrowly passed in the Senate. A similar bill, sponsored by the representative from Jo's state of California, passed in the House. The media—perhaps believing New Cubed would be difficult to understand by the mathematically challenged, a disproportionate segment of the US population—started calling it the New New Redo. With a lot less fanfare than the original, Whitney signed the bill into law at her desk in the Oval Office that afternoon, surrounded by business leaders, union representatives, and labor activists. Afterward, as the cameras of the White House press corps clicked, the three women—the president, the vice president, and the senator—held the document.

As she climbed the stairs, Whitney's mood was light. Mo and Jo had held up their end of the bargain. Arms had been twisted in both chambers of Congress. Cole Brennan had done his part, telling his listeners the bill's benefits and to contact their congressmen, multiple times if necessary.

Employers had started hiring in anticipation of the legislation's passing; unemployment would surely fall when Whitney received the next report. She imagined the discussions being held tonight between Senator Hampton and his lackey, Representative Howard Bell. Senator Sampson was no longer around to commiserate with them. As Sasha had expected, he had resigned last week.

A win. Finally.

Secret Service Agent Josh McPherson opened the door to the Residence and said, "Have a good evening, ma'am."

"You too, Josh."

He retreated.

Placing her briefcase on a stand in the foyer, she spotted the suitcase and travel bag.

Her eyes scanned the room until they met her husband's. Sitting on the sofa, he wore slacks, a white shirt, and jacket without a tie. A gin and tonic sat on the glass coffee table in front of him.

"Business trip?" she said, closing the door.

"No."

"Where are you going?"

"Home."

"This is your home."

"I'm needed in Missouri."

She hadn't moved. "Is it the bill?"

Put America Back to Work resurrected the infrastructure program from her defunct legacy legislation, allowing the federal government to administer grants and loans for building and repairing highways, bridges, parks, and low-income housing. Small and midsize businesses would be incentivized to bid on these projects. The increase of the minimum wage, on a regional basis, survived. Whitney still didn't know how Mo had convinced the conservative members of her party to agree to that provision.

Well, she had some idea.

"My brother's going to need some help figuring this out," Grayson said. "Our business—most businesses—won't be able to absorb the increased costs."

"When will you be back?"

"I don't know."

"What about the jobs initiative? Your commitment to the American people?"

"I can't let generations of my family's hard work go to waste," he said, standing. "You can find someone else to help the unemployed. Perhaps your new law will do the trick."

He stepped around the table and walked to the foyer. Hoisting the travel bag over his shoulder, he grabbed the handle of the suitcase.

She waved at the bags. "Grayson, someone can carry those for you."

He grabbed his newest fedora off the coat tree and perched it on his head. "As I said, I can handle my own business."

Whitney caught the double entendre.

He opened the door and turned to her, his expression unreadable. "Even though I don't agree with what you did, I love and support you, Madam President. But I must go."

"Of course. You're becoming an expert."

"At what?"

"Leaving."

CHAPTER FORTY-TWO

Seattle, Washington

THE FORD CROWN Victoria climbed a gigantic hill. Jade, sitting shotgun, hoped the traffic light would hold at green, for fear that they might roll backward. She breathed a sigh of relief as they passed under it, only then realizing she'd been rocking forward in her seat to help the car along.

At the top of Queen Anne Hill, a neighborhood north of downtown, the driver, a young agent from the Seattle FBI office named Brian Anderson, made a left on Galer Street, then a right on Fifth Avenue West. Parked cars lined both sides of the street, an inordinate number of them Subarus. Anderson drove slowly, periodically pulling over at an intersection, when a car headed toward them from the opposite direction. The agent finally found a parking spot around the corner from their destination.

Anderson, Jade, Max, Micah, and Dante exited the car and backtracked to a yellow two-story Craftsman house. They had staked out the address for a week, with no sighting of the object of their surveillance. The agents took turns watching the house, the off agents showering and sleeping at a hotel in Lower Queen Anne.

Dante had decided it was time to confront the person of interest.

On the porch, shoes of different sizes and styles—trainers, clogs, sneakers, loafers—were laid in a disorderly fashion just outside the front door. Two rocking chairs, in need of staining, faced the approaching sunset over the agents' shoulders.

A woman of about forty answered the door. "May I help you?"

Dante made the introductions. The woman examined their credentials.

"Does Jacob Collins live here?" Dante asked.

The woman pointed straight up. "He rents out the attic. We converted it into an apartment."

"We're here to ask him a few questions," he said. "Do you mind if we come in?"

He started to push past her to enter the house, but she didn't budge.

The woman gestured to the porch. "You're not very observant for an FBI agent."

"Ma'am, what are you talking about?"

She pointed. "You mind taking off your shoes?"

"I do," Dante said.

The woman looked at Jade, who nodded.

"Regulations," Jade said.

The woman frowned as she stepped back to open the door wider. "He comes in through a separate entrance, but you can come in this way. He's there now. I can hear him. Go up the stairs and turn left at the end of the hall. The last door on the left."

The agents filed past her and down the hallway with its hundred-year-old pine floors.

"What kind of trouble is he in?" the woman said from behind them.

"Don't know yet," Dante said as he started to climb.

"He's a person of interest in a criminal investigation," Jade clarified.

"It was only a matter of time," the homeowner said.

Jade stopped and turned. "Why do you say that?"

"Spends too much time up there alone, if you ask me. I've always wondered what he does up there. Friends never come over. He never goes out. Must be up to something."

"He could be playing video games. Virtual reality. Something like that." Jade thought about the killing sites: New York, Chicago, DC. "Does he travel?"

"Not much that I'm aware of. He works up there. Pays his rent on time and doesn't bother us, so we don't bother him."

"We'll need to talk to you as well."

The woman slipped on a Patagonia vest. "I'll be in my garden out back."

At the end of the hall, they opened the door, not bothering to knock, and climbed the narrow stairs to the attic. Jade's hand moved to the grip of her .40 Glock 23. She paused at the top. It opened to a living room with a green secondhand sofa behind a leaning, low metal coffee table. A thirty-six-inch TV rested on a simple stand. Against one wall, a small table served as a desk, with a desktop computer on it. The table's surface was littered with empty cups, Red Bull cans, and candy wrappers. It seemed The God of Veritas loved Snickers.

The apartment reeked of marijuana.

Above the table was a window you could only peer out of if you were standing. A body of water and snowcapped mountains were visible in the distance. The wind whispered outside.

The low, slanted ceilings, an inverted *V*, prevented Jade from standing at her full height.

A skinny white man in his early to midtwenties, wearing a faded Occupy Seattle T-shirt and jeans, came out of a back room, barefoot, chewing on a candy bar.

"Who the hell are you?"

Dante hunched over, stepped forward, and introduced himself and the other agents.

"Let me see some ID."

They flashed their badges. The man examined each badge, as if the agents were trying to access the San Francisco mint. When he finished, he still seemed unsatisfied.

"How did you get in?" he asked. "Don't you need a warrant or something?"

"Your landlord let us in," Dante said.

"She can do that?" When they didn't respond, he crossed to his computer and locked the screen. Turning his back to it, he said, "Why are you here?"

"We want to ask you some questions," Dante said, moving to the couch. "Take a seat."

"I'll stand, thank you."

"Suit yourself."

Jade and Max joined Dante on the sofa, while Anderson remained in front of the stairs. Micah grabbed a flimsy chair from the small kitchen table.

"What's your full name?" Dante said.

"I don't have to tell you that."

"We're here to talk to you," Jade said. "Or would you rather accompany us downtown to the FBI office and make this official?"

The man stared into Jade's eyes for less than a second before he decided to take the easier path. "Jacob Collins."

"Middle name?" Dante asked.

"Michael."

Pat had already determined his real name. They were testing him.

"Tell us about 'The God of Veritas,'" Dante said.

"How did you find me? My personal information on Twitter is private."

"Nothing is private," Dante said. "I'm waiting."

"I tweet. So what?"

"You tweet a lot."

Dante had obtained a search warrant for all of The God of Veritas's tweets, direct messages, photos, videos, and notifications. Jade had reviewed them on the plane ride west.

The young man shrugged. "Again, so what?"

"Are you the Shakespeare Killer?" asked Jade.

"What?" Collins's eyes bulged. He turned. A tremor was starting to develop in his hand as he pulled out the chair from the table behind him and sat. "Is that why you're here?"

"Answer the question," Dante said.

"Of course not."

"Then why is it," Jade said, "that every time you tweet about someone—especially someone wealthy—they end up dead?"

Sweat popped up on his pale forehead, despite the coolness of the room. "It's… it's a coincidence."

"Three coincidences is a lot, wouldn't you say?"

The curls of his medium-length brown hair began to shake. "That doesn't mean they're not coincidences. Besides, I tweet about a lot of people."

"I hope no one else you tweet about turns up dead," Dante said.

By now, Collins's eyes were ready to burst out of their sockets. "Do I need a lawyer?"

"Do you?" Dante asked.

His mouth opened and closed like a fish. "I don't think so. I didn't do anything. I just tweet, man."

"If you answer our questions truthfully," Jade said in a soothing tone, "you shouldn't need one."

He shot her a grateful look. "Okay."

"Where were you," Dante said, checking his notebook, "on the nights of January 3, January 17, and February 8 of this year?"

"I was here."

"Shouldn't you check a calendar?"

"I don't go anywhere, man. Honest. I'm an *online* activist. I spend most of my life online."

"What do you do," Jade asked, "for work?"

"I write a blog. Sell ads on my site. Generate affiliate income."

Dante took in the small apartment. "That's enough to make a living?"

"I get by."

"Seattle's an expensive place to live," Jade said. She knew this from the time she'd spent in Seattle last year.

Collins said, "This is getting by."

"Your tweets," Max said, "are aggressive. Almost threatening."

"Not to me. I write about stuff. Issues. Injustices. Try to keep our public leaders honest. But I don't *do* anything. I encourage other people to act."

"Like a consultant," Jade said helpfully. Out of the corner of her eye, she saw Max's lips twitch.

"What?" said Collins.

"What about your tweets about President Fairchild?" Jade asked.

The vitriol of his tweets had intensified over the last few months.

"She's a conservative," he said.

"Not a moderate?"

"There's no such thing. Today you must pick a side. It's us versus them. You can't compromise with the enemy."

She leaned forward, interested. "You see this as a war?"

"Of course it's a war. Only one side can win. The winner decides the course of this country for the next forty years. The loser risks oblivion."

"I thought this was the *United* States."

"You haven't been paying attention then," he said, his tone disdainful. "This nation is divided. More so now than at any time since the Civil War." He shook his head. "We use facts that only support our entrenched positions. Watch different news programs. Read different books. Recognize different histories. Live among our own kind. Unofficially, some states have already seceded. There are two Americas. We'll never be united again."

"If that's true," Jade said, "then what's the point?"

"What's the point of what?"

"Your tweets. Being an activist."

He blinked. After a moment, he said in a lame voice, "I still have to try. Even if it's a lost cause."

"How does Fairchild fit into all this?"

"She's a dinosaur. Like the rest of the old guard who've been in office forever. They need to go away and die."

As the other occupants in the room stiffened, Jacob Michael Collins realized he had just threatened the life of the president of the United States and members of other branches of the federal government while in a room full of federal agents.

He held up his hands. "Whoa! Everyone chill! It was a figure of speech." He dropped his hands. "What I meant was, she doesn't represent the progressivism of our party. Our generation."

Jade frowned. "That doesn't sound like the Fairchild I know."

This stopped Collins short. "You know her?"

"Yes, I do."

He seemed stumped.

Dante slid off the sofa. "We need to check out your apartment."

Max moved to the bedroom. Micah covered the kitchen. Dante checked out the bathroom. Jade remained seated on the sofa, studying the books stacked on the floor against the wall.

Collins jumped at the sudden activity.

"We need to take your computer," Jade said.

The God of Veritas backed up until his butt was on the table, his arms wide as if he were a basketball defender, blocking them from taking it. "You can't."

"We'll obtain a court order," Jade said.

Collins's shoulders slumped.

Jade signaled Anderson. With donned gloves, he picked up the computer and headed toward the stairs.

"What am I going to *do* until you return it?"

She thought for a moment. "*Something?*"

Collins looked at her, not understanding.

Jade stood, hitting her head on the ceiling.

That's what she got for being a smart-ass.

CHAPTER FORTY-THREE

The White House, Washington, DC

LEANING AGAINST THE back of the loveseat, Whitney puffed on a Cohiba cigar as she stared out the window at the Washington Monument. On the table was a glass of Pavillon Blanc du Château Margaux, the bottle next to it nearly empty.

After Grayson left, she'd gone to the Oval Library and perused her first editions: Louisa May Alcott, Maya Angelou, Jane Austen, Charlotte and Emily Brontë, Toni Morrison, Carson McCullers, Edith Wharton, and Virginia Woolf, among many others. She had kept Alcott's *Little Women,* a gift from Landon Phillips, despite everything he'd done. It wasn't the book's fault. It was one of her favorite stories growing up—Jo March, an early exposure to female independence. Plus, the book was in mint condition.

She had idled in the library, inhaling the calming, musty aroma. She had brought a few of the books back to the West Sitting Hall, but tonight, no matter which book she picked up, she couldn't concentrate on the words.

Whitney had known Grayson would be upset over the legislation. They'd discussed it beforehand, but he'd seemed nonplussed, perhaps thinking it wouldn't pass.

She'd never thought he would *leave* over it.

His company treated its employees fairly. He'd told her so many times. But not every employer acted like Fairchild Industries. Some required regulation to do the right thing. Didn't he believe every American worker deserved a living wage? He would respond that there was a better way. To let the free market work.

He didn't even need to be present for them to engage in this age-old argument.

The front door of the Residence burst open.

Hurriedly putting out the cigar in the ashtray, Whitney slipped both under the sofa cushion.

"Hey, Mom!"

Whitney rose. "Emma!"

Her daughter ran toward her but pulled up short.

"What's wrong?"

"Nothing."

"Are you crying?"

"No," Whitney said, rubbing imaginary sleep out of her eyes. "Long day."

She hugged Emma but stopped short herself.

Her daughter hadn't come alone.

"Hello," Whitney said to Emma's guest.

Skipping back to her friend, Emma pulled her forward.

"Surprise, Mom! This is Megan. My roommate."

There was trepidation on Emma's face. This young woman wasn't the same roommate that Whitney had met at the beginning of the school year, when she and Grayson had dropped Emma off. She shook Megan's hand.

"Hello, Megan."

"Madam President."

"I begged Josh to keep Megan's background check a secret," Emma explained, noticing the expression on Whitney's face. "Don't get him in trouble, Mother."

"We can talk about that later. Welcome, Megan. Please," Whitney said, gesturing toward the loveseat. As Whitney settled into one of the matching chairs, the two young women sat on the sofa, close enough that their bodies were almost touching.

Emma's roommate was dressed in a black T-shirt, green army jacket, scruffy jeans, and Birkenstocks, despite the cold weather. Her hair was the same length and style as Emma's. But where Emma's hair was light-brown with a tint of auburn, like Whitney's, Megan's hair was dyed black.

Turning to Emma, Whitney said, "This… is a surprise."

"We should've called," Emma said, missing the point, "but we were here for the Black Lives Still Matter march, and I wasn't sure we'd have time to visit." She gazed around the room. "Where's Dad?"

Whitney shifted her gaze to Megan. "Would you care for something to drink, Megan?"

The young woman's features were strong and feminine, her face unlined and without makeup. She shook her head. "I'm fine, ma'am."

Emma touched Megan's hand. "Are you sure? Don't be shy. She doesn't bite. Except when I bring home bad grades…"

Her hand remained on Megan's.

"Since I presume you're the same age as Emma, and not old enough to drink legally, how about some water? Or juice?"

"Actually," Megan said, "I'm old enough."

Whitney wondered how old she was.

"Do you have any cold-brewed coffee?" Megan asked. "In a can?"

"I'm sure we can scrounge one up." Whitney looked at Emma.

"The same."

"When did you—"

She refrained from completing her inquiry into when Emma had started drinking cold-brewed coffee, or any coffee for that matter, and instead picked up the phone to call the ground-floor kitchen.

"Mom, where's Dad?" Emma asked again.

"He returned to Clayton," Whitney said, tucking her legs beneath her. "Something to do with the business."

"Darn," Emma said. "I wanted him to meet Megan."

This must be serious.

"When did you become roommates?" Whitney asked. "I thought you were rooming with—"

Emma shifted on the sofa. "It didn't work out."

"I see."

After a knock on the door, a butler entered, setting a tray with two glasses of ice and two cans on the table in front of the young women.

"Thank you," Whitney said to him. He departed.

Megan poured coffee into a glass and handed it to Emma before pouring a glass for herself. Whitney gazed at her daughter's patrician nose, so much like Grayson's.

To Megan, Whitney asked, "Do you go to Princeton as well?"

"I do. I'm a senior. Majoring in social justice."

Whitney sipped her wine. "That's wonderful. How did you two meet?"

"At the library," Emma said.

"At an event," said Megan, almost at the same time.

Inclining her head, Whitney asked, "Which was it?"

The girls shared a glance.

"It was an event," Emma said. "At the library," they finished together.

"Em and I were working the same event," Megan clarified.

Em?

"I see," Whitney said.

Emma said, "Stop 'I seeing' us, Mom."

"What are you talking about?" Whitney asked.

"You 'I see' when you don't want to say how you really feel."

"I was unaware I did that."

"You do."

"I see," Whitney said, smiling, as she rose to retrieve another bottle of white wine from the refrigerator.

The occasion called for it.

Megan whispered to Emma, "Your mother's got jokes."

"She can be humorous in her own way," Emma whispered back.

When Whitney returned, she said to Emma, "How are your classes?"

"Fine. I declared my major."

"And?"

A slight lift of Emma's chin. "Politics."

Whitney sighed. "I failed both my children. Where did I go wrong?"

"I'm not going into politics," Emma said. "I'm going to be a lawyer."

"What kind?"

"Civil rights."

"I see."

"Mom! Stop!"

"Sorry, I forgot."

"We've been going to a lot of events. Talking to the people. Trying to understand their issues. Their concerns."

The people.

"What are they telling you?" Whitney asked.

"Things need to change. I want to help them."

"I…"—she almost said "see"—"I'm proud of you." She paused. "Are you staying here tonight?"

"Yeah."

"Your room is always ready," Whitney said.

Even though Chandler and Emma were in college at the time of Whitney's inauguration last year, it was important to her that they have their own rooms when they came "home." Emma's room was the West Bedroom; Chandler slept in the East Bedroom.

"Megan may sleep in the Queens' Bedroom," Whitney added.

She savored another sip of wine, her smile hidden behind the glass, while her daughter and her college roommate shared a disconcerting glance.

CHAPTER FORTY-FOUR

Washington, DC

JADE SPENT THE return trip from Seattle reading Veritas's blog. The topics ranged from free education, the environment, immigration, campaign finance reform, affordable housing, and income inequality.

While the others slept, she had turned to Max in the seat beside her. "You think he's good for it?"

Max shook his head. "He's too disorganized, for one thing. His tweets are reactive. He doesn't present sociopathic or psychopathic tendencies. Plus, he has a moral responsibility and a social conscience. I don't think he's our man."

Over the next week, Pat reported that Veritas hadn't made any trips via plane or train under his own name in the last year, but his alibis weren't airtight either. His landlord couldn't swear he was at home on the nights of the murders. The NSA tracked his phone to the apartment location, which didn't necessarily prove he was there. With no coworkers to interview, and seemingly no offline friends, they were hoping his computer could provide some answers. The activity on it provided an alibi of sorts. He or someone else had tweeted from his computer at the time of the murders. Other than that, the computer offered nothing helpful.

As Jade left the sandwich shop across the street, carrying her lunch, Christian ambled toward her. They stopped in the middle of the sidewalk outside FBI HQ.

"Hey, you," she said.

"Hey, yourself."

She shielded her eyes from the unexpected sunlight. It was supposed to rain today. "Anything new on Hurley?" Dante had left him behind to oversee the Finn Hurley investigation.

Christian shook his head.

"How are you and Dante getting along?"

"He's not you."

They were silent for a moment.

"What are your next steps?" she asked.

His gaze lifted upward as he prepared an answer. "Watch out!"

Christian grabbed her in a bear hug and tackled her to the ground as something crashed into the spot where she'd been standing. He lay on top of her, both of them staring at a chunk of concrete and some scattered pieces.

Shaken but trying not to show it, she said, "You're heavy."

He stood and offered her a hand.

She looked up at the netting installed to prevent an accident like this from occurring. There was a hole in it.

It was no secret that the FBI headquarters was falling apart. If the exterior was bad, the inside was worse. For years, agents had waited for Congress to appropriate funds to replace it with a building better suited for the twenty-first century and equipped for the never-ending war on terrorism. Jade had hoped the money appropriated from the infrastructure legislation would pay for construction of a new building, but those hopes were squashed with the repeal of the New New Deal Coalition Act. Her attitude regarding the president's latest legislative attempt was "wait and see."

After they brushed themselves off, she said, "That was close. Thanks." She told him about hitting her head in Veritas's apartment.

"Two times in one week," he said. "You might want to be more careful."

CHAPTER FORTY-FIVE

Washington, DC

DEV SAT ON a stool at the counter by the window, eating a turkey sandwich with cucumbers and sprouts and pretending to read the *Washington Post*. The proprietor was pounding a slab of meat at the back of the establishment. A young man, who resembled him, stood behind the register.

The door chimed as another customer entered.

Dev chanced a glance at Jade Harrington, who waited in line to place her order.

Tall. Striking. Intense. Confident. A formidable opponent.

Something stirred in Dev, a feeling unlike the competitive juices that flowed within her before a game. Before a kill.

The heralded FBI agent took in her surroundings. Dev averted her eyes by gazing out the window at the pedestrian traffic on Ninth Street. Nevertheless, Dev sensed the other woman's eyes lingering on the back of her head for a moment before moving on. When next Dev stole another glimpse of Harrington, the agent was placing her order.

Dev was in DC on a reconnaissance mission to study this FBI agent who hunted her. She knew of Harrington, of course, but had never met her.

Never worked with her.

Dev had just witnessed the blond agent, who looked like a linebacker, save Harrington from being hit by the concrete debris.

How ironic it would have been if the building in which the agent worked had dispatched Dev's nemesis for her.

Dev waited for the two agents to enter the employees' entrance of the Federal Bureau of Investigation before exiting the shop. She headed in the opposite direction toward Federal Triangle Station.

She had a plane to catch.

CHAPTER FORTY-SIX

Washington, DC

"I'M RESPONSIBLE FOR helping you try new things. Otherwise you'd eat the same thing every night."

Jade couldn't disagree with Zoe there. She chewed her spiced grilled chicken, savoring the different flavors. "Good call."

The two friends shared a late dinner at a bistro table for two, enjoying a variety of tapas. In addition to the chicken, they'd ordered the special written in trendy lettering on the sandwich board outside the front door: sautéed shrimp, patatas bravas, and roasted sweet corn. The Spanish restaurant was a new one in Logan Circle, a neighborhood just north of downtown.

"Qué pasa?" Zoe said.

"Not much. You?"

An unusual shadow crossed Zoe's angular face. "'Enough' didn't pass."

"Enough" was the legislation aimed at drastically reducing gun violence in the United States. Last year, a lone white male gunman—it was usually a lone white male gunman—had mowed down over one hundred and fifty elementary school children playing outside at recess. Enclosed in a fenced yard, the kids had offered him a human shooting gallery.

Zoe lowered her head. "I thought we had the votes this time."

"Memories are short," Jade said.

"Mine is long," Zoe said. "I can't forget about those kids. I don't want them to die in vain."

Jade remembered the images from the news: the young man and his vacant countenance, teachers and students scrambling for cover, teachers transforming themselves into human shields to protect their students. Most of the carnage was captured on the school's video surveillance system. A female teacher ended up tackling the gunman, saving an untold number of children's lives. Her heroism was rewarded with the loss of her own.

"It'll pass someday," Jade said. "Mass shootings won't cease on their own."

"Wouldn't it be fabulous to go to a movie theater or a concert or a school and not worry about getting shot?"

"Or a shopping mall."

Zoe cocked her head. "When was the last time you were in a mall?"

"Theoretically," Jade conceded.

"Remember when mass shootings occurred only at post offices?"

"They called it 'going postal,'" Jade said. Impulsively, she grabbed Zoe's hand and stared into her eyes. "You're on the right side of history on this, my friend. Don't give up."

She squeezed and let go. Zoe raised her hand to her heart and bowed her head in thanks. "I can't wait 'to provide new guards for their future security.'"

Not entirely sure what Zoe meant, Jade said, "We will."

The two friends ate in silence for a moment.

"Talked to Kyle lately?" Zoe said, her eyes narrowing, ready to scrutinize every nuance of Jade's response.

"No. The case is over."

"It's over? No one's been charged."

"That's true. Even so, there's no reason for me to talk to Kyle."

Zoe bit her lip to prevent herself from smiling.

Was that relief?

"You haven't heard," she said.

Jade sipped her sangria. "Heard what?"

"Kyle is seeing someone."

Swallowing with difficulty, Jade said, "Huh."

"They're engaged," Zoe said, still staring at Jade.

"Huh," Jade said again.

"Aren't you curious who it is?"

Jade popped a shrimp into her mouth. "Not really."

"It's Brittney Summers."

Jade didn't react outwardly, but she forcibly swallowed the shrimp and carefully placed her fork, tines down, on her plate.

Summers played in the WNBA, a point guard with the Seattle Storm, and was a former All-American at the University of Connecticut. Although Jade was a few years older, they had played against each other in AAU, college, and the pros. The rivalry was intense. They didn't hate each other, exactly, but they wouldn't hang out together after a game either.

Zoe searched her face. "Say something."

Jade picked up her glass again. "Good for them."

After dinner, Zoe left on her motorcycle, and Jade sauntered toward her car parked on a side street. She stopped on the sidewalk by a man sitting in front of Le Diplomat on Fourteenth Street. He appeared homeless.

"Do you got any money? I'm hungry."

She glanced at the expensive French restaurant, the scene epitomizing the American divide. Jade handed the man her leftovers. "It doesn't compare to the food in there, but it's pretty good."

He stared into her eyes. "Thank you, Chosen One."

She started at the reminder of what her father used to say to her. A phrase from the Bible. The Gospel of Matthew.

Later, as she drove across the Memorial Bridge, she listened to the eighties station on SiriusXM and softly sang the words to most of the songs, tapping her fingers on the steering wheel to the beat.

As the snow fell, she tried not to think of Kyle with someone else.

Jade didn't enjoy driving in the snow in DC. The transplants from New York and Boston drove too fast, to prove it wasn't a big deal. DC natives couldn't drive in the snow at all. And everyone else was caught in the middle. Fortunately, there weren't many cars on the bridge.

"It's Raining Men" came on.

Perfect.

She remembered the barista at the coffee shop singing it at the top of his lungs, oblivious to Kyle and Jade sitting at a table, his only audience.

She hadn't talked to Kyle since her surprise appearance at Jade's team celebration for closing the Robin Hood case. Kyle had been in DC on business. They hadn't talked much that night, and Kyle left the next day to fly home to Seattle.

Jade missed their conversations, a light sparring between two strong women. But Jade couldn't offer Kyle anything more. That was the problem.

Jade's life was here. With the FBI. With her team. With the victims and their families, who depended on her to seek justice for them. To find out the truth. Kyle's life was in Seattle. With her business. Her professional basketball team. Her political influencers. And so Kyle had moved on.

With Summers.

As Jade steered the car carefully over the bridge into Virginia, she changed the radio station to classical music.

CHAPTER FORTY-SEVEN

The White House, Washington, DC

"DON'T MINCE WORDS."

"It's bad," said Dr. Hayley Copeland, Whitney's chief economic advisor.

"Perhaps mince a little bit," Whitney said.

Copeland's face remained stoic. "Since the Sino-Russian trade agreement went into effect, our exports have fallen one percent, which might not sound like a lot…"

"But…"

"It equates to a hundred and thirty-eight billion dollars in lost revenue for US companies."

Hayley sat in a chair pulled up next to the *Resolute* desk in the Oval Office. Hayley and Whitney had met in college, at Northwestern University. Whitney had gone on to Harvard Law School while Hayley remained in Chicago, attaining a PhD in economics from the University of Chicago and then becoming a tenured professor. Whitney convinced her former classmate to leave academia and join the administration. Smart and attractive, Hayley knew her stuff, but the frustration of dealing with the negative effects of the trade agreement was evident on her middle-aged face.

"Which countries?" Whitney asked.

"Exports are down with all our trading partners, but the major ones have been hit the hardest: UK, Germany, France. Even our buddies to the north."

"Canada," Whitney said, disappointed.

"Canadians aren't any different from the rest. They don't care that their goods are made in China, as long as they're cheap."

"Options?"

"Companies will decrease prices. Promote more heavily. It'll be a downward spiral to the bottom. Not sure there's much we—the government—can do. Maybe talk to China again?"

Whitney shook her head. Min had made it clear that avenue was closed. "What about New Cubed?"

"We won't realize any significant benefits for a few months," Hayley added. "So the situation is bad but hopeful."

"Bad but hopeful. Have you found someone to replace Grayson yet?"

Hayley handed her a sheet of paper. "Here's a list of candidates—"

Sasha knocked and entered without an invitation, looking drained.

Whitney stood, knowing immediately that something was very, very wrong. "Sasha?"

"I need to speak with you," her chief of staff said. "Privately."

Whitney's eyes didn't leave Sasha's. "Hayley?"

Sasha's eyes followed the economic advisor until the door closed behind her. She stood in front of Whitney's desk. The two women stared at each other.

"What is it?"

"It's CJ Brennan," Sasha said.

"What happened?" Whitney asked. "Was he beaten up again?"

"No," said Sasha, sorrow in her brown eyes. "He committed suicide last night."

CHAPTER FORTY-EIGHT

Kensington, Maryland

JADE ATTENDED A lot of funerals, usually for the victims of the serial killers she chased.

CJ Brennan was a victim of a different sort. Bullied most of his short life, first because of his dad and then because he was gay, pretty, and could sing.

And he wasn't afraid to speak his mind.

Depression was a silent, lonely, and relentless killer. No one was immune from its tentacles' reach. No matter how beautiful or rich or famous you were.

Ever since he'd come out last year on a liberal cable news program, despite or because of his conservative father, CJ had become a mini-celebrity. He spoke out about gay and trans rights. His looks and his father's occupation proved a tantalizing combination for social media and the television talk-show circuit.

He'd also become a target for cruelty.

CJ's family sat on chairs set up in a row. The rest of the gathering stood behind them, Jade off to the side. She smelled the fresh flowers on top of the casket. Cole cried, unashamed, just as he had when Jade entered the church that morning.

The small Presbyterian church near the White House had been packed with a who's who of US politics and media. Cole Brennan, sitting in the front pew, stared at the large portrait of CJ next to the casket, the young man's hair blond and long. Jade touched Cole's arm, and he slowly turned. When he saw her, his face crumpled. Jade tried to take his hand. Instead, he stepped out into the aisle between the pews and wrapped her in a bear hug, which was oddly comforting for her.

And he wouldn't let go.

She peeked over his shoulder. Some of the other guests were looking at them in surprise. Jade guessed they'd never seen the most conservative white guy of them all hugging a black woman before.

After Jade hugged his wife, Ashley, and the children, Cole asked her to sit up front with the family. Jade demurred. During the service, she sat in a pew in the back of the church, flipping through the Bible she grabbed off the back of the pew in front of her, admiring the stained-glass windows high on the wall, studying the intricate sculpture of Jesus nailed to the cross over the altar, and glancing at the back of Cole's head.

Jade wasn't the only one in the church with tears in her eyes when members from CJ's high school glee club came together to sing "Over the Rainbow."

The last one to leave, Cole sat motionless in his pew, staring at the casket long after the funeral director had lowered the lid for the last time.

Now at the memorial park, Ashley sat next to him holding his beefy hand, with their five surviving children sitting next to her in chronological order: Colleen, Madeline, Ryan, Kaitlin, and Ronnie. All of them were crying, except for Kaitlin, who'd had a role in the TSK case.

It was cold but clear. The rain the forecasters predicted never materialized. The park was peaceful, with its manicured lawns, shrubs, and pine trees. The private graveside service included family, select coworkers, and exclusive guests. Mourners sniffled and cried.

Cole wept.

Ashley's face was pale and withered. The former model had aged ten years since Jade last saw her a year ago.

Jade kept her eyes on the family, ignoring the chaplain holding the Bible and tuning out his words of comfort. Looking at him or the casket dredged up memories of her parents' funeral.

After the service, Cole encircled his wife and children in a group hug.

Jade waited her turn and hugged Cole and Ashley again.

"He left a note," Cole said, wiping his nose with a handkerchief.

"Was it the bullying?" Jade asked.

"Partly," he said. "Mostly it was me. He never got over the fact that he let TSK into our home and almost got his sister killed."

"That wasn't your fault. Or his."

"TSK wanted to scare me or kill me. If it weren't for me, that godforsaken liberal killer wouldn't have been there."

Jade said nothing; it was true.

"Thanks for coming, little lady," Cole said, smiling through his pain, knowing she hated the nickname.

Ashley squeezed Jade's arm. "It means a lot."

Before Jade left, she needed to speak to one more person. She walked over.

"Madam President," Jade said.

The two hugged. Although they were separated in age by over twenty years, a kinship had blossomed between them. It was more than their being two alpha women trying to make it in a man's world—it was a strong relationship based on mutual trust and respect. These traits, at a time when they were most needed, were becoming less common between women.

"How's the new job?" President Whitney Fairchild asked her.

"It's been an adjustment," Jade said.

"That's what I like about you; you're always truthful with me."

"Don't know any other way to be." Jade tilted her head toward the grave site. "Like him."

The president nodded, her gaze drifting toward some departing mourners. Jade spotted Senators Hampton and Sampson, and Representative Howard Bell, walking away. Sampson's arm was around a woman's waist, presumably his wife's. "I wish you had taken me up on my offer."

"The FBI is in my blood, ma'am."

"We'll see," Fairchild said. "Well… you're the boss now. 'For unto whomsoever much is given, of him shall be much required.'"

With a faint smile, Jade said, "My father used to say that."

Fairchild cocked her head. "I would like to meet him."

Jade swallowed. "He's gone."

"I should have remembered. I'm sorry."

"No worries," Jade said. "You two would've had a lot to talk about."

A moment of silence.

"He's come around," the president said, waving her hand toward the inscription on the granite headstone.

COLE "CJ" BRENNAN JR.

LOVING SON AND BROTHER

WITH THE VOICE OF AN ANGEL

"What do you mean?"

"Cole never liked the nickname," Fairchild said. "He didn't want anyone to forget who his namesake was named after."

"As if anyone could."

"He also didn't appreciate that his son preferred singing in the glee club to running down a football field."

"Not everyone is destined to be a great athlete."

"No," the president said. "How boring would that be?"

Jade shrugged and smiled. "Well…"

Fairchild smiled. "Ah… right."

"He's come around in more ways than one," Jade said, inclining her head toward Cole, who was shaking hands with friends of CJ's, some prominent activists in the gay community.

Shifting her gaze back to Jade, Fairchild said, "Have you seen Blake?"

"No. How's he doing?"

"He's mending. I was hoping you two would…" She paused. "I must go, but we should get together soon." The president grasped both of Jade's hands in hers. "I miss our talks."

"Me too."

Fairchild started to walk away and then turned. "Agent Harrington?"

"Yes, Madam President?"

"Do you know the secret to success?"

"What?"

"Don't be afraid."

Afraid of what? Jade didn't ask.

"Ma'am, we need to go," said Josh McPherson, stepping toward Fairchild and nodding at Jade.

She was acquainted with him but didn't know him well.

He and the rest of the coterie of secret service agents escorted the president to her limousine, idling in the middle of a long line of limousines and black Suburban SUVs on the blocked-off street next to the cemetery. The throng of press waiting there started shouting questions at Fairchild.

Jade walked in the opposite direction.

As she crested the hill on her way to the cemetery's parking lot, from behind her came, "Mrs. Harrington! Wait!"

She turned. Kaitlin Brennan ran toward her. The girl came to an abrupt stop in front of Jade.

Jade crouched, her arms on her thighs, her eyes level with the girl's. She'd be about ten now.

"Yes?"

"I never thanked you for saving my life."

She wasn't sure how Kaitlin remembered, since she was unconscious by the time Jade had reached her on that fateful night. Her parents or siblings could have told her.

Jade smiled. "You don't need to thank me, Kaitlin. I was doing my job."

"When I have nightmares about that night, I think about you, and it makes me happy."

"Why is that?"

"Because you've got girl power. My daddy says you're strong and not afraid of anything."

"Did you tell your parents about these nightmares?"

The girl shook her head.

"Promise me you'll tell them," Jade said.

A solemn nod. "You're my shero."

*She*ro. Not *h*ero.

Kaitlin flung her arms around Jade's neck, almost knocking her off-balance. Jade hesitated, then hugged her back, the child's silky blond hair brushing Jade's cheek. She was surprised by the tears pressing against her own eyelids.

Pulling away, Kaitlin ran off to rejoin her family.

Jade didn't move. Despite all the accomplishments she'd achieved in her life—the trophies, medals, awards, press clippings, accolades—the simple gratitude of this young child might have been the most precious.

You couldn't put that in a box in the basement.

CHAPTER FORTY-NINE

Fairfax, Virginia

"YOU AGAIN?" SAID the skinny bartender with the punk-rock black hair. She leaned forward, her hands on the bar. Her rolled-up sleeves revealed a colorful tattoo on her right forearm. "You've got a new partner."

Micah looked from the bartender to Jade, confused. "You've been here with someone else?"

To Jade, the bartender said, "Will there be singing this time?"

Incredulous, Micah said, "You? Singing?" To the bartender, "Tell me more."

Jade said nothing. She gazed at the bartender with a look that said she didn't want to talk about the time she and Christian had gotten drunk in this very bar. By noon on that day, they were sitting on these same wooden stools, heads back, arms slung over each other's shoulders, singing "Bohemian Rhapsody" at the top of their lungs. The bartender gave her an imperceptible nod before turning to Micah. "A Brit?"

He nodded.

"Sweet," she said. "The first one for you is on the house. What can I get for you two? Guinness? Shots?"

She remembered.

"No," said Jade, more sharply than warranted. Softening her voice, she said, "A lager. English. Something on the lighter side."

"We'll take two Golden Glories," Micah said.

"You got it," the young woman said, pushing off the bar and grabbing two pint glasses. She slid one under a draft tap.

Jade eyed him. "Golden Glory?"

"Trust me," he said.

She held his gaze, wondering if she did trust him. Yesterday, after returning to the bureau from CJ's funeral, she'd run into Micah in the hallway. Noticing her subdued manner, he'd asked her what was wrong. When she told him, he invited her here. She protested that she had work to do. He said taking a few hours off from the case wouldn't hurt. She finally agreed.

Pictures of English royalty—including an American princess, political figures and celebrities—pennants of all the English Premier League teams, and English quotes and slogans covered almost every inch of the dark brown wood-paneled walls. An enormous Union Jack flag was displayed prominently on one wall.

The Stratford Arms was crowded because of the soccer game that was showing on every television in the place. Judging by the jerseys they wore, the patrons were evenly split by which team they supported.

"This is the quarterfinal of the FA Cup," Micah explained. "It's a big deal."

"I know," Jade said.

The bartender placed the glasses on cardboard coasters on the bar. Looking at Jade, she said, "Let me know when you get hungry. The fish and chips are ready this time."

She winked before moving away to help another customer.

"What's up with you two?" Micah asked.

"Nothing," Jade said, picking up her glass and holding it up for a toast. "I guess I'm cheering for Chelsea."

Micah picked up his glass. He looked like a soccer player, the formfitting red Arsenal jersey covering his upper body like a second skin.

"Always the contrarian," he said. "Cheers."

They clinked glasses and drank.

"Up for a bet?" he asked.

"Maybe."

"If my team wins, you have to sing the team fight song. And vice versa."

"I don't know the words."

Waving his arm, taking in the room, he said, "You'll have help."

Noncommittal, Jade changed the subject. "I like Mertens."

Micah nodded a few times at the name of Chelsea's versatile midfielder. "Me too. He just plays for the wrong team."

They sipped their beers as they watched the game on the flat-screen television high on the wall. The crowd in the bar cheered at every scoring chance, exceptional skill, and defensive stop, and groaned at every dispossession, errant pass, and uncalled foul.

At the half, Micah asked, "What do you think?"

"Chelsea is playing too far forward. They're susceptible to an overlap by a defender."

"They have to be. This is all or nothing."

"If they keep playing this way, it'll be nothing," she said. She took a sip of her pint. "Did you play?"

"A little."

Micah was almost as tight-lipped about his past as she was about hers. She didn't tell him she'd also played soccer.

The bartender slammed through the swinging saloon doors and placed two steaming cartons of fish and chips in front of them.

"To soak up the alcohol," she said. "On the house."

Micah followed her with his eyes as she went to help another customer. To Jade, he said, "I need to bring you here more often."

They both dug into their food. Jade hadn't realized she was ravenous. Between bites, she asked, "What are your thoughts on the case?"

"He's not leaving behind a lot of evidence. Almost as if he understands how a law enforcement officer investigates a crime. How are we ever going to find him?"

"Gathering evidence is not about finding him; it's about eliminating everyone else."

"We haven't eliminated anyone." He tilted his glass, staring into it. "I've been racking my brain about the Shakespeare connection. Is it an English bloke? If so, how is he connected to the victims? Why just the last two lines?"

"Go on."

"There's a reason he's leaving the couplet. It connects the victims in some way."

Jade sipped her beer. "I think you're right."

They ordered a few more rounds of beers and, along with the rest of the customers, cheered and groaned and shouted at the TVs. When Chelsea scored its first goal, Jade received a bear hug from the patron next to her, an older man with stale beer breath and a Chelsea jersey stretched tight over his proud beer belly.

During the second half, Micah's seat had moved closer to hers, their elbows occasionally touching.

Jade was feeling good. A little tipsy. She needed this.

"I like seeing you smile," Micah said.

"Don't get used to it."

He laughed and then, almost nonchalantly, said, "Are you still looking into the Robin Hood case?"

Jade shrugged.

"Any new leads?"

She shook her head. "Whoever stole that money was good. Really good."

He took a pull on his beer. "The idea, though, *was* good. Don't you think?"

"What do you mean?"

"The crime."

"Why would you say that?"

"Taking money from people who wouldn't miss it—money they, their children, and their children's children would never need—and giving it to the poor."

She swallowed her beer. "There're better ways to help the poor."

"I'm not saying that committing a crime was the right way to go about it. I think the intention was… noble."

"It was a crime. A lot of good that came out of it had to be undone."

He looked at her thoughtfully. "Do you always do the right thing?"

She stared into those mesmerizing gray eyes, a moment longer than was wise.

Finally, she said, "Nothing can happen between us. You know that, right?"

"Absolutely not," he said, taking a sip of his drink. "Nope. No way. No can do. Not if you were the last woman on earth."

Jade frowned. "Well, you don't have to go *that* far."

"I get it. We're mates."

"I'm not your mate, Micah. I'm your boss."

"Trust me," he mumbled. "I know."

He drained his beer and signaled the bartender, who was close by, for another round. "Don't worry, *boss*. I know my place. I'm a working-class bloke from London, after all."

Micah turned his attention back to the game. She thought about apologizing but decided against it. Better to squash any idea of a romantic future before it bloomed.

The bartender brought them two steaming cups. A tea for Micah and a coffee for Jade. She must have overheard the last part of their conversation. Jade eyed her, grateful. There would be no singing tonight.

At the ninetieth minute, the referee added one minute of stoppage time. The score was tied one to one.

"We're going into extra time," Micah said.

"We'll see," Jade said.

She sipped her coffee as an Arsenal defender dribbled the ball down the sideline. The opposing Chelsea defender, caught too far forward, turned and sprinted to catch up to the speedy Arsenal player. Ten yards from the end line, the Arsenal defender sent a left-footed cross to the team's forward, who left his feet and dove for the ball, heading it past the outstretched hand of Chelsea's six-foot-five goalie and inside the lower part of the goalpost.

As the forward sprinted to the flag in the corner of the field, he dropped to his knees, sliding most of the way. His teammates ran to him and fell on top of him in a heap of masculinity.

The referee blew his whistle to end the game.

Micah placed a hand on Jade's shoulder, his eyes wide with delight, the talk about their relationship forgotten.

"Brilliant!" he shouted. "How did you know?"

Not waiting for an answer, he hugged her, then hurriedly kissed her on the lips before flying out of his seat.

The kiss was an accident. He didn't even notice her reaction as he jumped up and down, fist-pumping, screaming, high-fiving, and bear-hugging his Arsenal compatriots in a bar in Virginia, a former colony far away from his native England.

She stared straight ahead while Micah joined them in the victory song, he forgetting about their bet, she trying to ignore the smell of his cologne.

Jade glanced at the bartender, who stood a few feet away.

To Jade, she mouthed, *He's fiiiiiiiiiine!*

Chapter Fifty

The White House, Washington, DC

A KNOCK. SASHA popped her head in, her hand remaining on the open door.

"You need to listen to something," she said.

She traversed the Oval Office and entered Whitney's study, not asking for permission nor waiting for Whitney to follow her. Whitney frowned at the unusual lack of protocol but followed her chief of staff just the same.

Sasha turned on the radio.

"It's always been a dream of mine," said a voice through the radio's speakers.

Whitney tensed.

"Why did it take you so long to run?" asked the talk-show host for Patriot News, his tone more subdued than usual. It was one of Cole Brennan's first broadcasts since his son's death.

"Life had other plans for me, I guess."

She envisioned the shrug and the boyish grin of Cole's guest. A grin she knew well.

"My daddy sold cars," the guest continued, "and I was expected to follow in his footsteps."

"I read about that in the *Washington Times*," Cole said. "The only legitimate paper in Washington, by the way. Then what happened?"

"I realized I wanted more out of life."

"You were a state legislator in Missouri," said Cole. "What made you run for Congress?"

"When I learned that Steven Barrett's death wasn't an accident," said the voice, tinged with anger, "and that the FBI covered it up, I had to do something. Congressman Barrett was a Missouri son. Born and raised. He represented our district and state faithfully for many years, and he deserved better than the investigation the federal government conducted for him."

"Those are strong accusations, my friend," Cole said. "Any proof?"

"Not yet, but I'll get it. How the FBI handled his murder was a travesty of justice and an injustice for the congressman's family. I won't rest until they receive the justice they deserve."

"Don't you find it ironic," Cole said, "that you and our president both come from the same district and were elected to the House because of a special election?"

A pause. Whitney held her breath, wondering if the guest would disclose their shared history.

"Her opportunity arose because of the suspicious death of Congressman Barrett," the guest responded. "I was elected after the governor appointed the congressman serving at the time to the president's vacant seat in the Senate. There's a difference."

"Are you implying," Cole said, his voice rising incredulously, "that the president of the United States was involved in Barrett's death?"

Another pause. "I didn't say that."

Sure you didn't.

"I know something about insinuation," Cole said, "and that sure sounded like it to me."

"All I'm saying is that it's a curious coincidence."

"If you say so. What are your plans now that you're in Congress?"

"There's plenty we need to do to take the country back, Cole. Decrease regulations, reduce the deficit, and create manufacturing jobs, to name a few."

"Couldn't agree more. Well, that's all the time we have today. Before I go, I want to thank all of you for your phone calls, letters, and emails about my son CJ. They mean a lot to Ashley and me. Now, I'm going to say something else some of you don't want to hear, but you need to. My son wasn't my gay son—he was just my son. Like your children. Depression doesn't happen to only one type of person. Anyone can become depressed: famous actors, celebrities, minorities, teenagers, middle schoolers, men. Anyone. If you or someone you love is depressed, please call the National Suicide Prevention Lifeline. Remember, you're not alone. This is Cole Brennan, protecting your life," he paused, "liberty, and pursuit of happiness. Join us again tomorrow for *The Conservative Voice*."

During the broadcast, Whitney had glanced at Sasha a few times. The chief of staff had listened intently. The president hadn't told Sasha her entire history, although with Sasha's "sources," Whitney believed she knew.

The guest on Cole's show was Cameron Kelly, the freshman representative from Missouri and Whitney's former high school boyfriend. She still hadn't told anyone, except for Grayson, that Cameron had once raped her.

"Cole didn't waste any time replacing Sampson as his puppet," Sasha said.

"He does sound smitten," Whitney agreed.

"Sounds as if Kelly has it in for you." Sasha looked at her. "Is there something you want to tell me about your colleague from the great state of Missouri?"

Whitney stared at the woman who had stood by her steadfastly the fourteen months she'd been in office.

"Yes," she said, "it's about time I do."

Washington, DC

IT HAD BEEN over two months since Sebastian Scofield's murder. The Shakespeare task force had interviewed—and sometimes reinterviewed—every witness to the three murders. In addition to driving back and forth across the Potomac River to and from Virginia, Dante and Micah had flown to New York and Chicago multiple times. At one point, Dante grudgingly asked Jade to review the case files again to see if she could spot something he'd missed.

If something was there, she couldn't find it either.

Max had created a psychological profile of the unsub. They knew the type of person they were looking for, but at least a million men fit that description.

Meanwhile, other murders wouldn't wait. Jade had no choice but to assign her team additional cases.

She locked her computer, calling it a day.

Standing, she began to stuff her briefcase with several folders from her desk. She stared at *The Complete Works of William Shakespeare* and grabbed it too.

CHAPTER FIFTY-TWO

Arlington, Virginia

THE VIBRATION WOKE her up.

Leaving one arm covering her closed eyes, she swiped her cell phone off the nightstand with the other. Jade didn't think she'd slept long. After leaving work, she'd texted Zoe for a recommendation for Indian food. Zoe was an encyclopedia of DC-area restaurants, her gift all the more remarkable given how often restaurants closed and opened in the city.

Jade had eaten her takeout while watching an episode of an HBO series that held the attention of everyone in the nation except her. Sleep still eluding her, she'd decided to go over the case files again. Sitting at the small desk in her bedroom, she gazed out the window at the unused patio furniture in her postage-stamp-size backyard surrounded by a faded wooden fence.

She fumbled with the phone. "Harrington."

"Coach," the caller said.

Immediately alert, Jade sat up in bed. Her cat, Card, jumped off her chest and onto the bed, circling before settling in next to her in a spot only he occupied.

The clock on the nightstand read 11:30 p.m. "LaKeisha, what is it?"

LaKeisha was the point guard on the high school spring league team that Jade coached every year. Their first practice wasn't until next week, and on top of that, LaKeisha had never called her before.

"I'm in trouble," the girl said simply.

Jade threw off the covers. "Where are you?"

@TheGodOfVeritas: Blayze Tishman may be generous and donate to a lot of causes, but he's also reaping the rewards from exploiting young black men. #shame

CHAPTER FIFTY-THREE

Washington, DC

JADE LEANED FORWARD, her arms resting on the steering wheel. She stared through the passenger-side window at the small, well-kept two-story row house on a street in Anacostia. Chain-link fences separated the lawns of the homes. This lower-income Southeast DC neighborhood had so far resisted the gentrification epidemic. Jade wondered what would happen to the residents when that day came.

She had some idea.

A basketball lay in the yard. A streetlight illuminated a solitary chair on the concrete front porch. No lights seemed to be on in the house.

Jade had never been to the house where LaKeisha grew up.

The young woman slouched in the passenger seat next to her. The litheness of last year had transformed into solid muscle. Only a couple of inches shorter than Jade, LaKeisha now outweighed her by twenty pounds.

A sophomore in high school, LaKeisha wore her black hair in long dreadlocks. Her bright smile, made brighter by her dark brown skin, was absent tonight.

Her second-year accomplishments on the hardwood exceeded her first. She was on her way to following in Jade's footsteps: a college scholarship, the WNBA, a professional contract overseas.

Jade wanted to keep it that way.

Although LaKeisha was smart and maintained a 3.0 grade point average, Jade didn't believe that LaKeisha's parents earned enough to pay for college or poor enough to receive sufficient financial aid. Athletics might be her only route to a college education.

When she saw LaKeisha play for the first time at an AAU tournament four years ago, Jade recognized something more than the twelve-year-old girl's talent and natural athletic ability. She had a will to win.

Now, she looked at LaKeisha. "You had one phone call."

The girl nodded.

"And you called me."

"Yeah."

"What happened?" Jade asked.

LaKeisha shifted in her seat. "Some of my friends… on my AAU team… got together to go see a movie. At Gallery Place." She paused. "After the movie, we were all hungry, so we went to a store. Kinda like a 7-Eleven." LaKeisha stopped.

Jade waited, resisting the urge to fill the silence. She wanted to give LaKeisha the time and space to tell the story in her own way.

"They started daring each other," she said. "Stuffing candy bars and snacks into their pockets. Their purses. A security guard came from the back of the store. He looked at all of us and grabbed me. I thought he was going to rip my arm out of the socket."

"And your teammates?"

"They didn't stick around. They ran. I was the only one taken to the station."

"I wonder why."

LaKeisha twisted the thin skin on the back of her hand.

"Ah," Jade said.

The DC Metropolitan PD had transported LaKeisha to the Youth Services Center on H Street NW. Since it was LaKeisha's first offense, CSS—Court Social Services—decided to release her to a guardian. Given their overflowing caseload, and that she was a federal law enforcement officer, Jade qualified. CSS would monitor LaKeisha for six months to make sure she didn't commit additional offenses.

"Did you tell them you didn't take anything?"

"They knew. They'd frisked me. They didn't care." LaKeisha laid her head against the headrest. "My parents are going to kill me."

"If you were my daughter, I would."

A slight smile flickered on the girl's face. After a moment, she said, "Do you know the worst part?"

"What?"

"It's not the getting arrested. Or the racism. Or my parents. It's that my quote-unquote *friends* weren't there for me. They *ran*." She broke eye contact. "They were never my friends."

"My dad used to say that you can count your true friends on one hand," Jade said.

LaKeisha held up her hand, large enough to palm a basketball, and spread her fingers. She retracted her thumb. "I used to count on my four teammates. Not anymore." Her hand dropped. "One reason I didn't take anything was because of you."

"Me?"

"I could never look you in the eye if I did something like that. I have dreams and goals because of you. I'm not going to mess up my future." She opened the passenger-side door. "Thanks for bailing me out, Coach. At least I can count on you. Always."

She slammed the car door shut.

"Always," Jade said into the silence.

Clayton, Missouri

"TAKE A COOKIE, dear."

Whitney's mother pushed the still-full plate toward her on the coffee table between them.

"Mom, I'm not hungry. Truly," Whitney said.

"I just baked them," her mother said, her tone scolding. "You're getting too thin. That job will be the death of you."

Whitney couldn't disagree on either count.

Hayden and Claire Churchill still lived in the same middle-class ranch in the St. Louis suburb where Whitney had grown up. Earlier, she'd walked through her brothers' and her old rooms. Nothing much had changed since they'd moved out decades ago. A *Grease* movie poster, depicting Olivia Newton-John and John Travolta clutching each other, still hung over her bed. Her cheerleading trophies and academic awards were still on the shelf over the window. Her little desk remained tidy, everything in its place.

Some of her clothes from her teenage years were in her closet. She could probably fit into them again.

Retired now, her father had once been an insurance agent, and her mother was his office manager. Her three brothers lived nearby with families of their own. Whitney didn't see them much and wouldn't have time during this visit. Sitting in a worn yellow chair, she gazed around the living room as she sipped lemonade from a glass. Unless one had been told, it would be hard to fathom that the occupants of this house were the parents of the most powerful person in the world.

"How's Grayson?" her mother asked from the couch across from her.

"He's fine."

"I hear he's back at work," her father said, dressed warmly in a gray-and-blue cardigan over a collared white shirt and dark pants. The house was almost as cold inside as it was outside. Despite her rare visit, he sat in a light-brown suede Barcalounger, reading the newspaper.

"He said the business needed him," Whitney said. "Washington can survive without him for a little while."

"What about you?" her mother said.

"I'm fine."

"I mean, can you survive without him for a little while?"

"Mom, I'm a grown woman. I don't need a man to survive." Whitney forced a laugh. "Besides, we've lived apart for so long over the years, I'm somewhat used to it."

"It can't be healthy for you or your marriage," her mother said.

"Mom, it's temporary. We're fine."

"A lot of 'fines,'" her father said, peering at her over the newspaper. He wore horn-rimmed glasses. "Why are you here? What's going on?"

Whitney said, "Not happy to see me?"

"Of course I am, but we haven't seen much of you since you left home." He paused. "Thirty years ago."

"We have some events in the Midwest, so I thought it would be a good opportunity to visit." Her parents looked unconvinced. "I wanted to see you," she said, simply.

I wanted to come home, she didn't say.

"Saw that Kelly boy on the news, yapping his mouth. He's on TV now almost as much as when he hawked cars."

"Hayden," her mother said, "I'm sure Whitney doesn't want to talk about him."

They knew Cameron had raped her. And did nothing. Instead, her liberal, marched-for-civil-rights-in-the-sixties parents had shipped her off to live with her father's sister, Mary, until the baby came. They didn't go to the police. They didn't take her to the hospital. They didn't confront the boy. Whitney dealt with the sexual assault and its aftermath on her own. As she had most situations in her life.

Her parents marched and protested and fought for everyone but her.

Some might say it was a different time then. A he-said, she-said situation. In a small town, where there was an inverse relationship between the maliciousness of the gossip and the size of the population, a girl had her reputation to protect. The boy's reputation would remain intact no matter what happened.

Her parents never explained their actions—or rather, inaction—to her.

"Cameron was an immature kid then," her mom said. "You know how boys are."

The heat rushed to Whitney's face. She placed her glass next to the plate of cookies. "I do."

She hadn't come to fight with her parents. They would never change. That she thought they would be here for her now, when they never were in the past, was the definition of insanity. "I'm going."

"Off to see Grayson?" her mother asked, oblivious to her daughter's feelings.

Whitney rose and went to them, bending over to kiss each of them on their soft, papery cheeks. Her hugs were brief, their bodies frailer than she remembered. She loved them despite their failures.

"I'll call you," she said.

In the Beast, the presidential limousine, Sasha said, "That good?"

Whitney shook her head.

Sasha continued to stare at her. "Are you all right?"

"Please… just head to the airport," Whitney said.

As Sasha picked up the phone to instruct the driver, Whitney donned sunglasses and stared straight ahead, even as the armored car passed the entrance to Fairchild Industries headquarters. The ten-story building and its twenty-acre campus were hard to ignore in this town.

Whitney chastised herself for seeking solace from her troubles at home with her parents. It had been a mistake.

She thought about the time she and Grayson had eaten ice cream in the ground-floor kitchen. It was one of the last romantic moments they had shared.

"Sasha," she said, "let's stop for some ice cream first."

"Ice cream?"

"My treat."

Sasha picked up the phone again.

CHAPTER FIFTY-FIVE

Seattle, Washington

SHE DIDN'T UNDERSTAND the last-minute addition. His name wasn't on the original list.

But her job wasn't to question. Or to reason. She was paid to carry out orders. Paid quite handsomely.

She waited.

Fifteen minutes after the appointed hour, a heavyset man tromped through the tall grass.

"Noah? Is that you?" he called out.

"Over here," she said, her voice noncommittal.

"Whew, it's dark! Why did you want to meet out here? You should've come over to the house." The man's loud voice sounded entitled and was already getting on her nerves. He finally reached her. "How was the slammer?" He looked into her eyes. "Wait, you're not—"

Pulling out the knife from behind her back, she stabbed him in the chest. She freed it and stabbed him again.

And again.

And again.

Blood sprayed her black pullover and running tights. She didn't care. She'd rented an Airbnb not far from here and would be ensconced in it soon.

As she continued to stab him, her mind drifted. She wasn't thinking of him as the gurgling sounds stopped.

He was dead.

But Dev was thinking about someone else. The woman who'd ruined her life.

Strike.

The woman who hadn't given her a chance to explain.

Strike.
Or a second chance.
Strike.
The woman who would pay.

CHAPTER FIFTY-SIX

Chantilly, Virginia

"WHAT?" JADE ASKED, removing her earplugs.

Max Stover stood ten yards away, sans coat and tie, dressed as if he'd come from the office. He walked past her to tap the smartpad on the wall. "I said you're losing your touch."

As the target drew closer, she scowled. Nine of her shots had gone through the heart. A small hole stood alone, an inch to the left of the others.

Max was right. Between thoughts of Micah's kiss and LaKeisha's troubles and CJ Brennan's suicide, she *had* lost her touch.

She reloaded the mag and clicked it into place.

"Send it back out," she told him, before putting the earplugs back in.

Comparable to the basketball that used to feel like a part of her hand, the heft of the weapon was familiar in Jade's grip. She steadied her breath, held it, and fired.

Jade and her mentor shot for thirty minutes, without speaking, at the range in Fairfax County. The place was crowded because of the unexpected pleasant day. The sounds of birds chirping—and bullets whizzing—filled the air.

She loved spending time on a range, whether here or at FBI HQ. She shot every other week to stay sharp and help take her mind off things. The death of CJ Brennan had hit her hard, although she hadn't known him, except for their brief encounter during the TSK case. Jade had gleaned most of what she knew about the young man from the media. She respected him for standing up for himself and not letting his father push him into being someone he wasn't.

She and Max sat across from each other at a picnic table in an outdoor area where customers took breaks in between rounds. Jade drank a Pepsi, and Max drank an Orange Crush.

"Any leads in the Shakespeare case?" he asked, sipping his drink.

"No leads. No activity. Nothing. At least there's some good news: no new murders."

"What about Veritas?"

"Nothing in the blogs helped. We spoke with all the advertisers; they didn't provide anything useful. He's no longer a person of interest."

"This isn't over," Max said.

She took a long pull of her soft drink. "I don't think so either."

"He's cooling off," he said, "if you call a month a cooling-off period. Perhaps he's gone back to his normal life. Might be years before he strikes again."

Jade raised an eyebrow. "You think?"

"No. He'll start missing the attention, if he doesn't already."

The elusive Shakespeare Killer was the source of rampant speculation on cable news and social media. MSNBC broadcasted a documentary reenacting the three murders. A sick individual had created a fake Twitter account for the killer. Women from all over the world professed their love to him, offering their bodies or proposals of marriage. These women didn't know or care whether he was married.

Or that he killed people.

What a crazy, crazy world. Or maybe it had always been this way, and the advent of social media only magnified people's basest behaviors and instincts.

"He doesn't want to be caught," she said.

Max nodded. "He likes killing too much. Every murder ups the tension, which can only be satisfied by another murder. Our man will strike again."

"Until he commits the perfect murder," Jade murmured. A perfectionist herself, she should know. "One that can't be topped." After a moment of silence, she said, "Guesses to motive?"

"Robbery has been ruled out," he said. "The murders don't appear to be random. All the victims are not only wealthy, but also major players in their respective fields."

"Don't forget white."

"Right. Did you find a connection?"

"Dante says no. Different industries. Different social circles. None belonged to the same associations or clubs or attended the same conferences."

They both sipped their drinks thoughtfully.

Max said, "How are you adjusting to being a supervisor?"

She didn't respond immediately.

"What is it?" he asked.

His white dress shirt, open at the collar, displayed an off-white under-shirt with a wrinkled crew neck. His sleeves were rolled up, exposing his slender arms.

"What if I'm not cut out for this?" she said ruefully. "I want to be where the action is. Not sitting behind a desk full time."

"You're a great agent."

"Maybe so," she said, "but I might suck as a boss."

"It's different," he said. "You're no longer a player. You're the coach."

"Player-coach."

"You've got to accept that it's not only about your success. Your success depends on others." He eyed her. "Is something else holding you back?"

Sheepish, she said, "Being a supervisor is boring."

Max chuckled. "I could see why you would think that." He paused. "How's Micah doing?"

"Not bad."

Max smiled.

"Okay," she conceded. "He's going to be good."

"I know. I taught him." Max wasn't bragging. He was stating a fact.

A man in a blue T-shirt and jeans walked by, his arm around his young son. They carried matching guns. Max followed them with his eyes. His wife had left him last year after thirty years of marriage. Was he thinking about being childless or something else entirely?

Still looking at the pair, he said, "I've watched you two in meetings."

We have a winner. Something else.

"Who?"

"You and Micah."

"Why would you do that?"

"That's what I do. Observe." He peered at her over the top of the soda can. "You two have become close."

Does he know about what happened at the pub?

She squinted at him. "What are you saying, Max?"

"Be careful, Jade."

Tamping down her temper, she said, "Give me some credit. I don't shit where I eat." She thought briefly of Kyle. *Well, not in the same restaurant.*

"You need to retain the respect of your staff. If they think you and Micah are—"

"I get it," she said tersely.

Jade wasn't sure what angered her about Max's suggestion. His observation?

The vibrating phone in the pocket of her black tracksuit pants saved her from continuing the conversation.

Pulling it out, she glanced at the display and smiled, even though the call surely portended bad news. She answered.

"It's been a long time," said the voice.

"My favorite detective. How are you?"

"I fell for that one before," said Detective Kurt McClaine.

"What's up?"

"Wish I weren't the bearer of bad news, but unfortunately, that seems to be the basis of our relationship."

"What've you got?"

He sighed. "One with your name written all over it."

"I've been promoted. I no longer work cases. Besides, I've spent way too much time in Seattle."

Two of Jade's most recent major cases had taken her to the Pacific Northwest city, where she'd worked with McClaine. And met Kyle.

Focus.

"You're going to want to come out here."

"Tell me why."

"I'm at a scene. The victim's name is Blayze Tishman."

She gasped.

Blayze Tishman retired last year as the CEO of a software company, the number three company in the Fortune 500. He'd recently bought a professional football team with plans to move it to the Bay Area.

"I'm listening," she said.

"It's bad," McClaine said. "The vic's messed up. The perp left a note."

"A sonnet?"

"Let me count the ways."

"That's Elizabeth Barrett Browning."

"Don't you know? I was never *good* in English," he said. "See you in Seattle."

He hung up.

Jade called Dante.

"Call the team together," she said when he answered, looking at Max, "and tell them to pack their bags. I'll meet you at Dulles."

Her next call was to Pat. "Check out Veritas's timeline for a tweet about Blayze Tishman."

Casper, Wyoming

"PRESIDENT RICHARD ELLISON and First Lady Nancy Ellison, President Timothy Hartman and First Lady Elizabeth Hartman, and President Edward Middleton and First Lady Barbara Middleton, I am honored and delighted to give the opening remarks today.

"I love to read, and libraries are one of my favorite places to spend my time." She paused. "Especially lately."

The one hundred people in attendance laughed. The troubles Whitney had experienced in the infancy of her presidency weren't a secret, nor was her love of reading. Although it was no longer news, the media still accompanied her on monthly trips to independent bookstores.

"Richard and I were involved in a hard-fought presidential campaign, but through it all, he comported himself with integrity and always treated me with respect and dignity. Although we don't agree on many issues—"

"None!" her predecessor joked, standing next to her, his tan, weathered face relaxed.

The crowd laughed again, harder this time.

Whitney joined in. "We weren't as far apart as he led you to believe. Richard was the rare breed of politician who put our country first, who considered issues on their merits rather than toeing the party line. He served as the governor of this great state of Wyoming, as its senator, and finally as our president. He loves his country, loves his family, and loves his ranch."

She remembered fondly her visit there last year. It wasn't far from where she stood now. She took in the scenery through the glass walls: miles of Wyoming dirt and cottonwood trees. A mountain in the distance. She scanned the guests, catching the eye of several familiar faces. Friends and foes alike.

"No matter how much you prepare for the presidency, you aren't truly prepared. A president, as soon as he or she"—she smiled—"sits behind the desk in the Oval Office, has a greater appreciation for all those who served before her. I want to thank Richard for being a resource for me, and now, a friend. This beautiful library represents him. Strong, angular, sturdy, and well crafted."

"You forgot out to pasture," he quipped.

She waited for the laughter to die down.

"The Richard Milhous Ellison Library is a monument to his legacy, for the benefit of his constituents and neighbors, and for posterity. God bless all of you and God bless the United States of America. Ladies and gentlemen, President Richard Ellison."

After the ribbon cutting, Whitney, Richard, and the other former presidents retired to a small room off the main one.

"What've you been up to?" asked former president Timothy Hartman. "Golf?"

Richard shook his head. "I'm not much of a golfer."

"Not sure how you can live out here."

"Casper too dull for you?"

"I've been here for only an afternoon," said Hartman. "It's great to see you again, but I'm ready to leave. I miss the buildings. The action. I want to see cars, not cattle."

Although Hartman had lived in California for most of his life, he'd moved to New York City after his term in office, where he now headed up a foundation named after him. He also jetted around the country, giving six-figure—sometimes seven-figure—speeches. He hadn't been president for over a decade, but the economic prosperity the country enjoyed during his presidency was still a reverent memory for the public.

The three men and Whitney comprised the most exclusive club in the world—the Presidents Club—an unofficial group of the current and former living US presidents. This was the first time during her presidency that all of them had been together.

"Don't talk about our cattle," Richard said. "Besides, the fresh air might do you some good."

"With all this dust? No thanks."

They quieted as a server placed four glasses on the table. He poured a dram into each glass and left the bottle of Macallan.

Whitney and Richard thanked him before he quietly retreated.

"Retirement treating you well?" Hartman asked.

"Can't complain."

The four presidents sat in white-cushioned chairs around a low square table. Despite the modern decor in the rest of the library, this room was bathed in beiges and browns. Built-in bookcases lined the walls with books and artifacts from Ellison's time in office.

They were alone, their secret service details just outside the door.

Hartman raised his glass. "To Richard!"

"To Richard," Whitney and Edward Middleton echoed. Richard nodded in appreciation. The three of them clinked glasses with Richard and each other. Swirling the scotch around in her glass, Whitney lifted it to her lips. She sniffed before taking a small sip, savoring the flavors of dried fruit, wood smoke, and spice.

Middleton looked at Richard. "Milhous, huh? Did your parents hate you?"

Richard Ellison laughed. "Nixon helped push through the Civil Rights Act of 1957 the year before I was born. My mother loved him. My father, not so much."

Middleton shook his head. "Richard Nixon, what a character." He turned to Whitney. "How's it going with you?"

"Slower than I expected," she said.

The three men laughed at the understatement. Her legislative achievements—except for the Equal Rights Amendment, the Anti-Bullying Act, and the slimmed-down New Cubed—were few.

"The job's getting harder," Middleton said. "Harder than in my day. With social media. The pace of the world. Terrorism. Cybercrime."

"Mass shootings," added Hartman.

Richard shook his head. "I disagree. Washington's experience was the toughest. He had no predecessor. Heck, he didn't even have a country—just a bunch of rebellious colonies. He had to make it up as he went along and set the precedent for all who came after him. If he'd messed up, who knows where this nation would've ended up."

"What about Franklin D.?" Hartman said. "He lifted us up out of the Great Depression and steered us through World War II."

"True," Whitney said. "And then there's Lincoln."

His accomplishments—including holding a divided country together—didn't need to be voiced.

"What about me?" Richard asked.

The three other presidents stared at him.

"You?" Middleton said.

Richard said, "Why do you all look surprised?"

"You didn't have it so hard," Hartman said.

"I had Cole Brennan always jabbering in my ear," Richard said, taking a sip of his drink.

"That's true," Middleton held up a hand, conceding.

"Good point," said Hartman.

"You got off easy," Richard continued, looking at Middleton, his Republican colleague. "At least you still had some moderates left in Congress."

After debating for a time who truly had it the toughest, Whitney said, "Perhaps my plight isn't so bad."

Richard leaned forward, reaching for the bottle. He refreshed their drinks, then sat back and crossed his legs, cradling his glass, looking at her. "How can we help?"

With which problem?

She thought about Grayson, Chandler, Emma, Min, Tamirov, and Cameron.

"Perhaps there is something you can do," she said.

"Name it," Richard said.

Seattle, Washington

JADE SLOWED HER pace to allow McClaine to catch up to her.

With his long blond hair and small silver star-shaped earring, McClaine didn't look like your typical detective. Over his slight frame, he wore jeans and his customary T-shirt, today's edition light blue with Safer in a Sanctuary City emblazoned in neon-green lettering. A tattoo snaked partway up his neck, reaching higher since the last time Jade saw him.

The footsteps of Dante, Micah, Max, Christian, and Brian Anderson, the local agent, crunched behind her.

McClaine had met Max and Christian during the Robin Hood case. Earlier today, Jade introduced him to Dante and Micah at the Seattle FBI office. He already knew Anderson.

Both cars were parked on the shoulder. Stepping over the guardrail, the detective and the five agents carefully waded their way down through the tall grass toward the water's edge.

"The vic was found there," McClaine said, pointing at a patch of trampled grass the size of a large man.

Jade crouched next to the indentation, the surrounding area littered with cigarette butts and craft beer cans. She didn't see any footprints. "Did it rain last night? Or was it that sprinkle stuff you Seattleites call rain."

McClaine smiled. "The sprinkle stuff."

"Not hard enough to wipe away footprints."

"No."

"Would have been lucky to find impressions in this grass." Jade stood, placing her hands on her hips. "Who found him?"

"UW rowing club," he said. "Women. They row Lake Washington every morning. Saw something on the bank. As they came closer, they realized that it was a body. They almost moved on, thinking it was a homeless person, sleeping."

"But they saw the blood," she said, scanning the drenched ground.

Next to her, Max was taking it all in. He met her eye but said nothing.

"Yep," McClaine said. "They rowed back to the Conibear Shellhouse"—he pointed to the other side of the lake—"and called us."

"Did they check to see if he was alive?"

"No. Claimed they didn't leave the boat."

She gazed out at a lone sailboat braving the cold. Small waves lapped against the shore. "Any witnesses?"

"None have come forward. We went house to house," he said, waving behind him at the houses on the hill overlooking them, "but no one saw anything. Still waiting on one resident to get back to us."

Veritas's house was still under surveillance. Although his real name had been confirmed as Jacob Michael Collins, Jade still thought of him as Veritas. Anderson had reported that he was home all night. NSA tracked his phone to his apartment. This morning, before Jade and the DC contingent arrived in Seattle, Anderson and another local agent paid a visit to Veritas. During the interview, he maintained his innocence. Anderson told her that all the defiance Veritas displayed during their previous trip had dissipated. He was scared. Shaking scared. Though he'd told them he wasn't going to stop tweeting.

Jade didn't think he was responsible for the murders, but the killer could be taking cues from him. She mentally kicked herself. They should have been monitoring his tweets.

She pulled out her phone and sent a text.

Pat's reply came within a minute: Cyber's on it.

Pocketing her phone, Jade inhaled the fresh air. Her eyes returned to the top of the hill. "What neighborhood is that?"

McClaine followed her gaze. "Madison Park."

"Gigantic houses. Great views."

"I should've gone into IT. Or coffee."

McClaine was referencing Seattle's tech hub, home to Amazon and Microsoft, of course, as well as hosting Google, Facebook, and Apple. Costco, Nordstrom, and Starbucks were all headquartered here too.

"You're dressed for it," she said.

"IT? Or coffee?"

"Both. TOD?"

"Coroner said between 10:00 p.m. and 1:00 a.m."

Jade surveyed the ground. "Any trace evidence?"

"Just the knife," McClaine said. "Oh… and a sonnet."

❋

Christian let out a breath. "Jesus."

Standing next to him, Jade said, "Why do you always say that?"

He invoked the Lord's name whenever he saw a naked, dead body.

In the morgue on Jefferson Street, just south of the First Hill neighborhood, the five agents and McClaine stared down at the body of Blayze Tishman on the stainless-steel table.

What remained of the body.

Stab wounds dotted his expansive pale torso, a macabre work of impressionist art.

Tishman's face and legs were unmarred. A tag with his identification information was tied around the big toe of his left foot.

Bright lights illuminated the chilly room, where the smell of antiseptic was overpowering.

Jade scrutinized the wounds. "How many?"

"Twenty-seven," McClaine said. "The victim ended up choking on his own blood."

Dante swallowed slowly. "Jesus is right."

"Such anger," Max murmured, his eyes scanning the body.

To Max, Dante said, "You think the perp knew him?"

"It's possible," came Max's noncommittal response.

"Or Tishman angered him in some way," said Micah.

"He could be abrasive," McClaine said. "It might've been drugs. Seattle has a huge opioid, mental health, and homelessness crisis. A dangerous combination. Or some guy thought the vic encroached on his turf. A quiet place to sleep."

"With a killer view," Dante said.

Jade looked at him. "You're becoming worse than Pat."

McClaine said, "I've seen victims murdered in this city for less."

DC too.

"But for the sonnet," she reminded him.

"But for the sonnet," McClaine said. "Let's go to my office."

❋

McClaine passed around copies of the sonnet and the police and autopsy reports to the team, who sat around the rectangular table in a conference room at the downtown precinct. He handed Jade the murder book containing the complete case file: autopsy report, crime scene photos, investigative notes, and witness interview reports.

He waited for the FBI agents to read through the materials.

Jade scanned the autopsy report. Tishman, fifty-eight, weighed two hundred twenty pounds. Manner of death: homicide. Under cause of death, each stab wound was listed. Pasta, tomato sauce, and a brownish liquid were found among the contents of his stomach.

"Tell us about his wife," Jade asked.

"Victoria Tishman. Married twenty-six years. She oversees their family foundation and, from what we've gathered, is very involved in her husband's business interests. She was his partner, personally and professionally. Formidable in her own right."

Jade flipped through the pages. "She give you anything?"

"Nothing helpful."

"We need to talk to her."

"Arranged," he said. "She's expecting us within the next couple of hours."

"Questions?" she asked her team, her eyes landing on Max.

Max looked thoughtful but didn't respond. She didn't press. He would tell her his thoughts when he was ready.

"Tishman was a big bloke," Micah said. "How did the perp overpower him?"

"Maybe he was a slow… bloke," Dante said. "Like Merritt."

Christian cut his eyes at Dante but refused to take the bait.

Jade placed the murder book on the table and picked up a copy of the sonnet.

For I am sham'd by that which I bring forth,
And so should you, to love things nothing worth.

—Bard of Avon

She checked the Shakespeare app on her phone, which she'd downloaded a few weeks ago, having left the tome in DC.

Sonnet LXXII.

Scanning the faces of her team, she said, "Seventy-two. Does this mean anything to anyone?"

Christian, Max, Dante, McClaine, and Anderson gave her blank looks.

"The last line," Micah said. "The perp might have thought Tishman cared about the wrong things. Wealth. Material things."

Jade stood, shaking her head. "Thank God for the Brit. Let's go talk to the wife."

CHAPTER FIFTY-NINE

The White House, Washington, DC

"WELL, HELL!" SENATOR Maureen McAllister said. "We're not going to make it."

Vice President Josephine Bates exhaled. "Damn."

"They're right," Sasha said.

A whiteboard set up on an easel had been erected in front of Whitney's desk in the Oval Office. Sasha had written the name of each of the fifty senators and his or her party affiliation—*R* or *D*—in parenthesis. There were no independents in the Senate. In two columns, under the headings "Aye" and "Nay," an *X* was marked next to each senator's name.

The Streamline Regulations Act had been more difficult to push through than Whitney expected, given that the GOP controlled both houses of Congress and deregulation had been a pillar of the party's platform for decades. If she were a Republican president, this legislation would have sailed through last year.

Earlier in the month, question marks accompanied quite a few names, but the Presidents Club had come through. Using their contacts, the weight of their former office, and leverage (read: subtle threats), they helped convert the votes of recalcitrant members of their parties. If successful, it would be the second major legislation passed in as many months.

The four women stood in a row, examining the easel. Although Whitney's high heels were under her desk where she'd kicked them off earlier, she towered over Mo standing next to her.

"Perhaps, if we stare long enough," Whitney said dryly, "the votes will change on their own."

"It'd make my job a lot easier," Sasha said. She'd spent a considerable amount of time on the Hill, persuading senators to change their minds.

Senator Mo looked up at Whitney. "Although I'm a firm believer in posi-tive thinking, I don't think that's going to help us."

Sasha, on the other side of Jo, said, "We need one more."

After a moment, Jo turned to Whitney. "Who owes you a favor?"

"That's cutting to the chase," Mo said.

"I've no time to waste," Jo said. "By the way, where's that moonshine?"

Whitney and Mo giggled. Sasha eyed them, understanding she wasn't privy to the joke, her body language indicating that she didn't want to be.

The laughter died as they all scanned the list again. Whitney went over every name with a "Nay" next to it. Her eyes rested on one halfway down. She pointed to it.

"Scott Harris," she said. "He might not owe me a favor, but he owes me."

CHAPTER SIXTY

Medina, Washington

AFTER SPEAKING INTO the intercom, McClaine closed the driver's side window and waited for the gate to open. He, Micah, and Dante drove through the entrance, the other agent's car following. The long driveway led to a circle in front of a humongous house of stone and siding and grand windows. The hedges and shrubs were manicured to perfection. Japanese maple trees dotted the lawn.

The Tishmans, like other former and current managers of Blayze's software company, lived in Medina, a city across Lake Washington from Seattle.

Many cars—Mercedes, BMWs, Porsches, a Jaguar, and a Subaru—were parked around the circle. The five-car garage must have been filled.

Max, Christian, Jade, and Anderson—their driver—sat in the car for a moment admiring the house.

"Wow," Christian said.

Max stared at the house but said nothing. Was he thinking about his own empty colonial in Virginia? He had told Jade that his ex-wife had moved in with her new partner.

An abundance of flowers greeted them on either side of the front door.

McClaine knocked. A woman in her midfifties opened the door.

"Detective Kurt McClaine," he said, proffering his badge. "I called earlier."

"Of course," she said. "I'm Victoria's sister, Margaret."

They stepped into a circular entryway with a black-and-white marble floor. A carpeted staircase led to the upper levels.

Margaret escorted them to a room off the foyer. A sitting room. Literally. The long rectangular space was filled with couches, chairs, and coffee and end tables in various groupings. Magnificent paintings hung on the walls. Jade stopped to examine one. A Renoir. It wasn't a reproduction. The soft carpet was identical in color to the carpet on the stairs. French doors led out to a side yard, where a fountain was surrounded by a circular stone path, with two iron benches, a gazebo, a swimming pool, a tennis court, and an outdoor seating area with a bar. The lake began where the lawn ended.

Wealth. This room screamed the word without making a sound. Tishman and Jared Carr could have run in the same circles.

"Please have a seat," Margaret said. "I'll fetch her."

She closed the white sliding door behind her.

Dante surveyed all the seating options. "Where should we sit?"

They selected an arrangement of two couches and two chairs in the center of the room.

The agents and McClaine sat. And waited.

After a while, Jade stood and paced.

Dante stood. "We should remind her that we're here."

"She's in mourning," Micah reminded him. "Tending to her guests. Poor woman."

"Poor my…" Dante started to respond and then saw Jade's expression. He swallowed the rest of his retort.

The door slid open.

Victoria Tishman took in the room with one glance. Also in her fifties, she had dyed blond hair and was dressed in black slacks and a black blouse, the severity of the clothing softened by the string of small pearls around her neck. Jade wondered if this was her mourning outfit or whether she regularly dressed this way. Her bearing was regal, despite her mourning, or, possibly, because of it.

The other agents and McClaine rose.

The woman extended her hand to McClaine. "Detective."

McClaine introduced her to the agents.

"Please sit," she said in a welcoming way. "Would you care for something to drink?"

"We're fine," McClaine said.

She sat in a chair across from one of the couches and leaned forward, her hands clasped. The biggest diamond that Jade had ever seen adorned the ring finger of her left hand.

After offering condolences, Jade asked, "What can you tell us about the night your husband was killed?"

Victoria briefly closed her eyes and exhaled. "I was at a function downtown. A women's group that I belong to. Blayze had called me earlier, telling me he was headed to the club."

"Which club was that?" Dante asked, before turning and widening his eyes at Micah, a request to take notes.

"The WAC," she said. "Washington Athletic Club. We've been members for decades. Our children practically grew up there with their friends. Whenever he was in town, Blayze played in the basketball league, which has several divisions for all levels of ability. Good thing." A slight smile. "He wasn't as good as he thought he was. He also swam. Worked out. Although, looking at him, you couldn't tell." Her words weren't meant to be hurtful. More of a shared memory with someone who could no longer share it.

"How do you think he ended up on the other side of the lake at that time of night?" Jade asked.

"Blayze loved the lake," the widow said, a tremor in her voice. She paused to compose herself. "One of his favorite things to do was to sit on the terrace off our bedroom upstairs, sipping whiskey and looking at the lake where he'd spent so much time. He used to row. At UW."

"What was he doing there that night?" Jade asked.

"I don't know."

"Thinking about his glory days?" Dante asked.

This made Victoria smile. "Probably. Although he's had a lot of glory days since then. To the world, my husband is a successful businessman and a loud-mouth owner of a professional sports team. To me, he's just Blayze. The same guy I met in college. Studied with. Went to parties and football games with. Fell in love with and married." She waved her hand, taking in the room. "Before we had all this." More quietly. "Before we had anything."

"Tell us about your children," Jade said.

"Our son, Patrick, lives here in Seattle. Our daughter Tara is in New York City, and our other daughter Lindsey lives in Phoenix. They arrived yesterday."

Children weren't mentioned in Sonnet LXXII, but it wouldn't hurt to investigate them. Jade made a mental note to have Pat check them out.

"Did you or your husband know Sebastian Scofield, Jared Carr, or Finn Hurley?" Dante asked.

Victoria Tishman's head jolted in his direction. "You think Blayze was murdered by the Shakespeare Killer?" She scanned the faces of the other agents. "I wondered why the FBI was involved."

"We're exploring every lead, ma'am."

She fingered her pearls. "We didn't socialize with any of them. Neither of us could stand Jared Carr or his politics. But… my husband's former company has dealings with Hurley Technologies."

"How so?"

"You should talk to the current CEO, but I think it had something to do with developing a joint product."

The White House, Washington, DC

"MADAM PRESIDENT."

Whitney's body woman, Sarah, stood just inside the door. Sasha paused handing out the day's agenda.

"I need a private word," Sarah said.

The members glanced at each other. What could be important enough to interrupt this meeting?

Whitney rose.

"Pardon me," she said to her cabinet, hustling out of the room. In the hallway, Josh McPherson closed the door behind her.

"What is it, Sarah?" Whitney said.

"It's about Senator Scott Harris."

I hope he hasn't died.

"What about him?"

Sarah looked around. There were only secret service agents positioned in the hall, staring straight ahead, studiously ignoring them.

"His son's been kidnapped."

❋

"Any news about your son?" Whitney said. She'd called Harris from the Oval Office.

"We haven't received a ransom note. No communication. Nothing." He paused. "I'm a US senator, and I feel helpless."

I know the feeling.

"How can I help?"

In a quiet voice, Senator Scott Harris said, "Just find my son."

"Perhaps we can help each other."

"What are you talking about?"

"I missed you last year, during the campaign. At Ohio State. You were supposed to attend and join me on stage before my speech."

"I had a conflict."

"Must have been important." *To stiff your party's nominee for president,* she didn't add.

"Why are you bringing this up?"

"We're one vote short for the SRA."

"Is that what this is all about?"

"What do you mean?"

"Are you holding my son hostage in exchange for my vote?"

Whitney's mouth parted in shock. "Of course not. How dare you?"

"Your timing is impeccable, Madam President." A long silence followed. Then he said, "I can't support the bill. I'm a Democrat. A real one."

He considered her a DINO. "As am I," she said.

It wasn't only through the efforts of the Presidents Club that the legislation was a success. Mo and Jo had worked tirelessly to help Whitney keep this campaign promise.

Cole Brennan had also done his part. Despite his grief, he'd talked to congressional members or called them out on his radio show. Between him and Mo, all the Republicans had fallen in line. They needed one more senator from the Democratic side.

Whitney believed Harris was her best bet. Although she felt badly about the timing, it couldn't be helped.

She crossed her legs. "This is a good bill, Scott. It will help our government work better and save money. This country is on a precipice. Many people believe that this government no longer works. Can no longer function. *Our* government. Let's show them that it still does." She paused. When he didn't respond, she added, "The money we save may be used for more progressive causes."

"Is that all you've got?"

"I'll mobilize the full strength of federal law enforcement to help locate your son."

"All right then," he said.

CHAPTER SIXTY-TWO

Seattle, Washington

THEY WERE MEETING at the local FBI office to debrief on the interview with Tishman's wife.

Jade received a call with a 202 area code. She recognized the number. "Excuse me," she said to the team.

"Hold please," she said into the phone as she strode down the hall looking for a vacant office. Finding one, she entered and shut the door. "Hello."

"Please hold for the president," the president's secretary said.

"Agent Harrington," the president said, her voice resonant, powerful.

"Yes, Madam President."

"I need a favor."

She listened, ending the call with, "We'll do our best."

Jade returned to the conference room, signaling Micah to join her in the hallway. She would give him an opportunity to show her how good he was.

"I need you to do something," she said, after he'd closed the conference room door behind him.

"Sure. What is it?"

Jade told him about the senator's son and the president's request.

"My plate's full." She searched his eyes. "Can you handle this?"

"I've got it."

"Make arrangements to return to DC tonight."

"No need," he said. "I just need a private room."

Puzzled, she gestured toward the office she'd just vacated.

"How are you going to take care of this from here?"

"Watch me."

"This is Iyanna Adey. With KIRO7?"

I need to change my number.

Holding the cell phone tighter, Jade sat up on the queen-size hotel bed. "Yes?"

"I heard you were in town investigating the Tishman murder. Anything you can tell me?"

"How did you get my number?"

"Agent Lawson gave it to me, remember?"

"I don't think he did."

"If you're here, this case is connected to the other Shakespeare murders. Did you find a sonnet?"

"No comment."

"Was the knife left in the body?"

She sat forward. "Where are you getting your information?"

No response. Adey had hung up.

Jade held the phone on her lap. Barringer? Who else could it be?

She remembered seeing Adey with Kyle and McClaine at the hearing and made a mental note to ask them about it.

She texted Pat: Check out Iyanna Adey with KIRO7.

A moment later, Pat responded: A reporter now too?

See if she's connected to someone at the FBI.

On it.

Jade stared at the phone for a moment, then placed the call. The professor answered on the first ring.

"How's your case going?" Bennett asked.

"The perpetrator's still at large," she said.

"So not well, I take it."

"No."

"I hoped that I had helped."

"You did. Professor Bennett, I want to email something to you. What's your address?"

"Only if you call me Alaia."

"Alaia."

"Are you always this stiff?"

Yes. "I'm working."

"Ah… hence the term 'working stiff.'"

This made Jade smile.

Bennett gave Jade her email address.

"Tell me when you've received it," Jade said.

"Just did. Give me a moment." Then she said, "Where did you find this one?"

"The victim lived in Seattle. Blayze Tishman. Former software CEO. Now the owner of a professional football team. Any thoughts?"

The professor paused. "I don't think the victims were selected at random. Your killer is decompensating."

Everyone's a profiler these days.

"I mean about the sonnet," Jade said. "This one doesn't include 'die' in it."

"But there's 'death,'" the professor pointed out. "Same concept. This is seventy-two. Shakespeare moved into a different period with Sonnets LXXI through LXXIV."

"What do you mean by 'a different period'?"

"These sonnets were about anticipated death."

Jade rolled her eyes. Shakespeare—the poet, not the killer—had had too much time on his hands.

While talking to the professor, she stared at the faux impressionist painting on the opposite wall. The elevator dinged out in the hallway. "Of whom? The recipient or the poet?"

"Excellent question. The answer might be both, but I think it's about the poet's impending death."

"Impending?"

"Remember when these sonnets were written. Death was pervasive in England at the time, not too far from a citizen's everyday thoughts. From the plague, which eradicated thousands of people in a short time, to the public execution of criminals and traitors."

Jade absorbed this. "Any other insight you can give me?"

"In the sonnet, 'shame' is mentioned twice and inferred once. The poet is shamed, but so is the recipient. Your killer and the victim might have done something shameful together. I would suggest looking into the victim's background. You might find your killer there."

The four walls of the hotel room were closing in. After her conversation with the professor, Jade needed a walk.

She eschewed an umbrella as well as the hood on her jacket, letting the rain fall on her hair and skin. She remembered Kyle telling her once that precipitation was cleansing.

Her mind was still. Maybe she would eventually get the hang of meditation after all.

She walked alone down Mercer Street. If she were accosted, her attackers would learn immediately that they'd picked the wrong target. At an underpass, she spotted a mural and stopped to admire it. It depicted the reality before her: tents surrounded by garbage bags and litter. A place where homeless people hunkered down for the evening. It was hard for her to grasp the extent of the homelessness crisis in Seattle, one of the wealthiest cities in the country, although DC was one of the most powerful cities in the world and it had the same problem. What was the answer?

She thought about it. And moved on.

Emerging from the underpass, she gazed at the decorative lights strung up on apartments and houses higher up the hill. The holidays were long over. Cranes—she counted at least nineteen—were decorated in bright colors, predominately green and blue, the colors of the Seattle Seahawks.

After talking to the professor, she'd sent Pat an email request to dig further into Blayze Tishman's background, including his current and past associates. Was there a relationship with the other victims that his wife wasn't aware of? Did his company supply software to their firms? Had he partnered with them in a venture? Or were they connected through the football team?

She also asked Pat to check out his children.

The wind picked up. A scrap of newspaper blew across her path, part of a full-page ad for the software company Tishman used to lead.

What product was Tishman's company working on with Hurley's?

Jade picked up the paper. Next to the ad was an article about Russia meddling in US elections.

A whisper from Tishman?

Balling it up, she tossed the paper into the next trash can and headed back to the hotel.

She had researched the bard's life. She knew more about him now than she ever thought she would. A poet, playwright, and actor, Shakespeare was still considered the greatest English-language writer of all time.

What in the hell did he have in common with modern-day wealthy Americans?

CHAPTER SIXTY-THREE

Bellevue, Washington

ON THE DRIVE east to Blayze Tishman's former company, Jade's phone vibrated in her pocket. Eyeing the number, she let it go to voicemail. When they arrived at the software company's campus, Jade said to the others, "I'll be there in a minute."

"Must be important," Christian said.

"Something I need to take care of."

She waited until Brian Anderson, Max, and Christian were out of hearing distance and hit the call back button.

"Hello," Kyle answered. A statement, not a question.

"Ms. Madison."

"Oh, we're back to that again?"

"How are you?" Jade said.

"I heard you were in Seattle. Since you're here, I presume it has to do with the Shakespeare Killer. Blayze?"

Jade might as well have rented a billboard advertising her arrival in Seattle. "Did you know him?"

"We were involved in a lot of charitable causes together. Attended the same events. Ran in the same political circles."

"Ah… one of Fairchild's army of small donors."

"Something like that."

It used to be a joke between them. Blayze Tishman wasn't a small donor. Neither was Kyle Madison.

"Is it true?" Kyle asked. "He was stabbed to death?"

Through the light fog, Jade admired the fir trees in the distance. Cars blazed by on the nearby freeway. Blaze. Blayze. "I can't discuss an ongoing investigation."

"Oh, right."

"Any idea who could've done this?"

"Always interrogating," she said. "That's the Jade I know."

"Well," Jade said, "since you're on the phone..."

A pause. Then, "Blayze always needed to prove how smart he was. He was loud. Boorish. Offensive. I'm sure anyone that successful developed some enemies along the way."

"Anyone specific?"

"Well..."

"Tell me."

"I hate to do this—he's been through so much—but Blayze never treated Noah very well. He was condescending, belittling to him. I'm sure Noah hated him."

"Enough to kill him?"

Kyle hesitated. "Conceivably."

"Do you know Iyanna Adey?"

"Who?"

"The reporter. Channel seven."

"I've seen her on TV."

"No. I saw you talking to her. At Noah's hearing."

A longer pause. "She interviewed me. For the trial."

"You, Adey, and McClaine seemed familiar with each other."

"We were all involved in Noah's case. Besides, despite its size, Seattle is a small town."

Jade didn't believe she'd misinterpreted what she saw.

The campus was right outside of Bellevue, a city near Medina. Locals called the area east of the lake the Eastside. The agents and McClaine spoke to the current CEO of the global software company, who wouldn't divulge the purpose of the joint project with Hurley Technologies without written authorization from US Cyber Command.

They also spoke to the human resources department. They had received threats targeted at Tishman over the years. The staff provided the names and addresses of all the now former employees involved.

Although described as brash and boorish, Tishman was well respected. The company's financial results spoke for themselves. Everyone agreed on the Tishmans' unparalleled generosity in their efforts to combat numerous social problems plaguing not only Seattle but cities and towns across the United States: homelessness, income disparity, and inequality in education funding.

The agents spent a few hours interviewing staff at all levels of the organization who'd worked with Tishman, but they learned nothing helpful.

Pat sent an email reporting that Tishman's kids were all successful in their own right. Tara was a corporate attorney, Lindsey an investment banker, and Patrick a product manager for Amazon. Victoria divulged that she was the sole heir of her husband's estate. Pat looked into her too, but so far hadn't come up with anything.

On the way back from Bellevue, Jade called AMB International and spoke with Augustus Mathias Blakeley, its CEO and Noah's father. He told her that Noah had moved to Panama shortly after he was exonerated.

To be with "his people."

CHAPTER SIXTY-FOUR

Seattle, Washington

LATER, BACK IN a conference room at the local FBI office, Jade, Dante, Max, Micah, Christian, McClaine, and Brian Anderson sat around an oval table discussing the interviews.

Anderson stood. "Anyone want anything? Coffee? Soda? Water?"

There were a few responses for water and coffee.

"Do you have tea, mate?" Micah asked.

"Teammate?" Dante said.

"No, I asked for tea from my mate here."

Shaking his head, Dante said, "A dude who drinks tea. God help me." To Anderson, "Can I have an espresso?"

Micah shook his head.

Once they had their drinks, Dante said to Jade, "We should leave Micah here to coordinate efforts among the locals, our office here, and the bureau."

Sitting across from Micah, she saw his eyes shift to McClaine.

Odd. Was Dante right about him? Was Micah gay? She thought of his kiss.

Definitely not gay.

"I need Micah in DC."

"What about Merritt?"

"I love how you're all talking about us as if we're not here," Micah said, sipping his hot tea out of a cup, his pinkie extended. Dante looked at him with disgust.

Christian rose abruptly and stood by the window, his arms crossed over his chest. She joined him.

As they both stared down on Third Avenue, she said, "I need someone here."

"I'm being forced out."

"That's not what this is."

He looked at her. "What happened to your 'rock'?"

She pushed him. He didn't budge. "See? You're still my rock. Coordinate things here and come back as soon as you can. You're an important member of this team and more valuable to me here."

After a moment, he nodded without looking at her.

They returned to the table.

Dante's head dropped, his expression one of pity. "Robin having trouble leaving Batman?"

Jade opened her mouth to give her usual response, but Christian beat her to it. In her tone of voice, he said, "Shut up, Dante."

The agents' laughter broke the tension.

After deciding on next steps, they stood to leave. McClaine came to stand next to Jade. "Until next time?"

"If you want to work with me so badly," she said, "why don't you move to DC?"

She started to smile, but McClaine's eyes shifted to Micah and Max, then back to her. It happened swiftly; perhaps she was mistaken.

"Maybe I will," he said.

"How do you know Iyanna Adey?"

An almost imperceptible tug of the eyes. "The reporter? She covers the crime beat, I think."

"I saw you talking to her and Kyle Madison at Noah Blakeley's hearing. The three of you seemed tight."

"Our police department prides itself on knowing the citizens in our community. That's what you saw. Safe travels, Agent Harrington."

He hugged her—he was a hugger—and left.

Retrieving her briefcase and rolling suitcase from against the wall, she said goodbye to Christian and Anderson and headed down the hallway, with Dante, Max, and Micah trailing behind her.

After the elevator doors closed, Jade turned to Micah.

"Do you and McClaine know each other?" Jade asked.

She sensed Max waiting for the answer too.

Micah stared up at the descending numbers. "Why do you ask?"

"A vibe I'm feeling," she said.

"As much as two guys can get to know each other during a car ride," he said. "He's a Sounders fan."

"I think Micah's sweet on him," Dante said.

"Are you jealous?" Micah looked at him. "You want a bromance, bro?"

"I'm serious, Micah," Jade said. "Have you worked with him?"

He turned to her. "Relax, Agent Harrington. We just met and clicked. There's no mystery here. Nothing for you to investigate."

She stared at his face, looking for tells.

There were none.

The car arrived at the lobby.

Micah's phone rang. "Alexander." He listened. "That's great news. Thank you."

He hung up. To Jade, he said, "It's about Senator Harris. We found his son."

"Is he—?"

"He's alive. And he's fine."

"Wow," she said, "good news."

That was fast.

CHAPTER SIXTY-FIVE

The White House, Washington, DC

"CONGRATULATIONS," SASHA SAID with a broad grin.

The Streamline Regulations Act had passed in the Senate by one vote. Scott Harris, surprising all the media pundits, signed on as a late sponsor of the bill.

In other news, his thirteen-year-old son had returned home unharmed. No ransom was demanded.

And there was no mention of who had abducted him.

Whitney would partake of a celebratory cigar after Sasha left.

Earlier that evening, they had enjoyed a steak dinner in the Residence dining room, prepared by the White House chef. Now, in the West Sitting Hall, Whitney sat on the sofa with her legs tucked under her; Sasha sat in a matching chair. The television in the corner was muted.

Raising her glass of wine, Whitney acknowledged the compliment. The bottle, three-quarters empty, rested on a side table next to the couch.

"How's the First Gentleman?"

"I wouldn't know," Whitney said as she poured more wine into Sasha's glass.

Sasha hesitated, then said, "'I have been driven many times upon my knees by the overwhelming conviction that I had nowhere else to go.'"

"Lincoln," said Whitney, who had read everything she could about the sixteenth president.

"'Look to the Lord and his strength.' 1 Chronicles. You should try it sometime. It might help."

"I guess if He helped Lincoln, He could help me."

Shaking her head in a tsk-tsk sort of way, Sasha said, "Don't shade scripture. Have you prayed about it?"

"No."

"Is he coming back?"

"I guess I shouldn't joke about whether that's a lowercase or uppercase *h*, but to answer your question… the decision isn't only up to him."

"Is he behaving himself?"

Sasha was referring to Grayson's previous affair.

Whitney shrugged.

Sasha had become more than just an employee during Whitney's first year in office. Whitney considered Sasha a friend, and, in her position, she didn't have many of those. The saying was true: it's lonely at the top. Regardless of how close they were, however, she was uncomfortable talking to Sasha about her relationship with her husband—or lack thereof.

Sasha took in the room. "I could get used to this."

Whitney raised an eyebrow. "Do you have aspirations?"

Sasha's smile was uncharacteristically vulnerable as she gazed into her glass. "Possibly."

Whitney raised her eyebrows. Sasha rubbed some people the wrong way; diplomacy wasn't her strong suit.

"I started out in politics," Sasha continued, "to give a voice to people who didn't have one, but over time, it's become something more."

"This job requires persistence," Whitney said. "A steady hand. Someone who keeps her head and can make decisions when everyone else around her is losing theirs." She paused. "You would make an excellent president."

Her chief of staff's eyes widened. "Thank you, Madam President."

Sasha understood that it was more than a compliment. It would take a strong, resilient, and persistent woman to be the first black woman president of the United States of America.

Something on the television caught Whitney's eye. She exhaled and said, "What is she up to now?"

Judy Porter stood in front of a dark, wooded area, speaking into an ABC microphone.

Reluctantly, Whitney grabbed the remote off the glass table and turned up the volume.

"As previously reported, coincidences and conspiracy theories have swirled around our current president during the campaign and throughout the infancy of her presidency: The death of her aunt. Her mysterious teenage pregnancy. Her meteoric rise in politics. But I believe it all started right here"—the reporter gestured behind her—"with the mysterious, and still unsolved, death of Congressman Steven Barrett."

Whitney stilled her face, not moving her eyes from the television, knowing Sasha's eyes were on her.

"A source within the local police department told me that the FBI's inquiry into the congressman's case was dropped, and all local efforts were to cease. The order came from up high. No reason given. Attempts by state legislator—now Congressman—Cameron Kelly from the 87th district to discover what happened were stonewalled. I wonder by whom?"

Judy scanned the forested area, then looked back into the camera's lens. "I will tell you this. I won't stop digging until I find out what happened here. Our viewers deserve to know. The American people deserve to know. This is Judy Porter reporting from Clayton, Missouri. Back to you, Glenn."

The camera cut to the anchorman in the studio.

Whitney forced a laugh as she picked up the remote and turned off the TV. "Speaking of persistence…"

Sasha shrugged. "She's a woman. She has to be."

As Whitney took another sip of her drink, Sasha swept her phone off the table and sent a quick message.

"Problem?" Whitney asked.

A shake of the head. Sasha set her phone facedown on the table and picked up her glass. Before taking a sip, she peered at Whitney over the rim of her glass. "Why won't she let this go, do you think?"

Biding time, Whitney poured herself some more wine. Sasha, her glass half full, waved away Whitney's offer for a refill.

"Perhaps she doesn't have a personal life," Whitney said, settling back into the sofa, "so she's consumed with mine."

Staring at the blank screen, the chief of staff mumbled something.

"What was that, Sasha?"

Sasha shook her head.

It had sounded like, "Or perhaps where there's smoke, there's fire."

CHAPTER SIXTY-SIX

Arlington, Virginia

JADE ENTERED HER townhouse and stood in the foyer for a moment. Waiting. The house was empty. The quietness enveloped her.

Her cat, Card, was staying with Zoe. It was weird when he wasn't there to greet her. With his unconditional love and complete dependence, he was more than a pet. He was her family.

She set her bag down and started down the hallway toward the kitchen. She'd fallen asleep during takeoff and hadn't eaten on the plane.

As she opened her refrigerator and peered at the slim pickings, her phone buzzed in her pocket.

Dante.

She'd just left him at the airport. Was there a lead in the Tishman case already? Did Pat find something?

"Don't bother unpacking," he said, his breath heavy from running or walking fast.

"I haven't, but I'm hungry."

"Grab something on the way. Shakespeare struck again."

She froze, her hunger pains replaced by a sinking sensation. Closing the refrigerator door, she said, "It hasn't been a week yet." Heading toward the front of the house so she could race upstairs to take a quick shower and pack some fresh clothes, she said, "Where are we going?"

"Missouri."

CHAPTER SIXTY-SEVEN

Clayton, Missouri

"WHAT'S HER NAME?" Jade said.

"Judy Porter. Washington driver's license."

"State?" asked Dante.

"DC," said the detective from the Clayton PD.

Jade, Dante, Max, and Micah gathered around the body. Jade had commissioned a private FBI plane, and they were on the ground in St. Louis three hours after she received Dante's call.

The local police had waited for them.

"As soon as we saw that"—the detective pointed to a piece of paper attached with a safety pin to the victim's shirt—"we called you in."

She scanned the area. A well-lit vacancy sign illuminated the front entrance. The body lay beside a dumpster in a parking lot behind the motel, where a putrid combination of trash, grease, and pizza filled the air. The asphalt was littered with needles, chip wrappers, cigarette butts, and dented soda cans. Dried blood formed a circle underneath the upper part of the victim's body.

"Who found her?" she asked.

"Maintenance guy. He was taking out the trash earlier tonight and spotted the body. He dropped the trash," he said, pointing at two large green bags, "and called us. Claimed he didn't touch the body."

"Print him?"

"Yep. He's in the manager's office, if you want to talk to him."

"We do."

She inclined her head toward the victim. "Was she staying here?"

"There's a room registered in her name, yes."

Something was missing. "Where's the murder weapon?"

"No sign of it."

The knife had been left in each of the other victims.

Jade crouched next to the body. Rigor mortis had set in. What appeared to be knife wounds marked the victim's left side. Her breath caught when she saw the auburn hair and pale face, the eyes void of life.

"Judy Porter," she said.

"That's what I said," the detective said roughly.

She looked up at him. "She's a reporter. From ABC News."

He stared at her blankly. "I only watch Fox."

"Why was she here?" Jade asked.

Shaking his head, he excused himself. He walked ten yards away, already on his cell phone.

Jade had never met the reporter and didn't watch her broadcasts often. She remembered the president telling her that ABC News was preparing an investigative report on her political ascendance after the mysterious death of Congressman Steven Barrett. Fairchild had privately asked Jade to find out what the network knew.

Judy Porter's presence wasn't a coincidence. Neither was her death.

Someone crouched down next to her.

"He's decompensating," Max said. "Organized killers plan their attacks. Planning is part of the fantasy. The other murders appeared to be planned." He pointed at the knife wounds. "This attack was sloppy. Disorganized. Unplanned."

"Judy was a reporter," Jade said, "albeit a national one, but I don't think she would be considered wealthy. At least not in the same class as the other victims. Unless she had money we haven't found out about yet."

"We need to catch him," Max said.

Jade stared at him. She understood. Looking over at the detective, she said, "Where's the manager's office?"

Clayton, Missouri

THE MAN IN the maintenance uniform sweated profusely. Although it was warm in the crowded manager's office, Jade suspected his discomfort was primarily due to the presence of law enforcement. In addition to Jade, Dante, Max, and Micah, there was the Clayton police detective, two police officers, and a pretty Hispanic woman in a motel uniform who worked at the front desk. After interviewing her, Jade realized she might be needed. The woman spoke fluent Spanish and English. Although Jade spoke passable Spanish, this interview was too important to allow any room for mistakes. She was grateful for the assistance.

The front desk clerk said Judy and her cameraman—or rather, "the woman and the guy with the bulky camera"—entered and left the motel several times over the past two days. The pair had not eaten in the motel's restaurant or swam in the small pool. Motel employees said Judy wasn't rude but intense; her mind always seemed focused elsewhere.

The motel's maintenance man was also Hispanic. Jade guessed Mexican. He was stocky, with black hair and a mole dotting his cheek. She pegged him for early forties. From his behavior, he might be working in the country illegally.

Or he was just nervous because he was brown.

"There are a lot of people in here," Jade said to him. "We're here to catch a murderer. That's all. You're not in any trouble. Do you understand?"

The woman translated. He still didn't respond.

Jade stared into his eyes and said to him in Spanish, "We're not ICE."

"I have children," he said.

Jade touched his hand. "I won't let anyone take you away from your children."

Or take your children away from you.

Seeing something in her eyes that convinced him to trust her, he gave her a slight nod.

He relayed the same story he'd told the detective. He hadn't seen anyone in the parking lot. After dropping the trash bags, he ran back to this office and told the manager about the dead woman.

"Close your eyes," Jade said, waiting. "Trust me, por favor."

He hesitated, then obeyed her instructions.

"Visualize the scene again," she said. "What do you see?"

He licked his lips.

The agents were quiet as they waited.

"A truck," he said in English, his eyes still closed. "Or an SUV. Black. Idling out on the street near the entrance. When I stopped near the body, it took off." The man opened his eyes in wonder. "I forgot all about that until now."

The front desk clerk started to repeat what he'd said, but Jade raised her hand. His English wasn't perfect, but it was perfectly understandable.

"In which direction?" Jade asked. "Where did it go?"

"Norte. North."

Dante, who'd been leaning against the wall, straightened. "Did you see the license plate? The driver?"

The man shook his head. "Too far away."

Jade thanked the witness and the woman. She tried to be patient as she waited for them to leave the room. A tingle had started in her fingertips and was spreading up her arm.

Their first break.

To the detective she said, "We need to find that vehicle."

❧

Dante used the key card the manager had given him to open the door to a second-floor room. All the motel's rooms faced the parking lot or the street, all the doors and staircases exposed to the elements. He flipped on the light switch.

Scanning the room, Jade wondered if the television network had fallen on hard times.

Why had Judy Porter stayed here?

The carpets were threadbare and stained, the furniture mismatched. Brown stains from past leaks blotched the ceiling tiles. A germaphobe, Jade gladly donned nitrile gloves as they spread out to examine the room. Micah took the closets, Dante checked out the bathroom, Max examined the bed, and Jade headed straight for the desk.

The room had been dusted for fingerprints, but Jade wasn't hopeful that anything useful would come back. A motel room contained hundreds, possibly thousands, of prints. And the killer might not have entered the room.

The desk's surface was spotted with water stains and cigarette burns. A laptop sat open next to a stack of papers. Jade shuffled through it. It appeared to be a transcript. After a cursory scan of the first page, she set it aside for later. A briefcase—one of those old, battered college professor ones—leaned against the desk. Sitting in the chair, Jade sifted through it. Nestled among the pens, Judy's press badge, pads of paper, and folders was a tape recorder. Jade took it out and set it on the desk.

She hit PLAY.

"I live in the neighborhood," said a male voice. "I was out walking my dog."

She turned up the volume to drown out the sounds of the TV in the next room and the traffic outside.

"What did you see?" said a woman's voice. Jade imagined the concerned-reporter expression on Judy's face.

"I was on the other side of the road."

"How far away were you?"

A pause. "Thirty yards. Fifty at the most."

"Tell me what happened."

"A car came toward me."

"Was it speeding?"

"Not really."

"And?"

"All of a sudden, an SUV came out of nowhere and sped up so it was even with the car. At first I thought it would pass, but then it almost seemed like..."

"What?"

"It wanted to race."

Silence from the recorder. While Jade had been listening, the other agents had gathered around her.

"And then?"

"Both of them sped up, as if they *were* racing. Then the SUV bumped the car. The car almost went into the ditch but corrected itself. The SUV bumped it harder. The car swerved again before righting itself. The SUV bumped it a third time. This time the car couldn't right itself. Not sure why the driver didn't use his brakes. The car slammed into a tree. It had been going at a good clip by this point. The car looked like one of those old musical instruments." Finger snaps. "An accordion. That's it."

"You said 'his brakes,'" Judy said. "Did you see the driver?"

"A woman wouldn't drive like that."

Judy paused. "What happened then?"

"The SUV stopped up the road. A man got out and walked back to the wreckage. He squatted and looked inside. I saw the airbag through the shattered window. Smoke came out from under the hood. Like it was going to blow. The man didn't try to help whoever was inside. He stared for a while and then walked back to the SUV and drove away."

"What did he look like?"

"I didn't get a good look. It gets dark out here. He was wearing a coat. It looked like leather. Dark slacks. Short hair. Military or ex-military."

"What did you do then?"

"I picked up my dog and ran back to my house."

"Did you call the police?"

"No."

"Why not?"

"Cell phone service isn't that great out here."

"Is that the reason—"

"I ran… because I was scared. Something about that guy screamed Special Forces. Or an assassin or something." Silence. "I have a family. A new grandson. Thought it best to mind my own business."

Jade let the recording continue, but the rest of the tape was dead air.

She was well aware of what she'd just heard.

Judy Porter was interviewing an eyewitness to the murder of United States Congressman Steven Barrett.

CHAPTER SIXTY-NINE

St. Louis, Missouri

For sweetest things turn sourest by their deeds:
Lilies that fester smell far worse than weeds.

—Bard of Avon

IT WAS EARLY or late, depending on how you looked at it.

Jade leaned against the headboard in a hotel room downtown. Dante thought it would be bad luck to stay in the same motel that Judy had stayed in. Jade agreed. Regardless, she wasn't keen to sleep in a motel one step up from seedy. Jade understood now why Judy had stayed there. It was the closest motel to the scene of the congressman's accident.

A pickle on a plate was all that remained from her room-service dinner of a double cheeseburger and fries. Sipping a Pepsi, she checked the Shakespeare app on her phone. The sonnet attached to Judy Porter was number ninety-four. She read it again.

What did it mean? What did any of them mean? How did the reporter fit in? Had she gotten too close? To what?

This last question made Jade sit up.

Was Judy's investigation connected to the Shakespeare murders? Was the killer acquainted with all his victims? Jade agreed with the professor; she didn't think they were selected at random. What was the glue? Were they looking for an English professor? Teacher? How many serial-killing English teachers could there be in America?

She chuckled. She was tired and being silly.

Earlier, she'd reviewed Veritas's timeline on Twitter, but she couldn't locate a single tweet about Judy Porter during the last month. She made a mental note to tell Pat to check further back and submit another court order to the social media company in case the tweet had been deleted.

Assuming he hadn't tweeted about Judy, why the break in pattern?

She laid each of the partial sonnets in a neat row in front of her on the bedspread and the full texts in a row above them. She wrote the numbers down: 1, 3, 7, 72, 94. After a moment, she wrote their equivalent Roman numerals: I, III, VII, LXXII, and XCIV. She sent Pat a text about the court order and the sonnet numbers, hoping the analysts would find a pattern.

Jade had read every sonnet in its entirety—all hundred and fifty-four of them—along with the online CliffsNotes and SparkNotes analyses of each one. Although she understood the poems better, she hadn't discovered any clues as to their connection with the victims or to the identity of the perpetrator or where he'd strike next.

Her cell phone buzzed. Expecting Dante, she swiped to accept the call without looking at the display.

"What's up?" she asked.

"Pardon me?"

"Oh…"

"It's Blake."

She remembered that he didn't want to see her. "Okay."

"Are you in town?"

"No."

"I want to explain."

She squinted at the generic painting on the opposite wall. It looked like the one in her hotel room in Seattle.

"You're up late," she said.

"I don't sleep much these days."

"Why?"

"It hurts." A pause. "How've you been?"

She glanced down at the sonnets. "Puzzled."

Despite his condition, he'd asked her how she was doing. She imagined the remonstrations of her mother for forgetting her manners.

"How are you feeling?" she asked.

"Been better. I'm home. Finally. I would like to see you sometime, but… not yet."

"I understand." And she did. She wasn't sure she'd want him to visit her under similar circumstances.

"Anything new on who's responsible? For the terrorist attack?"

"No," she said. She'd been too busy with her team's cases to check on his. "Have you found out anything?"

"No."

"I'll check with Counterterrorism."

"No need," he said. "I have my own sources."

The president.

"But that's not why I called," he continued.

"Oh?"

"I heard about Judy Porter."

"I haven't told the president yet."

"Her husband called me."

"How do you—wait!" Jade grabbed the notebook on the nightstand. "You knew her."

"She was in the press corps. We weren't friends and didn't drink together, but we saw each other at events. That's how I met her husband, David."

"What did you think of her?"

"A fine reporter. Did her homework. Practiced journalism the way it's supposed to be. I respected her tremendously. It's a loss for the profession."

"Are you okay?"

"That's not why I called either." He paused. "Did you watch her broadcast the other night?"

"Not yet."

"You should."

"Because…"

"I don't think the Shakespeare Killer killed her. I think it had something to do with Congressman Barrett's murder."

"What makes you say that?"

"Just a feeling," he said. "I'm going to keep digging."

"Blake, you should leave the investigating to the investigators. To me."

"I want to help." Another pause. "I have nothing but time on my hands."

"As a law enforcement officer, I should dissuade you from pursing this matter further."

"Perhaps, but I would pursue it in any event."

CHAPTER SEVENTY

St. Louis, Missouri

"IT'S LATE. ANOTHER murder?"

"Yes," Jade said into her cell phone.

"Which sonnet?"

"Ninety-four."

"'For sweetest things turn sourest by their deeds,'" quoted the professor. "Lilies that fester smell far worse than weeds.'"

"That's it."

"At first blush," Alaia Bennett said, "ninety-four is similar to the sonnet preceding it, contrasting virtue with appearance. This one, however, contains no reference to the poet or the young man."

"What's it about then?"

"The difference between outward appearance and inner worth. Or, as my grandma used to say, just because it looks good doesn't mean it's good for you."

How did this sonnet apply to Judy? Was there more to her, or to what she was investigating, than met the eye?

Jade was tired but not sleepy. She stuffed another pillow behind her head. "How did you become a professor?"

"I went to Spelman—the best historically black college in the country, by the way—and loved it. I was an activist before and after graduation, but I realized that no matter how hard I worked or how passionate I was, I wasn't making any progress. *We* weren't making any progress. I decided I could better serve the cause by teaching the next generation about *our* history."

"Through literature?" Jade asked, not bothering to mask her skepticism.

"I don't teach only Shakespeare," Bennett said, "and the other great white writers. I expose my students to the writings of James Baldwin, Zora Neale Hurston, Langston Hughes, Maya Angelou, Richard Wright, Toni

Morrison, Ralph Ellison, Octavia Butler, Alex Haley, Alice Walker, and Lorraine Vivian Hansberry."

"Who is Lorraine Vivian Hansberry?"

The professor tsked. "You need to know your history. We are descended from kings and queens. We are their wildest dreams."

Jade thought of her parents. Sounded about right. "Tell me about Hansberry."

"An African-American playwright. She was the first black woman to write a play performed on Broadway. *A Raisin in the Sun*. Heard of it?"

"Sure."

"She was also a civil rights activist in the fifties and sixties. A little militant. Believed that black people should fight back using any means at their disposal, whether legal or illegal, violent or nonviolent, passive or aggressive."

"Do you agree with her?"

"Absolutely. There's no playbook for a revolution."

"Sounds like a formidable woman."

"She was. Married to a Jewish guy. And a closeted lesbian."

Jade wasn't sure what to say to that.

"Have you read any of the other authors?"

"I read *The Color Purple*," Jade said, "and some Toni Morrison in school. *Invisible Man*."

"Pitiful," the professor said. "It's because of people like you that I teach." She paused. "You should take my class."

"Maybe I should."

CHAPTER SEVENTY-ONE

The White House, Washington, DC

WHITNEY SPOONED A small wedge of grapefruit into her mouth, her eyes falling on the empty place setting.

She and Grayson had developed a routine of having breakfast and reading major newspapers from around the globe together in the Residence kitchen before heading to their offices in the West Wing.

After he had left, almost two months ago now, whenever they'd called each other, they discussed only the children or their work. They hadn't discussed their relationship.

He hadn't called recently.

She hadn't called him either.

Every day, she ate breakfast alone. In truth, she enjoyed the solitude.

After finishing the grapefruit, she placed her dishes in the sink.

The phone rang.

She moved to the counter to answer it.

Only a handful of people in the world could reach her directly. Whitney glanced at the clock: 5:30 a.m. The sun wouldn't rise for another hour. This wasn't good news.

"Madam President, Jade Harrington."

"Agent Harrington. I presume this isn't a social call."

"No, it isn't. I'm in Clayton, Missouri."

Whitney gripped the handset tighter. Grayson lived in Clayton. As did her parents. Her brothers and their families. Were her children visiting? Her mind spun with all the horrendous possibilities.

"I'm listening," she said.

"Judy Porter was murdered here last night."

"My God! I watched her on television the other night. Why was she still in Clayton?" That was the wrong question to ask. "Sorry, this is such a shock. What happened?"

"She was working on a story about Congressman Steven Barrett's accident. She was found dead in the parking lot of the motel where she was staying."

"Why couldn't she let it go?" Whitney murmured.

"Let what go?" the agent asked.

Did I say that aloud?

"How did it happen?"

"She was stabbed."

"How awful. Judy was a fine reporter. I truly respected her. She will be missed."

"What couldn't she let go, Madam President?"

Whitney paused, thinking. "A story. Any story."

Silence on the other end. Then, "I wanted you to hear it from me before you heard it on the news." Other voices in the background. Jade said to someone else, "I'll be right there." Into the phone, she said, "Ma'am, I've gotta go."

"Thank you for this call. Please keep me informed."

The agent didn't respond before hanging up.

Whitney slowly replaced the receiver.

She made a mental note to call the reporter's family. Whitney had met her husband once—Daniel? Dylan? David!—and that was the extent of what she knew about Judy's private life.

Judy had kept digging into Whitney's past long after most reporters would have quit.

Despite her sadness for the reporter's family, she would no longer need to worry about Judy Porter.

Whitney's past could finally be buried.

CHAPTER SEVENTY-TWO

Washington, DC

JADE FLEW HOME a few hours after talking to Fairchild, leaving Dante and the rest of the team to finish the initial investigation into Judy Porter's murder. They interviewed the motel's guests, Judy's cameraman, and the neighbors that lived along the road where Barrett was killed. Finding the witness to the congressman's death was a top priority.

She thought about the president's question.

Why couldn't she let it go?

What was Judy Porter after?

And was she killed for it?

After landing at Reagan, Jade went home for a quick shower and change of clothes.

She dialed the number on the way to work.

"You rang, your highn-ass?"

"Good morning to you too. Why are you still in bed?"

"What time is it?" asked Zoe.

"Eight."

"Damn. I overslept. Where are you?"

"Just flew in from St. Louis. On my way to the office. How's Card?"

"He's fine. Been sleeping with me. Really cramping my style. I put his name on the mailbox, by the way."

"Funny," Jade said, turning right on E Street. "I'm picking up my baby tonight."

"Ooh… am I your baby?"

"My furry one."

"Damn," Zoe said. "We'll be here. Let us know if you'll be joining us for dinner. I'm going back to sleep. Why is the snooze button for only nine minutes?"

"Don't know. I've got my own mysteries to figure out."

She pressed the button near the radio to end the call.

In her office, Jade booted up her computer. An email from Pat, with all of Judy's broadcasts for the past year, awaited her.

She considered Blake's suspicion that Judy's death was a copycat killing, that it wasn't the Shakespeare Killer.

Blake said he had a feeling. Jade made decisions based on evidence, but she, too, placed a great deal of faith in her intuition. She should have dissuaded him from helping her. Despite his investigative reporting skills, he was a civilian. She ignored the small part of her that looked forward to spending more time with him.

Jade clicked on the video that Blake had recommended she watch. Judy Porter stood by the side of the road adjacent to a wooded area, speaking into a microphone, describing the circumstances of the congressman's car accident. She also described the coincidences concerning his death and the special election to replace him. Nothing Jade hadn't heard before. No mention of the witness. Judy might have been trying to locate someone else who could corroborate his story.

She tensed when Judy mentioned that although the death was ruled a homicide, the FBI had dropped its inquiry. Jade paused the recording and leaned back in her chair, closing her eyes. Thinking back to the dinner she'd had with the president in the White House Residence, she remembered that Fairchild asked her to investigate the accident. Jade had delegated the assignment to Pat. Pat discovered that the single-car crash wasn't an accident. The car's brakes were tampered with. The congressman had no chance of navigating the sharp turn or avoiding the oak tree. Since the car was totaled and the family believed it was an accident, they'd sold it to a mechanic, who sold it for parts.

The perpetrator of Jade's first major case, the Talk-Show Killer, happened to be in the area at the time. Judy was right. Many coincidences surrounded this case. Jade didn't believe in coincidences, and she suspected that the reporter hadn't either.

Something wasn't right.

Amid everything else going on, she hadn't kept track of the outcome of the congressman's case.

She called Pat. "How's the court order for Twitter coming?"

"Still waiting."

"Anything back on Adey?"

"No luck so far."
"Whatever happened to your inquiry into Congressman Barrett's death?"
Pat hesitated. "I was told to stop."
Jade had been Pat's direct supervisor at the time.
"I don't recall telling you to stop."
"You didn't."
"Who then?"
Even as she asked, the answer came to Jade.
"Barringer," Pat said.

CHAPTER SEVENTY-THREE

The White House, Washington, DC

AFTER ANOTHER DINNER alone, Whitney retreated to the Treaty Room on the second floor of the Residence. Like many of her predecessors, she used the room as a study when she worked late.

The room and the table were named by former first lady Jacqueline Kennedy in honor of the numerous treaties signed there: from the end of the Spanish American War in 1898 to the peace treaty between Egypt and Israel in 1979.

Whitney set the pen down next to the briefing book, still thinking about Judy Porter. Instead of relief, unease weighed on her.

At the knock on her door, she beckoned. "Come in, Sasha."

Sasha had called fifteen minutes ago, asking to see her.

The chief of staff crossed the room and stood looking at the stack of books on the table: biographies (Mikhail Gorbachev, Catherine the Great, and Leo Tolstoy), a book on Russian history, another on Russian politics, and a young adult novel squeezed among them.

"Homework?" Sasha asked.

"'If you know the enemy and know yourself, you need not fear the result of a hundred battles. If you know yourself but not the enemy, for every victory gained you will also suffer a defeat. If you know neither the enemy nor yourself, you will succumb in every battle.'"

"Sun Tzu. *The Art of War*. When do you have time to read all those books?"

Whitney glanced at them. "Reading helped me to get here"—she swept her arm in a gesture that took in the entire White House—"and is sometimes my only salvation. How did it go?"

"Fine. She's at home, resting. Scared more than anything else."

Sasha had flown home to Texas two days ago. Her mother had showed symptoms of a heart attack.

"I'm glad it was just a scare."

"Thank you." Then, her face neutral, Sasha said, "Awful about what happened to Judy."

Whitney sat back in her leather chair and crossed her legs. "Such a tragedy. She was a good reporter."

Sasha held her eyes. "Like a dog with a bone."

"She *was* persistent."

"It was more than that, though."

What was she implying?

Sasha continued, "Well, you won't need to worry about her any longer."

Was her relief that obvious?

"That's an awful thing to say, Sasha!"

"Yes, it is." Sasha handed Whitney a sheaf of papers. "Here are your remarks for tomorrow."

She turned to leave, then turned back. "Since you're always quoting people, I've got one of mine I want to share with you. It's not the dead you need to worry about. It's the living."

Sasha left.

"That's all I ever do," Whitney said to the empty room.

Arriving early to the Oval Office the next day, she finished up her morning briefing with a high-ranking analyst from the Office of the Director of National Intelligence. She was distracted the entire time; her thoughts kept drifting to the conversation with Sasha the night before.

At 8:00 a.m., Sean buzzed her.

"Cole Brennan is on the line."

"Did he say what he wanted?"

"No. He's becoming a regular Chatty Cathy, isn't he?"

She smiled. "Put him through, Sean." Then, "Good morning, Cole."

"I'm getting ready to go on the air, but I have a message for you."

"Oh?"

"I ate breakfast with Congressman Cameron Kelly this morning to discuss the next election."

"Don't you think you're placing your bet too early?" Whitney asked, her tone dry.

"It's never too soon to start. We're up against a formidable opponent."

"Cole, are you complimenting me?"

"I tell it like it is."

"Thank you. What's the message?"

"He wants a meeting with you. Since the two of you are from the same district, I thought it was a good idea and agreed to set it up."

Whitney didn't trust herself to speak. After a moment, she said, "I don't have time."

"I haven't told you when," he said. His media instincts kicked in. "Is there some reason you don't want to meet with him?"

"When?" she managed to say.

"How about tonight?"

Washington, DC

FOR THE REMAINDER of the afternoon, Jade viewed the rest of Judy's broadcasts on the computer in her office. The reporter never said it outright, but she insinuated that the president hid her teenage pregnancy from the American people during the presidential campaign because she believed her child had grown up to be the Talk-Show Killer. Judy further implied that then state legislator Whitney Fairchild was involved in Congressman Barrett's death and, as president, had ordered the FBI to cover it up.

Impeachment implications. World-shattering ramifications. Possible criminal charges. Could a sitting president be indicted and sent to jail while in office?

Jade believed so, although it hadn't happened in the United States. Yet.

She stopped herself. What about innocent until proven guilty? This was one reporter's unproven allegations.

Did this jive with the Whitney Fairchild Jade knew?

Judy Porter was the only victim who'd had the knife removed from her body.

It still hadn't been recovered.

The task force hadn't released the detail about the knives being left in the bodies of the first four victims. Not even to local law enforcement agencies. Had Judy Porter's murder been staged to look like the work of the Shakespeare Killer because she possessed incriminating information about the president of the United States?

Jade turned her attention to the file on her desk: a dossier on Judy Porter prepared by Pat.

Judy Porter wasn't wealthy, but she came from money. Her father was the CEO of Adams Appliances, a firm in business for over one hundred years. His great-grandfather started the business in 1905 in a small town in Southern Illinois. The company went from being a small local business to a regional one until the "go-go sixties," when Judy's father took the company public and it became national, and then, in the 1990s, international. As far as Pat could determine, Judy was never involved in the business.

But she ended up investigating the company through her job.

Judy Adams left Illinois after high school to study journalism at Syracuse University. After college, she landed in Chicago and started as an intern at ABC7, the local ABC affiliate. On a Tuesday, the day after the stock market crashed on October 19, 1987—known as Black Monday—she interviewed David Porter, an assistant professor of economics at the University of Chicago and later a full professor at Georgetown University.

Over the next seven years, Judy continued to pay her dues, moving to wherever in the United States the network needed her. She broke the story of accounting shenanigans and possible insider trading at her father's company, forcing the Securities and Exchange Commission to investigate. The SEC had difficulty proving its case against her father's team of high-priced lawyers. No charges were ever filed.

At one of the many interminable DC cocktail parties of political movers and shakers, Judy ran into David Porter. By this time, she was ensconced in the White House press corps and shocked—according to her friends—when the shy economist asked her out for a private drink afterward.

Married almost nine years to the day from when they met on the University of Chicago campus, they now had two grown children. David eventually became the vice chairman of the Board of Governors of the Federal Reserve System in Washington, DC, appointed by President Edward Middleton. The Federal Reserve System was critical to the smooth functioning of the US economy. Although Judy's husband was in a powerful position, and most people would say the same about her, their dual incomes didn't place them in the same strata of wealth as the other Shakespeare victims.

Jade sprang from her chair, left her office, and strode over to Pat's cubicle.

"Adams Appliances," Jade said without preamble. "Find out who took the company public."

"Will do." Pat tapped the reminder on her computer. "Court order came through. I received a listing of all of Veritas's deleted tweets. Nothing about Judy Porter."

"So either his tweets are coincidental or we're dealing with a copycat killer."

"Or he forgot to tweet about it." Pat stopped typing. "I also discovered that a private investigator kept tabs on Jared Carr."

"Who hired him?"

"His brother, Jason."

"Why?"

"Apparently they kept tabs on each other. Sued each other over their inheritance. They signed a decree seven years ago to stop suing each other, but I guess it didn't stop them from spying."

"What else did you find out?"

"The discrimination suits didn't end with their father. Many of the Carr brothers' properties were found to contain hazardous substances. Their tenants got sick. Jared authorized the falsification of documents and intimidation of witnesses, fired whistleblowers, and bribed government officials. Employees hurt on the job were denied workers' comp claims. Some died. He never paid restitution to the families. Not a nice guy, that one."

"Doesn't sound like it."

"Jason's gay."

Jade's eyebrow rose. She knew what their foundation stood for. "How did Jared feel about that?"

"Since Jared's dead, there's only one way to find out."

Washington, DC

WHITNEY FOLLOWED JOSH McPherson into the Capital Grille, a restaurant on Pennsylvania Avenue, about nine blocks from the White House. He scanned the interior, confirming again that it was empty of patrons, then led her to a private room in the back. A lone man sat at a table for ten with place settings for two.

He wore a dark suit and purple tie. She hadn't been this close to him in almost thirty-four years. His brown hair was graying at the temples. The lines on his forehead and around his eyes didn't detract from the twinkle in them. He was heavier than he'd been in high school, but not by much. Still handsome, and he knew it.

"Thanks, Josh," she said to the secret service agent. He eyed her before backing away. She had instructed him to leave the door ajar.

"Hello, Whitney," Cameron said, standing. "I'm sorry." He bowed slightly. "Madam President."

She did not want to be here. To face him. Still, it was better to meet him away from all the prying eyes—and cameras—at the White House.

Her house.

Know thy enemy.

"What do you want?" she said.

"Please." He moved to pull out a chair for her.

"I'll stand."

Cameron frowned and returned to his seat.

"I met with Cole this morning," he said. A boyish grin. The one that used to melt her insides, make her stomach flip. Now it made her want to throw up. "He's been supportive in my freshman year."

A server joined them, proffering the wine list to Cameron.

To her, Cameron said, "Do you mind if I choose?"

"Not at all, since you'll be the only one drinking."

His nostrils flared. Pointing at the menu, he said, "This one. A glass."

The server retreated.

"Can you please sit down?" Cameron said, looking up at her.

She didn't budge.

He cleared his throat. "We've come a long way since high school." Picking up his fork, he rubbed the handle between his thumb and index finger. "I never knew why you left that year. I thought we had something special. That we were getting serious. Then one day you were gone."

"There's nothing special about rape."

He dropped the fork, his mouth gaping open. "Rape? I didn't rape you. Might've been a little aggressive. But I was young. Didn't know what I was doing. Now"—he grinned—"I do."

If not for the width of the table between them, she would have slapped him. He made her skin crawl.

How could this man make her feel this way? She was the president of the United States.

"I'm leaving." She took a step toward the door.

"Wait a minute." He rose quickly from his chair, trying to block her way.

Josh got there first.

His hand shot to Cameron's chest, pushing him back.

Josh looked at her. "Is there a problem, Madam President?"

To Cameron, she said, "Congressman Kelly?"

Cameron held up both hands. "No problem. I need another minute."

She stared at him. It was better to know what he was thinking than not. She nodded at Josh.

He pressed once on Cameron's chest before backing up to just outside the door.

"Say what you have to say," she said to Cameron, who remained standing.

"I waited for you. I could've had lots of girls, but I stayed single my junior year. When you came back for our senior year, you wouldn't even talk to me. I started seeing someone else, but I wanted to be with you."

Whitney remained silent. She remembered avoiding him their last year of high school. Wouldn't take his calls. This was before cell phones. He wouldn't dare drop by the house and risk running into one of her brothers.

Whitney was relieved when he started dating her eventual neighbor in Missouri. She'd heard they broke up in college.

"I've thought about you over the years," he said. "About getting back in touch. Trying again. Then I met my future wife, and..."

He shrugged his shoulders.

"A lucky woman," Whitney said, hoping he would pick up on the sarcasm but knowing he wouldn't. "And now I really must be going."

Something in his eyes changed. "Like I said, I've been thinking about that time you were away. And why. About nine months, wasn't it?"

Whitney kept her face composed. Inside she roiled. "I don't recall."

"I think you do," he said. "Whitney, where's my child?"

CHAPTER SEVENTY-SIX

Chicago, Illinois

JADE AND MICAH took the first flight out to Chicago the next morning. Dante stayed in DC to oversee the investigation.

The pressure to solve the case had heightened, not only from Barringer but also from the press. Some reporters speculated that Jade had lost her touch.

"Special Agents Harrington and Alexander to see Jason Carr."

"I need to see ID," said the rent-a-cop manning the marble counter in the well-appointed, tasteful lobby of the fifty-five-story office building.

After the security guard examined their IDs and badges with an undue amount of care, they moved away from him to wait.

A few minutes later, a fit, handsome, well-dressed man materialized. Jade pegged him for late twenties and of Filipino ancestry.

"Agent Harrington? I'm Benjie Bautista, Mr. Carr's assistant. Right this way."

Bautista led them to the elevator. The car had one button. The three of them were silent as they ascended. Both men wore cologne; each scent was pleasant, almost complementary. A soft ding greeted them as they reached the top. The doors opened on to another lobby, the entire floor surrounded by glass windows, affording a 360-degree view of the cloudless day. In addition to the waiting room, there were two gigantic offices. Glass walls allowed their occupants to observe everything happening on the floor.

The lobby contained a sofa, a chair, and a glass coffee table, on top of which sat thick glossy magazines. Jade and Micah declined Bautista's offer of refreshments.

On the phone in one of the offices, Jason Carr motioned to his assistant to bring them in.

The furniture was sleek and modern. Jason finished the call and indicated for them to sit in two of the six guest chairs in front of his desk.

"Agent Harrington. This is a surprise. What are you doing in Chicago?"

"We came to ask you a few more questions."

"Shall I ring my mother and my sister-in-law?"

"That won't be necessary."

"Oh. Did you… find my brother's murderer?"

Jade ignored his question. "I want to ask you something."

"What's that?"

"Did Jared know you were gay?"

He stiffened, but after a moment, he said, "I believe so, although I never came out to him."

"Your organization was opposed to homosexuality."

"I kept silent. I didn't grow up in the type of family where you could easily express yourself."

"What changed your brother's mind?"

"I'm not sure. We never discussed it, but I noticed at some point that he became less vocal about his opposition to marriage equality. Then he removed references to it from our marketing materials." He paused. "I assumed it was because of me."

"You hired a private investigator to tail your brother. For years. What were you hoping to find?"

A brief tightening of the eyes, but otherwise no reaction.

"My brother and I were in business together, but that didn't mean we trusted each other. Not many people understand what it's like when there's this much money involved."

"Tell me."

He hesitated before shaking his head. "It would come across as first-world problems." His eyes strayed briefly to his assistant working at a desk adjacent to his office. "Let's just say there was a lot of pressure from our father."

"What about the lawsuits against each other?" Micah asked.

Jason waved this detail away. "We sued each other like other brothers play fantasy football. It was a game to us. To see who could bring the best case against the other one. It didn't mean anything. We bugged each other's offices. I watched him from here, but I wanted to know what he was saying to his visitors and on the phone."

Money never meant much to Jade. Did Jason want them to feel sorry for him? She did, but not in the way he intended. She'd rather be broke than rich and surrounded by people she couldn't trust.

"Do you still have the recordings? From bugging his phone?"

Jason shook his head. "I'd listen to them the same night and delete them."

"There were many lawsuits against the company," Jade said. "A lot of cases ended unfavorably for the plaintiffs. Do you think any of them would want to kill your brother?"

Jason laughed. "No doubt. Probably all of them. Me too. If you want to investigate all of Jared's enemies, it'll take you twenty years to solve this case." He rose. "Although it's been a pleasure, I have business to attend to. I'm the sole chairman and CEO now. It's difficult to accommodate drop-ins."

A glint in his eye, like a second-born son with a slim chance of becoming king. Jason had surmounted the odds.

A motive.

Did Jason know that Jared would have died from pancreatic cancer?

Jade and Micah remained seated.

"I'm sure it is," Jade said. "If you'd rather, we can finish this conversation in the local FBI office. I'm sure *they* can accommodate us."

Jason sat back down.

Before he got comfortable, Jade asked, "Did you have your brother killed, Jason?"

He didn't bother looking upset. "Truth is, Agent Harrington, I didn't like my brother much. I wished him dead a million times." He smiled. "But I didn't kill him."

CHAPTER SEVENTY-SEVEN

Washington, DC

THE NEXT MORNING, on the way to her office, Jade stopped by Dante's office to update him on the interview with Jason Carr.

Dante leaned back in his chair. "Even if you peg him for Jared, what's his motive for the other murders?"

"Good question. I need you to take a deeper dive. Bank accounts, associations. We're missing something. And check out Benjie Bautista."

"Who's he?"

"Jason's assistant."

"Right."

"Another motive."

"In what way?"

"I think he's Jason's lover."

"Jesus Christ." He threw up his hands. "Is everyone gay?"

"I don't know," she said. "Do you have something to tell me?"

She left his office before he could respond and stopped by Pat's cubicle next.

"I found out who took Adams Appliances public," Pat said.

Jade raised an eyebrow.

"Goldman Sachs," Pat said. "But what's more important is that Judy Porter's father, Eli Adams, invested his personal funds with Scofield Asset Management."

"You think there's a there there?"

"Maybe. But that's still not the most interesting part."

"You're killing me, Pat."

"Jared Carr."

"Jared Carr what?"

"He invested his personal funds with Scofield too."

Jade took a moment to absorb this. "What about Jason?"

Pat shook her head. "Scofield belonged to a club also. In New York."

"What was it called?"

"The Club."

"Creative. Any affiliation with the Carrs' club in Chicago?"

"No."

"What about the sonnet numbers?" asked Jade. "Did the analysts find anything?"

"If there's a relationship among the numbers, they couldn't find it."

"Roman numerals?"

"Nothing."

"What about Judy Porter's computer?"

Pat's fingers stilled on her keyboard.

"What?" Jade said.

Pat glanced over her shoulder at the other agents working in their cubicles. Some were in conversation or speaking on the phone. "Let's go to your office."

Locking her computer, she got up and walked away from her desk. Stunned by the request, Jade, for once in her life, followed.

She entered her office and closed the door behind her, gesturing for Pat to take a guest chair, while she took the other.

"What's with the cloak-and-dagger?" Jade said.

"Judy Porter's computer contained a lot of information on Fairchild's stay in Chicago when she was a teenager. Her time with the aunt and at the convent. The adoption records, even a picture of the baby. Also, Landon's work history with the president. That he paged for her in high school. What she didn't have was proof that Fairchild knew—or believed—that he was TSK."

"I still don't understand all the secrecy."

Pat eyed Jade's desk phone, as if it might be bugged. She lowered her voice. "I discovered the identity of the witness."

"What's his name?"

"Joseph Miller."

"Got an address?"

Pat nodded.

"That's great," Jade said. "Why didn't you tell me this earlier?" She sprung from her chair and went behind her desk, grabbing the handset. "I'll call Dante. We can be in St. Louis in a few hours."

Pat walked around the desk, took the phone out of Jade's hand, and returned it to its cradle.

Pat held out her hand. "Where's your cell phone?"

Jade fished her phone out of her pants pocket and handed it to Pat. She took both of their phones and put them in one of Jade's desk drawers.

"You're starting to freak me out," Jade said.

The wrinkles around Pat's eyes seemed to multiply. "Maybe we should be. I'm not sure who's listening."

"What's going on?"

"We don't need Miller's address," Pat said, "because he's not going to be there."

"Did he move?"

"No," she said. "He's dead."

"What happened?"

Pat stared into her eyes. Jade saw fear in them for the first time. Pat motioned for Jade to bend down toward her.

"A car accident," Pat whispered. "Same stretch of road as the congressman, and he hit the same—"

"Tree," Jade finished for her.

❋

After Pat left, Jade paced while she deliberated on next steps. She collapsed in her chair and leaned over the desk, resting her forehead on her arms. She couldn't remember the last time she'd slept through the night.

Jade believed that her current supervisor, Warren Barringer, had halted a federal investigation into the murder of a US congressman, and an eyewitness to that murder who was in a similar accident as Steven Barrett was now dead too. Judy Porter, who'd dogged President Fairchild throughout her candidacy and her time in office, was also dead.

Should she confront Fairchild? Jade didn't have any proof that the president was involved.

Should she confront Barringer?

It would be career suicide.

She picked up the phone. "I need to see him."

Moments later, she marched toward the elevator. Photographs of the many agents who'd served the FBI over the last century hung on the corridor's walls. Some had fallen in the line of duty. Almost all of them were heroes.

Micah jumped up from his cubicle chair and ran to catch up to her. He fell into step. "Where are you going?"

"Headed up to Barringer's office. Why?"

"I wanted to show you something. On the Shakespeare case."

"I can't now."

"It's important."

"I'll be back."

He held her arm, stopping her. "I want to show you now."

Looking into his eyes, she remembered when he'd warned her off reopening the Blakeley case in the bureau's parking garage.

He'd brought up the case at the English bar. What was his interest in it?

Jade looked at his hand, waiting for him to remove it. After he did, she said, "What's this about, Micah? It's almost as if you're trying to stop me from seeing Barringer."

She forced herself not to look away from those damn eyes.

"I can't imagine anyone stopping you from doing anything you want to do," he said. "What I want to show you is more important."

"I'll be the judge of that."

"May I at least walk you to the lift?"

"I can walk myself."

She brushed by him. After she entered the elevator, Jade pressed the button and turned around.

Micah stood in the hallway, staring at her, as the doors closed.

CHAPTER SEVENTY-EIGHT

Washington, DC

"WHEN DID YOU last speak to your son?" Sasha asked quietly.

They were ensconced in the back of the Beast. Sarah sat in the adjacent sofa seat, making changes to Whitney's daily schedule. Whitney wanted to spend more time at her next stop, necessitating that they rearrange the entire day.

They were bound for a suburban Maryland elementary school, where Whitney would be giving a speech on the urgent need for girls to pursue STEM careers. The US needed more scientists, technologists, engineers, and mathematicians.

The United States needed women.

Whitney didn't understand the concern on Sasha's face. Perhaps it was because of Whitney's dysfunctional home life. Sasha probably suspected that something was wrong. Grayson resided in Missouri, and neither of her children had visited the White House in a long time.

Immersed in shame, Whitney hadn't spoken to her son since he walked out on them at Camp David.

"I don't recall," Whitney said simply.

"A source tells me that Chandler started a new job."

"Sampson's replacement?" Whitney said. "What of it? I'm glad he no longer works for Sampson. I didn't think he represented his state or the legislative branch well, and I certainly didn't think he was the proper role model for my son."

Sasha pursed her lips. "Lord knows I agree with you. Money doesn't buy class. But you're not going to be happy about his new employer."

"I can live with Hampton, if that's what you're implying. It's not optimal, but at least he possesses some principles and is a master of parliamentary procedure, which could prove helpful if, God forbid, Chandler decides to remain in politics."

"It's not Sampson's replacement, and it's not Senator Eric Hampton."

"Who then?"

"Your son," Sasha said, "is the newest legislative aide for Congressman Cameron Kelly."

Washington, DC

ASSISTANT DIRECTOR, CRIMINAL Investigative Division Warren Barringer's spacious office looked out on Pennsylvania Avenue. Unlike Ethan's office, with the FBI motto displayed behind the desk, photographs of Barringer with the who's who of Washington—President Fairchild, former president Richard Ellison, Senators Eric Hampton and Paul Sampson, Representative Howard Bell—decorated the walls.

After being waved in, Jade walked behind his desk, surveying the photographs.

She pointed at one. "Who's this?"

Barringer strained to turn his bulk in the chair and glance over his shoulder. "That's my latest addition. Congressman Cameron Kelly."

"From what state?"

"Missouri."

Jade thought for a moment. "Which district?"

"Who cares?" he said. "He's a good man. Let's get to it, shall we? I'm meeting with the director in fifteen minutes."

Jade moved to a chair across from him. "Actually, Missouri is what I want to talk to you about."

Barringer shuffled some papers on his desk. "What about it?"

"There was an inquiry. About a congressman from there. Car accident. One of my agents said that you directed her to stop any further inquiries into the case."

"I don't remember that."

"You don't remember the case or calling her off it?"

"Neither."

She pointed at his computer. "Can you check?"

Barringer stopped shuffling. "No, I can't. I'm busy."

"This might be important."

"I decide what's important, and you're working on a major case already, which, I'll remind you, isn't going that well. You don't have time to mess around with an old closed case."

"That's the point. It shouldn't be closed. I think—"

Barringer stood. "I don't care what you think. You've got a job to do, and I expect you to do it."

"I'm doing my job."

"So you say. To be clear, I'm ordering you to drop any further inquiries into Congressman Steven Barrett's death."

The heat flashed in Jade's face. "Ordering?"

"That's what I said, princess."

She stood still.

Motionless.

Stared at him.

"Why did you call me that?"

"It's just a term. I didn't mean anything by it. Don't go charging me with sexual harassment or assault or any of that foolishness."

Jade wasn't angry at the inappropriate endearment. She was stunned. Only her father called her princess.

Striding to the door, she turned back to him. "Given that you don't remember the case, it's funny that you know his name."

She made sure to slam the door on her way out.

On the way back from Barringer's office, Jade stopped by Micah's cubicle, which was decorated with photos of Arsenal football players. A new photo had been added: a beautiful black woman who looked like a model. Jade peered closer. "That's new. Who is it?"

"What do you Yanks say? Noneya?"

"Okay," Jade said, feigning disinterest. She realized for the first time that aside from his love of the English Premier League team, she didn't know much about Special Agent Micah Alexander. "What were you going to tell me?"

Still fuming, she wanted to distract herself from the disturbing conversation with Barringer.

"You said it wasn't important."

"I'll be the judge of that," she said without humor.

He shook his head. "It was about Hurley. She went to the Carr Summit years ago."

She leaned against the edge of his cubicle wall. "What's that?"

"It's where a bunch of conservative blokes and ladies congregate, donate a lot of money, and carve up the world."

"Any of the other victims there?"

He shrugged. "I only know Hurley was there, because she told her ex-husband."

"We need the list of attendees," Jade said.

"That'll be hard to do. Not only is the invitation list a secret, but so is the event itself. If you tell anyone that you've been invited or discuss anything that takes place there, you'll never be invited back."

"You learned all this from her ex?"

"Hurley sometimes got drunk and would call him late at night. I guess being a CEO, she didn't have a lot of people to speak freely with. He said he's never told anyone."

"And now it doesn't matter that she won't be invited back," she said. "Solid, Micah."

"Told you."

She turned to go.

"That wasn't all," he said. "I found a link between Scofield and Carr."

"Pat told me Scofield handled Carr's money."

"Did she also tell you that they went to prep school together?" He checked his notes. "The Phillips Academy in Andover, Massachusetts."

CHAPTER EIGHTY

The White House, Washington, DC

WHITNEY OCCUPIED A lounge chair on the Truman Balcony just off the Yellow Oval Room, which afforded a view of the South Lawn, the National Mall, the Washington Monument, and the Lincoln Memorial. A few small trees and fresh flowers were interspersed with chairs, couches, and tables grouped in various arrangements. The balcony was used for entertaining foreign heads of state, diplomats, members of the other branches of government, and celebrities.

It was becoming Whitney's favorite spot in the White House. She enjoyed breakfast out here on the weekends, and, on warm nights, she worked or read.

The phone rang. She picked up the extension on a side table.

"Madam President," Sasha said, her voice tight, "you're needed in the Situation Room. Now."

"Sasha, what's happened?"

"Reports are coming in that a number of power plants and electrical grids are down along the West Coast."

"What's the cause?"

"We don't know yet."

"You don't think it's a coincidence?"

"No."

"Tamirov."

"Or Min. Or both."

China and Russia had reportedly infiltrated the electrical grid of the US back in 2009, leaving behind software that could disrupt several regions of the country.

"We've received word that at least three large corporations were breached.

Social security numbers, email addresses, personal information. Cyber Command thinks there will be more."

"My God," Whitney said. "I'll be right there."

She hung up.

Whitney looked longingly at her glass before picking it and the bottle up and heading inside. She poured the remaining wine in the glass down the sink and capped the bottle, returning it to the wine refrigerator.

She called the ground-floor kitchen for a pot of coffee to be delivered to the Situation Room.

Time to go to work.

❋

Whitney scanned the intense faces around the table.

"Dani?" she said.

"Electric power grids, water systems, and energy were impacted on the West Coast," said Danielle Oliver, the secretary of energy.

"Ditto for telecommunications and transportation," said Julio Casillas from transportation.

"Automatic cars crashed. Interstate trucking has been impacted. Grocery stores won't receive deliveries on time, if at all. If this goes on a lot longer, they'll run out of food. Same with gas stations."

Oliver said, "Blackouts in LA, San Francisco, Seattle, Las Vegas, and Portland."

"I'm worried about the inner cities," Vice President Josephine Bates said.

"What time did this happen?" Whitney asked no one in particular.

"Midnight," responded several of them.

Energy Secretary Oliver caught her eye. "Exactly midnight."

"Personal computers and cell phones aren't working at all," Transportation Secretary Casillas said. "Some are displaying gibberish."

"Manufacturing facilities have been infiltrated," said Tucker Price, secretary of labor. The sweat from his underarms formed gray semicircles on his white shirt.

Smaller than most citizens imagined, the Situation Room now smelled of a mix of sweat, cologne, perfume, and coffee.

Secretary of Homeland Security Maricela Salcedo said, "Several banks and credit card companies were hit with denial-of-service attacks. Corporate servers, ISPs are down. Folks will panic when they can't email, Skype, text, or conduct online transactions. Even the RainForest, which provides cloud-based solutions that support many businesses around the world, including eighty percent of the Fortune 500, was hit. When the public starts realizing what's happening… we need to be prepared. For possible violence."

"This will disproportionately hit poor people," Jo said. "Minorities. They'll freak the fuck out."

"Everyone's going to freak out," wailed Price. "It's a fuckin' mess."

"Calm down, Tucker," Whitney said.

Jo said to him, "Why are you always so emotional?"

Whitney cut her a look. "Jo. Please."

"Asian markets are plummeting," said London James, secretary of the treasury. "I expect US markets to plunge. Thousands of points." She paused. "Should we stop the market from opening?"

"No," Whitney said. "The world needs to know that the United States of America is open for business."

"How can we be open for business when a quarter of the country is in the dark?" said Oliver.

Good question.

She turned to James. "What's the impact?"

London James was the first female CEO in Goldman Sachs's history and another in a long succession of former Goldman Sachs CEOs to join presidential cabinets. Whitney liked the tenaciousness it took for James to claw her way to the top spot at the top investment bank in the world.

"Daily?"

Whitney nodded.

James shrugged. "Trillions."

"Go on," Whitney said.

"Banks will shut down. Customers won't be able to access cash or credit. People will panic. Demand for food, gas, and other necessities will outstrip supply. A US panic will cause a global panic. Demand for the dollar will plummet. Inflation will rise. If it goes on for long, hyperinflation will ensue. Interest rates will increase. Investors will invest in other currencies. Shall I continue?"

Whitney held up her hand. "Who benefits?"

"China most likely. They can fill the void. No one else."

Whitney turned to Edison Banks, secretary of health and human services. "Hospitals?"

"It's a crisis. Medical care facilities rely on power. We'll need to move people soon."

Whitney eyed Pravir Ratta, her secretary of education.

"Nothing's come in so far," he said.

"Media?"

"No reports that they've been hit," Energy Secretary Oliver said.

"But what do we tell them?" asked Lena, the acting press secretary.

"Nothing for now," Whitney said. "Until we know our plan."

Lena leaned forward. "With all due respect, Madam President, the East Coast is asleep now, but they won't be for much longer. Some people might still be up—

"As we are," murmured Secretary of Commerce Ashton Crawford.

"—trying to contact loved ones on the West Coast. We won't be able to keep this under wraps for long."

Whitney turned to Secretary of Defense Leyton Quinn. "Military systems?" She shook her head.

Breathing a sigh of relief, Whitney shuddered to think of the consequences of the infiltration of their nuclear or missile systems.

"Winters, what's your assessment? Did you see this coming?"

General Malachi Winters was the chairman of the US Cyber Command and head of the NSA. Now, in addition to land, sea, air, and space, his responsibilities included a new battlefield: cyberspace. Cyber Command's mission was to neutralize cyberattacks and defend military computer network systems.

"We had an inkling," Winters said, shaking his head. Deep lines furrowed his dark forehead. "But nothing like this. I would've told you. Do you want my resignation?"

Whitney waved this thought away. "Options?"

"At first," said Defense Secretary Quinn, "we thought it was a massive outage, but now I think…"

"What?" Whitney asked.

"It was a military attack," Quinn said.

Her words silenced the room.

After a moment, she added, "This was an act of war."

"By whom?" said Winters. "A sovereign state? A nonstate? A bunch of teenagers playing a game?"

"Or a fat guy lying on his bed," said Commerce Secretary Crawford.

The nervous giggles died quickly.

Whitney eyed a woman dressed in a military uniform decorated with five stars on her shoulder straps. "General?"

Chairwoman of the Joint Chiefs of Staff, General Frances Wilkerson was the first woman to hold the title. Possessing a high standard of integrity, she guided the military with restraint. She despised partisan politics, especially when they got in the way of doing the right thing. Whitney trusted her completely.

The general gazed at her, calm and unflappable. "At your command, we are ready."

Whitney broke the stare and scanned the cabinet members' faces again. "Is there any good news?"

No one met her eyes. Some of them doodled on the notepads in front of them. Some stared off into the distance.

"I think it was Tamirov," said Defense Secretary Quinn.

Russia had done something like this before. A decade ago, to Ukraine. Ukraine, however, was not the most powerful country in the world.

"Could be Min," said Maricela Salcedo from Homeland Security.

"He possesses a hacker army of hundreds of thousands of private citizens," Winters said, "while we employ a few thousand civil servants to protect us. It's not a fair fight." He hesitated, then looked at Salcedo. "Could it be both?"

Whitney thought it was plausible.

"Let's talk to Min," she said, nodding at Secretary of State Park Chui. "Instead of mutually assured destruction, we want mutually assured restraint. Otherwise, this will not end well. For anyone."

"What about Tamirov?" asked Leyton Quinn, the defense secretary.

"I'll talk to him," Whitney said. She looked at her team again. "Come up with a plan for bringing our citizens back online." She stood. "I want it on my desk within the hour."

"An hour?" said Oliver, voicing—if their expressions were any indication—the concern shared by most of the other members.

"One hour," said Whitney. "We're at war."

"With all due respect, Madam President," Winters said, "we've been in a cyberwar for a long time, and we're losing. Most Americans just don't know it."

Washington, DC

SHE WASN'T SURE how she'd ended up here.

Well, she knew how, but not why.

Jade had spent that afternoon discussing next steps on the Shakespeare case with Dante and dealing with other matters. The conversation with Barringer continued to bother her.

When she called it a night, Jade didn't feel like going home, and she wasn't up for Zoe's upbeat company. Zoe lit up a room, but the energy she needed to fuel herself could drain those around her.

Instead, Jade stopped by a small dive bar in Capitol Hill, a place where she hoped no one would recognize her. A jazz trio played near the entrance. Photographs of jazz and blues artists—recent and seasoned, young and old—dotted the walls. When she arrived, there were no vacant seats at the bar, but there was an empty semicircle booth for two in the back.

She removed her suit jacket, laid it next to her, and ordered a Heineken.

Taking a pull on the beer, she closed her eyes, allowing her head to bob to the music.

"Is this seat taken?"

Jade opened her eyes. A woman stood across the table. She was about five eight, with light-brown hair, attractive in an androgynous sort of way.

"No."

"This place is always crowded. Do you mind?"

Jade moved her jacket closer to her. The woman slid into the booth.

"You look familiar," Jade said.

"I live nearby, so you might've seen me here." To the server, "I'll have what she's having."

"Glass?" the server asked.

The woman glanced at Jade's bottle. "No."

The server left.

The woman smiled, embarrassed. "Forgive me. My name's Brooklyn. My friends call me Brook."

"Jade."

They shook hands.

After receiving her beer, Brooklyn raised her glass. "To jazz?"

"To jazz."

They clinked bottles and drank.

"Thanks for letting me share your table."

The two women listened to the music and sipped their drinks.

"What do you do?" Brooklyn asked.

If this woman didn't recognize her, Jade wasn't going to be the one to inform her.

"Security," Jade said. "You?"

A pause. "Customer service."

Brook turned to face the band. Her neck was taut, her forearms sinewy.

Jade sipped her beer. "Athlete?"

The woman turned back to her. "Volleyball. Setter."

"Do you still play?"

Brooklyn shook her head as she signaled for two more beers. "I'm more of a triathlete now."

"Impressive."

The two women talked as they listened to the first set. Brooklyn was also a fan of all the DC sports teams, including soccer, and they discussed the prospects for DC United this season. Jade was enjoying herself immensely. She hadn't talked sports with another woman in a long time. For the moment, she forgot about Barringer, Shakespeare, Judy Porter, and Whitney Fairchild.

They ordered a bucket of Heinekens and stayed for the second set.

That was several hours ago.

The bedroom was dark.

"Brook, I gotta go," Jade said. "Thanks for tonight."

Brooklyn turned to face her, her head still on the pillow. "It was nice."

Jade rolled out of the bed, gathered her clothes, which were scattered all over the floor, and dressed hurriedly.

She quietly let herself out of the Capitol Hill townhouse.

Driving home, Jade realized she didn't know Brook's last name.

Chapter Eighty-Two

Washington, DC

"CRAZY WHAT HAPPENED on the West Coast last night," Pat said, looking up from her computer.

"What happened?" Jade asked.

"Where were you? Sleeping under a rock?"

Sort of.

Early the next morning, head pounding, she'd stopped by Pat's cubicle on the way to her office. Jade still hadn't processed her feelings about sleeping with Brooklyn.

"Tell me," she said.

Pat told her about the blackouts.

"Sounds like a test," Jade said.

Pat ceased her typing and squinted up at her. "You okay?"

Jade yawned. "Late night."

Pat looked hopeful.

"Noneya," Jade said.

Pat raised both of her arms, as if Jade had hit a three-pointer. "Yes!"

Christian looked over from his cubicle. Since he'd returned from Seattle the night before, Jade had told him to take the day off. He'd come in anyway.

"What's up, Pat?" he called over.

"Jade got some last night!"

He lumbered over. "Really? Who!?"

Jade's face flushed. "Noneya. Chill."

Dante came out of his office. "What's going on?"

"Shit," Jade said under her breath.

"Boss got some," Pat and Christian answered, almost simultaneously.

"It's about time. Maybe now you can get off my back," Dante said. He raised his hand to give her a high five. "Male, female, or both?"

Jade ignored him. "Can you all get back to work? I'm talking to Pat."

"We're happy for you, that's all," Christian said, grinning.

A parting, suggestive smile from Dante. "Can't wait to hear more."

As she watched Christian return to his cubicle, her gaze landed on Micah. Still seated at his desk chair, he glared at her, his jaw clenched, his face a mask. He averted his eyes and turned to face his computer.

Jade couldn't help him.

To Pat, she said sarcastically, "Thanks."

"Sorry." Pat suppressed a smile. "Couple of things for you. After running into a dead end with the Barrett witness—"

"Pat," Jade warned.

"—I found out that the SUV used in the Porter killing was out of range of the motel's camera, which pointed toward the parking lot."

"But..."

"A traffic light camera caught it. The license plate turned out to be fake. Indiana. Unregistered. They still haven't been able to locate the vehicle."

"I wonder if it's the same SUV as the one used to kill Barrett."

"I doubt it. That was a long time ago. Plus, there aren't any cameras on that country road, and our only witness is dead."

"Unless we lifted something off the congressman's car."

"Which is in pieces and part of other vehicles now."

"True. What else?"

"Sebastian Scofield also attended the Carr Summit. He and Hurley belonged to the Carrs' billion-dollar donor club."

"Someone might be targeting the attendees. These people are at risk. Micah tried to obtain a list. Can you check it out?"

Pat rolled her chair a few paces to the other end of the desk. She returned, handing Jade a file.

Jade opened it to find a list of attendees. "All righty then. Tishman and Porter on the list?"

"No. Tishman was a progressive. Still unsure how he fits in. Or Porter. She had no connection to the other victims. She wasn't a conservative. Quite the opposite. Her husband said she voted for Fairchild. She was a strong supporter and respected the president tremendously, but she hid it behind journalistic impartiality. He said she felt sick breaking the news about the first man's affair."

Jade closed the file; she'd review it later. It was a long list. "Come with me."

Once they were both seated in her office, Jade said, "I need a favor."

Pat's arms were on the guest chair's armrest, her hands clasped. "Sure."

"I need you to explore Barrett's death again." Jade straightened the already-straightened items on her desk. Without looking at Pat, she said, "Also, find out why Barringer would want us to stop the investigation."

"Are you sure?" Pat said. "You're treading on dangerous territory, Jade. We could lose our jobs."

We.

Pat just called her Jade. She didn't remember the last time that Pat called her by her given name. If she ever had.

"I've thought a lot about this," Jade said. "Some things are more important than a job. We swore to obey the Constitution with uncompromising integrity. That case stinks. Something's not right."

"We're not only talking about losing our jobs here," Pat said in a quiet voice.

"I know."

The older woman gazed down at the floor, then raised her head. "I'm in."

"This stays between us."

"I got it, boss."

Shit. Now Dante has everyone saying it.

Jade had secretly started to like it.

"I need you to do something else for me," she said. She spun around in her chair and grabbed a sheet of blank paper from the stack next to the printer.

Placing the paper on her desk, she sketched two objects from memory.

When she finished, Pat gave her a puzzled look. "A tree?"

Jade nodded. "Find out what kind it is."

Pat pointed. "What about this symbol? It looks Japanese."

進捗

"I believe it's 'progress,'" Jade said, "but find out for sure. My Japanese is a little rusty."

Jade's mother was Japanese, and at one time, Jade spoke it fluently. With her mother gone, she no longer spoke it every day. Another piece of her parents that she'd allowed to slip away.

While Jade ruminated about them, Pat grabbed the sketches and left her office.

CHAPTER EIGHTY-THREE

Washington, DC

"WHAT'S THE LATEST?"

Sasha stood in front of Whitney's desk in the Oval Office, looking no worse for wear. "Power grids, water systems, and energy are back online. Transportation is up and running, although with significant delays."

"Roads?"

"Cleanup has commenced on the highways." Sasha paused. "Although the cars were driverless, it doesn't mean they were without passengers. At least five hundred deaths and counting. We were blessed that the event happened at midnight, or there would have been more. Many more."

"There were enough."

Sasha gave her a solemn nod. "Thank God there weren't many planes in the sky."

"I wonder if that was why that particular time was selected. To minimize casualties."

"Several planes made emergency landings. Reports of injuries—some severe—but no deaths. Factories are up and running. A lot of wasted product, but otherwise no long-term damage."

"What else?"

"Internet's back up. Most personal computers and cell phones are working, but…"

"What?"

"We're encouraging the public to download antivirus software on their computers, servers, and smart TVs to combat any malware installed during this event. There's no guarantee that people will do it."

"Likely adding identities to the list of casualties," Whitney said, leaning back in her chair.

Sasha waited.

"It was a test," Whitney said.

She was more convinced that Russia was the culprit.

The former Soviet Union hadn't forgotten that the CIA had planted the computer malware that blew up part of the Trans-Siberian pipeline back in 1982, causing the biggest non-nuclear explosion the world had ever seen. The country didn't publicly blame the US at the time.

"I think you're right." Sasha cocked her head. "Did you sleep?"

"No. I took a cold shower. You?"

"I tried to sleep on the couch in my office, but it was clearly made for a skinny girl, not a voluptuous woman like me."

Whitney held up her hand. "Don't start shimmying. Care to watch the opening bell with me? Instead of Breakfast at Wimbledon, let's enjoy Breakfast at Wall Street." She punched the speakerphone, not waiting for Sasha's answer. "Sean, please bring breakfast into my study. Something hearty. For two."

"Has the First Gentleman returned?" he said, hopeful.

"Thank you, Sean," Whitney said, hanging up.

Twenty minutes later, a butler wheeled in a cart with several covered trays. He lifted each cover and described the tray's contents before departing.

The two women sat a table in front of the television eating eggs and bacon and toast—Sasha asked Whitney to call back and add pancakes to the order—as they watched the negative red numbers light up the screen.

"We should do this every day," said Sasha. "Not that,"—she pointed her forkful of eggs at the television—"this." She slipped the fork into her mouth.

The Dow dropped two thousand points by 9:31 a.m.

By 9:35, the New York Stock Exchange halted trading.

Whitney dabbed her mouth with a white linen napkin. "I guess you should call Lena in here."

"She can wait a few minutes." Sasha lifted a tray cover, heaping another helping of eggs onto her plate. "We need to fortify ourselves. It's going to be a long day."

Whitney looked at the second helping on Sasha's plate, suddenly not hungry. "By all means. Any word from Chui?"

"He said that Min categorically denies any involvement and is open to further discussions of mutually assured restraint." Sasha chewed and swallowed. "Tamirov?"

"Still waiting for him to call me back."

"Normally he's available to take your calls or responds immediately." Sasha eyed her. "I always thought he was sweet on you."

Whitney was saved from responding—and analyzing why this comment pleased her—by Sean's voice coming over the speakerphone. "Madam President, President Tamirov is on the line."

She gave Sasha a "this is it" look before moving behind her desk and picking up the handset.

"Andrei."

"Whitney, good morning. I hear you are having difficulty keeping the lights on."

"With your help?"

"Why would you think I was involved in your recent troubles?"

She sat in her chair. "I could think of a thousand reasons. Were you?"

"Your recovery has been swift. Impressive. It seems the rumors of the decline of the alleged greatest nation on earth are vastly exaggerated."

"You shouldn't listen to rumors."

"Maybe so," he said, "but unlike you Americans, Russians have suffered throughout history. The unforgiving cold weather. The wars and endless conflicts. The revolutions. The scarcity. Nevertheless, we always come through every challenge better off because of it."

"Why are you telling me this?"

"We are a proud people, and we don't forget even the smallest of slights. We are also patient."

"Andrei, if I have slighted you in some way—"

"That," he said, "was for the pipeline."

PART III

CHAPTER EIGHTY-FOUR

Washington, DC

JADE STRODE DOWN a path near the reflecting pool. She spotted Pat sitting on a bench underneath a shade tree, eating a hot dog.

"Late lunch?" Jade said.

"You work me too hard."

Jade smiled before glancing around the crowded National Mall. On one of the first days of spring, people were out eating, walking, and running. Workers pecked away on their laptops. Students relaxed on the grass, studying, their backpacks lying next to them. Groups of color-coordinated tourists trekked up the Lincoln Memorial stairs.

"Here," Pat said, handing a hot dog to Jade. "You work yourself too hard too."

"Thanks. I forgot to eat."

"You usually do."

Jade took a bite of the dog, which was still warm and loaded with melted cheese and chili. "That's good. Thank you."

Pat waved behind her. "Food truck. One of my go-to places."

The two ate in silence.

Finally, Jade said, "Why did you call me out here, Pat? It wasn't to eat lunch together."

"You're right," she said, lifting a file from her lap and handing it to Jade. "I found your tree."

Jade scanned the document inside the folder. She looked at Pat. "The Liberty Tree?"

"It was an elm tree planted in Boston in 1646, on the only road into or out of the city. After the British Parliament passed the Stamp Act in 1765, a band of merchants and artisans formed a radical secret society called the Sons of Liberty, or the Loyal Nine. They hung items on the tree, including an image in effigy of the tax collector. A mob gathered and started breaking into houses, destroying furniture, raiding liquor cabinets, that sort of thing. For the next decade, Boston's angriest demonstrations took place there, symbolizing the violent aspect of the Revolutionary War—a side that the colonists we're still too sensitive to see."

Jade said, "What happened to the tree?"

"The British Army chopped it down in 1775, which is why most Americans haven't heard of it. Towns throughout the colonies planted Liberty Trees in protest. One of the founding fathers, Thomas Paine, wrote a song about the tree and its importance to all Americans." She glanced down at the folder that now lay on the bench between them. "The lyrics are in there."

"Anything else?"

"Thomas Jefferson tried to make the Liberty Tree a lasting metaphor." Pat quoted from memory, "'The tree of liberty must be refreshed from time to time with the blood of patriots and tyrants.'"

"Sounds dangerous," Jade said.

Pat searched her face. "What's this about?"

Why would Zoe tattoo the Liberty Tree on her wrist?

"What about the symbol?" Jade asked, ignoring Pat's question.

"You were right. It's the Japanese word for 'progress.'"

"What else?"

"I've also looked into Barrett's death, as you asked. You're right about that too—it stinks."

"How so?"

"I obtained a copy of the original airplane manifest and compared it to the one we had on file. It'd been altered."

Jade stopped chewing. "What?"

"Rick Cheney, the alias that Caleb Hewitt used on that flight, appeared on the second manifest, but not the first."

"Meaning…"

"Rick Cheney didn't replace another passenger. He was an addition."

"So we would deduce that it was an alias for Hewitt."

"Correct. I don't think Hewitt was in St. Louis at the time of the murder."

"Then where was he?"

"I don't know," Pat said. "There's more."

"Go on."

"Since the manifest for the flight from Philadelphia to St. Louis was altered, I decided to check out the flight from Newark to Chicago."

Caleb Hewitt had used the alias Walker G. Bush on that flight, putting him in the vicinity around the time the president's aunt, Mary Churchill, was killed.

A sense of foreboding settled over Jade. "And?"

"That manifest was altered too."

No longer hungry, Jade balled up the uneaten remainder of the hot dog in its wrapper and lobbed it into the trash can a few feet away. Swish. Nothing but net.

"Hewitt hated the Bush administration," Jade recalled. "Rick Cheney represented Dick Cheney. Walker G. Bush was obviously George W. Bush. We copped Hewitt for both murders, tying them in with the TSK murders. Someone handed us a gift wrapped with a bow."

"And we opened it," Pat said.

Jade paused. "It's more than that. Evidence tampering of this magnitude would need to come from the highest of levels."

Pat nodded. "That's why we're eating lunch out here."

"And Barringer asked us to stop looking into the Barrett case."

The two women looked at each other for a moment.

Pat stood. "Be careful, Jade."

She walked away.

Jade glanced down at the folder.

A feeling of dread came to life in the pit of her stomach. And, if she were being honest, not a small amount of fear.

CHAPTER EIGHTY-FIVE

Arlington, Virginia

"HEY," BLAKE SAID.

Jade had been shooting around on the court at the park by her house. It was dusk, the basket swathed in shadows. During her routine, she thought about her conversation with Pat earlier that afternoon. Holding the basketball in one hand and her phone in the other, she sat cross-legged underneath the basket. No need to worry about being hit by a stray ball. She was the only one on the court.

She was disappointed that none of the usual crowd had showed up. She loved playing ball with the fellas. Well-earned respect reflected in their eyes when they realized—or knew—that she could (still) hold her own. It gave her a sense of pride. And she could use a vigorous game about now.

Blake's call surprised her.

"Hey, yourself," she said.

"How's your investigation going?"

Instead of the Shakespeare case, she contemplated the Barrett and Churchill cases. Which weren't officially her cases. Or open ones, for that matter.

"It's going. Still at home?"

"Yes," Blake said, "in bed, where I've been spending a lot of time."

"Are you up for visitors yet?"

"No," he said in a quiet voice. "I'm still not ready."

"When are you returning to work?"

He sighed. "Not sure I'm ready for the pressures of the White House yet either."

"I hear you."

She enjoyed the quiet of the park. The crickets chirped. Through the trees, she saw lights coming on in some of the townhouses. A squirrel darted onto the court and stopped to look at her. Finding nothing of interest, he moved on.

"I've been doing a little digging into what Judy was working on."

"Blake…"

"She *was* onto something."

"Such as?"

"I'm not sure I should tell you."

"You did call."

"Right." He hesitated. "I don't think Congressman Barrett's death was an accident."

Of course it wasn't. "Why do you say that?"

"At first I believed the news reports. An unfortunate accident for him, and serendipity for the future president. I checked in with the police in Clayton, Missouri. They're now saying that it wasn't an accident, but they are tight-lipped about the details. After the congressman died, Fairchild ran and won the special election to replace him."

"Everyone knows about the special election. Are you saying there's a connection?"

"I think there is. Yes."

"There was no assurance she would win," Jade pointed out.

"Maybe not," he said, "but a significant amount of money for her poured in from outside the state. I'm still trying to track down the sources of the contributions, but it was a disproportionate amount for a special election House race, especially back then for an unknown, unproven candidate."

"You're talking about the president." She paused. "Your boss."

"I don't like corruption. Something about this stinks. My boss and mo—" He hesitated. "Notwithstanding."

"And what?"

"Nothing."

"You think someone was behind her getting elected?"

"Someone," he said, "or something."

❁

Jade picked up Card from the sheet of paper on the couch next to her. The cat possessed an uncanny ability to sit on whatever she was about to read. Kissing him on the top of his head, she placed him in her lap.

She reread Thomas Paine's song about the Liberty Tree, which ended:

But hear, O ye swains ('tis a tale most profane),
How all the tyrannical powers,
Kings, Commons, and Lords, are uniting amain
To cut down this guardian of ours.
From the East to the West blow the trumpet to arms,
Thro' the land let the sound of it flee:
Let the far and the near all unite with a cheer,
In defense of our Liberty Tree.

She'd heard of Thomas Paine, of course, and read *Common Sense* in high school. That didn't mean she remembered any of it. Tapping a key to bring her laptop to life, she googled his name and clicked on his Wikipedia page.

Common Sense was originally titled *Plain Truth*.

Was this connected to Veritas?

After a few hours of reading about the man and his work, she understood why Zoe identified with him. A lot of his views were progressive: human rights, progressive taxation to combat poverty, egalitarian society, world peace, social security for the elderly and the poor, the evils of arbitrary government, combating illiteracy, the need for insurances against unemployment. Paine was staunchly antislavery and believed in religious tolerance.

"'Every religion is good that teaches man to be good,'" Jade read aloud.

She liked that.

Paine sounded like Zoe's kind of founding father. Was that why she'd tatted the Liberty Tree on her wrist? Zoe didn't need a reason to do anything, but a tattoo was a permanent declaration. At least, until it was removed.

The tattoo must represent something political. Politics was Zoe's life. Why was she seeking liberty?

And progress.

Jade's eyes drifted to the wooden triangle frame perched on a shelf of her bookcase. Jonathan Harrington's sacrifice. A soldier had handed the flag to her at her parents' funeral.

What did Zoe say that time? Something about a new guard for future security? She googled this phrase and got a hit on the first link:

… it is their right, it is their duty, to throw off such Government, and to provide new Guards for their future security.

Part of a sentence from the Declaration of Independence.

Jade leaned back, frowning.

Her doorbell rang.

Visitors to her home, unannounced or otherwise, were rare. She set Card and the paper aside. Looking through the peephole, she saw Pat Turner glancing over both shoulders.

Jade opened the door. "How do you know where I live?"

Pat gave her a look that said *I know everything.* "I need to talk to you," she said.

Jade opened the door wider. "Come in."

Pat shook her head. "No. Let's go to that park you're always talking about." She mouthed, *Leave your phone.*

Grabbing her keys, Jade pulled a light jacket over her Stanford Women's Basketball T-shirt and Adidas track pants. The night was cool but pleasant. The two women didn't speak as they walked along the sidewalk, then cut between a break in the townhouses to travel the short distance to the park.

Pat didn't stop walking until she'd arrived at the center of the court. The lights surrounding the court were off. Jade could barely make out Pat's face.

"I found an encrypted file hidden on Judy Porter's computer," Pat whispered.

"What was in it?" Jade whispered back.

"I haven't been able to open it yet."

Jade put her hands on her hips. "Then why are we here?"

"Because of the name of the file."

"Which is?"

"Paine," Pat said.

Washington, DC

"DO YOU THINK that's a good idea?" Dante asked the next morning.

Jade stood in Dante's doorway, as he used to when she occupied this office.

Christian slid in next to her. "Morning. What were you talking about when I got here?"

"What we can do to flush out Shakespeare," she said.

"That rhymed," said Micah, standing with them in the now crowded hallway. "Almost sounds like a couplet." He rapped: "What were you talking about when I got here? What we can do to flush out Shakespeare."

"She's a poet and doesn't know it," said Dante.

Christian moved his head to an imaginary beat. "Don't mess with Jade if you can't abade."

Micah looked puzzled. "Is 'abade' a word?"

"I might have just made it up," Christian replied.

Jade rolled her eyes. "I'm leaving."

She turned, hiding her smile, and headed down the hallway, while her team continued to make up rhymes behind her.

She'd been thinking about this plan for some time. She was desperate. There hadn't been any movement on the Shakespeare Killer case. Barrington was still griping about her solve rate. The drumbeat of his impatience—and the public's—rumbled louder.

Picking up the handset in her office, she checked the Seattle number and dialed.

Three rings. She was about to hang up when he answered.

"Yeah."

"This is Agent Jade Harrington."

"What do you want?"

"Now that's not very nice. Not even 'Seattle nice.'"

He didn't laugh.

"I need you to do something for me," she said.

"What?"

She told him.

There was silence for several moments.

"If I do it, will you get off my case?"

"Yes," she said.

"I can do that," said The God of Veritas.

"Tell me about the Liberty Tree," Jade said.

Zoe, puzzled, said, "What are you talking about?"

Jade pointed at Zoe's wrist. "That."

Zoe scoffed. "It's a tree. I like trees."

"Since when?"

"I'm an environmentalist. Always have been. What of it? Why are you questioning my tattoo? I can tat whatever I want on *my* body. A naked woman or a—"

Jade held up her hand. "Stop."

Zoe closed her mouth.

"The tree is significant," Jade said. "It's a symbol of the American Revolution. Rebellion. Of a dark side of US history. Why is it tatted on your wrist?"

Zoe examined her wrist, pouting, a look Jade had seen many times before. "I wanted a tree. It's no big deal."

"I think it's a big deal and means a lot to you." Jade leaned forward and placed her hands on the counter that separated Zoe's kitchen from the rest of her Adams Morgan apartment. "Who's the artist?"

Zoe swept her arm toward the living room. "Can we at least sit down?"

She went to sprawl on her favorite circular wicker chair with beige cushions, perching her feet on the coffee table. Jade sat on the couch. For once, she didn't grab the round orange pillow and start shooting it like a basketball. Zoe looked at the pillow and back at Jade.

"This *must* be serious," Zoe said.

In contrast to the minimalist decor in Jade's townhouse, Zoe's apartment was eclectic: walls of indigo, eggplant, and lime. Bookshelves crowded with African knickknacks obtained during her time in the Peace Corps.

The aroma of patchouli incense did not put Jade at ease today.

She gazed at the new posters on the wall. One had a 1950s-looking woman flexing her bicep above the words "ERA Amendment Now," the legislation that passed during Fairchild's first year in office. The other showed an arcade gallery from the point of view of someone holding an assault rifle. People were the rotating targets. Underneath was the word "Enough," the name of the gun reform bill that didn't pass after the elementary school shooting.

Zoe pointed up. "Do you hear what's playing?"

"Sade," Jade said.

"Thought you would like that, being from your era and all. Do you want to order takeout? There's a great new Japanese restaurant in Dupont Circle that delivers."

"You know I don't eat Japanese food."

"Why not? You're half Japanese. Your mother—"

"Zoe," Jade said, "this isn't a social visit."

She placed a blown-up drawing of Zoe's tree tattoo on the coffee table between them.

"What is this?" asked Zoe, sitting up.

Jade placed another drawing on the table and tapped it. "The Japanese symbol for 'progress.'"

Zoe's eyes became huge. "How do you know about that?"

"I saw it. Last year. When you covered me with a blanket."

"I need to wear tighter clothes," Zoe muttered to herself.

"These tats are related to some cases I'm working on. Who's the artist?"

Zoe stood. "This is crazy. Are you investigating *me*? Again? What for? I thought we were friends. Best friends. If this is the way you treat me, I feel sorry for your enemies. Isn't this abuse of power or something? Doesn't a crime have to be committed?"

"We are friends," Jade said, standing as well. "That's why I'm here. Alone. This is your chance to tell me the truth." Jade picked up the photographs and returned them to her briefcase. "Crimes have been committed, and I think you're involved. Do you have something to tell me? I can get you immunity."

"I still have no idea what you're talking about."

"Were you involved with the death of Congressman Barrett or setting up Noah Blakeley? You were a hacker in college. A good one. All along, we've thought foreign agents were responsible, but now I think you were involved in one or both cases."

Jade's eyes never left Zoe's face.

She looked for a sign that Zoe was lying: A shifting of the eyes. Swallowing. Clearing of the throat. Grooming gestures. A pause before responding.

Zoe paused, swallowed, cleared her throat, and ran her hand through her short hair. Her eyes blinked rapidly.

The FBI believed that only a sophisticated hacker—or hackers—had the ability to pull off the Robin Hood heist of millions of dollars from corporate and individual bank accounts. All the ill-gotten funds had been used to help people by providing low-income housing, jobs, and education. All good causes. All causes that Zoe believed in.

Cyber didn't believe the perp kept any money for himself.

Or herself.

In college, Stanford had suspended Zoe for two weeks for changing everyone's grades in her poli-sci class to As. The reason: she wanted everyone to be a winner. She was reinstated only when she agreed to join the university's information security department, assist with counter-cyberthreat efforts, and promise never to use her skills improperly at the university again. As far as Jade knew, Zoe had kept her promise.

And Jade should know; she'd been Zoe's roommate.

Although Zoe was capable of committing the Robin Hood heist and altering the manifests in the Barrett case, she didn't possess the resources to pull off these crimes alone.

Jade hadn't told anyone of her suspicions. Her friend deserved a chance to come clean first.

Zoe's silence spoke volumes.

"Who are you working for?" Jade asked.

"My organization helps pro—"

Jade stepped closer, looking down at her friend. "Zoe, who do you really work for?"

"Get out!"

The two women stared at each other for what felt to Jade like minutes.

Placing a hand on Zoe's shoulder, she said, "I'm worried about you. Are you in over your head? If so, I can get you out. But if you don't tell me, I might not be able to protect you."

Anger flitted across Zoe's face before compassion took its place. She placed her hand over Jade's. "You're my best friend, and I love you. I can't tell you *anything*, but I will tell you that you need to stop investigating me or anything else to do with the Robin Hood and Barrett cases."

Something in Zoe's words reminded Jade of what Micah had said at the conclusion of the Robin Hood case: "Move on."

It wasn't a suggestion. It was a command.

"Do you know Micah Alexander?"

Zoe blinked. "No."

Jade yelled, "Why are you lying to me?"

Zoe put her hands over her ears. "Stop! Stop with the questions. Or else!"

"Or else what? Is that a threat?"

Sighing, Zoe pulled her hands away and shook her head. Her eyes beseeched Jade's.

"It's not a threat, Jade. It's a warning."

@TheGodOfVeritas: President Fairchild invited some important people to a Kennedy Center Gala next week. Why doesn't she ever invite the common people? #shame

CHAPTER EIGHTY-SEVEN

Washington, DC

JADE READ THE paragraph again, still disturbed by her conversation with Zoe the night before. A chasm had erupted between them, and Jade wasn't sure it could be crossed.

Movement at her office door made Jade shift her gaze from the email she'd been reading.

A man poked his head in. "I love what you've done with the place."

Jade laughed—she hadn't done anything. It still looked the same as when he'd occupied it. "Ethan!"

Hopping out of her chair—*his* chair—she ran to him, giving him an uncharacteristic hug.

He hesitated, then hugged her back.

She pulled away from him. "What are you doing here?"

He was dressed impeccably, as always, in a black suit, pressed white shirt, and—she knew without looking—suspenders underneath his jacket. She could see her reflection in his polished shoes.

Looking rested and fit, he smiled. "Running, as a pastime, is overrated. I'm ready to get to work. And I want my office back."

※

Jade sipped champagne in the small red-and-gold room adjacent to the presidential box at the Kennedy Center. She had come alone and was unacquainted with the other invitees. She watched them mingle with each other.

She wasn't one for mingling.

She was still thinking of Zoe. Had she been too hard on her? But Zoe was involved somehow in whatever was going on with the president as well as the Robin Hood case.

She and Zoe hadn't spoken today.

The door opened, and she started to rise, expecting President Whitney Fairchild. Instead, Kyle Madison entered, wearing her customary tailored black pantsuit and crisp white shirt, an outfit that cost more than Jade's monthly rent. Kyle's medium-length shampoo-commercial hair shimmered as her green eyes found Jade's. Jade froze momentarily midrise and then stood to greet Kyle, who smiled. Jade started to respond in kind until she realized Kyle wasn't alone.

Following close behind Kyle was Brittney Summers, with her sandy complexion and long blond braids. She sort of looked like Prince in her purple women's tux.

"I'm surprised you're here, Agent Harrington." Kyle held out her hand, squeezing Jade's hand firmly before letting go.

There was a diamond on the ring finger of her other hand.

"Same here, Ms. Madison," Jade said.

"Being one of her minor donors has its privileges," she said, smiling. "I believe you've met Brittney."

Jade locked eyes with Summers, the tension between the baller and former baller on display like a scene from a bad teen movie.

Jade shook Summers's hand. "How's it going?" she said.

Summers raised her chin. "What's up?"

This had been the extent of their conversations when they played against each other.

As the mature adult, Jade broke eye contact first.

"I love the symphony," Kyle said, seeming to enjoy the tension. "Don't you?"

Jade wouldn't know. This was her first time. Before she could respond, an older woman made an entrance. And it was an entrance. Jade recognized her from television. She wore a black fitted dress, her neck wrapped in gold. Her bracelets tinkled as she made a beeline for Jade.

"Hello, I'm Senator Maureen McAllister, but you may call me Mo." The tiny woman hugged Jade, and Jade awkwardly hugged her back. The senator pulled away. "I don't believe in highfalutin titles. Do you? You're that famous agent I've read so much about. What a pleasure to meet you. You're prettier in person. Where's your family from?"

Slightly off-balance in the wake of the senator's staccato delivery, Jade responded, "Uh… I'm an army brat, so… everywhere."

"Well, thank you and your family for your service. This here is my husband, Jimmy." Mo patted his chest. "We call him Nub. He doesn't want to be here, but he knows who wears the dresses in the family." She winked at Jade.

Jimmy's eyes sparkled—he was a man who liked a good time. The way he looked at his wife reminded Jade of how her father used to look at her mother.

"How're you doing, darlin'?"

Jade pointed at the small Mississippi State pin on his collar. "Basketball or football?"

He grinned. "All sports. But women's basketball is my favorite."

"Good man," she said.

Mo and her husband moved on to introduce themselves to Kyle and her fiancée and the others in the box.

Next to enter was an attractive middle-aged black woman also wearing a black dress. She, too, came straight over to Jade.

Jade was anxious to meet her as well.

"Vice President Bates," Jade said. "Truly an honor."

"Oh, put your hand down and give me a hug. I'm a fan of yours. Please call me Jo. All my friends do."

Jade glanced over at Mo and back at her. "The three of you are the real deal. You, the senator, and the president are as close as it appears on TV."

"If we were younger, the press would call us Charlie's Angels, but at our age, they'll probably call us the Golden Girls. And we're just getting started. You haven't seen anything yet."

"I bet," Jade said.

A man stepped into the box. "Ladies and gentlemen, the President of the United States of America."

Everyone turned to face the door. Entering alone, Fairchild wore a gorgeous blue evening gown with a diamond necklace and earrings. She was followed closely by Secret Service Agent Josh McPherson.

Fairchild shook hands with the other guests in the box before approaching Jade. After exchanging pleasantries, she asked quietly, "Any progress on the Shakespeare Killer?"

"Not yet. I hope to have something to report soon."

Hopefully tomorrow.

As the president asked to be kept informed, Jade gazed over Fairchild's shoulder; there was movement by the door.

Another secret service agent had entered.

Jade stared open-mouthed at the agent.

The president followed Jade's gaze.

"Remember me?"

The agent wasn't speaking to Jade, but to Fairchild, who appeared confused.

The agent whipped a gun from behind her back and pointed it at the president.

For Jade, everything slowed down.

"What are you doing here?" someone yelled. It sounded like Kyle.

Jade wondered the same thing. She had a brief vision of a woman coming up to her table at the jazz club on Capitol Hill, and another of eyes meeting hers across the pillows.

Jade pushed the president to the floor. Josh dove to cover Fairchild as Jade lunged for the gun.

Don't be afraid, the president had said at CJ's funeral.

A loud boom filled the enclosed space.

Something pinged into Jade's chest.

A grunt, sounding as if it came from her, preceded a burning sensation that radiated to other parts of her body. She slammed into the floor where the agent had stood.

Why would Brook be dressed up like a secret service agent?

Why would she try to kill the president?

Kill me?

Screaming. Footsteps. Someone shouting Jade's name. Sounded like Kyle again.

Suddenly she felt tired. So tired.

Touching her chest, she gazed at the dark liquid on her fingers.

She needed to stay awake.

The pain was unbearable.

I need to close my eyes. Just for a little while.

She saw her parents' faces.

I can't wait to see you.

Then she felt nothing.

CHAPTER EIGHTY-EIGHT

The White House, Washington, DC

"HOW'S OUR FRIEND?"

"The same."

"I hope she makes it," he said.

"Me too." Whitney spun in her chair to look out the window at the Rose Garden. "What's on your mind, Cole?"

He never called to chat.

"Wanted to tell you something before you heard it from one of those busybodies in Washington."

Whitney's heart dropped. Was it about Cameron?

Keeping her voice light, she said, "Present company excluded?"

"Ashley's pregnant."

"Oh… that's wonderful news."

"Speak for yourself. I'm too old to have another kid."

"You have some control over that, you know."

He laughed. "That I do. By the time this kid graduates from college, I'll be seventy-eight years old. They'll be wheeling me in on a gurney to his graduation ceremony. If I make it that long."

"Age gives us perspective," she said.

"Tell that to my body."

"You're a good dad."

His breathing heavy, he said, "I miss my boy. CJ. I should've been more understanding, but I didn't understand him. He was different from the boys I hung out with growing up. From me. I won't make the same mistakes this time."

"All parents make mistakes, Cole. No one provided us with a manual. You can only do your best."

"I don't feel like I did my best with CJ."

He sniffed. She gave him a moment.

"But that's not the only reason I called."

She braced herself. "Oh?"

"We've selected a name, regardless of sex."

Whitney was perplexed. Perhaps he *did* just want to chat. "Okay…"

"Reagan Fairchild Brennan, after our two favorite presidents. You're Ashley's, by the way, so don't get the wrong idea. I'm not sure what you said to her when she came to visit you at the White House. Girl power stuff, I bet."

Caught off guard, Whitney teared up. This time, she needed a moment. "I'm speechless. Honored. And it's women power, Cole."

"Oh brother," he said. "We're not going to let the kid tell anyone his middle name. It'll be one of those old embarrassing family names that no one ever talks about."

She smiled. "Even so."

"And that's not all. You know how every time there's a mass shooting, and we conservatives say we need to put money toward mental health, but we never do it?"

She didn't bother to answer.

"Let's do something about it. For real this time. In honor of my son. What do you say?"

"I say yes."

He clapped. "Hot dog! I'll start twisting some arms on my side of the aisle. Have a good evening, Madam President."

"You too. And thank you, Cole. Give Ashley my best."

❋

Whitney packed her briefcase. Grayson, Chandler, and Emma were upstairs in the Residence. After the assassination attempt, the Secret Service had located each of them and brought them back to the White House as a precaution.

Josh McPherson waited for her just outside the door to the Oval Office. He opened it for her as she approached.

He held an envelope.

She stepped outside. "Is that what I think it is?"

He tried to hand it to her.

She gripped her briefcase handle in front of her with both hands, not taking it.

"It's my fault. She was one of ours."

"Any news on her whereabouts?"

"Not yet."

"As I've told you every day since the… attempt, I won't accept your resignation. So put that away."

He held it out for a second longer, then slid the letter into a pocket inside his suit jacket.

"And I don't want to see it again," she said, holding his gaze, "until the next time you allow one of my children to bring home a date I haven't met."

He grinned. "Your daughter can be persuasive."

"So can I," she said. "Walk with me."

Whitney and Josh strolled along the West Wing Colonnade. The evening was balmy. Summer was coming.

"How are your children, Josh?"

His brown eyes lit up. "They're fine, ma'am. Ava and Mia are almost two."

"Ah… the terrible twos."

"I'm ready."

She shook her head at the muscular agent. "No, you're not."

They shared a smile.

She stopped walking. "Jade Harrington risked her life for me. For all of us. Without hesitation. Without a thought to her own well-being. She… reacted."

"It was her duty."

She looked at him. "Would you do the same for me?"

"Without a thought."

CHAPTER EIGHTY-NINE

Washington, DC

KURT MCCLAINE, IYANNA Adey, and Kyle Madison stood in the hallway of the Seattle courthouse. Jade couldn't hear their conversation from the other end of the hall. She crept closer, as she used to do as a kid when she spied on her parents.

Kyle did nearly all the talking. She was giving instructions, not being interviewed as Adey had told her. McClaine and Adey eventually left.

After a time, Zoe joined Kyle.

What is she doing here?

By now, Jade hovered next to them, but for some reason, they couldn't see her.

"She's getting close," Zoe said. "I'm not sure how long I can hold out."

"You'd better find a way."

"I hate lying to her."

Why would you lie to me?

"It can't be helped."

A sob. "What if she never comes out of the coma? What if she dies?"

"She won't."

"If she does, Paine won't be happy."

"Don't ever say that name in public again."

Jade was falling away from them. She could no longer hear their voices.

Paine?

Darkness enveloped her again.

❁

She was treading water. It felt warm and embracing. Above her she saw a glimmer of light. She knew she must swim toward it.

If she didn't, she would die.

She'd never backed away from a challenge. A fight. Her dad used to say, "For many are called, but few are chosen." A passage from the Bible. Although he wasn't a religious man, it was the code he lived by. The way he wanted her to live.

He would want her to fight.

Did they fight when they were trapped in a car at the bottom of a ravine off the Pacific Coast Highway? Did they try to come back to her? For her?

When Jade was a child, her mom would sometimes take her to the convenience store and allow her to buy a bag of M&M's. But she would let Jade eat only one M&M a day, no matter how much she begged for more. Her mother wanted Jade to learn self-control.

When her mom wasn't looking, her dad would sneak the rest of the bag to her.

Jade wanted to be with them. But she wasn't ready. Yet.

She started to swim.

Fifty yards. Twenty yards. Ten. Five. Three. Two. One. She broke through the water's surface.

And opened her eyes.

"Blimey!" a voice with a British accent said. "She's awake!"

Hazy. Everything hazy. Thankfully it wasn't too bright. She tried to say something, but her mouth wasn't working. It felt as if it were stuffed with cotton balls.

The person who'd spoken dashed out of the room. A moment later, a woman in a white coat stood in his place.

"Welcome back," said the woman. She had a friendly voice, and her English was precise with a slight Indian accent. "I am Dr. Sati Sangha, the president's personal physician. And now, it seems, yours as well. You're in the George Washington University Hospital."

"Wa—"

The doctor reached toward the bedside table and produced a clear plastic cup. She bent the straw to Jade's lips. The water burned her throat on the way down.

Jade swallowed. "The president?"

"She's fine. Thanks to you. She's been by to see you. She's quite worried."

"How long?" Jade croaked.

"You've been out for a few days."

"Damage?"

"Nothing permanent. You won't be working for a while. Or playing basketball." The doctor patted her arm. "I want you to rest now. You've had a lot of visitors."

"Who?"

Jade couldn't wait for the answer. She fell back asleep.

CHAPTER NINETY

Washington, DC

"I THOUGHT YOU were angry at me."

"I was," Zoe said. "I am. But you almost died, so I forgive you. Besides, you're a hero. Again. It's hard sometimes, being best friends with all this greatness. May I have some of that?"

Jade was sitting up in bed. Bandages were wrapped around her chest and left arm. She shifted the bowl of Jell-O away from Zoe. "No."

The room resembled a living room from a TV sitcom. There was a recliner near the bed, a couch, and a small round table with four chairs. The beeping and hissing noises from the medical equipment were muted.

"You were lucky. The bullet barely missed your heart."

Jade spooned some Jell-O into her mouth.

"Kyle was there," Zoe continued. "How was that?"

Jade stared at her snack as if it were a work of art, while Zoe examined her face for any sign of interest in Kyle.

"I don't really remember."

Zoe frowned. "That's too bad. I wanted to hear how it went with Brittney."

She regaled Jade of the press coverage from her exploits, how Jade had trended on Twitter for almost an entire day, with people of all ages posting videos of themselves diving into the air and landing on the floor or the ground ("Jading"), and that she had been named one of *People* magazine's Most Beautiful People.

"Must be a down year," Jade said.

"You're really famous now!"

Jade eventually tuned her friend out. Something tugged at her. Something about Kyle. And Zoe.

What was it?

A few minutes after Zoe left, there was a knock at her hospital room door.

Kyle Madison popped her head in. "Up for another visitor?"

"Of course."

At least Zoe had left. What a disaster that would've been.

Kyle entered with a dozen roses.

The clack of Kyle's high heels stopped as she looked around the room. "Oh my."

Most of the horizontal surfaces were covered with get-well cards and flower arrangements from friends, coworkers, former teammates, other students from the tae kwon do school, and the president of the United States of America.

Shifting some vases from other well-wishers, Kyle placed hers in a prominent position on the table.

She sat in the chair next to the bed and leaned forward, hands clasped, arms resting on her legs. She wore a gray shirt with black pants. Her makeup and hair were impeccable.

"I finally saw you in action," Kyle said. "You saved her life. All our lives." She touched Jade's hand. The skin on Kyle's finger was lighter where the engagement ring had been. "I, for one, will be forever grateful. Thank you."

"I was only doing my job," Jade said.

Kyle tilted her head. "I thought that was the Secret Service's job."

"Yeah… well," Jade said.

"When in Rome?"

"Something like that." Jade paused. "Did you know her?"

"Who?"

"Brooklyn."

"Who?"

"The secret service agent."

Kyle pulled her hand away. "No."

"You yelled at her."

"Everyone was yelling."

They were silent for a moment.

"In town on business?" Jade said.

Kyle didn't answer at first, turning instead to gaze out the window. She turned back to Jade. "I haven't gone home. I've been here since… the assassination attempt."

"Why?" Jade said. "What about your businesses?"

"That's what technology is for."

"I still don't understand why you're here."

"Because of you, silly."

Jade wasn't sure what to say, so she did what she did best: deflected. "Is Summers here too?"

Kyle crossed her legs, resting her elbow on her thigh, chin in hand. "I wouldn't know."

Silence again.

Jade said, "I enjoyed the time we spent together in Seattle, but—"

"When I saw you lying there," Kyle said, "I didn't know whether you were alive or dead. Whether you would live or die. Things suddenly became clear to me. My feelings became clear." She gazed at Jade, her eyes as blue as a perfect sea. "I told Brittney about my feelings for you."

Jade was speechless.

"Don't say a word. We'll talk about this later. I've realized tomorrow isn't promised."

Jade looked at Kyle. She felt… nothing.

"I—"

They both turned at the knock on the door. Kyle was agitated at the interruption. Jade was relieved.

At the threshold stood Professor Alaia Bennett, carrying a stack of books. Jade smiled. "Hi."

Mouth parted, Kyle looked from Alaia to Jade. "Did I realize it too late?"

CHAPTER NINETY-ONE

The White House, Washington, DC

WHITNEY KNOCKED ON Emma's bedroom door.

"Hello?" said a female voice that was not her daughter's.

She frowned. "Emma?"

Talking to Cole the night before had made her think of mistakes she'd made with her own children. Chandler had been avoiding her, staying in his room and leaving it only for work. They still hadn't spoken. She should have made more of an effort. How could she bring a divided country together if she couldn't do the same for her family? She was a mother first. Other mothers found the time.

The door cracked open, revealing half of Megan's face. Emma had insisted that Megan come with her to the White House. "Are you looking for Em?"

"Well, yes."

"Hold on a minute, Madam President. She's just getting out of the shower."

Whitney debated whether to leave but remained where she was.

Megan called out to Emma. "It's your mom!"

A moment later, Emma emerged from her room, closing the door behind her. Her hair was dry. "Mom."

"I wanted to make sure you're all right."

"I'm fine. We were studying."

Did college students typically study in the shower these days?

"I'll let you… study."

"That reminds me, Mom, I have something to tell you."

Whitney looked at her, questioning.

Her daughter hesitated. "Megan and I are sort of a couple."

"Sort of."

"Well, we are a couple."

Emma's secret service detail must know. Who else? Obviously the press hadn't caught on yet.

"I see."

Emma exhaled. "There you go again."

"Forgive me, but my daughter just came out to me." She glanced around the hall. There was no one there. "Perhaps we should talk about this some other time."

"Will there ever be a good time?"

The news wasn't a total surprise. The noise that Whitney heard last night—the same noise she'd heard last time Emma and Megan had spent the night in the White House—was Emma sneaking off to the Queens' Bedroom.

A mother knew.

After a moment, Emma said, "I didn't think so. I thought you would be cool with it, given your politics. Or is tolerance reserved for your base?"

"I don't care that you're gay. I'm upset that you didn't tell me." She paused. "We used to be close."

"We're still close, Mom. Just because we don't talk every day doesn't mean I don't love you."

"Emma," Whitney said, placing her hands on both of her daughter's shoulders, "I love you, and I respect who you are. I'm proud to be your mother, and I can't wait to become better acquainted with Megan."

"That's great, Mom," Emma said, "because I have something else to tell you."

"Oh?"

"Megan and I… we're going to live together, after the semester is over."

❋

"When you weren't in your library, I thought I might find you here."

Whitney remained in the plank position. "I wanted to be alone."

Her husband took a step into the White House Residence gym. "Where's Nicki?"

Nicki was her private yoga instructor.

"As I said, I wanted to be alone."

"Even from me?"

"I will not repeat myself again."

Grayson crossed the room and stopped a few feet away from her. He sat cross-legged on the floor.

Whitney clenched her butt cheeks and sucked in her stomach. Her palms pressed into the yoga mat, a small tremor shooting up her forearms. She had been holding the pose for a while.

She lowered herself, not wanting him to see her shake. Matching his cross-legged position, she faced him.

Classical spa music played through the in-wall speakers, the relaxing sounds juxtaposed by the tension between them.

"While I've been here," he said, "I've had time to think. About what's important."

She waited.

"You. Us. I'm back."

"What about… ?"

"It's nothing."

"Another mistake?" she said.

He opened his mouth, then closed it.

The first time he engaged in an affair with their next-door neighbor in Missouri, he claimed it was a one-night stand. It was a mistake, the result of consuming too much wine.

Now Grayson's eyes beseeched hers. "It's over. For good this time. I've learned that I need to keep the politics and our relationship separate. I won't make the same mistake again."

That word. Again.

She stared at the face of the man she had loved for most of her life. The father of two of her children. Her best friend.

"No," she said, "you won't."

He exhaled with relief. "Thank you. I promise to be the husband I should've been."

"I hope she appreciates that, since you weren't for me. Every time it got hard, you left, and I had to get through it alone. And now I've realized that I don't need you." Rising, she walked by him without looking down. "Now get the fuck out of my house."

CHAPTER NINETY-TWO

Washington, DC

"HI."

Jade looked up from the novel she was reading, *Their Eyes Were Watching God* by Zora Neale Hurston.

She hadn't seen him in almost six months. His face still showed the aftermath of the Rockefeller Center bombing, although the scars were healing.

"Hi," she said, setting the open book facedown beside her on the bed.

Entering the room, he sat in the chair that Alaia Bennett had vacated an hour ago.

He took in the books on the nightstand: *The Bluest Eye* by Toni Morrison. *Native Son* by Richard Wright. *Kindred* by Octavia Butler.

"Light reading," he said. "I detect a theme."

"A friend brought them over," she said. "You look great."

"Liar. I'm supposed to be saying that to you. Thanks for seeing me."

"At least I put you on the list," she said, teasing. Then, "I can't wait to get out of here."

"I know the feeling. I can't imagine that lying here all day suits you."

She smiled. "No. How's it going?"

"My doctor said I should make a complete recovery. Additional surgery will take care of the rest." He surveyed her bandages. "We make quite a pair, don't we?"

"I'm glad you came."

He shrugged. "I missed you."

She should respond in kind, but instead she allowed the silence to drag on too long.

Finally she asked, "Back at work?"

"Not yet. But it won't be long. President Fairchild thinks it's important to show the public that terrorism didn't win." He pointed to his face. "I'm going to need lots of makeup."

As the White House press secretary, Blake gave on-camera daily briefings to the American people.

She decided to trust him. She needed to.

"I've been thinking a lot about our discussions," she said. "About the coincidences. Your conspiracy theories. I think it's a good thing you're back at work."

"Why?" he said.

She told him about Zoe's tattoos, her reaction when Jade confronted her, and her warning. Blake had worked with Zoe on political campaigns.

Jade stared at him, gauging his reaction to what she was going to say next.

"I think Fairchild had something to do with Judy Porter's murder."

He looked into her eyes, his tone flat. "I do too."

❋

"Hey, Coach."

Taking a hesitant step into the room, LaKeisha smiled, but it wasn't as bright as it once was.

She glanced around as she sat in the chair next to the hospital bed. "Nicer than my house."

"Mine too."

"How can you afford this?"

"I can't," Jade said, looking around the room herself. "Let's just say our president is grateful."

"You're the best FBI agent ever. You're friends with the president. You were a great basketball player. And you're not a bad coach either."

"Thanks. I think."

"Some of my AAU teammates can't believe you're my coach. You're the truth. It means you're the shit." LaKeisha grinned. "Oops. Sorry, Coach."

Jade smiled. "I know what it means."

Jade thought about her plan with Veritas to flush out the killer. It almost worked. Too well.

"Are you in pain?"

Jade shook her head. "The nurses are taking care of me." She felt groggy from the medication; the nurses had administered the drugs before the next round of pain could commence. "Sorry I couldn't coach the spring league team this year."

"No worries. We knew you were busy."

"How's AAU going?"

"We're going to nationals next month. New Orleans."

"Next time you find yourself in a potentially compromising situation, leave."

"Don't worry about me, Coach." Subdued, she said, "I learned my lesson." Jade studied her face.

"What lesson is that?"

"I need to pick better friends," LaKeisha said, forcing a laugh.

"No, really," Jade said. Although this girl looked tough, she held a lot of things inside. Jade needed to draw her out.

LaKeisha looked down at her red long-sleeve Adidas T-shirt and black track pants. "That it's different for me. Because of what I look like. How I dress." She pulled at a braid. "My hair."

"It can be. Yes."

LaKeisha's eyes met hers. "Is it that way for you, Coach?"

Jade wondered if LaKeisha would ever trust the system again. Jade had been fortunate that she hadn't suffered much racism during her life, but she wasn't immune.

She believed Barringer was a racist, for example.

"Sometimes. As a black person, your standards must be higher."

The girl's expression was anguished behind her cool facade. "How do you deal with it?"

Jade thought for a moment, not wanting to give LaKeisha a pat answer. "I try to focus on me. What I'm trying to do. Being the best me I can be." Jade held her eyes. "Racism isn't about you. There isn't anything wrong with you. Or the color of your skin. It's about them. Something is wrong with *them*. Their insecurity. Their fear of uncertainty. You need to keep doing you." She thought about what Alaia had said to her. "You're descended from kings and queens. You are their wildest dreams."

LaKeisha's eyes shone. "I'm focusing on my game. Scholarship offers are coming in."

"Let me know if you ever want to talk about that. I've been through the process."

"I'll take you up on that."

"You should focus on your studies."

"I will."

"And don't worry about the charges," Jade said. "They've been dropped. Your record was expunged."

Jade had called in a favor at CSS before the assassination attempt. She hadn't had a chance to tell LaKeisha until now.

The girl swallowed hard, about to cry. She didn't. Instead, she stood and extended her hand. Jade slapped LaKeisha's hand and held it.

"No matter if you coach me or not," the girl said, "you'll always be my coach."

The White House, Washington, DC

IN THE ROSE Garden the next morning, Whitney stood at the podium set up for the occasion. She was flanked on either side by Senator Maureen McAllister and Vice President Josephine Bates. Next to Jo stood radio talk-show host Cole Brennan. The two women wore smart suits with skirts. Cole's tan suit fit. He had lost weight.

The weather was perfect, the arrival of the suffocating DC humidity still a month away.

She gazed out over the assembled audience.

Whitney concluded her speech, "Suicides are at an all-time high in this country. This legislation will not prevent a mass murderer from easily obtaining a gun, but it will decrease the number of suicides. Especially among our teens." She turned to Cole. "It won't bring CJ back, but I believe he would have liked this bill. He fought for the causes he believed in, like his daddy... although he chose the right side."

Cole laughed. "Not going to debate you here, Madam President, but you're right. CJ would have liked this bill." He gave her a slight bow. "Thank you."

The CJ Brennan Mental Health Act would create a department within the executive branch to coordinate mental health programs across federal, state, and local agencies in order to help Americans in need find care, housing, job assistance, and other services.

She moved to the small mahogany table with the presidential seal affixed to its front and waited for Mo, Jo, Cole, Sasha, and several other supportive members of Congress to gather behind her. Selecting one of the many Cross Townsend pens, Whitney signed the act using one pen for every two to three letters of her name. When she finished, she stood and gave one pen to Jo, one to Mo, and one to Sasha. The last three pens she handed to Cole.

"One for you. One for Ashley. And one for CJ."

Tears fell from Cole's eyes, and he pulled her toward him in a bear hug. Josh McPherson took a step toward her, but she held out a hand to stop him.

After a moment, she disengaged and slipped her arms around the waists of Mo and Jo. The four of them posed as the press pool cameras clicked away.

"Cole, I want one with just the women."

He made a face, pretending to be offended. "Aren't you always complaining about sexism and discrimination?"

"It's *our* turn," she said simply.

Raising his arms in surrender, Cole walked away.

As she posed for the cameras, Cole went to stand by Cameron Kelly.

And her son, Chandler.

What is Cameron doing here?

After the last photo was taken, she said to Mo and Jo, "Thank you both. I could not have done this without you."

"We should do it again," said Jo. "We're on a roll."

"It was a hoot!" said Mo. "I love working with you two."

"We *should* get together again," Whitney said, "but for fun. Dinner. Once a month. Just us. What do you say?"

"I'm in," said Jo.

"I'll bring the moonshine!" said Mo.

"I would certainly hope so," Whitney said, smiling.

I don't need him.

A weight she had borne for as long as she could remember had lifted. There was life—a good life—after Grayson.

"Madam President, a few questions!" said one of the White House press corps.

Whitney returned to the podium. She spotted Judy's replacement at ABC and pointed at the reporter.

"What's your question, Mike?"

"You said this mental health act would've helped CJ Brennan. Can you think of a time in your life when it would've helped you?"

The conversational noise ceased. Everyone looked at her, waiting for her answer.

It was time.

"Yes, Mike, I can. When I was a junior in high school, I went to live with my aunt, Mary Churchill, and transferred to a school in a suburb outside of Chicago. Winters there can be frigid. I wore bulky coats and sweaters every day. For the last three months of my stay, I lived at a convent where my aunt volunteered."

She paused.

A few reporters raised their hands, some shouting "Madam President!" or "President Fairchild!"

Holding up a hand, she said, "Let me finish. There's been a lot of speculation out there. You've waited a long time for this story. It's my story; let me tell it. If you're patient, I'll answer most of your questions."

"I doubt it!" shouted one reporter.

The others laughed.

She waited for the laughter to subside.

"The entire experience was a painful one. Living away from my family and friends. Attending a new school where I knew no one, with only my aunt for company. I was all alone. It would have been helpful to have someone to talk to. A professional.

"Being there wasn't a choice. At least, not my choice. It was my parents' decision. They believed they needed to protect me and my reputation from the inevitable small-town gossip.

"I had a secret, you see. I was pregnant." The reporters started to murmur. "After the baby was born, I held him once before I signed the papers giving him up for adoption. Before he was taken away from me forever. I was promised he would be brought up in a good home. With parents who would love him. And I returned home to Missouri.

"My story is far from unique. There are women across this country and around the world with similar stories. Similar situations that happened *to* them. Not because of anything they did or the clothes they wore, but because they are women. I applaud the brave women speaking out. Remember, what happened to you is not your fault.

"Over a decade ago, an African-American civil rights activist named Tarana Burke started a movement called Me Too." She stared at Cameron Kelly. "I stand here today to tell you that I was raped. I am your president, and I am a survivor. Yes. Me too."

The press corps and other guests were silent. Stunned. A bird chirped.

Chandler looked from Whitney to Cameron and then backed to Whitney. He roared: "You!"

An ugly look consumed her son's face, now inches from Cameron's. Chandler's hands encircled Cameron's neck and squeezed. Cameron's face turned red as the two men fell to the ground. Whitney took a step toward them before

Josh grasped her wrist and held her in place. Two secret service agents sprinted past him, each of them grabbing one of Chandler's arms.

They pulled him off Cameron.

"You fucking asshole!" Chandler tried to shake off the agents, his face also a deep shade of red. Spittle leaked out of the corner of his mouth. "You raped my mother! And you hired me anyway? You goddamn—"

"Josh," Whitney said to her lead agent. "I have to do something. I need to protect my baby."

Josh stared at her. He looked around and called two agents over. "Watch her."

Sasha yelled at the press corps, "Stop taking pictures!"

Sprinting toward Chandler, Josh encircled her son in his powerful arms. Chandler struggled all the way as Josh carried him into the White House.

Cameron staggered to his feet, holding his neck and coughing.

"Did you see what that little fucker did?" he gasped to Cole.

Cole looked at him. "Is it true? Did you rape the president?"

Cameron was caught off guard by the question. And then he grinned. "She begged for it."

"Did she now?" Cole was agile for a big man. His right arm shot out, making contact with Cameron's jaw. Whitney's ex-boyfriend fell backward with the impact of the knock-out punch.

Sasha continued to yell at the camera people and everyone who had pulled out their smartphones.

To no avail.

CHAPTER NINETY-FOUR

Washington, DC

"AREN'T YOU TIRED of lazing around?" Dante said. "You need to get back to work, boss."

He was followed into the hospital room by Micah, Pat, Christian, Max, and Ethan. Micah moved the metal IV stand and LED heart monitor out of the way so the six of them could gather around the bed.

Jade lifted her chin toward the equipment. "I hope I won't need that." She scanned their faces. "Can you help bust me out of here?"

"Don't tempt them," Max said.

Christian surveyed the room and spotted the refrigerator.

"How are you feeling?" Ethan asked.

"Bored. Any sign of the perp?"

He shook his head.

Jade finally asked the question that had consumed her for the last several days. "Who is she?"

"Her name's Devon Mattix," said Dante, "a former secret service agent."

"Secret Service?" she said.

Christian returned, popping open a Pepsi. "She was fired from the first daughter's detail last year when Emma Fairchild sneaked out of her dorm."

"I remember that. And she blamed Fairchild?"

"She wanted revenge," Dante said.

With a proud smile, Micah said, "Told you she was in law enforcement."

"You also thought she was a he," she reminded him. He frowned. "Nine millimeter?"

"Ruger LC9s," Dante said.

"You should've worn a vest," Max said, his voice soft.

"Didn't think I'd need one at the symphony," she said. "How did she get the gun in?"

Dante plopped himself in the recliner. "She had help. One of the president's secret service detail disappeared the night of the assassination attempt."

That was too scary to contemplate. She sat up higher in the bed. "We should inform the—"

"We're on it," Dante said. "Every law enforcement agency in the country is looking for both of them."

"McPherson wasn't in on it, right?"

"No."

She exhaled. She thought of Josh as one of the good guys. If he were dirty, it would've shaken her worldview. "What's new with the Shakespeare case?"

"Not much," Dante said.

"Did you find anything tying Brook—Mattix to the murders?" she asked.

Her talkative team became silent. Christian looked up at the ceiling. Micah studied the books on her nightstand. Max gazed out the window. Pat studied her cell phone. Dante and Ethan stared down at the floor.

Dante looked at her. "What if she was hired to kill them?"

Doubtful, Christian said, "Contract killings?"

Jade remembered what Brooklyn had said she did for a living.

Customer service.

"Thought of something?" Max asked.

"I might—"

She should tell them she'd already "caught" Mattix. Or rather, Mattix had caught her. Seduced her.

Why?

She could tell them where Mattix lived, but she wasn't sure of the address. Only the neighborhood.

Jade closed her mouth, averting her gaze. "I thought I did, but it's gone."

"A contract killing does seem farfetched," Micah said.

"Does it?" Dante said. "She was a well-trained agent out for revenge."

"And fit," Jade said.

"How do you know that?" Micah asked.

"Uh… I got a glimpse of her before she shot me."

"That still doesn't answer why," Ethan said. "Or who took out the contracts."

"We've examined Mattix's bank accounts," Pat said, "and haven't come up with any unusual or significant deposits."

"Doesn't prove anything," Dante said. "She could have offshore accounts."

"We're working on that," Pat said.

As Micah opened his mouth to say something, his hand accidentally knocked into the rolling table that Jade used to eat her meals. A stainless-steel tray clattered to the floor.

Jade yelled, "Everybody down!"

Her heart pounded as she glanced around wildly at her colleagues.

"It was just a tray, Jade," Micah said, bending to pick it up.

Concern was etched on the faces of her fellow agents.

Laughing it off, she said, "It was so loud."

Silence descended.

"We should go," Ethan said.

"Pat and Max," Jade said, "can you stay for a moment?"

Micah frowned.

Christian, Ethan, and Dante hugged her and shuffled out.

Micah stared down at her, concern still evident in those gray eyes. "You sure you're going to be all right?"

"I'll be beating your butt up the Lincoln steps in no time."

Micah looked unconvinced. "Can't wait." Glancing at Max, he hugged her. "See ya, Jade."

He sauntered out of the room.

Jade watched him leave.

Her heart pounded again, as if it would bust out of her gown.

But not in a lovelorn way.

She had never seen Micah shirtless. But when he leaned over, she happened to peek under his open-collared shirt. A chill went through her as she caught a glimpse of the tattoo on his chest.

The same as Zoe's.

In the exact same place.

進捗

CHAPTER NINETY-FIVE

The White House, Washington, DC

"HOW BAD IS it?"

"Actually," Sasha said, sitting in the chair alongside Whitney's desk in the study, "it's quite the opposite. Your approval ratings are up."

Whitney shook her head. "Of course they are."

That morning, the headline of the *Washington Post* was "The Melee in the Rose Garden." The entire front page comprised stories about Whitney and her family: Whitney's confession, Chandler fighting with Cameron, Cole punching Cameron, and speculation—once again—about the identity of Whitney's baby. The passing of the mental health act warranted two small paragraphs in the lower right corner.

Cameron declared he wouldn't press charges against either Chandler or Cole, probably figuring it wasn't a wise career move.

Women took to social and traditional media to tell their stories of sexual assault using the hashtag #MeTooWhitney.

"You just have to look outside," Sasha said.

Earlier, from the Residence, Whitney had looked out the window at the many women standing just outside the White House fence, most of them holding signs. In addition to #MeTooWhitney, there was #MeToo, #IBelieveYou, and #ItsNeverTooLateToBeFree.

Whitney wasn't sure why it had taken her so long to speak out about what had happened to her. None of her reasons seemed to matter now.

She *was* free.

"Cole's on."

"Turn it up," Whitney said.

"It's been quite a week," Cole said. "Who knew White House press conferences could be so lively? Thank you all for the cards and emails. Yes, my hand is fine, and no, I shouldn't have hit him harder. I apologize to you folks that

I was such a bad judge of character. I thought Kelly was a better man. I want to tell the fellas something. Are you listening? Come closer to the radio or the computer. Are you ready?

"No means no. It's not code for yes. Guys like Cameron Kelly have no place in the Republican Party or in Congress.

"If he should run again when he's up for reelection, I promise to God I will do everything in my power to defeat him. Are you with me?

"We need to pay the bills now, but after the break, my guest will be a former legislative aide to Cameron Kelly, Chandler Fairchild. Yes, that Chandler Fairchild. Stay tuned."

Whitney looked at Sasha. "You knew?"

Sasha cocked her head and pursed her lips.

After the intermission, Cole introduced Chandler.

"What are you going to do now, champ?" Cole asked.

"I'm not sure yet, Mr. Brennan. I might take a break from politics."

"Why?"

"My last two bosses weren't very good."

Cole's high-pitched laugh squealed over the airwaves. "That's true. How did you feel when you realized the truth about Kelly?"

"Blindsided. This guy hired me, showed an interest in my career, in me. Now I know it was to spite her."

"Not very nice of him."

"I was just as bad. A real sh—jerk to my mom."

"Who knows, son? She might be listening. You do listen to my show, President Fairchild, don't you?"

Whitney smiled.

"What would you say to her," Cole said, "if she were listening?"

"Mom, I love you, and I'm so proud of you and all your accomplishments. I'm sorry I ever went to work for that douchebag."

"What do you think about your mom? After what she went through."

"She's a badass. I should've been there for her like she's always been there for me. Chosen her over politics. Sons are supposed to protect their mothers."

"Are you going to switch parties?"

"I'm still a Republican, but I respect my mom's views, as she's always respected mine."

"She has?"

"Well… most of the time."

"We need a loyal guy like you at the network."

Chandler paused. "Have your people call my people."

Cole laughed. "We'll leave it right there for today. Thank you, Chandler Fairchild. Good luck to you, young man."

"Thank you, Mr. Brennan."

Cole signed off.

Sasha turned off the radio. Whitney wiped her eyes.

"Sounds as if you've got your son back," Sasha said.

Chopin's Nocturne in E-flat major, op. 55, no. 2 trilled from Whitney's cell phone. A ringtone she hadn't heard in a while.

"I need to take this, Sasha," Whitney said.

Her younger son was calling.

After she hung up with Chandler, she returned to the paperwork on her desk. She caught herself humming. She was happy.

She glanced at the credenza. Sasha had left her purse.

Whitney picked up the handset to ask Sean to retrieve it, then set it back down. She needed to stretch her legs. She could return the purse to her chief of staff's office herself.

As she got closer, she noticed that the black patent leather purse was open.

She peered inside. A sheet of parchment paper.

A familiar color.

The texture was familiar to her touch.

Pulling it out, she unfolded it, already knowing its contents.

A letter addressed to her. From Landon Phillips.

Worn from the many times she had read it.

The same letter stolen from Whitney's purse several months ago.

Sasha had known all along that Landon believed he was Whitney's son.

Why did Sasha take the letter?

Why hadn't she returned it?

What else was she keeping from Whitney?

A heaviness overcame her. She slipped the letter back inside Sasha's purse and picked up the phone to call Sean.

Washington, DC

"MAY I SPEAK to Pat first?" Jade said to Max.

"Of course," he said.

She waited for the wide hospital room door to close behind him. "Anything new on Barrett?"

The other woman shook her head.

Jade looked at Pat for a long time, then said, "'For sweetest things turn sourest by their deeds.'"

"Ninety-four," Pat said. "The sonnet left with Judy Porter. What of it?"

"I think it's a message."

"Meaning?"

"I need you to run a check on someone."

"Sure. Who?"

Jade put a finger to her lips. She scribbled a name and an address on a sheet of paper from a notepad on her nightstand and held it up.

"Memorize it."

Pat's eyes narrowed. "Isn't that your friend?"

Jade nodded.

Pat stared at the paper and then nodded.

Jade ripped off the piece of paper with Zoe's name and address and handed it to Pat. "Flush it."

Pat did as she was asked.

Jade thought about seeing Kyle, McClaine, and Iyanna Adey at the Seattle courthouse. There was something between them. Something involving Zoe.

But what?

"Look into Kyle Madison."

"We ran a check on her for the Robin Hood case."

"Do it again," Jade said. "We missed something. And one more thing."

Pat looked at her, questioning.
"There's another person I need information on."
"Who?"
"Micah."

943

CHAPTER NINETY-SEVEN

Washington, DC

"THIS IS UNEXPECTED," Blake said.

He stood in the doorway, his normally styled hair tousled. He was barefoot and dressed in a plain black T-shirt and jeans.

"I was just visiting Jade," Whitney said.

"How's she doing?"

"You haven't seen her?"

"I have."

This pleased her. "Aren't you going to invite me in?"

"Uh… sure."

She entered Blake's condo, which opened to a living and dining room area. The furniture was modern, the walls gray and white. Crossing the cherry floors, she gazed out the window at the George Washington University Hospital across the street and listened to the rhythm of the city outside.

"How convenient," she said.

"I could've walked home."

Behind her, he picked up papers and files from the sofa and rectangular wooden coffee table. She turned, watching him. "What are you working on?"

"Nothing," he said, cradling all the material in his arms. "Trying to catch up on what I missed while I was out. Please sit down. I'll be right back."

He walked past her to where there were two other rooms: his bedroom and the guest room he used as an office.

Sitting on the sofa, she admired the white marble flecked with gray that surrounded the fireplace.

He wasn't gone long.

"Your fireplace is beautiful," she said.

"I lucked out, finding a place like this close to the White House. Would you like something to drink?"

"I'm fine."

Opting to sit on a chair across from her, he crossed his legs at the ankles.

"I can imagine the traffic jam you're causing outside," he said.

"I won't be long. I suppose you're wondering why I'm here."

"You've never visited me at home before."

"It's about what happened in the Rose Garden."

"Sorry to miss all the excitement. Do you want me to write up a statement?"

"This has nothing to do with your job," she said. "It's about you."

"What about me?"

"It's time."

He sat up straighter. "Time?"

"For us to tell everyone who you are."

"Why?"

"It will come out eventually. We need to craft the story the way we want it to be told."

"Okay." He dragged the word out, unconvinced.

"Your life is about to change," she said, noticing his discomfort. "Everything you do will be scrutinized and commented on, worse than in your role as press secretary. You'll receive protection from the Secret Service."

He looked sharply at her, as if he hadn't considered this.

"I don't want their protection."

"It's a hassle sometimes," she said, "but you'll get used to it."

"I'm of age. I can decline it."

"Given what happened to me, I wouldn't recommend that. Everyone will come after you."

Standing, he moved to the window behind him, gazing down at the traffic jam around Washington Circle.

"I like my life the way it is," he said.

She came and stood by him, following his gaze.

"You are my son. This is your life now."

CHAPTER NINETY-EIGHT

Washington, DC

"HOW LONG?" MAX said upon reentering the room after Pat had departed. He sat down in the chair next to the bed.

"How long what?"

"Have you been jumpy like this."

She started to blow him off, then looked at him. "Ever since it happened."

"Is there anything else that's different?" Max asked.

She thought about it for a moment. She was exhausted from all the visitors. "My chest hurts before it rains."

"Nightmares?"

"Every night. But not about that night."

"About what then?"

"My parents."

His brow furrowed. "What about them?"

"I'm trying to find them."

The last word hung in the air. After a while, Max said, "I looked into their deaths. At the time. I met with the local chief of police and the detective in charge of the case." He stared into her eyes. "It was officially ruled an accident, Jade. They're gone."

She was never satisfied with that conclusion. They died in a one-car accident on the Pacific Coast Highway. There were other tread marks at the scene. The police thought that it might have been a hit-and-run. The other car was never found.

Fire had consumed her parents' car. There were no remains. Their caskets, laid to rest in Arlington National Cemetery, were empty.

Glancing down, she said, "I blamed myself. Believed that the accident was somehow my fault. That I could've prevented it."

"You've never told me that," Max said. Then, quieter, "I miss your parents too. I'm your godfather for a reason." A pause. "Did you know your dad was a spiritual man?"

"We never went to church."

"But he read the Bible. Every day. 'For unto whomsoever much is given, of him shall be much required.' He believed privilege bestowed responsibility."

"I know," she said. "He told me that many times." She paused. "I want to get back to it, Max."

"It's going to take some time before they'll allow it," he said. "Even a desk job."

"Can't you pull some strings?"

"You need to rest."

"Being here has given me a lot of time to think," she said.

"About?"

"I'm not ready to sit behind a desk."

"I could've told you that."

"I miss my previous job. Being an ASAC. I miss the hunt."

"It's what you were born to do."

"Did my father say that too?"

Max hesitated. "Possibly."

"I'm glad Ethan's back," she said, fiddling with her hospital wristband.

His expression changed. "So am I."

She wondered what that was about. "Did you have something to do with that?"

"I don't possess that type of pull. I should go, let you rest. When will they discharge you?"

"Tomorrow?"

"Need a ride?"

"Zoe's coming." She hesitated. She wanted to tell him her suspicions about the president. About Zoe. Something made her hold back. She wasn't sure what. Max was one of the few people in her life whom she'd always trusted.

He'd always been there.

"What about you?" she asked.

"What about me?"

"How are you doing?"

"I'm fine," he said. "I started writing."

This made Jade sit up. "Writing what?"

"Fiction."

"Crime fiction?"

"No," he said. "A historical thriller. Set during the Shakespearean era."

"Can't let all that research go to waste."

"That," he said, "and it fills the hours." Max was never one to rush to fill silences, even awkward ones. He surprised her. "We need to talk about Micah."

She looked at him. "What about him?"

"The way he looks at you." Max pushed his glasses farther up on his nose. "You shouldn't let him be so attached."

Jade didn't like anyone telling her what to do. "He works for me."

"All the more reason to keep it professional."

"We *are* professional," she said. "Is there more to this? What's going on, Max?"

"Just take my word for it."

"What've you got against Micah?" Jade said, eyeing him with suspicion. "Isn't he your platinum child? I thought you'd want us to be close. Your two protégés. You know something about him that I don't?"

He stared at her for a long while, an inner debate taking place.

"I do."

"What? Tell me."

Max swallowed. "He's your brother."

CHAPTER NINETY-NINE

The White House, Washington, DC

WHITNEY STEPPED TO the podium.

Gathered before her in the James S. Brady Press Briefing Room, the press corps sensed a major announcement forthcoming.

"Good afternoon, ladies and gentlemen," she said into the microphone. "I want to share something with you. Please hold your questions until the end.

"After the Rockefeller Center terrorist attack, Blake Haynes, who stands here before you every day speaking on my behalf, needed a blood transfusion. Without it, he would have died. Blake has a rare blood type, shared by few people. My chief of staff, Sasha Scott, led the effort to find someone with a match. It turned out I was one of those people."

The press started to murmur.

She plowed on. "I donated my blood to him." She turned to the wings and motioned to him. "Come out here, Blake."

He came and stood next to her, smiling bashfully at his colleagues.

"When are you coming back to work, Blake?" shouted a male reporter. "We miss you!"

"I bet," Blake said.

Whitney held up a hand. "Please. During this process, our DNA was tested." The murmurs were getting louder. She glanced at the empty chair where Judy used to sit, her colleagues still leaving it vacant in her honor. "It was confirmed that Blake Haynes is not only a valuable member of the White House staff, but he is also my biological son.

"And now," she said, "I'd like to bring out his brother and sister."

Chandler and Emma joined them on stage. She placed her arms around Blake's and Emma's waists. Chandler stood on the other side of Blake, his arm around his brother's shoulders.

They'd met their new brother at dinner the night before. They'd listened as Blake told them about his upbringing. He listened as Chandler and Emma told him how much it sucked to be the president's children.

"Where's your husband?" shouted Mike from ABC News.

Whitney gave a wry smile. "I'll leave that for another press conference. Thank you, everyone. I hope I've answered all your questions."

Every reporter's hand was raised, all of them shouting questions at her.

Whitney looked at her three children.

And laughed.

✳

Sasha crossed the Oval Office and handed Whitney some papers. "It's good to see you happy."

Whitney hadn't forgotten Sasha's betrayal, but she believed that it was best to keep her friends close and her enemies closer. Her frenemies, even more so.

"I *am* happy," Whitney said.

Sasha cocked her head. "It's not awkward?"

"A little. For all of us. Chandler and Blake are attending a Nationals game tonight." Whitney held up the papers. "Anything important? I want to spend some time with Emma before she heads back to school."

Sasha shook her hand. "It can wait. Have a good night, Madam President."

"You too, Sasha."

Sasha left.

Whitney retrieved her purse from her desk, leaving her briefcase on the credenza.

No work tonight.

Her phone rang. "Yes, Sean."

"Secretary Salcedo is here."

Whitney frowned. The secretary of homeland security didn't usually drop by unannounced.

"Send her in. And get Sasha back here, will you?"

"Will do."

The secretary entered a few moments later, followed by Sasha.

Salcedo stopped a few paces from her. Glancing at the purse in Whitney's hand, she said, "Madam President, sorry to disturb you. It's about the Rockefeller Center bombing."

"Someone claimed responsibility?"

"There's been an arrest."

Whitney laid her purse on her desk and returned to her seat. "That's excellent."

"I hadn't heard," Sasha said. "Who?"

"Isaiah and Jeremiah Johnson, ages twenty-four and twenty, respectively. They're brothers."

Whitney's mouth parted in surprise. "American?"

Salcedo nodded. "Members of a white nationalist organization with a grudge against the cable network."

"My God!" Whitney said.

"Terrorism knows no color," said Sasha.

"The FBI director is on his way."

"What do we know?" asked Whitney.

"FBI Counterterrorism traced significant payments to their personal bank accounts."

"Any idea who was behind it?"

Salcedo hesitated. "We believe that it was the Carr brothers. The FBI office in Chicago is en route to pick up Jason Carr."

Whitney's mind raced as she tried to absorb what she had just learned. "Any connection with the Shakespeare Killer?"

"We're not sure," Salcedo said, "but there's more. The brothers received financial backing from another party. We don't know for sure if the Carrs were cognizant of the other funding source."

"Who was it?"

Salcedo's stare didn't waver. "Russia."

The bear never forgets.

Whitney picked up the phone to say goodbye to her daughter.

Washington, DC

"NICE DIGS," HE said as she let him into the Ritz-Carlton suite in Georgetown.

"My home away from home for the moment. Charming earring. What is it, a star?"

"It's a tree. How is she?"

"She's going to be fine. She knows you're here?"

"No. I was asked to check on the situation. Jade would think it was odd if I visited her."

"Are you hungry?" She waved a hand toward the dining room. "We can have something brought in. Or eat downstairs."

"I'm not sure if being seen together here is a good idea," he said.

"You're right. I believe that Jade's already suspicious. We can order in."

"I'm not that hungry."

She gestured to the living room. "Well, then, have a seat."

"I'll stand, thanks. I've been sitting for five hours."

"It is a long flight." She moved to a beige chair by the unlit fireplace. "I'll sit, if you don't mind."

"Suit yourself," he said. "I see that Collins stopped tweeting."

"The silly little activist served his purpose."

"You paid him to tweet to throw off the feds. And then what? Were you going to set him up as the fall guy?"

"He was paid handsomely for his insignificant efforts."

"Were the sonnets supposed to throw them off too?"

She nodded. "I tried to select the most appropriate sonnet for each victim, but I knew the media and the FBI wouldn't be able to resist murders with a literary connection. Zoe, of all people, gave me the idea. Before she came up with the name Astrea, she was going to name the program Dark Lady."

"She knows what you've been up to?"

"She didn't. She might've figured it out by now, though."

He seemed to consider this.

"It was a means to accomplish our goals while throwing law enforcement off the scent," she continued. "They were looking for a serial killer with a passion for Shakespeare. While we were eliminating the enemies of the republic one by one."

"'Our goals.'"

"The end justified the means."

"Why Hurley? You did the Russians a favor."

"She's the CEO of a public company. She can be replaced."

"And Tishman? He brokered the deal with Hurley to create a product to protect our election system. Didn't you think he was of some utility?"

She shrugged. "I never liked him."

"Seems rash."

"Good riddance. But Judy Porter wasn't me."

"I know," he said. "What about Fairchild? Was assassinating her a means to an end?"

"God, no," she said, horrified. "That wasn't part of the plan. How was I to know she'd go rogue?"

"How did you connect with her?"

"Dev? We knew each other from another life."

"You dated?"

"We went to school together."

"Paine isn't happy," he said, stepping forward to admire the painting over the fireplace, his hands behind his back. "*You* shouldn't have gone rogue."

"It had to be done." She shook her head, her hair cascading over her shoulders and down her back. "Besides, it was a one-time thing. It won't happen again."

"You're right about that." Detective Kurt McClaine touched the silencer to the middle of Kyle Madison's forehead. "Hurley isn't the only one who can be replaced."

He fired.

THE END

Acknowledgments

It takes a team to produce a book. My novels would not have been published without the support, morale boosts, and constructive criticism I received along the way.

MANY THANKS TO:

- My editors: Leah Wohl-Pollack, Michael Manahan, Christina Tinling, Jim Thomsen, and Alan Rinzler.

- Dan Schlosser for always being there to answer my questions and provide wise guidance.

- Damonza for their awesome formatting and cover design prowess.

- An early reader of Don't Speak, Sherron Bates.

- My writing companions: my cats, Fitzgerald and Duke.

- My children, Travis, Brandon, and Jaz for their support and always being there.

- My parents who never let me settle and instilled the work ethic in me to become an author. My mother placed a book in my hand when I was three; I've carried one ever since. Our weekly trips to the library are one of my fondest memories.

- My amazing wife, manager, and editor, Audi. She encouraged me to write Don't Speak, reads and comments on every draft of every manuscript, and supports me throughout each project. She is with me on every page.

- My readers. I am overwhelmed and honored by the positive reaction to Jade's story. It means so much to me. Thank you.

About the Author

Julie L. Brown is the author of the historical fiction, *Bend, Don't Break*, the alternative-history novel, *No One Will Save Us*, and the creator, under the pen name J. L. Brown, of the Jade Harrington series, political thrillers which include the novels, *Don't Speak, Rule of Law,* and *The Divide*, and the short story, "Few Are Chosen."

Julie earned an MFA in Creative Writing from the Stonecoast program at the University of Southern Maine. She resides with her family in the Pacific Northwest, where she is working on her next novel.

You can find her on:
Website: julielbrown.com
Instagram: @julielbrownwrites

If you would like to receive an email when I release my next book and other exclusive offers and updates, you may sign up for my newsletter at bit.ly/JLBNews. Your privacy is important. Your address will never be shared, and you can unsubscribe at any time.

Thank you for reading *The Jade Harrington Series*, Books 1-3 and don't forget to leave a short review on Goodreads and your favorite bookstore's website.